CONTEMPORARY AMERICAN
SHORT STORIES

DOUGLAS ANGUS was born in Nova Scotia, the son of a fur trader. He received his B.A. from Acadia University (Canada), his M.A. from the University of Maine, and his Ph.D. from Ohio State University. He has taught at several universities, been Fulbright Lecturer at the Uinversity of Istanbul, and is now Charles A. Dana Professor Emeritus at St. Lawrence University. He is the author of four novels, editor of four short story anthologies, and contributor to numerous magazines and critical journals.

SYLVIA ANGUS was born in Brooklyn, attended Cornell and George Washington universities, and received an M.A. from St. Lawrence University. Like her husband, she has taught at several universities, including the University of Istanbul, and is currently Professor of English at The State University of New York at Potsdam. She is the author of four novels, a textbook, and co-editor with her husband of three story anthologies. She has also written numerous articles and short stories for magazines.

CONTEMPORARY AMERICAN SHORT STORIES

Selected and Introduced by
DOUGLAS and SYLVIA ANGUS

FAWCETT PREMIER • NEW YORK

Cover art: Detail of painting by Edward Hopper   High Road. 1931. Watercolor on paper. 20 x 28 inches. Collection of Whitney Museum of American Art. Bequest of Josephine N. Hopper.

CONTEMPORARY AMERICAN SHORT STORIES

Published by Fawcett Premier Books, CBS Educational and Professional Publishing, a division of CBS Inc.

A Fawcett Premier Original

The editors and publishers wish to thank all those who have contributed to this volume. Acknowledgments for individual short stories will be found on the first page of each selection.

ISBN: 0-449-30832-4

First Fawcett Premier printing: October 1967

Printed in the United States of America

30 29 28 27 26 25 24 23 22 21 20 19 18 17

CONTENTS

There can be little doubt that the Second World War interrupted the creative life of America more than the first, but what happened during World War II was actually far more shattering to the human soul than anything that took place in World War I, and its aftermath may already be stirring the creative mind more profoundly. In the second war, mankind saw whole nations converted to barbarism, witnessed the awesome power of mass-media propaganda to enslave masses of humanity, and saw the breakthrough to the ultimate weapon by which man could at last destroy himself. Perhaps the sheer immensity of these revelations temporarily distracted artistic creativity in both America and Europe. However, some very fine short stories were written in America during and closely following World War II, while the past decade has witnessed the appearance of a number of exciting young writers whose daring experimentalism may herald a new movement in fiction every bit as brilliant as that of the twenties. This new fiction has a maturity, sophistication, and philosophical depth that even the best fiction of the twenties lacked, and although the great modern revolution in style seems to be largely completed in most of the arts, it seems to be revitalized in the all-out symbolism and expression of such young writers of the sixties as Tillie Olsen, Stanley Elkin, Jack Ludwig, James Purdy, and Donald Barthelme.

The main themes attracting the attention of short story writers in this period are the continuing social inertia of the South, where it is still possible in 1967 to be arrested for teaching Darwinian evolution; the new explosive phase of the Negro racial issue; the new cosmopolitanism of Americans, their endless traveling and world involvement; the rebellion of the young; the problems of the aged; the plight of the illiterate, all at once an anomaly in the modern technological state; life in suburbia; and nostalgia for yesterday, the day before the new technology passed its wand over the old, worn, romantic, natural world and changed it into a world of power, speed, gadgetry, luxury, vast organization, and widespread alienation.

Among those writers who have enhanced the "Southern Gothic" school in the fifties and sixties, none are quite so brilliant as the three represented here, Eudora Welty, Peter Taylor, and the late Flannery O'Connor. In their writing, impressionism has reached a remarkable richness and refinement. It is as if among the backwaters of the South the force of life turning inward has produced a luxuriant flowering of character—quaint, exotic, exuberant, even at times luridly evil, subject matter magnificently suited to Chekhovian impressionism. Yet these writers go beyond impressionism. In the works of Flannery O'Connor, potential violence is never far from the surface. Eudora Welty's stories deal less with violence than with subtle nuances of emotion, but some of them, like "Why I Live at the P.O.," are remarkable for their objectivity and comic insight. Peter Taylor's stories, even when brilliantly alive in the present, as is "The Fancy Woman," give the reader the feeling that they are haunted by evocations from a Southern past that will not die, that lives on, distorted, in the actions of today.

It is curious that the three white writers mentioned above seem to deal more often with the problems within the Southern white culture than with what we think of more specifically as "race" problems. Negro writers Ralph Ellison and James Baldwin, and the gifted young Texan Georgia McKinley, on the other hand, have concentrated upon both the open violence and the inner, emotional dislocation produced by racial difference. Ellison's story "Battle Royal," used later as the opening chapter of his famous novel *Invisible Man,* is one of the most shocking portraits of the brutalization of the Negro by corrupt white men in all of twentieth-century fiction. In a different vein, James Baldwin's "Come Out the Wilderness" probes the subtle emotional difficulties that disintegrate a Negro-white love affair. Georgia McKinley, in "The Crime," explores with remarkable insight the way in which a Negro is forced defensively to live out the lie demanded by the white man's conception of his race. All three stories illustrate the agony of our racial crisis with far more depth of understanding than did many older stories that concentrated on the more obvious horrors of physical brutality.

The stories about Negro life and those about Jewish life are often lumped together because both deal with problems of oppression and minority status. The differences between them, however, are more striking than the similarities. A minority group like the Negroes, the Jews in the United States suffer from a less obvious persecution. The pogrom is not an element of the American scene. The Jewish writers, whose number reflects their literary importance, are urban, cosmopolitan, sophisticated, deeply concerned with the spiritual search for identity and with the problems of maintaining cultural entity in a society whose aim is to break down racial and cultural barriers. Their stories question their own past and try to make sense of their present. They are full of the characteristic irony of a people accustomed to turning humor in on themselves as a device for survival.

Bernard Malamud's "The Last Mohican" is an ironic picture of a cosmopolitan scholar in Italy coming up sharply and unexpectedly against the immutability of his own Jewish cultural ties. Jack Ludwig's story "A Woman of Her Age" explores with tenderness and insight the life of an old woman whose wealth in a fast-moving technical society has kept her from attaining the simple, traditional joys of the Jewish mother. Finally, Philip Roth, in a story of sparkling humor, gives us the Jewish boy debating the illogicalities of religious dogma from the rooftop of his Hebrew school.

One of the most fascinating sources of fiction during this

period is provided by the denizens of the new cloud-cuckoo-land of suburbia and their prototypes, the well-heeled sophisticates who live in the towering metropolitan apartment houses—the "elevated" people. John Cheever, Mary McCarthy, and John Updike have all written with consistent brilliance about these people trapped and stereotyped among the curious artifices of the environment in which affluence and scientific technology have placed them. McCarthy and Updike write with great stylistic flair and much humor. Updike is particularly fascinated by the emotional tangles of young married people and by the idealisms and illusions of adolescents in an adult world that seems to stifle those qualities. "A & P" is a striking example of the latter theme. Mary McCarthy is a contemporary master of irony, writing with a pen dipped in acid. The clean-cut, aphoristic style and sustained wit of her story "Cruel and Barbarous Treatment" make it a little masterpiece. Cheever, less the virtuoso, is more meditative and penetrating. His great story "The Country Husband" gathers slowly to a denouement whose mournful mockery reverberates in the reader's mind long after he has put the story down. All three writers describe the problems of people who, seemingly, should not have any —the prosperous, comfortable Americans who suffer from a spiritual malaise no less real for seeming slightly absurd in a world still plagued by war, starvation, and misery.

Among those stories in which the author looks backward to that strangely sweet and simple life that preceded the great technological revolution of our time, three highly original and memorable stories have been selected for this collection. Two of them, Delmore Schwartz's "In Dreams Begin Responsibilities" and Dorothy Canfield's "Sex Education," illustrate brilliant solutions to the problem of how to keep unity of time in a short story covering more than one generation. In the Schwartz story, the young narrator watches as in a dream a cinema in which his parents act out the day on which his father proposes. There are in the story two moments of special poignance. In one of these, thinking of all the troubles in his family, he has an impulse to shout out across time to his parents not to get married at all. The other moment comes a little later, when a small quarrel threatens the whole courtship, and he experiences a sudden rush of terror as he realizes that his whole existence depends upon his parents' ability to heal this little breach between them. Within the dream, then, the narrator discovers how precious is his sorrow-threaded life.

In "Sex Education," a woman retells a single incident of her youth, at three different times in her life. In each telling, the story has subtly changed. These changes in the way a small event is interpreted show the psychological growth of a whole lifetime.

Katherine Anne Porter's "Holiday" also involves reminiscence and illumination, though technically its method is more straightforward. The whole story is a wonderfully detailed memory of a long-ago vacation on a Texas farm, during which the narrator, who is seeking a haven from emotional problems of her own, shares the simple life of a peasant family as it goes through the life cycle of birth, marriage, natural disasters, and death. In the course of her relations with the family, and particularly with its crippled daughter, she comes to understand and accept the inevitability of suffering as a natural part of human life. As in the Schwartz and Canfield stories, the backward glance illuminates the present.

Also full of reflections on the past, but existing too vividly in the present to quite fit into the above grouping, is Wright Morris' moving story "The Ram in the Thicket." Here Morris satirizes with a tender touch many of the frailties of American life: the dominating wife and mother, the fixation on cleanliness, the "organization" woman, the inarticulate relationship between father and son, the deadly formalities of patriotism. But the story is not a burlesque. It becomes, in Morris' rich prose, a deeply felt evocation of a man's complex relationships with his wife and his dead son. The biblical allusion of the title is only partly ironic. It also suggests a sobering parallel.

One of the special categories of fiction that has emerged since the Second World War is the sociological story, sociological in the sense that the author has invented a whole society for purposes of comparative criticism or to depict archetypal themes. Shirley Jackson's "The Lottery," William Golding's *Lord of the Flies,* and Florence Randall's "The Watchers" are interesting examples of this genre. "Among the Dangs" by George P. Elliott is a *tour de force* of this type. Through his account of the sojourn of a young American Negro anthropologist among a tribe of savages called the Dangs, the author burlesques both anthropology and all the stories ever written about civilized man and the savage. Every society's taboos and mores are potentially comical to the outsider, and Elliott fully exploits this rich vein of comedy. The high point of the mockery comes when the hero escapes death at the hands of his savage captors by recounting the great myth of his own culture, the passion of Christ, over and over until the Dangs believe it and accept him as a great prophet. In his mystical agony of fear, however, he almost surrenders to the myth the way the Dangs have. Instead he escapes home to America. Looking back on the adventure, he sees that he could have become a Christ among the Dangs and so, as he now feels, have "lost" himself "utterly."

One of the best stories written since the war on the subject of Americans abroad is Saul Bellow's "The Gonzaga Manuscripts." In this story, a young American, while passionately engaged in a pilgrimage to Spain to find a dead Spanish poet's lost poems, is maliciously persecuted and called to task for all the sins that America is conventionally accused of—the atomic bomb, too much wealth, materialism, and bad taste. Since the young man is using his time and limited resources to save something beautiful that his persecutors have lost, forgotten, and never appreciated,

INTRODUCTION 13

the irony of the situation is devastating. Subtly the story reminds the world that the high-brow American has not only caught up with Europeans in aesthetic taste but has become less materialistic and more civilized than many of those Europeans who continue to mock and scorn American philistinism.

Of writers who have specialized in one facet of contemporary culture the most successful is J. F. Powers, whose quiet, intimate, sympathetic satire on the life of the Roman Catholic clergy is a unique and precious contribution to the literature of this period. "Prince of Darkness" is one of the most detailed of these stories, all of which are distinguished by their elaborate re-creation of this island of scholastic, ritualistic monasticism persisting in the midst of America's boisterous, worldly pursuit of life, liberty, and happiness.

Critics have continued to ponder over the mystery of the short story's continued vitality in the presence of such limited commercial reward. Actually, this freedom of the short story from commercial controls is its great strength. It costs at least a hundred thousand dollars to produce a play on Broadway and ten thousand dollars to publish a novel, a situation that makes producers and publishers conservative, but a highly experimental short story, if it has value at all, can usually find publication in some low-budgeted, avant-garde magazine. It should not be surprising, then, that the spirit of revolt and experimentation abroad among young artists in all fields during the sixties should be especially evident in the stories of a group of writers who have recently begun to attract attention.

One of the first of these innovators to be noticed is James Purdy, whose work clearly marks a fresh departure from traditional modernism. Admittedly his style is simple and awkward, yet an effect is achieved of starkness, unaffectedness, and directness that is a refreshing change from the overworked styles and familiar attitudes of those who still imitate the innovations of the twenties. As his story "Encore" illustrates, there invariably gathers within his narrative a surge of powerful pathos made more effective by the low-pitched key of his bare style.

No story by these young writers of the sixties has aroused such immediate acclaim as Tillie Olsen's "Tell Me a Riddle," and indeed, it has been some time since a new writer has used narrative prose with such confidence, originality, and flourish. Discarding the customary transitions as she moves easily from the inner dialogue of the mind to spoken dialogue, Miss Olsen seems to have broken through to a fiction of increased fluidity and density of emotion. Intuitively she has exploited the natural poetry of the uninhibited broken English of first-generation Americans, and this poetic effect is heightened by the replacement of conventional or logical sequence by a symphonic unfolding of scenes that is continually and excitingly surprising. But this young author's genius is not limited to style; the theme of this story is unusual and deeply moving. There is tremendous pathos in hearing within the pain-torn, bitter musings of an old woman—robbed by husband, children, and circumstance of the right to read, and so to develop her fine intelligence—such penetrating and ruthless insight into the ways the New World can corrupt the old values.

Another young writer of great promise is Stanley Elkin, whose unusual story "I Look Out for Ed Wolfe" is included here. In his stories there is little plot in the ordinary sense, but rather a series of ritualistic actions in which the frustration, tension, and anguish of unfulfilled contemporary man are continuously exorcised. These stories may be framed by some kind of time limitation or the final ritualistic act may be climactic or anticlimactic, and although this final action does wrap things up, the structure of the story is symphonic rather than mechanical. Rarely can the themes of Elkin's stories be neatly paraphrased. This is because they are an emotional purgation rather than a rational, critical analysis of life. In the story included here, Ed Wolfe is a guilt-ridden individual who finds release in sadism; thus the ideal job for him is ruthless bill-collecting for a loan company. When his overzealous efforts get him fired, he falls compulsively into an elaborate ritual in which he turns all his possessions into cash. When he has thus converted all his assets, that is, himself, into cash, he gets drunk and gives his own life (his money) to buy the freedom of a poor Negress, who seems to have been forced into prostitution. As a result of this act of atonement, Ed Wolfe gets rid of his guilt-ridden old self and is free and whole again.

The writer making the most drastic break of all with realism, however, is Donald Barthelme. Barthelme, like Kafka, Beckett, and Genet, experiments with the absurd in order to mock the clichés and shibboleths of our twentieth-century gadget world. Nowhere is that world more absurd than in TV land, where "A Shower of Gold" takes us, where, indeed, showers of gold today seduce the innocents below. But the reference of the hero, Peterson, to the old Greek myth about Zeus suggests that the godlike in man may yet be regenerated if we will only turn off our TV sets.

Altogether these stories present a fascinating psychological record of what may best be termed "The Age of Crisis," the age in which modern man finds himself teetering on a fine edge of destiny, when his own fateful decisions will take him either to hell or to paradise.

SYLVIA ANGUS and DOUGLAS ANGUS

April, 1967

GREENLEAF

by Flannery O'Connor

Flannery O'Connor (1925–1964), in her short lifetime, achieved remarkable distinction as both short
story writer and novelist. Born in Savannah,
Georgia, she did her undergraduate work at the
Woman's College of Georgia and received an
MFA from the State University of Iowa. A professional writer all her adult life, Miss O'Connor
has contributed significantly to the high position
held by Southern writers in modern America. Outstanding among her works have been *Wise Blood*
(1952), *A Good Man Is Hard To Find* (1955),
The Violent Bear It Away (1960), and the posthu-
mously published *Everything That Rises Must
Converge* (1965).

Mrs. May's bedroom window was low and faced on the east
and the bull, silvered in the moonlight, stood under it, his
head raised as if he listened—like some patient god come
down to woo her—for a stir inside the room. The window
was dark and the sound of her breathing too light to be carried outside. Clouds crossing the moon blackened him and
in the dark he began to tear at the hedge. Presently they
passed and he appeared again in the same spot, chewing
steadily, with a hedgewreath that he had ripped loose for
himself caught in the tips of his horns. When the moon

drifted into retirement again, there was nothing to mark his place but the sound of steady chewing. Then abruptly a pink glow filled the window. Bars of light slid across him as the venetian blind was slit. He took a step backward and lowered his head as if to show the wreath across his horns.

For almost a minute there was no sound from inside, then as he raised his crowned head again, a woman's voice, guttural as if addressed to a dog, said, "Get away from here, Sir!" and in a second muttered, "Some nigger's scrub bull."

The animal pawed the ground and Mrs. May, standing bent forward behind the blind, closed it quickly lest the light make him charge into the shrubbery. For a second she waited, still bent forward, her nightgown hanging loosely from her narrow shoulders. Green rubber curlers sprouted neatly over her forehead and her face beneath them was smooth as concrete with an egg-white paste that drew the wrinkles out while she slept.

She had been conscious in her sleep of a steady rhythmic chewing as if something were eating one wall of the house. She had been aware that whatever it was had been eating as long as she had had the place and had eaten everything from the beginning of her fence line up to the house and now was eating the house and calmly with the same steady rhythm would continue through the house, eating her and the boys, and then on, eating everything but the Greenleafs, on and on, eating everything until nothing was left but the Greenleafs on a little island all their own in the middle of what had been her place. When the munching reached her elbow, she jumped up and found herself, fully awake, standing in the middle of her room. She identified the sound at once: a cow was tearing at the shrubbery under her window. Mr. Greenleaf had left the lane gate open and she didn't doubt that the entire herd was on her lawn. She turned on the dim pink table lamp and then went to the window and slit the blind. The bull, gaunt and long-legged, was standing about four feet from her, chewing calmly like an uncouth country suitor.

For fifteen years, she thought as she squinted at him fiercely, she had been having shiftless people's hogs root up her oats, their mules wallow on her lawn, their scrub bulls breed her cows. If this one was not put up now, he would be over the fence, ruining her herd before morning—and Mr. Greenleaf was soundly sleeping a half mile down the road in the tenant house. There was no way to get him unless she dressed and got in her car and rode down there and woke him up. He would come but his expression, his whole figure, his every pause, would say: "Hit looks to me like one or both of them boys would not make their maw ride out in the middle of the night thisaway. If hit was my boys, they would have got thet bull up theirself."

The bull lowered his head and shook it and the wreath slipped down to the base of his horns where it looked like a menacing prickly crown. She had closed the blind then; in a few seconds she heard him move off heavily.

Mr. Greenleaf would say, "If hit was my boys they would never have allowed their maw to go after hired help in the middle of the night. They would have did it theirself."

Weighing it, she decided not to bother Mr. Greenleaf. She returned to bed thinking that if the Greenleaf boys had risen in the world it was because she had given their father employment when no one else would have him. She had had Mr. Greenleaf fifteen years but no one else would have had him five minutes. Just the way he approached an object was enough to tell anybody with eyes what kind of a worker he was. He walked with a high-shouldered creep and he never appeared to come directly forward. He walked on the perimeter of some invisible circle and if you wanted to look him in the face, you had to move and get in front of him. She had not fired him because she had always doubted she could do better. He was too shiftless to go out and look for another job; he didn't have the initiative to steal, and after she had told him three or four times to do a thing, he did it; but he never told her about a sick cow until it was too late to call the veterinarian and if her barn had caught on fire, he would have called his wife to see the flames before he began to put them out. And of the wife, she didn't even like to think. Beside the wife, Mr. Greenleaf was an aristocrat.

"If it had been my boys," he would have said, "they would have cut off their right arm before they would have allowed their maw to . . ."

"If your boys had any pride, Mr. Greenleaf," she would like to say to him some day, "there are many things that they would not *allow* their mother to do."

The next morning as soon as Mr. Greenleaf came to the back door, she told him there was a stray bull on the place and that she wanted him penned up at once.

"Done already been here three days," he said, addressing his right foot which he held forward, turned slightly as if he were trying to look at the sole. He was standing at the bottom of the three back steps while she leaned out the kitchen door, a small woman with pale near-sighted eyes and grey hair that rose on top like the crest of some disturbed bird.

"Three days!" she said in the restrained screech that had become habitual with her.

Mr. Greenleaf, looking into the distance over the near pasture, removed a package of cigarets from his shirt pocket and let one fall into his hand. He put the package back and stood for a while looking at the cigaret. "I put him in the bull pen but he torn out of there," he said presently. "I didn't see him none after that." He bent over the cigaret and lit it and then turned his head briefly in her direction. The upper part of his face sloped gradually into the lower which was long and narrow, shaped like a rough chalice. He had deepset fox-colored eyes shadowed under a grey felt hat that he wore slanted forward following the line of his nose. His build was insignificant.

"Mr. Greenleaf," she said, "get that bull up this morning before you do anything else. You know he'll ruin the breeding schedule. Get him up and keep him up and the next time there's a stray bull on this place, tell me at once. Do you understand?"

"Where you want him put at?" Mr. Greenleaf asked.

"I don't care where you put him," she said. "You are supposed to have some sense. Put him where he can't get out. Whose bull is he?"

For a moment Mr. Greenleaf seemed to hesitate between silence and speech. He studied the air to the left of him. "He must be somebody's bull," he said after a while.

"Yes, he must!" she said and shut the door with a precise little slam.

She went into the dining room where the two boys were eating breakfast and sat down on the edge of her chair at the head of the table. She never ate breakfast but she sat with them to see that they had what they wanted. "Honestly!" she said, and began to tell about the bull, aping Mr. Greenleaf saying, "It must be *somebody's* bull."

Wesley continued to read the newspaper folded beside his plate but Scofield interrupted his eating from time to time to look at her and laugh. The two boys never had the same reaction to anything. They were as different, she said, as night and day. The only thing they did have in common was that neither of them cared what happened on the place. Scofield was a business type and Wesley was an intellectual.

Wesley, the younger child, had had rheumatic fever when he was seven and Mrs. May thought that this was what had caused him to be an intellectual. Scofield, who had never had a day's sickness in his life, was an insurance salesman. She would not have minded his selling insurance if he had sold a nicer kind but he sold the kind that only Negroes buy. He was what Negroes call a "policy man." He said there was more money in nigger-insurance than any other kind, and before company, he was very loud about it. He would shout, "Mamma don't like to hear me say it but I'm the best nigger-insurance salesman in this county!"

Scofield was thirty-six and he had a broad pleasant smiling face but he was not married. "Yes," Mrs. May would say, "and if you sold decent insurance, some *nice* girl would be willing to marry you. What nice girl wants to marry a nigger-insurance man? You'll wake up some day and it'll be too late."

And at this Scofield would yodel and say, "Why Mamma, I'm not going to marry until you're dead and gone and then I'm going to marry me some nice fat farm girl that can take over this place!" And once he had added, "—some nice lady like Mrs. Greenleaf." When he had said this, Mrs. May had risen from her chair, her back stiff as a rake handle, and had gone to her room. There she had sat down on the edge of her bed for some time with her small face drawn. Finally she had whispered, "I work and slave, I struggle and sweat to keep this place for them and soon as I'm dead, they'll marry trash and bring it in here and ruin everything. They'll marry trash and ruin everything I've done," and she had made up her mind at that moment to change her will. The next day she had gone to her lawyer and had had the property entailed so that if they married, they could not leave it to their wives.

The idea that one of them might marry a woman even remotely like Mrs. Greenleaf was enough to make her ill. She had put up with Mr. Greenleaf for fifteen years, but the only way she had endured his wife had been by keeping entirely out of her sight. Mrs. Greenleaf was large and loose. The yard around her house looked like a dump and her five girls were always filthy; even the youngest one dipped snuff. Instead of making a garden or washing their clothes, her preoccupation was what she called "prayer healing."

Every day she cut all the morbid stories out of the newspaper—the accounts of women who had been raped and criminals who had escaped and children who had been burned and of train wrecks and plane crashes and the divorces of movie stars. She took these to the woods and dug a hole and buried them and then she fell on the ground over them and mumbled and groaned for an hour or so, moving her huge arms back and forth under her and out again and finally just lying down flat and, Mrs. May suspected, going to sleep in the dirt.

She had not found out about this until the Greenleafs had been with her a few months. One morning she had been out to inspect a field that she had wanted planted in rye but that had come up in clover because Mr. Greenleaf had used the wrong seeds in the grain drill. She was returning through a wooded path that separated two pastures, muttering to herself and hitting the ground methodically with a long stick she carried in case she saw a snake. "Mr. Greenleaf," she was saying in a low voice, "I cannot afford to pay for your mistakes. I am a poor woman and this place is all I have. I have two boys to educate. I cannot . . ."

Out of nowhere a guttural agonized voice groaned, "Jesus! Jesus!" In a second it came again with a terrible urgency. "Jesus! Jesus!"

Mrs. May stopped still, one hand lifted to her throat. The sound was so piercing that she felt as if some violent unleashed force had broken out of the ground and was charging toward her. Her second thought was more reasonable: somebody had been hurt on the place and would sue her for everything she had. She had no insurance. She rushed forward and turning a bend in the path, she saw Mrs. Greenleaf sprawled on her hands and knees off the side of the road, her head down.

"Mrs. Greenleaf!" she shrilled, "what's happened?"

Mrs. Greenleaf raised her head. Her face was a patchwork of dirt and tears and her small eyes, the color of two field peas, were red-rimmed and swollen, but her expression was as composed as a bulldog's. She swayed back and forth on her hands and knees and groaned, "Jesus! Jesus!"

Mrs. May winced. She thought the word, Jesus, should be kept inside the church building like other words inside the bedroom. She was a good Christian woman with a large respect for religion, though she did not, of course, believe any of it was true. "What is the matter with you?" she asked sharply.

"You broken my healing," Mrs. Greenleaf said, waving her aside. "I can't talk to you until I finish."

Mrs. May stood, bent forward, her mouth open and her stick raised off the ground as if she were not sure what she wanted to strike with it.

"Oh Jesus, stab me in the heart!" Mrs. Greenleaf shrieked. "Jesus, stab me in the heart!" and she fell back flat in the dirt, a huge human mound, her legs and arms spread out as if she were trying to wrap them around the earth.

Mrs. May felt as furious and helpless as if she had been insulted by a child. "Jesus," she said, drawing herself back, "would be *ashamed* of you. He would tell you to get up from there this instant and go wash your children's clothes!" and she had turned and walked off as fast as she could.

Whenever she thought of how the Greenleaf boys had advanced in the world, she had only to think of Mrs. Greenleaf sprawled obscenely on the ground, and say to herself, "Well, no matter how far they *go*, they *came* from that."

She would like to have been able to put in her will that when she died, Wesley and Scofield were not to continue to employ Mr. Greenleaf. She was capable of handling Mr. Greenleaf; they were not. Mr. Greenleaf had pointed out to her once that her boys didn't know hay from silage. She had pointed out to him that they had other talents, that Scofield was a successful business man and Wesley a successful intellectual. Mr. Greenleaf did not comment, but he never lost an opportunity of letting her see, by his expression or some simple gesture, that he held the two of them in infinite contempt. As scrub-human as the Greenleafs were, he never hesitated to let her know that in any like circumstance in which his own boys might have been involved, they—O. T. and E. T. Greenleaf—would have acted to better advantage.

The Greenleaf boys were two or three years younger than the May boys. They were twins and you never knew when you spoke to one of them whether you were speaking to O. T. or E. T., and they never had the politeness to enlighten you. They were long-legged and raw-boned and red-skinned, with bright grasping fox-colored eyes like their father's. Mr. Greenleaf's pride in them began with the fact that they were twins. He acted, Mrs. May said, as if this were something smart they had thought of themselves. They were energetic and hardworking and she would admit to anyone that they had come a long way—and that the Second World War was responsible for it.

They had both joined the service and, disguised in their uniforms, they could not be told from other people's children. You could tell, of course, when they opened their mouths but they did that seldom. The smartest thing they had done was to get sent overseas and there to marry French wives. They hadn't married French trash either. They had married nice girls who naturally couldn't tell that they murdered the king's English or that the Greenleafs were who they were.

Wesley's heart condition had not permitted him to serve his country but Scofield had been in the army for two years. He had not cared for it and at the end of his military service, he was only a Private First Class. The Greenleaf boys were both some kind of sergeants, and Mr. Greenleaf, in those days, had never lost an opportunity of referring to them by their rank. They had both managed to get wounded and now they both had pensions. Further, as soon as they were released from the army, they took advantage of all the benefits and went to the school of agriculture at the university—the taxpayers meanwhile supporting their French wives. The two of them were living now about two miles down the highway on a piece of land that the government had helped them to buy and in a brick duplex bungalow that the government had helped to build and pay for. If the war had made anyone, Mrs. May said, it had made the Greenleaf boys. They each had three little children apiece, who spoke Greenleaf English and French, and who, on account of their mothers' background, would be sent to the convent school and brought up with manners. "And in twenty years," Mrs. May asked Scofield and Wesley, "do you know what those people will be?"

"*Society*," she said blackly.

She had spent fifteen years coping with Mr. Greenleaf and, by now, handling him had become second nature with her. His disposition on any particular day was as much a factor in what she could and couldn't do as the weather was, and she had learned to read his face the way real country people read the sunrise and sunset.

She was a country woman only by persuasion. The late Mr. May, a business man, had bought the place when land was down, and when he died it was all he had to leave her. The boys had not been happy to move to the country to a broken-down farm, but there was nothing else for her to do. She had the timber on the place cut and with the proceeds had set herself up in the dairy business after Mr. Greenleaf had answered her ad. "i seen yor ad and i will come have 2 boys," was all his letter said, but he arrived the next day in a pieced-together truck, his wife and five daughters sitting on the floor in back, himself and the two boys in the cab.

Over the years they had been on her place, Mr. and Mrs. Greenleaf had aged hardly at all. They had no worries, no responsibilities. They lived like the lilies of the field, off the fat that she struggled to put into the land. When she was dead and gone from overwork and worry, the Greenleafs, healthy and thriving, would be just ready to begin draining Scofield and Wesley.

Wesley said the reason Mrs. Greenleaf had not aged was because she released all her emotions in prayer healing. "You ought to start praying, Sweetheart," he had said in the voice that, poor boy, he could not help making deliberately nasty.

Scofield only exasperated her beyond endurance but Wesley caused her real anxiety. He was thin and nervous and bald and being an intellectual was a terrible strain on his disposition. She doubted if he would marry until she died but she was certain that then the wrong woman would get him. Nice girls didn't like Scofield but Wesley didn't like nice girls. He didn't like anything. He drove twenty miles every day to the university where he taught and twenty miles back every night, but he said he hated the twenty-mile drive and he hated the second-rate university and he hated the morons who attended it. He hated the country and he hated the life he lived; he hated living with his mother and his idiot brother and he hated hearing about the damn dairy and the damn help and the damn broken machinery. But in spite of all he said, he never made any move to leave. He talked about Paris and Rome but he never went even to Atlanta.

"You'd go to those places and you'd get sick," Mrs. May would say. "Who in Paris is going to see that you get a salt-free diet? And do you think if you married one of those odd numbers you take out that *she* would cook a salt-free diet for you? No indeed, she would not!" When she took this line, Wesley would turn himself roughly around in his chair and ignore her. Once when she had kept it up too long, he had snarled, "Well, why don't you do something practical, Woman? Why don't you pray for me like Mrs. Greenleaf would?"

"I don't like to hear you boys make jokes about religion," she had said. "If you would go to church, you would meet some nice girls."

But it was impossible to tell them anything. When she looked at the two of them now, sitting on either side of the table, neither one caring the least if a stray bull ruined her herd—which was their herd, their future—when she looked at the two of them, one hunched over a paper and the other teetering back in his chair, grinning at her like an idiot, she wanted to jump up and beat her fist on the table and shout, "You'll find out one of these days, you'll find out what *Reality* is when it's too late!"

"Mamma," Scofield said, "don't you get excited now but I'll tell you whose bull that is." He was looking at her wickedly. He let his chair drop forward and he got up. Then with his shoulders bent and his hands held up to cover his head, he tiptoed to the door. He backed into the hall and pulled the door almost to so that it hid all of him but his face. "You want to know, Sugarpie?" he asked.

Mrs. May sat looking at him coldly.

"That's O. T. and E. T.'s bull," he said. "I collected from their nigger yesterday and he told me they were missing it," and he showed her an exaggerated expanse of teeth and disappeared silently.

Wesley looked up and laughed.

Mrs. May turned her head forward again, her expression unaltered. "I am the only *adult* on this place," she said. She leaned across the table and pulled the paper from the side of his plate. "Do you see how it's going to be when I die and you boys have to handle him?" she began. "Do you see why he didn't know whose bull that was? Because it was theirs. Do you see what I have to put up with? Do you see that if I hadn't kept my foot on his neck all these years, you boys might be milking cows every morning at four o'clock?"

Wesley pulled the paper back toward his plate and staring at her full in the face, he murmured, "I wouldn't milk a cow to save your soul from hell."

"I know you wouldn't," she said in a brittle voice. She sat back and began rapidly turning her knife over at the side of her plate. "O. T. and E. T. are fine boys," she said. "They ought to have been my sons." The thought of this was so horrible that her vision of Wesley was blurred at once by a wall of tears. All she saw was his dark shape, rising quickly from the table. "And you two," she cried, "you two should have belonged to that woman!"

He was heading for the door.

"When I die," she said in a thin voice, "I don't know what's going to become of you."

"You're always yapping about when-you-die," he growled as he rushed out, "but you look pretty healthy to me."

For some time she sat where she was, looking straight

ahead through the window across the room into a scene of indistinct greys and greens. She stretched her face and her neck muscles and drew in a long breath but the scene in front of her flowed together anyway into a watery grey mass. "They needn't think I'm going to die any time soon," she muttered, and some more defiant voice in her added: I'll die when I get good and ready.

She wiped her eyes with the table napkin and got up and went to the window and gazed at the scene in front of her. The cows were grazing on two pale green pastures across the road and behind them, fencing them in, was a black wall of trees with a sharp sawtooth edge that held off the indifferent sky. The pastures were enough to calm her. When she looked out any window in her house, she saw the reflection of her own character. Her city friends said she was the most remarkable woman they knew, to go, practically penniless and with no experience, out to a rundown farm and make a success of it. "Everything is against you," she would say, "the weather is against you and the dirt is against you and the help is against you. They're all in league against you. There's nothing for it but an iron hand!"

"Look at Mamma's iron hand!" Scofield would yell and grab her arm and hold it up so that her delicate blue-veined little hand would dangle from her wrist like the head of a broken lily. The company always laughed.

The sun, moving over the black and white grazing cows, was just a little brighter than the rest of the sky. Looking down, she saw a darker shape that might have been its shadow cast at an angle, moving among them. She uttered a sharp cry and turned and marched out of the house.

Mr. Greenleaf was in the trench silo, filling a wheelbarrow. She stood on the edge and looked down at him. "I told you to get up that bull. Now he's in with the milk herd."

"You can't do two thangs at oncet," Mr. Greenleaf remarked.

"I told you to do that first."

He wheeled the barrow out of the open end of the trench toward the barn and she followed close behind him. "And you needn't think, Mr. Greenleaf," she said, "that I don't know exactly whose bull that is or why you haven't been in any hurry to notify me he was here. I might as well feed O. T. and E. T.'s bull as long as I'm going to have him here ruining my herd."

Mr. Greenleaf paused with the wheelbarrow and looked behind him. "Is that them boys' bull?" he asked in an incredulous tone.

She did not say a word. She merely looked away with her mouth taut.

"They told me their bull was out but I never known that was him," he said.

"I want that bull put up now," she said, "and I'm going to drive over to O. T. and E. T.'s and tell them they'll have to come get him today. I ought to charge for the time he's been here—then it wouldn't happen again."

"They didn't pay but seventy-five dollars for him," Mr. Greenleaf offered.

"I wouldn't have had him as a gift," she said.

"They was just going to beef him," Mr. Greenleaf went on, "but he got loose and run his head into their pickup truck. He don't like cars and trucks. They had a time getting his horn out the fender and when they finally got him loose, he took off and they was too tired to run after him—but I never known that was him there."

"It wouldn't have paid you to know, Mr. Greenleaf," she said. "But you know now. Get a horse and get him."

In a half hour, from her front window she saw the bull, squirrel-colored, with jutting hips and long light horns, ambling down the dirt road that ran in front of the house. Mr. Greenleaf was behind him on the horse. "That's a Greenleaf bull if I ever saw one," she muttered. She went out on the porch and called, "Put him where he can't get out."

"He likes to bust loose," Mr. Greenleaf said, looking

with approval at the bull's rump. "This gentleman is a sport."

"If those boys don't come for him, he's going to be a dead sport," she said. "I'm just warning you."

He heard her but he didn't answer.

"That's the awfullest looking bull I ever saw," she called but he was too far down the road to hear.

It was mid-morning when she turned into O. T. and E. T.'s driveway. The house, a new red-brick, low-to-the-ground building that looked like a warehouse with windows, was on top of a treeless hill. The sun was beating down directly on the white roof of it. It was the kind of house that everybody built now and nothing marked it as belonging to Greenleafs except three dogs, part hound and part spitz, that rushed out from behind it as soon as she stopped her car. She reminded herself that you could always tell the class of people by the class of dog, and honked her horn. While she sat waiting for someone to come, she continued to study the house. All the windows were down and she wondered if the government could have air-conditioned the thing. No one came and she honked again. Presently a door opened and several children appeared in it and stood looking at her, making no move to come forward. She recognized this as a true Greenleaf trait—they could hang in a door, looking at you for hours.

"Can't one of you children come here?" she called.

After a minute they all began to move forward, slowly. They had on overalls and were barefooted but they were not as dirty as she might have expected. There were two or three that looked distinctly like Greenleafs; the others not so much so. The smallest child was a girl with untidy black hair. They stopped about six feet from the automobile and stood looking at her.

"You're mighty pretty," Mrs. May said, addressing herself to the smallest girl.

There was no answer. They appeared to share one dispassionate expression between them.

"Where's your Mamma?" she asked.

There was no answer to this for some time. Then one of them said something in French. Mrs. May did not speak French.

"Where's your daddy?" she asked.

After a while, one of the boys said, "He ain't hyar neither."

"Ahhhh," Mrs. May said as if something had been proven. "Where's the colored man?"

She waited and decided no one was going to answer. "The cat has six little tongues," she said. "How would you like to come home with me and let me teach you how to talk?" She laughed and her laugh died on the silent air. She felt as if she were on trial for her life, facing a jury of Greenleafs. "I'll go down and see if I can find the colored man," she said.

"You can go if you want to," one of the boys said.

"Well, thank you," she murmured and drove off.

The barn was down the lane from the house. She had not seen it before but Mr. Greenleaf had described it in detail for it had been built according to the latest specifications. It was a milking parlor arrangement where the cows are milked from below. The milk ran in pipes from the machines to the milk house and was never carried in no bucket, Mr. Greenleaf said, by no human hand. "When you gonter get you one?" he had asked.

"Mr. Greenleaf," she said, "I have to do for myself. I am not assisted hand and foot by the government. It would cost me $20,000 to install a milking parlor. I barely make ends meet as it is."

"My boys done it," Mr. Greenleaf had murmured, and then—"but all boys ain't alike."

"No indeed!" she had said. "I thank God for that!"

"I thank Gawd for ever-thang," Mr. Greenleaf had drawled.

You might as well, she had thought in the fierce silence that followed; you've never done anything for yourself.

She stopped by the side of the barn and honked but no one appeared. For several minutes she sat in the car, observing the various machines parked around, wondering how many of them were paid for. They had a forage harvester and a rotary hay baler. She had those too. She decided that since no one was here, she would get out and have a look at the milking parlor and see if they kept it clean.

She opened the milking room door and stuck her head in and for the first second she felt as if she were going to lose her breath. The spotless white concrete room was filled with sunlight that came from a row of windows head-high along both walls. The metal stanchions gleamed ferociously and she had to squint to be able to look at all. She drew her head out of the room quickly and closed the door and leaned against it, frowning. The light outside was not so bright but she was conscious that the sun was directly on top of her head, like a silver bullet ready to drop into her brain.

A Negro carrying a yellow calf-feed bucket appeared from around the corner of the machine shed and came toward her. He was a light yellow boy dressed in the cast-off army clothes of the Greenleaf twins. He stopped at a respectable distance and set the bucket on the ground.

"Where's Mr. O. T. and Mr. E. T.?" she asked.

"Mist O. T. he in town, Mist E. T. he off yonder in the field," the Negro said, pointing first to the left and then to the right as if he were naming the position of two planets.

"Can you remember a message?" she asked, looking as if she thought this doubtful.

"I'll remember it if I don't forget it," he said with a touch of sullenness.

"Well, I'll write it down then," she said. She got in her car and took a stub of pencil from her pocketbook and began to write on the back of an empty envelope. The Negro came and stood at the window. "I'm Mrs. May," she said as she wrote. "Their bull is on my place and I want him off *today*. You can tell them I'm furious about it."

"That bull lef here Sareday," the Negro said, "and none of us ain't seen him since. We ain't knowed where he was."

"Well, you know now," she said, "and you can tell Mr. O. T. and Mr. E. T. that if they don't come and get him today, I'm going to have their daddy shoot him the first thing in the morning. I can't have that bull ruining my herd." She handed him the note.

"If I knows Mist O. T. and Mist E. T.," he said, taking it, "they goin to say you go ahead on and shoot him. He done busted up one of our trucks already and we be glad to see the last of him."

She pulled her head back and gave him a look from slightly bleared eyes. "Do they expect me to take my time and my worker to shoot their bull?" she asked. "They don't want him so they just let him loose and expect somebody else to kill him? He's eating my oats and ruining my herd and I'm expected to shoot him too?"

"I speck you is," he said softly. "He done busted up . . ."

She gave him a very sharp look and said, "Well, I'm not surprised. That's just the way some people are," and after a second she asked, "Which is boss, Mr. O. T. or Mr. E. T.?" She had always suspected that they fought between themselves secretly.

"They never quarls," the boy said. "They like one man in two skins."

"Hmp. I expect you just never heard them quarrel."

"Nor nobody else heard them neither," he said, looking away as if this insolence were addressed to some one else.

"Well," she said, "I haven't put up with their father for fifteen years not to know a few things about Greenleafs."

The Negro looked at her suddenly with a gleam of recognition. "Is you my policy man's mother?" he asked.

"I don't know who your policy man is," she said sharply. "You give them that note and tell them if they don't come for that bull today, they'll be making their father shoot it tomorrow," and she drove off.

She stayed at home all afternoon waiting for the Greenleaf twins to come for the bull. They did not come. I might as well be working for them, she thought furiously. They are simply going to use me to the limit. At the supper table, she went over it again for the boys' benefit because she wanted them to see exactly what O. T. and E. T. would do. "They don't want that bull," she said, "—pass the butter— so they simply turn him loose and let somebody else worry about getting rid of him for them. How do you like that? I'm the victim. I've always been the victim."

"Pass the butter to the victim," Wesley said. He was in a worse humor than usual because he had had a flat tire on the way home from the university.

Scofield handed her the butter and said, "Why Mamma, ain't you ashamed to shoot an old bull that ain't done nothing but give you a little scrub strain in your herd? I declare," he said, "with the Mamma I got it's a wonder I turned out to be such a nice boy!"

"You ain't her boy, Son," Wesley said.

She eased back in her chair, her fingertips on the edge of the table.

"All I know is," Scofield said, "I done mighty well to be as nice as I am seeing what I come from."

When they teased her they spoke Greenleaf English but Wesley made his own particular tone come through it like a knife edge. "Well lemme tell you one thang, Brother," he said, leaning over the table, "that if you had half a mind you would already know."

"What's that, Brother?" Scofield asked, his broad face grinning into the thin constricted one across from him.

"That is," Wesley said, "that neither you nor me is her boy . . . ," but he stopped abruptly as she gave a kind of hoarse wheeze like an old horse lashed unexpectedly. She reared up and ran from the room.

"Oh, for God's sake," Wesley growled. "What did you start her off for?"

"I never started her off," Scofield said. "You started her off."

"Hah."

"She's not as young as she used to be and she can't take it."

"She can only give it out," Wesley said. "I'm the one that takes it."

His brother's pleasant face had changed so that an ugly family resemblance showed between them. "Nobody feels sorry for a lousy bastard like you," he said and grabbed across the table for the other's shirtfront.

From her room she heard a crash of dishes and she rushed back through the kitchen into the dining room. The hall door was open and Scofield was going out of it. Wesley was lying like a large bug on his back with the edge of the overturned table cutting him across the middle and broken dishes scattered on top of him. She pulled the table off him and caught his arm to help him rise but he scrambled up and pushed her off with a furious charge of energy and flung himself out of the door after his brother.

She would have collapsed but a knock on the back door stiffened her and she swung around. Across the kitchen and back porch, she could see Mr. Greenleaf peering eagerly through the screenwire. All her resources returned in full strength as if she had only needed to be challenged by the devil himself to regain them. "I heard a thump," he called, "and I thought the plastering might have fell on you."

If he had been wanted someone would have had to go on a horse to find him. She crossed the kitchen and the porch and stood inside the screen and said, "No, nothing happened but the table turned over. One of the legs was weak," and without pausing, "the boys didn't come for the bull so tomorrow you'll have to shoot him."

The sky was crossed with thin red and purple bars and behind them the sun was moving down slowly as if it were descending a ladder. Mr. Greenleaf squatted down on the step, his back to her, the top of his hat on a level with her feet. "Tomorrow I'll drive him home for you," he said.

"Oh no, Mr. Greenleaf," she said in a mocking voice, "you drive him home tomorrow and next week he'll be back here. I know better than that." Then in a mournful tone, she said, "I'm surprised at O. T. and E. T. to treat me this way. I thought they'd have more gratitude. Those boys spent some mighty happy days on this place, didn't they, Mr. Greenleaf?"

Mr. Greenleaf didn't say anything.

"I think they did," she said. "I think they did. But they've forgotten all the nice little things I did for them now. If I recall, they wore my boys' old clothes and played with my boys' old toys and hunted with my boys' old guns. They swam in my pond and shot my birds and fished in my stream and I never forgot their birthday and Christmas seemed to roll around very often if I remember it right. And do they think of any of those things now?" she asked. "NOOOOO," she said.

For a few seconds she looked at the disappearing sun and Mr. Greenleaf examined the palms of his hands. Presently as if it had just occurred to her, she asked, "Do you know the real reason they didn't come for that bull?"

"Naw I don't," Mr. Greenleaf said in a surly voice.

"They didn't come because I'm a woman," she said. "You can get away with anything when you're dealing with a woman. If there were a man running this place . . ."

Quick as a snake striking Mr. Greenleaf said, "You got two boys. They know you got two men on the place."

The sun had disappeared behind the tree line. She looked down at the dark crafty face, upturned now, and at the wary eyes, bright under the shadow of the hatbrim. She waited long enough for him to see that she was hurt and then she said, "Some people learn gratitude too late, Mr. Greenleaf, and some never learn it at all," and she turned and left him sitting on the steps.

Half the night in her sleep she heard a sound as if some large stone were grinding a hole on the outside wall of her brain. She was walking on the inside, over a succession of beautiful rolling hills, planting her stick in front of each step. She became aware after a time that the noise was the sun trying to burn through the tree line and she stopped to watch, safe in the knowledge that it couldn't, that it had to sink the way it always did outside of her property. When she first stopped it was a swollen red ball, but as she stood watching it began to narrow and pale until it looked like a bullet. Then suddenly it burst through the tree line and raced down the hill toward her. She woke up with her hand over her mouth and the same noise, diminished but distinct, in her ear. It was the bull munching under her window. Mr. Greenleaf had let him out.

She got up and made her way to the window in the dark and looked out through the slit blind, but the bull had moved away from the hedge and at first she didn't see him. Then she saw a heavy form some distance away, paused as if observing her. This is the last night I am going to put up with this, she said, and watched until the iron shadow moved away in the darkness.

The next morning she waited until exactly eleven o'clock. Then she got in her car and drove to the barn. Mr. Greenleaf was cleaning milk cans. He had seven of them standing up outside the milk room to get the sun. She had been telling him to do this for two weeks. "All right, Mr. Greenleaf," she said, "go get your gun. We're going to shoot that bull."

"I thought you wanted theseyer cans . . ."

"Go get your gun, Mr. Greenleaf," she said. Her voice and face were expressionless.

"That gentleman torn out of there last night," he murmured in a tone of regret and bent again to the can he had his arm in.

"Go get your gun, Mr. Greenleaf," she said in the same triumphant toneless voice. "The bull is in the pasture with the dry cows. I saw him from my upstairs window. I'm going to drive you up to the field and you can run him into the empty pasture and shoot him there."

He detached himself from the can slowly. "Ain't nobody ever ast me to shoot my boys' own bull!" he said in a high rasping voice. He removed the rag from his back pocket and began to wipe his hands violently, then his nose.

She turned as if she had not heard this and said, "I'll wait for you in the car. Go get your gun."

She sat in the car and watched him stalk off toward the harness room where he kept a gun. After he had entered the room, there was a crash as if he had kicked something out of his way. Presently he emerged again with the gun, circled behind the car, opened the door violently and threw himself onto the seat beside her. He held the gun between his knees and looked straight ahead. He'd like to shoot me instead of the bull, she thought, and turned her face away so that he could not see her smile.

The morning was dry and clear. She drove through the woods for a quarter of a mile and then out into the open where there were fields on either side of the narrow road. The exhilaration of carrying her point had sharpened her senses. Birds were screaming everywhere, the grass was almost too bright to look at, the sky was an even piercing blue. "Spring is here!" she said gaily. Mr. Greenleaf lifted one muscle somewhere near his mouth as if he found this the most asinine remark ever made. When she stopped at the second pasture gate, he flung himself out of the car door and slammed it behind him. Then he opened the gate and she drove through. He closed it and flung himself back in, silently, and she drove around the rim of the pasture until she spotted the bull, almost in the center of it, grazing peacefully among the cows.

"The gentleman is waiting on you," she said and gave Mr. Greenleaf's furious profile a sly look. "Run him into that next pasture and when you get him in, I'll drive in behind you and shut the gate myself."

He flung himself out again, this time deliberately leaving

the car door open so that she had to lean across the seat and close it. She sat smiling as she watched him make his way across the pasture toward the opposite gate. He seemed to throw himself forward at each step and then pull back as if he were calling on some power to witness that he was being forced. "Well," she said aloud as if he were still in the car, "it's your own boys who are making you do this, Mr. Greenleaf." O. T. and E. T. were probably splitting their sides laughing at him now. She could hear their identical nasal voices saying, "Made Daddy shoot our bull for us. Daddy don't know no better than to think that's a fine bull he's shooting. Gonna kill Daddy to shoot that bull!"

"If those boys cared a thing about you, Mr. Greenleaf," she said, "they would have come for that bull. I'm surprised at them."

He was circling around to open the gate first. The bull, dark among the spotted cows, had not moved. He kept his head down, eating constantly. Mr. Greenleaf opened the gate and then began circling back to approach him from the rear. When he was about ten feet behind him, he flapped his arms at his sides. The bull lifted his head indolently and then lowered it again and continued to eat. Mr. Greenleaf stooped again and picked up something and threw it at him with a vicious swing. She decided it was a sharp rock for the bull leapt and then began to gallop until he disappeared over the rim of the hill. Mr. Greenleaf followed at his leisure.

"You needn't think you're going to lose him!" she cried and started the car straight across the pasture. She had to drive slowly over the terraces and when she reached the gate, Mr. Greenleaf and the bull were nowhere in sight. This pasture was smaller than the last, a green arena, encircled almost entirely by woods. She got out and closed the gate and stood looking for some sign of Mr. Greenleaf but he had disappeared completely. She knew at once that his plan was to lose the bull in the woods. Eventually, she would see him emerge somewhere from the circle of trees and come limping toward her and when he finally reached her, he would say, "If you can find that gentleman in them woods, you're better than me."

She was going to say, "Mr. Greenleaf, if I have to walk into those woods with you and stay all afternoon, we are going to find that bull and shoot him. You are going to shoot him if I have to pull the trigger for you." When he saw she meant business he would return and shoot the bull quickly himself.

She got back into the car and drove to the center of the pasture where he would not have so far to walk to reach her when he came out of the woods. At this moment she could picture him sitting on a stump, marking lines in the ground with a stick. She decided she would wait exactly ten minutes by her watch. Then she would begin to honk. She got out of the car and walked around a little and then sat down on the front bumper to wait and rest. She was very tired and she lay her head back against the hood and closed her eyes. She did not understand why she should be so tired when it was only mid-morning. Through her closed eyes, she could feel the sun, red-hot overhead. She opened her eyes slightly but the white light forced her to close them again.

For some time she lay back against the hood, wondering drowsily why she was so tired. With her eyes closed, she didn't think of time as divided into days and nights but into past and future. She decided she was tired because she had been working continuously for fifteen years. She decided she had every right to be tired, and to rest for a few minutes before she began working again. Before any kind of judgement seat, she would be able to say: I've worked, I have not wallowed. At this very instant while she was recalling a lifetime of work, Mr. Greenleaf was loitering in the woods and Mrs. Greenleaf was probably flat on the ground, asleep over her holeful of clippings. The woman had got worse over the years and Mrs. May believed that now she was actually demented. "I'm afraid your wife has let religion warp her," she said once tactfully to Mr. Greenleaf. "Everything in moderation, you know."

"She cured a man oncet that half his gut was eat out with worms," Mr. Greenleaf said, and she had turned away, half-sickened. Poor souls, she thought now, so simple. For a few seconds she dozed.

When she sat up and looked at her watch, more than ten minutes had passed. She had not heard any shot. A new thought occurred to her: suppose Mr. Greenleaf had aroused the bull chunking stones at him and the animal had turned on him and run him up against a tree and gored him? The irony of it deepened: O. T. and E. T. would then get a shyster lawyer and sue her. It would be the fitting end to her fifteen years with the Greenleafs. She thought of it almost with pleasure as if she had hit on the perfect ending for a story she was telling her friends. Then she dropped it, for Mr. Greenleaf had a gun with him and she had insurance.

She decided to honk. She got up and reached inside the car window and gave three sustained honks and two or three shorter ones to let him know she was getting impatient. Then she went back and sat down on the bumper again.

In a few minutes something emerged from the tree line, a black heavy shadow that tossed its head several times and then bounded forward. After a second she saw it was the bull. He was crossing the pasture toward her at a slow gallop, a gay almost rocking gait as if he were overjoyed to find her again. She looked beyond him to see if Mr. Greenleaf was coming out of the woods too but he was not. "Here he is, Mr. Greenleaf!" she called and looked on the other side of the pasture to see if he could be coming out there but he was not in sight. She looked back and saw that the bull, his head lowered, was racing toward her. She remained perfectly still, not in fright, but in a freezing unbelief. She stared at the violent black streak bounding toward her as if she had no sense of distance, as if she could not decide at once what his intention was, and the bull had buried his head in her lap, like a wild tormented lover, before her expression changed. One of his horns sank until it pierced her heart and the other curved around her side and held her in an unbreakable grip. She continued to stare straight ahead but the entire scene in front of her had changed—the tree line was a dark wound in a world that was nothing but sky—and she had the look of a person whose sight had been suddenly restored but who finds the light unbearable.

Mr. Greenleaf was running toward her from the side with his gun raised and she saw him coming though she was not looking in his direction. She saw him approaching on the outside of some invisible circle, the tree line gaping behind him and nothing under his feet. He shot the bull four times through the eye. She did not hear the shots but she felt the quake in the huge body as it sank, pulling her forward on its head, so that she seemed, when Mr. Greenleaf reached her, to be bent over whispering some last discovery into the animal's ear.

WHY I LIVE AT THE P.O.

by Eudora Welty

Eudora Welty (1909–   ) was born in Jackson, Mississippi, the scene of much of her work. Miss Welty's early ambition to paint gave way to an interest in writing when she was still quite young. She attended the Mississippi State College for Women before going North to take her bachelor's degree from the University of Wisconsin. In 1941 her first book of short stories, *A Curtain of Green,* was enthusiastically received by the critics. She has since published many stories and four novels, *Delta Wedding* (1946), *The Ponder Heart* (1953), *Losing Battles* (1970), and *The Optimist's Daughter* (1972) for which she was awarded the Pulitzer Prize for fiction. One of our most distinguished Southern writers, her work has received many honors and awards, including the Howells Medal, awarded every five years for outstanding fiction.

I was getting along fine with Mama, Papa-Daddy and Uncle Rondo until my sister Stella-Rondo just separated from her husband and came back home again. Mr. Whitaker! Of course I went with Mr. Whitaker first, when he first appeared here in China Grove, taking "Pose Yourself" photos, and Stella-Rondo broke us up. Told him I was one-sided. Bigger on one side than the other, which is a deliberate, calculated falsehood: I'm the same. Stella-Rondo is exactly twelve months to the day younger than I am and for that reason she's spoiled.

She's always had anything in the world she wanted and then she'd throw it away. Papa-Daddy gave her this gorgeous Add-a-Pearl necklace when she was eight years old and she threw it away playing baseball when she was nine, with only two pearls.

So as soon as she got married and moved away from home the first thing she did was separate! From Mr. Whitaker! This photographer with the popeyes she said she trusted. Came home from one of those towns up in Illinois and to our complete surprise brought this child of two.

Mama said she like to made her drop dead for a second. "Here you had this marvelous blonde child and never so much as wrote your mother a word about it," says Mama. "I'm thoroughly ashamed of you." But of course she wasn't.

Stella-Rondo just calmly takes off this *hat*, I wish you could see it. She says, "Why, Mama, Shirley-T.'s adopted, I can prove it."

"How?" says Mama, but all I says was, "H'm!" There I was over the hot stove, trying to stretch two chickens over five people and a completely unexpected child into the bargain, without one moment's notice.

"What do you mean—'H'm'?" says Stella-Rondo, and Mama says, "I heard that, Sister."

I said that oh, I didn't mean a thing, only that whoever Shirley-T. was, she was the spit-image of Papa-Daddy if he'd cut off his beard, which of course he'd never do in the world. Papa-Daddy's Mama's papa and sulks.

Stella-Rondo got furious! She said, "Sister, I don't need to tell you you got a lot of nerve and always did have and I'll thank you to make no future reference to my adopted child whatsoever."

"Very well," I said. "Very well, very well. Of course I noticed at once she looks like Mr. Whitaker's side too. That frown. She looks like a cross between Mr. Whitaker and Papa-Daddy."

"Well, all I can say is she isn't."

"She looks exactly like Shirley Temple to me," says Mama, but Shirley-T. just ran away from her.

So the first thing Stella-Rondo did at the table was turn Papa-Daddy against me.

"Papa-Daddy," she says. He was trying to cut up his meat. "Papa-Daddy!" I was taken completely by surprise. Papa-Daddy is about a million years old and's got this long-long beard. "Papa-Daddy, Sister says she fails to understand why you don't cut off your beard."

So Papa-Daddy l-a-y-s down his knife and fork! He's real rich. Mama says he is, he says he isn't. So he says, "Have I heard correctly? You don't understand why I don't cut off my beard?"

"Why," I says, "Papa-Daddy, of course I understand, I did not say any such of a thing, the idea!"

He says, "Hussy!"

I says, "Papa-Daddy, you know I wouldn't any more want you to cut off your beard than the man in the moon. It was the farthest thing from my mind! Stella-Rondo sat there and made that up while she was eating breast of chicken."

But he says, "So the postmistress fails to understand why I don't cut off my beard. Which job I got you through my influence with the government. 'Bird's nest'—is that what you call it?"

, Not that it isn't the next to smallest P.O. in the entire state of Mississippi.

I says, "Oh, Papa-Daddy," I says, "I didn't say any such of a thing, I never dreamed it was a bird's nest, I have always been grateful though this is the next to smallest P.O. in the state of Mississippi, and I do not enjoy being referred to as a hussy by my own grandfather."

But Stella-Rondo says, "Yes, you did say it too. Anybody in the world could of heard you, that had ears."

"Stop right there," says Mama, looking at *me*.

So I pulled my napkin straight back through the napkin ring and left the table.

As soon as I was out of the room Mama says, "Call her back, or she'll starve to death," but Papa-Daddy says, "This is the beard I started growing on the Coast when I was fifteen years old." He would of gone on till nightfall if Shirley-T. hadn't lost the Milky Way she ate in Cairo.

So Papa-Daddy says, "I am going out and lie in the hammock, and you can all sit here and remember my words: I'll never cut off my beard as long as I live, even one inch, and I don't appreciate it in you at all." Passed right by me in the hall and went straight out and got in the hammock.

It would be a holiday. It wasn't five minutes before Uncle Rondo suddenly appeared in the hall in one of Stella-Rondo's flesh-colored kimonos, all cut on the bias, like something Mr. Whitaker probably thought was gorgeous.

"Uncle Rondo!" I says. "I didn't know who that was! Where are you going?"

"Sister," he says, "get out of my way, I'm poisoned."

"If you're poisoned stay away from Papa-Daddy," I says. "Keep out of the hammock. Papa-Daddy will certainly beat you on the head if you come within forty miles of him. He thinks I deliberately said he ought to cut off his beard after he got me the P.O., and I've told him and told him and told him, and he acts like he just don't hear me. Papa-Daddy must of gone stone deaf."

"He picked a fine day to do it then," says Uncle Rondo, and before you could say "Jack Robinson" flew out in the yard.

What he'd really done, he'd drunk another bottle of that prescription. He does it every single Fourth of July as sure as shooting, and it's horribly expensive. Then he falls over in the hammock and snores. So he insisted on zigzagging right on out to the hammock, looking like a half-wit.

Papa-Daddy woke up with this horrible yell and right there without moving an inch he tried to turn Uncle Rondo against me. I heard every word he said. Oh, he told Uncle Rondo I didn't learn to read till I was eight years old and he didn't see how in the world I ever got the mail put up at the P.O., much less read it all, and he said if Uncle Rondo could only fathom the lengths he had gone to to get me that job! And he said on the other hand he thought Stella-Rondo had a brilliant mind and deserved credit for getting out of town. All the time he was just lying there swinging as pretty as you please and looping out his beard, and poor Uncle Rondo was *pleading* with him to slow down the hammock, it was making him as dizzy as a witch to watch it. But that's what Papa-Daddy likes about a hammock. So Uncle Rondo was too dizzy to get turned against me for the time being. He's Mama's only brother and is a good case of a one-track mind. Ask anybody. A certified pharmacist.

Just then I heard Stella-Rondo raising the upstairs window. While she was married she got this peculiar idea that it's cooler with the windows shut and locked. So she has to raise the window before she can make a soul hear her outdoors.

So she raises the window and says, *"Oh!"* You would have thought she was mortally wounded.

Uncle Rondo and Papa-Daddy didn't even look up, but kept right on with what they were doing. I had to laugh.

I flew up the stairs and threw the door open! I says, "What in the wide world's the matter, Stella-Rondo? You mortally wounded?"

"No," she says, "I am not mortally wounded but I wish you would do me the favor of looking out that window there and telling me what you see."

So I shade my eyes and look out the window.

"I see the front yard," I says.

"Don't you see any human beings?" she says.

"I see Uncle Rondo trying to run Papa-Daddy out of the hammock," I says. "Nothing more. Naturally, it's so suffocating-hot in the house, with all the windows shut and locked, everybody who cares to stay in their right mind will

have to go out and get in the hammock before the Fourth
of July is over."

"Don't you notice anything different about Uncle Rondo?" asks Stella-Rondo.

"Why no, except he's got on some terrible-looking flesh-
colored contrapticn I wouldn't be found dead in, is all I can
see," I says.

"Never mind, you won't be found dead in it, because it
happens to be part of my trousseau, and Mr. Whitaker took
several dozen photographs of me in it," says Stella-Rondo.
"What on earth could Uncle Rondo *mean* by wearing part
of my trousseau out in the broad open daylight without saying so much as 'Kiss my foot,' *knowing* I only got home this
morning after my separation and hung my negligee up on
the bathroom door, just as nervous as I could be?"

"I'm sure I don't know, and what do you expect me to do
about it?" I says. "Jump out the window?"

"No, I expect nothing of the kind. I simply declare that
Uncle Rondo looks like a fool in it, that's all," she says. "It
makes me sick to my stomach."

"Well, he looks as good as he can," I says. "As good as
anybody in reason could." I stood up for Uncle Rondo,
please remember. And I said to Stella-Rondo, "I think I
would do well not to criticize so freely if I were you and
came home with a two-year-old child I had never said a
word about, and no explanation whatever about my
separation."

"I asked you the instant I entered this house not to refer
one more time to my adopted child, and you gave me your
word of honor you would not," was all Stella-Rondo would
say, and started pulling out every one of her eyebrows with
some cheap Kress tweezers.

So I merely slammed the door behind me and went down
and made some green-tomato pickle. Somebody had to do it.
Of course Mama had turned both the niggers loose; she always said no earthly power could hold one anyway on the
Fourth of July, so she wouldn't even try. It turned out that

Jaypan fell in the lake and came within a very narrow limit of drowning.

So Mama trots in. Lifts up the lid and says, "H'm! Not very good for your Uncle Rondo in his precarious condition, I must say. Or poor little adopted Shirley-T. Shame on you!"

That made me tired. I says, "Well, Stella-Rondo had better thank her lucky stars it was her instead of me came trotting in with that very peculiar-looking child. Now if it had been me that trotted in from Illinois and brought a peculiar-looking child of two, I shudder to think of the reception I'd of got, much less controlled the diet of an entire family."

"But you must remember, Sister, that you were never married to Mr. Whitaker in the first place and didn't go up to Illinois to live," says Mama, shaking a spoon in my face. "If you had I would of been just as overjoyed to see you and your little adopted girl as I was to see Stella-Rondo, when you wound up with your separation and came on back home."

"You would not," I says.

"Don't contradict me, I would," says Mama.

But I said she couldn't convince me though she talked till she was blue in the face. Then I said, "Besides, you know as well as I do that that child is not adopted."

"She most certainly is adopted," says Mama, stiff as a poker.

I says, "Why, Mama, Stella-Rondo had her just as sure as anything in this world, and just too stuck up to admit it."

"Why, Sister," said Mama. "Here I thought we were going to have a pleasant Fourth of July, and you start right out not believing a word your own baby sister tells you!"

"Just like Cousin Annie Flo. Went to her grave denying the facts of life," I reminded Mama.

"I told you if you ever mentioned Annie Flo's name I'd slap your face," says Mama, and slaps my face.

"All right, you wait and see," I says.

"I," says Mama, "*I* prefer to take my children's word for

anything when it's humanly possible." You ought to see Mama, she weighs two hundred pounds and has real tiny feet.

Just then something perfectly horrible occurred to me.

"Mama," I says, "can that child talk?" I simply had to whisper! "Mama, I wonder if that child can be—you know —in any way? Do you realize," I says, "that she hasn't spoken one single, solitary word to a human being up to this minute? This is the way she looks," I says, and I looked like this.

Well, Mama and I just stood there and stared at each other. It was horrible!

"I remember well that Joe Whitaker frequently drank like a fish," says Mama. "I believed to my soul he drank *chemicals*." And without another word she marches to the foot of the stairs and calls Stella-Rondo.

"Stella-Rondo? O-o-o-o-o! Stella-Rondo!"

"What?" says Stella-Rondo from upstairs. Not even the grace to get up off the bed.

"Can that child of yours talk?" asks Mama.

Stella-Rondo says, "Can she what?"

"Talk! Talk!" says Mama. "Burdyburdyburdyburdy!"

So Stella-Rondo yells back, "Who says she can't talk?"

"Sister says so," says Mama.

"You didn't have to tell me, I know whose word of honor don't mean a thing in this house," says Stella-Rondo.

And in a minute the loudest Yankee voice I ever heard in my life yells out, "OE'm Pop-OE the Sailor-r-r-r Ma-a-an!" and then somebody jumps up and down in the upstairs hall. In another second the house would of fallen down.

"Not only talks, she can tap-dance!" calls Stella-Rondo. "Which is more than some people I won't name can do."

"Why, the little precious darling thing!" Mama says, so surprised. "Just as smart as she can be!" Starts talking baby talk right there. Then she turns on me. "Sister, you ought to be thoroughly ashamed! Run upstairs this instant and apologize to Stella-Rondo and Shirley-T."

"Apologize for what?" I says. "I merely wondered if the child was normal, that's all. Now that she's proved she is, why, I have nothing further to say."

But Mama just turned on her heel and flew out, furious. She ran right upstairs and hugged the baby. She believed it was adopted. Stella-Rondo hadn't done a thing but turn her against me from upstairs while I stood there helpless over the hot stove. So that made Mama, Papa-Daddy and the baby all on Stella-Rondo's side.

Next, Uncle Rondo.

I must say that Uncle Rondo has been marvelous to me at various times in the past and I was completely unprepared to be made to jump out of my skin, the way it turned out. Once Stella-Rondo did something perfectly horrible to him—broke a chain letter from Flanders Field—and he took the radio back he had given her and gave it to me. Stella-Rondo was furious! For six months we all had to call her Stella instead of Stella-Rondo, or she wouldn't answer. I always thought Uncle Rondo had all the brains of the entire family. Another time he sent me to Mammoth Cave, with all expenses paid.

But this would be the day he was drinking that prescription, the Fourth of July.

So at supper Stella-Rondo speaks up and says she thinks Uncle Rondo ought to try to eat a little something. So finally Uncle Rondo said he would try a little cold biscuits and ketchup, but that was all. So *she* brought it to him.

"Do you think it wise to disport with ketchup in Stella-Rondo's flesh-colored kimono?" I says. Trying to be considerate! If Stella-Rondo couldn't watch out for her trousseau, somebody had to.

"Any objections?" asks Uncle Rondo, just about to pour out all the ketchup.

"Don't mind what she says, Uncle Rondo," says Stella-Rondo. "Sister has been devoting this solid afternoon to sneering out my bedroom window at the way you look."

"What's that?" says Uncle Rondo. Uncle Rondo has got

the most terrible temper in the world. Anything is liable to make him tear the house down if it comes at the wrong time.

So Stella-Rondo says, "Sister says 'Uncle Rondo certainly does look like a fool in that pink kimono!' "

Do you remember who it was really said that?

Uncle Rondo spills out all the ketchup and jumps out of his chair and tears off the kimono and throws it down on the dirty floor and puts his foot on it. It had to be sent all the way to Jackson to the cleaners and re-pleated.

"So that's your opinion of your Uncle Rondo, is it?" he says. "I look like a fool, do I? Well, that's the last straw. A whole day in this house with nothing to do, and then to hear you come out with a remark like that behind my back!"

"I didn't say any such of a thing, Uncle Rondo," I says, "and I'm not saying who did, either. Why, I think you look all right. Just try to take care of yourself and not talk and eat at the same time," I says. "I think you better go lie down."

"Lie down my foot," says Uncle Rondo. I ought to of known by that he was fixing to do something perfectly horrible.

So he didn't do anything that night in the precarious state he was in—just played Casino with Mama and Stella-Rondo and Shirley-T. and gave Shirley-T. a nickel with a head on both sides. It tickled her nearly to death, and she called him "Papa." But at 6:30 A.M. the next morning, he threw a whole five-cent package of some unsold one-inch firecrackers from the store as hard as he could into my bedroom and they every one went off. Not one bad one in the string. Anybody else, there'd be one that wouldn't go off.

Well, I'm just terribly susceptible to noise of any kind, the doctor has always told me I was the most sensitive person he had ever seen in his whole life, and I was simply prostrated. I couldn't eat! People tell me they heard it as far as the cemetery, and old Aunt Jep Patterson, that had been holding her own so good, thought it was Judgment Day and she was going to meet her whole family. It's usually so quiet here.

And I'll tell you it didn't take me any longer than a minute to make up my mind what to do. There I was with the whole entire house on Stella-Rondo's side and turned against me. If I have anything at all I have pride.

So I just decided I'd go straight down to the P.O. There's plenty of room there in the back, I says to myself.

Well! I made no bones about letting the family catch on to what I was up to. I didn't try to conceal it.

The first thing they knew, I marched in where they were all playing Old Maid and pulled the electric oscillating fan out by the plug, and everything got real hot. Next I snatched the pillow I'd done the needle-point on right off the davenport from behind Papa-Daddy. He went "Ugh!" I beat Stella-Rondo up the stairs and finally found my charm bracelet in her bureau drawer under a picture of Nelson Eddy.

"So that's the way the land lies," says Uncle Rondo. There he was, piecing on the ham. "Well, Sister, I'll be glad to donate my army cot if you got any place to set it up, providing you'll leave right this minute and let me get some peace." Uncle Rondo was in France.

"Thank you kindly for the cot and 'peace' is hardly the word I would select if I had to resort to firecrackers at 6:30 A.M. in a young girl's bedroom," I says back to him. "And as to where I intend to go, you seem to forget my position as postmistress of China Grove, Mississippi," I says. "I've always got the P.O."

Well, that made them all sit up and take notice.

I went out front and started digging up some four-o'clocks to plant around the P.O.

"Ah-ah-ah!" says Mama, raising the window. "Those happen to be my four-o'clocks. Everything planted in that star is mine. I've never known you to make anything grow in your life."

"Very well," I says. "But I take the fern. Even you,

Mama, can't stand there and deny that I'm the one watered that fern. And I happen to know where I can send in a box top and get a packet of one thousand mixed seeds, no two the same kind, free."

"Oh, where?" Mama wants to know.

But I says, "Too late. You 'tend to your house, and I'll 'tend to mine. You hear things like that all the time if you know how to listen to the radio. Perfectly marvelous offers. Get anything you want free."

So I hope to tell you I marched in and got that radio, and they could of all bit a nail in two, especially Stella-Rondo, that it used to belong to, and she well knew she couldn't get it back, I'd sue for it like a shot. And I very politely took the sewing-machine motor I helped pay the most on to give Mama for Christmas back in 1929, and a good big calendar, with the first-aid remedies on it. The thermometer and the Hawaiian ukulele certainly were rightfully mine, and I stood on the stepladder and got all my watermelon-rind preserves and every fruit and vegetable I'd put up, every jar. Then I began to pull the tacks out of the bluebird wall vases on the archway to the dining room.

"Who told you you could have those, Miss Priss?" says Mama, fanning as hard as she could.

"I bought 'em and I'll keep track of 'em," I says. "I'll tack 'em up one on each side of the post-office window, and you can see 'em when you come to ask me for your mail, if you're so dead to see 'em."

"Not I! I'll never darken the door to that post office again if I live to be a hundred," Mama says. "Ungrateful child! After all the money we spent on you at the Normal."

"Me either," says Stella-Rondo. "You can just let my mail lie there and *rot,* for all I care. I'll never come and relieve you of a single, solitary piece."

"I should worry," I says. "And who you think's going to sit down and write you all those big fat letters and postcards, by the way? Mr. Whitaker? Just because he was the only man ever dropped down in China Grove and you got him——

unfairly—is he going to sit down and write you a lengthy correspondence after you come home giving no rhyme nor reason whatsoever for your separation and no explanation for the presence of that child? I may not have your brilliant mind, but I fail to see it."

So Mama says, "Sister, I've told you a thousand times that Stella-Rondo simply got homesick, and this child is far too big to be hers," and she says, "Now, why don't you all just sit down and play Casino?"

Then Shirley-T. sticks out her tongue at me in this perfectly horrible way. She has no more manners than the man in the moon. I told her she was going to cross her eyes like that some day and they'd stick.

"It's too late to stop me now," I says. "You should have tried that yesterday. I'm going to the P.O. and the only way you can possibly see me is to visit me there."

So Papa-Daddy says, "You'll never catch me setting foot in that post office, even if I should take a notion into my head to write a letter some place." He says, "I won't have you reachin' out of that little old window with a pair of shears and cuttin' off any beard of mine. I'm too smart for you!"

"We all are," says Stella-Rondo.

But I said, "If you're so smart, where's Mr. Whitaker?"

So then Uncle Rondo says, "I'll thank you from now on to stop reading all the orders I get on postcards and telling everybody in China Grove what you think is the matter with them," but I says, "I draw my own conclusions and will continue in the future to draw them." I says, "If people want to write their inmost secrets on penny postcards, there's nothing in the wide world you can do about it, Uncle Rondo."

"And if you think we'll ever *write* another postcard you're sadly mistaken," says Mama.

"Cutting off your nose to spite your face then," I says. "But if you're all determined to have no more to do with the U. S. mail, think of this: What will Stella-Rondo do now, if she wants to tell Mr. Whitaker to come after her?"

"Wah!" says Stella-Rondo. I knew she'd cry. She had a conniption fit right there in the kitchen.

"It will be interesting to see how long she holds out," I says. "And now—I am leaving."

"Good-bye," says Uncle Rondo.

"Oh, I declare," says Mama, "to think that a family of mine should quarrel on the Fourth of July, or the day after, over Stella-Rondo leaving old Mr. Whitaker and having the sweetest little adopted child! It looks like we'd all be glad!"

"Wah!" says Stella-Rondo, and has a fresh conniption fit.

"*He* left *her*—you mark my words," I says. "That's Mr. Whitaker. I know Mr. Whitaker. After all, I knew him first. I said from the beginning he'd up and leave rer. I foretold every single thing that's happened."

"Where did he go?" asks Mama.

"Probably to the North Pole, if he knows what's good for him," I says.

But Stella-Rondo just bawled and wouldn't say another word. She flew to her room and slammed the door.

"Now look what you've gone and done, Sister," says Mama. "You go apologize."

"I haven't got time, I'm leaving," I says.

"Well, what are you waiting around for?" asks Uncle Rondo.

So I just picked up the kitchen clock and marched off, without saying "Kiss my foot" or anything, and never did tell Stella-Rondo good-bye.

There was a nigger girl going along on a little wagon right in front.

"Nigger girl," I says, "come help me haul these things down the hill, I'm going to live in the post office."

Took her nine trips in her express wagon. Uncle Rondo came out on the porch and threw her a nickel.

And that's the last I've laid eyes on any of my family or my family laid eyes on me for five solid days and nights. Stella-Rondo may be telling the most horrible tales in the world about Mr. Whitaker, but I haven't heard them. As I tell everybody, I draw my own conclusions.

But oh, I like it here. It's ideal, as I've been saying. You see, I've got everything cater-cornered, the way I like it. Hear the radio? All the war news. Radio, sewing machine, book ends, ironing board and that great big piano lamp—peace, that's what I like. Butter-bean vines planted all along the front where the strings are.

Of course, there's not much mail. My family are naturally the main people in China Grove, and if they prefer to vanish from the face of the earth, for all the mail they get or the mail they write, why, I'm not going to open my mouth. Some of the folks here in town are taking up for me and some turned against me. I know which is which. There are always people who will quit buying stamps just to get on the right side of Papa-Daddy.

But here I am, and here I'll stay, I want the world to know I'm happy.

And if Stella-Rondo should come to me this minute, on bended knees, and *attempt* to explain the incidents of her life with Mr. Whitaker, I'd simply put my fingers in both my ears and refuse to listen.

THE FANCY WOMAN

by Peter Taylor

Peter Taylor (1917–   ). Born in Trenton, Tennessee, Taylor attended Vanderbilt University and Kenyon College, and has taught creative writing courses at Ohio State University and at the University of North Carolina at Greensboro. His stories have appeared in many literary quarterlies and in *The New Yorker,* and in several collections of his work, notably *Miss Leonora When Last Seen* and *In the Miro District and Other Stories.*

He wanted no more of her drunken palaver. Well, sure enough. Sure enough. And he had sent her from the table like she were one of his half-grown brats. *He,* who couldn't have walked straight around to her place if she *hadn't* been lady enough to leave, sent *her* from the table like either of the half-grown kids he was so mortally fond of. At least she hadn't turned over three glasses of perfectly good stuff during one meal. Talk about vulgar. She fell across the counterpane and slept.

She awoke in the dark room with his big hands busying with her clothes, and she flung her arms about his neck. "Not a stitch on y', have you?" she said. And she said, "You marvelous, fattish thing."

His hoarse voice was in her ear, "You like it?" He chuckled deep in his throat, and she whispered:

"You're an old thing-a-ma-gig, George."

Reprinted by permission of the author.

Her eyes opened in the midday sunlight, and she felt the back of her neck soaking in her own sweat on the counterpane. She saw the unfamiliar cracks in the ceiling and said, "Whose room's this?" She looked at the walnut dresser and the wardrobe and said, "Oh, the kids' room"; and as she laughed, saliva bubbled up and fell back on her upper lip. She shoved herself up with her elbows and was sitting in the middle of the bed. Damn him! Her blue silk dress was twisted about her body, and a thin army blanket covered her lower half. "He didn't put that over me, I know damn well. One of those tight-mouth niggers sneaking around!" She sprang from the bed, slipped her bare feet into her white pumps and stepped toward the door. Oh, God! She beheld herself in the dresser mirror.

She stalked to the dresser with her eyes closed and felt about for a brush. There was nothing but a tray of collar buttons there. She grabbed a handful of them and screamed as she threw them to bounce off the mirror, "This ain't my room!" She ran her fingers through her hair and went out into the hall and into her room next door. She rushed to her little dressing table. There was the bottle half full. She poured out a jigger and drank it. Clearing her throat as she sat down, she said, "Oh, what's the matter with me?" She combed her hair back quite carefully, then pulled the yellow strands out of the amber comb; and when she had greased and wiped her face and had rouged her lips and the upper portions of her cheeks, she smiled at herself in the mirror. She looked flirtatiously at the bottle but shook her head and stood up and looked about the room. It was a long, narrow room with two windows at the end. A cubbyhole beside the kids' room! Yet it *was* a canopied bed with yellow ruffles that matched the ruffles on the dressing table and on the window curtains. She went over and turned back the covers and mussed the pillow. It might not have been the niggers! She poured another drink and went down to get some nice, hot lunch.

The breakfast room was one step lower than the rest of the house, and it was all windows. But the Venetian blinds were lowered all round, and she sat at a big circular table. "I can't make out about this room," she said to the negress who was refilling her coffee-cup. She lit a cigarette and questioned the servant, "What's the crazy table made out of, Amelia?"

"It makes a good table, 'spite all."

"It sure enough does make a strong table, Amelia." She kicked the toe of her shoe against the brick column which supported the table top. "But what *was* it, old dearie?" She smiled invitingly at the servant and pushed her plate away and pulled her coffee in front of her. She stared at the straight scar on Amelia's wrist as Amelia reached for the plate. What big black buck had put it there? A lot these niggers had to complain of in her when every one of them was all dosed up.

Amelia said that the base of the table was the old cistern. "He brung that top out f'om Memphis when he done the po'ch up this way for breakfast and lunch."

The woman looked about the room, thinking, "I'll get some confab out of this one yet." And she exclaimed, "Oh, and that's the old bucket to it over there, then, with the vines on it, Amelia!"

"No'm," Amelia said. Then after a few seconds she added, "They brung that out f'om town and put it there like it was it."

"Yeah . . . yeah . . . go on, Amelia. I'm odd about old-fashioned things. I've got a lot of interest in any antiques."

"That's all."

The little negro woman started away with the coffee-pot and the plate, dragging the soft soles of her carpet slippers over the brick floor. At the door she lingered, and, too cunning to leave room for a charge of impudence, she added to the hateful "That's all" a mutter, "Miss Josephine."

And when the door closed, Miss Josephine said under her

breath, "If that black bitch hadn't stuck that on, there wouldn't be another chance for her to sneak around with army blankets."

George, mounted on a big sorrel and leading a small dapple-gray horse, rode onto the lawn outside the breakfast room. Josephine saw him through the slits of the blinds looking up toward her bedroom window. "Not for me," she said to herself. "He'll not get *me* on one of those animals." She swallowed the last of her coffee on her feet and then turned and stomped across the bricks to the step-up into the hallway. There she heard him calling:

"Josie! Josie! Get out-a that bed!"

Josephine ran through the long hall cursing the rugs that slipped under her feet. She ran the length of the hall looking back now and again as though the voice were a beast at her heels. In the front parlor she pulled up the glass and took a book from the bookcase nearest to the door. It was a red book, and she hurled herself into George's chair and opened to page sixty-five:

> pity, with anxiety, and with pity. Hamilcar was rubbing himself against my legs, wild with delight.

She closed the book on her thumb and listened to George's bellowing:

"I'm coming after you!"

She could hear the noise of the hoofs as George led the horses around the side of the house. George's figure moved outside the front windows. Through the heavy lace curtains she could see him tying the horses to the branch of a tree. She heard him on the veranda and then in the hall. Damn him! God damn him, he couldn't make her ride! She opened to page sixty-five again as George passed the doorway. But he saw her, and he stopped. He stared at her for a moment, and she looked at him over the book. She rested her head on the back of the chair sullenly. Her eyes were fixed on his hairy arms, on the little bulk in his rolled sleeves, then on the white shirt over his chest, on the brown jodhpurs, and finally on the blackened leather of his shoes set apart on the polished hall floor. Her eyelids were heavy, and she longed for a drink of the three-dollar whiskey that was on her dressing table.

He crossed the carpet with a smile, showing, she guessed, his delight at finding her. She smiled. He snatched the book from her hands and read the title on the red cover. His head went back, and as he laughed she watched through the open collar the tendons of his throat tighten and take on a purplish hue.

At Josephine's feet was a needlepoint footstool on which was worked a rust-colored American eagle against a background of green. George tossed the red book onto the stool and pulled Josephine from her chair. He was still laughing, and she wishing for a drink.

"Come along, come along," he said. "We've only four days left, and you'll want to tell your friend-girls you learned to ride."

She jerked one hand loose from his hold and slapped his hard cheek. She screamed, "Friend-girl? You never heard me say Friend-girl. What black nigger do you think you're talking down to?" She was looking at him now through a mist of tears and presently she broke out into furious weeping. His laughter went on as he pushed her across the room and into the hall, but he was saying:

"Boochie, Boochie. Wotsa matter? Now, old girl, old girl. Listen: You'll want to tell your girl-friends, your *girl-friends,* that you learned to ride." That was how George was! He would never try to persuade her. He would never pay any attention to what she said. He wouldn't argue with her. He wouldn't mince words! The few times she had seen him before this week there had been no chance to talk much. When they were driving down from Memphis, Saturday, she had gone through the story about how she was tricked by Jackie Briton and married Lon and how he had left her right away and the pathetic part about the baby she never even saw in the hospital. And at the end of it she realized that George had been smiling at her as he probably would at one of his half-grown kids. When she stopped the story quickly, he had reached over and patted her hand (but still smiling) and right away had started talking about the sickly-looking tomato crops along the highway. After lunch on Saturday when she'd tried to talk to him again and he had deliberately commenced to play the victrola, she said, "Why won't you take me seriously?" But he had, of course, just laughed at her and kissed her and they had already begun drinking then. She couldn't resist him (more than other men, he could just drive her wild), and he would hardly look at her, never had. He either laughed at her or cursed her or, of course, at night would pet her. He hadn't hit her.

He was shoving her along the hall, and she had to make herself stop crying.

"Please, George."

"Come on, now! That-a girl."

"Honest to God, George. I tell you to let up, stop it."

"Come on. *Up* the steps. *Up! Up!*"

She let herself become limp in his arms but held with one hand to the banister. Then he grabbed her. He swung her up into his arms and carried her up the stair which curved around the back end of the hall, over the doorway to the breakfast room. Once in his arms she didn't move a muscle, for she thought, "I'm no featherweight, and we'll both go tumbling down these steps and break our skulls." At the top he fairly slammed her to her feet and, panting for breath, he said without a trace of softness:

"Now, put on those pants, Josie, and I'll wait for you in the yard." He turned to the stair, and she heard what he said to himself: "I'll sober her. I'll sober her up."

As he pushed Josephine onto the white, jumpy beast he must have caught a whiff of her breath. She knew that he must have! He was holding the reins close to the bit while she tried to arrange herself in the flat saddle. Then he grasped her ankle and asked her, "Did you take a drink, upstairs?" She laughed, leaned forward in her saddle and whispered: "Two. Two jiggers."

She wasn't afraid of the horse now, but she was dizzy. "George, let me down," she said faintly. She felt the horse's flesh quiver under her leg and looked over her shoulder when it stomped one rear hoof.

George said, "Confound it, I'll sober you." He handed her the reins, stepped back and slapped the horse on the flank. "Hold on!" he called, and her horse cantered across the lawn.

Josie was clutching the leather straps tightly, and her face was almost in the horse's mane. "I could kill him for this," she said, slicing out the words with a sharp breath. God damn it! The horse was galloping along a dirt road. She saw nothing but the yellow dirt. The hoofs rumbled over a three-plank wooden bridge, and she heard George's horse on the other side of her. She turned her face that way and saw George through the hair that hung over her eyes. He was smiling. "You dirty bastard," she said.

He said, "You're doin' all right. Sit up, and I'll give you some pointers." She turned her face to the other side. Now she wished to God she hadn't taken those two jiggers. George's horse quickened his speed and hers followed. George's slowed and hers did likewise. She could feel George's grin in the back of her neck. She had no control over her horse.

They were galloping in the hot sunlight, and Josie stole glances at the flat fields of strawberries. "If you weren't drunk, you'd fall off," George shouted. Now they were passing a cotton field. ("The back of my neck'll be blistered," she thought. "Where was it I picked strawberries once? At Dyersburg when I was ten, visiting some God-forsaken relations.") The horses turned off the road into wooded bottom land. The way now was shaded by giant trees, but here and there the sun shone between the foliage. Once after riding thirty feet in shadow, watching dumbly the cool blue-green underbrush, Josie felt the sun suddenly on her neck. Her stomach churned, and the eggs and coffee from breakfast burnt her throat as it all gushed forth, splattering her pants-leg and the brown saddle and the horse's side. She looked over the horse at George.

But there was no remorse, no compassion and no humor in George's face. He gazed straight ahead and urged on his horse.

All at once the horses turned to the right. Josie howled. She saw her right foot flying through the air, and after the thud of the fall and the flashes of light and darkness she lay on her back in the dirt and watched George as he approached on foot, leading the two horses.

"Old girl——" he said.

"You get the hell away from me!"

"Are you hurt?" He kneeled beside her, so close to her that she could smell his sweaty shirt.

Josie jumped to her feet and walked in the direction from which they had ridden. In a moment George galloped past her, leading the gray horse and laughing like the son-of-a bitch he was.

"Last night he sent me upstairs! But this is more! I'm not gonna have it." She walked through the woods, her lips moving as she talked to herself. "He wants no more of my drunken palaver!" Well, he was going to get no more of her drunken anything now. She had had her fill of him and everybody else and was going to look out for her own little sweet self from now on.

That was her trouble, she knew. She'd never made a good thing of people. "That's why things are like they are now," she said. "I've never made a good thing out of anybody." But it was real lucky that she realized it now, just exactly when she had, for it was certain that there had never been one whom more could be made out of than George. "God damn him," she said, thinking still of his riding by her like that. "Whatever it was I liked about him is gone now."

She gazed up into the foliage and branches of the trees, and the great size of the trees made her feel really small, and young. If Jackie or Lon had been different she might have learned things when she was young. "But they were both of 'em easy-goin' and just slipped out on me." They *were* sweet. She'd never forget how sweet Jackie always was. "Just plain sweet." She made a quick gesture with her right hand: "If only they didn't all get such a hold on me!"

But she was through with George. This time *she* got through first. He was no different from a floorwalker. He had more sense. "He's educated, and the money he must have!" George had more sense than a floorwalker, but he didn't have any manners. He treated her just like the floorwalker at Jobe's had that last week she was there. But George was worth getting around. She would find out what it was. She wouldn't take another drink. She'd find out what was wrong inside him, and somehow get a hold on him. Little Josephine would make a place for herself at last. She just wouldn't think about him as a man.

At the edge of the wood she turned onto the road, and across the fields she could see his house. That house was just simply as old and big as they come, and wasn't a cheap house. "I wonder if he looked after getting it fixed over and remodeled." Not likely. She kept looking at the whitewashed brick and shaking her head. "No, by Jesus," she exclaimed. *"She* did it!" George's wife.

All of her questions seemed to have been answered. The wife had left him for his meanness, and he was lonesome. There was, then, a place to be filled. She began to run along the road. "God, I feel like somebody might step in before I get there." She laughed, but then the heat seemed to strike her all at once. Her stomach drew in. She vomited in the ditch, and, by God, it was as dry as cornflakes!

She sat still in the grass under a little maple tree beside the road, resting her forehead on her drawn-up knees. All between Josie and her new life seemed to be the walk through the sun in these smelly, dirty clothes. Across the fields and in the house was a canopied bed and a glorious new life, but she daren't go into the sun. She would pass out cold. "People kick off in weather like this!"

Presently Josie heard the voices of niggers up the road. She wouldn't look up, she decided. She'd let them pass, without looking up. They drew near to her and she made out the voices of a man and a child. Then the man said, "Hursh!" and the voices ceased. There was only the sound of their feet padding along the dusty road.

The noise of the padding grew fainter. Josie looked up and saw that the two had cut across the fields toward George's house. Already she could hear the niggers mouthing it about the kitchen. That little yellow Henry would look at her over his shoulder as he went through the swinging door at dinner tonight. If she heard them grumbling once more, as she did Monday, calling her "she," Josie decided that she was going to come right out and ask Amelia about the scar. Right before George. But the niggers were the least of her worries now.

All afternoon she lay on the bed, waking now and then to look at the bottle of whiskey on the dressing table and to wonder where George had gone. She didn't know whether it had been George or the field nigger who sent Henry after her in the truck. Once she dreamed that she saw George at the head of the stair telling Amelia how he had sobered Miss Josephine up. When she awoke that time she said, "I ought to get up and get myself good and plastered before George comes back from wherever he is." But she slept again and dreamed this time that she was working at a hat sale at Jobe's and that she had to wait on Amelia who picked up a white turban and asked Josie to model it for her. And the dream ended with Amelia telling Josie how pretty she was and how much she liked her.

Josie had taken another hot bath (to ward off soreness from the horseback ride) and was in the sitting room, which everybody called the back parlor, playing the electric victrola and feeling just prime when George came in. She let him go through the hall and upstairs to dress for dinner without calling to him. She chuckled to herself and rocked to the time of the music.

George came with a real mint julep in each hand. His hair was wet and slicked down over his head; the part, low on the left side, was straight and white. His cheeks were shaven and were pink with new sunburn. He said, "I had myself the time of my life this afternoon."

Josie smiled and said that she was glad he had enjoyed himself. George raised his eyebrows and cocked his head to one side. She kept on smiling at him, and made no movement toward taking the drink that he held out to her.

George set the glass on the little candle stand near her chair and switched off the victrola.

"George, I was listening . . ."

"Ah, now," he said, "I want to tell you about the cockfight."

"Let me finish listening to that piece, George."

George dropped down into an armchair and put his feet on a stool. His pants and shirt were white, and he wore a blue polka dot tie.

"You're nice and clean," she said, as though she had forgotten the victrola.

"Immaculate!" There was a mischievous grin on his face, and he leaned over one arm of the chair and pulled the victrola plug from the floor socket. Josie reached out and took the glass from the candle stand, stirred it slightly with a shoot of mint and began to sip it. She thought, "I *have* to take it when he acts this way."

At the dinner table George said, "You're in better shape tonight. You look better. Why don't you go easy on the bottle tonight?"

She looked at him between the two candles burning in the center of the round table. "I didn't ask you for that mint julep, I don't think."

"And you ain't gettin' any more," he said, winking at her

as he lifted his fork to his lips with his left hand. This, she felt, was a gesture to show his contempt for her. Perhaps he thought she didn't know the difference, which, of course, was even more contemptuous.

"Nice manners," she said. He made no answer, but at least he could be sure that she had recognized the insult. She took a drink of water, her little finger extended slightly from the glass, and over the glass she said, "You didn't finish about the niggers having a fight after the chickens did."

"Oh, yes." He arranged his knife and fork neatly on his plate. "The two nigs commenced to watch each other before their chickens had done scrapping. And when the big rooster gave his last hop and keeled over, Ira Blakemoor jumped over the two birds onto Jimmy's shoulders. Jimmy just whirled round and round till he threw Ira the way the little mare did you this morning." George looked directly into Josie's eyes between the candles, defiantly unashamed to mention that event, and he smiled with defiance and yet with weariness. "Ira got up and the two walked around looking at each other like two black games before a fight." Josie kept her eyes on George while the story, she felt, went on and on and on.

That yellow nigger Henry was paused at the swinging door, looking over his shoulder toward her. She turned her head and glared at him. He was not even hiding this action from George, who was going on and on about the niggers' fighting. This Henry was the worst hypocrite of all. He who had slashed Amelia's wrist (it was surely Henry who had done it), and probably had raped his own children, the way niggers do, was denouncing her right out like this. Her heart pounded when he kept looking, and then George's story stopped.

A bright light flashed across Henry's face and about the room which was lit by only the two candles. Josie swung her head around, and through the front window she saw the lights of automobiles that were coming through the yard.

She looked at George, and his face said absolutely nothing for itself. He moistened his lips with his tongue.

"Guests," he said, raising his eyebrows. And Josie felt that in that moment she had seen the strongest floorwalker weaken. George had scorned and laughed at everybody and every situation. But now he was ashamed. He was ashamed of her. On her behavior would depend his comfort. She was cold sober and would be *up* to whatever showed itself. It was her real opportunity.

From the back of the house a horn sounded, and above other voices a woman's voice rose, calling "Whoohoo!" George stood up and bowed to her beautifully, like something she had never seen, and said, "You'll excuse me?" Then he went out through the kitchen without saying "scat" about what she should do.

She drummed on the table with her fingers and listened to George's greetings to his friends. She heard him say, "Welcome, Billy, and welcome, Mrs. Billy!" They were the only names she recognized. It was likely the Billy Colton she'd met with George one night.

Then these *were* Memphis Society people. Here for the night, at least! She looked down at her yellow linen dress and straightened the lapels at the neck. She thought of the women with their lovely profiles and soft skin and natural-colored hair. What if she had waited on one of them once at Jobe's or, worse still, in the old days at Burnstein's? But they had probably never been to one of those cheap stores. What if they stayed but refused to talk to her, or even to meet her? They could be mean bitches, all of them, for all their soft hands and shaved legs. Her hand trembled as she rang the little glass bell for coffee.

She rang it, and no one answered. She rang it again, hard, but now she could hear Henry coming through the breakfast room to the hall, bumping the guests' baggage against the doorway. Neither Amelia nor Mammy, who cooked the evening meal, would leave the kitchen during dinner, Josie knew. "I'd honestly like to go out in the kitchen and ask

'em for a cup of coffee and tell 'em just how scared I am."
But too well she could imagine their contemptuous, accusing gaze. "If only I could get something on them! Even
catch 'em toting food just once! That Mammy's likely killed
enough niggers in her time to fill Jobe's basement."

Josie was even afraid to light a cigarette. She went over
to the side window and looked out into the yard; she could
see the lights of the automobile shining on the green leaves
and on the white fence around the house lot.

And she was standing thus when she heard the voices and
the footsteps in the long hall. She had only just turned
around when George stood in the wide doorway with the
men and women from Memphis. He was pronouncing her
name first: "Miss Carlson, this is Mr. Roberts, Mrs. Roberts,
Mr. Jackson, Mrs. Jackson and Mr. and Mrs. Colton."

Josie stared at the group, not trying to catch the names.
She could think only, "They're old. The women are old and
plump. George's wife is old!" She stared at them, and when
the name Colton struck her ear, she said automatically and
without placing his face, "I know Billy."

George said, in the same tone in which he had said,
"You'll excuse me? . . . Josie, will you take the ladies upstairs to freshen up while the men and I get some drinks
started? We'll settle the rooming question later." George was
the great floorwalker whose wife was old and who had now
shown his pride to Josie Carlson. He had shown his shame.
Finally he had decided on a course and was following it, but
he had given 'way his sore spots. Only God knew what he
had told his friends. Josie said to herself, "It's plain he don't
want 'em to know who I am."

As Josie ascended the stair, followed by those she had
already privately termed the "three matrons," she watched
George and the three other men go down the hall to the
breakfast room. The sight of their white linen suits and brown
and white shoes in the bright hall seemed to make the climb
a soaring. At the top of the stair she stopped and let the
three women pass ahead of her. She eyed the costume of each

as they passed. One wore a tailored seersucker dress. Another wore a navy blue linen dress with white collar and cuffs, and the third wore a striped linen skirt and silk blouse. On the wrist of this last was a bracelet from which hung a tiny silver dog, a lock, a gold heart.

Josie observed their grooming: their fingernails, their lipstick, their hair in tight curls. There was gray in the hair of one, but not one, Josie decided now, was much past forty. Their figures were neatly corseted, and Josie felt that the little saggings under their chins and under the eyes of the one in the navy blue made them more charming; were, indeed, almost a part of their smartness. She wanted to think of herself as like them. They were, she realized, at least ten years older than she, but in ten years, beginning tonight, she might become one of them.

"Just go in my room there," she said. She pointed to the open door and started down the steps, thinking that this was the beginning of the new life and thinking of the men downstairs fixing the drinks. And then she thought of the bottle of whiskey on her dressing table in the room where the matrons had gone!

"Oh, hell," she swore under her breath. She had turned to go up the two steps again when she heard the men's voices below. She heard her own name being pronounced carefully: "Josie Carlson." She went down five or six steps on tiptoe and stood still to listen to the voices that came from the breakfast room.

"You said to come any time, George, and never mentioned having this thing down here."

George laughed. "Afraid of what the girls will say when you get home? I can hear them. 'In Beatrice's own lovely house,' " he mocked.

"Well, fellow, you've a shock coming, too," one of them said. "Beatrice has sent your boys down to Memphis for a month with you. They say she has a beau."

"And in the morning," one said, "your sister Kate's sending them down here. She asked us to bring them, and then decided to keep them one night herself."

"You'd better get *her* out, George."

George laughed. Josie could hear him dropping ice into glasses.

"We'll take her back at dawn, if you say."

"What would the girls say to that?" He laughed at them as he laughed at Josie.

"The girls are gonna be decent to her. They agreed in the yard."

"Female curiosity?" George said.

"Your boys'll have curiosity, too. Jock's seventeen."

Even the clank of the ice stopped. "You'll every one of you please to remember," George said slowly, "that Josie's a friend of yours and that she met the girls here by appointment."

Josie tiptoed down the stair, descending, she felt, once more into her old world. "He'll slick me some way if he has to for his kids, I think." She turned into the dining-room at the foot of the stair. The candles were burning low, and she went and stood by the open window and listened to the counterpoint of the crickets and the frogs while Henry, who had looked over his shoulder at the car lights, rattled the silver and china and went about clearing the table.

Presently George had come and put his hand on her shoulder. When she turned around she saw him smiling and holding two drinks in his left hand. He leaned his face close to hers and said, "I'm looking for the tears."

Josie said, "There aren't any to find, fellow"; and she thought it odd, really odd, that he had expected her to cry. But he was probably poking fun at her again.

She took one of the drinks and clinked glasses with George. To herself she said, "I bet they don't act any better than I do after they've got a few under their belts." At least she showed her true colors! "I'll keep my eyes open for their true ones."

If only they'd play the victrola instead of the radio. She liked the victrola so much better. She could play "Louisville Lady" over and over. But, *no*. They all wanted to switch the radio about. To get Cincinnati and Los Angeles and Bennie this and Johnny that. If they liked a piece, why did they care who played it. For God's sake! They wouldn't dance at first, either, and when she first got George to dance with her, they sat smiling at each other, grinning. They had played cards, too, but poker didn't go so well after George slugged them all with that third round of his three-dollar-whiskey drinks. Right then she had begun to watch out to see who slapped whose knee.

She asked George to dance because she so liked to dance with him, and she wasn't going to care about what the others did any more, she decided. But finally when two of them had started dancing off in the corner of the room, she looked about the sitting-room for the other four and saw that Billy Colton had disappeared not with his own wife but with that guy Jackson's. And Josie threw herself down into the armchair and laughed aloud, so hard and loud that everybody begged her to tell what was funny. But she stopped suddenly and gave them as mean a look as she could manage and said, "Nothin'. Let's dance some more, George."

But George said that he must tell Henry to fix more drinks, and he went out and left her by the radio with Roberts and Mrs. Colton. She looked at Mrs. Colton and thought, "Honey, you don't seem to be grieving about Billy."

Then Roberts said to Josie, "George says you're from Vicksburg."

"I was raised there," she said, wondering why George hadn't told her whatever he'd told them.

"He says you live there now."

Mrs. Colton, who wore the navy blue and was the fattest of the three matrons, stood up and said to Billy, "Let's dance in the hall where there are fewer rugs." And she gave a kindly smile to Josie, and Josie spit out a "Thanks." The couple skipped into the hall, laughing, and Josie sat alone by the radio wishing she could play the victrola and wishing that George would come and kiss her on the back of her neck. "And I'd slap him if he did," she said. Now and again she would cut her eyes around to watch Jackson and Mrs. Roberts dancing. They were at the far end of the room and were dancing slowly. They kept rubbing against the heavy blue drapery at the window and they were talking into each other's ears.

But the next piece that came over the radio was a hot one, and Jackson led Mrs. Roberts to the center of the room and whirled her round and round, and the trinkets at her wrist tinkled like little bells. Josie lit a cigarette and watched them dance. She realized then that Jackson was showing off for her sake.

When George came with a tray of drinks he said, "Josie, move the victrola," but Josie sat still and glared at him as if to say, What on earth are you talking about? Are you nuts? He set the tray across her lap and turned and picked up the little victrola and set it on the floor.

"Oh, good God!" Josie cried in her surprise and delight. "It's a portable."

George, taking the tray from her, said, "It's not for you to port off, old girl."

The couple in the center of the room had stopped their whirling and had followed George. "We like to dance, but there are better things," Jackson was saying.

Mrs. Roberts flopped down on the broad arm of Josie's chair and took a drink from George. Josie could only watch the trinkets on the bracelet, one of which she saw was a little gold book. George was telling Jackson about the cockfight again, and Mrs. Roberts leaned over and talked to Josie. She tried to tell her how the room seemed to be whirling around. They both giggled, and Josie thought, "Maybe we'll get to be good friends, and she'll stop pretending to be so swell." But she couldn't think of anything to say to her, partly because she just never did have anything to say to women and partly because Jackson, who was not at all a bad-looking little man, was sending glances her way.

It didn't seem like more than twenty minutes or half an hour more before George had got to that point where he ordered her around and couldn't keep on his own feet. He finally lay down on the couch in the front parlor, and as she and Mrs. Roberts went up the stair with their arms about each other's waists, he called out something that made Mrs. Roberts giggle. But Josie knew that little Josephine was at the point where she could say nothing straight, so she didn't even ask to get the portable victrola. She just cursed under her breath.

The daylight was beginning to appear at the windows of Josie's narrow little room when waking suddenly she sat up in bed and then flopped down again and jerked the sheet about her. "That little sucker come up here," she grumbled, "and cleared out, but where was the little sucker's wife?" Who was with George, by damn, all night? After a while she said, "They're none of 'em any better than the niggers. I knew they couldn't be. Nobody is. By God, nobody's better than I am. Nobody can say anything to me." Everyone would like to live as free as she did! There was no such thing as . . . There was no such thing as what the niggers and the whites liked to pretend they were. She was going to let up, and do things in secret. Try to look like an angel. It wouldn't be as hard since there was no such thing.

It was all like a scene from a color movie, like one of the musicals. It was the prettiest scene ever. And they were like two of those lovely wax models in the boys' department at Jobe's. Like two of those models, with the tan skin and blond hair, come to life! And to see them in their white shorts springing about the green grass under the blue, blue sky, hitting the little feather thing over the high net, made Josie go weak all over. She went down on her knees and rested her elbows on the window sill and watched them springing about before the people from Memphis; these were grouped under a tree, sitting in deck chairs and on the grass. George stood at the net like a floorwalker charmed by his wax models which had come to life.

It had been George's cries of "Outside, outside!" and the jeers and applause of the six spectators that awakened Josie. She ran to the window in her pajamas, and when she saw the white markings on the grass and the net that had sprung up there overnight, she thought that this might be a dream. But the voices of George and Mrs. Roberts and Phil Jackson were completely real, and the movements of the boys' bodies were too marvelous to be doubted.

She sank to her knees, conscious of the soreness which her horseback ride had left. She thought of her clumsy self in the dusty road as she gazed down at the graceful boys on the lawn and said, "Why, they're actually pretty. Too pretty." She was certain of one thing: She didn't want any of their snobbishness. She wouldn't have it from his two kids.

One boy's racket missed the feather thing. George shouted, "Game!" The group under the tree applauded, and the men pushed themselves up from their seats to come out into the sunlight and pat the naked backs of the boys.

When the boys came close together, Josie saw that one was six inches taller than the other. "Why, that one's grown!" she thought. The two of them walked toward the house, the taller one walking with the shorter's neck in the crook of his elbow. George called to them, "You boys get dressed for lunch." He ordered them about just as he did her, but they went off smiling.

Josie walked in her bare feet into the little closet-like bathroom which adjoined her room. She looked at herself in the mirror there and said, "I've never dreaded anything so much in all my life before. You can't depend on what kids'll say." But were they kids? For all their prettiness, they were too big to be called kids. And nobody's as damn smutty as a smart-alecky shaver.

Josephine bathed in the little, square, maroon bathtub. There were maroon-and-white checkered tile steps built up around the tub, so that it gave the effect of being sunken. After her bath, she stood on the steps and powdered her whole soft body. Every garment which she put on was absolutely fresh. She went to her closet and took out her new white silk dress and slipped it over her head. She put on white shoes first, but, deciding she looked too much like a trained nurse, she changed to her tan pumps. Josie knew what young shavers thought about nurses.

She combed her yellow hair till it lay close to her head, and put on rouge and lipstick. Someone knocked at the bedroom door. "Yeah," she called. No answer came, so she went to the door and opened it. In the hall stood one of the boys. It was the little one.

He didn't look at her; he looked past her. And his eyes *were* as shiny and cold as those on a wax dummy!

"Miss Carlson, my dad says to tell you that lunch is ready. And I'm Buddy."

"Thanks." She didn't know what the hell else she could say. "Tell him, all right," she said. She stepped back into her room and shut the door.

Josie paced the room for several times. "He didn't so much as look at me." She was getting hot, and she went and put her face to the window. The people from Memphis had come indoors, and the sun shone on the brownish-green grass and on the still trees. "It's a scorcher," she said. She walked the length of the room again and opened the door. Buddy was still there. Standing there in white, his shirt open at the collar, and his white pants, long pants. He was leaning against the banister.

"Ready?" he said, smiling.

As they went down the steps together, he said, "It's nice that you're here. We didn't know it till just a few minutes ago." He was a Yankee kid, lived with his mother somewhere, and rolled his r's, and spoke as though there was a

lot of meaning behind what he said. She gave him a quick
glance to see what he meant by that last remark. He smiled,
and this time looked right into her eyes.

After lunch, which Josie felt had been awful embarrassing,
they traipsed into the back parlor, and George showed off
the kids again. She had had a good look at the older one
during lunch and could tell by the way the corners of his
mouth drooped down that he was a surly one, unless maybe
he was only trying to keep from looking so pretty. And all he
said to the questions which George asked him about girls
and his high school was "Yeah," or "Aw, naw." When
Henry brought in the first round of drinks, and he took one,
his daddy looked at him hard and said, "Jock?" And the
boy looked his daddy square in the eye.

Buddy only shook his head and smiled when Henry
offered him a drink, but he was the one that had started all
the embarrassment for her at lunch. When they came into
the dining-room he pulled her chair out, and she looked back
at him—knowing how kids like to jerk chairs. Everybody
laughed, but she kept on looking at him. And then she
knew that she blushed, for she thought how big her behind
must look to him with her bent over like she was.

The other thing that was awful was the question that Mrs.
Jackson, the smallest matron and the one with the gray
streak in her hair, asked her, "And how do *you* feel this
morning, Miss Carlson?" It was the fact that it was Jackson's wife which got her most. But then the fool woman
said, "Like the rest of us?" And Josie supposed that she
meant no meanness by her remark, but she had already
blushed; and Jackson, across the table, looked into his plate.
Had this old woman and George been messing around? She
wondered. Probably Mrs. Jackson hadn't meant anything.

As they all lounged about the sitting-room after lunch,
she even felt that she was beginning to catch on to these
people and that she was going to start a little pretense of her
own and make a good thing out of old Georgie. It was

funny the way her interest in him, any real painful interest was sort of fading. "I've never had so much happen to me at one time," she said to herself. She sat on the floor beside George's chair and put her hand on the toe of his brown-and-white shoe.

Then George said, "Buddy, you've got to give us just one recitation." And Buddy's face turned as red as a traffic light. He was sitting on a footstool and looking down at his hands.

Jock reached over and touched him on the shoulder and said: "Come on, Buddy, the one about 'if love were like a rose.'" Buddy shook his head and kept his eyes on his hands.

Josie said to herself, "The kid's honestly timid." It gave her the shivers to see anybody so shy and ignorant of things. But then he began to say the poetry without looking up. It was something about a rose and a rose leaf, but nobody could hear him very good.

George said, "Louder! Louder!" The boy looked at him and said a verse about "sweet rain at noon." Next he stood up and moved his hands about as he spoke, and the blushing was all gone. He said the next one to Mrs. Roberts, and it began:

> If you were life, my darling,
> And I, your love, were death . . .

That verse ended with something silly about "fruitful breath." He went to Billy Colton's wife, and the verse he said to her was sad. The boy *did* have a way with him! His eyes were big and he could look sad and happy at the same time. "And I were page to joy," he said. He actually looked like one of the pages they have in stores at Christmas.

But now the kid was perfectly sure of himself, and he had acted timid at first. It was probably all a show. She could just hear him saying dirty "limricks." She realized that he was bound to say a verse to her if he knew that many, and she listened carefully to the one he said to Mrs. Jackson:

If you were April's lady,
And I were lord in May,
We'd throw with leaves for hours
And draw for days with flowers,
Till day like night were shady
And night were bright like day;
If you were April's lady,
And I were lord in May.

He turned to Josie in his grandest manner:

If you were queen of pleasure,
And I were king of pain,
We'd hunt down love together,
Pluck out his flying-feather
And teach his feet a measure,
And find his mouth a rein;
If you were queen of pleasure,
And I were king of pain.

And Josie sat up straight and gave the brat the hardest look she knew how. It was too plain. "Queen of pleasure" sounded just as bad as whore! Especially coming right after the verse about "April's lady." The boy blushed again when she glared at him. No one made a noise for a minute. Josie looked at George, and he smiled and began clapping his hands, and everybody clapped. Buddy bowed and ran from the room.

"He's good, George. He's good," Jackson said, squinting his beady little eyes. Jackson was really a puny-looking little guy in the light of day! And he hadn't thought the boy was any better than anybody else did. It was just that he wanted to be the first to say something.

"He's really very good," Mrs. Jackson said.

George laughed. "He's a regular little actor," he said. "Gets it from Beatrice, I guess." Everybody laughed.

George's wife was an actress, then! She'd probably been

the worst of the whole lot. There was no telling what this child was really like.

"How old is he, Jock?" Jackson asked. How that man liked to hear his own voice!

"Fourteen and a half," Jock said. "Have you seen him draw?" He talked about his kid brother like he was his own child. Josie watched him. He was talking about Buddy's drawings, about the likenesses. She watched him, and then he saw her watching. He dropped his eyes to his hands as Buddy had done. But in a minute he looked up; and as the talking and drinking went on he kept his eyes on Josephine.

It wasn't any of George's business. It wasn't any of his or anybody's how much she drank, and she knew very well that *he* didn't really give a damn! But it *was* smarter 'n hell of him to take her upstairs, because the boys had stared at her all afternoon and all through supper. That was really why she had kept on taking the drinks when she had made up her mind to let up. She had said, "You're jealous. You're jealous, George." And he had put his hand over her mouth, saying, "Careful, Josie." But she was sort of celebrating so much's happening to her, and she felt good, and she was plain infuriated when George kissed her and went back downstairs. "He was like his real self comin' up the steps," she said. He had told her that she didn't have the gumption God gave a crabapple.

Josie went off to sleep with her lips moving and awoke in the middle of the night with them moving again. She was feeling just prime and yet rotten at the same time. She had a headache and yet she had a happy feeling. She woke up saying, "Thank God for small favors." She had been dreaming about Jock. He was all right. She had dreamed that together she and Jock had watched a giant bear devouring a bull, and Jock had laughed. He was all right. She was practically sure. His eyes were like George's, and he was as stubborn.

It would have been perfectly plain to everybody if supper hadn't been such an all-round mess. What with Jackson's smutty jokes and his showing off (trying to get her to look at him), and Mrs. Colton's flirting with her husband (holding his hand on the table!), nobody but George paid any attention to Jock. And she was glad that she had smacked Jackson when he tried to carry her up the stair, for it made Jock smile his crooked smile.

"They all must be in bed," she thought. The house was so quiet that she could hear a screech owl, or something, down in the woods.

She thought she heard a noise in her bathroom. She lay still, and she was pretty sure she had heard it again. She supposed it was a mouse, but it might be something else; she had never before thought about where that door beside the bathtub might lead. There was only one place it could go. She got up and went in her stocking feet to the bathroom. She switched on the light and watched the knob. She glanced at herself in the mirror. Her new white silk dress was twisted and wrinkled. "Damn him," she whispered to herself. "He *could* have made me take off *this* dress." Then she thought she had seen the knob move, move as though someone had released it. She stood still, but there wasn't another sound that night.

In the morning when she turned off the bathroom light, she was still wondering. She looked out of the window; the high net was down. No one was in sight.

What they all did was to slip out on her before she woke up! And in the breakfast room that morning Amelia wanted to talk, but Josephine wasn't going to give the nigger the chance. There was no telling what they had let the niggers hear at breakfast. Amelia kept coming to the breakfast room door and asking if everything was all right, if Miss Josephine wanted this or wanted that, but Josephine would only shake her head and say not a word after Amelia had once answered, "They've went back to Memphis." For all she knew, George and the kids had gone too. It would have been like him to leave her and send after her, just because he had promised her she could stay a week. (He talked like it was such a great treat for her. She hadn't given a copper about the place at first. It had been *him*.) But he'd damned well better not have left her. She'd got a taste of this sort of thing for its own sake now, and she'd stay for good!

Buddy opened the outside door of the breakfast room. "Good morning, Miss Carlson," he said.

"Hello," Josie said. She did wonder what Jock had told Buddy, what he had guessed to tell him. Buddy wasn't at dinner last night, or she couldn't remember him there.

He was wearing khaki riding pants and a short-sleeved shirt. He sat down across the table from her. "I guess we're all that's left," he said. He picked up the sugar bowl and smiled as he examined it. The corners of his mouth turned up like in a picture kids draw on a blackboard.

"Did Jock and George go to Memphis? Did they?"

"Jock did."

"He did?"

"Yes, he did. And Henry told me he didn't much want to go. I was off riding when they all got up this morning. Daddy wanted me to go, but I wasn't here." He smiled again, and Josie supposed he meant that he'd been hiding from them.

"Where's your dad?"

"He? Oh, he went to the village to see about some hams. What are you going to do now?"

Josie shrugged her shoulders and began to drink her coffee. Jock was gone! He might have just been scorning her with those looks all the time. She should have got that door open somehow and found out what was what. "Why didn't Jock want to go?" she asked Buddy.

"Our pleasant company, I suppose," he said. "Or yours."

She looked at him and he laughed. She wondered could this brat be poking fun at her? "Queen of pleasure!" she said out loud, not meaning to at all.

"Did you like that poem?" he asked. It was certain that he wasn't timid when he was alone with somebody, not at least when alone with her.

"I don't know," she said. Then she looked at him. "I don't like the one you picked for me."

"That's not one of the best, is it?"

Neither of them spoke while Josie finished her coffee. She put in another spoonful of sugar before taking the last few swallows, and Buddy reddened when she motioned for him to give up the sugar bowl. Amelia came and removed the breakfast plate and the butter plate. She returned for Josie's coffeecup, and, finding it not quite ready, she stood behind Buddy's chair and put her hands on his shoulders. The scar was right beside his cheek. Buddy smiled and beat the back of his head against her ribs playfully. Finally Josie put her cup down and said, "That's all."

She went upstairs to her room. Jock had tried to get in through her bathroom last night, or he had been so on her mind that her ears and eyes had made up the signs of it. Maybe Buddy had caught Jock trying to open the door and had told George. At any rate George had sent Jock away. If he sent him away, then Jock had definitely had notions. Josie smiled over that. She was sitting on the side of her little canopied bed, smoking a red-tipped cigarette. There was the noise of an automobile motor in the yard. George was back! Josie went to her dressing table and drank the last of her whiskey.

She sat on the stool before her dressing table, with her eyes on the hall door. She listened to George's footsteps on the stair, and sat with her legs crossed, twitching the left foot, which dangled. George came in and closed the door behind him.

"I've bought you a ticket on the night train, Josie. You're goin' back tonight."

So he wasn't such a stickler for his word, after all! Not in this case! He was sending her home. Well, what did he expect her to say? Did he think she would beg to stay on? She would clear out, and she wasn't the one beaten. George was beaten. One of his kids that he was so mortally fond of, one for sure had had notions. "Almost for sure." George opened the door and left Josie staring after him. In a few minutes she heard his horse gallop past the house and out onto the dirt road.

She folded her white dress carefully and laid it on the bottom of her traveling bag. She heard Buddy somewhere in the house, singing. She wrapped her white shoes in toilet paper and stuck them at the ends of the bag. Buddy seemed to be wandering through the house, singing. His voice was high like a woman's, never breaking as she sometimes thought it did in conversation. It came from one part of the house and then another. Josie stopped her packing. "There's no such thing," she said.

She went down the steps like a child, stopping both feet on each step, then stepping to the next. One hand was on her hip, the other she ran along the banister. She walked through the front parlor with its bookcases and fancy chairs with the eagles worked in the needlepoint, and through the back parlor with the rockingchairs and the silly candle stand and the victrola. She stepped down into the breakfast room where the sunlight came through the blinds and put stripes on the brick wall. She went into the kitchen for the first time. Mammy, with a white dust cap on the back of her head, had already started supper. She stood by the big range, and Amelia sat in the corner peeling potatoes. Josie wasn't interested in the face of either. She went through the dark pantry and into the dining-room. She looked through the windows there, but no one was in the yard. She went into the hall.

Buddy was near the top of the stairway which curved around the far end of the long hall, looking down at her. "Why don't you come up here?" He pronounced every word sharply and rolled his *r*'s. But his voice was flat, and his words seemed to remain in the hall for several minutes. His question seemed to float down from the ceiling, down through the air like a feather.

"How did he get up there without me hearing him?" Josie mumbled. She took the first two steps slowly, and Buddy hopped up to the top of the stair.

The door to the kids' room was open and Josie went in. Buddy shut the white paneled door and said, "Don't you think it's time you did something nice for me?"

Josie laughed, and she watched Buddy laugh. Queen of pleasure indeed!

"I want to draw you," he said.

"Clothes and all, Bud . . . ?"

"No. That's not what I mean!"

Josie forced a smile, and she suddenly felt afraid and thought she was going to be sick again.

"That's not what I mean," she heard the kid say again, without blinking an eye, without blushing. "I didn't know you were that sort of nasty thing here. I didn't know you were a fancy woman. Go away. Go on out of here. Go on out of here!" he ordered her.

As Josie went down the steps she kept puckering her lips and nodding her head. She was trying to talk to herself about how many times she had been up and down the steps, but she could still see the smooth brown color of his face and his yellow hair, and she could also see her hand trembling on the banister. It seemed like five years since she had come up the steps with the matrons from Memphis.

In the breakfast room she tore open the frail door to George's little liquor cabinet and took a quart of Bourbon from the shelf. Then she stepped up into the hall and went into the sitting-room and took the portable victrola and that record. As she stomped back into the hall, Buddy came running down the steps. He opened the front door and ran out across the veranda and across the lawn. His yellow hair was like a ball of gold in the sunlight as he went through the gate. But Josie went upstairs.

She locked her door and threw the big key across the room. She knocked the bottle of toilet water and the amber brush off her dressing table as she made room for the victrola. When she had started "Louisville Lady" playing she sat on the stool and began to wonder. "The kid's head was like a ball of gold, but I'm not gonna think about him ever once I get back to Memphis," she told herself. "No, by damn, but I wonder just what George'll do to me." She broke the blue seal of the whiskey with her fingernail, and it didn't seem like more than twenty minutes or half an hours before George was beating and kicking on the door, and she was sitting on the stool and listening and just waiting for him to break the door, and wondering what he'd do to her.

BATTLE ROYAL

by Ralph Ellison

Ralph Ellison (1914–   ) is a distinguished
novelist whose book *Invisible Man* has become a
classic in his own lifetime. A spokesman for
American-Negro life, Ellison has lectured widely
at universities and conferences. His critical writing
has appeared in *Saturday Review, Partisan Review, Harper's,* and many other magazines. The
story included here was originally conceived and
published as a separate story, although later it
formed the first chapter of *Invisible Man,* which
won the National Book Award for fiction.

It goes a long way back, some twenty years. All my life
I had been looking for something, and everywhere I turned
someone tried to tell me what it was. I accepted their answers too, though they were often in contradiction and even
self-contradictory. I was naïve. I was looking for myself and
asking everyone except myself questions which I, and only I,
could answer. It took me a long time and much painful
boomeranging of my expectations to achieve a realization
everyone else appears to have been born with: That I am
nobody but myself. But first I had to discover that I am an
invisible man!

And yet I am no freak of nature, nor of history. I was in
the cards, other things having been equal (or unequal)
eighty-five years ago. I am not ashamed of my grandparents

for having been slaves. I am only ashamed of myself for having at one time been ashamed. About eighty-five years ago they were told that they were free, united with others of our country in everything pertaining to the common good, and, in everything social, separate like the fingers of the hand. And they believed it. They exulted in it. They stayed in their place, worked hard, and brought up my father to do the same. But my grandfather is the one. He was an odd old guy, my grandfather, and I am told I take after him. It was he who caused the trouble. On his deathbed he called my father to him and said, "Son, after I'm gone I want you to keep up the good fight. I never told you, but our life is a war and I have been a traitor all my born days, a spy in the enemy's country ever since I give up my gun back in the Reconstruction. Live with your head in the lion's mouth. I want you to overcome 'em with yeses, undermine 'em with grins, agree 'em to death and destruction, let 'em swoller you till they vomit or bust wide open." They thought the old man had gone out of his mind. He had been the meekest of men. The younger children were rushed from the room, the shades drawn and the flame of the lamp turned so low that it sputtered on the wick like the old man's breathing. "Learn it to the younguns," he whispered fiercely; then he died.

But my folks were more alarmed over his last words than over his dying. It was as though he had not died at all, his words caused so much anxiety. I was warned emphatically to forget what he had said and, indeed, this is the first time it has been mentioned outside the family circle. It had a tremendous effect upon me, however. I could never be sure of what he meant. Grandfather had been a quiet old man who never made any trouble, yet on his deathbed he had called himself a traitor and a spy, and he had spoken of his meekness as a dangerous activity. It became a constant puzzle which lay unanswered in the back of my mind. And whenever things went well for me I remembered my grandfather and felt guilty and uncomfortable. It was as though I was carrying out his advice in spite of myself. And to make

it worse, everyone loved me for it. I was praised by the most
lily-white men of the town. I was considered an example of
desirable conduct—just as my grandfather had been. And
what puzzled me was that the old man had defined it as
treachery. When I was praised for my conduct I felt a guilt
that in some way I was doing something that was really
against the wishes of the white folks, that if they had understood they would have desired me to act just the opposite,
that I should have been sulky and mean, and that that really
would have been what they wanted, even though they were
fooled and thought they wanted me to act as I did. It made
me afraid that some day they would look upon me as a
traitor and I would be lost. Still I was more afraid to act
any other way because they didn't like that at all. The old
man's words were like a curse. On my graduation day I
delivered an oration in which I showed that humility was
the secret, indeed, the very essence of progress. (Not that I
believed this—how could I, remembering my grandfather?
—I only believed that it worked.) It was a great success.
Everyone praised me and I was invited to give the speech at
a gathering of the town's leading white citizens. It was a triumph for our whole community.

It was in the main ballroom of the leading hotel. When I
got there I discovered that it was on the occasion of a
smoker, and I was told that since I was to be there anyway I
might as well take part in the battle royal to be fought by
some of my schoolmates as part of the entertainment. The
battle royal came first.

All of the town's big shots were there in their tuxedoes,
wolfing down the buffet foods, drinking beer and whiskey
and smoking black cigars. It was a large room with a high
ceiling. Chairs were arranged in neat rows around three sides
of a portable boxing ring. The fourth side was clear, revealing a gleaming space of polished floor. I had some misgiv-
ings over the battle royal, by the way. Not from a distaste for
fighting, but because I didn't care too much for the other
fellows who were to take part. They were tough guys who

seemed to have no grandfather's curse worrying their minds. No one could mistake their toughness. And besides, I suspected that fighting a battle royal might detract from the dignity of my speech. In those pre-invisible days I visualized myself as a potential Booker T. Washington. But the other fellows didn't care too much for me either, and there were nine of them. I felt superior to them in my way, and I didn't like the manner in which we were all crowded together into the servants' elevator. Nor did they like my being there. In fact, as the warmly lighted floors flashed past the elevator we had words over the fact that I, by taking part in the fight, had knocked one of their friends out of a night's work.

We were led out of the elevator through a rococo hall into an anteroom and told to get into our fighting togs. Each of us was issued a pair of boxing gloves and ushered out into the big mirrored hall, which we entered looking cautiously about us and whispering, lest we might accidentally be heard above the noise of the room. It was foggy with cigar smoke. And already the whiskey was taking effect. I was shocked to see some of the most important men of the town quite tipsy. They were all there—bankers, lawyers, judges, doctors, fire chiefs, teachers, merchants. Even one of the more fashionable pastors. Something we could not see was going on up front. A clarinet was vibrating sensuously and the men were standing up and moving eagerly forward. We were a small tight group, clustered together, our bare upper bodies touching and shining with anticipatory sweat; while up front the big shots were becoming increasingly excited over something we still could not see. Suddenly I heard the school superintendent, who had told me to come, yell, "Bring up the shines, gentlemen! Bring up the little shines!"

We were rushed up to the front of the ballroom, where it smelled even more strongly of tobacco and whiskey. Then we were pushed into place. I almost wet my pants. A sea of faces, some hostile, some amused, ringed around us, and in the center, facing us, stood a magnificent blonde—stark naked. There was dead silence. I felt a blast of cold air chill me. I tried to back away, but they were behind me and around me. Some of the boys stood with lowered heads, trembling. I felt a wave of irrational guilt and fear. My teeth chattered, my skin turned to goose flesh, my knees knocked. Yet I was strongly attracted and looked in spite of myself. Had the price of looking been blindness, I would have looked. The hair was yellow like that of a circus kewpie doll, the face heavily powdered and rouged, as though to form an abstract mask, the eyes hollow and smeared a cool blue, the color of a baboon's butt. I felt a desire to spit upon her as my eyes brushed slowly over her body. Her breasts were firm and round as the domes of East Indian temples, and I stood so close as to see the fine skin texture and beads of pearly perspiration glistening like dew around the pink and erected buds of her nipples. I wanted at one and the same time to run from the room, to sink through the floor, or go to her and cover her from my eyes and the eyes of the others with my body; to feel the soft thighs, to caress her and destroy her, to love her and murder her, to hide from her, and yet to stroke where below the small American flag tattooed upon her belly her thighs formed a capital V. I had a notion that of all in the room she saw only me with impersonal eyes.

And then she began to dance, a slow sensuous movement, the smoke of a hundred cigars clinging to her like the thinnest of veils. She seemed like a fair bird-girl girdled in veils calling to me from the angry surface of some gray and threatening sea. I was transported. Then I became aware of the clarinet playing and the big shots yelling at us. Some threatened us if we looked and others if we did not. On my right I saw one boy faint. And now a man grabbed a silver pitcher from a table and stepped close as he dashed ice water upon him and stood him up and forced two of us to support him as his head hung and moans issued from his thick bluish lips. Another boy began to plead to go home. He was the largest of the group, wearing dark red fighting trunks much too small to conceal the erection which projected from him as though in answer to the insinuating low-registered moaning of the clarinet. He tried to hide himself with his boxing gloves.

And all the while the blonde continued dancing, smiling faintly at the big shots who watched her with fascination, and faintly smiling at our fear. I noticed a certain merchant who followed her hungrily, his lips loose and drooling. He was a large man who wore diamond studs in a shirtfront which swelled with the ample paunch underneath, and each time the blonde swayed her undulating hips he ran his hand through the thin hair of his bald head and, with his arms upheld, his posture clumsy like that of an intoxicated panda, wound his belly in a slow and obscene grind. This creature was completely hypnotized. The music had quickened. As the dancer flung herself about with a detached expression on her face, the men began reaching out to touch her. I could see their beefy fingers sink into the soft flesh. Some of the others tried to stop them and she began to move around the floor in graceful circles, as they gave chase, slipping and sliding over the polished floor. It was mad. Chairs went crashing, drinks were spilt, as they ran laughing and howling after her. They caught her just as she reached a door, raised her from the floor, and tossed her as college boys are tossed at a hazing, and above her red, fixed-smiling lips I saw the terror and disgust in her eyes, almost like my own terror and that which I saw in some of the other boys. As I watched, they tossed her twice and her soft breasts seemed to flatten against the air and her legs flung wildly as she spun. Some of the more sober ones helped her to escape. And I started off the floor, heading for the anteroom with the rest of the boys.

Some were still crying and in hysteria. But as we tried to leave we were stopped and ordered to get into the ring. There was nothing to do but what we were told. All ten of us climbed under the ropes and allowed ourselves to be blindfolded with broad bands of white cloth. One of the men seemed to feel a bit sympathetic and tried to cheer us up as we stood with our backs against the ropes. Some of us tried to grin. "See that boy over there?" one of the men said. "I want you to run across at the bell and give it to him right in the belly. If you don't get him, I'm going to get you. I don't like his looks." Each of us was told the same. The blindfolds were put on. Yet even then I had been going over my speech. In my mind each word was as bright as flame. I felt the cloth pressed into place, and frowned so that it would be loosened when I relaxed.

But now I felt a sudden fit of blind terror. I was unused to darkness. It was as though I had suddenly found myself in a dark room filled with poisonous cottonmouths. I could hear the bleary voices yelling insistently for the battle royal to begin.

"Get going in there!"

"Let me at that big nigger!"

I strained to pick up the school superintendent's voice, as though to squeeze some security out of that slightly more familiar sound.

"Let me at those black sonsabitches!" someone yelled.

"No, Jackson, no!" another voice yelled. "Here, somebody, help me hold Jack."

"I want to get at that ginger-colored nigger. Tear him limb from limb," the first voice yelled.

I stood against the ropes trembling. For in those days I was what they called ginger-colored, and he sounded as though he might crunch me between his teeth like a crisp ginger cookie.

Quite a struggle was going on. Chairs were being kicked about and I could hear voices grunting as with a terrific effort. I wanted to see, to see more desperately than ever before. But the blindfold was tight as a thick skin-puckering scab and when I raised my gloved hands to push the layers of white aside a voice yelled, "Oh, no you don't, black bastard! Leave that alone!"

"Ring the bell before Jackson kills him a coon!" someone boomed in the sudden silence. And I heard the bell clang and the sound of the feet scuffling forward.

A glove smacked against my head. I pivoted, striking out stiffly as someone went past, and felt the jar ripple along the length of my arm to my shoulder. Then it seemed as though all nine of the boys had turned upon me at once. Blows pounded me from all sides while I struck out as best I could. So many blows landed upon me that I wondered if I were not the only blindfolded fighter in the ring, or if the man called Jackson hadn't succeeded in getting me after all.

Blindfolded, I could no longer control my motions. I had no dignity. I stumbled about like a baby or a drunken man. The smoke had become thicker and with each new blow it seemed to sear and further restrict my lungs. My saliva became like hot bitter glue. A glove connected with my head, filling my mouth with warm blood. It was everywhere. I could not tell if the moisture I felt upon my body was sweat or blood. A blow landed hard against the nape of my neck. I felt myself going over, my head hitting the floor. Streaks of blue light filled the black world behind the blindfold. I lay prone, pretending that I was knocked out, but felt myself seized by hands and yanked to my feet. "Get going, black boy! Mix it up!" My arms were like lead, my head smarting from blows. I managed to feel my way to the ropes and held on, trying to catch my breath. A glove landed in my mid-section and I went over again, feeling as though the smoke had become a knife jabbed into my guts. Pushed this way and that by the legs milling around me, I finally pulled erect and discovered that I could see the black, sweat-washed forms weaving in the smoky-blue atmosphere like drunken dancers weaving to the rapid drum-like thuds of blows.

Everyone fought hysterically. It was complete anarchy. Everybody fought everybody else. No group fought together for long. Two, three, four, fought one, then turned to fight each other, were themselves attacked. Blows landed below the belt and in the kidney, with the gloves open as well as closed, and with my eye partly opened now there was not so much terror. I moved carefully, avoiding blows, although not too many to attract attention, fighting from group to group. The boys groped about like blind, cautious crabs crouching to protect their mid-sections, their heads pulled in short against their shoulders, their arms stretched nervously before them, with their fists testing the smoke-filled air like the knobbed feelers of hypersensitive snails. In one corner I glimpsed a boy violently punching the air and heard him scream in pain as he smashed his hand against a ring post. For a second I saw him bent over holding his hand, then going down as a blow caught his unprotected head. I played one group against the other, slipping and throwing a punch then stepping out of range while pushing the others into the melee to take the blows blindly aimed at me. The smoke was agonizing and there were no rounds, no bells at three minute intervals to relieve our exhaustion. The room spun round me, a swirl of lights, smoke, sweating bodies surrounded by tense white faces. I bled from both nose and mouth, the blood spattering upon my chest.

The men kept yelling, "Slug him, black boy! Knock his guts out!"

"Uppercut him! Kill him! Kill that big boy!"

Taking a fake fall, I saw a boy going down heavily beside me as though we were felled by a single blow, saw a sneaker-clad foot shoot into his groin as the two who had knocked him down stumbled upon him. I rolled out of range, feeling a twinge of nausea.

The harder we fought the more threatening the men became. And yet, I had begun to worry about my speech again. How would it go? Would they recognize my ability? What would they give me?

I was fighting automatically when suddenly I noticed that one after another of the boys was leaving the ring. I was surprised, filled with panic, as though I had been left alone with an unknown danger. Then I understood. The boys had arranged it among themselves. It was the custom for the two men left in the ring to slug it out for the winner's prize. I discovered this too late. When the bell sounded two men in tuxedoes leaped into the ring and removed the blindfold. I found myself facing Tatlock, the biggest of the gang. I felt sick at my stomach. Hardly had the bell stopped ringing in my ears than it clanged again and I saw him moving swiftly toward me. Thinking of nothing else to do I hit him smash on the nose. He kept coming, bringing the rank sharp violence of stale sweat. His face was a black blank of a face, only his eyes alive—with hate of me and aglow with a feverish terror from what had happened to us all. I became anxious. I wanted to deliver my speech and he came at me as though he meant to beat it out of me. I smashed him again and again, taking his blows as they came. Then on a sudden impulse I struck him lightly and as we clinched, I whispered, "Fake like I knocked you out, you can have the prize."

"I'll break your behind," he whispered hoarsely.

"For *them?*"

"For *me,* sonofabitch!"

They were yelling for us to break it up and Tatlock spun me half around with a blow, and as a joggled camera sweeps in a reeling scene, I saw the howling red faces crouching tense beneath the cloud of blue-gray smoke. For a moment the world wavered, unraveled, flowed, then my head cleared and Tatlock bounced before me. That fluttering shadow before my eyes was his jabbing left hand. Then falling forward, my head against his damp shoulder, I whispered,

"I'll make it five dollars more."

"Go to hell!"

But his muscles relaxed a trifle beneath my pressure and I breathed, "Seven!"

"Give it to your ma," he said, ripping me beneath the heart.

And while I still held him I butted him and moved away. I felt myself bombarded with punches. I fought back with hopeless desperation. I wanted to deliver my speech more than anything else in the world, because I felt that only these men could judge truly my ability, and now this stupid clown was ruining my chances. I began fighting carefully now, moving in to punch him and out again with my greater speed. A lucky blow to his chin and I had him going too—until I heard a loud voice yell, "I got my money on the big boy."

Hearing this, I almost dropped my guard. I was confused. Should I try to win against the voice out there? Would not this go against my speech, and was not this a moment for humility, for nonresistance? A blow to my head as I danced about sent my right eye popping like a jack-in-the-box and settled my dilemma. The room went red as I fell. It was a dream fall, my body languid and fastidious as to where to land, until the floor became impatient and smashed up to meet me. A moment later I came to. An hypnotic voice said FIVE emphatically. And I lay there, hazily watching a dark red spot of my own blood shaping itself into a butterfly, glistening and soaking into the soiled gray world of the canvas.

When the voice drawled TEN I was lifted and dragged to a chair. I sat dazed. My eye pained and swelled with each throb of my pounding heart and I wondered if now I would be allowed to speak. I was wringing wet, my mouth still bleeding. We were grouped along the wall now. The other boys ignored me as they congratulated Tatlock and speculated as to how much they would be paid. One boy whimpered over his smashed hand. Looking up front, I saw attendants in white jackets rolling the portable ring away and placing a small square rug in the vacant space surrounded by chairs. Perhaps, I thought, I will stand on the rug to deliver my speech.

Then the M.C. called to us, "Come on up here boys and get your money."

We ran forward to where the men laughed and talked in their chairs, waiting. Everyone seemed friendly now.

"There it is on the rug," the man said. I saw the rug

covered with coins of all dimensions and a few crumpled bills. But what excited me, scattered here and there, were the gold pieces.

"Boys, it's all yours," the man said. "You get all you grab."

"That's right, Sambo," a blond man said, winking at me confidentially.

I trembled with excitement, forgetting my pain. I would get the gold and the bills, I thought. I would use both hands. I would throw my body against the boys nearest me to block them from the gold.

"Get down around the rug now," the man commanded, "and don't anyone touch it until I give the signal."

"This ought to be good," I heard.

As told, we got around the square rug on our knees. Slowly the man raised his freckled hand as we followed it upward with our eyes.

I heard, "These niggers look like they're about to pray!"

Then, "Ready," the man said. "Go!"

I lunged for a yellow coin lying on the blue design of the carpet, touching it and sending a surprised shriek to join those rising around me. I tried frantically to remove my hand but could not let go. A hot, violent force tore through my body, shaking me like a wet rat. The rug was electrified. The hair bristled up on my head as I shook myself free. My muscles jumped, my nerves jangled, writhed. But I saw that this was not stopping the other boys. Laughing in fear and embarrassment, some were holding back and scooping up the coins knocked off by the painful contortions of the others. The men roared above us as we struggled.

"Pick it up, goddamnit, pick it up!" someone called like a bass-voiced parrot. "Go on, get it!"

I crawled rapidly around the floor, picking up the coins, trying to avoid the coppers and to get greeenbacks and the gold. Ignoring the shock by laughing, as I brushed the coins off quickly, I discovered that I could contain the electricity —a contradiction, but it works. Then the men began to push

us onto the rug. Laughing embarrassedly, we struggled out
of their hands and kept after the coins. We were all wet and
slippery and hard to hold. Suddenly I saw a boy lifted into
the air, glistening with sweat like a circus seal, and dropped,
his wet back landing flush upon the charged rug, heard him
yell and saw him literally dance upon his back, his elbows
beating a frenzied tattoo upon the floor, his muscles twitching like the flesh of a horse stung by many flies. When he
finally rolled off, his face was gray and no one stopped him
when he ran from the floor amid booming laughter.

"Get the money," the M.C. called. "That's good hard
American cash!"

And we snatched and grabbed, snatched and grabbed. I
was careful not to come too close to the rug now, and when
I felt the hot whiskey breath descend upon me like a cloud
of foul air I reached out and grabbed the leg of a chair. It
was occupied and I held on desperately.

"Leggo, nigger! Leggo!"

The huge face wavered down to mine as he tried to push
me free. But my body was slippery and he was too drunk. It
was Mr. Colcord, who owned a chain of movie houses and
"entertainment palaces." Each time he grabbed me I slipped
out of his hands. It became a real struggle. I feared the rug
more than I did the drunk, so I held on, surprising myself
for a moment by trying to topple *him* upon the rug. It was
such an enormous idea that I found myself actually carrying it out. I tried not to be obvious, yet when I grabbed his
leg, trying to tumble him out of the chair, he raised up roaring with laughter, and, looking at me with soberness dead
in the eye, kicked me viciously in the chest. The chair leg
flew out of my hand and I felt myself going and rolled. It
was as though I had rolled through a bed of hot coals. It
seemed a whole century would pass before I would roll
free, a century in which I was seared through the deepest
levels of my body to the fearful breath within me and the
breath seared and heated to the point of explosion. It'll all

be over in a flash, I thought as I rolled clear. It'll all be over in a flash.

But not yet, the men on the other side were waiting, red faces swollen as though from apoplexy as they bent forward in their chairs. Seeing their fingers coming toward me I rolled away as a fumbled football rolls off the receiver's fingertips, back into the coals. That time I luckily sent the rug sliding out of place and heard the coins ringing against the floor and the boys scuffling to pick them up and the M.C. calling, "All right, boys, that's all. Go get dressed and get your money."

I was limp as a dish rag. My back felt as though it had been beaten with wires.

When we had dressed the M.C. came in and gave us each five dollars, except Tatlock, who got ten for being last in the ring. Then he told us to leave. I was not to get a chance to deliver my speech, I thought. I was going out into the dim alley in despair when I was stopped and told to go back. I returned to the ballroom, where the men were pushing back their chairs and gathering in groups to talk.

The M.C. knocked on a table for quiet. "Gentlemen," he said, "we almost forgot an important part of the program. A most serious part, gentlemen. This boy was brought here to deliver a speech which he made at his graduation yesterday . . ."

"Bravo!"

"I'm told that he is the smartest boy we've got out there in Greenwood. I'm told that he knows more big words than a pocket-sized dictionary."

Much applause and laughter.

"So now, gentlemen, I want you to give him your attention."

There was still laughter as I faced them, my mouth dry, my eye throbbing. I began slowly, but evidently my throat was tense, because they began shouting, "Louder! Louder!"

"We of the younger generation extol the wisdom of that great leader and educator," I shouted, "who first spoke these flaming words of wisdom: 'A ship lost at sea for many days suddenly sighted a friendly vessel. From the mast of the unfortunate vessel was seen a signal: "Water, water; we die of thirst!" The answer from the friendly vessel came back: "Cast down your bucket where you are." The captain of the distressed vessel, at last heeding the injunction, cast down his bucket, and it came up full of fresh sparkling water from the mouth of the Amazon River.' And like him I say, and in his words, 'To those of my race who depend upon bettering their condition in a foreign land, or who underestimate the importance of cultivating friendly relations with the Southern white man, who is his next-door neighbor, I would say: "Cast down your bucket where you are"— cast it down in making friends in every manly way of the people of all races by whom we are surrounded . . .'"

I spoke automatically and with such fervor that I did not realize that the men were still talking and laughing until my dry mouth, filling up with blood from the cut, almost strangled me. I coughed, wanting to stop and go to one of the tall brass, sand-filled spittoons to relieve myself, but a few of the men, especially the superintendent, were listening and I was afraid. So I gulped it down, blood, saliva and all, and continued. (What powers of endurance I had during those days! What enthusiasm! What a belief in the rightness of things!) I spoke even louder in spite of the pain. But still they talked and still they laughed, as though deaf with cotton in dirty ears. So I spoke with greater emotional emphasis. I closed my ears and swallowed blood until I was nauseated. The speech seemed a hundred times as long as before, but I could not leave out a single word. All had to be said, each memorized nuance considered, rendered. Nor was that all. Whenever I uttered a word of three or more syllables a group of voices would yell for me to repeat it. I used the phrase "social responsibility" and they yelled:

"What's that word you say, boy?"

"Social responsibility," I said.

"What?"

"Social . . ."

"Louder."

". . . responsibility."

"More!"

"Respon—"

"Repeat!"

"sibility."

The room was filled with the uproar of laughter until, no doubt, distracted by having to gulp down my blood, I made a mistake and yelled a phrase I had often seen denounced in newspaper editorials, heard debated in private.

"Social . . ."

"What?" they yelled.

". . . equality—"

The laughter hung smokelike in the sudden stillness. I opened my eyes, puzzled. Sounds of displeasure filled the room. The M.C. rushed forward. They shouted hostile phrases at me. But I did not understand.

A small dry mustached man in the front row blared out, "Say that slowly, son!"

"What, sir?"

"What you just said!"

"Social responsibility, sir," I said.

"You weren't being smart were you, boy?" he said, not unkindly.

"No, sir!"

"You sure that about 'equality' was a mistake?"

"Oh, yes sir," I said. "I was swallowing blood."

"Well, you had better speak more slowly so we can understand. We mean to do right by you, but you've got to know your place at all times. All right, now, go on with your speech."

I was afraid. I wanted to leave but I wanted also to speak and I was afraid they'd snatch me down.

"Thank you, sir," I said, beginning where I had left off, and having them ignore me as before.

Yet when I finished there was a thunderous applause. I

was surprised to see the superintendent come forth with a package wrapped in white tissue paper, and, gesturing for quiet, address the men.

"Gentlemen, you see that I did not overpraise this boy. He makes a good speech and some day he'll lead his people in the proper paths. And I don't have to tell you that that is important in these days and times. This is a good, smart boy, and so to encourage him in the right direction, in the name of the Board of Education I wish to present him a prize in the form of this . . ."

He paused, removing the tissue paper and revealing a gleaming calfskin brief case.

". . . in the form of this first-class article from Shad Whitmore's shop."

"Boy," he said, addressing me, "take this prize and keep it well. Consider it a badge of office. Prize it. Keep developing as you are and some day it will be filled with important papers that will help shape the destiny of your people."

I was so moved that I could hardly express my thanks. A rope of bloody saliva forming a shape like an undiscovered continent drooled upon the leather and I wiped it quickly away. I felt an importance that I had never dreamed.

"Open it and see what's inside," I was told.

My fingers a-tremble, I complied, smelling the fresh leather and finding an official-looking document inside. It was a scholarship to the state college for Negroes. My eyes filled with tears and I ran awkwardly off the floor.

I was overjoyed. I did not even mind when I discovered that the gold pieces I had scrambled for were brass pocket tokens advertising a certain make of automobile.

When I reached home everyone was excited. Next day the neighbors came to congratulate me. I even felt safe from grandfather, whose deathbed curse usually spoiled my triumphs. I stood beneath his photograph with my brief case in hand and smiled triumphantly into his stolid black peasant's face. It was a face that fascinated me. The eyes seemed to follow everywhere I went.

That night I dreamed I was at a circus with him and that he refused to laugh at the clowns no matter what they did. Then later he told me to open my brief case and read what was inside and I did, finding an official envelope stamped with the state seal; and inside the envelope I found another and another, endlessly and I thought I would fall of weariness. "Them's years," he said. "Now open that one." And I did and in it I found an engraved document containing a short message in letters of gold, "Read it," my grandfather said. "Out loud!"

"To Whom It May Concern," I intoned. "Keep This Nigger-boy Running."

I awoke with the old man's laughter in my ears.

(It was a dream I was to remember and dream again for many years after. But at that time I had no insight into its meaning. First I had to attend college.)

COME OUT THE WILDERNESS

by James Baldwin

James Baldwin (1924–   ). Born in New York
City, Baldwin has had a distinguished career as
short story writer, novelist, and essayist. He has
been a Saxton, Rosenwald, Guggenheim, and Partisan Review Fellow, has won the National Institute of Arts and Letters award, and has been a
Ford grantee. His first novel, *Go Tell It on the
Mountain*, appeared in 1953 and was widely acclaimed for its powerful and moving picture of
Negro life. *Giovanni's Room*, appearing in 1958,
was a controversial novel about homosexuality.
Collections of Mr. Baldwin's essays, notably *Notes
of a Native Son*, *Nobody Knows My Name*, and
The Fire Next Time, have raised a critical furor.
His stories have appeared in many magazines and
in prize story collections.

Paul did not yet feel her eyes on him. She watched him.
He went to the window, peering out between the slats in the
Venetian blinds. She could tell from his profile that it did
not look like a pleasant day. In profile, all of the contradic-
tions that so confounded her seemed to be revealed. He had
a boy's long, rather thin neck but it supported a head that
seemed even more massive than it actually was because of
its plantation of thickly curling black hair, hair that was always a little too long or else, cruelly, much too short. His

forehead was broad and high but this austerity was contradicted by a short, blunt, almost ludicrously upturned nose. And he had a large mouth and very heavy, sensual lips, which suggested a certain wry cruelty when turned down but looked like the mask of comedy when he laughed. His body was really excessively black with hair, which proved, she said, since Negroes were generally less hairy than whites, which race, in fact, had moved farthest from the ape. Other people did not see his beauty, which always mildly astonished her—it was like thinking that the sun was ordinary. He was sloppy about the way he stood and sat, that was true, and so his shoulders were already beginning to be round. And he was a poor man's son, a city boy, and so his body could not really remind anyone of a Michelangelo statue as she— "fantastically," he said—claimed; it did not have that luxury or that power. It was economically tense and hard and testified only to the agility of the poor, who are always dancing one step ahead of the devil.

He stepped away from the window, looking worried. Ruth closed her eyes. When she opened them he was disappearing away from her down the short, black hall that led to the bathroom. She wondered what time he had come in last night; she wondered if he had a hang-over; she heard the water running. She thought that he had probably not been home long. She was very sensitive to his comings and goings and had often found herself abruptly upright and wide awake a moment after he, restless at two-thirty in the morning, had closed the door behind him. Then there was no more sleep for her. She lay there on a bed that inexorably became a bed of ashes and hot coals, while her imagination dwelt on every conceivable disaster, from his having forsaken her for another woman to his having, somehow, ended up in the morgue. And as the night faded from black to gray to daylight, the telephone began to seem another presence in the house, sitting not far from her like a great, malevolent black cat that might, at any moment, with one shrill cry, scatter her life like dismembered limbs all over this tiny room. There were places she could have called, but she would have died first. After all—he had only needed to point it out once, he would never have occasion to point it out again—they were not married. Often she had pulled herself out of bed, her loins cold and her body trembling, and gotten dressed and had coffee and gone to work without seeing him. But he would call her in the office later in the day. She would have had several stiff drinks at lunch and so could be very offhand over the phone, pretending that she had only supposed him to have gotten up a little earlier than herself that morning. But the moment she put the receiver down she hated him. She made herself sick with fantasies of how she would be revenged. Then she hated herself; thinking into what an iron maiden of love and hatred he had placed her, she hated him even more. She could not help feeling that he treated her this way because of her color, because she was a colored girl. Then her past and her present threatened to engulf her. She knew she was being unfair; she could not help it; she thought of psychiatry; she saw herself transformed, at peace with the world, herself, her color, with the male of indeterminate color she would have found. Always, this journey round her skull ended with tears, resolutions, prayers, with Paul's face, which then had the power to reconcile her even to the lowest circle of hell.

After work, on the way home, she stopped for another drink, or two or three; bought Sen-Sen to muffle the odor, wore the most casually glowing of smiles as he casually kissed her when she came through one door.

She knew that he was going to leave her. It was in his walk, his talk, his eyes. He wanted to go. He had already moved back, crouching to leap. And she had no rival. He was not going to another woman. He simply wanted to go. It would happen today, tomorrow; three weeks from today; it was over, she could do nothing about it; neither could she save herself by jumping first. She had no place to go, she only wanted him. She had tried to want other men, and she was still young, only twenty-six, and there was no real lack of opportunity. But all she knew about other men was that they were not Paul.

Through the gloom of the hallway he came back into the room and, moving to the edge of the bed, lit a cigarette. She smiled up at him.

"Good morning," she said. "Would you light one for me too?"

He looked down at her with a sleepy and slightly shame-faced grin. Without a word he offered her his freshly lit cigarette, lit another, and then got into bed, shivering slightly.

"Good morning," he said then. "Did you sleep well?"

"Very well," she said lightly. "Did you? I didn't hear you come in."

"Ah, I was very quiet," he said teasingly, curling his great body toward her and putting his head on her breast. "I didn't want to wake you up. I was afraid you'd hit me with something."

She laughed. "What time *did* you come in?"

"Oh"—he raised his head, dragging on his cigarette, and half-frowned, half-smiled—"about an hour or so ago."

"What did you do? Find a new after-hours joint?"

"No. I ran into Cosmo. We went over to his place to look at a couple new paintings he's done. He had a bottle, we sat around."

She knew Cosmo and distrusted him. He was about forty and he had had two wives; he did not think women were worth much. She was sure that Cosmo had been giving Paul advice as to how to be rid of her; she could imagine, or believed she could, how he had spoken about her, and she felt her skin tighten. At the same moment she became aware of the warmth of Paul's body.

"What did you talk about?" she asked.

"Oh. Painting. His paintings, my paintings, all God's chillun's paintings."

During the day, while she was at work, Paul painted in

the back room of this cramped and criminally expensive Village apartment, where the light was bad and where there was not really room enough for him to step back and look at his canvas. Most of his paintings were stored with a friend. Still, there were enough, standing against the wall, piled on top of the closet and on the table, for a sizable one-man show. "If they were any good," said Paul, who worked very hard. She knew this, despite the fact that he said so rather too often. She knew by his face, his distance, his quality, frequently, of seeming to be like a spring, unutterably dangerous to touch. And by the exhaustion, different in kind from any other, with which he sometimes stretched out in bed.

She thought—of course—that his paintings were very good, but he did not take her judgment seriously. "You're sweet, funnyface," he sometimes said, "but, you know, you aren't really very bright." She was scarcely at all mollified by his adding, "Thank heaven. I hate bright women."

She remembered, now, how stupid she had felt about music all the time she had lived with Arthur, a man of her own color who had played a clarinet. She was still finding out today, so many years after their breakup, how much she had learned from him—not only about music, unluckily. If I stay on this merry-go-round, she thought, I'm going to become very accomplished, just the sort of girl no man will ever marry.

She moved closer to Paul, the fingers of one hand playing with his hair. He lay still. It was very silent.

"Ruth." he said finally, "I've been thinking . . ."

At once she was all attention. She drew on her cigarette, her fingers still drifting through his hair, as though she were playing with water. "Yes?" she prompted.

She had always wondered, when the moment came, if she would make things easy for him, or difficult. She still did not know. He leaned up on one elbow, looking down at her. She met his eyes, hoping that her own eyes reflected nothing but calm curiosity. He continued to stare at her and put one hand on her short, dark hair. Then, "You're a nice girl," he said, irrelevantly, and leaned down and kissed her.

With a kiss! she thought.

"My father wouldn't think so," she said, "if he could see me now. What is it you've been thinking?"

He still said nothing but only looked down at her, an expression in his eyes that she could not read.

"I've been thinking," he said, "that it's about time I got started on that portrait of you. I ought to get started right away."

She felt, very sharply, that his nerve had failed him. But she felt, too, that his decision now to do a portrait of her was a means of moving far enough away from her to be able to tell her the truth. Also, he had always said that he could do something wonderful with her on canvas—it would be foolish to let the opportunity pass. Cosmo had probably told him this. She had always been flattered by his desire to paint her but now she hoped that he would suddenly go blind.

"Anytime," she said, and could not resist, "Am I to be part of a gallery?"

"Yeah. I'll probably be able to sell you for a thousand bucks," he said, and kissed her again.

"That's not a very nice thing to say," she murmured.

"You're a funny girl. What's not nice about a thousand dollars?" He leaned over her to put out his cigarette in the ash tray near the bed; then took hers and put it out too. He fell back against her and put his hand on her breast.

She said tentatively: "Well, I suppose if you do it often enough, I could stop working."

His arms tightened but she did not feel that this was due entirely to desire; it might be said that he was striving, now, to distract her. "If I do *what* enough?" he grinned.

"Now, now," she smiled, "you just said that I was a nice girl."

"You're one of the nicest girls I ever met," said Paul soberly. "Really you are. I often wonder . . ."

"You often wonder what?"

"What's going to become of you."

She felt like a river trying to run two ways at once: she felt herself shrinking from him, yet she flowed toward him too; she knew he felt it. "But as long as you're with me," she said, and she could not help herself, she felt she was about to cry; she held his face between her hands, pressing yet closer against him. "As long as you're with me." His face was white, his eyes glowed: there was a war in him too. Everything that divided them charged, for an instant, the tiny space between them. Then the veils of habit and desire covered both their eyes.

"Life is very long," said Paul at last. He kissed her. They both sighed. And slowly she surrendered, opening up before him like the dark continent, made mad and delirious and blind by the entry of a mortal as bright as the morning, as white as milk.

When she left the house he was sleeping. Because she was late for work and because it was raining, she dropped into a cab and was whirled out of the streets of the Village —which still suggested, at least, some faint memory of the individual life—into the grim publicities of mid-town Manhattan. Blocks and squares and exclamation marks, stone and steel and glass as far as the eye could see; everything towering, lifting itself against, though by no means into, heaven. The people, so surrounded by heights that they had lost any sense of what heights were, rather resembled, nevertheless, these gray rigidities and also resembled, in their frantic motion, people fleeing a burning town. Ruth, who was not so many years removed from trees and earth, had felt in the beginning that she would never be able to live on an island so eccentric; she had, for example, before she arrived, dreamed of herself as walking by the river. But apart from the difficulties of realizing this ambition, which were not inconsiderable, it turned out that a lone girl walking by the river was simply asking to be victimized by both the disturbers and the defenders of the public peace. She retreated into the interior and this dream was abandoned—along with others. For her as for most of Manhattan, trees and water ceased to be realities; the nervous, trusting landscape of the city began to be the landscape of her mind. And soon her mind, like life on the island, seemed to be incapable of flexibility, of moving outward, could only shriek upward into meaningless abstractions or drop downward into cruelty and confusion.

She worked for a life insurance company that had only recently become sufficiently progressive to hire Negroes. This meant that she worked in an atmosphere so positively electric with interracial good will that no one ever dreamed of telling the truth about anything. It would have seemed, and it quite possibly would have been a spiteful act. The only other Negro there was male, a Mr. Davis, who was very highly placed. He was an expert, it appeared, in some way about Negroes and life insurance, from which Ruth had ungenerously concluded that he was the company's expert on how to cheat more Negroes out of more money and not only remain within the law but also be honored with a plaque for good race relations. She often—but not always—took dictation from him. The other girls, manifesting a rough, girl-scoutish camaraderie that made the question of their sincerity archaic, found him "marvelous" and wondered if he had a wife. Ruth found herself unable to pursue these strangely overheated and yet eerily impersonal speculations with anything like the indicated vehemence. Since it was extremely unlikely that any of these girls would ever even go dancing with Mr. Davis, it was impossible to believe that they had any ambition to share his couch, matrimonial or otherwise, and yet, lacking this ambition, it was impossible to account for their avidity. But they were all incredibly innocent and made her ashamed of her body. At the same time it demanded, during their maddening coffee breaks, a great deal of will power not to take Paul's photograph out of her wallet and wave it before them saying, *"You'll never*

lay a finger on Mr. Davis. But look what I took from you!"
Her face at such moments allowed them to conclude that
she was planning to ensnare Mr. Davis herself. It was perhaps this assumption, despite her phone calls from Paul,
that allowed them to discuss Mr. Davis so freely before her,
and they also felt, in an incoherent way, that these discussions were proof of their democracy. She did not find Mr.
Davis "marvelous," though she thought him good-looking
enough in a square, stocky, gleaming, black-boyish sort of
way.

Near her office, visible from her window and having the
air of contraband in Caesar's market place, was a small gray
chapel. An ugly neon cross jutted out above the heads of
passers-by, proclaiming "Jesus Saves." Today, as the lunch
hour approached and she began, as always, to fidget, debating whether she should telephone Paul or wait for Paul to
telephone her, she found herself staring in some irritation at
this cross, thinking about her childhood. The telephone rang
and rang, but never for her; she began to feel the need of
a drink. She thought of Paul sleeping while she typed and
became outraged, then thought of his painting and became
maternal; thought of his arms and paused to light a cigarette,
throwing the most pitying of glances toward the girl who
shared her office, who still had a crush on Frank Sinatra.
Nevertheless, the sublimatory tube still burning, the smoke
tickling her nostrils and the typewriter bell clanging at brief
intervals like signals flashing by on a railroad track, she re-
lapsed into bitterness, confusion, fury: for she was trapped,
Paul was a trap. She wanted a man of her own and she
wanted children and all she could see for herself today was
a lifetime of typing while Paul slept or a lifetime of typing
with no Paul. And she began rather to envy the stocky girl
with the crush on Frank Sinatra, since she would settle one
day, obviously, for a great deal less, and probably turn out
children as Detroit turned out cars and never sigh for an
instant for what she had missed, having indeed never, and

especially with a lifetime of moviegoing behind her, missed anything.

"Jesus Saves." She began to think of the days of her innocence. These days had been spent in the South, where her mother and father and older brother remained. She had an older sister, married and with several children, in Oakland, and a baby sister who had become a small-time night club singer in New Orleans. There were relatives of her father's living in Harlem and she was sure that they wrote to him often complaining that she never visited them. They, like her father, were earnest churchgoers, though, unlike her father, their religion was strongly mixed with an opportunistic respectability and with ambitions to better society and their own place in it, which her father would have scorned. Their ambitions vitiated in them what her father called the "true" religion, and what remained of this religion, which was principally vindictiveness, prevented them from understanding anything whatever about those concrete Northern realities that made them at once so obsequious and so venomous.

Her innocence. It was many years ago. She remembered their house, so poor and plain, standing by itself, apart from other houses, as nude and fragile on the stony ground as an upturned cardboard box. And it was nearly as dark inside as it might have been beneath a box, it leaked when the rain fell, froze when the wind blew, could scarcely be entered in July. They tried to coax sustenance out of a soil that had long ago gone out of the business. As time went on they grew to depend less and less on the soil and more on the oyster boats, and on the wages and leftovers brought home by their mother, and then herself, from the white kitchens in town. And her mother still struggled in these white kitchens, humming sweet hymns, tiny, mild-eyed and bent, her father still labored on the oyster boats; after a lifetime of labor, should they drop dead tomorrow, there would not be a penny for their burial clothes. Her brother, still unmarried, nearing thirty now, loitered through the town with his dangerous reputation, drinking and living off the women he murdered with his love-making. He made her parents fearful but they reiterated in each letter that they had placed him, and all their children, in the hands of God. Ruth opened each letter in guilt and fear, expecting each time to be confronted with the catastrophe that had at last overtaken her kin; anticipating too, with a selfish annoyance that added to her guilt, the enforced and necessary journey back to her home in mourning; the survivors gathered together to do brief honor to the dead, whose death was certainly, in part, attributable to the indifference of the living. She often wrote her brother asking him to come North, and asked her sister in Oakland to second her in this plea. But she knew that he would not come North—because of her. She had shamed him and embittered him, she was one of the reasons he drank.

Her mother's song, which she, doubtless, still hummed each evening as she walked the old streets homeward, began with the question, *How did you feel when you come out the wilderness?*

And she remembered her mother, half-humming, half-singing, with a steady, tense beat that would have made any blues singer sit up and listen (though she thought it best not to say this to her mother):

Come out the wilderness,
Come out the wilderness.
How did you feel when you come out the wilderness,
Leaning on the Lord?

And the answers were many: *Oh, my soul felt happy!* or, *I shouted hallelujah!* or, *I do thank God!*

Ruth finished her cigarette, looking out over the stone-cold, hideous New York streets, and thought with a strange new pain of her mother. Her mother had once been no older than she, Ruth, was today, she had probably been pretty, she had also wept and trembled and cried beneath the rude thrusting that was her master and her life, and children had knocked in her womb and split her as they came crying out. Out, and into the wilderness: she had placed them in the hands of God. She had known nothing but labor and sorrow, she had had to confront, every day of her life, the everlasting, nagging, infinitesimal details, it had clearly all come to nothing, how could she be singing still?

"Jesus Saves." She put out her cigarette and a sense of loss and disaster wavered through her like a mist. She wished, in that moment, from the bottom of her heart, that she had never left home. She wished that she had never met Paul. She wished that she had never been touched by his whiteness. She should have found a great, slow, black man, full of laughter and sighs and grace, a man at whose center there burned a steady, smokeless fire. She should have surrendered to him and been a woman, and had his children, and found, through being irreplaceable, despite whatever shadows life might cast, peace that would enable her to endure.

She had left home practically by accident; it had been partly due to her brother. He had grown too accustomed to thinking of her as his prized, adored litle sister to recognize the changes that were occurring within her. This had had something to do with the fact that his own sexual coming of age had disturbed his peace with her—he would, in good faith, have denied this, which did not make it less true. When she was seventeen her brother had surprised her alone in a barn with a boy. Nothing had taken place between herself and this boy, though there was no saying what might not have happened if her brother had not come in. She, guilty though she was in everything but the act, could scarcely believe and had not, until today, ever quite

forgiven his immediate leap to the obvious conclusion.
She began screaming before he hit her, her father had had
to come running to pull her brother off the boy. And she
had shouted their innocence in a steadily blackening despair,
for the boy was too badly beaten to be able to speak and
it was clear that no one believed her. She bawled at last:
"Goddamit, I wish I had, I wish I had, I might as well of
done it!" Her father slapped her. Her brother gave her a
look and said: "You dirty . . . you dirty . . . you black
and dirty——" Then her mother had had to step between
her father and her brother. She turned and ran and sat
down for a long time in the darkness, on a hillside, by herself, shivering. And she felt dirty, she felt that nothing
would ever make her clean.

After this she and her brother scarcely spoke. He had
wounded her so deeply she could not face his eyes. Her
father dragged her to church to make her cry repentance but
she was as stubborn as her father, she told him she had
nothing to repent. And she avoided them all, which was
exactly the most dangerous thing that could have happened,
for when she met the musician, Arthur, who was more than
twenty years older than she, she ran away to New York with
him. She lived with him for more than four years. She did
not love him all that time, she simply did not know how
to escape his domination. He had never made the big-time
himself and he therefore wanted her to become a singer;
and perhaps she had ceased to love him when it became
clear that she had no talent whatever. He was very disappointed, but he was also very proud, and he made her
go to school to study shorthand and typing, and made her
self-conscious about her accent and her grammar, and took
great delight in dressing her. Through him, she got over
feeling that she was black and unattractive and as soon
as this happened she was able to leave him. In fleeing Harlem and her relatives there, she drifted downtown to the
Village, where, eventually, she found employment as a
waitress in one of those restaurants with candles on the

tables. Here, after a year or so, and several increasingly disastrous and desperate liaisons, she met Paul.

The telephone rang several desks away from her and, at the same instant, she was informed that Mr. Davis wanted her in his office. She was sure that it was Paul telephoning but she picked up her pad and walked into Mr. Davis' cubbyhole. Someone picked up the receiver, cutting off the bell, and she closed the door of Mr. Davis' office behind her.

"Good morning," she said.

"Good morning," he answered. He looked out of his window. "Though, between you and me, I've seen better mornings. This morning ain't half trying."

They both laughed, self-consciously amused and relieved by his "ain't."

She sat down, her pencil poised, looking at him questioningly.

"How do you like your job?" he asked her.

She had not expected his question, which she immediately distrusted and resented, suspecting him, on no evidence whatever, of acting now as a company spy.

"It's quite pleasant," she said in a guarded, ladylike tone, and stared hypnotically at him as though she believed that he was about to do her mischief by magical means and she had to resist his spell.

"Are you intending to be a career girl?"

He was giving her more attention this morning than he ever had before, with the result that she found herself reciprocating. A tentative friendliness wavered in the air between them. She smiled. "I guess I ought to say that it depends on my luck."

He laughed—perhaps rather too uproariously, though, more probably, she had merely grown unaccustomed to his kind of laughter. Her brother bobbed briefly to the surface of her mind.

"Well," he said, "does your luck seem likely to take you out of this office anytime in the near future?"

"No," she said, "it certainly doesn't look that way," and they laughed again. But she wondered if he would be laughing if he knew about Paul.

"If you don't mind my saying so, then," he said, *"I'm* lucky." He quickly riffled some papers on his desk, putting on a business air as rakishly as she had seen him put on his hat. "There's going to be some changes made around here—I reckon you have heard that." He grinned. Then, briskly: "I'm going to be needing a secretary. Would you like it? You get a raise"—he coughed—"in salary, of course."

"Why, I'd love it," she heard herself saying before she had had time for the bitter reflection that this professional advance probably represented the absolute extent of her luck. And she was ashamed of the thought, which she could not repress, that Paul would probably hang on a little longer if he knew she was making more money.

She resolved not to tell him and wondered how many hours this resolution would last.

Mr. Davis looked at her with an intentness almost personal. There was a strained, brief silence. "Good," he said at last. "There are a few details to be worked out, like getting me more office space"—they both smiled—"but you'll be hearing directly in a few days. I only wanted to sound you out first." He rose and held out his hand. "I hope you're going to like working with me," he said. "I think I'm going to like working with you."

She rose and shook his hand, bewildered to find that something in his simplicity had touched her very deeply. "I'm sure I will," she said, gravely. "And thank you very much." She reached backward for the doorknob.

"Miss Bowman,". he said sharply—and paused. "Well, if I were you I wouldn't mention it yet to"—he waved his hand uncomfortably—"the girls out there." Now he really did look rather boyish. "It looks better if it comes from the front office."

"I understand," she said quickly.

"Also, I didn't ask for you out of any—racial—considerations," he said. "You just seemed the most *sensible* girl available."

"I understand," she repeated; they were both trying not to smile. "And thank you again." She closed the door of his office behind her.

"A man called you," said the stocky girl. "He said he'd call back."

"Thank you," Ruth said. She could see that the girl wanted to talk so she busily studied some papers on her desk and retired behind the noise of her typewriter.

The stocky girl had gone out to lunch and Ruth was reluctantly deciding that she might as well go too when Paul called again.

"Hello. How's it going up there?"

"Dull. How are things down there? Are you out of bed already?"

"What do you mean, already?" He sounded slightly nettled and was trying not to sound that way, the almost certain signal that a storm was coming. "It's nearly one o'clock. I got work to do too, you know."

"Yes, I know." But neither could she quite keep the sardonic edge out of her voice.

There was a silence.

"You coming straight home from work?"

"Yes. Will you be there?"

"Yeah, I got to go uptown with Cosmo this afternoon, talk to some gallery guy, Cosmo thinks he might like my stuff."

"Oh"—thinking *Damn Cosmo!*—"that's wonderful, Paul. I hope something comes of it."

Nothing whatever would come of it. The gallery owner would be evasive—*if* he existed, if they ever got to his gallery—and then Paul and Cosmo would get drunk. She would hear, while she ached to be free, to be anywhere else, *with* anyone else, from Paul, all about how stupid art dealers were, how incestuous the art world had become, how impossible it was to *do* anything—his eyes, meanwhile, focusing with a drunken intensity, his eyes at once arrogant and defensive.

Well. Most of what he said was true, and she knew it, it was not his fault.

Not his fault. "Yeah, I sure hope so. I thought I'd take up some of my water colors, some small sketches—you know, all the most *obvious* things I've got."

This policy did not, empirically, seem to be as foolproof as everyone believed but she did not know how to put her uncertain objections into words. "That sounds good. What time have you got to be there?"

"Around three. I'm meeting Cosmo now for lunch."

"Oh"—lightly—"why don't you two, just this once, order your lunch before you order your cocktails?"

He laughed too and was clearly no more amused than she. "Well, Cosmo'll be buying, he'll have to, so I guess I'll leave it up to him to order."

Touché. Her hand, holding the receiver, shook. "Well, I hope you two make it to the gallery without falling flat on your faces."

"Don't worry." Then, in a rush, she recognized the tone before she understood the words, it was his you-can't-say-I-haven't-been-honest-with-you-tone: "Cosmo says the gallery owner's got a daughter."

I hope to God she marries you, she thought. I hope she marries you and takes you off to Istanbul forever, where I will never have to hear of you again, so I can get a breath of air, so I can get out from under.

They both laughed, a laugh conspiratorial and sophisticated, like the whispered, whisky laughter of a couple in a night club. "Oh?" she said. "Is she pretty?"

"She's probably a pig. She's had two husbands already, both artists."

She laughed again. "Where has she buried the bodies?"

"Well"—really amused this time, but also rather grim—

"one of them ended up in the booby hatch and the other turned into a fairy and was last seen dancing with some soldiers in Majorca."

Now they laughed together and the wires between them hummed, almost, with the stormless friendship they both hoped to feel for each other someday. "A powerful pig. Maybe you *better* have a few drinks."

"You see what I mean? But Cosmo says she's not such a fool about painting."

"She doesn't seem to have much luck with painters. Maybe you'll break the jinx."

"Maybe. Wish me luck. It sure would be nice to unload some of my stuff on somebody."

You're doing just fine, she thought. "Will you call me later?"

"Yeah. Around three-thirty, four o'clock, as soon as I get away from there."

"Right. Be good."

"You too. Good-by."

"Good-by."

She put down the receiver, still amused and still trembling. After all, he had called her. But he would probably not have called her if he were not actually nourishing the hope that the gallery owner's daughter might find him interesting: in that case he would have to tell Ruth about her and it was better to have the way prepared. Paul was always preparing the way for one unlikely exploit or flight or another, it was the reason he told Ruth "everything." To tell everything is a very effective means of keeping secrets. Secrets hidden at the heart of midnight are simply waiting to be dragged to the light, as, on some unlucky high noon, they always are. But secrets shrouded in the glare of candor are bound to defeat even the most determined and agile inspector for the light is always changing and proves that the eye cannot be trusted. So Ruth knew about Paul nearly all there was to know, knew him better than anyone else on earth ever had or probably ever would, only—she did not know him well enough to stop him from being Paul.

While she was waiting for the elevator she realized, with mild astonishment, that she was actually hoping that the gallery owner's daughter would take Paul away. This hope resembled the desperation of someone suffering from a toothache who, in order to bring the toothache to an end, was almost willing to jump out of a window. But she found herself wondering if love really ought to be like a toothache. Love ought—she stepped out of the elevator, really wondering for a moment which way to turn—to be a means of being released from guilt and terror. But Paul's touch would never release her. He had power over her not because she was free but because she was guilty. To enforce his power over her he had only to keep her guilt awake. This did not demand malice on his part, it scarcely demanded perception—it only demanded that he have, as, in fact, he overwhelmingly did have, an instinct for his own convenience. His touch, which should have raised her, lifted her roughly only to throw her down hard; whenever he touched her, she became blacker and dirtier than ever; the loneliest place under heaven was in Paul's arms.

And yet—she went into his arms with such eagerness and such hope. She had once thought herself happy. Was this because she had been proud that he was white? But—it was she who was insisting on these colors. Her blackness was not Paul's fault. Neither was her guilt. She was punishing herself for something, a crime she could not remember. *You dirty . . . you black and dirty . . .*

She bumped into someone as she passed the cigar stand in the lobby and, looking up to murmur, "Excuse me," recognized Mr. Davis. He was stuffing cigars into his breast pocket—though the gesture was rather like that of a small boy stuffing his pockets with cookies, she was immediately certain that they were among the most expensive cigars that could be bought. She wondered what he spent on his clothes

—it looked like a great deal. From the crown of rakishly tilted, deafeningly conservative hat to the tips of his astutely dulled shoes, he glowed with a very nearly vindictive sharpness. There were no flies on Mr. Davis. He would always be the best-dressed man in *any*body's lobby.

He was just about the last person she wanted to see. But perhaps his lunch hour was over and he was coming in.

"Miss Bowman!" He gave her a delighted grin. "Are you just going to lunch?"

He made her want to laugh. There was something so incongruous about finding that grin behind all that manner and under all those clothes.

"Yes," she said. "I guess you've had your lunch?"

"No, I ain't had no lunch," he said. "I'm hungry, just like you." He paused. "I'd be delighted to have your company, Miss Bowman."

Very courtly, she thought, amused, and the smile is extremely wicked. Then she realized that she was pleased that a man was *being* courtly with her, even if only for an instant in a crowded lobby, and, at the same instant, made the discovery that what was so widely referred to as a "wicked" smile was really only the smile, scarcely ever to be encountered any more, of a man who was not afraid of women.

She thought it safe to demur. "Please don't think you have to be polite."

"I'm never polite about food," he told her. "Almost drove my mamma crazy." He took her arm. "I know a right nice place nearby." His stride and his accent made her think of home. She also realized that he, like many Negroes of his uneasily rising generation, kept in touch, so to speak, with himself by deliberately affecting, whenever possible, the illiterate speech of his youth. "We going to get on real well, you'll see. Time you get through being my secretary, you likely to end up with Alcoholics Anonymous."

The place "nearby" turned out to be a short taxi ride away, but it was, as he had said, "right nice." She doubted that Mr. Davis could possibly eat there every day, though it was clear that he was a man who liked to spend money.

She ordered a dry Martini and he a bourbon on the rocks. He professed himself astonished that she knew what a dry Martini was. "I thought you was a country girl."

"I *am* a country girl," she said.

"No, no," he said, "no more. You a country girl who came to the city and that's the dangerous kind. Don't know if it's safe, having you for my secretary."

Underneath all this chatter she felt him watching her, sizing her up.

"Are you afraid your wife will object?" she asked.

"You ought to be able to look at me," he said, "and tell that I ain't got a wife."

She laughed. "So you're *not* married. I wonder if I should tell the girls in the office?"

"I don't care what you tell them," he said. Then: "How do you get along with them?"

"We get along fine," she said. "We don't have much to talk about except whether or not you're married but that'll probably last until you *do* get married and then we can talk about your wife."

But, thinking; For God's sake let's get off this subject, she added, before he could say anything: "You called me a country girl. Aren't you a country boy?"

"I am," he said, "but *I* didn't *change* my drinking habits when I come North. If bourbon was good enough for me down yonder, it's good enough for me up here."

"*I* didn't have any drinking habits to change, Mr. Davis," she told him. "I was too young to be drinking when I left home."

His eyes were slightly questioning but he held his peace, while she wished she had held hers. She concentrated on sipping her Martini, suddenly remembering that she was sitting opposite a man who knew more about why girls left home than could be learned from locker room stories. She wondered if he had a sister and tried to be amused at finding herself still so incorrigibly old-fashioned. But he did not, really, seem to be much like her brother. She met his eyes again.

"Where I come from," he said, with a smile, "*nobody* was too young to be drinking. Toughened them up for later life," and he laughed.

By the time lunch was over she had learned that he was from a small town in Alabama, was the youngest of three sons (but had no sisters), had gone to college in Tennessee, was a reserve officer in the Air Force. He was thirty-two. His mother was living, his father was dead. He had lived in New York for two years but was beginning, now, to like it less than he had in the beginning.

"At first," he said, "I thought it would be fun to live in a city where didn't nobody know you and you didn't know nobody and where, look like, you could just do anything you was big and black enough to do. But you get tired not knowing nobody and there ain't really that many things you want to do alone."

"Oh, but you must have friends," she said, "uptown."

"I don't live uptown. I live in Brooklyn. Ain't *nobody* in Brooklyn got friends."

She laughed with him, but distrusted the turn the conversation was taking. They were walking back to the office. He walked slowly, as though in deliberate opposition to the people around them, although they were already a little late—at least *she* was late, but, since she was with one of her superiors, it possibly didn't matter.

"Where do you live?" he asked her. "Do you live uptown?"

"No," she said. "I live downtown on Bank Street." And after a moment: "That's in the Village, Greenwich Village."

He grinned. "Don't tell me you studying to be a writer or a dancer or something?"

"No. I just found myself there. It used to be cheap."

He scowled. "Ain't nothing cheap in this town no more, not even the necessities."

His tone made clear to which necessities he referred and

she would have loved to tease him a little, just to watch him laugh. But she was beginning, with every step they took, to be a little afraid of him. She was responding to him with parts of herself that had been buried so long she had forgotten they existed. In his office that morning, when he shook her hand, she had suddenly felt a warmth of affection, of nostalgia, of gratitude even—and again in the lobby—he had somehow made her feel safe. It was his friendliness that was so unsettling. She had grown used to unfriendly people.

Still, she did not *want* to be friends with him; still less did she desire that their friendship should ever become anything more. Sooner or later he would learn about Paul: He would look at her differently then. It would not be—so much—because of Paul as a man, perhaps not even Paul as a white man. But it would make him bitter, it would make her ashamed, for him to see how she was letting herself be wasted—for Paul, who did not love her.

This was the reason she was ashamed and wished to avoid the scrutiny of Mr. Davis. She was doing something to herself—out of shame?—that he would be right in finding indefensible. She was punishing herself. For what? She looked sideways at his Black Sambo profile under the handsome lightweight Dobbs hat and wished that she could tell him about it, that he would turn his head, holding it slightly to one side, and watch her with those eyes that had seen and that had learned to hide so much. Eyes that had seen so many girls like her taken beyond the hope of rescue, while all the owner of the eyes could do—perhaps she wore Paul the way Mr. Davis wore his hat. And she looked away from him, half-smiling and yet near tears, over the furious streets on which, here and there, like a design, colored people also hurried, thinking, *And we were slaves here once*.

"Do you like music?" he asked her abruptly. "I don't necessarily mean Carnegie Hall."

Now was the time to stop him. She had only to say, "Mr. Davis, I'm living with someone." It would not be necessary to say anything more than that.

She met his eyes. "Of course I like music," she said faintly.

"Well, I know a place I'd like to take you one of these evenings, after work. Not going to be easy, being my secretary."

His smile forced her to smile with him. But, "Mr. Davis," she said, and stopped. They were before the entrance of their office building.

"What's the matter?" he asked. "You forget something?"

"No." She looked down, feeling big, black and foolish. "Mr. Davis," she said, "you don't know anything about me."

"You don't know anything about me, either," he said.

"That's not what I mean," she said.

He sounded slightly angry. "I ain't asked you nothing yet," he said. "Why can't you wait till you're asked?"

"Well," she stammered, "it may be too late then."

They stared hard at each other for a moment. "Well," he said, "if it turns out to be too late, won't be nobody to blame but me, will it?"

She stared at him again, almost hating him. She blindly felt that he had no right to do this to her, to cause her to feel such a leap of hope, if he was only, in the end, going to give her back all her shame.

"You know what they say down home," she said slowly. "If you don't know what you doing, you better ask somebody." There were tears in her eyes.

He took her arm. "Come on in this house, girl," he said. "We got insurance to sell."

They said nothing to each other in the elevator on the way upstairs. She wanted to laugh and she wanted to cry. He, ostentatiously, did not watch her; he stood next to her, humming *Rocks in My Bed*.

She waited all afternoon for Paul to telephone, but although, perversely enough, the phone seemed never to cease ringing, it never rang for her. At five-fifteen, just before she left the office, she called the apartment. Paul was not there.

She went downstairs to a nearby bar and ordered a drink and called again at a quarter to six. He was not there. She resolved to have one more drink and leave this bar, which she did, wandering a few blocks north to a bar frequented by theatre people. She sat in a booth and ordered a drink and at a quarter to seven called again. He was not there.

She was in a reckless, desperate state, like flight. She knew that she could not possibly go home and cook supper and wait in the empty apartment until his key turned in the lock. He would come in, breathless and contrite—or else, truculently, *not* contrite—probably a little drunk, probably quite hungry. He would tell her where he had been and what he had been doing. Whatever he told her would probably be true—there are so many ways of telling the truth! And whether it was true or not did not matter and she would not be able to reproach him for the one thing that *did* matter: that he had left her sitting in the house alone. She could not make the reproach because, after all, leaving women sitting around in empty houses had been the specialty of all men for ages. And, for ages, when the men arrived women bestirred themselves to cook supper—luckily, it was not yet common knowledge that many a woman had narrowly avoided committing murder by calmly breaking a few eggs.

She wondered where it had all gone to—the ease, the pleasure they had had together once. At one time their evenings together, sitting around the house, drinking beer or reading or simply laughing and talking, had been the best part of all their days. Paul, reading, or walking about with a can of beer in his hand, talking, gesturing, scratching his chest; Paul, stretched out on the sofa, staring at the ceiling; Paul, cheerful, with that lowdown, cavernous chuckle and that foolish grin, Paul grim, with his mouth turned down and his eyes burning; Paul doing anything whatever, Paul with his eyelids sealed in sleep, drooling and snoring, Paul lighting her cigarette, touching her elbow, talking, talking, talking, in his million ways, to her, had been the light that lighted up her world. Now it was all gone, it would never come again, and that face which was like the heavens was darkening against her.

These present days, after supper, when the chatter each used as a cover began to show dangerous signs of growing thinner, there would be no choice but sleep. She might, indeed, have preferred a late movie, or a round of the bars, lights, noise, other people, but this would scarcely be Paul's desire, already tired from his day. Besides—after all, she had to face the office in the morning. Eventually, therefore, bed; perhaps he or she or both of them might read awhile; perhaps there would take place between them what had sometimes been described as the act of love. Then sleep, black and dreadful, like a drugged state, from which she would be rescued by the scream of the alarm clock or the realization that Paul was no longer in bed.

Ah. Her throat ached with tears of fury and despair. In the days before she had met Paul men had taken her out, she had laughed a lot, she had been young. She had not wished to spend her life protecting herself, with laughter, against men she cared nothing about; but she could not go on like this either, drinking in random bars because she was afraid to go home; neither could she guess what life might bring her when Paul was gone.

She wished that she had never met him. She wished that he, or she, or both of them were dead. And for a moment she really wished it, with a violence that frightened her. Perhaps there was always murder at the very heart of love; the strong desire to murder the beloved, so that one could at last be assured of privacy and peace and be as safe and unchanging as the grave. Perhaps this was why disasters, thicker and more malevolent than bees, circled Paul's head whenever he was out of her sight. Perhaps in those moments when she had believed herself willing to lay down her life for him she had only been presenting herself with a metaphor for her peace, his death; death, which would be an inadequate revenge for the color of his skin, for his failure, by not loving her, to release her from the prison of her own.

The waitress passed her table and Ruth ordered another drink. After this drink she would go. The bar was beginning to fill up, mostly, as she judged, with theatre people, some of them, possibly, on their way to work, most of them drawn here by habit and hope. For the past few moments, without realizing it, she had been watching a lean, pale boy at the bar, whose curly hair leaned electrically over his forehead like a living, awry crown. Something about him, his stance, his profile or his grin, prodded painfully at her attention. But it was not that he reminded her of Paul. He reminded her of a boy she had known, briefly, a few years ago, a very lonely boy, who was now a merchant seaman, probably, wherever he might be on the globe at this moment, whoring his unbearably unrealized, mysteriously painful life away. She had been fond of him but loneliness in him had been like a cancer, it had really unfitted him for human intercourse, and she had not been sorry to see him go. She had not thought of him for years; yet, now, this stranger at the bar, whom she was beginning to recognize as an actor of brief but growing reputation, abruptly brought him back to her; brought him back encrusted, as it were, with the anguish of the intervening years. She remembered things she thought she had forgotten and wished that she had been wiser then—then she smiled at herself, wishing she were wiser now.

Once, when he had done something to hurt her, she had told him, trying to be calm but choked and trembling with rage: "Look. This is the twentieth century. We're not down on a plantation, you're not the master's son, and I'm not the black girl you can just sleep with when you want to and kick about as you please!"

His face, then, had held something, held many things—bitterness, amusement, fury; but the startling element was pain, his pain, with which she now invested the face of the actor at the bar. It made her wish that she had held her tongue.

"Well," he said at last, "I guess I'll get on back to the big house and leave you down here with the pickaninnies."

They had seen each other a few times thereafter but that was really the evening on which everything had ended between them.

She wondered if that boy had ever found a home.

The actor at the bar looked toward her briefly, but she knew he was not seeing her. He looked at his watch, frowned, she saw that he was not as young as he looked; he ordered another drink and looked downward, leaning both elbows on the bar. The dim lights played on his crown of hair. He moved his head slightly, with impatience, upward, his mouth slightly open, and in that instant, somehow, his profile was burned into her mind. He reminded her then of Paul, of the vanished boy, of others, of others she had seen and never touched, of an army of boys—boys forever!—an army she feared and hated and loved. In that gesture, that look upward, with the light so briefly on his face, she saw the bones that held his face together and the sorrow beginning to corrode his brow, the blood beating like butterfly wings against the cage of his heavy neck. But there was no name for something blind, cruel, lustful, lost, intolerably vulnerable in his eyes and mouth. She knew that in spite of everything, his color, his power or his coming fame, he was lost. He did not know what had happened to his life. And never would. This was the pain she had seen on the face of that boy so long ago, and it was this that had driven Paul into her arms, and now away. The sons of the masters were roaming the world, looking for arms to hold them. And the arms that might have held them—could not forgive.

A sound escaped her; she was astonished to realize it was a sob. The waitress looked at her sharply. Ruth put some money on the table and hurried out. It was dark now and the rain that had been falling intermittently all day spangled the air and glittered all over the streets. It fell against her face and mingled with her tears and she walked briskly through the crowds to hide from them and from herself the fact that she did not know where she was going.

THE CRIME

by Georgia McKinley

Georgia McKinley (1917–   ) was born in
Dallas and graduated from the University of
Texas. Her fiction, often set in the Southwest she
knows so well, has appeared in many quarterlies
and such periodicals as *The Paris Review, Kenyon
Review,* and *Southwest Review. The Mighty Distance,* a collection of her short stories, was published in 1965.

Some Saturdays the two white men did not hunt, but would
sit nearly motionless on the front porch of the little lodge,
with the Bourbon and the bucket of ice cubes between them
on the floor, staring somberly off toward the rows of houses
which had crept out from the city to menace their land. On
such days they were short-tempered and mean as old dogs
sitting in the sun, snapping at each other and at Leroy, the
Negro whom they always brought with them to carry and
clean the game.

Leroy had gone on these excursions for so long that in
some ways he knew the men better than anyone else did,
including their wives, and he could predict what their mood
would be from the moment they picked him up in town. This
winter noon the very blast of their horn in the street outside

Reprinted from *The Mighty Distance,* by permission of the publisher,
Houghton Mifflin Company.

alarmed him. He had just sat down in the kitchen to eat a
plate of grits and bacon fat for lunch, when, too soon and
too loud, the deep note rolled through his daughter's flimsy
little house as though to level it. Leroy rose straight up from
the table, propelled on the sound. "They here!" he said, his
hands fluttering before him in quieting motions. "Oh Lord,
oh shush," he muttered, but again the horn called.

Of course everyone in the house, everyone in the neighborhood had heard. His daughter, with whom he lived, now
appeared in the doorway. "Well, you friends is here again,
Poppa," she said, her voice buttery and rich with sarcasm.
"You white friends come to call for you, Poppa, and they
seems anxious. Better hurry on—" She planted herself
across his path and in spite of the racket outside, held him
motionless with her stubborn presence.

"Well, I *hears* 'em," he said, and bending his head sulkily,
hoping she didn't mean to start anything, he noticed his own
hands hanging limply on the air. The skin of his hands was
turning grey with age; once they had been a deep solid,
brown, but now they looked as if they had been coated with
a bluish-white powder which would not come off. He
scrubbed them against his shirt and held them up, then
looked over at his daughter but she was still there, looking
up at him with her twitching, middle-aged face.

"Where you goin', Poppa?" she said.

He stared at her. "I goin' with *them*, of course, and I got
to *go*, Irma."

"You goin' with them white men *again?*" she said in a
sudden loud voice.

He hung his head. He could never understand Irma,
touchy and nervous as she was, always talking anxiously
over the telephone about a committee or a meeting. Ever
since his wife had died and he had moved in with her, it
had been a shame for him to do what he had done all his
life: to work for whatever white people offered to pay him;
to take their old clothes; to go to backdoors for handouts
on Christmas and Easter and Thanksgiving and to go with

the two men outside whenever and wherever they wanted.

"I not gonna have 'em come down here no *mo'*," she said. "Roaring in down here in they big car honking and hollering. My neighbors is respectable and they don't like it."

"Well, I tell 'em I meet 'em somewheres else," he said in a little, bright voice. It sounded like a child's lie and they both knew it.

"Now I'm thinkin' about *you,* Poppa, ever bit as much as me," she went on warningly.

"Well, don't you ever worry about me, I *always* get along with 'em."

Her face drew in and became smaller and more pointed, marked by deep lines, and her eyes grew sharp at the centers and soft with black tears around the edges. "Self-respeck," she said in a ragged whisper as though the word had lodged in her throat, "I'm talkin' about self-respeck."

"Um-hum," he said affirmatively and stood looking down at her, waiting.

Then she shrugged, sighed, and stepped barely out of his path. "You a white man's nigger," she said to him very gently and without any particular interest as he passed.

The little house was long and narrow as a railroad car and the kitchen was at the far end; he had still to walk the whole length of it and somewhere ahead of him his grandchildren were waiting. Light came in a thin yellow strip through the front door and as he walked toward it, he passed the three children crowded darkly together in the shadows. They let him pass in silence. They were ready to go to the white men's schools when the time should come and too self-involved to notice him.

Outside, he turned uneasily to look back and saw that they were all watching him. The house was so narrow that, seen from the front door, they seemed to be standing close together in one group, and against the brown wallpaper, from the yellow crowded dimness of the house, their black faces looked after him, unmoving and touched with sadness.

He lifted his hand in a confused movement of farewell

and turned away, then stopped to get himself together: rubbed down his hair, looked at his cracked shoes and wiped them against his pants legs. Under his feet on the dirt path was a pulp of mashed chinaberries from the tree overhead, their thick meal sending up a sweetish smell. He lifted his eyes from this grey and yellow mess to the white men's car. There was the Cadillac, huge and gay in the winter scene of grey leafless trees and grey paintless houses. Amid the crumble and decay of the little yards, between the garbage and mud, the car struck hard and solid against his eyes and shone before him, silver and glistening blue. There was now a deep solemn quiet across the neighborhood as if everyone were waiting in the houses, watching from hiding as he approached the car. In a sudden fever of excitement, he thought, "Someone goan throw a rock," and carefully scraping the chinaberries off his feet, he got into the car.

"Mr. Underwood, Mr. McIntire," he murmured politely, but after all the noise they had made, they were bent above a newspaper open between them and did not seem to notice he had come.

He sank into the back seat, out of sight, he hoped, of the people in the houses, but he was still aware of them. He was oddly aware even of what the one among them felt who was going to throw something; the heft of a solid object seemed to run along his own arm. "Come on, please, Mr. Underwood, let's get out of here," he said.

The man at the wheel turned and gave him a sly look. "What's matter, Leroy, your daughter been after you again?" he said, as he started the car.

"Yessuh," Leroy said with a ghostly, high, crackling laugh. It had been the white men's idea, while his wife was alive, that she held a rolling pin over his head, and now his daughter had stepped into her place. This had nothing to do with the truth, just as his crazy cackle was not his real laughter, but both pleased the white men and gave them something to talk about. It would never have occurred to him to tell them anything about his daughter that was true: he would have felt it was none of their business. The white men and his daughter were simply *there* for him to deal with from time to time and he was happy and relieved when he was able to do so in such a way as to make one or all of them happy. So now, in the car, the unpleasantness at his daughter's house was past, before him was whatever the afternoon might bring; but now blessedly, there was nothing to think about, nothing to do but wait. He folded his hands drily in his lap and his mind, with a rush, floated free.

When he was a child he had been hired out in cotton-picking seasons to a family of Negroes who lived in east Texas. The house in which he had stayed stood in the middle of a field with the cotton rows planted up against its walls, so that a child had only to step through the door or roll out a window to be in the field and at work. It was there that he had first learned to snatch a moment when he was not at work for blank rest of mind and body. After so many years and so much hard work, when he was not dealing directly with a tool and a task in hand, he did not think. The higher centers of his brain were still.

Now the winter sun, still high in the sky, was on his side of the car; the glass of the window concentrated the rays to his old chilled bones. With his head back on the cushions, his nose awoke and found the smell high up in the big car, thin, sour and delicious—beer! The white men had been drinking beer. He breathed in dreamily, warmed by the sun, the white men moving dimly in their own world, thousands of miles away in the front seat.

Mr. McIntire, the little nervous one, kept twisting about, looking out the front, the side window, the back, up, down, anywhere, everywhere, and talking talking. Mr. Underwood sat heavily around the wheel as if grown upon it, his big face flat and vacant from the side, giving nothing. Leroy had gone on hunting trips far and near with them for over thirty years, and although at least half of what they said always lay in his mind unused, a great waste pile of white words, still he had his own feelings and lights in which they were clearly reflected.

It was partly because of Mr. Underwood's name, but more because of his nature, that Leroy, almost ever since he had known him, had thought of him as being like a big and solid tree, a hard, rough trunk of a man, never to be moved from the exact place in which he had made his slow and stubborn growth. Mr. McIntire, so happy and careless, had little weight beside him, and merely ran like a squirrel in Mr. Underwood's branches, always looking brightly around and chattering.

Leroy found Mr. McIntire only amusing, and though he almost never listened to his words, he enjoyed hearing him talk. The man spoke in crazy spurts, the speed of his own nervous thoughts straining against his soft and whining southern speech.

"Look at that, look at that," Mr. McIntire was saying, "They're putting up another damned motel here . . ."

Mr. Underwood did not look aside from the highway but said slowly, "We used to shoot quail there, you remember that?"

But Mr. McIntire was busy at the window. "Now will you look, will you just *look* at that?"

Leroy looked lazily out the window. There where the flat land had lain so long in black plowed fields or empty prairie grasslands (they *had* shot quail here a few times) now there was a whole city of bright little houses, row upon row, acre upon acre, off to the edge of sight.

"Now isn't that a *damnable* shame," Mr. Underwood said suddenly in great bitterness.

They had passed this addition and others like it almost all the way out to the hunting lodge every Saturday now for three or four years—five, six, seven years they had been building out from town in this direction, coming in with bulldozers and piles of bright new wood, and leaving behind them the finished boxes. Still, every time they passed, something new had been started or finished and that got on the white men's nerves, but Leroy could not understand why they should seem to be so angry about it now. They were in a bad mood about something, he thought, that was for sure. Reluctantly, he roused and gathered himself to pay a little more attention to them.

Fifteen years ago, the men would have laughed at all this, packed up and gone off to wild country. Only ten years ago the three of them had gone to the Grand Tetons and hunted moose above the timberline. Since then, though they had planned many trips, they had never quite made one—there was something a little wrong about Mr. Underwood's heart, Mr. McIntire said he had an ulcer. Still the men had their two hundred acres which they kept stocked with birds and small game, and they had a fine lake full of fish on the property, but the little box houses had almost reached them now, and already the County had cut a highway straight across their land, slicing open the red clay earth with machines and leaving it healed with a wide grey macadam scar. It seemed unlikely that a wild duck would ever land on the lake again and day to day nothing was quite the same as it had been the day before.

Presently Mr. McIntire said wildly, "Look, look at that; now there's their damned Zeppelin!"

"Their what?" Mr. Underwood gnawed out.

Mr. McIntire had rolled down the glass and was leaning away out the window. "It said—in the paper—they were going to have a Zeppelin," he yelled over his shoulder. "They'll play searchlights on it tonight."

Leroy looked out too. There in the great blue sky floated the peaceful silver sausage, out just in the direction they were going.

Mr. Underwood spoke in his blank voice. "Leroy."

"Yessuh?" He sat up straight. "Mr. Underwood?"

"They're opening a new supermarket out by the hunting property today. Got the Zeppelin there. You want to go over?"

"You want me git you sumthin?" he asked carefully.

"Hell no. I mean *you* want to go? They're gonna have a hillybilly band and free corsages for ladies. White and colored invited. It said so in the paper."

Leroy stirred on his bony hips and rubbed his hands with a sound of paper, puzzled that Mr. Underwood should seem to be blaming him for the supermarket. "No *suh*, I don't wanna go there," he said quickly. "Not to *no* supermarket. Ah gets so lost and bamboozled in them places. Why I 'member once—" He gave his cracked and crazy laugh but there was no response from the front seat.

"Lots of colored folks be there, Leroy," Mr. Underwood said. "Lots of colored moving into that area."

"Yessuh," he said and rubbed down his grey hair. "I guess so." And then they left him and passed on to other things. There was a Negro settlement building up out there, they said; one big block of the houses you could see from the hunting lodge belonged to Negroes; other solid blocks belonged to white people and they were building at the edges of all the areas so that they grew closer and closer together.

"They'll meet," Mr. Underwood was saying. "Have to come a street with new white houses on one side and new colored houses on the other."

"Boy, I'd hate to be there when that happens," Mr. McIntire said, bouncing around.

"Yeh," said Mr. Underwood. He brooded over the wheel for a few minutes. "Hell, don't kid yourself," he said, "the first thing you know it'll be possible, it'll be *legal,* for some black son of a bitch to move in next door to any of us."

Leroy looked up and saw Mr. Underwood's eyes, a bright clean blue, standing fixed on him in the rear-view mirror.

He dropped his own eyes quickly. In the front seat the white men went on with their jabbering as though nothing had happened, but Leroy sat quietly, his eyes on his folded hands.

He thought of all the years he had gotten along so fine with them—how they had kidded and laughed at and taken care of him. He could get almost anything he wanted from them by telling a long, pitiful story of trouble, or by making himself look so silly with some rambling crazy tale that they would laugh to bust their sides and do whatever he wanted. He thought now with quiet relish of some of these occasions and laughed noiselessly to himself.

But the car had been turned ferociously off the highway and onto the torn and rutted red clay road that led up to the hunting lodge and when they had lurched to a stop behind the little house, Mr. Underwood and Mr. McIntire left the car immediately, walked around to the front and stared intently off into the wide sunny distance. For a moment Leroy thought they had gone to look for a duck on the lake below or the rise of a bird, as they had done so often in the past. Then, getting out himself, he saw their eyes were fixed beyond the sweet empty brown slopes and valleys of their own property, off toward the flag-decorated building with the silver sausage floating above it and the highway where clots of little cars were moving in both directions. "Got a nice big crowd," Mr. McIntire said in a voice like spitting.

"Colored and white invited," Mr. Underwood said, and lifted his arms widely to the horizon.

Then they went into the house but instead of loading their guns, Leroy heard them rattling out ice cubes into a bucket. In a few minutes, they brought the makings of their drinks and came out onto the porch. He saw Mr. Underwood kick a chair viciously into place and they sat glumly down, facing out toward the small far hills.

He sighed. There would be no hunting today, for they would never touch a gun after having drunk whiskey. There would be nothing for him to do, for his sole duty was to clean the game, and he shrugged and gathered up his hands like a couple of awkward parcels and sat down at his usual place, a broken-down wooden bench in the yard. He liked to clean the game as well as anything he ever did, holding the small soft bodies in his loose hands, making the feathers or the scales fly, and he took seriously his job of seeing that it was equally divided between them. For as long as he could remember they had kidded him about stealing their game from them, but in fact it was he who kept them from cheating each other. However, none of that joking today, but only the white men sitting on the porch growing crosser and meaner as the afternoon wore on.

Feeling lonely, he looked sadly out before him. The near fields, warm and still, he knew foot by foot; all the sweep of winter grass, the clumps of cedar or mesquite, the gray bare lake. Sluggishly his eyes rose to where the hated houses stood line on line across the hills like rows of little white teeth, gnawing off the distance that lay between them and him. "They coming," he thought unhappily, "they sure gonna spoil the hunting."

There was nothing he could do about it. Slowly, helplessly he dropped his eyes from the hills, down down, until they rested upon a small circle of ground at his feet and found there many comfortable and familiar things: scalloped brown leaves and tiny acorns from the scrub oak trees, shining stalks of dry grass, some wing feathers of a mallard and everywhere whorls of soft gray breast feathers from birds, and right in the middle, a good big cluster of dried horse droppings, all smelling warmly, dustily of earth. He knew that if you sat still in the direct sun, even in winter, you could pull its heat straight through your skin until you had a pool of warmth inside you. This he did now and the voices on the porch diminished for him and disappeared. Gradually he leaned forward, head closer to the ground, until he felt the sun also touch the back of his neck. He did not sleep, he merely peacefully existed.

There was no time for him then; he would have noted the movement of hours only when the sun had set and left him cold. He could not have said how much later it was when he realized the white men were talking about him. There was a drunken rise and whine to their voices which had not been there when he heard them last.

"Now take Leroy," Mr. Underwood was saying. "There's

a fine example of the new Negro—alert, intelligent—a real ball o'fire, ain't he?"

"Hard to keep him still—mighty peppy, full of fight," Mr. McIntire said and laughed a long, soughing laugh.

"The new Negro," Mr. Underwood mused, and then his voice rose sharply. "Why the hell you suppose he thinks we bring him out here? For his beauty, or his sweet smell, or just because he's so nice and black and shiny?"

"Why hell," Mr. McIntire said, "he just thinks we want him to sit with us so we won't be lonely for him. *That's* what they think now—they think we just want to be with them all the time and everywhere we go—on the buses, you know, and in the schools, and come to dinner with us, and marry our young girls so we'll all really be together—"

"*Lee*roy," Mr. Underwood suddenly howled out like a banshee. "What you doing?"

His eyes rose dead blank. "I been sittin' here a spell, Mistah Underwood. Ain't no game to clean. What I goan do?"

"Well, you can get up off your black ass and go in there and start cleaning up this house."

Leroy looked at him in hopeless puzzlement. "This house?" he said tonelessly. Then with gathering force, he said, "But Mistah Underwood, I ain't never *done* that before."

"Well, times are changing, Leroy," Mr. Underwood said, "and we got to change with 'em, so *git* going."

He arose stiffly, went around the house and leaned in dignity against the back screen. All his life he had been kept so busy following the white men's rules that he had never had time to think much about them. It did not seem queer that while he slept in the same room with them, and occasionally, on cold nights, under the same blanket with them on hunting trips, he would be an unwelcomed next-door neighbor. It had never bothered him to be cursed or called a thief or a liar by the white men but today, for the first time, they had called him a Negro. In the years he had known them, they had never before mentioned the color of his skin, avoiding it so completely that he had come to realize without knowing it that this was the one thing which none of them must talk about.

So he knew now they did not want him to clean the house, nor mind if he sat still in the sun—they were after something else entirely. They wanted him to fight with them; this much he now understood. He saw that they had pushed and would keep pushing him back until he did something—some unknown and unthought of thing. Frightened by the strangeness of the situation and remembering all the years he had been with them, he could not think now how to be against them. But the fact of his long servitude came newly to his mind and he thought of all he had taken from them—all the laughing and the cursing and the dirty nigger work they had given him to do—and now this. Lonely and chilled in the waning light, he leaned against the door driving his mind before him past the outer edges of his own experience, determined that he must act, since they wanted him to, but not realizing how little of himself had been left him to act with.

And then the answer came to him; rose complete in his brain from outside himself, formed of ideas which were not his own. He would steal from them; that was what he would do. He had always known that some Negroes did steal from the whites; he had always known that white people expected Negroes to steal. It was the old and accepted way to get back. Now he knew that this was what he too must do and he stood for a moment in a sudden sweat of relief, thankful that he had been able to think of just the right thing.

Then going quickly into the house, he rummaged in the bathroom closet, found the laundry bag, and taking it into the kitchen, put it down in the middle of the floor. He looked wonderingly about the rough kitchen and decided to start with the liquor closet, both because he knew the whiskey was expensive and because it was something he would never have wanted for himself. Foraging among the bottles, he took out one each of Bourbon, Scotch and cognac, respectfully wiped off the dirty shoulders on his pants, and put them into his sack. Now that he had begun to steal, laying his hands for the first time on things which did not belong to him, he passed into a kind of coma of excitement. At the thought of his own courage, his hands trembled wildly, and his thoughts seemed to come to him with dazzling clarity, like balls of colored light which rose up through his brain and burst, giving out ideas, "Take the toaster," "Better get the guns," "No—finish the kitchen first." Now in his excitement, he slammed the liquor closet door and turned to the food cabinet, but the lower shelves contained only good inexpensive food, cans of soup and pork-and-beans. Dutifully he climbed up onto the counter to reach the delicacies on the higher shelves. He was standing there, brooding among the odd-shaped tins and crockery jars, wondering what was worth stealing, when the white men came out to see what the noise was about. He looked down, his big hands full of cans, and saw them.

They were staring up at him in dazed solemnity. "What the hell do you think you're doing?" Mr. McIntire asked in genuine amazement.

"Why, I'se stealing," he said politely, as if in answer to a stupid question, but unexpectedly, on the last syllable, his voice quavered off to a higher note. The men looked astonished, as if they had not expected anything like this at all and their surprise was mirrored in him. "That stuff there," he explained, trying to get his bearings.

Mr. Underwood jerked the sack open and they stood for a moment looking down into it at the odd assortment: the three clean bottles, the greasy old toaster, and a few worthless odds and ends of bar equipment, including a bottle cork with a laughing pottery head. After a moment, Mr. Underwood raised a round, blank face and his eyes roamed off, wild and unfocused, around the kitchen and then back up to Leroy. "What you doing up there, Roy?" he asked.

The sweat broke out on Leroy's face. "I'se stealing, Mr. Underwood," he said. "I'se just stealing."

Now Mr. McIntire's little eyes swept up and over Leroy with bright curiosity and he looked down at the sack and nodded reasonably. "That's right," he said, "he's stealing."

But Mr. Underwood broke out in a wounded, enraged roar. "But Leroy, you never *done* that before." He raised his red hands, grabbed fiercely at the air, and lunging toward Leroy, stumbled and half fell across the sack.

As he struggled to his feet, Mr. McIntire caught hold of his arm and pulled him toward the door. "Come on," he said, "no use to get yourself excited over a nigger stealing. We'll go out on the porch and talk it over."

When they had left the room, Leroy crumpled down from his place somewhere near the ceiling and crouched on the counter, the cans dangling in his hands. He had had no thought beyond this. The shooting lights which had guided him died out in his head; whatever had seized him left as suddenly as it had come, leaving behind it nothing, hardly even any memory of itself. He knew that he was in deep trouble from which formless horrors would flow.

His mind lay still in a hollow of fright, while all around it, he heard the men's voices, coming wordlessly from the porch, Mr. Underwood's howling out in brutal fury, Mr. McIntire's breaking anxiously across it, as if trying to calm him down. In his interior misery, it seemed to Leroy that Mr. Underwood would now be sure to have a heart attack, that there was nothing to stop that, too, from following.

Squatting on the counter, after a time his knee joints began to ache but still he did not move. He would not have moved if they had, as he expected, gone to the phone to call the police, or even if the police had burst into the kitchen, keeping himself removed to the last moment from what was going to happen, but suddenly he heard a sound which was so unexpected that it fixed his attention. At first, as though he had never heard it before, he wasn't sure just what it was. Then he realized that someone was laughing.

He let himself down from his counter and crept closer to them out into the living room which adjoined the porch.

It was Mr. McIntire who was laughing, with the sound rising in a long, high-pitched yowl.

"What the hell's the matter with you?" Mr. Underwood asked him. "You lost *your* mind, too?" He had begun his question in scorn and amazement but before he had finished there was the slightest rippling and bubbling through the hard surface of his own voice, as if from something rising from below.

"Oh I can't help it—it strikes me funny," Mr. McIntire said, still laughing. "I was just thinking that all those years we been *kidding* Leroy about stealing, he probably really was. Because now it seems like he's got so used to it he doesn't even bother hiding it any more—just stands in the middle of the kitchen and fills up his sack—"

Harshly, reluctantly, Mr. Underwood laughed too. "All these years—you really think so?" He spoke in a voice filled with wonder and something akin to appreciation. "Well, I'll be goddam, the crazy nigger," he said, and chuckled.

"We could tell the police he's been stealing from us for thirty years and we finally got good and tired of it." Mr. McIntire snickered.

"Well, I ought to teach him a lesson," Mr. Underwood said sullenly. But then suddenly all the mirth which had threatened his control began to flow through in long, hard brays of laughter. "Well, I'll be goddam," he said again. "How do you suppose he expected to get it home? Were we supposed to drive him there and he'd get out with his sack and thank us for the ride—I mean, *how* did he have it figured? Can you just tell me that?"

"Why, you can't understand them," Mr. McIntire said reasonably.

"I don't know about that," Mr. Underwood said slowly. "You've just got to remember that they're like children— these people are just like children." Filaments of tenderness clotted wetly in his voice so that he cleared his throat largely.

"It's those damned smart Yankee organizers cause the trouble!" he said. "Our southern Negroes are just like children. Oh *Lee*-roy," he called out, "come out here."

Leroy scuttled forward out of the living room and stood in the doorway to the porch, blinking crazily out at them. The sunny porch, with the men lounging at rest in the wicker chairs was so usual that it seemed totally strange, like something he had never seen before. He was weak and unnerved with the anticipation of trouble that did not come.

But the men were sprawled out at their ease, looking casually, without interest, out at the wide circle of the world. He leaned cautiously against the door and shuffled his feet to get their attention. "Hi Leroy," Mr. Underwood said without looking around.

"Are you gonna call the police now?" he asked. His voice came out louder than usual; in fact, in his surprise that he had spoken at all, it seemed to him almost as though his voice ran crying out before him down the little hills.

"Oh now, Leroy," Mr. Underwood said, "of course we're not gonna call the police. I tell you what," he added, "we're gonna give you those things you put in your sack—you just go right ahead and take 'em."

"Oh no," Leroy cried out, appalled, "I don't want them things—what I goan do with 'em?" But he felt tired. He sagged against the door and ceased to speak or listen. Now the sun was very low, the long rays running across the porch and striking back into the house, but the men sat looking straight into it, their faces shallow and expressionless, the empty slopes of their own property before them. He stood behind them, no longer thinking of them or of anything else. Then with a start he became aware that their ears stood from their heads pinkly shining in the late light, rosy-red, purple-veined, a strange and unnatural color.

But Mr. Underwood turned his round eyes sweetly upon him and said coaxingly, like a child at bedtime. "Come on, Leroy, come on out and sit down with us and tell us about this great big robbery you pulled off . . ."

For a moment, his eyes flitted about as if he were looking for another place to go, but his feet moved him out toward them. He sat down at the extreme edge of a chair and his eyes went wearily backward into his head, seeking invention, and then slowly his hands rose up before him, the gray fingers spread and rigid, as though they held the form of the story he had devised. From deep within him, creaky and flawed, there rose his old crazy cackle. "Well now, gentmun, I tell you," he began . . .

THE LAST MOHICAN

by Bernard Malamud

Bernard Malamud (1914–   ), a native of
Brooklyn, was graduated from City College and
received an M.A. from Columbia in 1942. Like
many other distinguished American literary men,
Malamud has combined university teaching and
writing in his professional career. His work has
received many awards, including the Ford Fellowship, the Rosenthal Award, the 1959 National
Book Award for *The Magic Barrel* (the first of
two collections of his short stories), and the 1967
National Book Award and the Pulitzer Prize for
The Fixer. His novels include *The Natural, The
Assistant, The Fixer,* and *Dubin's Lives*.

Fidelman, a self-confessed failure as a painter, came to Italy
to prepare a critical study of Giotto, the opening chapter of
which he had carried across the ocean in a new pigskin
leather briefcase, now gripped in his perspiring hand. Also
new were his gum-soled oxblood shoes, a tweed suit he had
on despite the late-September sun slanting hot in the Roman
sky, although there was a lighter one in his bag; and a Da-
cron shirt and set of cotton-Dacron underwear, good for
quick and easy washing for the traveler. His suitcase, a
bulky, two-strapped affair which embarrassed him slightly,
he had borrowed from his sister Bessie. He planned, if he

Reprinted from *The Magic Barrel* by Bernard Malamud, by permission of
Farrar, Straus & Giroux, Inc. Copyright © 1958 by Bernard Malamud.

had any money left at the end of the year, to buy a new one in Florence. Although he had been in not much of a mood when he had left the U.S.A., Fidelman picked up in Naples, and at the moment, as he stood in front of the Rome railroad station, after twenty minutes still absorbed in his first sight of the Eternal City, he was conscious of a certain exaltation that devolved on him after he had discovered that directly across the many-vehicled piazza stood the remains of the Baths of Diocletian. Fidelman remembered having read that Michelangelo had had a hand in converting the baths into a church and convent, the latter ultimately changed into the museum that presently was there. "Imagine," he muttered. "Imagine all that history."

In the midst of his imagining, Fidelman experienced the sensation of suddenly seeing himself as he was, to the pinpoint, outside and in, not without bittersweet pleasure; and as the well-known image of his face rose before him he was taken by the depth of pure feeling in his eyes, slightly magnified by glasses, and the sensitivity of his elongated nostrils and often tremulous lips, nose from lips divided by a mustache of recent vintage that looked, Fidelman thought, as if it had been sculptured there, adding to his dignified appearance although he was stockily built and not tall. But almost at the same moment, this unexpectedly intense sense of his being—it was more than appearance—faded, exaltation having gone where exaltation goes, and Fidelman became aware that there was an exterior source to the strange, almost tridimensional reflection of himself he had felt as well as seen. Behind him, a short distance to the right, he had noticed a stranger—give a skeleton a couple of pounds—loitering near a bronze statue on a stone pedestal of the heavy-dugged Etruscan wolf suckling the infant Romulus and Remus, the man contemplating Fidelman already acquisitively so as to suggest to the traveler that he had been mirrored (lock, stock, barrel) in the other's gaze for some time, perhaps since he had stepped off the train. Casually studying him though pretending no, Fidelman beheld a person of about his own height, oddly dressed in brown knickers and black, knee-length woolen socks drawn up over slightly bowed, broomstick legs, these grounded in small, porous, pointed shoes. His yellowed shirt was open at the gaunt throat, both sleeves rolled up over skinny, hairy arms. The stranger's high forehead was bronzed, his black hair thick behind small ears, the dark, close-shaven beard tight on the face; his experienced nose was weighted at the tip, and the soft brown eyes, above all, *wanted*. Though his expression suggested humility, he all but licked his lips as he approached the ex-painter.

"Shalom," he greeted Fidelman.

"Shalom," the other hesitantly replied, uttering the word— so far as he recalled—for the first time in his life. My God, he thought, a handout for sure. My first hello in Rome and it has to be a schnorrer.

The stranger extended a smiling hand. "Susskind," he said, "Shimon Susskind."

"Arthur Fidelman." Transferring his briefcase to under his left arm while standing astride the big suitcase, he shook hands with Susskind. A blue-smocked porter came by, glanced at Fidelman's bag, looked at him, then walked away.

Whether he knew it or not Susskind was rubbing his palms contemplatively together.

"Parla italiano?"

"Not with ease, although I read it fluently. You might say I need the practice."

"Yiddish?"

"I express myself best in English."

"Let it be English then." Susskind spoke with a slight British intonation. "I knew you were Jewish," he said, "the minute my eyes saw you."

Fidelman, who did not look particularly Jewish, chose to ignore the remark. "Where did you pick up your knowledge of English?"

"In Israel."

Israel interested Fidelman. "You live there?"

"Once, not now," Susskind answered vaguely. He seemed suddenly bored.

"How so?"

Susskind twitched a shoulder. "Too much heavy labor for a man of my modest health. Also I couldn't stand the suspense."

Fidelman nodded.

"Furthermore, the desert air makes me constipated. In Rome I am lighthearted."

"A Jewish refugee from Israel, no less," Fidelman said good-humoredly.

"I'm always running," Susskind answered mirthlessly. If he was lighthearted, he had yet to show it.

"Where else from, if I may ask?"

"Where else but Germany, Hungary, Poland? Where not?"

"Ah, that's so long ago." Fidelman then noticed the gray in the man's hair. "Well, I'd better be going," he said. He picked up his bag as two porters hovered uncertainly nearby.

But Susskind offered certain services. "You got a hotel?"

"All picked and reserved."

"How long are you staying?"

What business is it of his? However, Fidelman courteously replied, "Two weeks in Rome, the rest of the year in Florence, with a few side trips to Sienna, Assisi, Padua and maybe also Venice."

"You wish a guide in Rome?"

"Are you a guide?"

"Why not?"

"No," said Fidelman. "I'll look as I go along to museums, libraries, et cetera."

This caught Susskind's attention. "What are you, a professor?"

Fidelman couldn't help blushing. "Not exactly, really just a student."

"From which institution?"

He coughed a little. "By that I mean a professional student, you might say. Call me Trofimov, from Chekhov. If there's something to learn I want to learn it."

"You have some kind of a project?" the other persisted. "A grant?"

"No grant. My money is hard earned. I worked and saved a long time to take a year in Italy. I made certain sacrifices. As for a project, I'm writing on the painter Giotto. He was one of the most important—"

"You don't have to tell me about Giotto," Susskind interrupted with a little smile.

"You've studied his work?"

"Who doesn't know Giotto?"

"That's interesting to me," said Fidelman, secretly irritated. "How do you happen to know him?"

"How do you?"

"I've given a good deal of time and study to his work."

"So I know him, too."

I'd better get this over with before it begins to amount up to something, Fidelman thought. He set down his bag and fished with a finger in his leather coin purse. The two porters watched with interest, one taking a sandwich out of his pocket, unwrapping the newspaper, and beginning to eat.

"This is for yourself," Fidelman said.

Susskind hardly glanced at the coin as he let it drop into his pants pocket. The porters then left.

The refugee had an odd way of standing motionless, like a cigar store Indian about to burst into flight. "In your luggage," he said vaguely, "would you maybe have a suit you can't use? I could use a suit."

At last he comes to the point. Fidelman, though annoyed, controlled himself. "All I have is a change from the one you now see me wearing. Don't get the wrong idea about me, Mr. Susskind. I'm not rich. In fact, I'm poor. Don't let a few new clothes deceive you. I owe my sister money for them."

Susskind glanced down at his shabby, baggy knickers. "I

haven't had a suit for years. The one I was wearing when I ran away from Germany fell apart. One day I was walking around naked."

"Isn't there a welfare organization that could help you out—some group in the Jewish community, interested in refugees?"

"The Jewish organizations wish to give me what they wish, not what I wish," Susskind replied bitterly. "The only thing they offer me is a ticket back to Israel."

"Why don't you take it?"

"I told you already, here I feel free."

"Freedom is a relative term."

"Don't tell me about freedom."

He knows all about that, too, Fidelman thought. "So you feel free," he said, "but how do you live?"

Susskind coughed, a brutal cough.

Fidelman was about to say something more on the subject of freedom but left it unsaid. Jesus, I'll be saddled with him all day if I don't watch out.

"I'd better be getting off to the hotel." He bent again for his bag.

Susskind touched him on the shoulder and when Fidelman exasperatedly straightened up, the half dollar he had given the man was staring him in the eye.

"On this we both lose money."

"How do you mean?"

"Today the lira sells six-twenty-three on the dollar, but for specie they only give you five hundred."

"In that case, give it here and I'll let you have a dollar." From his billfold Fidelman quickly extracted a crisp bill and handed it to the refugee.

"Not more?" Susskind sighed.

"Not more," the student answered emphatically.

"Maybe you would like to see Diocletian's Bath? There are some enjoyable Roman coffins inside. I will guide you for another dollar."

"No thanks." Fidelman said goodbye, and lifting the suitcase, lugged it to the curb. A porter appeared and the student, after some hesitation, let him carry it toward the line of small dark-green taxis in the piazza. The porter offered to carry the briefcase too, but Fidelman wouldn't part with it. He gave the cabdriver the address of the hotel, and the taxi took off with a lurch. Fidelman at last relaxed. Susskind, he noticed, had disappeared. Gone with his breeze, he thought. But on the way to the hotel he had an uneasy feeling that the refugee, crouched low, might be clinging to the tire on the back of the cab; however, he didn't look out to see.

Fidelman had reserved a room in an inexpensive hotel not far from the station with its very convenient bus terminal. Then, as was his habit, he got himself quickly and tightly organized. He was always concerned with not wasting time, as if it were his only wealth—not true, of course, though Fidelman admitted he was an ambitious person—and he soon arranged a schedule that made the most of his working hours. Mornings he usually visited the Italian libraries, searching their catalogues and archives, read in poor light, and made profuse notes. He napped for an hour after lunch, then at four. when the churches and museums were reopening, hurried off to them with lists of frescoes and paintings he must see. He was anxious to get to Florence, at the same time a little unhappy at all he would not have time to take in in Rome. Fidelman promised himself to return again if he could afford it, perhaps in the spring, and look at anything he pleased.

After dark he managed to unwind himself and relax. He ate as the Romans did, late, enjoyed a half liter of white wine and smoked a cigarette. Afterward he liked to wander —especially in the old sections near the Tiber. He had read that here, under his feet, were the ruins of Ancient Rome. It was an inspiring business, he, Arthur Fidelman, after all, born a Bronx boy, walking around in all this history. History was mysterious, the remembrance of things unknown, in a way burdensome, in a way a sensuous experience. It uplifted and depressed, why he did not know, except that it excited his thoughts more than he thought good for him. This kind of excitement was all right up to a point, perfect maybe for a creative artist, but less so for a critic. A critic, he thought, should live on beans. He walked for miles along the winding river, gazing at the star-strewn skies. Once, after a couple of days in the Vatican Museum, he saw flights of angels—gold, blue, white—intermingled in the sky. My God, I got to stop using my eyes so much, Fidelman said to himself. But back in his room he sometimes wrote till morning.

Late one night, about a week after his arrival in Rome, as Fidelman was writing notes on the Byzantine style mosaics he had seen during the day, there was a knock on the door, and though the student, immersed in his work, was not conscious he had said "Avanti," he must have, for the door opened, and instead of an angel, in came Susskind in his shirt and baggy knickers.

Fidelman, who had all but forgotten the refugee, certainly never thought of him, half rose in astonishment. "Susskind," he exclaimed, "how did you get in here?"

Susskind for a moment stood motionless, then answered with a weary smile. "I'll tell you the truth, I know the desk clerk."

"But how did you know where I live?"

"I saw you walking in the street so I followed you."

"You mean you saw me accidentally?"

"How else? Did you leave me your address?"

Fidelman resumed his seat. "What can I do for you, Susskind?" He spoke grimly.

The refugee cleared his throat. "Professor, the days are warm but the nights are cold. You see how I go around naked." He held forth bluish arms, goosefleshed. "I came to ask you to reconsider about giving away your old suit."

"And who says it's an old suit?" Despite himself, Fidelman's voice thickened.

"One suit is new, so the other is old."

"Not precisely. I am afraid I have no suit for you, Susskind. The one I presently have hanging in the closet is a little more than a year old and I can't afford to give it away. Besides, it's gabardine, more like a summer suit."

"On me it will be for all seasons."

After a moment's reflection, Fidelman drew out his billfold and counted four single dollars. These he handed to Susskind.

"Buy yourself a warm sweater."

Susskind also counted the money. "If four," he said, "why not five?"

Fidelman flushed. The man's warped nerve. "Because I happen to have four available," he answered. "That's twenty-five hundred lire. You should be able to buy a warm sweater and have something left over besides."

"I need a suit," Susskind said. "The days are warm but the nights are cold." He rubbed his arms. "What else I need I won't say."

"At least roll down your sleeves if you're so cold."

"That won't help me."

"Listen, Susskind," Fidelman said gently, "I would gladly give you the suit if I could afford to, but I can't. I have barely enough money to squeeze out a year for myself here. I've already told you I am indebted to my sister. Why don't you try to get yourself a job somewhere, no matter how menial? I'm sure that in a short while you'll work yourself up into a decent position."

"A job, he says," Susskind muttered gloomily. "Do you know what it means to get a job in Italy? Who will give me a job?"

"Who gives anybody a job? They have to go out and look for it."

"You don't understand, professor. I am an Israeli citizen, and this means I can only work for an Israeli company. How many Israeli companies are there here?—maybe two, El Al and Zim, and even if they had a job, they wouldn't give it to me because I have lost my passport. I would be better off now if I were stateless. A stateless person shows his *laissez passer* and sometimes he can find a small job."

"But if you lost your passport why didn't you put in for a duplicate?"

"I did, but did they give it to me?"

"Why not?"

"Why not? They say I sold it."

"Had they reason to think that?"

"I swear to you somebody stole it from me."

"Under such circumstances," Fidelman asked, "how do you live?"

"How do I live?" He chomped his teeth. "I eat air."

"Seriously?"

"Seriously, on air. I also peddle," he confessed, "but to peddle you need a license, and that the Italians won't give me. When they caught me peddling I was interned for six months in a work camp."

"Didn't they attempt to deport you?"

"They did, but I sold my mother's old wedding ring that I kept in my pocket so many years. The Italians are a humane people. They took the money and let me go but they told me not to peddle any more."

"So what do you do now?"

"I peddle. What should I do, beg?—I peddle. But last spring I got sick and gave my little money away to the doctors. I still have a bad cough." He coughed fruitily. "Now I have no capital to buy stock with. Listen, professor, maybe we can go in partnership together? Lend me twenty thousand lire and I will buy ladies' nylon stockings. After I sell them I will return you your money."

"I have no funds to invest, Susskind."

"You will get it back, with interest."

"I honestly am sorry for you," Fidelman said, "but why don't you at least do something practical? Why don't you go to the Joint Distribution Committee, for instance, and ask them to assist you? That's their business."

"I already told you why. They wish me to go back, but I wish to stay here."

"I still think going back would be the best thing for you."

"No," cried Susskind angrily.

"If that's your decision, freely made, then why pick on me? Am I responsible for you then, Susskind?"

"Who else?" Susskind loudly replied.

"Lower your voice, please, people are sleeping around here," said Fidelman, beginning to perspire. "Why should I be?"

"You know what responsibility means?"

"I think so."

"Then you are responsible. Because you are a man. Because you are a Jew, aren't you?"

"Yes, goddamn it, but I'm not the only one in the whole wide world. Without prejudice, I refuse the obligation. I am a single individual and can't take on everybody's personal burden. I have the weight of my own to contend with."

He reached for his billfold and plucked out another dollar.

"This makes five. It's more than I can afford, but take it and after this please leave me alone. I have made my contribution."

Susskind stood there, oddly motionless, an impassioned statue, and for a moment Fidelman wondered if he would stay all night, but at last the refugee thrust forth a stiff arm, took the fifth dollar and departed.

Early the next morning Fidelman moved out of the hotel into another, less convenient for him, but far away from Shimon Susskind and his endless demands.

This was Tuesday. On Wednesday, after a busy morning in the library, Fidelman entered a nearby trattoria and ordered a plate of spaghetti with tomato sauce. He was reading his *Messaggero,* anticipating the coming of the food, for he was unusually hungry, when he sensed a presence at the table. He looked up, expecting the waiter, but beheld instead Susskind standing there, alas, unchanged.

Is there no escape from him? thought Fidelman, severely vexed. Is this why I came to Rome?

"Shalom, professor," Susskind said, keeping his eyes off the table. "I was passing and saw you sitting here alone, so I came in to say shalom."

"Susskind," Fidelman said in anger, "have you been following me again?"

"How could I follow you?" asked the astonished Susskind. "Do I know where you live now?"

Though Fidelman blushed a little, he told himself he owed nobody an explanation. So he had found out he had moved—good.

"My feet are tired. Can I sit five minutes?"

Susskind drew out a chair. The spaghetti arrived, steaming hot. Fidelman sprinkled it with cheese and wound his fork into several tender strands. One of the strings of spaghetti seemed to stretch for miles, so he stopped at a certain point and swallowed the forkful. Having foolishly neglected to cut the long spaghetti string he was left sucking it, seemingly endlessly. This embarrassed him.

Susskind watched with rapt attention.

Fidelman at last reached the end of the long spaghetti, patted his mouth with a napkin, and paused in his eating.

"Would you care for a plateful?"

Susskind, eyes hungry, hesitated. "Thanks," he said.

"Thanks yes or thanks no?"

"Thanks no." The eyes looked away.

Fidelman resumed eating, carefully winding his fork; he had had not too much practice in this sort of thing and was soon involved in the same dilemma with the spaghetti. Seeing Susskind still watching him, he became tense.

"We are not Italians, professor," the refugee said. "Cut it in small pieces with your knife. Then you will swallow it easier."

"I'll handle it as I please," Fidelman responded testily. "This is my business. You attend to yours."

"My business," Susskind sighed, "don't exist. This morning I had to let a wonderful chance get away from me. I had a chance to buy ladies' stockings at three hundred lire if I had money to buy half a gross. I could easily sell them for five hundred a pair. We would have made a nice profit."

"The news doesn't interest me."

"So if not ladies' stockings, I can also get sweaters, scarves, men's socks, also cheap leather goods, ceramics—whatever would interest you."

"What interests me is what you did with the money I gave you for a sweater."

"It's getting cold, professor," Susskind said worriedly. "Soon comes the November rains, and in winter the tramontana. I thought I ought to save your money to buy a couple of kilos of chestnuts and a bag of charcoal for my burner. If you sit all day on a busy street corner you can sometimes make a thousand lire. Italians like hot chestnuts. But if I do this I will need some warm clothes, maybe a suit."

"A suit," Fidelman remarked sarcastically, "why not an overcoat?"

"I have a coat, poor that it is, but now I need a suit. How can anybody come in company without a suit?"

Fidelman's hand trembled as he laid down his fork. "To my mind you are utterly irresponsible and I won't be saddled with you. I have the right to choose my own problems and the right to my privacy."

"Don't get excited, professor, it's bad for your digestion. Eat in peace." Susskind got up and left the trattoria.

Fidelman hadn't the appetite to finish his spaghetti. He paid the bill, waited ten minutes, then departed, glancing around from time to time to see if he were being followed. He headed down the sloping street to a small piazza where he saw a couple of cabs. Not that he could afford one, but he wanted to make sure Susskind didn't tail him back to his new hotel. He would warn the clerk at the desk never to allow anybody of the refugee's name or description even to make inquiries about him.

Susskind, however, stepped out from behind a splashing

fountain at the center of the little piazza. Modestly addressing the speechless Fidelman, he said, "I don't wish to take only, professor. If I had something to give you, I would gladly give it to you."

"Thanks," snapped Fidelman, "just give me some peace of mind."

"That you have to find yourself," Susskind answered.

In the taxi Fidelman decided to leave for Florence the next day, rather than at the end of the week, and once and for all be done with the pest.

That night, after returning to his room from an unpleasurable walk in the Trastevere—he had a headache from too much wine at supper—Fidelman found his door ajar and at once recalled that he had forgotten to lock it, although he had as usual left the key with the desk clerk. He was at first frightened, but when he tried the armadio in which he kept his clothes and suitcase, it was shut tight. Hastily unlocking it, he was relieved to see his blue gabardine suit—a one-button jacket affair, the trousers a little frayed on the cuffs, but all in good shape and usable for years to come—hanging amid some shirts the maid had pressed for him; and when he examined the contents of the suitcase he found nothing missing, including, thank God, his passport and traveler's checks. Gazing around the room, Fidelman saw all in place. Satisfied, he picked up a book and read ten pages before he thought of his briefcase. He jumped to his feet and began to search everywhere, remembering distinctly that it had been on the night table as he had lain on the bed that afternoon, rereading his chapter. He searched under the bed and behind the night table, then again throughout the room, even on top of and behind the armadio. Fidelman hopelessly opened every drawer, no matter how small, but found neither the briefcase, nor, what was worse, the chapter in it.

With a groan he sank down on the bed, insulting himself for not having made a copy of the manuscript, for he had more than once warned himself that something like this might happen to it. But he hadn't because there were some revisions he had contemplated making, and he had planned to retype the entire chapter before beginning the next. He thought now of complaining to the owner of the hotel, who lived on the floor below, but it was already past midnight and he realized nothing could be done until morning. Who could have taken it? The maid or hall porter? It seemed unlikely they would risk their jobs to steal a piece of leather goods that would bring them only a few thousand lire in a pawnshop. Possibly a sneak thief? He would ask tomorrow if other persons on the floor were missing something. He somehow doubted it. If a thief, he would then and there have ditched the chapter and stuffed the briefcase with Fidelman's oxblood shoes, left by the bed, and the fifteen-dollar R. H. Macy sweater that lay in full view of the desk. But if not the maid or porter or a sneak thief, then who? Though Fidelman had not the slightest shred of evidence to support his suspicions he could think of only one person—Susskind. This thought stung him. But if Susskind, why? Out of pique, perhaps, that he had not been given the suit he had coveted, nor was able to pry it out of the armadio? Try as he would, Fidelman could think of no one else and no other reason. Somehow the peddler had followed him home (he suspected their meeting at the fountain) and had got into his room while he was out to supper.

Fidelman's sleep that night was wretched. He dreamed of pursuing the refugee in the Jewish catacombs under the ancient Appian Way, threatening him a blow on the presumptuous head with a seven-flamed candelabrum he clutched in his hand; while Susskind, clever ghost, who knew the ins and outs of all the crypts and alleys, eluded him at every turn. Then Fidelman's candles all blew out, leaving him sightless and alone in the cemeterial dark; but when the student arose in the morning and wearily drew up the blinds, the yellow Italian sun winked him cheerfully in both bleary eyes.

Fidelman postponed going to Florence. He reported his loss to the Questura, and though the police were polite and eager to help, they could do nothing for him. On the form on which the inspector noted the complaint, he listed the briefcase as worth ten thousand lire, and for "valore del manuscritto" he drew a line. Fidelman, after giving the matter a good deal of thought, did not report Susskind; first, because he had absolutely no proof, for the desk clerk swore he had seen no stranger around in knickers; second, because he was afraid of the consequences for the refugee if he were written down "suspected thief" as well as "unlicensed peddler" and "inveterate refugee." He tried instead to rewrite the chapter, which he felt sure he knew by heart, but when he sat down at the desk, there were important thoughts, whole paragraphs, even pages, that went blank in the mind. He considered sending to America for his notes for the chapter but they were in a barrel in his sister's attic in Levittown, among many notes for other projects. The thought of Bessie, a mother of five, poking around in his things, and the work entailed in sorting the cards, then getting them packaged and mailed to him across the ocean, wearied Fidelman unspeakably; he was certain she would send the wrong ones. He laid down his pen and went into the street, seeking Susskind. He searched for him in neighborhoods where he had seen him before, and though Fidelman spent hours looking, literally days, Susskind never appeared; or if he perhaps did, the sight of Fidelman caused him to vanish. And when the student inquired about him at the Israeli consulate, the clerk, a new man on the job, said he had no record of such a person or his lost passport; on the other hand, he was known at the Joint Distribution Committee, but by name and address only—an impossibility, Fidelman thought. They gave him a number to go to but the place had long since been torn down to make way for an apartment house.

Time went without work, without accomplishment. To put an end to this appalling waste Fidelman tried to force himself back into his routine of research and picture viewing. He moved out of the hotel, which he now could not

stand for the harm it had done him (leaving a telephone
number and urging he be called if the slightest clue turned
up), and he took a room in a small pensione near the
Stazione and here had breakfast and supper rather than go
out. He was much concerned with expenditures and carefully recorded them in a notebook he had acquired for the
purpose. Nights, instead of wandering in the city, feasting
himself upon its beauty and mystery, he kept his eyes glued
to paper, sitting steadfastly at his desk in an attempt to recreate his initial chapter, because he was lost without a beginning. He had tried writing the second chapter from notes
in his possession but it had come to nothing. Always Fidelman needed something solid behind him before he could
advance, some worth-while accomplishment upon which to
build another. He worked late, but his mood, or inspiration,
or whatever it was, had deserted him, leaving him with
growing anxiety, almost disorientation; of not knowing—it
seemed to him for the first time in months—what he must
do next, a feeling that was torture. Therefore he again took
up his search for the refugee. He thought now that once he
had settled it, knew that the man had or hadn't stolen his
chapter—whether he recovered it or not seemed at the moment immaterial—just the knowing of it would ease his
mind and again he would *feel* like working, the crucial
element.

Daily he combed the crowded streets, searching for Susskind wherever people peddled. On successive Sunday mornings he took the long ride to the Porta Portese market and
hunted for hours among the piles of secondhand goods and
junk lining the back streets, hoping his briefcase would
magically appear, though it never did. He visited the open
market at Piazza Fontanella Borghese, and observed the
ambulant venders at Piazza Dante. He looked among fruit
and vegetable stalls set up in the streets, whenever he
chanced upon them, and dawdled on busy street corners
after dark, among beggars and fly-by-night peddlers. After
the first cold snap at the end of October, when the chestnut

sellers appeared throughout the city, huddled over pails of glowing coals, he sought in their faces the missing Susskind. Where in all of modern and ancient Rome was he? The man lived in the open air—he had to appear somewhere. Sometimes when riding in a bus or tram, Fidelman thought he had glimpsed somebody in a crowd, dressed in the refugee's clothes, and he invariably got off to run after whoever it was—once a man standing in front of the Banco di Santo Spirito, gone when Fidelman breathlessly arrived; and another time he overtook a person in knickers, but this one wore a monocle. Sir Ian Susskind?

In November it rained. Fidelman wore a blue beret with his trench coat and a pair of black Italian shoes, smaller, despite their pointed toes, than his burly oxbloods which overheated his feet and whose color he detested. But instead of visiting museums he frequented movie houses, sitting in the cheapest seats and regretting the cost. He was, at odd hours in certain streets, several times accosted by prostitutes, some heartbreakingly pretty, one a slender, unhappy-looking girl with bags under her eyes whom he desired mightily, but Fidelman feared for his health. He had got to know the face of Rome and spoke Italian fairly fluently, but his heart was burdened, and in his blood raged a murderous hatred of the bandy-legged refugee—although there were times when he bethought himself he might be wrong—so Fidelman more than once cursed him to perdition.

One Friday night, as the first star glowed over the Tiber, Fidelman, walking aimlessly along the left riverbank, came upon a synagogue and wandered in among a crowd of Sephardim with Italianate faces. One by one they paused before a sink in an antechamber to dip their hands under a flowing faucet, then in the house of worship touched with loose fingers their brows, mouths, and breasts as they bowed to the Arc, Fidelman doing likewise. Where in the world am I? Three rabbis rose from a bench and the service began, a long prayer, sometimes chanted, sometimes accompanied by invisible organ music, but no Susskind anywhere. Fidelman sat at a desklike pew in the last row, where he could inspect the congregants yet keep an eye on the door. The synagogue was unheated and the cold rose like an exudation from the marble floor. The student's freezing nose burned like a lit candle. He got up to go, but the beadle, a stout man in a high hat and short caftan, wearing a long thick silver chain around his neck, fixed the student with his powerful left eye.

"From New York?" he inquired, slowly approaching.

Half the congregation turned to see who.

"State, not city," answered Fidelman, nursing an active guilt for the attention he was attracting. Then, taking advantage of a pause, he whispered, "Do you happen to know a man named Susskind? He wears knickers."

"A relative?" The beadle gazed at him sadly.

"Not exactly."

"My own son—killed in the Ardeatine Caves." Tears stood forth in his eyes.

"Ah, for that I'm sorry."

But the beadle had exhausted the subject. He wiped his wet lids with pudgy fingers and the curious Sephardim turned back to their prayer books.

"Which Susskind?" the beadle wanted to know.

"Shimon."

He scratched his ear. "Look in the ghetto."

"I looked."

"Look again."

The beadle walked slowly away and Fidelman sneaked out.

The ghetto lay behind the synagogue for several well-packed, crooked blocks, encompassing aristocratic palazzi ruined by age and unbearable numbers, their discolored façades strung with lines of withered wet wash, the fountains in the piazzas, dirt-laden, dry. And dark stone tenements, built partly on centuries-old ghetto walls, inclined toward one another across narrow, cobblestoned streets. In and among the impoverished houses were the wholesale establishments of wealthy Jews, dark holes ending in jeweled interiors, silks and silver of all colors. In the mazed streets wandered the present-day poor, Fidelman among them, oppressed by history, although, he joked to himself, it added years to his life.

A white moon shone upon the ghetto, lighting it like dark day. Once he thought he saw a ghost he knew by sight, and hastily followed him through a thick stone passage to a blank wall where shone in white letters under a tiny electric bulb: VIETATO URINARE. Here was a smell but no Susskind.

For thirty lire the student bought a dwarfed, blackened banana from a street vender (not S.) on a bicycle, and stopped to eat. A crowd of ragazzi gathered to watch.

"Anybody here know Susskind, a refugee wearing knickers?" Fidelman announced, stooping to point with the banana where the pants went beneath the knees. He also made his legs a trifle bowed but nobody noticed.

There was no response until he had finished his fruit, then a thin-faced boy with brown liquescent eyes out of Murillo, piped: "He sometimes works in the Cimitero Verano, the Jewish section."

There too? thought Fidelman. "Works in the cemetery?" he inquired. "With a shovel?"

"He prays for the dead," the boy answered, "for a small fee."

Fidelman bought him a quick banana and the others dispersed.

In the cemetery, deserted on the Sabbath—he should have come Sunday—Fidelman went among the graves, reading legends carved on tombstones, many topped with small brass candelabra, while withered yellow chrysanthemums lay on the stone tablets of other graves, dropped stealthily, Fidelman imagined, on All Souls' Day—a festival in another part of the cemetery—by renegade sons and daughters unable to bear the sight of their dead bereft of flowers while the crypts of the goyim were lit and in bloom. Many were burial places, he read on the stained stones, of those who, for one reason or another, had died in the late large war, including an empty place, it said under a six-pointed star engraved upon a marble slab that lay on the ground, for "My beloved father/Betrayed by the damned Fascists/Murdered at Auschwitz by the barbarous Nazis/*O Crime Orribile.*" But no Susskind.

Three months had gone by since Fidelman's arrival in Rome. Should he, he many times asked himself, leave the city and this foolish search? Why not off to Florence, and there, amid the art splendors of the world, be inspired to resume his work? But the loss of his first chapter was like a spell cast over him. There were times he scorned it as a man-made thing, like all such, replaceable; other times he feared it was not the chapter per se, but that his volatile curiosity had become somehow entangled with Susskind's strange personality—Had he repaid generosity by stealing a man's lifework? Was he so distorted? To satisfy himself, to know man, Fidelman had to know, though at what a cost in precious time and effort. Sometimes he smiled wryly at all this; ridiculous, the chapter grieved him for itself only—the precious thing he had created then lost—especially when he got to thinking of the long diligent labor, how painstakingly he had built each idea, how cleverly mastered problems of order, form, how impressive the finished product, Giotto reborn! It broke the heart. What else, if after months he was here, still seeking?

And Fidelman was unchangingly convinced that Susskind had taken it, or why would he still be hiding? He sighed much and gained weight. Mulling over his frustrated career, on the backs of envelopes containing unanswered letters from his sister Bessie he aimlessly sketched little angels flying. Once, studying his minuscule drawing, it occurred to him that he might someday return to painting, but the thought was more painful than Fidelman could bear.

One bright morning in mid-December, after a good night's sleep, his first in weeks, he vowed he would have another look at the Navicella and then be off to Florence. Shortly before noon he visited the porch of St. Peter's, trying, from his remembrance of Giotto's sketch, to see the mosaic as it had been before its many restorations. He hazarded a note or two in shaky handwriting, then left the church and was walking down the sweeping flight of stairs when he beheld at the bottom—his heart misgave him, was he still seeing pictures, a sneaky apostle added to the overloaded boatful?—ecco, Susskind! The refugee, in beret and long green GI raincoat, from under whose skirts showed his black-stockinged, rooster's ankles—indicating knickers going on above though hidden—was selling black and white rosaries to all who would buy. He held several strands of beads in one hand, while in the palm of the other a few gilded medallions glinted in the winter sun. Despite his outer clothing, Susskind looked, it must be said, unchanged, not a pound more of meat or muscle, the face though aged, ageless. Gazing at him, the student ground his teeth in remembrance. He was tempted quickly to hide, and unobserved observe the thief; but his impatience, after the long unhappy search, was too much for him. With controlled trepidation he approached Susskind from his left as the refugee was busily engaged on the right, urging a sale of beads upon a woman drenched in black.

"Beads, rosaries, say your prayers with holy beads."

"Greetings, Susskind," Fidelman said, coming shakily down the stairs, dissembling the Unified Man, all peace and contentment. "One looks for you everywhere and finds you here. Wie gehts?"

Susskind, though his eyes flickered, showed no surprise to speak of. For a moment his expression seemed to say he had no idea who was this, had forgotten Fidelman's existence, but then at last remembered—somebody long ago from another country, whom you smiled on, then forgot.

"Still here?" he perhaps ironically joked.

"Still." Fidelman was embarrassed at his voice slipping.

"Rome holds you?"

"Rome," faltered Fidelman, "—the air." He breathed deep and exhaled with emotion.

Noticing the refugee was not truly attentive, his eyes roving upon potential customers, Fidelman, girding himself, remarked, "By the way, Susskind, you didn't happen to notice—did you?—the briefcase I was carrying with me around the time we met in September?"

"Briefcase—what kind?" This he said absently, his eyes on the church doors.

"Pigskin. I had in it—" here Fidelman's voice could be heard cracking—"a chapter of a critical work on Giotto I was writing. You know, I'm sure, the Trecento painter?"

"Who doesn't know Giotto?"

"Do you happen to recall whether you saw, if, that is—" He stopped, at a loss of words other than accusatory.

"Excuse me—business." Susskind broke away and bounced up the steps two at a time. A man he approached shied away. He had beads, didn't need others.

Fidelman had followed the refugee. "Reward," he muttered up close to his ear. "Fifteen thousand for the chapter, and who has it can keep the brand-new briefcase. That's his business, no questions asked. Fair enough?"

Susskind spied a lady tourist, including camera and guidebook. "Beads—holy beads." He held up both hands, but she was just a Lutheran, passing through.

"Slow today," Susskind complained as they walked down the stairs, "but maybe it's the items. Everybody has the same. If I had some big ceramics of the Holy Mother, they go like hot cakes—a good investment for somebody with a little cash."

"Use the reward for that," Fidelman cagily whispered, "buy Holy Mothers."

If he heard, Susskind gave no sign. At the sight of a family of nine emerging from the main portal above, the refugee, calling "Addio" over his shoulder, fairly flew up the steps. But Fidelman uttered no response. I'll get the rat yet. He went off to hide behind a high fountain in the square. But the flying spume raised by the wind wet him, so he retreated behind a massive column and peeked out at short intervals to keep the peddler in sight.

At two o'clock, when St. Peter's closed to visitors, Susskind dumped his goods into his raincoat pockets and locked up shop. Fidelman followed him all the way home, indeed the ghetto, although along a street he had not consciously been on before, which led into an alley where the refugee pulled open a left-handed door, and without transition, was "home." Fidelman, sneaking up close, caught a dim glimpse of an overgrown closet containing bed and table. He found no address on wall or door, nor, to his surprise, any door lock. This for a moment depressed him. It meant Susskind had nothing worth stealing. Of his own, that is. The student promised himself to return tomorrow, when the occupant was elsewhere.

Return he did, in the morning, while the entrepreneur was out selling religious articles, glanced around once and was quickly inside. He shivered—a pitch-black freezing cave. Fidelman scratched up a thick match and confirmed bed and table, also a rickety chair, but no heat or light except a drippy candle stub in a saucer on the table. He lit the yellow candle and searched all over the place. In the table drawer a few eating implements plus safety razor, though where he shaved was a mystery, probably a public toilet. On a shelf above the thin-blanketed bed stood half a flask of red wine, part of a package of spaghetti, and a hard panino. Also an unexpected little fish bowl with a bony gold fish swimming around in Arctic seas. The fish, reflecting the candle flame, gulped repeatedly, thrashing its frigid tail as Fidelman watched. He loves pets, thought the student. Under the bed he found a chamber pot, but nowhere a briefcase with a fine critical chapter in it. The place was not more than an icebox someone probably had lent the refugee to come in out of the rain. Alas, Fidelman sighed. Back in the pensione, it took a hot-water bottle two hours to thaw him out; but from the visit he never fully recovered.

In this latest dream of Fidelman's he was spending the

day in a cemetery all crowded with tombstones when up out of an empty grave rose this long-nosed brown shade, Virgilio Susskind, beckoning.

Fidelman hurried over.

"Have you read Tolstoy?"

"Sparingly."

"Why is art?" asked the shade, drifting off.

Fidelman, willy-nilly, followed, and the ghost, as it vanished, led him up steps going through the ghetto and into a marble synagogue.

The student, left alone, for no reason he could think of lay down upon the stone floor, his shoulders keeping strangely warm as he stared at the sunlit vault above. The fresco therein revealed this saint in fading blue, the sky flowing from his head, handing an old knight in a thin red robe his gold cloak. Nearby stood a humble horse and two stone hills.

Giotto. *San Francesco dona le vesti al cavaliere povero.*

Fidelman awoke running. He stuffed his blue gabardine into a paper bag, caught a bus, and knocked early on Susskind's heavy portal.

"Avanti." The refugee, already garbed in beret and raincoat (probably his pajamas), was standing at the table, lighting the candle with a flaming sheet of paper. To Fidelman the paper looked like the underside of a typewritten page. Despite himself, the student recalled in letters of fire his entire chapter.

"Here, Susskind," he said in a trembling voice, offering the bundle, "I bring you my suit. Wear it in good health."

The refugee glanced at it without expression. "What do you wish for it?"

"Nothing at all." Fidelman laid the bag on the table, called goodbye and left.

He soon heard footsteps clattering after him across the cobblestones.

"Excuse me, I kept this under my mattress for you." Susskind thrust at him the pigskin briefcase.

Fidelman savagely opened it, searching frenziedly in each compartment, but the bag was empty. The refugee was already in flight. With a bellow the student started after him. "You bastard, you burned my chapter!"

"Have mercy," cried Susskind, "I did you a favor."

"I'll do you one and cut your throat."

"The words were there but the spirit was missing."

In a towering rage, Fidelman forced a burst of speed, but the refugee, light as the wind in his marvelous knickers, his green coattails flying, rapidly gained ground.

The ghetto Jews, framed in amazement in their medieval windows, stared at the wild pursuit. But in the middle of it, Fidelman, stout and short of breath, moved by all he had lately learned, had a triumphant insight.

"Susskind, come back," he shouted, half sobbing. "The suit is yours. All is forgiven."

He came to a dead halt but the refugee ran on. When last seen he was still running.

A WOMAN OF HER AGE

by Jack Ludwig

Jack Ludwig (1922–   ). Born in Canada, Ludwig took his Ph.D. from the University of California and has since settled in the United States, where he has taught at Williams, Bard College, and the State University of New York at Stony Brook. Ludwig received the Atlantic First Award for 1960, and his stories have been chosen for Martha Foley's *Best American Short Stories for 1961* and for the *O'Henry Award Prize Stories for 1961*. In addition to his stories, Ludwig has published *Confusions* (1963) and *Recent American Novelists* (1962). He has been co-editor of *The Noble Savage* magazine and of *Stories, British and American.*

Once a week, even now, Mrs Goffman makes that chauffeur drive her slowly down from the mountain, back to St Lawrence Boulevard and Rachel Street; she doesn't want any old cronies who might still be alive spotting her in that hearse of a limousine, so she gets out a couple of blocks from the Market and walks the rest of the way, not in her Persian lamb or her warm beaver, but in that worn cloth coat she bought at Eaton's Basement years ago, the black one. Long, gaunt as a late afternoon shadow, Mrs Goffman concentrates on smiling. Otherwise she looks like a spook. At seventy-five you can feel warm, sweet, girlish even, but an old old face has trouble expressing soft feelings. Those reddish-brown eyebrows that didn't turn white with the rest of her hair, they're to blame, so bushy, so fierce, with an ironic twist that was snappy when she was a hot young radical, but now, when she's old enough to be a great-grandmother, who needs it?

"Wordsworth," her son Jimmy used to call her. In a drugstore window she sees reflected Wordsworth's broad forehead, deep-set eyes, small mouth, short chin. By God, she tells herself, this is a darned good face. Jimmy had this face. Her father had it too—who knows how far back these purplish lips go, or the dark rings under eyes, or the pale olive complexion? Moses might have had similar coloring. Her nose gives a sly twitch to call attention to itself: Wordsworth's large humped nose she has too, and it deserves the dominant spot it earned for itself on Mrs Goffman's face. She judges everything by its smell. That's why the ambassador's mansion she lives in flunks so badly—it's not only quiet as a church, it smells like a church. Six days a week her nose puts up with that dry lonely quiet smell, does what a nose is supposed to do in Westmount, breathe a little: on St Lawrence Boulevard a nose is for smelling, and Mrs Goffman doesn't miss a sniff. Families are getting ready for sabbath.

Doba, catch that goose roasting, her nose seems to say. Hey, poppyseed cookies! *Real* stuffed fish! St Lawrence Boulevard, I love you!

2

Mitchell the "Kosher Butcher" nodded his usual pitying nod as she walked past his full window—fresh-killed ducks and chickens hanging by their feet, cows' brains in pools, tongues like holsters, calves' feet signed by the Rabbi's indelible pencil. Mrs Goffman nodded her black-turbaned head at Mitchell but he'd already given *his* nod, and only stared back, open-mouthed, his hands pressed against his slaughter-house-looking apron. Naturally Mitchell has her pegged: doesn't he know this shopping trip is a fake, that Mrs Grosney, the cook, does Mrs Goffman's buying and cooking? Mitchell knows about the Persian lamb coat she doesn't wear to Market. Mitchell knew her dead husband well. Mitchell, like all of Montreal, knows the story of her dead son Jimmy.

When Simon-may-he-rest-in-peace was still alive the Goffmans lived down here, among people, in life. Now life was a novelty to Mrs Goffman. Six days to Westmount, one to St Lawrence and Rachel Street, what idiotic arrangement was that? Some day she'd get real tough with her son Sidney. Marry him off. Make him sell the ambassador's mansion and lead a normal life.

Her eyebrows went into their ironic arch. You, Doba, they seemed to mock her, when could you get your kids to do anything?

3

In front of Bernstein's Kiddies' Korner a young girl pressed her lovely dark face against the window, her hand nervously rocking a baby carriage. Black hair, heavy lips, nursing breasts, what a beauty of a mother, Mrs Goffman thought; she could double for Jimmy's Shirley! By rights Mrs Goffman should have a grand-daughter this girl's age. One? A dozen!

What would it hurt if she *pretended* she had come to Kiddies' Korner to buy something or other for her grand-daughter and great-grandchild? The thought made her feel wonderful.

"Dear," she said, "good morning, dear. How's baby?"

The girl nodded absently. She had eyes only for a white bunting in the window. If she wanted pink or blue I'd know at least if my grandchild was a boy or girl, Mrs Goffman thought. In her low Russian-sounding voice she cooed at the baby, tried to make her grand-daughter look at her.

"Dear," she tried again, "what do you think is nice, eh, dear?"

"That bunting," the girl said, still not looking at her grandmother, "but what a high price!"

"Twenty-five bucks! Highway robbery," Mrs Goffman said in a loud voice, thinking she'd better not ham it up too much. Her purse was lined with dough—a few fifties, four or five twenties, a dozen tens, fives, ones, even a two—Mrs Goffman was never too neat about money. Every handbag was loaded this way, and what Montreal bank didn't have Doba Goffman as an account? Money to her was like a big soup: you cooked it in a vat but then came the problem of how to store it. You pour in one jar, then another, then another—except that with Sidney or Jimmy there was no end to what she had to put in jars. The faster she stored money away the faster they brought her more. No matter what she did to get rid of it—charities, trips to New York every week to see shows, an opera, flights to Israel, Hawaii, buying those bozos Sulka ties at fifty bucks a crack—no matter how fast she gave it, they stuffed her accounts, lined handbags, papered the walls, those successes of hers, those imbeciles!

Bernstein's clerk poked his head out the door.

"Highway robbery, is that what you call it, *babbe?*" he said in a hurt voice. "Come inside. I'll show you my cost."

Years ago Mrs Goffman felt offended when people called her *babbe,* grandmother, but not now. She turned her head and gave the man a mirthless smile.

"Honey," he said to the girl, "let your *babbe* stay out here with the baby. You come in. I've got a real bargain for the kid."

The girl didn't seem to hear.

"Go 'head, dear," Mrs Goffman said warmly. "I'll rock baby."

The girl wheeled the carriage around and hurried towards the Market. Mrs Goffman followed quickly.

4

At the corner of Rachel and St Lawrence Mrs Goffman stopped to let a horse-drawn wagon go by. What a wonderful stink an old nag gave off! Wheels creaking was a melody to her deafish ear. Across the way was Simon's old store, the "upstairs" they used to live in. Dimly, like an imagination, Mrs Goffman made out the "S. Goffman and Sons" which "J. Olin and Brother" had been painted over. Her nose sniffed at the rubber and leather smell coming from the old store. Those French perfumes Sidney gave her should only smell so nice!

Crossing the street she hurried after her grand-daughter, but, suddenly, without warning, tears gushed from Mrs Goffman's eyes, biting, salty tears mixed in with the heady fish fragrance around the Rachel Street Market stalls. Stop it, old fool, she told herself, but the tears kept running.

She pretended she was buying, dropped her eyes, rubbed a cold slimy fish with her manicured fingernails, poked open a carp's small-toothed mouth, combed its stiff freezing fins with her wrinkled hand. Next to Simon's gold wedding band was the hideous ruby Sidney gave her for her birthday last year; above them both was Jimmy's gift, a diamond-studded watch.

"Babbe, babbe," a gentle voice said to her, "why are you crying?"

She didn't have to open her eyes to know the man was new on the job: everybody on Rachel Street knew why Mrs Goffman cried.

"A Cold," she said.

"In the eyes?" the voice said skeptically. "Then maybe you shouldn't handle my fish?"

"Listen," Mrs Goffman said wildly, "give me two large carp and three nice whitefish!"

"There's an order!" the man clapped his hands together.

"Only your generation, eh, *babbe?* Big families need a full table!"

The girl with the baby wheeled up beside Mrs Goffman, hefted a small pike, looked wistful. Mrs Goffman moved over to give her grand-daughter more room.

"Mister," she said to the fishman, "I've got lots of time. Look after the mother with the baby first."

The girl had turned around and was poking at the baby's blankets. The fishman grabbed at a floppy-tailed carp beating its fins on the damp wood stall.

"Today's girl," he laughed, "can wait longer than you, *babbe*. Your generation grinds, stuffs, cooks—just like my ma-may-she-rest-in-peace—two dozen people at *shabbes* table wasn't too much. But these kids?" He pointed at Mrs Goffman's grand-daughter. "She'll toss a pike in a frying pan and one, two, it's *shabbes.*"

A second carp, big as a shark, fell with a splat against the first; three dancing whitefish got buried in a wad of newspapers.

"Dear," Mrs Goffman said sweetly, "he's ready to take your order."

Again she didn't look up. Mrs Goffman wanted to holler —"Hey, sleeping beauty, can't you even answer when your *babbe* talks to you?"

"*Babbe*," the fishman said, "this parcel's too heavy. You live right around here somewheres? St Dominique maybe? I'll deliver you the fish myself."

"I'm a strong woman," Mrs Goffman said, holding out her arms.

"I can see, *babbe*. I only wish I should be in your shape at your age," the man said enthusistically. "Have a good sabbath. Enjoy the kiddies. You deserve the best. I can tell!"

"Good-bye, dear," Mrs Goffman said to her grand-daughter.

"Good-bye, good-bye," the fishman answered, clapping his hands together. "Next?"

5

The moment the fish touched her arms they seemed to re-vive and start swimming—twenty, thirty pounds writhing in her helpless arms! Fish? Who needed fish? When did she cook fish last! That last batch stunk up Sidney's limousine so badly he had to sell it for next to nothing!

The newspaper parcel was leaking all over her coat. Let it bust and she'd be chased by every cat in Montreal! Was she out of her mind? Seventy-five years in this world and still not able to resist the most foolish impulse!

Her arms hurt, her face turned red, her heart beat crazily. Leave it to an old Radical to act like a nut! Two blocks away is that healthy horse of a chauffeur sitting on his fanny and sunning himself. Two blocks? She'd never make it. But where could she dump this useless stuff? In the empty baby carriages scattered around St Lawrence Boulevard? She thought of letting it fall casually on the sidewalk, like a lost handkerchief. Maybe she could slip it into the empty mov-ing van she saw across the street. Who but a woman loaded with money could afford such grandstand plays?

Fish water soaked her gloves, dribbled down her coat front: a bit of fin slipped through the dissolving newspaper, a sappy fish-eye made peek-a-boo. In a shop window Mrs Goffman caught sight of herself—a black streak, a bundle, eyebrows. Get sloppy sentimental and this is the result!

Triminiuk's. She suddenly came up with a brain-wave: Captain Triminiuk would save her! Giggling, panting, giddy, red-faced, she staggered across the street and into Trimini-uk's Delicatessen.

The fish hit the counter like an explosion; the whitefish, wild as Cossacks, danced out of their covering.

"Come save an old sap, Gershon," Mrs Goffman called to the back of the store. "I overstocked myself with fish."

She wiped her coat with orange wrappers, fell back, laugh-ing helplessly, into one of Gershon's old chairs. Only Captain Triminiuk's Delicatessen still had these small round marble-top tables with wire legs and matching chairs with backs like wire carpet-beaters. The air inside was like a home-made mist—garlic, pickles, pastrami, salami, sauerkraut, fresh rye bread, Triminiuk himself, who smelled like a real smokehouse.

Marching—he never walked—one-eyed Triminiuk came toward her, disapproving, as usual, everything about her. He stood at attention, his black cuff-guards up to his armpits, tieless collar buttoned at the neck, vest unbuttoned, also part of his pants. One of his eyes was almost closed, the other bright as turqoise, his moustache bristly, yellowed with tobacco.

Forty years ago, when she and Simon first met the old bluffer, he was just out of the Russian army, a cook who lost an eye from splattering fat. Since then Triminiuk, in recognition of himself, every ten years or so gave himself a promotion. Now he was a captain. Now the missing eye was a result of a sabre in the Russo-Japanese War.

"Fish?" he sniffed.

"Be a pal. Take it off my hands, Gershon," she said flirtatiously.

"I need charity, Doba?"

"Don't play poor mouth with me, you bandit," she laughed. "You want to be independent, give me a tea with lemon."

He didn't budge. Long ago she had given up trying to explain things to a stubborn old bluffer like Triminiuk. All he saw was that Doba Goffman, the hot-headed young Radical, became Mrs S. Goffman, prominent member of an Orthodox synagogue, patroness of the foolishness her sons' success brought her. Try to convince Gershon that she'd joined the Orthodoxes in protest against her sons' becoming Anglican-like Reform Jews? If those characters had stayed on St Lawrence Boulevard she would never have set foot in a synagogue. But when they climbed Westmount, bought that enormous mansion from the Ambassador, bragged about looking out on Nuns' Island, took her to Temple where the Rabbi pursed his lips in such a way that everybody should know he learned Hebrew not at home but in a University, then she, in protest, became again a Jew! Gershon should have seen the lousy Jewish-style cooking she, a Radical who had nothing to do with kitchens, forced her bigshot sons to eat—he should only know she got her Jewish recipes from *Better Homes and Gardens!*

Gershon accepted no explanations. He considered her a traitor. Worse. Maybe even a Zionist!

"My tea, captain," Mrs Goffman said.

Triminiuk looked toward the door.

A fat woman, hair messy, hands dug deep in the ripped pockets of an old flowered housecoat, drove several kids into the store in front of her, stood for a second sighing, muttering, scratching herself under the pockets. Corns stuck out of her pink-and-aqua wedgies.

"Captain," she said in a high nasal whine, "my kids came to eat me up alive again. Let a mouse try to find a crumb by me, let. Herbie's wetters, Gertie's soilers, four five already, and Gertie's carrying again, you've heard about such misfortunes? They act like Westmount millionaires. You can't afford kids, don't have, I keep telling."

Triminiuk, Mrs Goffman saw, was trying to shut the woman up.

"Lady," he said in his military voice, "what can I get for you?"

One of the children, about seven, a girl with black hair, black eyes, front teeth out, stared at Mrs Goffman.

"Ma," Mrs Goffman's deafish ears heard her whisper, "why's the old lady all in black?"

"Gimme a couple rye loaves to stop up the mouths quickly," the woman said shrilly, "a salami, a few slices lox—"

"Ma," the little girl stole behind her mother's housecoat and peeked at Mrs Goffman, "is it a witch?"

"Tammy, stop botherin'," the woman said absently, fingering the fish on the counter. "Captain, how can you make today's kid stop carrying? It's living here with the French that makes 'em like this, hah?"

"Lady," Triminiuk snapped, "is this everything?"

"Ma," the little girl tugged at her mother's sleeve, "I'm afraid of her—"

"Let me be," the woman whined, shoving the child at Mrs Goffman. Hard as Mrs Goffman's old face tried, it couldn't come up with a look to reassure the child.

"You're very sweet, dear," she said softly.

The child seemed to shudder.

"What did you say?" the woman mumbled.

"She's a very sweet little girl," Mrs Goffman said.

"Listen, you want her? She's yours, the pest. You can have these others in the bargain," the woman said without a smile.

"Two dollars and five cents," Triminiuk all but shouted.

"What's he getting sore for? Don't I pay in time? Here," she threw down a dollar bill, "payday I'll give the rest."

"Gramma," the smallest kid in the store said quietly, "can each of us have a sucker?"

"I got no money for suckers," the woman said nastily, missing with a slap she'd aimed at the kid. Tammy, the little girl, frightened, jumped toward Mrs Goffman, grew more frightened, jumped back, catching her grandmother's corns with her shoe.

"For godssake, pests!" the woman shouted, slapping Tammy across the cheek. "Get out of this store!"

"Don't cry, dear," Mrs Goffman tried to make Tammy hear.

"I'm sorry these crazy kids bothered you, lady," the woman said as she shooed them out the door. "With these pests gone you can have peace."

Triminiuk went to get her her tea.

That kid Tammy was right, Mrs Goffman thought as she caught sight of herself in Triminiuk's small calendar mirror. A witch. Black. What sentimental soft-headedness made her dress this way? What right did she have to dump her mourning on St Lawrence Boulevard? In her old age was she becoming a professional widow, a dopey eccentric? Tomorrow she'd go down to one of those fancy French shops on Sherbrooke and get gussied up in pink, violet, maybe even yellow.

Sentimentality, respectability, a tough old Radical like Mrs Goffman had been had, by America. How else did a revolutionary become a quiet-spoken tea-sipper dumb with good taste? By God, an old-fashioned St Dominique Street ma would have chased her kids out of the house with a broom, made their lives so miserable they would *have* to marry, in self-defence. And when Simon died, what stopped her from marrying again? Loyalty. Love. Now, when the time for praying was past and with the lock on the synagogue door, now she realized that love too was smaller than life. A stepfather would have been another way of getting her boys into life on their own. Jimmy had been a bachelor till forty-five, just a year before his death. Poor Sidney, still unmarried, fifty-three, a pill-swallower, complained his way from hotel to hotel crossing three continents.

Waste, Mrs Goffman thought with a sinking feeling, waste is the law of America—too much money, too much talent, even too much fish. Getting stuck with something useless like money and fish was a judgement against her and her sons.

Triminiuk came shuffling toward her, balancing a cup of tea in one hand, a glass in the other. Should she say something? I've done too much damage with silence, Mrs Goffman thought.

"Listen here, Capatanchik," she said nastily, "what's the big idea bringing me tea in a cup and yourself in a glass?"

"Westmount ladies drink from china cups," the old bluffer said without batting an eye.

"Turn right around, you pirate, and get me a glass," Mrs Goffman said, hitting her palm against the marble top. "To hell with Westmount!"

"I only got one glass," Triminiuk came back.

"Then it's for me," Mrs Goffman said in triumph. "Hand it over."

To show he was a winner, Triminiuk poured his tea into a saucer and sipped noisy, like a roughneck.

"How's the rich son?" he asked. She couldn't tell for sure if he was being nasty.

"Sidney's fine," she lied. One thing Sidney never was was fine, specially since without Jimmy he was a total loss in the world. He hadn't been with a woman in over a year. Women weren't Sidney's line—his hair was red and thin, his face chubby and round, his eyes watery and always blinking, his lower lip ready to blubber.

But Jimmy!

Elegant, taller than his tall mother, with her face, her colouring, dressed like a British diplomat, smooth with continental manners, chased by every woman in Montreal, and for what, what for? "Fun," he called it, and what came of his fun? Ashes, dust. The dopiest kid on St Dominique Street had more claim on life than her handsome successful Jimmy. He drove a Bentley, wore a white leather raincoat, a British vest with brass buttons, a Parisian necktie— what he wore Montreal copied, the gals he took out were immediately stamped with approval. "Lover boy" the high-school year-book nicknamed him. "Lover man" was what they called him at McGill, and "Don Giovanni". Women, women, hundreds upon hundreds of women, affairs without number, and what came of it all? "Listen to me, bozos," she had said years ago, when they'd first moved to the Ambassador's mansion, "let's get down to life now, eh? At sixty I'm *entitled* to grandchildren. Who'll mourn me when I'm dead, our bankers?"

Mrs. Goffman's eyes filled, blood rushed to her face, in anger and despair she beat her ringed hand against the marble table. Jimmy, the poor fool Jimmy, marrying at forty-five, and how, with a nineteen-year-old who'd been living with another man since sixteen!

Triminiuk put his hand on her shoulder.

"What are you aggravating yourself for?" His blind eye looked like the dead fish's.

"Gershon, the worst thing is for people to die out of their own generation."

"If people died neatly," Triminiuk said, raising his face from the tilted saucer, "we'd both be long buried by now."

A little French girl barged into the store, wiggling her hips, pushing out her breasts. Her hair was tight with nasty bobby pin curls that gave Mrs Goffman the pip, her skin was broken out, badly powdered and rouged. She chewed gum with an open mouth. Her arms, though, were lovely and slim, and her legs were shapely. Even you, you tramp, Mrs Goffman thought as she watched Triminiuk give the girl a package of Sweet Caporal, even a gum-chewing slut like you I would have taken for a daughter-in-law at the end, when I saw what the score was.

"Bye, Cap," the girl said with a wink. Triminiuk dismissed her with a wave.

"What were you saying, Doba?"

"I was being depressed," she reminded him with a smile, "and you were trying to snap me out of it."

"Why should you be depressed?" Triminiuk said after a long slurp. "The boy died a big success. It should happen to all my grandchildren, such a success."

All his grandchildren—Gershon, big-shot, atheist, lived by "increase and multiply" the Bible's way. He *was* a success. Eight or nine kids, twenty-five grandchildren. Jimmy and Sidney took "increase and multiply" to mean mergers, expansion, deals, transactions. Hundreds of thousands Jimmy left his mother, and bonds, and buildings, and tracts of land—ashes, dust, because neither his loins nor Sidney's produced a child.

She felt the blood rush to her face again. Imbecility, America's imbecility. Jimmy galloping after success while life runs off right under his feet. Mocking, teasing. His Shirley was a born mother, gorgeous, built to bear children.

Not Jimmy's, though. On Jimmy's money Shirley, the most beautiful widow in Montreal, married that childhood sweetheart of hers. For him Shirley became a mother.

"Your tea's cold, I betcha," she heard Triminiuk's voice say gruffly.

"I'll be your guest," said Mrs Goffman. Triminiuk gave her a searching look, nodded briskly, shuffled with a military swagger to the back of the store.

He understood everything. Sitting with Gershon was comfortable, even in silence. Their conversations were one-quarter open, three-quarters between the lines, as it used to be with Simon. But the other kind of silence, the silence that buzzed in her deafish ears in the Ambassador's mansion, that kind Mrs Goffman couldn't stand. That silence frightened her more than the loudest noise. That silence was the noise of death.

"Look how a *madamchikeh* can't wait for a glass of tea," the old man scolded, but she noticed he was coming back in a big hurry.

"Gershon," she said as he sat down, "if we're lucky in life we *see,* if only for a split second. Life or death, there's no other issue, Gershon. Jimmy learned it too late. Not till the end could he stop for life, but he had to stop for death."

"Doba," Triminiuk said bluntly, "you're beginning to sound religious."

"What religious, when religious?" she cried out, "in those clear moments blindness drops from us, we see and know everything!"

Twice I knew, she thought: once when Shirley's lover turned up at Jimmy's funeral in Jimmy's clothes. The other time too was at a funeral.

"So cut away my blindness," Triminiuk said gently, poking at his inert gluey eye.

"'*Touché,*" she said, hiding her face behind the tea glass. Triminiuk didn't press his advantage.

She glanced quickly at him and imagined him naked. She

flushed. His face was weather-beaten, sketched over with tiny red-and-blue blood vessels, but his body would be blue-white, his back rounded, his rib-cage prominent as a starving man's. Mrs Goffman grew conscious of her own body—so long, so gaunt, so like a stranger's now the skin was dry and criss-crossed, now her breasts were flat with colour faded out of the nipples. Her nails didn't grow much, or her hair. Whatever was shrivelled in a man like Gershon was spent, whatever shrivelled on her was wasted.

Wisdom was overrated. It had little to do with life. She was wise, but powerless. When she had power she must have been stupid. Pride, shyness, loyalty to Simon's memory seemed so important years ago. Now Mrs Goffman knew she should have married even a gargoyle of a man, and had more children. But by the time she caught on to what Jimmy's and Sidney's fate was, it was too late for her to do anything for them, or herself. "Fun," Jimmy said, relying on his mother's Radical tolerance, sneaking beauty after beauty into the house and his bed—for what, what for? All those gorgeous Rachels, but never a fruitful Leah.

"Gershon," Mrs Goffman suddenly said, "blaming is for innocents. I don't blame Shirley. I don't even blame Doba Goffman."

Shirley dressed like a Hollywood star for the funeral—a large black picture-hat, dark glasses, elbow-length black gloves, a clinging sheath dress so open down the front the gravediggers scattered dirt in all directions trying to stay in position to stare at her. Her lover wore Jimmy's black Italian silk suit. They whispered together. Shirley didn't pretend to cry. She didn't even carry a handkerchief.

Sidney, for once in his tired life, got hot, wanted to throw himself at the two of them. Mrs Goffman wouldn't let him. What was Shirley's lower-animal foolishness compared to the horrible truth—Jimmy in the ground without a child to mourn for him! Who was left, Mrs Goffman, an old woman with teeth falling out of her head?

"I get such a cold feeling," she whispered to Triminiuk. "We throw life aside like a rag. When we die it's an end— papa's line, Simon's line—a crime, Gershon, a crime against the whole human race."

Triminiuk nodded stiffly, like an officer commending a subordinate.

It *was* a crime against the whole human race. Life wasn't something to be kicked aside just because you happened to have it. In crowds, on the street, Mrs Goffman felt the difference bitterly—not she alone, not Sidney alone, a whole strain in the human race was dying in them! Simon's stubborn look was finished! Her pa's bass voice. Jimmy's way of greeting you—a *hello,* his arm thrown in front of his eyes as if you were the sun and so brilliant he couldn't absorb you. Jimmy made you feel that you were morning. Even Sidney had qualities the race shouldn't lose. Character, size, shape, all human magnificence, all possibility dying, dying, dying.

Mrs Goffman thought she would pass out.

"Doba, Doba," Triminiuk's voice sounded urgent in her ear, "stop aggravating, I said. Look on St Lawrence. The kids are coming home from school."

He steered her into the doorway, made her look out on the boulevard. Dabs and specks of red, green, blue danced in the distance, faint squeals and shrieks washed terror of silence away from her ears. Gershon knew his onions. Bending down—Triminiuk was the same size as Simon, a peanut—she kissed him on his wrinkled forehead. He shook her off, stood rigid at attention, nodded her away.

"Thanks for taking the fish off my hands," she said.

"Don't do it again," he answered gruffly.

7

Mrs Goffman concluded she would have to change her life, and immediately. She ordered her chauffeur to drive her to Fifi's, Shmifi's—a fancy French place for clothes-horses. It would be a double victory—she'd get spiffed up and stop scaring kids, she'd unload most of the money choking in her handbag.

Not all the perfumes of Paris could overcome the fish smell as Mrs Goffman entered the shop. Only her liveried chauffeur and that funeral car parked in front saved her from being tossed out on her ear. She gave the salesgirls, who sniffed usually just from snobbery, something real to sniff about!

"That coat," she said, in a voice as military as Triminiuk's.

A salesgirl hid her nose in a useless frilly hankie and came at Mrs Goffman sideways. The coat was a Marlene Dietrich type—magenta. Mrs Goffman made a trade. The girl almost passed out.

"A Gloria Swanson hat—burn the coat, dollie, don't cling to the rag." Mrs Goffman dismissed the salesgirl, who was greenish and crampy-looking from the fish smell. "Get me a flapper number. And a handbag too." With one motion she dumped all her money on the counter. The salesgirl's eyes, sick as they had been, bugged with the proper respect money always got.

"I look like a big popsicle, eh Josef?" Mrs Goffman said to her chauffeur. If kids didn't get scared to death by this number, they were still in danger of laughing themselves to death looking at her.

"Take, take," Mrs Goffman waved the girl onward to the pile of bills on the counter. "Put what's left in my new bag, dollie."

Without bitterness Mrs Goffman reflected how easy it was in America to buy everything you don't want.

She left the store, salespeople bowing to her right and to her left as if she were Queen Mary, gave them a queenly wave while her nose triumphantly recorded that in the air, wistful, fleeting, elusive as Chanel Number Five, was Rachel Street Fish.

8

Josef put down her arm-rest, adjusted a small reading-light over her newspaper—Sidney's style. Headlines shimmered in front of her eyes, and the usual faces—Khrushchev the hearty liar. Dulles's sour face set permanently in a "no," Eisenhower with that puzzled look which meant if his press secretary didn't say something fast he was a goner. What was it Jimmy said? Everybody in Eisenhower's cabinet was a millionaire except for Martin Durkin and God Almighty. The headlines recorded imbecile explosions, tests in Siberia, Nevada. Sincere falseness in Ottawa, Washington, false sincerity in Moscow. Idiots! Suckers! At least Jimmy at the end *knew:* these crumbs would never know!

"Josef, go home the long way," she said gently. Those French put their cemeteries right in the middle of the city—gray crosses stamped on the sky, cold stone saints, wreaths of dark artificial flowers. Silence was loudest near cemeteries.

What the heck was she doing going back up there anyway? Rachel Street was like a wonderful party she couldn't stand to see end. Six more days of nothing was coming.

"Josef, drive your slowest," she requested.

Every stage in her kids' success mocked her on these trips home. Goffman buildings, Goffman businesses. The banks their money was in. The houses they'd lived in during their climb to the top of Westmount and the Ambassador's mansion. I dragged my feet, Mrs Goffman remembered with sadness, but I didn't interfere. A young Radical became an old dishrag! Good taste left a bad taste in her mouth.

In her small vanity mirror she made a John Foster Dulles face and laughed herself back into a better humour.

9

The limousine passed the Mount Royal Hotel. Cabs lined

up, people were running, some school kids tumbled out of a car and skipped giggling toward St Catherine Street. Mrs Goffman wanted to try her new outfit on a kid and see what the reaction would be. She still felt bad about frightening that young girl Tammy.

Brighten up, sister, she told herself, but the Mount Royal had done its damage already: Jimmy first saw Shirley at a Mount Royal New Year's Eve Frolic—he loved to tell about it, to begin with.

The Mount Royal was Jimmy's home ground, a perfect setting for his style. He had Sally Rossen with him that night —a Toronto deb type, gorgeous, crazy for Jimmy, hot and burning. They danced every dance, drank champagne, moved arm in arm through the ballroom, visiting parties in different rooms, Jimmy in terrific shape, gay, gallant, witty, full of life. Then he saw Shirley. Sally was out.

How his eyes lighted up when he talked about Shirley— her hair he said was like a quiet waterfall in total darkness; her black eyes with that heavy fringe of eyelashes skimmed over Jimmy; she was in white, bare shouldered, proud of her beautiful young full breasts, her sexy body, her slow slow walk. Elegant Jimmy lost his manners. Clumsy as an ox he bumped his way across the floor, leaving Sally standing all alone. Up went Jimmy's arm in that gesture all Montreal knew—Shirley's beauty was blinding, he couldn't look.

Shirley cut him dead.

Sucker! He should have quit! Shirley's lover said something nasty—Jimmy heard—about "old enough to be your father." Shirley giggled, leaned on her boy, Maxie, and left Jimmy standing just as he had left Sally! Don Giovanni, huh? Mrs Goffman thought in her agitation. Big shot lover? He couldn't quit.

"My dance, beautiful," he said, almost chasing after her through the crowd. He gave the old flourish, poured on the charm.

"My card is filled," Shirley said coldly; they had him.

Like a crack had appeared in a great building. He didn't

fall apart then and there, where Westmount society surrounded him, where he was familiar, where his ways could get a gentle response. Later it started, at home, when she caught him in front of a mirror.

"Since when did you pull out grey hair, Jimmy?" she had asked. Jimmy didn't answer.

"Grey hair makes you look distinguished."

"Distinguished, and old," Jimmy said with a wink.

Lines on his face from laughing, character lines which made Jimmy the handsome guy he was, he couldn't stand them now. He wanted to rub everything out, be as young-looking as that pimply-faced Maxie who had the only woman who had ever denied Jimmy anything at all. Didn't his mother see Jimmy's reaction? He started to take out younger and younger girls—one was seventeen, not even out of high school! A photographer told him his left side was more handsome than his right, so the dope sat with his right side hidden, as if it had been burned! He sent Shirley flowers, pins, necklaces, phoned her, wired her—what a set-up for those two kids! Jimmy would spend a fortune on Shirley, but Maxie would spend the night!

Mrs Goffman smiled to herself: in a way—if Jimmy's end wasn't so horrible—there was justice in it. The most brilliant lawyer and financier in Montreal getting trimmed down to his BVD's by a couple of snot-nosed kids! Shirley had been sleeping with Maxie for four or five years, but not till her eighth date with Jimmy did she let him so much as peck her on the cheek. Don Giovanni?

Late one night Mrs Goffman had overheard a conversation that made her want to ring bells and blow whistles.

"Jimmy, you, getting married?" Sidney had said—he couldn't have been more shocked if Jimmy had grown side-curls and turned Hassidic.

"I can't get it from her any way else," Don Giovanni admitted.

Didn't she know he was going to get trimmed? But what did she care about money by that time? Life—a child—that was at stake, not Jimmy's lousy fortune. Marry even a prostitute for all Mrs Goffman cared by then—but get married. Why, when Marie the upstairs maid got pregnant, didn't Mrs Goffman hope one of her boys had done it? To hell with Westmount's ways! She knew. She had seen the truth by then. So who has to be the knocker-up, this chauffeur Josef!

"Drive more slowly," she said savagely, thinking how many snot-nosed kids this overgrown squash of a driver must have already brought into the world.

Josef looked back at her, startled.

"Please, I mean," she added.

A child—she was a lunatic on the subject. After the wedding she nagged, coaxed, threatened, whined. "Kids, go home early." "Shirley, maybe you're late this month, eh, dollie?" Vulgar and rude and coarse—her father's line, Simon's that's what the stakes were! Sidney was past praying for, she herself couldn't have kids. Everything was up to Jimmy. And he wanted a child too—that was the heartbreaking thing! Jimmy knew, saw, understood everything.

Mrs Goffman felt herself suffocating in the closed car. Her ears pulsed, her heart beat fast, she felt cold all over. Weakly, falteringly, she rolled down the window.

If only a child *had* come out of that marriage. Suffering was a man's lot in life. Everybody suffered, but not senselessly, like Jimmy. His suffering did nothing, made nothing, was worse than death. Noises made him jump. Coffee made him nervous. He began gobbling Sidney's pills. How could a hot-looking girl turn out so cold? He was repulsive, old, a mark, a fool—his nerve went.

Every bourgeois cliché that she as a Radical had scoffed at came thudding home—*you only live once,* what was more ghastly than that realization? *You're not getting any younger,* how that mocked Jimmy! What good was Mrs Goffman to her suffering son? Could she reverse her campaign to make him want a child? Could she destroy what he felt for Shirley just by telling him exactly what he knew anyway—

that he was a cinch, a target, a bankroll, but feeling his age and growing helpless?

Mrs Goffman began to cough, gasp, and with a great effort pushed her face close to the open window.

"Madam, what is it?" Josef said, slowing down.

"I'm alright," she lied, "don't stop."

It was as if life and time couldn't hold back their revenge. Shirley sneaked ties to Maxie, money, let him put things on Jimmy's charge accounts. Flagrant, open, Jimmy was Montreal's parlour-car joke. And Mrs Doba Goffman watched and waited, hoping hoping hoping.

Shirley never did bear Jimmy a child.

10

The limousine made a sudden swoop, a turn, a halt, then began its progress up the hill. Mrs Goffman craned her head, trying to get a last look at what wasn't Westmount. Her nose behaved like a pair of opera glasses after the opera, folding itself up awaiting the next liberation. Streets were empty, windows heavily draped so you couldn't see a sign of movement. Closer to the Ambassador's house there were no sidewalks, black limousines sped out of hidden driveways. Like this one, Mrs Goffman thought, sickening.

What a terrible death! Her confident Jimmy, worrying about flat tires all the time, stopping the car a dozen times to make Josef check, or getting out himself. Nothing was ever wrong, only Jimmy's shot nerves—he was half-destroyed when he stepped into the fog on Summit Circle. A limousine crushed him against his rear bumper and finished the job! Upstairs in the Ambassador's mansion, Mrs Goffman heard the smash and Jimmy's screams—horrible, horrible!

Mrs Goffman writhed, pinned her new hat against her ears, tears streaming from her eyes. Like a tiny boy Jimmy shrieked for her, screaming, screaming, and she ran into the cold dark mist, barefoot, in her nightgown, seeing nothing, hearing nothing but silence. That silence. Death's.

She'd screamed too—slapped at Josef, called him pig, ingrate, block, crook, shirker—why didn't he get out of the car instead of Jimmy? But now, when everything was past blaming, Mrs Goffman conceded the truth: Josef had more claim to life than Jimmy, much as she loved her son, great as his success had been.

She pulled wet terrified eyes away from the limousine floor and looked out at the houses on Summit Circle.

Right here! On this spot! She closed her eyes again and waited.

11

You fake, she chided herself. A real Radical would never cry. What a way to louse up this new magenta outfit—streaming eyes, a shiny shnozzola! You'd think she'd spent her afternoon at a Yiddish tear-jerker.

As Josef turned into the driveway Mrs Goffman touched her sulking nose with a powder puff, dried her eyes, made her old face smile. When there was hope it was O.K. to despair, but now hope was gone, what was the point of it? She winked at herself.

Sidney's worried face peeked out from her heavy drapes, his wristwatch close to his bad eyes. Why depress Sidney? She'd jolly him up a little, tell him how ridiculous she looked carrying the fish, how she stunk up that ritzy dress shop good.

She shielded her eyes, sighed, smiled more broadly, seeing past Josef's shoulder Nuns' Island. It was for sale. A million bucks they wanted.

By rights, Mrs Goffman thought as she looked toward her door, they shouldn't sell it. Nuns should stay on an island.

THE CONVERSION OF THE JEWS

by Philip Roth

Philip Roth (1933–   ). Although still quite young, Roth has already had a distinguished career as a writer. He was born in Newark and received a masters degree from the University of Chicago in 1955. His stories have appeared frequently in *Best American Short Stories* and in the *O'Henry Prize Stories*. He has been Writer-in-Residence at Princeton University and a Guggenheim Fellow. *Goodbye, Columbus* won the National Book Award in 1960. His novels, daring and original, have roused a furor, especially *Portnoy's Complaint*. His most recent books have been *The Ghost Writer* and *Zuckerman Unbound*.

"You're a real one for opening your mouth in the first place," Itzie said. "What do you open your mouth all the time for?"

"I didn't bring it up, Itz, I didn't," Ozzie said.

"What do you care about Jesus Christ for anyway?"

"I didn't bring up Jesus Christ. He did. I didn't even know what he was talking about. Jesus is historical, he kept saying. Jesus is historical." Ozzie mimicked the monumental voice of Rabbi Binder.

"Jesus was a person that lived like you and me," Ozzie continued. "That's what Binder said—"

"Yeah? . . . So what! What do I give two cents whether

Reprinted from *Goodbye, Columbus*, 1959. Reprinted by permission of the publisher, Houghton Mifflin Company.

he lived or not. And what do you gotta open your mouth!"
Itzie Lieberman favored closed-mouthedness, especially
when it came to Ozzie Freedman's questions. Mrs. Freedman had to see Rabbi Binder twice before about Ozzie's
questions and this Wednesday at four-thirty would be the
third time. Itzie preferred to keep *his* mother in the kitchen;
he settled for behind-the-back subtleties such as gestures,
faces, snarls and other less delicate barnyard noises.

"He was a real person, Jesus, but he wasn't like God, and
we don't believe he is God." Slowly, Ozzie was explaining
Rabbi Binder's position to Itzie, who had been absent from
Hebrew School the previous afternoon.

"The Catholics," Itzie said helpfully, "they believe in
Jesus Christ, that he's God." Itzie Lieberman used "the
Catholics" in its broadest sense—to include the Protestants.

Ozzie received Itzie's remark with a tiny head bob, as
though it were a footnote, and went on. "His mother was
Mary, and his father probably was Joseph," Ozzie said.
"But the New Testament says his real father was God."

"His *real* father?"

"Yeah," Ozzie said, "that's the big thing, his father's
supposed to be God."

"Bull."

"That's what Rabbi Binder says, that it's impossible—"

"Sure it's impossible. That stuff's all bull. To have a baby
you gotta get laid," Itzie theologized. "Mary hadda get
laid."

"That's what Binder says: 'The only way a woman can
have a baby is to have intercourse with a man.' "

"He said *that,* Ozz?" For a moment it appeared that Itzie
had put the theological question aside. "He said that, intercourse?" A little curled smile shaped itself in the lower half
of Itzie's face like a pink mustache. "What you guys do,
Ozz, you laugh or something?"

"I raised my hand."

"Yeah? Whatja say?"

"That's when I asked the question."

Itzie's face lit up. "Whatja ask about—intercourse?"

"No, I asked the question about God, how if He could create the heaven and earth in six days, and make all the animals and the fish and the light in six days—the light especially, that's what always gets me, that He could make the light. Making fish and animals, that's pretty good—"

"That's damn good." Itzie's appreciation was honest but unimaginative: it was as though God had just pitched a one-hitter.

"But making light . . . I mean when you think about it, it's really something," Ozzie said. "Anyway, I asked Binder if He could make all that in six days, and He could *pick* the six days he wanted right out of nowhere, why couldn't He let a woman have a baby without having intercourse."

"You said intercourse, Ozz, to Binder?"

"Yeah."

"Right in class?"

"Yeah."

Itzie smacked the side of his head.

"I mean, no kidding around," Ozzie said, "that'd really be nothing. After all that other stuff, that'd practically be nothing."

Itzie considered a moment. "What'd Binder say?"

"He started all over again explaining how Jesus was historical and how he lived like you and me but he wasn't God. So I said I under*stood* that. What I wanted to know was different."

What Ozzie wanted to know was always different. The first time he had wanted to know how Rabbi Binder could call the Jews "The Chosen People" if the Declaration of Independence claimed all men to be created equal. Rabbi Binder tried to distinguish for him between political equality and spiritual legitimacy, but what Ozzie wanted to know, he insisted vehemently, was different. That was the first time his mother had to come.

Then there was the plane crash. Fifty-eight people had been killed in a plane crash at La Guardia. In studying a

casualty list in the newspaper his mother had discovered
among the list of those dead eight Jewish names (his grandmother had nine but she counted Miller as a Jewish name);
because of the eight she said the plane crash was "a tragedy."
During free-discussion time on Wednesday Ozzie had
brought to Rabbi Binder's attention this matter of "some of
his relations" always picking out the Jewish names. Rabbi·
Binder had begun to explain cultural unity and some other
things when Ozzie stood up at his seat and said that what he
wanted to know was different. Rabbi Binder insisted that he
sit down and it was then that Ozzie shouted that he wished
all fifty-eight were Jews. That was the second time his
mother came.

"And he kept explaining about Jesus being historical, and
so I kept asking him. No kidding, Itz, he was trying to make
me look stupid." ·

"So what he finally do?"

"Finally he starts screaming that I was deliberately
simple-minded and a wise guy, and that my mother had to
come, and this was the last time. And that I'd never get bar-
mitzvahed if he could help it. Then, Itz, then he starts talking in that voice like a statue, real slow and deep, and he says
that I better think over what I said about the Lord. He told
me to go to his office and think it over." Ozzie leaned his
body towards Itzie. "Itz, I thought it over for a solid hour,
and now I'm convinced God could do it."

Ozzie had planned to confess his latest transgression to his
mother as soon as she came home from work. But it was a
Friday night in November and already dark, and when Mrs.
Freedman came through the door she tossed off her coat,
kissed Ozzie quickly on the face, and went to the kitchen
table to light the three yellow candles, two for the Sabbath
and one for Ozzie's father.

When his mother lit the candles she would move her two
arms slowly towards her, dragging them through the air, as
though persuading people whose minds were half made up.
And her eyes would get glassy with tears. Even when his

father was alive Ozzie remembered that her eyes had gotten glassy, so it didn't have anything to do with his dying. It had something to do with lighting the candles.

As she touched the flaming match to the unlit wick of a Sabbath candle, the phone rang, and Ozzie, standing only a foot from it, plucked it off the receiver and held it muffled to his chest. When his mother lit candles Ozzie felt there should be no noise; even breathing, if you could manage it, should be softened. Ozzie pressed the phone to his breast and watched his mother dragging whatever she was dragging, and he felt his own eyes get glassy. His mother was a round, tired, gray-haired penguin of a woman whose gray skin had begun to feel the tug of gravity and the weight of her own history. Even when she was dressed up she didn't look like a chosen person. But when she lit candles she looked like something better; like a woman who knew momentarily that God could do anything.

After a few mysterious minutes she was finished. Ozzie hung up the phone and walked to the kitchen table where she was beginning to lay the two places for the four-course Sabbath meal. He told her that she would have to see Rabbi Binder next Wednesday at four-thirty, and then he told her why. For the first time in their life together she hit Ozzie across the face with her hand.

All through the chopped liver and chicken soup part of the dinner Ozzie cried; he didn't have any appetite for the rest.

On Wednesday, in the largest of the three basement classrooms of the synagogue, Rabbi Marvin Binder, a tall, handsome, broad-shouldered man of thirty with thick strong-fibered black hair, removed his watch from his pocket and saw that it was four o'clock. At the rear of the room Yakov Blotnik, the seventy-one-year-old custodian, slowly polished the large window, mumbling to himself, unaware that it was four o'clock or six o'clock, Monday or Wednesday. To most of the students Yakov Blotnik's mumbling, along with his brown curly beard, scythe nose, and two heel-trailing black cats, made of him an object of wonder, a foreigner, a relic, towards whom they were alternately fearful and disrespectful. To Ozzie the mumbling had always seemed a monotonous, curious prayer; what made it curious was that old Blotnik had been mumbling so steadily for so many years, Ozzie suspected he had memorized the prayers and forgotten all about God.

"It is now free-discussion time," Rabbi Binder said. "Feel free to talk about any Jewish matter at all—religion, family, politics, sports—"

There was silence. It was a gusty, clouded November afternoon and it did not seem as though there ever was or could be a thing called baseball. So nobody this week said a word about that hero from the past, Hank Greenberg—which limited free discussion considerably.

And the soul-battering Ozzie Freedman had just received from Rabbi Binder had imposed its limitation. When it was Ozzie's turn to read aloud from the Hebrew book the rabbi had asked him petulantly why he didn't read more rapidly. He was showing no progress. Ozzie said he could read faster but that if he did he was sure not to understand what he was reading. Nevertheless, at the rabbi's repeated suggestion Ozzie tried, and showed a great talent, but in the midst of a long passage he stopped short and said he didn't understand a word he was reading, and started in again at a drag-footed pace. Then came the soul-battering.

Consequently when free-discussion time rolled around none of the students felt too free. The rabbi's invitation was answered only by the mumbling of feeble old Blotnik.

"Isn't there anything at all you would like to discuss?" Rabbi Binder asked again, looking at his watch. "No questions or comments?"

There was a small grumble from the third row. The rabbi requested that Ozzie rise and give the rest of the class the advantage of his thought.

Ozzie rose. "I forget it now," he said, and sat down in his place.

Rabbi Binder advanced a seat towards Ozzie and poised himself on the edge of the desk. It was Itzie's desk and the rabbi's frame only a dagger's-length away from his face snapped him to sitting attention.

"Stand up again, Oscar," Rabbi Binder said calmly, "and try to assemble your thoughts."

Ozzie stood up. All his classmates turned in their seats and watched as he gave an unconvincing scratch to his forehead.

"I can't assemble any," he announced, and plunked himself down.

"Stand up!" Rabbi Binder advanced from Itzie's desk to the one directly in front of Ozzie; when the rabbinical back was turned Itzie gave it five-fingers off the tip of his nose, causing a small titter in the room. Rabbi Binder was too absorbed in squelching Ozzie's nonsense once and for all to bother with titters. "Stand up, Oscar. What's your question about?"

Ozzie pulled a word out of the air. It was the handiest word. "Religion."

"Oh, now you remember?"

"Yes."

"What is it?"

Trapped, Ozzie blurted the first thing that came to him. "Why can't He make anything He wants to make!"

As Rabbi Binder prepared an answer, a final answer, Itzie, ten feet behind him, raised one finger on his left hand, gestured it meaningfully towards the rabbi's back, and brought the house down.

Binder twisted quickly to see what had happened and in the midst of the commotion Ozzie shouted into the rabbi's back what he couldn't have shouted to his face. It was a loud, toneless sound that had the timbre of something stored inside for about six days.

"You don't know! You don't know anything about God!"

The rabbi spun back towards Ozzie. "What?"

"You don't know—you don't—"

"Apologize, Oscar, apologize!" It was a threat.

"You don't—"

Rabbi Binder's hand flicked out at Ozzie's cheek. Perhaps it had only been meant to clamp the boy's mouth shut, but Ozzie ducked and the palm caught him squarely on the nose.

The blood came in a short, red spurt on to Ozzie's shirt front.

The next moment was all confusion. Ozzie screamed, "You bastard, you bastard!" and broke for the classroom door. Rabbi Binder lurched a step backwards, as though his own blood had started flowing violently in the opposite direction, then gave a clumsy lurch forward and bolted out the door after Ozzie. The class followed after the rabbi's huge blue-suited back, and before old Blotnik could turn from his window, the room was empty and everyone was headed full speed up the three flights leading to the roof.

If one should compare the light of day to the life of man: sunrise to birth; sunset—the dropping down over the edge—to death; then as Ozzie Freedman wiggled through the trapdoor of the synagogue roof, his feet kicking backwards bronco-style at Rabbi Binder's outstretched arms—at that moment the day was fifty years old. As a rule, fifty or fifty-five reflects accurately the age of late afternoons in November, for it is in that month, during those hours, that one's awareness of light seems no longer a matter of seeing, but of hearing: light begins clicking away. In fact, as Ozzie locked shut the trapdoor in the rabbi's face, the sharp click of the bolt into the lock might momentarily have been mistaken for the sound of the heavier gray that had just throbbed through the sky.

With all his weight Ozzie kneeled on the locked door; any instant he was certain that Rabbi Binder's shoulder would fling it open, splintering the wood into shrapnel and catapulting his body into the sky. But the door did not move and below him he heard only the rumble of feet, first loud then dim, like thunder rolling away.

A question shot through his brain. "Can this be *me?*" For a thirteen-year-old who had just labeled his religious leader a bastard, twice, it was not an improper question. Louder and louder the question came to him—"Is it me? Is it me?" —until he discovered himself no longer kneeling, but racing crazily towards the edge of the roof, his eyes crying, his throat screaming, and his arms flying everywhichway as though not his own.

"Is it me? Is it me Me ME ME ME! It has to be me—but is it!"

It is the question a thief must ask himself the night he jimmies open his first window, and it is said to be the question with which bridegrooms quiz themselves before the altar.

In the few wild seconds it took Ozzie's body to propel him to the edge of the roof, his self-examination began to grow fuzzy. Gazing down at the street, he became confused as to the problem beneath the question: was it, is-it-me-who-called-Binder-a-bastard? or, is-it-me-prancing-around-on-the-roof? However, the scene below settled all, for there is an instant in any action when whether it is you or somebody else is academic. The thief crams the money in his pockets and scoots out the window. The bridegroom signs the hotel register for two. And the boy on the roof finds a streetful of people gaping at him, necks stretched backwards, faces up, as though he were the ceiling of the Hayden Planetarium. Suddenly you know it's you.

"Oscar! Oscar Freedman!" A voice rose from the center of the crowd, a voice that, could it have been seen, would have looked like the writing on scroll. "Oscar Freedman, get down from there. Immediately!" Rabbi Binder was pointing one arm stiffly up at him; and at the end of that arm, one finger aimed menacingly. It was the attitude of a dictator, but one—the eyes confessed all—whose personal valet had spit neatly in his face.

Ozzie didn't answer. Only for a blink's length did he look towards Rabbi Binder. Instead his eyes began to fit together the world beneath him, to sort out people from places, friends from enemies, participants from spectators. In little jagged starlike clusters his friends stood around Rabbi Binder, who was still pointing. The topmost point on a star compounded not of angels but of five adolescent boys was Itzie. What a world it was, with those stars below, Rabbi Binder below . . . Ozzie, who a moment earlier hadn't been able to control his own body, started to feel the meaning of the word control: he felt Peace and he felt Power.

"Oscar Freedman, I'll give you three to come down."

Few dictators give their subjects three to do anything; but, as always, Rabbi Binder only looked dictatorial.

"Are you ready, Oscar?"

Ozzie nodded his head yes, although he had no intention in the world—the lower one or the celestial one he'd just entered—of coming down even if Rabbi Binder should give him a million.

"All right then," said Rabbi Binder. He ran a hand through his black Samson hair as though it were the gesture prescribed for uttering the first digit. Then, with his other hand cutting a circle out of the small piece of sky around him, he spoke. "One!"

There was no thunder. On the contrary, at that moment, as though "one" was the cue for which he had been waiting, the world's least thunderous person appeared on the synagogue steps. He did not so much come out the synagogue door as lean out, onto the darkening air. He clutched at the doorknob with one hand and looked up at the roof.

"Oy!"

Yakov Blotnik's old mind hobbled slowly, as if on crutches, and though he couldn't decide precisely what the boy was doing on the roof, he knew it wasn't good—that is, it wasn't-good-for-the-Jews. For Yakov Blotnik life had fractionated itself simply: things were either good-for-the-Jews or no-good-for-the-Jews.

He smacked his free hand to his in-sucked cheek, gently. "Oy, Gut!" And then quickly as he was able, he jacked down his head and surveyed the street. There was Rabbi Binder (like a man at an auction with only three dollars in his pocket, he had just delivered a shaky "Two!"); there were the students, and that was all. So far it-wasn't-so-bad-for-the-Jews. But the boy had to come down immediately, before anybody saw. The problem: how to get the boy off the roof?

Anybody who has ever had a cat on the roof knows how to get him down. You call the fire department. Or first you call the operator and you ask her for the fire department. And the next thing there is great jamming of brakes and clanging of bells and shouting of instructions. And then the cat is off the roof. You do the same thing to get a boy off the roof.

That is, you do the same thing if you are Yakov Blotnik and you once had a cat on the roof.

When the engines, all four of them, arrived, Rabbi Binder had four times given Ozzie the count of three. The big hook-and-ladder swung around the corner and one of the firemen leaped from it, plunging headlong towards the yellow fire hydrant in front of the synagogue. With a huge wrench he began to unscrew the top nozzle. Rabbi Binder raced over to him and pulled at his shoulder.

"There's no fire . . ."

The fireman mumbled back over his shoulder and, heatedly, continued working at the nozzle.

"But there's no fire, there's no fire . . ." Binder shouted. When the fireman mumbled again, the rabbi grasped his face with both his hands and pointed it up at the roof.

To Ozzie it looked as though Rabbi Binder was trying to tug the fireman's head out of his body, like a cork from a bottle. He had to giggle at the picture they made: it was a family portrait—rabbi in black skullcap, fireman in red fire hat, and the little yellow hydrant squatting beside like a kid brother, bareheaded. From the edge of the roof Ozzie waved at the portrait, a one-handed, flapping, mocking wave; in doing it his right foot slipped from under him. Rabbi Binder covered his eyes with his hands.

Firemen work fast. Before Ozzie had even regained his balance, a big, round, yellowed net was being held on the synagogue lawn. The firemen who held it looked up at Ozzie with stern, feelingless faces.

One of the firemen turned his head towards Rabbi Binder. "What, is the kid nuts or something?"

Rabbi Binder unpeeled his hands from his eyes, slowly, painfully, as if they were tape. Then he checked: nothing on the sidewalk, no dents in the net.

"Is he gonna jump, or what?" the fireman shouted.

In a voice not at all like a statue, Rabbi Binder finally answered. "Yes, Yes, I think so . . . He's been threatening to . . ."

Threatening to? Why, the reason he was on the roof, Ozzie remembered, was to get away; he hadn't even thought about jumping. He had just run to get away, and the truth was that he hadn't really headed for the roof as much as he'd been chased there.

"What's his name, the kid?"

"Freedman," Rabbi Binder answered. "Oscar Freedman."

The fireman looked up at Ozzie. "What is it with you, Oscar? You gonna jump, or what?"

Ozzie did not answer. Frankly, the question had just arisen.

"Look, Oscar, if you're gonna jump, jump—and if you're not gonna jump, don't jump. But don't waste our time, willya?"

Ozzie looked at the fireman and then at Rabbi Binder. He wanted to see Rabbi Binder cover his eyes one more time.

"I'm going to jump."

And then he scampered around the edge of the roof to

the corner, where there was no net below, and he flapped his arms at his sides, swishing the air and smacking his palms to his trousers on the downbeat. He began screaming like some kind of engine, "Wheeeee . . . wheeeeee," and leaning way out over the edge with the upper half of his body. The fireman whipped around to cover the ground with the net. Rabbi Binder mumbled a few words to Somebody and covered his eyes. Everything happened quickly, jerkily, as in a silent movie. The crowd, which had arrived with the fire engines, gave out a long, Fourth-of-July fireworks oooh-aahhh. In the excitement no one had paid the crowd much heed, except, of course, Yakov Blotnik, who swung from the doorknob counting heads. "Fier und tsvansik . . . finf und tsvantsik . . . Oy, Gut!" It wasn't like this with the cat.

Rabbi Binder peeked through his fingers, checked the sidewalk and net. Empty. But there was Ozzie racing to the other corner. The firemen raced with him but were unable to keep up. Whenever Ozzie wanted to he might jump and splatter himself upon the sidewalk, and by the time the firemen scooted to the spot all they could do with their net would be to cover the mess.

"Wheeeee . . . wheeeee . . ."

"Hey, Oscar," the winded fireman yelled, "What the hell is this, a game or something?"

"Wheeeee . . . wheeeee . . ."

"Hey, Oscar—"

But he was off now to the other corner, flapping his wings fiercely. Rabbi Binder couldn't take it any longer—the fire engines from nowhere, the screaming suicidal boy, the net. He fell to his knees, exhausted, and with his hands curled together in front of his chest like a little dome, he pleaded, "Oscar, stop it, Oscar. Don't jump, Oscar. Please come down . . . Please don't jump."

And further back in the crowd a single voice, a single young voice, shouted a lone word to the boy on the roof.

"Jump!"

It was Itzie. Ozzie momentarily stopped flapping.

"Go ahead, Ozz—jump!" Itzie broke off his point of the star and courageously, with the inspiration not of a wise-guy but of a disciple, stood alone. "Jump, Ozz, jump!"

Still on his knees, his hands still curled, Rabbi Binder twisted his body back. He looked at Itzie, then, agonizingly, back to Ozzie.

"Oscar, Don't jump! Please, Don't jump . . . please please . . ."

"Jump!" This time it wasn't Itzie but another point of the star. By the time Mrs. Freedman arrived to keep her four-thirty appointment with Rabbi Binder, the whole little upside down heaven was shouting and pleading for Ozzie to jump, and Rabbi Binder no longer was pleading with him not to jump, but was crying into the dome of his hands.

Understandably Mrs. Freedman couldn't figure out what her son was doing on the roof. So she asked.

"Ozzie, my Ozzie, what are you doing? My Ozzie, what is it?"

Ozzie stopped wheeeeeing and slowed his arms down to a cruising flap, the kind birds use in soft winds, but he did not answer. He stood against the low, clouded darkening sky—light clicked down swiftly now, as on a small gear—flapping softly and gazing down at the small bundle of a woman who was his mother.

"What are you doing, Ozzie?" She turned towards the kneeling Rabbi Binder and rushed so close that only a paper-thickness of dusk lay between her stomach and his shoulders.

"What is my baby doing?"

Rabbi Binder gaped up at her but he too was mute. All that moved was the dome of his hands; it shook back and forth like a weak pulse.

"Rabbi, get him down! He'll kill himself. Get him down, my only baby . . ."

"I can't," Rabbi Binder said, "I can't . . ." and he turned his handsome head towards the crowd of boys behind him. "It's them. Listen to them."

And for the first time Mrs. Freedman saw the crowd of boys, and she heard what they were yelling.

"He's doing it for them. He won't listen to me. It's them." Rabbi Binder spoke like in a trance.

"For them?"

"Yes."

"Why for them?"

"They want him to . . ."

Mrs. Freedman raised her two arms upward as though she were conducting the sky. "For them he's doing it!" And then in a gesture older than pyramids, older than prophets and floods, her arms came slapping down to her sides. "A martyr I have. Look!" She tilted her head to the roof. Ozzie was still flapping softly. "My martyr."

"Oscar, come down, *please*," Rabbi Binder groaned.

In a startlingly even voice Mrs. Freedman called to the boy on the roof. "Ozzie, come down, Ozzie. Don't be a martyr, my baby."

As though it was a litany, Rabbi Binder repeated her words. "Don't be a martyr, my baby. Don't be a martyr."

"Gawhead, Ozz—*be* a Martin!" It was Itzie. "Be a Martin, be a Martin," and all the voices joined in singing for Martindom, whatever *it* was. "Be a Martin, be a Martin . . ."

Somehow when you're on a roof the darker it gets the less you can hear. All Ozzie knew was that two groups wanted two new things: his friends were spirited and musical about what they wanted; his mother and the rabbi were even-toned, chanting, about what they didn't want. The rabbi's voice was without tears now and so was his mother's.

The big net stared up at Ozzie like a sightless eye. The big, clouded sky pushed down. From beneath it looked like a gray corrugated board. Suddenly, looking up into that unsympathetic sky, Ozzie realized all the strangeness of what these people, his friends, were asking: they wanted him to jump, to kill himself; they were singing about it now—it made them that happy. And there was an even greater strangeness: Rabbi Binder was on his knees, trembling. If there was a question to be asked now it was not "Is it me?" but rather "Is it us? . . . Is it us?"

Being on the roof, it turned out, was a serious thing. If he jumped would the singing become dancing? Would it? What would jumping stop? Yearningly, Ozzie wished he could rip open the sky, plunge his hands through, and pull out the sun; and on the sun, like a coin, would be stamped JUMP or DON'T JUMP.

Ozzie's knees rocked and sagged a little under him as though they were setting him for a dive. His arms tightened, stiffened, froze, from shoulders to fingernails. He felt as if each part of his body were going to vote as to whether he should kill himself or not—and each part as though it were independent of *him*.

The light took an unexpected click down and the new darkness, like a gag, hushed the friends singing for this and the mother and rabbi chanting for that.

Ozzie stopped counting votes, and in a curiously high voice, like one who wasn't prepared for speech, he spoke.

"Mamma?"

"Yes, Oscar."

"Mamma, get down on your knees, like Rabbi Binder."

"Oscar—"

"Get down on your knees," he said, "or I'll jump."

Ozzie heard a whimper, then a quick rustling, and when he looked down where his mother had stood he saw the top of a head and beneath that a circle of dress. She was kneeling beside Rabbi Binder.

He spoke again. "Everybody kneel." There was the sound of everybody kneeling.

Ozzie looked around. With one hand he pointed towards the synagogue entrance. "Make *him* kneel."

There was a noise, not of kneeling, but of body-and-cloth stretching. Ozzie could hear Rabbi Binder saying in a gruff whisper, ". . . or he'll *kill* himself," and when next he looked there was Yakov Blotnik off the doorknob and for the first time in his life upon his knees in the Gentile posture of prayer.

As for the firemen—it is not as difficult as one might imagine to hold a net taut when you are kneeling.

Ozzie looked around again; and then he called to Rabbi Binder.

"Rabbi?"

"Yes, Oscar."

"Rabbi Binder, do you believe in God."

"Yes."

"Do you believe God can do Anything?" Ozzie leaned his head out into the darkness. "Anything?"

"Oscar, I think—"

"Tell me you believe God can do Anything."

There was a second's hesitation. Then: "God can do Anything."

"Tell me you believe God can make a child without intercourse."

"He can."

"Tell me!"

"God," Rabbi Binder admitted, "can make a child without intercourse."

"Mamma, you tell me."

"God can make a child without intercourse," his mother said.

"Make *him* tell me." There was no doubt who *him* was.

In a few moments Ozzie heard an old comical voice say something to the increasing darkness about God.

Next, Ozzie made everybody say it. And then he made them all say they believed in Jesus Christ—first one at a time, then all together.

When the catechizing was through it was the beginning of evening. From the street it sounded as if the boy on the roof might have sighed.

"Ozzie?" A woman's voice dared to speak. "You'll come down now?"

There was no answer, but the woman waited, and when

a voice finally did speak it was thin and crying, and exhausted as that of an old man who has just finished pulling the bells.

"Mamma, don't you see—you shouldn't hit me. He shouldn't hit me. You shouldn't hit me about God, Mamma. You should never hit anybody about God—"

"Ozzie, please come down now."

"Promise me, promise me you'll never hit anybody about God."

He had asked only his mother, but for some reason everyone kneeling in the street promised he would never hit anybody about God.

Once again there was silence.

"I can come down now, Mamma," the boy on the roof finally said. He turned his head both ways as though checking the traffic lights. "Now I can come down . . ."

And he did, right into the center of the yellow net that glowed in the evening's edge like an overgrown halo.

A & P

by John Updike

John Updike (1932–   ), a native of Pennsylvania, graduated from Harvard. His stories began
appearing very shortly thereafter in *The New
Yorker*, and he was already well known for them
before he was twenty-five. Several volumes of them
have been published, including *The Same Door*
(1959) and *Pigeon Feathers and Other Stories*
(1962), and *Museums and Women* (1973). A
great stylist, Updike has also been widely praised
for his novels which include *The Poorhouse Fair*,
Rabbit, Run, *The Centaur*, *Rabbit Redux*, and
Rabbit Is Rich.

In walks these three girls in nothing but bathing suits. I'm
in the third checkout slot, with my back to the door, so I
don't see them until they're over by the bread. The one that
caught my eye first was the one in the plaid green two-
piece. She was a chunky kid, with a good tan and a sweet
broad soft-looking can with those two crescents of white
just under it, where the sun never seems to hit, at the top
of the backs of her legs. I stood there with my hand on a
box of HiHo crackers trying to remember if I rang it up
or not. I ring it up again and the customer starts giving me
hell. She's one of these cash-register-watchers, a witch
about fifty with rouge on her cheekbones and no eyebrows,
and I know it made her day to trip me up. She'd been

watching cash registers for fifty years and probably never seen a mistake before.

By the time I got her feathers smoothed and her goodies into a bag—she gives me a little snort in passing, if she'd been born at the right time they would have burned her over in Salem—by the time I get her on her way the girls had circled around the bread and were coming back, without a pushcart, back my way along the counters, in the aisles between the checkouts and the Special bins. They didn't even have shoes on. There was this chunky one, with the two-piece—it was bright green and the seams on the bra were still sharp and her belly was still pretty pale so I guessed she just got it (the suit)—there was this one, with one of those chubby berry-faces, the lips all bunched together under her nose, this one, and a tall one, with black hair that hadn't quite frizzed right, and one of these sunburns right across under the eyes, and a chin that was too long—you know, the kind of girl other girls think is very "striking" and "attractive" but never quite makes it, as they very well know, which is why they like her so much—and then the third one, that wasn't quite so tall. She was the queen. She kind of led them, the other two peeking around and making their shoulders round. She didn't look around, not this queen, she just walked straight on slowly, on these long white prima-donna legs. She came down a little hard on her heels, as if she didn't walk in her bare feet that much, putting down her heels and then letting the weight move along to her toes as if she was testing the floor with every step, putting a little deliberate extra action into it. You never know for sure how girls' minds work (do you really think it's a mind in there or just a little buzz like a bee in a glass jar?) but you got the idea she had talked the other two into coming in here with her, and now she was showing them how to do it, walk slow and hold yourself straight.

She had on a kind of dirty-pink—beige maybe, I don't know—bathing suit with a little nubble all over it and, what got me, the straps were down. They were off her shoulders looped loose around the cool tops of her arms, and I guess as a result the suit had slipped a little on her, so all around the top of the cloth there was this shining rim. If it hadn't been there you wouldn't have known there could have been anything whiter than those shoulders. With the straps pushed off, there was nothing between the top of the suit and the top of her head except just *her*, this clean bare plane of the top of her chest down from the shoulder bones like a dented sheet of metal tilted in the light. I mean, it was more than pretty.

She had sort of oaky hair that the sun and salt had bleached, done up in a bun that was unravelling, and a kind of prim face. Walking into the A & P with your straps down, I suppose it's the only kind of face you *can* have. She held her head so high her neck, coming up out of those white shoulders, looked kind of stretched, but I didn't mind. The longer her neck was, the more of her there was.

She must have felt in the corner of her eye me and over my shoulder Stokesie in the second slot watching, but she didn't tip. Not this queen. She kept her eyes moving across the racks, and stopped, turned so slow it made my stomach rub the inside of my apron, and buzzed to the other two, who kind of huddled against her for relief, and then they all three of them went up the cat-and-dog-food-breakfast-cereal-macaroni-rice-raisins-seasonings-spreads-spaghetti-soft-drinks-crackers-and-cookies aisle. From the third slot I look straight up this aisle to the meat counter, and I watched them all the way. The fat one with the tan sort of fumbled with the cookies, but on second thought she put the package back. The sheep pushing their carts down the aisle—the girls were walking against the usual traffic (not that we have one-way signs or anything)—were pretty hilarious. You could see them, when Queenie's white shoulders dawned on them, kind of jerk, or hop, or hiccup, but their eyes snapped back to their own baskets and on they pushed. I bet you could set off dynamite in an A & P and the people would by and large keep reaching and checking oatmeal off their lists and muttering "Let me see, there was a third thing, began with A, asparagus, no, ah, yes, applesauce!" or whatever it is they do mutter. But there was no doubt, this jiggled them. A few houseslaves in pin curlers even looked around after pushing their carts past to make sure what they had seen was correct.

You know, it's one thing to have a girl in a bathing suit down on the beach, where what with the glare nobody can look at each other much anyway, and another thing in the cool of the A & P, under the fluorescent lights, against all those stacked packages, with her feet paddling along naked over our checker-board green-and-cream rubber-tile floor.

"Oh Daddy," Stokesie said beside me. "I feel so faint."

"Darling," I said. "Hold me tight." Stokesie's married, with two babies chalked up on his fuselage already, but as far as I can tell that's the only difference. He's twenty-two, and I was nineteen this April.

"Is it done?" he asks, the responsible married man finding his voice. I forgot to say he thinks he's going to be manager some sunny day, maybe in 1990 when it's called the Great Alexandrov and Petrooshki Tea Company or something.

What he meant was, our town is five miles from a beach, with a big summer colony out on the Point, but we're right in the middle of town, and the women generally put on a shirt or shorts or something before they get out of the car into the street. And anyway these are usually women with six children and varicose veins mapping their legs and nobody, including them, could care less. As I say, we're right in the middle of town, and if you stand at our front doors you can see two banks and the Congregational church and the newspaper store and three real-estate offices and about twenty-seven old freeloaders tearing up Central Street because the sewer broke again. It's not as if we're on the Cape; we're north of Boston and there's people in this town haven't seen the ocean for twenty years.

The girls had reached the meat counter and were asking McMahon something. He pointed, they pointed, and they shuffled out of sight behind a pyramid of Diet Delight peaches. All that was left for us to see was old McMahon patting his mouth and looking after them sizing up their joints. Poor kids, I began to feel sorry for them, they couldn't help it.

Now here comes the sad part of the story, at least my family says it's sad, but I don't think it's so sad myself. The store's pretty empty, it being Thursday afternoon, so there was nothing much to do except lean on the register and wait for the girls to show up again. The whole store was like a pinball machine and I didn't know which tunnel they'd come out of. After a while they come around out of the far aisle, around the light bulbs, records at discount of the Caribbean Six or Tony Martin Sings or some such gunk you wonder they waste the wax on, sixpacks of candy bars, and plastic toys done up in cellophane that fall apart when a kid looks at them anyway. Around they come, Queenie still leading the way, and holding a little gray jar in her hand. Slots Three through Seven are unmanned and I could see her wondering between Stokes and me, but Stokesie with his usual luck draws an old party in baggy gray pants who stumbles up with four giant cans of pineapple juice (what do these bums *do* with all that pineapple juice? I've often asked myself) so the girls come to me. Queenie puts down the jar and I take it into my fingers icy cold. Kingfish Fancy Herring Snacks in Pure Sour Cream: 49¢. Now her hands are empty, not a ring or a bracelet, bare as God made them, and I wonder where the money's coming from. Still with that prim look she lifts a folded dollar bill out of the hollow at the center of her nubbled pink top. The jar went heavy in my hand. Really, I thought that was so cute.

Then everybody's luck begins to run out. Lengel comes in from haggling with a truck full of cabbages on the lot

and is about to scuttle into that door marked MANAGER
behind which he hides all day when the girls touch his eye.
Lengel's pretty dreary, teaches Sunday school and the rest,
but he doesn't miss that much. He comes over and says,
"Girls, this isn't the beach."

Queenie blushes, though maybe it's just a brush of sunburn I was noticing for the first time, now that she was so
close. "My mother asked me to pick up a jar of herring
snacks." Her voice kind of startled me, the way voices do
when you see the people first, coming out so flat and dumb
yet kind of tony, too, the way it ticked over "pick up" and
"snacks." All of a sudden I slid right down her voice into
her living room. Her father and the other men were standing around in ice cream coats and bow ties and the women
were in sandals picking up herring snacks on toothpicks off
a big glass plate and they were all holding drinks the color
of water with olives and sprigs of mint in them. When my
parents have somebody over they get lemonade and if it's
a real racy affair Schlitz in tall glasses with "They'll Do It
Every Time" cartoons stencilled on.

"That's all right," Lengel said. "But this isn't the beach."
His repeating this struck me as funny, as if it had just occurred to him, and he had been thinking all these years the
A & P was a great big dune and he was the head lifeguard.
He didn't like my smiling—as I say he doesn't miss much
—but he concentrates on giving the girls that sad Sunday-
school-superintendent stare.

Queenie's blush is no sunburn now, and the plump one
in plaid, that I liked better from the back—a really sweet
can—pipes up. "We weren't doing any shopping. We just
came in for the one thing."

"That makes no difference," Lengel tells her, and I could
see from the way his eyes went that he hadn't noticed she
was wearing a two-piece before. "We want you decently
dressed when you come in here."

"We *are* decent," Queenie says suddenly, her lower lip

pushing, getting sore now that she remembers her place, a place from which the crowd that runs the A & P must look pretty crummy. Fancy Herring Snacks flashed in her very blue eyes.

"Girls, I don't want to argue with you. After this come in here with your shoulders covered. It's our policy." He turns his back. That's policy for you. Policy is what the kingpins want. What the others want is juvenile delinquency.

All this while, the customers had been showing up with their carts but, you know, sheep, seeing a scene, they had all bunched up on Stokesie, who shook open a paper bag as gently as peeling a peach, not wanting to miss a word. I could feel in the silence everybody getting nervous, most of all Lengel, who asks me, "Sammy, have you rung up their purchase?"

I thought and said "No" but it wasn't about that I was thinking. I go through the punches, 4, 9, GROC, TOT—it's more complicated than you think, and after you do it often enough, it begins to make a little song, that you hear words to, in my case "Hello (*bing*) there, you (*gung*) hap-py *pee*-pul (*splat*)!"—the *splat* being the drawer flying out. I uncrease the bill, tenderly as you may imagine, it just having come from between the two smoothest scoops of vanilla I had ever known were there, and pass a half and a penny into her narrow pink palm, and nestle the herrings in a bag and twist its neck and hand it over, all the time thinking.

The girls, and who'd blame them, are in a hurry to get out, so I say "I quit" to Lengel quick enough for them to hear, hoping they'll stop and watch me, their unsuspected hero. They keep right on going, into the electric eye; the door flies open and they flicker across the lot to their car, Queenie and Plaid and Big Tall Goony-Goony (not that as raw material she was so bad), leaving me with Lengel and a kink in his eyebrow.

"Did you say something, Sammy?"

"I said I quit."

"I thought you did."

"You didn't have to embarrass them."

"It was they who were embarrassing us."

I started to say something that came out "Fiddle-de-doo." It's a saying of my grandmother's, and I know she would have been pleased.

"I don't think you know what you're saying," Lengel said.

"I know you don't," I said. "But I do." I pull the bow at the back of my apron and start shrugging it off my shoulders. A couple customers that had been heading for my slot begin to knock against each other, like scared pigs in a chute.

Lengel sighs and begins to look very patient and old and gray. He's been a friend of my parents for years. "Sammy, you don't want to do this to your Mom and Dad," he tells me. It's true. I don't. But it seems to me that once you begin a gesture it's fatal not to go through with it. I fold the apron, "Sammy" stitched in red on the pocket, and put it on the counter, and drop the bow tie on top of it. The bow tie is theirs, if you've ever wondered. "You'll feel this for the rest of your life," Lengel says, and I know that's true, too, but remembering how he made that pretty girl blush makes me so scrunchy inside I punch the No Sale tab and the machine whirs "pee-pul" and the drawer splats out. One advantage to this scene taking place in summer, I can follow this up with a clean exit, there's no fumbling around getting your coat and galoshes, I just saunter into the electric eye in my white shirt that my mother ironed the night before, and the door heaves itself open, and outside the sunshine is skating around on the asphalt.

I look around for my girls, but they're gone, of course. There wasn't anybody but some young married screaming with her children about some candy they didn't get by the door of a powder-blue Falcon station wagon. Looking back in the big windows, over the bags of peat moss and aluminum lawn furniture stacked on the pavement, I could see

Lengel in my place in the slot, checking the sheep through. His face was dark gray and his back stiff, as if he'd just had an injection of iron, and my stomach kind of fell as I felt how hard the world was going to be to me hereafter.

CRUEL AND BARBAROUS TREATMENT

by Mary McCarthy

Mary McCarthy (1912–) has been essayist, drama critic, teacher, and editor of the *Partisan Review*. Twice a Guggenheim Fellow, she has been called one of the wittiest women writing in America today. She is the author of a number of brilliantly satirical novels, the most widely known of which have been *The Groves of Academe* and, *The Group*, from which an award-winning movie was made. Her essay and art book, *The Stones of Florence*, is a handsome evocation of that fascinating city. In recent years, she has written widely on political and literary subjects.

She could not bear to hurt her husband. She impressed this on the Young Man, on her confidantes, and finally on her husband himself. The thought of Telling Him actually made her heart turn over in a sudden and sickening way, she said. This was true, and yet she knew that being a potential divorcee was deeply pleasurable in somewhat the same way that being an engaged girl had been. In both cases, there was at first a subterranean courtship, whose significance it was necessary to conceal from outside observers. The concealment of the original, premarital courtship had, however, been a mere superstitious gesture,

Reprinted by permission of Brandt & Brandt, from *The Company She Keeps*, published by Harcourt, Brace & World, Inc. Copyright © 1967, 1939 by Mary McCarthy.

briefly sustained. It had also been, on the whole, a private secretiveness, not a partnership of silence. One put one's family and one's friends off the track because one was still afraid that the affair might not come out right, might not lead in a clean, direct line to the altar. To confess one's aspirations might be, in the end, to publicize one's failure. Once a solid understanding had been reached, there followed a short intermission of ritual bashfulness, in which both parties awkwardly participated, and then came the Announcement.

But with the extramarital courtship, the deception was prolonged where it had been ephemeral, necessary where it had been frivolous, conspiratorial where it had been lonely. It was, in short, serious where it had been dilettantish. That it was accompanied by feelings of guilt, by sharp and genuine revulsions, only complicated and deepened its delights, by abrading the sensibilities, and by imposing a sence of outlawry and consequent mutual dependence upon the lovers. But what this interlude of deception gave her, above all, she recognized, was the opportunity, unparalleled in her experience, for exercising feelings of superiority over others. For her husband she had, she believed, only sympathy and compunction. She got no fun, she told the Young Man, out of putting horns on her darling's head, and never for a moment, she said, did he appear to her as the comic figure of the cuckolded husband that one saw on the stage. (The Young Man assured her that his own sentiments were equally delicate, that for the wronged man he felt the most profound respect, tinged with consideration.) It was as if by the mere act of betraying her husband, she had adequately bested him; it was supererogatory for her to gloat, and, if she gloated at all, it was over her fine restraint in not-gloating, over the integrity of her moral sense, which allowed her to preserve even while engaged in sinfulness the acute realization of sin and shame. Her overt superiority feelings she reserved for her friends. Lunches and teas, which had been time-killers, matters of routine, now became perilous and dramatic adventures. The Young Man's name was a bright, highly explosive ball which she bounced casually back and forth in these feminine tête-à-têtes. She would discuss him in his status of friend of the family, speculate on what girls he might have, attack him or defend him, anatomize him, keeping her eyes clear and impersonal, her voice empty of special emphasis, her manner humorously detached. *While all the time . . . !*

Three times a week or oftener, at lunch or tea, she would let herself tremble thus on the exquisite edge of self-betrayal, involving her companions in a momentous game whose rules and whose risks only she herself knew. The Public Appearances were even more satisfactory. To meet at a friend's house by design and to register surprise, to strike just the right note of young-matronly affection at cocktail parties, to treat him formally as "my escort" at the theater during intermissions—these were triumphs of stage management, more difficult of execution, more nerve-racking than the lunches and teas, because *two* actors were involved. His overardent glance must be hastily deflected; his too-self-conscious readings of his lines must be entered in the debit side of her ledger of love, in anticipation of an indulgent accounting in private.

The imperfections of his performance were, indeed, pleasing to her. Not, she thought, because his impetuosities, his gaucheries, demonstrated the sincerity of his passion for her, nor because they proved him a new hand at this game of intrigue, but rather because the high finish of her own acting showed off well in comparison. "I should have gone on the stage," she could tell him gaily, "or been a diplomat's wife or an international spy," while he would admiringly agree. Actually, she doubted whether she could ever have been an actress, acknowledging that she found it more amusing and more gratifying to play herself than to interpret any character conceived by a dramatist. In these private theatricals it was her own many-faceted nature that she put on exhibit, and the audience, in this case unfortunately limited to two, could applaud both her skill of projection and her intrinsic variety. Furthermore, this was a play in which the donnée was real, and the penalty for a missed cue or an inopportune entrance was, at first anyway, unthinkable.

She loved him, she knew, for being a bad actor, for his docility in accepting her tender, mock-impatient instruction. Those superiority feelings were fattening not only on the gullibility of her friends, but also on the comic flaws of her lover's character, and on the vulnerability of her lover's position. In this particular hive she was undoubtedly queen bee.

The Public Appearances were not exclusively duets. They sometimes took the form of a trio. On these occasions the studied and benevolent carefulness which she always showed for her husband's feelings served a double purpose. She would affect a conspicuous domesticity, an affectionate conjugal demonstrativeness, would sprinkle her conversation with "Darlings," and punctuate it with pats and squeezes till her husband would visibly expand and her lover plainly and painfully shrink. For the Young Man no retaliation was possible. These endearments of hers were sanctioned by law, usage, and habit; they belonged to her rôle of wife and could not be condemned or paralleled by a young man who was himself unmarried. They were clear provocations, but they could not be called so, and the Young Man preferred not to speak of them. *But she knew.* . . . Though she was aware of the sadistic intention of these displays, she was not ashamed of them, as she was sometimes twistingly ashamed of the hurt she was preparing to inflict on her husband. Partly she felt that they were punishments which the Young Man richly deserved for the wrong he was doing her husband, and that she herself in contriving them was acting, quite fittingly, both as judge and accused. Partly, too, she believed herself justified in playing the fond wife, whatever the damage to her lover's ego, because, in a sense, she actually was a fond wife. She *did* have these feelings, she insisted, whether she was exploiting them or not.

Eventually, however, her reluctance to wound her husband and her solicitude for his pride were overcome by an inner conviction that her love affair must move on to its next preordained stage. The possibilities of the subterranean courtship had been exhausted; it was time for the Announcement. She and the Young Man began to tell each other in a rather breathless and literary style that the Situation Was Impossible, and Things Couldn't Go On This Way Any Longer. The ostensible meaning of these flurried laments was that, under present conditions, they were not seeing enough of each other, that their hours together were too short and their periods of separation too dismal, that the whole business of deception had become morally distasteful to them. Perhaps the Young Man really believed these things; she did not. For the first time, she saw that the virtue of marriage as an institution lay in its public character. Private cohabitation, long continued, was, she concluded, a bore. Whatever the coziness of isolation, the warm delights of having a secret, a love affair finally reached the point where it needed the glare of publicity to revive the interest of its protagonists. Hence, she thought, the engagement parties, the showers, the big church weddings, the presents, the receptions. These were simply socially approved devices by which the lovers got themselves talked about. The gossip-value of a divorce and remarriage was obviously far greater than the gossip-value of a mere engagement, and she was now ready, indeed hungry, to hear What People Would Say.

The lunches, the teas, the Public Appearances were getting a little flat. It was not, in the end, enough to be a Woman With A Secret, if to one's friends one appeared to be a woman without a secret. The bliss of having a secret required, in short, the consummation of telling it, and she looked forward to the My-dear-I-had-no-idea's, the I-thought-you-and-Bill-were-so-happy-together's, the How-did-you-keep-it-so-dark's with which her intimates would greet her announcement. The audience of two no longer sufficed her; she required a larger stage. She tried it first, a little nervously, on two or three of her closest friends, swearing them to secrecy. "Bill must hear it first from me," she declared. "It would be too terrible for his pride if he found out afterwards that the whole town knew it before he did. So you mustn't tell, even later on, that I told you about this today. I felt I had to talk to someone." After these lunches she would hurry to a phone booth to give the Young Man the gist of the conversation, just as a reporter, sent to cover a fire, telephones in to the city desk. "She certainly was surprised," she could always say with a little gush of triumph. "But she thinks it's fine." *But did they actually?* She could not be sure. Was it possible that she sensed in these luncheon companions, her dearest friends, a certain reserve, a certain unexpressed judgment?

It was a pity, she reflected, that she was so sensitive to public opinion. "I couldn't really love a man," she murmured to herself once, "if everybody didn't think he was wonderful." Everyone seemed to like the Young Man, of course. *But still.* . . . She was getting panicky, she thought. Surely it was only common sense that nobody is admired by everybody. And even if a man were universally despised, would there not be a kind of defiant nobility in loving him in the teeth of the whole world? There would, certainly, but it was a type of heroism that she would scarcely be called upon to practice, for the Young Man was popular, he was invited everywhere, he danced well, his manners were ingratiating, he kept up intellectually. But was he not perhaps *too* amiable, *too* accommodating? Was it for this that her friends seemed silently to criticize him?

At this time a touch of acridity entered into her relations with the Young Man. Her indulgent scoldings had an edge to them now, and it grew increasingly difficult for her to keep her make-believe impatience from becoming real. She would look for dark spots in his character and drill away at them as relentlessly as a dentist at a cavity. A compulsive didacticism possessed her: no truism of his, no cliché, no ineffectual joke could pass the rigidity of her censorship. And, hard as she tried to maintain the character of charming schoolmistress, the Young Man, she saw, was taking alarm. She suspected that, frightened and puzzled, he contemplated flight. She found herself watching him with scientific interest, speculating as to what course he would take, and she was relieved but faintly disappointed when it became clear that he ascribed her sharpness to the tension of the situation and had decided to stick it out.

The moment had come for her to tell her husband. By this single, cathartic act, she would, she believed, rid herself of the doubts and anxieties that beset her. If her husband were to impugn the Young Man's character, she could answer his accusations and at the same time discount them as arising from jealousy. From her husband, at least, she might expect the favor of an open attack to which she could respond with the prepared defense that she carried, unspoken, about with her. Further, she had an intense, childlike curiosity as to How Her Husband Would Take It, a curiosity which she disguised for decency's sake as justifiable apprehension. The confidences already imparted to her friends seemed like pale dress rehearsals of the supreme confidence she was about to make. Perhaps it was toward this moment that the whole affair had been tending, for this moment that the whole affair had been designed. This would be the ultimate testing of her husband's love, its final, rounded, quintessential expression. Never, she thought, when you live with a man do you feel the full force of his love. It is gradually rationed out to you in an impure state, compounded with all the other elements of daily existence, so that you are hardly sensible of receiving it. There is no single point at which it is concentrated; it spreads out into the past and the future until it appears as a nearly imperceptible film over the surface of your life. Only face to face with its own annihilation could it show itself wholly, and, once shown, drop into the category of completed experiences.

She was not disappointed. She told him at breakfast in a fashionable restaurant, because, she said, he would be better able to control his feelings in public. When he called at once for the check, she had a spasm of alarm lest in an access of brutality or grief he leave her there alone, conspicuous, and, as it were, unfulfilled. But they walked out of the restaurant together and through the streets, hand in hand, tears streaming "unchecked," she whispered to herself, down their faces. Later they were in the Park, by an artificial lake, watching the ducks swim. The sun was very bright, and she felt a kind of superb pathos in the careful and irrelevant attention they gave to the pastoral scene. This was, she knew, the most profound, the most subtle, the most idyllic experience of her life. All the strings of her nature were, at last, vibrant. She was both doer and sufferer: she inflicted pain and participated in it. And she was, at the same time, physician, for, as she was the weapon that dealt the wound, she was also the balm that could assuage it. Only she could know the hurt that engrossed him, and it was to her that he turned for the sympathy she had ready for him. Finally, though she offered him his discharge slip with one hand, with the other she beckoned him to approach. She was wooing him all over again, but wooing him to a deeper attachment than he had previously experienced, to an unconditional surrender. She was demanding his total understanding of her, his compassion, and his forgiveness. When at last he answered her repeated and agonized I-love-you's by grasping her hand more tightly and saying gently, "I know," she saw that she had won him over. She had drawn him into a truly mystical union. Their marriage was complete.

Afterwards everything was more prosaic. The Young Man had to be telephoned to and summoned to a conference

a trois, a conference, she said, of civilized, intelligent people. The Young Man was a little awkward, even dropped a
tear or two, which embarrassed everyone else, but what
after all, she thought, could you expect? He was in a difficult position; his was a thankless part. With her husband
behaving so well, indeed, so gallantly, the Young Man
could not fail to look a trifle inadequate. The Young Man
would have preferred it, of course, if her husband had made
a scene, had bullied or threatened her, so that he himself
might have acted the chivalrous protector. She, however,
did not hold her husband's heroic courtesy against him: in
some way, it reflected credit on herself. The Young Man,
apparently, was expecting to Carry Her Off, but this she
would not allow. "It would be too heartless," she whispered
when they were alone for a moment. "We must all go somewhere together."

So the three went out for a drink, and she watched with
a sort of desperation her husband's growing abstraction,
the more and more perfunctory attention he accorded the
conversation she was so bravely sustaining. "He is bored,"
she thought. "He is going to leave." The prospect of being
left alone with the Young Man seemed suddenly unendurable. If her husband were to go now, he would take with
him the third dimension that had given the affair depth, and
abandon her to a flat and vulgar love scene. Terrified, she
wondered whether she had not already prolonged the drama beyond its natural limits, whether the confession in the
restaurant and the absolution in the Park had not rounded
off the artistic whole, whether the sequel of divorce and
remarriage would not, in fact, constitute an anticlimax. Already she sensed that behind her husband's good manners
an ironical attitude toward herself had sprung up. Was it
possible that he had believed that they would return from
the Park and all would continue as before? It was conceivable that her protestations of love had been misleading, and
that his enormous tenderness toward her had been based,
not on the idea that he was giving her up, but rather on the

idea that he was taking her back—with no questions asked. If that were the case, the telephone call, the conference, and the excursion had in his eyes been a monstrous gaffe, a breach of sensibility and good taste, for which he would never forgive her. She blushed violently. Looking at him again, she thought he was watching her with an expression which declared: I have found you out: now I know what you are like. For the first time, she felt him utterly alienated.

When he left them she experienced the let-down she had feared but also a kind of relief. She told herself that it was as well that he had cut himself off from her: it made her decision simpler. There was now nothing for her to do but to push the love affair to its conclusion, whatever that might be, and this was probably what she most deeply desired. Had the poignant intimacy of the Park persisted, she might have been tempted to drop the adventure she had begun and return to her routine. But that was, looked at coldly, unthinkable. For if the adventure would seem a little flat after the scene in the Park, the resumption of her marriage would seem even flatter. If the drama of the triangle had been amputated by her confession, the curtain had been brought down with a smack on the drama of wedlock.

And, as it turned out, the drama of the triangle was not quite ended by the superficial rupture of their marriage. Though she had left her husband's apartment and been offered shelter by a confidante, it was still necessary for her to see him every day. There were clothes to be packed, and possessions to be divided, love letters to be reread and mementos to be wept over in common. There were occasional passionate, unconsummated embraces; there were endearments and promises. And though her husband's irony remained, it was frequently vulnerable. It was not, as she had at first thought, an armor against her, but merely a sword, out of *Tristan and Isolde,* which lay permanently between them and enforced discretion.

They met often, also, at the houses of friends, for, as she said, "What can I do? I know it's not tactful, but we all know the same people. You can't expect me to give up my friends." These Public Appearances were heightened in interest by the fact that these audiences, unlike the earlier ones, had, as it were, purchased librettos, and were in full possession of the intricacies of the plot. She preferred, she decided, the evening parties to the cocktail parties, for there she could dance alternately with her lover and her husband to the accompaniment of subdued gasps on the part of the bystanders.

This interlude was at the same time festive and heart-rending: her only dull moments were the evenings she spent alone with the Young Man. Unfortunately, the Post-Announcement period was only too plainly an interlude and its very nature demanded that it be followed by something else. She could not preserve her anomalous status indefinitely. It was not decent, and, besides, people would be bored. From the point of view of one's friends, it was all very well to entertain a Triangle as a novelty; to cope with it as a permanent problem was a different matter. Once they had all three gotten drunk, and there was a scene, and, though everyone talked about it afterwards, her friends were, she thought, a little colder, a little more critical. People began to ask her when she was going to Reno. Furthermore, she noticed that her husband was getting a slight edge in popularity over the Young Man. It was natural, of course, that everyone should feel sorry for him, and be especially nice. *But yet. . . .*

When she learned from her husband that he was receiving invitations from members of her own circle, invitations in which she and the Young Man unaccountably were not included, she went at once to the station and bought her ticket. Her good-bye to her husband, which she had privately allocated to her last hours in town, took place prematurely, two days before she was to leave. He was rushing off to what she inwardly feared was a Gay Weekend in the country; he had only a few minutes; he wished her a pleasant trip; and he would write, of course. His highball was drained while her glass still stood half full; he sat forward nervously on his chair; and she knew herself to be acting the Ancient Mariner, but her dignity would not allow her to hurry. She hoped that he would miss his train for her, but he did not. He left her sitting in the bar, and that night the Young Man could not, as he put it, do a thing with her. There was nowhere, absolutely nowhere, she said passionately, that she wanted to go, nobody she wanted to see, nothing she wanted to do. "You need a drink," he said with the air of a diagnostician. "A drink," she answered bitterly. "I'm sick of the drinks we've been having. Gin, whiskey, rum, and what else is there?" He took her into a bar, and she cried, but he bought her a fancy mixed drink, something called a Ramos gin fizz, and she was a little appeased because she had never had one before. Then some friends came in, and they all had another drink together, and she felt better. "There," said the Young Man, on the way home, "don't I know what's good for you? Don't I know how to handle you?" "Yes," she answered in her most humble and feminine tones, but she knew that they had suddenly dropped into a new pattern, that they were no longer the cynosure of a social group, but merely another young couple with an evening to pass, another young couple looking desperately for entertainment, wondering whether to call on a married couple or to drop in somewhere for a drink. This time the Young Man's prescription had worked, but it was pure luck that they had chanced to meet someone they knew. A second or a third time they would scan the faces of the other drinkers in vain, would order a second drink and surreptitiously watch the door, and finally go out alone, with a quite detectable air of being unwanted.

When, a day and a half later, the Young Man came late to take her to the train, and they had to run down the platform to catch it, she found him all at once detestable. He would ride to 125th Street with her, he declared in a burst of gallantry, but she was angry all the way because she was afraid there would be trouble with the conductor. At 125th

Street, he stood on the platform blowing kisses to her and shouting something that she could not hear through the glass. She made a gesture of repugnance, but, seeing him flinch, seeing him weak and charming and incompetent, she brought her hand reluctantly to her lips and blew a kiss back. The other passengers were watching, she was aware, and though their looks were doting and not derisive, she felt herself to be humiliated and somehow vulgarized. When the train began to move, and the Young Man began to run down the platform after it, still blowing kisses and shouting alternately, she got up, turned sharply away from the window and walked back to the club car. There she sat down and ordered a whiskey and soda.

There were a number of men in the car, who looked up in unison as she gave her order; observing that they were all the middle-aged, small-business-men who "belonged" as inevitably to the club car as the white-coated porter and the leather-bound *Saturday Evening Post,* she paid them no heed. She was now suddenly overcome by a sense of depression and loss that was unprecedented for being in no way dramatic or pleasurable. In the last half hour she had seen clearly that she would never marry the Young Man, and she found herself looking into an insubstantial future with no signpost to guide her. Almost all women, she thought, when they are girls never believe that they will get married. The terror of spinsterhood hangs over them from adolescence on. Even if they are popular they think that no one really interesting will want them enough to marry them. Even if they get engaged they are afraid that something will go wrong, something will intervene. When they do get married it seems to them a sort of miracle, and, after they have been married for a time, though in retrospect the whole process looks perfectly natural and inevitable, they retain a certain unarticulated pride in the wonder they have performed. Finally, however, the terror of spinsterhood has been so thoroughly exorcised that they forget ever having been haunted by it, and it is at this stage that they contemplate divorce. "How could I have forgotten?" she said to herself and began to wonder what she would do.

She could take an apartment by herself in the Village. She would meet new people. She would entertain. But, she thought, if I have people in for cocktails, there will always come the moment when they have to leave, and I will be alone and have to pretend to have another engagement in order to save embarrassment. If I have them to dinner, it will be the same thing, but at least I will not have to pretend to have an engagement. I shall give dinners. Then, she thought, there will be the cocktail parties, and, if I go alone, I shall always stay a little too late, hoping that a young man or even a party of people will ask me to dinner. And if I fail, if no one asks me, I shall have the ignominy of walking out alone, trying to look as if I had somewhere to go. Then there will be the evenings at home with a good book when there will be no reason at all for going to bed, and I shall perhaps sit up all night. And the mornings when there will be no point in getting up, and I shall perhaps stay in bed till dinnertime. There will be the dinners in tea rooms with other unmarried women, tea rooms because women alone look conspicuous and forlorn in good restaurants. And then, she thought, I shall get older.

She would never, she reflected angrily, have taken this step, had she felt that she was burning her bridges behind her. She would never have left one man unless she had had another to take his place. But the Young Man, she now saw, was merely a sort of mirage which she had allowed herself to mistake for an oasis. "If the Man," she muttered, "did not exist, the Moment would create him." This was what had happened to her. She had made herself the victim of an imposture. But, she argued, with an accent of cheerfulness, if this were true, if out of the need of a second, a new, husband she had conjured up the figure of one, she had possibly been impelled by unconscious forces to behave more intelligently than appearances would indicate. She was perhaps acting out in a sort of hypnotic trance a ritual whose meaning had not yet been revealed to her, a ritual which required that, first of all, the Husband be eliminated from the cast of characters. Conceivably, she was designed for the rôle of *femme fatale,* and for such a personage considerations of safety, provisions against loneliness and old age, were not only Philistine but irrelevant. She might marry a second, a third, a fourth time, or she might never marry again. But, in any case for the thrifty bourgeois love-insurance, with its daily payments of patience, forbearance, and resignation, she was no longer eligible. She would be, she told herself delightedly, a bad risk.

She was, or soon would be, a Young Divorcee, and the term still carried glamor. Her divorce decree would be a passport conferring on her the status of citizeness of the world. She felt gratitude toward the Young Man for having unwittingly effected her transit into a new life. She looked about her at the other passengers. Later she would talk to them. They would ask, of course, where she was bound for; that was the regulation opening move of train conversations. But it was a delicate question what her reply should be. To say "Reno" straight out would be vulgar; it would smack of confidences too cheaply given. Yet to lie, to say "San Francisco" for instance, would be to cheat herself, to minimize her importance, to mislead her interlocutor into believing her an ordinary traveler with a commonplace destination. There must be some middle course which would give information without appearing to do so, which would hint at a *vie galante* yet indicate a barrier of impeccable reserve. It would probably be best, she decided, to say "West" at first, with an air of vagueness and hesitation. Then, when pressed, she might go so far as to say "Nevada." But no farther.

THE COUNTRY HUSBAND

by John Cheever

John Cheever (1912–   ) is a New Englander born and bred. A native of Quincy, Massachusetts, Cheever studied at the Thayer Academy. He has settled in the suburban area of the Hudson Valley, which he has made peculiarly his own in a series of distinguished novels and short stories, dealing most often with the subterranean lives and frustrations of the upper middle class. He was the winner of the Howells Fiction Medal, and the National Book Award for 1958, which he received for *The Wapshot Chronicle. The Wapshot Scandal* appeared in 1964, followed by *Bullet Park, The World of Apples,* and *Falconer.* His short stories have appeared frequently in *The New Yorker* and have been collected in several volumes, most recently in *The Stories of John Cheever* (1979).

To begin at the beginning, the airplane from Minneapolis in which Francis Weed was travelling East ran into heavy weather. The sky had been a hazy blue, with the clouds below the plane lying so close together that nothing could be seen of the earth. Then mist began to form outside the windows, and they flew into a white cloud of such density that it reflected the exhaust fires. The color of the cloud darkened to grey, and the plane began to rock. Francis had been in heavy weather before, but he had never been shaken up so much. The man in the seat beside him pulled a

Reprinted from *Stories* by John Cheever, by permission of Farrar, Straus & Giroux, Inc. Copyright 1954 by The New Yorker Magazine, Inc. Copyright © 1956 by Farrar, Straus & Cudahy, Inc.

flask out of his pocket and took a drink. Francis smiled at his neighbor, but the man looked away; he wasn't sharing his painkiller with anyone. The plane had begun to drop and flounder wildly. A child was crying. The air in the cabin was overheated and stale, and Francis' left foot went to sleep. He read a little from a paper book that he had bought at the airport, but the violence of the storm divided his attention. It was black outside the ports. The exhaust fires blazed and shed sparks in the dark, and, inside, the shaded lights, the stuffiness, and the window curtains gave the cabin the atmosphere of intense and misplaced domesticity. Then the lights flickered and went out. "You know what I've always wanted to do?" the man beside Francis said suddenly. "I've always wanted to buy a farm in New Hampshire and raise beef cattle." The stewardess announced that they were going to make an emergency landing. All but the child saw in their minds the spreading wings of the Angel of Death. The pilot could be heard singing faintly, "I've got sixpence, jolly, jolly sixpence. I've got sixpence to last me all my life . . ." There was no other sound.

The loud groaning of the hydraulic valves swallowed up the pilot's song, and there was a shrieking high in the air, like automobile brakes, and the plane hit flat on its belly in a cornfield and shook them so violently that an old man up forward howled, "Me kidneys! Me kidneys!" The stewardess flung open the doors, and someone opened an emergency door at the back, letting in the sweet noise of their continuing mortality—the idle splash and smell of a heavy rain. Anxious for their lives, they filed out of the doors and scattered over the cornfield in all directions, praying that the thread would hold. It did. Nothing happened. When it was clear that the plane would not burn or explode, the crew and the stewardess gathered the passengers together and led them to the shelter of a barn. They were not far from Philadelphia, and in a little while a string of taxis took them into the city. "It's just like the Marne," someone said, but there was surprisingly little relaxation of that suspiciousness with which many Americans regard their fellow-travellers.

In Philadelphia, Francis Weed got a train to New York. At the end of that journey, he crossed the city and caught, just as it was about to pull out, the commuting train that he took five nights a week to his home in Shady Hill.

He sat with Trace Bearden. "You know, I was in that plane that just crashed outside Philadelphia," he said. "We came down in a field . . ." He had travelled faster than the newspapers or the rain, and the weather in New York was sunny and mild. It was a day in late September, as fragrant and shapely as an apple. Trace listened to the story, but how could he get excited? Francis had no powers that would let him recreate a brush with death—particularly in the atmosphere of a commuting train, journeying through a sunny countryside where already, in the slum gardens, there were signs of harvest. Trace picked up his newspaper, and Francis was left alone with his thoughts. He said good night to Trace on the platform at Shady Hill and drove in his second-hand Volkswagen up to the Blenhollow neighborhood, where he lived.

The Weeds' Dutch Colonial house was larger than it appeared to be from the driveway. The living room was spacious and divided like Gaul into three parts. Around an ell to the left as one entered from the vestibule was the long table, laid for six, with candles and a bowl of fruit in the centre. The sounds and smells that came from the open kitchen door were appetizing, for Julia Weed was a good cook. The largest part of the living room centered around a fireplace. On the right were some bookshelves and a piano. The room was polished and tranquil, and from the windows that opened to the west there was some late-summer sunlight, brilliant and as clear as water. Nothing here was neglected; nothing had not been burnished. It was not the kind of household where, after prying open a stuck cigarette box, you would find an old shirt button and a tarnished nickel. The hearth was swept, the roses on the piano were reflected in the polish of the broad top, and there was an album of Schubert waltzes on the rack. Louisa Weed, a pretty girl of nine, was looking out the western windows. Her younger brother Henry was standing beside her. Her still younger brother, Toby, was studying the figures of some tonsured monks drinking beer on the polished brass of the wood box. Francis, taking off his hat and putting down his paper, was not consciously pleased with the scene; he was not that reflective. It was his element, his creation, and he returned to it with that sense of lightness and strength with which any creature returns to its home. "Hi, everybody," he said. "The plane from Minneapolis . . ."

Nine times out of ten, Francis would be greeted with affection, but tonight the children are absorbed in their own antagonisms. Francis has not finished his sentence about the plane crash before Henry plants a kick in Louisa's behind. Louisa swings around saying "*Damn* you!" Francis makes the mistake of scolding Louisa for bad language before he punishes Henry. Now Louisa turns on her father and accuses him of favoritism. Henry is always right; she is persecuted and lonely; her lot is helpless. Francis turns to his son, but the boy has justification for the kick—she hit him first; she hit him on the ear, which is dangerous. Louisa agrees with this passionately. She hit him on the ear, and she *meant* to hit him on the ear, because he messed up her china collection. Henry says that this is a lie. Little Toby turns away from the wood box to throw in some evidence for Louisa. Henry claps his hands over little Toby's mouth. Francis separates the two boys but accidentally pushes Toby into the wood box. Toby begins to cry. Louisa is already crying. Just then, Julia Weed comes into that part of the room where the table is laid. She is a pretty, intelligent woman, and the white in her hair is premature. She does not seem to notice the fracas. "Hello, darling," she says serenely to Francis. "Wash your hands, everyone. Dinner is ready." She strikes a match and lights the six candles in this vale of tears.

This simple announcement, like the war cries of the Scottish chieftains, only refreshes the ferocity of the combatants. Louisa gives Henry a blow on the shoulder. Henry, although he seldom cries, has pitched nine innings and is tired. He bursts into tears. Little Toby discovers a splinter in his hand and begins to howl. Francis says loudly that he has been in a plane crash and that he is tired. Julia appears again, from the kitchen, and, still ignoring the chaos, asks Francis to go upstairs and tell Helen that everything is ready. Francis is happy to go; it is like getting back to headquarters company. He is planning to tell his oldest daughter about the airplane crash, but Helen is lying on her bed reading a *True Romance* magazine, and the first thing Francis does is to take the magazine from her hand and remind Helen that he has forbidden her to buy it. She did not buy it, Helen replies. It was given to her by her best friend, Bessie Black. Everybody reads *True Romance*. Bessie Black's father reads *True Romance*. There isn't a girl in Helen's class who doesn't read *True Romance*. Francis expresses his detestation of the magazine and then tells her that dinner is ready—although from the sounds downstairs it doesn't seem so. Helen follows him down the stairs. Julia has seated herself in the candlelight and spread a napkin over her lap. Neither Louisa nor Henry has come to the table. Little Toby is still howling, lying face down on the floor. Francis speaks to him gently: "Daddy was in a plane crash this afternoon, Toby, don't you want to hear about it?" Toby goes on crying. "If you don't come to the table now, Toby," Francis says, "I'll have to send you to bed without any supper." The little boy rises, gives him a cutting look, flies up the stairs to his bedroom, and slams the door. "Oh dear," Julia says, and starts to go after him. Francis says that she will spoil him. Julia says that Toby is ten pounds underweight and has to be encouraged to eat. Winter is coming, and he will spend the cold months in bed unless he has his dinner. Julia goes upstairs. Francis sits down at the table with Helen. Helen is suffering from the dismal feeling of having read too intently on a fine day, and she gives her father and the room a jaded look. She doesn't understand about the plane crash, because there wasn't a drop of rain in Shady Hill.

Julia returns with Toby, and they all sit down and are served: "Do I have to look at that big, fat slob?" Henry says of Louisa. Everybody but Toby enters into this skirmish, and it rages up and down the table for five minutes. Toward the end, Henry puts his napkin over his head and tries to eat that way, spills spinach all over his shirt. Francis asks Julia if the children couldn't have their dinner earlier. Julia's guns are loaded for this. She can't cook two dinners and lay two tables. She paints with lightning strokes that panorama of drudgery in which her youth, her beauty, and her wit have been lost. Francis says that he must be understood; he was nearly killed in an airplane crash, and he doesn't like to come home every night to a battlefield. Now Julia is deeply committed. Her voice trembles. He doesn't come home every night to a battlefield. The accusation is stupid and mean. Everything was tranquil until he arrived. She stops speaking, puts down her knife and fork, and looks into her plate as if it is a gulf. She begins to cry. "Poor Mummy!" Toby says, and when Julia gets up from the table, Toby goes to her side. "Poor Mummy," he says. "Poor Mummy!" And they climb the stairs together. The other children drift away from the battlefield, and Francis goes into the back garden for a cigarette and some air.

It was a pleasant garden, with walks and flower beds and places to sit. The sunset had nearly burned out, but there was still plenty of light. Put into a thoughtful mood by the crash and the battle, Francis listened to the evening sounds of Shady Hill. "Varmints! Rascals!" old Mr. Nixon shouted to the squirrels in his bird-feeding station. "Avaunt and quit my sight!" A door slammed. Someone was playing tennis on the Babcocks' court; someone was cutting grass.

Then Donald Goslin, who lived at the corner, began to play the "Moonlight Sonata." He did this nearly every night. He threw the tempo out the window and played it *rubato* from beginning to end, like an outpouring of tearful petulance, lonesomeness, and self-pity—of everything it was Beethoven's greatness not to know. The music rang up and down the street beneath the trees like an appeal for love, for tenderness, aimed at some lonely housemaid—some fresh-faced, homesick girl from Galway, looking at old snapshots in her third-floor room. "Here, Jupiter, here, Jupiter," Francis called to the Mercers' retriever. Jupiter crashed through the tomato vines with the remains of a felt hat in his mouth.

Jupiter was an anomaly. His retrieving instincts and his high spirits were out of place in Shady Hill. He was as black as coal, with a long, alert, intelligent, rakehell face. His eyes gleamed with mischief, and he held his head high. It was the fierce, heavily collared dog's head that appeared in heraldry, in tapestry, and that used to appear on umbrella handles and walking sticks. Jupiter went where he pleased, ransacking wastebaskets, clotheslines, garbage pails, and shoe bags. He broke up garden parties and tennis matches, and got mixed up in the processional at Christ's Church on Sunday, barking at the men in red dresses. He crashed through old Mr. Nixon's rose garden two or three times a day, cutting a wide swath through the Condesa de Sastagos, and as soon as Donald Goslin lighted his barbecue fire on Thursday nights, Jupiter would get the scent. Nothing the Goslins did could drive him away. Sticks and stones and rude commands only moved him to the edge of the terrace, where he remained, with his gallant and heraldic muzzle, waiting for Donald Goslin to turn his back and reach for the salt. Then he would spring onto the terrace, lift the steak lightly off the fire, and run away with the Goslins' dinner. Jupiter's days were numbered. The Wrightsons' German gardener or the Farquarsons' cook would soon poison him. Even old Mr. Nixon might put some arsenic in the garbage that Jupiter loved. "Here, Jupiter, Jupiter!" Francis called, but the dog pranced off, shaking the hat in his white teeth. Looking in at the windows of his house, Francis saw Julia had come down and was blowing out the candles.

Julia and Francis Weed went out a great deal. Julia was well liked and gregarious, and her love of parties sprang from a most natural dread of chaos and loneliness. She went through her morning mail with real anxiety, looking for invitations, and she usually found some, but she was insatiable, and if she had gone out seven nights a week, it would not have cured her of a reflective look—the look of someone who hears distant music—for she would always suppose that there was a more brilliant party somewhere else. Francis limited her to two week-night parties, putting a flexible interpretation on Friday, and rode through the weekend like a dory in a gale. The day after the airplane crash, the Weeds were to have dinner with the Farquarsons.

Francis got home late from town, and Julia got the sitter while he dressed, and then hurried him out of the house. The party was small and pleasant, and Francis settled down to enjoy himself. A new maid passed the drinks. Her hair was dark, and her face was round and pale and seemed familiar to Francis. He had not developed his memory as a sentimental faculty. Wood smoke, lilac, and other such perfumes did not stir him, and his memory was something like his appendix—a vestigial repository. It was not his limitation at all to be unable to escape the past; it was perhaps his limitation that he had escaped it so successfully. He might have seen the maid at other parties, he might have seen her taking a walk on Sunday afternoons, but in either case he would not be searching his memory now. Her face was, in a wonderful way, a moon face—Norman or Irish—but it was not beautiful enough to account for his feeling that he had seen her before, in circumstances that he ought to be able to remember. He asked Nellie Farquarson who she was. Nellie said that the maid had come through an agency, and that her home was Trénon, in Normandy—a small place with a church and a restaurant that Nellie had once visited. While Nellie talked on about her travels abroad, Francis realized where he had seen the woman before. It had been at the end of the war. He had left a replacement depot with some other men and taken a three-day pass in Trénon. On their second day, they had walked out to a crossroads to see the public chastisement of a young woman who had lived with the German commandant during the Occupation.

It was a cool morning in the fall. The sky was overcast, and poured down onto the dirt crossroads a very discouraging light. They were on high land and could see how like one another the shapes of the clouds and the hills were as they stretched off toward the sea. The prisoner arrived sitting on a three-legged stool in a farm cart while the mayor read the accusation and the sentence. Her head was bent and her face was set in that empty half smile behind which the whipped soul is suspended. When the major was finished, she undid her hair and let it fall across her back. A little man with a grey mustache cut off her hair with shears and dropped it on the ground. Then, with a bowl of soapy water and a straight razor, he shaved her skull clean. A woman approached and began to undo the fastenings of her clothes, but the prisoner pushed her aside and undressed herself. When she pulled the chemise over her head and threw it on the ground, she was naked. The women jeered; the men were still. There was no change in the falseness or the plaintiveness of the prisoner's smile. The cold wind made her white skin rough and hardened the nipples of her breasts. The jeering ended gradually, put down by the recognition of their common humanity. One woman spat on her, but some inviolable grandeur in her nakedness lasted through the ordeal. When the crowd was quiet, she turned—she had begun to cry—and with nothing on but a pair of worn black shoes and stockings, walked down the dirt road alone, away from the village. The round white face had aged a little, but there was no question but that the maid who passed his cocktails and later served Francis his dinner was the woman who had been punished at the crossroads.

The war now seemed so distant and that world where the cost of partisanship had been death or torture so long ago. Francis had lost track of the men who had been with him in Vésey. He could not count on Julia's discretion. He could not tell anyone. And if he had told the story now, at the dinner table, it would have been a social as well as a human error. The people in the Farquarsons' living room seemed united in their tacit claim that there had been no past, no war—that there was no danger or trouble in the world. In the recorded history of human arrangements, this extraordinary meeting would have fallen into place, but the atmosphere of Shady Hill made the memory unseemly and impolite. The prisoner withdrew after passing the coffee, but the encounter left Francis feeling languid; it had opened his memory and his senses, and left them dilated. He and Julia drove home when the party ended, and Julia went into the house. Francis stayed in the car to take the sitter home.

Expecting to see Mrs. Henlein, the old lady who usually stayed with the children, he was surprised when a young girl opened the door and came out onto the lighted stoop. She stayed in the light to count her textbooks. She was frowning and beautiful. Now, the world is full of beautiful young girls, but Francis saw here the difference between beauty and perfection. All those endearing flaws, moles, birthmarks, and healed wounds were missing, and he experienced in his consciousness that moment when music breaks glass, and felt a pang of recognition as strange, deep, and wonderful as anything in his life. It hung from her frown, from an impalpable darkness in her face—a look that impressed him as a direct appeal for love. When she had counted her books, she came down the steps and opened the car door. In the light, he saw that her cheeks were wet. She got in and shut the door.

"You're new," Francis said.

"Yes. Mrs. Henlein is sick. I'm Anne Murchison."

"Did the children give you any trouble?"

"Oh, no, no." She turned and smiled at him unhappily in the dim dashboard light. Her light hair caught on the collar of her jacket, and she shook her head to set it loose.

"You've been crying."

"Yes."

"I hope it was nothing that happened in our house."

"No, no, it was nothing that happened in your house." Her voice was bleak. "It's no secret. Everybody in the village knows. Daddy's an alcoholic, and he just called me from some saloon and gave me a piece of his mind. He thinks I'm immoral. He called just before Mrs. Weed came back."

"I'm sorry."

"Oh, *Lord!*" she gasped and began to cry. She turned toward Francis, and he took her in his arms and let her cry on his shoulder. She shook in his embrace, and this movement accentuated his sense of the fineness of her flesh and bone. The layers of their clothing felt thin, and when her shuddering began to diminish, it was so much like a paroxysm of love that Francis lost his head and pulled her roughly against him. She drew away. "I live on Belleview Avenue," she said. "You go down Lansing Street to the railroad bridge."

"All right." He started the car.

"You turn left at that traffic light. . . . Now you turn right here and go straight on toward the tracks."

The road Francis took brought him right out of his own neighborhood, across the tracks, and toward the river, to a street where the near-poor lived, in houses whose peaked gables and trimmings of wooden lace conveyed the purest feelings of pride and romance, although the houses themselves could not have offered much privacy or comfort, they were all so small. The street was dark, and, stirred by the grace and beauty of the troubled girl, he seemed, in turning into it, to have come to the deepest part of some submerged memory. In the distance, he saw a porch light burning. It was the only one, and she said that the house with the light was where she lived. When he stopped the car, he could see beyond the porch light into a dimly lighted hallway with an old-fashioned clothes tree. "Well, here we are," he said, conscious that a young man would have said something different.

She did not move her hands from the books, where they were folded, and she turned and faced him. There were tears of lust in his eyes. Determinedly—not sadly—he opened the door on his side and walked around to open hers. He took her free hand, letting his fingers in between hers, climbed at her side the two concrete steps, and went up a narrow walk through a front garden where dahlias, marigolds, and roses— things that had withstood the light frosts—still bloomed, and made a bittersweet smell in the night air. At the steps, she freed her hand and then turned and kissed him swiftly. Then she crossed the porch and shut the door. The porch light went out, then the light in the hall. A second later, a light went on upstairs at the side of the house, shining into a tree that was still covered with leaves. It took her only a few minutes to undress and get into bed, and then the house was dark.

Julia was asleep when Francis got home. He opened a second window and got into bed to shut his eyes on that night, but as soon as they were shut—as soon as he had dropped off to sleep—the girl entered his mind, moving with perfect freedom through its shut doors and filling chamber after chamber with her light, her perfume, and the music of her voice. He was crossing the Atlantic with her on the old Mauretania and, later, living with her in Paris. When he woke from this dream, he got up and smoked a cigarette at the open window. Getting back into bed, he cast around in his mind for something he desired to do that would injure no one, and he thought of skiing. Up through the dimness in his mind rose the image of a mountain deep in snow. It was late in the day. Wherever his eyes looked, he saw broad and heartening things. Over his shoulder, there was a snow-filled valley, rising into wooded hills where the trees dimmed the whiteness like a sparse coat of hair. The cold deadened all sound but the loud, iron clanking of the lift machinery. The light on the trails was blue, and it was harder than it had been a minute or two earlier to pick the turns, harder to judge—now that the snow was all deep blue—the crust, the ice, and the bare spots, and the deep piles of dry powder. Down the mountain he swung, matching his speed against the contours of a slope that had been formed in the first ice age, seeking with ardor some simplicity of feeling and circumstances. Night fell then, and he drank a Martini with some old friend in a dirty country bar.

In the morning, Francis's snow-covered mountain was gone, and he was left with vivid memories of Paris and the Mauretania. He had been bitten gravely. He washed his body, shaved his jaws, drank his coffee, and missed the seven-thirty-one. The train pulled out just as he brought his car to the station, and the longing he felt for the coaches as they drew stubbornly away from him reminded him of the humors of love. He waited for the eight-two, on what was now an empty platform. It was a clear morning; the morning seemed thrown like a gleaming bridge of light over his mixed affairs. His spirits were feverish and high. The image of the girl seemed to put him into a relationship to the world that was mysterious and enthralling. Cars were beginning to fill up the parking lot, and he noticed that those that had driven down from the high land above Shady Hill were white with hoarfrost. This first clear sign of autumn thrilled him. An express train—a night train from Buffalo or Albany—came down the tracks between the platforms, and he saw that the roofs of the foremost cars were covered with a skin of ice. Struck by the miraculous physicalness of everything, he smiled at the passengers in the dining car, who could be seen eating eggs and wiping their mouths with napkins as they travelled. The sleeping-car compartments, with their soiled bed linen, trailed through the fresh morning like a string of rooming-house windows. Then he saw an extraordinary thing; at one of the bedroom windows sat an unclothed woman of exceptional beauty, combing her golden hair, and Francis followed her with his eyes until she was out of sight. Then old Mrs. Wrightson joined him on the platform and began to talk.

"Well, I guess you must be surprised to see me here the third morning in a row," she said, "but because of my window curtains I'm becoming a regular commuter. The curtains I bought on Monday I returned on Tuesday, and the curtains I bought Tuesday I'm returning today. On Monday, I got exactly what I wanted—it's a wool tapestry with roses and birds—but when I got home, I found they were the wrong length. Well, I exchanged them yesterday, and when I got them home, I found they were still the wrong length. Now I'm praying to high Heaven that the decorator will have them in the right length, because you know my house, you *know* my living-room windows, and you can imagine what a problem they present. I don't know what to do with them."

"I know what to do with them," Francis said.

"What?"

"Paint them black on the inside, and shut up."

There was a gasp from Mrs. Wrightson, and Francis looked down at her to be sure that she knew he meant to be rude. She turned and walked away from him, so damaged in spirit that she limped. A wonderful feeling enveloped him, as if light were being shaken about him, and he thought again of Venus combing and combing her hair as she drifted through the Bronx. The realization of how many years had passed since he had enjoyed being deliberately impolite sobered him. Among his friends and neighbors, there were brilliant and gifted people—he saw that—but many of them, also, were bores and fools, and he had made the mistake of listening to them all with equal attention. He had confused a lack of discrimination with Christian love, and the confusion seemed general and destructive. He was grateful to the girl for this bracing sensation of independence. Birds were singing—cardinals and the last of the robins. The sky shone like enamel. Even the smell of ink from his morning paper honed his appetite for life, and the world that was spread out around him was plainly a paradise.

If Francis believed in some hierarchy of love—in spirits armed with hunting bows, in the capriciousness of Venus or Eros—or even in magical potions, philtres, and stews, in scapulae and quarters of the moon, it might have explained his susceptibility and his feverish high spirits. The autumnal loves of middle age are well publicized, and he guessed he was face to face with one of these, but there was not a trace of autumn in what he felt. He wanted to sport in the green woods, scratch where he itched, and drink from the same cup.

His secretary, Miss Rainey, was late that morning—she went to a psychiatrist three mornings a week—and when she came in, Francis wondered what advice a psychiatrist would have for him. But the girl promised to bring back into his life something like the sound of music. The realization that this music might lead him straight to a trial at the county courthouse collapsed his happiness. The photograph of his four children laughing into the camera on the beach at Gay Head reproached him. On the letterhead of his firm there was a drawing of the Laocoön, and the figure of the priest and his sons in the coils of the snake appeared to him to have the deepest meaning.

He had lunch with Pinky Trabert, who told him a couple of dirty stories. At a conversational level, the mores of his friends were robust and elastic, but he knew that the moral card house would come down on them all—on Julia and the children as well—if he got caught taking advantage of a baby sitter. Looking back over the recent history of Shady Hill for some precedent, he found there was none. There was no turpitude; there had not been a divorce since he lived there; there had not even been a breath of scandal. Things seemed arranged with more propriety even than in the Kingdom of Heaven. After leaving Pinky, Francis went to a jeweller's and bought the girl a bracelet. How happy this clandestine purchase made him, how stuffy and comical the jeweller's clerks seemed, how sweet the women who passed at his back smelled! On Fifth Avenue, passing Atlas with his shoulders bent under the weight of the world, Francis thought of the strenuousness of containing his physicalness within the patterns he had choesn.

He did not know when he would see the girl next. He had the bracelet in his inside pocket when he got home. Opening the door of his house, he found her in the hall. Her back was to him, and she turned when she heard the door close. Her smile was open and loving. Her perfection stunned him like a fine day—a day after a thunderstorm. He seized her and covered her lips with his, and she struggled but she did not have to struggle for long, because just then little Gertrude Flannery appeared from somewhere and said, "Oh, Mr. Weed . . ."

Gertrude was a stray. She had been born with a taste for exploration, and she did not have it in her to centre her life with her affectionate parents. People who did not know the Flannerys concluded from Gertrude's behavior that she was the child of a bitterly divided family, where drunken quarrels were the rule. This was not true. The fact that little Gertrude's clothing was ragged and thin was her own triumph over her mother's struggle to dress her warmly and neatly. Garrulous, skinny, and unwashed, she drifted from house to house around the Blenhollow neighborhood, forming and breaking alliances based on an attachment to babies, animals, children her own age, adolescents, and sometimes adults. Opening your front door in the morning, you would find Gertrude sitting on your step. Going into the bathroom to shave, you would find Gertrude using the toilet. Looking into your son's crib, you would find it empty, and, looking further, you would find that Gertrude had pushed him in his baby carriage into the next village. She was helpful, pervasive, honest, hungry and loyal. She never went home of her own choice. When the time to go arrived she was indifferent to all its signs. "Go home, Gertrude" people could be heard saying in one house or another, night after night. "Go home, Gertrude." "It's time for you to go home now, Gertrude." "You had better go home and get your supper, Gertrude." "I told you to go home twenty minutes ago, Gertrude." "Your mother will be worrying about you, Gertrude," "Go home, Gertrude, go home."

There are times when the lines around the human eye seem like shelves of eroded stone and when the staring eye itself strikes us with such a wilderness of animal feeling that we are at a loss. The look Francis gave the little girl was ugly and queer, and it frightened her. He reached into his pocket—his hands were shaking—and took out a quarter. "Go home, Gertrude, go home, and don't tell anyone. Gertrude. Don't—" He choked and ran into the living room as Julia called down to him from upstairs to hurry up and dress.

The thought that he would drive Anne Murchison home later that night ran like a golden thread through the events of the party that Francis and Julia went to, and he laughed uproariously at dull jokes, dried a tear when Mabel Mercer told him about the death of her kitten, and stretched, yawned, sighed, and grunted like any other man with a rendezvous at the back of his mind. The bracelet was in his pocket. As he sat talking, the smell of grass was in his nose, and he was wondering where he would park the car. Nobody lived in the old Parker mansion, and the driveway was used as a lover's lane. Townsend Street was a dead end, and he could park there, beyond the last house. The old lane that used to connect Elm Street to the riverbanks was overgrown, but he had walked there with his children, and he could drive his car deep enough into brushwoods to be concealed.

The Weeds were the last to leave the party, and their

host and hostess spoke of their own married happiness while they all four stood in the hallway saying good night. "She's my girl," their host said, squeezing his wife. "She's my blue sky. After sixteen years, I still bite her shoulders. She makes me feel like Hannibal crossing the Alps."

The Weeds drove home in silence. Francis brought his car up to the driveway and sat still, with the motor running. "You can put the car in the garage," Julia said as she got out. "I told the Murchison girl she could leave at eleven. Someone drove her home." She shut the door, and Francis sat in the dark. He would be spared nothing then, it seemed, that a fool was not spared: ravening, lewdness, jealousy, this hurt to his feelings that put tears in his eyes, even scorn—for he could see clearly the image he now presented, his arms spread over the steering wheel and his head buried in them for love.

Francis had been a dedicated Boy Scout when he was young, and, remembering the precepts of his youth, he left his office early the next afternoon and played some round-robin squash, but, with his body toned up by exercise and a shower, he realized that he might better have stayed at his desk. It was a frosty night when he got home. The air smelled sharply of change. When he stepped into the house, he sensed an unusual stir. The children were in their best clothes, and when Julia came down she was wearing a lavender dress and her diamond sunburst. She explained the stir: Mr. Hubber was coming at seven to take their photograph for the Christmas card. She had put out Francis' blue suit and a tie with some color in it, because the picture was going to be in color this year. Julia was light hearted at the thought of being photographed for Christmas. It was the kind of ceremony she enjoyed.

Francis went upstairs to change his clothes. He was tired from the day's work and tired with longing, and sitting on the edge of the bed had the effect of deepening his weariness. He thought of Anne Murchison, and the physical need to express himself, instead of being restrained by the pink lamps on Julia's dressing table, engulfed him. He went to Julia's desk, took a piece of writing paper, and began to write on it: "Dear Anne, I love you, I love you, I love you . . ." No one would see the letter, and he used no restraint. He used phrases like "Heavenly bliss," and "love nest." He salivated, sighed, and trembled. When Julia called him to come down, the abyss between his fantasy and the practical world opened so wide that he felt it affect the muscles of his heart.

Julia and the children were on the stoop, and the photographer and his assistant had set up a double battery of floodlights to show the family and architectural beauty of the entrance to their house. People who had come home on a late train slowed their cars to see the Weeds being photographed for their Christmas card. A few waved and called to the family. It took half an hour of smiling and wetting their lips before Mr. Hubber was satisfied. The heat of the lights made an unfresh smell in the frosty air, and when they were turned off, they lingered on the retina of Francis' eyes.

Later that night, while Francis and Julia were drinking their coffee in the living room, the doorbell rang. Julia answered the door and let in Clayton Thomas. He had come to pay her for some theater tickets that she had given his mother some time ago, and that Helen Thomas had scrupulously insisted on paying for, though Julia had asked her not to. Julia invited him in to have a cup of coffee. "I won't have any coffee," Clayton said, "but I will come in for a minute." He followed her into the living room, said good evening to Francis, and sat down awkwardly in a chair.

Clayton's father had been killed in the war, and the young man's fatherlessness surrounded him like an element. This may have been conspicuous in Shady Hill because the Thomases were the only family that lacked a piece; all the other marriages were intact and productive. Clayton was in his second or third year of college, and he and his mother lived alone in a large house which she hoped to sell. Clayton had once made some trouble. Years ago, he had stolen some money and run away; he had got to California before they caught up with him. He was tall and homely, wore horn-rimmed glasses, and spoke in a deep voice.

"When do you go back to college, Clayton?" Francis asked.

"I'm not going back," Clayton said. "Mother doesn't have the money, and there's no sense in all this pretense. I'm going to get a job, and if we sell the house, we'll take an apartment in New York."

"Won't you miss Shady Hill?" Julia asked.

"No," Clayton said. "I don't like it."

"Why not?" Francis asked.

"Well, there's a lot here I don't approve of," Clayton said gravely. "Things like the club dances. Last Saturday night, I looked in toward the end and saw Mr. Granner trying to put Mrs. Minot into the trophy case. They were both drunk. I disapprove of so much drinking."

"It was Saturday night," Francis said.

"And all the dovecotes are phony," Clayton said. "And the way people clutter up their lives. I've thought about it a lot, and what seems to me to be really wrong with Shady Hill is that it doesn't have any future. So much energy is spent in perpetuating the place—in keeping out undesirables, and so forth—that the only idea of the future anyone has is just more and more commuting trains and more parties. I don't think that's healthy. I think people ought to be able to dream big dreams about the future. I think people ought to be able to dream great dreams."

"It's too bad you couldn't continue with college," Julia said.

"I wanted to go to divinity school," Clayton said.

"What's your church?" Francis asked.

"Unitarian, Theosophist, Transcendentalist, Humanist," Clayton said.

"Wasn't Emerson a transcendentalist?" Julia asked.

"I mean the English transcendentalists," Clayton said. "All the American transcendentalists were goops."

"What kind of job do you expect to get?" Francis added.

"Well, I'd like to work for a publisher," Clayton said. "But everyone tells me there's nothing doing. But it's the kind of thing I'm interested in. I'm writing a long verse play about good and evil. Uncle Charlie might get me into a bank, and that would be good for me. I need the discipline. I have a long way to go in forming my character. I have some terrible habits. I talk too much. I think I ought to take vows of silence. I ought to try not to speak for a week, and discipline myself. I've thought of making a retreat at one of the Episcopalian monasteries, but I don't like Trinitarianism."

"Do you have any girl friends?" Francis asked.

"I'm engaged to be married," Clayton said. "Of course, I'm not old enough or rich enough to have my engagement observed or respected or anything, but I bought a simulated emerald for Anne Murchison with the money I made cutting lawns this summer. We're going to be married as soon as she finishes school."

Francis recoiled at the mention of the girl's name. Then a dingy light seemed to emanate from his spirit, showing everything—Julia, the boy, the chairs—in their true colorlessness. It was like a bitter turn of the weather.

"We're going to have a large family," Clayton said. "Her father's a terrible rummy, and I've had my hard times, and we want to have lots of children. Oh, she's wonderful, Mr. and Mrs. Weed, and we have so much in common. We like all the same things. We sent out the same Christmas card last year without planning it, and we both have an allergy to tomatoes, and our eyebrows grow together in the middle. Well, good night."

Julia went to the door with him. When she returned, Francis said that Clayton was lazy, irresponsible, affected, and smelly. Julia said that Francis seemed to be getting intolerant; the Thomas boy was young and should be given a chance. Julia had noticed other cases where Francis had been short-tempered. "Mrs. Wrightson has asked everyone in Shady Hill to her anniversary party but us," she said.

"I'm sorry, Julia."

"Do you know why they didn't ask us?"

"Why?"

"Because you insulted Mrs. Wrightson."

"Then you know about it?"

"June Masterson told me. She was standing behind you."

Julia walked in front of the sofa with a small step that expressed, Francis knew, a feeling of anger.

"I did insult Mrs. Wrightson, Julia, and I meant to. I've never liked her parties, and I'm glad she's dropped us."

"What about Helen?"

"How does Helen come into this?"

"Mrs. Wrightson's the one who decides who goes to assemblies."

"You mean she can keep Helen from going to the dances?"

"Yes."

"I hadn't thought of that."

"Oh, I knew you hadn't thought of it." Julia cried, thrusting hilt-deep into this chink of his armor. "And it makes me furious to see this kind of stupid thoughtlessness wreck everyone's happiness."

"I don't think I've wrecked anyone's happiness."

"Mrs. Wrightson runs Shady Hill and has run it for the last forty years. I don't know what makes you think that in a community like this you can indulge every impulse you have to be insulting, vulgar, and offensive."

"I have very good manners," Francis said, trying to give the evening a turn toward the light.

"Damn you, Francis Weed!" Julia cried, and the spit of her words struck him in the face. "I've worked hard for the social position we enjoy in this place, and I won't stand by and see you wreck it. You must have understood when you settled here that you couldn't expect to live like a bear in a cave."

"I've got to express my likes and dislikes."

"You can conceal your dislikes. You don't have to meet everything head-on, like a child. Unless you're anxious to be a social leper. It's no accident that we get asked out a great deal. It's no accident that Helen has so many friends. How would you like to spend your Saturday nights at the movies? How would you like to spend your Sundays raking up dead leaves? How would you like it if your daughter spent the assembly nights sitting at her window, listening to the music from the club? How would you like it—" He did something then that was, after all, not so unaccountable, since her words seemed to raise up between them a wall so deadening that he gagged: he struck her full in the face. She staggered and then, a moment later, seemed composed. She went up the stairs to their room. She didn't slam the door. When Francis followed, a few minutes later, he found her packing a suitcase.

"Julia, I'm very sorry."

"It doesn't matter," she said. She was crying.

"Where do you think you're going?"

"I don't know. I just looked at the timetable. There's an eleven-sixteen into New York. I'll take that."

"You can't go, Julia."

"I can't stay. I know that."

"I'm sorry about Mrs. Wrightson, Julia, and I'm—"

"It doesn't matter about Mrs. Wrightson. That isn't the trouble."

"What is the trouble?"

"You don't love me."

"I do love you, Julia."

"No, you don't."

"Julia, I do love you, and I would like to be as we were —sweet and bawdy and dark—but now there are so many people."

"You hate me."

"I don't hate you, Julia."

"You have no idea of how much you hate me. I think it's subconscious. You don't realize the cruel things you've done."

"What cruel things, Julia?"

"The cruel acts your subconscious drives you to in order to express your hatred for me."

"What, Julia?"

"I've never complained."

"Tell me."

"Your clothes."

"What do you mean?"

"I mean the way you leave your dirty clothes around in order to express your subconscious hatred for me."

"I don't understand."

"I mean your dirty socks and your dirty pajamas and your dirty underwear and your dirty shirts!" She rose from kneeling by the suitcase and faced him, her eyes blazing and her voice ringing with emotion. "I'm talking about the fact that you've never learned to hang up anything. You just leave your clothes all over the floor where they drop, in order to humiliate me. You do it on purpose!" She fell on the bed, sobbing.

"Julia, darling!" he said, but when she felt his hand on her shoulder she got up.

"Leave me alone," she said. "I have to go." She brushed past him to the closet and came back with a dress. "I'm not taking any of the things you've given me," she said. "I'm leaving my pearls and the fur jacket."

"Oh, Julia!" Her figure, so helpless in its self-deceptions, bent over the suitcase made him nearly sick with pity. She did not understand how desolate her life would be without him. She didn't understand the hours that working women have to keep. She didn't understand that most of her friendships existed within the framework of their marriage, and that without this she would find herself alone. She didn't understand about travel, about hotels, about money. "Julia,

I can't let you go! What you don't understand, Julia, is that you've come to be dependent on me."

She tossed her head back and covered her face with her hands. "Did you say I was dependent on *you?*" she asked. "Is that what you said? And who is it that tells you what time to get up in the morning and when to go to bed at night? Who is it that prepares your meals and picks up your dirty closet and invites your friends to dinner? If it weren't for me your neckties would be greasy and your clothing would be full of moth holes. You were alone when I met you, Francis Weed, and you'll be alone when I leave. When mother asked you for a list to send out invitations to our wedding, how many names did you have to give her? Fourteen!"

"Cleveland wasn't my home, Julia."

"And how many of your friends came to the church? Two!"

"Since I'm not taking the fur jacket," she said quietly, "you'd better put it back into storage. There's an insurance policy in the pearls that comes due in January. The name of the laundry and the maid's telephone number—all those things are in my desk. I hope you won't drink too much, Francis. I hope that nothing bad will happen to you. If you do get into serious trouble, you can call me."

"Oh my darling, I can't let you go!" Francis said. "I can't let you go, Julia!" He took her in his arms.

"I guess I'd better stay and take care of you for a little while longer," she said.

Riding to work in the morning. Francis saw the girl walk down the aisle of the coach. He was surprised; he hadn't realized that the school she went to was in the city, but she was carrying books, she seemed to be going to school. His surprise delayed his reaction, but then he got up clumsily and stepped into the aisle. Several people had come between them, but he could see her ahead of him, waiting for somone to open the car door, and then, as the train swerved, putting out her hand to support herself as she crossed the

platform into the next car. He followed her through that
car and halfway through another before calling her name—
"Anne! Anne!"—but she didn't turn. He followed her into
still another car, and she sat down in an aisle seat. Coming
up to her, all his feelings warm and bent in her direction, he
put his hand on the back of her seat—even this touch
warmed him—and leaning down to speak to her, he saw
that it was not Anne. It was an older woman wearing
glasses. He went on deliberately into another car, his face
red with embarrassment and the much deeper feeling of
having his good sense challenged; for if he couldn't tell one
person from another, what evidence was there that his life
with Julia and the children had as much reality as his
dreams of iniquity in Paris or the litter, the grass smell, and
the cave-shaped trees in Lover's Lane.

Late that afternoon, Julia called to remind Francis that
they were going out for dinner. A few minutes later Trace
Bearden called. "Look fellar," Trace said. "I'm calling for
Mrs. Thomas. You know, Clayton, that boy of hers doesn't
seem to be able to get a job and I wondered if you could
help. If you'd call Charlie Bell—I know he's indebted to
you—and say a good word for the kid, I think Charlie
would—"

"Trace, I hate to say this," Francis said, "but I don't feel
that I can do anything for that boy. The kid's worthless. I
know it's a harsh thing to say, but it's a fact. Any kindness
done for him would backfire in everybody's face. He's just
a worthless kid, Trace, and there's nothing to be done
about it. Even if we got him a job, he wouldn't be able to
keep it for a week. I know that to be a fact. It's an awful
thing, Trace, and I know it is, but instead of recommend-
ing that kid, I'd feel obliged to warn people against him—
people who knew his father and would naturally want to
step in and do something. I'd feel obliged to warn them.
He's a thief . . ."

The moment this conversation was finished, Miss Rainey
came in and stood by his desk. "I'm not going to be able to

work for you any more, Mr. Weed," she said. "I can stay until the seventeenth if you need me, but I've been offered a whirlwind of a job, and I'd like to leave as soon as possible."

She went out, leaving him to face alone the wickedness of what he had done to the Thomas boy. His children in their photograph laughed and laughed, glazed with all the bright colors of summer, and he remembered that they had met a bagpiper on the beach that day and he had paid the piper a dollar to play them a battle song of the Black Watch. The girl would be at the house when he got home. He would spend another evening among his kind neighbors, picking and choosing dead-end streets, cart tracks, and the driveways of abandoned houses. There was nothing to mitigate his feeling—nothing that laughter or a game of softball with his children would change—and, thinking back over the plane crash, the Farquarsons' new maid, and Anne Murchison's difficulties with her drunken father, he wondered how he could have avoided arriving at just where he was. He was in trouble. He had been lost once in his life, coming back from a trout stream in the north woods, and he had now the same bleak realization that no amount of cheerfulness or hopefulness or valor or perseverance could help him find, in the gathering dark, the path that he had lost. He smelled the forest. The feeling of bleakness was intolerable, and he saw clearly that he had reached the point where he would have to make a choice.

He could go to a psychiatrist, like Miss Rainey; he could go to church and confess his lusts; he could go to a Danish massage parlor in the West Seventies that had been recommended by a salesman; he could rape the girl or trust that he would somehow be prevented from doing this; or he could get drunk. It was his life, his boat, and, like every other man, he was made to be the father of thousands, and what harm could there be in a tryst that would make them both feel more kindly toward the world? This was the wrong train of thought, and he came back to the first, the psychiatrist. He had the telephone number of Miss Rainey's doctor, and he called and asked for an immediate appointment. He was insistent with the doctor's secretary—it was his manner in business—and when she said that the doctor's schedule was full for the next few weeks, Francis demanded an appointment that day and was told to come at five.

The psychiatrist's office was in a building that was used mostly by doctors and dentists and the hallways were filled with the candy smell of mouth-wash and the memories of pain. Francis' character had been formed upon a series of private resolves—resolves about cleanliness, about going off the high diving board or repeating any other feat that challenged his courage, about punctuality, honesty, and virtue. To abdicate the perfect loneliness in which he had made his most vital decisions shattered his concept of character and left him now in a condition that felt like shock. He was stupefied. The scene for his *miserere mei Deus* was, like the waiting room of so many doctors' offices, a crude token gesture toward the sweets of domestic bliss: a place arranged with antiques, coffee tables, potted plants, and etchings of snow-covered bridges and geese in flight, although there were no children, no marriage bed, no stove, even, in this travesty of a house, where no one had ever spent the night and where the curtained windows looked straight onto a dark air shaft. Francis gave his name and address to a secretary and then saw, at the side of the room, a policeman moving toward him. "Hold it, hold it," the policeman said. "Don't move. Keep your hands where they are."

"I think it's all right, Officer," the secretary began. "I think it will be—"

"Let's make sure," the policeman said, and he began to slap Francis' clothes, looking for what—pistols, knives, an icepick? Finding nothing, he went off, and the secretary began a nervous apology: "When you called on the telephone, Mr. Weed, you seemed very excited, and one of the doctor's patients has been threatening his life, and we have to be careful. If you want to go in now?" Francis pushed open a door connected to an electrical chime, and in the doctor's lair set down heavily, blew his nose into a handkerchief, searched in his pockets for cigarettes, for matches, for something, and said hoarsely, with tears in his eyes, "I'm in love, Dr. Herzog."

It is a week or ten days later in Shady Hill. The seven-fourteen has come and gone, and here and there dinner is finished and the dishes are in the dish washing machine. The village hangs, morally and economically, by its thread in the evening light. Donald Goslin has begun to worry the "Moonlight Sonata" again. *Marcatoma sempre pianissimo!* He seems to be wringing out a wet bath towel, but the housemaid does not heed him. She is writing a letter to Arthur Godfrey. In the cellar of his house, Francis Weed is building a coffee table. Dr. Herzog recommended woodwork as a therapy, and Francis finds some true consolation in the simple arithmetic involved and in the holy smell of new wood. Francis is happy. Upstairs, little Toby is crying, because he is tired. He puts off his cowboy hat, gloves and fringed jacket, unbuckles the belt studded with gold and rubies, the silver bullets and holsters, slips off his suspenders, his checked shirt, and Levis, and sits on the edge of his bed to pull off his high boots. Leaving this equipment in a heap, he goes to the closet and takes his space suit off a nail. It is a struggle for him to get into the long tights, but he succeeds. He loops the magic cape over his shoulders and, climbing onto the footboard of his bed, he spreads his arms and flies the short distance to the floor, landing with a thump that is audible to everyone in the house but himself.

"Go home, Gertrude, go home," Mrs. Masterson says. "I told you to go home an hour ago, Gertrude. It's way past your suppertime and your mother will be worried. Go home!" A door on the Babcocks' terrace flies open, and out comes Mrs. Babcock without any clothes on, pursued by her naked husband. (Their children are away at boarding school, and their terrace is screened by a hedge.) Over the terrace they go and in at the kitchen door, as passionate and handsome a nymph and satyr as you will find on any wall in Venice. Cutting the last of her roses in her garden, Julia hears old Mr. Nixon shouting at the squirrels in his bird-feeding station. "Rapscallions! Varmits! Avaunt and quit my sight!" A miserable cat wanders into the garden, sunk in spiritual and physical discomfort. Tied to its head is a small straw hat—a doll's hat—and it is securely buttoned into a doll's dress, from the skirts of which protrudes its long, hairy tail. As it walks, it shakes its feet, as if it had fallen into water.

"Here, pussy, pussy, pussy!" Julia calls.

"Here, pussy, here, poor pussy!" But the cat gives her a skeptical look and stumbles away in its skirts. The last to come is Jupiter. He prances through the tomato vines, holding in his generous mouth the remains of an evening slipper. Then it is dark; it is a night where kings in golden suits ride elephants over the mountains.

IN DREAMS BEGIN
RESPONSIBILITIES

by Delmore Schwartz

Delmore Schwartz (1913–1966). Known perhaps primarily as a poet, Schwartz was also a distinguished and original short story writer. He was born in Brooklyn and educated at New York University and at Harvard. He was editor of *Partisan Review,* poetry editor of *The New Republic,* and recipient of many awards, including Guggenheim and Kenyon Review fellowships, the *Poetry* magazine award for 1950 and 1959, and the Bollingen poetry prize for 1959. In addition to his poetry collections, he published *Successful Love and Other Stories* (1962) and many stories and critical articles in major magazines.

I think it is the year 1909. I feel as if I were in a motion picture theatre, the long arm of light crossing the darkness and spinning, my eyes fixed on the screen. This is a silent picture as if an old Biograph one, in which the actors are dressed in ridiculously old-fashioned clothes, and one flash succeeds another with sudden jumps. The actors too seem to jump about and walk too fast. The shots themselves are full of dots and rays, as if it were raining when the picture was photographed. The light is bad.

It is Sunday afternoon, June 12th, 1909, and my father is walking down the quiet streets of Brooklyn on his way to visit my mother. His clothes are newly pressed and his tie is too tight in his high collar. He jingles the coins in his pockets, thinking of the witty things he will say. I feel as if I had by now relaxed entirely in the soft darkness of the theatre; the organist peals out the obvious and approximate emotions on which the audience rocks unknowingly. I am anonymous, and I have forgotten myself. It is always so when one goes to the movies, it is, as they say, a drug.

My father walks from street to street of trees, lawns and houses, once in a while coming to an avenue on which a streetcar skates and gnaws, slowly progressing. The conductor, who has a handle-bar mustache, helps a young lady wearing a hat like a bowl with feathers on to the car. She lifts her long skirts slightly as she mounts the steps. He leisurely makes change and rings his bell. It is obviously Sunday, for everyone is wearing Sunday clothes, and the street-car's noises emphasize the quiet of the holiday. Is not Brooklyn the City of Churches? The shops are closed and their shades drawn, but for an occasional stationery store or drug-store with great green balls in the window.

My father has chosen to take this long walk because he likes to walk and think. He thinks about himself in the future and so arrives at the place he is to visit in a state of mild exaltation. He pays no attention to the houses he is passing, in which the Sunday dinner is being eaten, nor to the many trees which patrol each street, now coming to their full leafage and the time when they will room the whole street in cool shadow. An occasional carriage passes, the horse's hooves falling like stones in the quiet afternoon, and once in a while an automobile, looking like an enormous upholstered sofa, puffs and passes.

My father thinks of my mother, of how nice it will be to introduce her to his family. But he is not yet sure that he wants to marry her, and once in a while he becomes panicky about the bond already established. He reassures himself by thinking of the big men he admires who are married: William Randolph Hearst, and William Howard Taft, who has just become President of the United States.

My father arrives at my mother's house. He has come too early and so is suddenly embarrassed. My aunt, my mother's sister, answers the loud bell with her napkin in her hand, for the family is still at dinner. As my father enters, my grandfather rises from the table and shakes hands with him. My mother has run upstairs to tidy herself. My grandmother asks my father if he has had dinner, and tells him that Rose will be downstairs soon. My grandfather opens the conversation by remarking on the mild June weather. My father sits uncomfortably near the table, holding his hat in his hand. My grandmother tells my aunt to take my father's hat. My uncle, twelve years old, runs into the house, his hair touseled. He shouts a greeting to my father, who has often given him a nickel, and then runs upstairs. It is evident that the respect in which my father is held in this household is tempered by a good deal of mirth. He is impressive, yet he is very awkward.

2

Finally my mother comes downstairs, all dressed up, and my father being engaged in conversation with my grandfather becomes uneasy, not knowing whether to greet my mother or continue the conversation. He gets up from the chair clumsily and says "hello" gruffly. My grandfather watches, examining their congruence, such as it is, with a critical eye, and meanwhile rubbing his bearded cheek roughly, as he always does when he reflects. He is worried; he is afraid that my father will not make a good husband for his oldest daughter. At this point something happens to the film, just as my father is saying something funny to my mother; I am awakened to myself and my unhappiness just as my interest was rising. The audience begins to clap impatiently. Then the trouble is cared for but the film has been returned to a portion just shown, and once more I see my grandfather rubbing his bearded cheek and pondering my father's character. It is difficult to get back into the picture once more and forget myself, but as my mother giggles at my father's words, the darkness drowns me.

My father and mother depart from the house, my father shaking hands with my mother once more, out of some unknown uneasiness. I stir uneasily also, slouched in the hard chair of the theatre. Where is the older uncle, my mother's older brother? He is studying in his bedroom upstairs, studying for his final examination at the College of the City of New York, having been dead of rapid pneumonia for the last twenty-one years. My mother and father walk down the same quiet streets once more. My mother is holding my father's arm and telling him of the novel which she has been reading; and my father utters judgments of the characters as the plot is made clear to him. This is a habit which he very much enjoys, for he feels the utmost superiority and confidence when he approves and condemns the behavior of other people. At times he feels moved to utter a brief "Ugh,"—whenever the story becomes what he would call sugary. This tribute is paid to his manliness. My mother feels satisfied by the interest which she has awakened; she is showing my father how intelligent she is, and how interesting.

They reach the avenue, and the street-car leisurely arrives. They are going to Coney Island this afternoon, although my mother considers that such pleasures are inferior. She has made up her mind to indulge only in a walk on the boardwalk and a pleasant dinner, avoiding the riotous amusements as being beneath the dignity of so dignified a couple.

My father tells my mother how much money he has made in the past week, exaggerating an amount which need not have been exaggerated. But my father has always felt that actualities somehow fall short. Suddenly I begin to weep. The determined old lady who sits next to me in the theatre is annoyed and looks at me with an angry face, and being intimidated, I stop. I drag out my handkerchief and dry my face, licking the drop which has fallen near my lips. Meanwhile I have missed something, for here are my mother and father alighting at the last stop, Coney Island.

3

They walk toward the boardwalk, and my father commands my mother to inhale the pungent air from the sea. They both breathe in deeply, both of them laughing as they do so. They have in common a great interest in health, although my father is strong and husky, my mother is frail. Their minds are full of theories of what is good to eat and not good to eat, and sometimes they engage in heated discussions of the subject, the whole matter ending in my father's announcement, made with a scornful bluster, that you have to die sooner or later anyway. On the boardwalk's flagpole, the American flag is pulsing in an intermittent wind from the sea.

My father and mother go to the rail of the boardwalk and look down on the beach where a good many bathers are casually walking about. A few are in the surf. A peanut whistle pierces the air with its pleasant and active whine, and my father goes to buy peanuts. My mother remains at the rail and stares at the ocean. The ocean seems merry to her; it pointedly sparkles and again and again the pony waves are released. She notices the children digging in the wet sand, and the bathing costumes of the girls who are her own age. My father returns with the peanuts. Overhead the sun's lightning strikes and strikes, but neither of them are at all aware of it. The boardwalk is full of people dressed in their Sunday clothes and idly strolling. The tide does not reach as far as the boardwalk, and the strollers would feel no danger if it did. My mother and father lean on the rail of the boardwalk and absently stare at the ocean. The ocean is becoming rough; the waves come in slowly, tugging strength from far back. The moment before they somersault, the moment when they arch their backs so beautifully, showing green and white veins amid the black, that moment is intolerable. They finally crack, dashing fiercely upon the sand, actually driving, full force downward, against the sand, bouncing upward and forward, and at last petering out into a small stream which races up the beach and then is recalled. My parents gaze absentmindedly at the ocean, scarcely interested in its harshness. The sun overhead does not disturb them. But I stare at the terrible sun which breaks up sight, and the fatal, merciless, passionate ocean, I forget my parents. I stare fascinated and finally, shocked by the indifference of my father and mother, I burst out weeping once more. The old lady next to me pats me on the shoulder and says "There, there, all of this is only a movie, young man, only a movie," but I look up once more at the terrifying sun and the terrifying ocean, and being unable to control my tears, I get up and go to the men's room, stumbling over the feet of the other people seated in my row.

4

When I return, feeling as if I had awakened in the morning sick for lack of sleep, several hours have apparently passed and my parents are riding on the merry-go-round. My father is on a black horse, my mother on a white one, and they seem to be making an eternal circuit for the single purpose of snatching the nickel rings which are attached to the arm of one of the posts. A hand-organ is playing; it is one with the ceaseless circling of the merry-go-round.

For a moment it seems that they will never get off the merry-go-round because it will never stop. I feel like one who looks down on the avenue from the 50th story of a building. But at length they do get off; even the music of the hand-organ has ceased for a moment. My father has acquired ten rings, my mother only two, although it was my mother who really wanted them.

They walk on along the boardwalk as the afternoon descends by imperceptible degrees into the incredible violet of dusk. Everything fades into a relaxed glow, even the ceaseless murmuring from the beach, and the revolutions of the merry-go-round. They look for a place to have dinner. My father suggests the best one on the boardwalk and my mother demurs, in accordance with her principles.

However they do go to the best place, asking for a table near the window, so that they can look out on the boardwalk and the mobile ocean. My father feels omnipotent as he places a quarter in the waiter's hand as he asks for a table. The place is crowded and here too there is music, this time from a kind of string trio. My father orders dinner with a fine confidence.

As the dinner is eaten, my father tells of his plans for the future, and my mother shows with expressive face how interested she is, and how impressed. My father becomes exultant. He is lifted up by the waltz that is being played, and his own future begins to intoxicate him. My father tells my mother that he is going to expand his business, for there is a great deal of money to be made. He wants to settle down. After all, he is twenty-nine, he has lived by himself since he was thirteen, he is making more and more money, and he is envious of his married friends when he visits them in the cozy security of their homes, surrounded it seems, by the calm domestic pleasures, and by delightful children, and then, as the waltz reaches the moment when all the dancers swing madly, then, then with awful daring, then he asks my mother to marry him, although awkwardly enough and puzzled, even in his excitement, at how he had arrived at the proposal, and she, to make the whole business worse, begins to cry, and my father looks nervously about, not knowing at all what to do now, and my mother says: "It's all I've wanted from the moment I saw you," sobbing, and he finds all of this very difficult, scarcely to his taste, scarcely as he had thought it would be, on his long walks over Brooklyn Bridge in the revery of a fine cigar, and it was then that I stood up in the theatre and shouted: "Don't do it. It's not too late to change your minds, both of you. Nothing good will come of it, only remorse, hatred, scandal, and two children whose characters are monstrous." The whole audience turned to look at me, annoyed, the usher came hurrying down the aisle flashing his searchlight, and the old lady next to me tugged me down into my seat, saying: "Be quiet. You'll be put out, and you paid thirty-five cents to come in." And so I shut my eyes because I could not bear to see what was happening. I sat there quietly.

5

But after awhile I begin to take brief glances, and at length I watch again with thirsty interest, like a child who wants to maintain his sulk although offered the bribe of candy. My parents are now having their picture taken in a photographer's booth along the boardwalk. The place is shadowed in the mauve light which is apparently necessary. The camera is set to the side on its tripod and looks like a Martian man. The photographer is instructing my parents in how to pose. My father has his arm over my mother's shoulder, and both of them smile emphatically. The photographer brings my mother a bouquet of flowers to hold in her hand but she holds it at the wrong angle. Then the photographer covers himself with the black cloth which drapes the camera and all that one sees of him is one protruding arm and his hand which clutches the rubber ball which he will squeeze when the picture is finally taken. But he is not satisfied with their appearance. He feels with certainty that somehow there is something wrong in their pose. Again and again he issues from his hidden place with new directions. Each suggestion merely makes matters worse. My father is becoming impatient. They try a seated pose. The photographer explains that he has pride, he is not interested in all of this for the money, he wants to make beautiful pictures. My father says: "Hurry up, will you? We haven't got all night." But the photographer only scurries about apologetically, and issues new directions. The photographer charms me. I approve of him with all my heart, for I know just how he feels, and as he criticizes each revised pose according to some unknown idea of rightness, I become quite hopeful. But then my father says angrily: "Come on, you've had enough time, we're not going to wait any longer." And the photographer, sighing unhappily, goes back under his black covering, holds out his hand, says: "One, two, three, Now!", and the picture is taken, with my father's smile turned to a grimace and my mother's bright and false. It takes a few minutes for the picture to be developed and as my parents sit in the curious light they become quite depressed.

6

They have passed a fortune-teller's booth and my mother wishes to go in, but my father does not. They begin to argue about it. My mother becomes stubborn, my father once more impatient, and then they begin to quarrel, and what my father would like to do is walk off and leave my mother there, but he knows that that would never do. My mother refuses to budge. She is near to tears, but she feels an uncontrollable desire to hear what the palm-reader will say. My father consents angrily, and they both go into a booth which is in a way like the photographer's, since it is draped in black cloth and its light is shadowed. The place is too warm, and my father keeps saying this is all nonsense, pointing to the crystal ball on the table. The fortune-teller, a fat, short woman, garbed in what are supposed to be Oriental robes, comes into the room from the back and greets them, speaking with an accent. But suddenly my father feels that the whole thing is intolerable; he tugs at my mother's arm, but my mother refuses to budge. And then, in terrible anger, my father lets go of my mother's arm and strides out, leaving my mother stunned. She moves to go after my father, but the fortune-teller holds her arm tightly and begs her not to do so, and I in my seat am shocked more than can ever be said, for I feel as if I were walking a tight-rope a hundred feet over a circus-audience and suddenly the rope is showing signs of breaking, and I get up from my seat and begin to shout once more the first words I can think of to communicate my terrible fear and once more the usher comes hurrying down the aisle flashing his searchlight, and the old lady pleads with me, and the shocked audience has turned to stare at me and I keep shouting: "What are they doing? Don't they know what they are doing? Why doesn't my mother go after my father? If she does not do that, what will she do? Doesn't my father know what he is doing?"—But the usher has seized my arm and is dragging me away, and as he does so, he says: "What are *you* doing? Don't you know that you can't do whatever you want to do? Why should a young man like you, with your whole life before you, get hysterical like this? Why don't you *think* of what you're doing? You can't act like this even if other people aren't around! You will be sorry if you do not do what you should do, you can't carry on like this, it is not right, you will find that out soon enough, everything you do matters too much," and he said that dragging me through the lobby of the theatre into the cold light, and I woke up into the bleak winter morning of my 21st birthday, the windowsill shining with its lip of snow, and the morning already begun.

SEX EDUCATION

by Dorothy Canfield

> Dorothy Canfield (1879–1958) was a Kansan by
> birth but a Vermonter by adoption. A distin-
> guished scholar, Miss Canfield took a Ph.D. in
> Romance Languages from Columbia University
> in 1904 and has written several books on educa-
> tional problems. After her marriage to John R.
> Fisher, she settled permanently in Arlington, Ver-
> mont, the setting for many of her novels and short
> stories, including *Hillsboro People, The Brimming
> Cup,* and *Memories of Arlington.*

It was three times—but at intervals of many years—that I
heard my Aunt Minnie tell about an experience of her girl-
hood that had made a never-to-be-forgotten impression on
her. The first time was in her thirties, still young. But she
had been married for ten years, so that to my group of
friends all in the early teens, she seemed quite of another
generation.

The day she told us the story, we had been idling on one
end of her porch as we made casual plans for a picnic supper in the woods. Darning stockings at the other end, she
paid no attention to us until one of the girls said, "Let's
take blankets and sleep out there. It'd be fun."

"No," Aunt Minnie broke in sharply, "you mustn't do
that."

"Oh, for goodness' sakes, why not!" said one of the younger girls, rebelliously, "the boys are always doing it. Why can't we, just once."

Aunt Minnie laid down her sewing. "Come here, girls," she said, "I want you should hear something that happened to me when I was your age."

Her voice had a special quality which, perhaps, young people of today would not recognize. But we did. We knew from experience that it was the dark voice grownups used when they were going to say something about sex.

Yet at first what she had to say was like any dull family anecdote; she had been ill when she was fifteen; and afterwards she was run down, thin, with no appetite. Her folks thought a change of air would do her good, and sent her from Vermont out to Ohio—or was it Illinois? I don't remember. Anyway, one of those places where the corn grows high. Her mother's Cousin Ella lived there, keeping house for her son-in-law.

The son-in-law was the minister of the village church. His wife had died some years before, leaving him a young widower with two little girls and a baby boy. He had been a normally personable man then, but the next summer, on the Fourth of July when he was trying to set off some fireworks to amuse his children, an imperfectly manufactured rocket had burst in his face. The explosion had left one side of his face badly scarred. Aunt Minnie made us see it, as she still saw it, in horrid detail: the stiffened scarlet scar tissue distorting one cheek, the lower lip turned so far out at one corner that the moist red mucous-membrane lining always showed, one lower eyelid hanging loose, and watering.

After the accident, his face had been a long time healing. It was then that his wife's elderly mother had gone to keep house and take care of the children. When he was well enough to be about again, he found his position as pastor of the little church waiting for him. The farmers and village people in his congregation, moved by his misfortune, by

his faithful service and by his unblemished character, said
they would rather have Mr. Fairchild, even with his scarred
face, than any other minister. He was a good preacher,
Aunt Minnie told us, "and the way he prayed was kind of
exciting. I'd never known a preacher, not to live in the
same house with him, before. And when he was in the pulpit, with everybody looking up at him, I felt the way his
children did, kind of proud to think we had just eaten
breakfast at the same table. I liked to call him 'Cousin
Malcolm' before folks. One side of his face was all right,
anyhow. You could see from that that he *had* been a good-
looking man. In fact, probably one of those ministers that
all the women—" Aunt Minnie paused, drew her lips together, and looked at us uncertainly.

Then she went back to the story as it happened—as it
happened that first time I heard her tell it. "I thought he
was a saint. Everybody out there did. That was all *they*
knew. Of course, it made a person sick to look at that awful
scar—the drooling corner of his mouth was the worst. He
tried to keep that side of his face turned away from folks.
But you always knew it was there. That was what kept him
from marrying again, so Cousin Ella said. I heard her say
lots of times that he knew no woman would touch any man
who looked the way he did, not with a ten-foot pole.

"Well, the change of air did do me good. I got my appetite back, and ate a lot and played outdoors a lot with
my cousins. They were younger than I (I had my sixteenth
birthday there) but I still liked to play games. I got taller
and laid on some weight. Cousin Ella used to say I grew
as fast as the corn did. Their house stood at the edge of the
village. Beyond it was one of those big cornfields they have
out West. At the time when I first got there, the stalks were
only up to a person's knee. You could see over their tops.
But it grew like lightning, and before long, it was the way
thick woods are here, way over your head, the stalks growing so close together it was dark under them.

"Cousin Ella told us youngsters that it was lots worse for

getting lost in than woods, because there weren't any land-marks in it. One spot in a cornfield looked just like any other. 'You children keep out of it,' she used to tell us al-most every day, *especially you girls.* It's no place for a decent girl. You could easy get so far from the house no-body could hear you if you hollered. There are plenty of men in this town that wouldn't like anything better than—' she never said what.

"In spite of what she said, my little cousins and I had figured out that if we went across one corner of the field, it would be a short cut to the village, and sometimes, without letting on to Cousin Ella, we'd go that way. After the corn got really tall, the farmer stopped cultivating, and we soon beat down a path in the loose dirt. The minute you were inside the field it was dark. You felt it as if you were miles from anywhere. It sort of scared you. But in no time the path turned and brought you out on the far end of Main Street. Your breath was coming fast, maybe, but that was what made you like to do it.

"One day I missed the turn. Maybe I didn't keep my mind on it. Maybe it had rained and blurred the tramped-down look of the path. I don't know what. All of a sudden, I knew I was lost. And the minute I knew that, I began to run, just as hard as I could run. I couldn't help it, any more than you can help snatching your hand off a hot stove. I didn't know what I was scared of, I didn't even know I *was* running, till my heart was pounding so hard I had to stop.

"The minute I stood still, I could hear Cousin Ella say-ing, 'There are plenty of men in this town that wouldn't like anything better than—' I didn't know, not really, what she meant. But I knew she meant something horrible. I opened my mouth to scream. But I put both hands over my mouth to keep the scream in. If I made any noise, one of those men would hear me. I thought I heard one just be-hind me, and whirled around. And then I thought another one had tiptoed up behind me, the other way, and I spun around so fast I almost fell over. I stuffed my hands hard up against my mouth. And then—I couldn't help it—I ran again—but my legs were shaking so I soon had to stop. There I stood, scared to move for fear of rustling the corn and letting the men know where I was. My hair had come down, all over my face. I kept pushing it back and looking around, quick, to make sure one of the men hadn't found out where I was. Then I thought I saw a man coming towards me, and I ran away from him—and fell down, and burst some of the buttons off my dress, and was sick to my stomach—and thought I heard a man close to me and got up and staggered around, knocking into the corn because I couldn't even see where I was going.

"And then, off to one side, I saw Cousin Malcolm. Not a man. The minister. He was standing still, one hand up to his face thinking. He hadn't heard me.

"I was so *terrible* glad to see him, instead of one of those men, I ran as fast as I could and just flung myself on him, to make myself feel how safe I was."

Aunt Minnie had become strangely agitated. Her hands were shaking, her face was crimson. She frightened us. We could not look away from her. As we waited for her to go on, I felt little spasms twitch at the muscles inside my body. "And what do you think that *saint,* that holy minister of the Gospel, did to an innocent child who clung to him for safety? The most terrible look came into his eyes—you girls are too young to know what he looked like. But once you're married, you'll find out. He grabbed hold of me— that dreadful face of his was *right on mine*—and began clawing the clothes off my back."

She stopped for a moment, panting. We were too frightened to speak. She went on, "He had torn my dress right down to the waist before I—then I *did* scream—all I could —and pulled away from him so hard I almost fell down, and ran and all of a sudden I came out of the corn, right in the back yard of the Fairchild house. The children were staring at the corn, and Cousin Ella ran out of the kitchen door. They had heard me screaming. Cousin Ella shrieked out, 'What is it? What happened? Did a man scare you?' And I said, 'Yes, yes, yes, a man—I ran—!' And then I fainted away. I must have. The next thing I knew I was on the sofa in the living room and Cousin Ella was slapping my face with a wet towel."

She had to wet her lips with her tongue before she could go on. Her face was gray now. "There! that's the kind of thing girls' folks ought to tell them about—so they'll know what men are like."

She finished her story as if she were dismissing us. We wanted to go away, but we were too horrified to stir. Finally one of the youngest girls asked in a low trembling voice, "Aunt Minnie, did you tell on him?"

"No, I was ashamed to," she said briefly. "They sent me home the next day anyhow. Nobody ever said a word to me about it. And I never did either. Till now."

By what gets printed in some of the modern child-psychology books, you would think that girls to whom such a story had been told would never develop normally. Yet, as far as I can remember what happened to the girls in that group, we all grew up about like anybody. Most of us married, some happily, some not so well. We kept house. We learned—more or less—how to live with our husbands, we had children and struggled to bring them up right—we went forward into life, just as if we had never been warned not to.

Perhaps, young as we were that day, we had already had enough experience of life so that we were not quite blank paper for Aunt Minnie's frightening story. Whether we thought of it then or not, we couldn't have failed to see that at this very time, Aunt Minnie had been married for ten years or more, comfortably and well married, too. Against what she tried by that story to brand into our minds stood the cheerful home life in that house, the good-natured, kind, hard-working husband, and the children—

the three rough-and-tumble, nice little boys, so adored by their parents, and the sweet girl baby who died, of whom they could never speak without tears. It was such actual contact with adult life that probably kept generation after generation of girls from being scared by tales like Aunt Minnie's into a neurotic horror of living.

Of course, since Aunt Minnie was so much older than we, her boys grew up to be adolescents and young men while our children were still little enough so that our worries over them were nothing more serious than whooping cough and trying to get them to make their own beds. Two of our aunt's three boys followed, without losing their footing, the narrow path which leads across adolescence into normal adult life. But the middle one, Jake, repeatedly fell off into the morass. "Girl trouble," as the succinct family phrase put it. He was one of those boys who have "charm," whatever we mean by that, and was always being snatched at by girls who would be "all wrong" for him to marry. And once, at nineteen, he ran away from home, whether with one of these girls or not we never heard, for through all her ups and downs with this son, Aunt Minnie tried fiercely to protect him from scandal that might cloud his later life.

Her husband had to stay on his job to earn the family living. She was one who went to find Jake. When it was gossiped around that Jake was in "bad company" his mother drew some money from the family savings-bank account, and silent, white-cheeked, took the train to the city where rumor said he had gone.

Some weeks later he came back with her. With no girl. She had cleared him of that entanglement. As of others, which followed, later. Her troubles seemed over when, at a "suitable" age, he fell in love with a "suitable" girl, married her and took her to live in our shire town, sixteen miles away, where he had a good position. Jake was always bright enough.

Sometimes, idly, people speculated as to what Aunt Minnie had seen that time she went after her runaway son, wondering where her search for him had taken her—very queer places for Aunt Minnie to be in, we imagined. And how could such an ignorant, homekeeping woman ever have known what to say to an errant willful boy to set him straight?

Well, of course, we reflected, watching her later struggles with Jake's erratic ways, she certainly could not have remained ignorant, after seeing over and over what she probably had; after talking with Jake about the things which, a good many times, must have come up with desperate openness between them.

She kept her own counsel. We never knew anything definite about the facts of those experiences of hers. But one day she told a group of us—all then married women—something which gave us a notion about what she had learned from them.

We were hastily making a layette for a not-especially welcome baby in a poor family. In those days, our town had no such thing as a district-nursing service. Aunt Minnie, a vigorous woman of fifty-five, had come in to help. As we sewed, we talked, of course; and because our daughters were near or in their teens, we were comparing notes about the bewildering responsibility of bringing up girls.

After a while, Aunt Minnie remarked. "Well, I hope you teach your girls some *sense*. From what I read, I know you're great on telling them 'the facts,' facts we never heard of when we were girls. Like as not, some facts I don't know, now. But knowing the facts isn't going to do them any more good than not knowing the facts ever did, unless they have some sense taught them, too."

"What do you mean, Aunt Minnie?" one of us asked her uncertainly.

She reflected, threading a needle, "Well, I don't know but what the best way to tell you what I mean is to tell you about something that happened to me, forty years ago. I've never said anything about it before. But I've thought about it a good deal. Maybe—"

She had hardly begun when I recognized the story—her visit to her Cousin Ella's Midwestern home, the widower with his scarred face and saintly reputation and, very vividly, her getting lost in the great cornfield. I knew every word she was going to say—to the very end, I thought.

But no, I did not. Not at all.

She broke off, suddenly, to exclaim with impatience, "Wasn't I the big ninny? But not so big a ninny as that old cousin of mine. I could wring her neck for getting me in such a state. Only she didn't know any better, herself. That was the way they brought young people up in those days, scaring them out of their wits about the awfulness of getting lost, but not telling them a thing about how *not* to get lost. Or how to act, if they did.

"If I had had the sense I was born with, I'd have known that running my legs off in a zigzag was the worst thing I could do. I couldn't have been more than a few feet from the path when I noticed I wasn't on it. My tracks in the loose plow dirt must have been perfectly plain. If I'd h' stood still, and collected my wits, I could have looked down to see which way my footsteps went and just walked back over them to the path and gone on about my business.

"Now I ask you, if I'd been told how to do that, wouldn't it have been a lot better protection for me—if protection was what my aunt thought she wanted to give me—than to scare me so at the idea of being lost that I turned deef-dumb-and-blind when I thought I was?

"And anyhow that patch of corn wasn't as big as she let on. And she knew it wasn't. It was no more than a big field in a farming country. I was a well-grown girl of six-teen, as tall as I am now. If I couldn't have found the path, I could have just walked along one line of cornstalks—*straight*—and I'd have come out somewhere in ten minutes. Fifteen at the most. Maybe not just where I wanted to go. But all right, safe, where decent folks were living."

She paused, as if she had finished. But at the inquiring blankness in our faces, she went on, "Well, now, why isn't teaching girls—and boys, too, for the Lord's sake don't forget they need it as much as the girls—about this man-and-woman business, something like that? If you give them the idea—no matter whether it's *as* you tell them the facts, or as you *don't* tell them the facts, that it is such a terribly scary thing that if they take a step into it, something's likely to happen to them so awful that you're ashamed to tell them what—well, they'll lose their heads and run around like crazy things, first time they take one step away from the path.

"For they'll be trying out the paths, all right. You can't keep them from it. And a good thing too. How else are they going to find out what it's like? Boys' and girls' going to-gether is a path across one corner of growing up. And when they go together, they're likely to get off the path some. Seems to me, it's up to their folks to bring them up so when they do, they don't start screaming and running in circles, but stand still, right where they are, and get their breath and figure out how to get back.

"And anyhow, you don't tell 'em the truth about sex" (I was astonished to hear her use the actual word, taboo to women of her generation) "if they get the idea from you that it's all there is to living. It's not. If you don't get to where you want to go in it, well, there's a lot of landscape all around it a person can have a good time in.

"D'you know, I believe one thing that gives girls and boys the wrong idea is the way folks *look!* My old cousin's face, I can see her now, it was as red as a rooster's comb when she was telling me about men in that cornfield. I be-lieve now she kind of *liked* to talk about it."

(Oh, Aunt Minnie—and yours! I thought.)

Someone asked, "But how *did* you get out, Aunt Minnie?"

She shook her head, laid down her sewing. "More foolishness. That minister my mother's cousin was keeping house for—her son-in-law—I caught sight of him, down along one of the aisles of cornstalks, looking down at the ground, thinking, the way he often did. And I was so glad to see him I rushed right up to him, and flung my arms around his neck and hugged him. He hadn't heard me coming. He gave a great start, put one arm around me and turned his face full towards me—I suppose for just a second he had forgotten how awful one side of it was. His expression, his eyes—well, you're all married women, you know how he looked, the way any able-bodied man thirty-six or -seven, who'd been married and begotten children, would look—for a minute anyhow, if a full-blooded girl of sixteen, who ought to have known better, flung herself at him without any warning, her hair tumbling down, her dress half unbuttoned, and hugged him with all her might.

"I was what they called innocent in those days. That is, I knew just as little about what men are like as my folks could manage I should. But I was old enough to know all right what that look meant. And it gave me a start. But of course the real thing of it was that dreadful scar of his, so close to my face—that wet corner of his mouth, his eye drawn down with the red inside of the lower eyelid showing—

"It turned me so sick, I pulled away with all my might, so fast that I ripped one sleeve nearly loose, and let out a screech like a wildcat. And ran. Did I run? And in a minute, I was through the corn and had come out in the back yard of the house. I hadn't been more than a few feet from it, probably, any of the time. And then I fainted away. Girls were always fainting away; it was the way our corset strings were pulled tight, I suppose, and then— oh, a lot of fuss.

"But anyhow," she finished, picking up her work and going on setting neat, firm stitches with steady hands, "there's one thing, I never told anybody it was Cousin Malcolm I had met in the cornfield. I told my cousin that 'a man had scared me.' And nobody said anything more about it to me, not ever. That was the way they did it in those days. They thought if they didn't let on about something, maybe it wouldn't have happened. I was sent back to Vermont right away and Cousin Malcolm went on being minister of the church. I've always been," said Aunt Minnie moderately, "kind of proud that I didn't go and ruin a man's life for just one second's slip-up. If you could have called it that. For it *would* have ruined him. You know how hard as stone people are about other folks' letdowns. If I'd have told, not one person in that town would have had any charity. Not one would have tried to understand. One slip, *once,* and they'd have pushed him down in the mud. If I had told, I'd have felt pretty bad about it, later— when I came to have more sense. But I declare, I can't see how I came to have the decency, dumb as I was then, to know that it wouldn't be fair."

It was not long after this talk that Aunt Minnie's elderly husband died, mourned by her, by all of us. She lived alone then. It was peaceful October weather for her, in which she kept a firm roundness of face and figure, as quiet-living country-women often do, on into her sixties.

But then Jake, the boy who had had girl trouble, had wife trouble. We heard he had taken to running after a young girl, or was it that she was running after him? It was something serious. For his nice wife left him and came back with the children to live with her mother in our town. Poor Aunt Minnie used to go see her for long talks which made them both cry. And she went to keep house for Jake, for months at a time.

She grew old, during those years. When finally she (or something) managed to get the marriage mended so that Jake's wife relented and went back to live with him, there was no trace left of her pleasant brisk freshness. She was stooped and slow-footed and shrunken. We, her kinspeople, although we would have given our lives for any one of our own children, wondered whether Jake was worth what it had cost his mother to—well, steady him, or reform him. Or perhaps just understand him. Whatever it took.

She came of a long-lived family and was able to go on keeping house for herself well into her eighties. Of course we and the other neighbors stepped in often to make sure she was all right. Mostly, during those brief calls, the talk turned on nothing more vital than her geraniums. But one midwinter afternoon, sitting with her in front of her cozy stove, I chanced to speak in rather hasty blame of someone who had, I thought, acted badly. To my surprise this brought from her the story about the cornfield which she had evidently quite forgotten telling me, twice before.

This time she told it almost dreamily, swaying to and fro in her rocking chair, her eyes fixed on the long slope of snow outside her window. When she came to the encounter with the minister she said, looking away from the distance and back into my eyes, "I know now that I had been, all along, kind of *interested* in him, the way any girl as old as I was would be, in any youngish man living in the same house with her. And a minister, too. They have to have the gift of gab so much more than most men, women get to thinking they are more alive than men who can't talk so well. I *thought* the reason I threw my arms around him was because I had been so scared. And I certainly had been scared, by my old cousin's horrible talk about the cornfield being full of men waiting to grab girls. But that wasn't all the reason I flung myself at Malcolm Fairchild and hugged him. I know that now. Why in the world shouldn't I have been taught *some* notion of it then? 'Twould do girls good to know that they are just like everybody else—human nature *and* sex, all mixed up together. I didn't have to hug him. I wouldn't have, if he'd been dirty or fat and old, or chewed tobacco."

I stirred in my chair, ready to say, "But it's not so simple as all that to tell girls—" and she hastily answered my unspoken protest. "I know, I know, most of it can't be put into words. There just aren't any words to say something that's so both-ways-at-once all the time as this man-and-woman business. But look here, you know as well as I do that there are lots more ways than in words to teach young folks what you want 'em to know."

The old woman stopped her swaying rocker to peer far back into the past with honest eyes. "What was in my mind back there in the cornfield—partly anyhow—was what had been there all the time I was living in the same house with Cousin Malcolm—that he had long straight legs, and broad shoulders, and lots of curly brown hair, and was nice and flat in front, and that one side of his face was good-looking. But most of all, that he and I were really alone, for the first time, without anybody to see us.

"I suppose, if it hadn't been for that dreadful scar, he'd have drawn me up, tight, and—most any man would— kissed me. I know how I must have looked, all red and hot and my hair down and my dress torn open. And, used as he was to big cornfields, he probably never dreamed that the reason I looked that way was because I was scared to be by myself in one. He may have thought—you know what he may have thought.

"Well—if his face had been like anybody's—when he looked at me the way he did, the way a man does look at a woman he wants to have, it would have scared me—some. But I'd have cried, maybe. And probably he'd have kissed me again. You know how such things go. I might have come out of the cornfield halfway engaged to marry him. Why not? I was old enough, as people thought then. That would have been nature. That was probably what he thought of, in that first instant.

"But what did I do? I had one look at his poor, horrible face, and started back as though I'd stepped on a snake. And screamed and ran.

"What do you suppose *he* felt, left there in the corn? He

must have been sure that I would tell everybody he had attacked me. He probably thought that when he came out and went back to the village he'd already be in disgrace and put out of the pulpit.

"But the worst must have been to find out, so rough, so plain from the way I acted—as if somebody had hit him with an ax—the way he would look to any woman he might try to get close to. That must have been—" she drew a long breath, "well, pretty hard on him."

After a silence, she murmured pityingly, "Poor man!"

HOLIDAY

by Katherine Anne Porter

Katherine Anne Porter (1894–1980). A Texan by birth, Miss Porter was educated at home and in Southern girls' schools. She was a professional writer and teacher most of her life. Although her collected work is relatively small in quantity, the list of literary awards and honors she received is very long. She won the Guggenheim Medal for *Pale Horse, Pale Rider,* a Ford grant, and first prize in the 1962 *O'Henry Prize Stories,* and a Pulitzer Prize, among other recognitions. She was also a Fellow of the Library of Congress. Her short stories and novellas have been collected in several volumes, and her 1962 novel *Ship of Fools* was an international success and the basis of an award-winning film.

At that time I was too young for some of the troubles I was having, and I had not yet learned what to do with them. It no longer can matter what kind of troubles they were, or what finally became of them. It seemed to me then there was nothing to do but run away from them, though all my tradition, background, and training had taught me unanswerably that no one except a coward ever runs away from anything. What nonsense! They should have taught me the difference between courage and foolhardiness, instead of leaving me to find it out for myself. I learned finally that

if I still had the sense I was born with, I would take off
like a deer at the first warning of certain dangers. But this
story I am about to tell you happened before this great
truth impressed itself upon me—that we do not run from
the troubles and dangers that are truly ours, and it is
better to learn what they are earlier than later, and if we
don't run from the others, we are fools.

I confided to my friend Louise, a former schoolmate
about my own age, not my troubles but my little problem:
I wanted to go somewhere for a spring holiday, by myself,
to the country, and it should be very simple and nice and,
of course, not expensive, and she was not to tell anyone
where I had gone; but if she liked, I would send her word
now and then, if anything interesting was happening. She
said she loved getting letters but hated answering them; and
she knew the very place for me, and she would not tell anybody anything. Louise had then—she has it still—something near to genius for making improbable persons, places,
and situations sound attractive. She told amusing stories
that did not turn grim on you until a little while later, when
by chance you saw and heard for yourself. So with this
story. Everything was just as Louise had said, if you like,
and everything was, at the same time, quite different.

"I know the very place," said Louise, "a family of real
old-fashioned German peasants, in the deep blackland
Texas farm country, a household in real patriarchal style—
the kind of thing you'd hate to live with but is very nice to
visit. Old father, God Almighty himself, with whiskers and
all; Old mother, matriarch in men's shoes; endless daughters and sons and sons-in-law and fat babies falling about
the place; and fat puppies—my favorite was a darling little
black thing named Kuno—cows, calves, and sheep and
lambs and goats and turkeys and guineas roaming up and
down the shallow green hills, ducks and geese on the ponds.
I was there in the summer when the peaches and water-
melons were in——"

"This is the end of March," I said, doubtfully.

"Spring comes early there," said Louise. "I'll write to the Müllers about you, you just get ready to go."

"Just where is this paradise?"

"Not far from the Louisiana line," said Louise. "I'll ask them to give you my attic—oh, that was a sweet place! It's a big room, with the roof sloping to the floor on each side, and the roof leaks a little when it rains, so the shingles are all stained in beautiful streaks, all black and grey and mossy green, and in one corner there used to be a stack of dime novels, *The Duchess,* Ouida, Mrs. E.D.E.N. Southworth, Ella Wheeler Wilcox's poems—one summer they had a lady boarder who was a great reader, and she went off and left her library. I loved it! And everybody was healthy and good-hearted, and the weather was perfect. . . . How long do you want to stay?"

I hadn't thought of this, so I said at random, "About a month."

A few days later I found myself tossed off like an express package from a dirty little crawling train onto the sodden platform of a country station, where the stationmaster emerged and locked up the waiting room before the train had got round the bend. As he clumped by me he shifted his wad of tobacco to his cheek and asked, "Where you goin'?"

"To the Müller farm," I said, standing beside my small trunk and suitcase with the bitter wind cutting through my thin coat.

"Anybody meet you?" he asked, not pausing.

"They *said* so."

"All right," he said, and got into his little ragged buckboard with a sway-backed horse and drove away.

I turned my trunk on its side and sat on it facing the wind and the desolate mud-colored shapeless scene and began making up my first letter to Louise. First I was going to tell her that unless she was to be a novelist, there was no excuse for her having so much imagination. In daily life, I was going to tell her, there are also such useful things as the plain facts that should be stuck to, through thick and thin. Anything else led to confusion like this. I was beginning to enjoy my letter to Louise when a sturdy boy about twelve years old crossed the platform. As he neared me, he took off his rough cap and bunched it in his thick hand, dirt-stained at the knuckles. His round cheeks, his round nose, his round chin were a cool healthy red. In the globe of his face, as neatly circular as if drawn in bright crayon, his narrow, long, tip-tilted eyes, clear as pale-blue water, seemed out of place, as if two incompatible strains had collided in making him. They were beautiful eyes, and the rest of the face was not to be taken seriously. A blue woollen blouse buttoned up to his chin ended abruptly at his waist as if he would outgrow it in another half hour, and his blue drill breeches flapped about his ankles. His old clodhopper shoes were several sizes too big for him. Altogether, it was plain he was not the first one to wear his clothes. He was a cheerful, detached, self-possessed apparition against the tumbled brown earth and ragged dark sky, and I smiled at him as well as I could with a face that felt like wet clay.

He smiled back slightly without meeting my eye, motioning for me to take up my suitcase. He swung my trunk to his head and tottered across the uneven platform, down the steps slippery with mud where I expected to see him crushed beneath his burden like an ant under a stone. He heaved the trunk into the back of his wagon with a fine smash, took my suitcase and tossed it after, then climbed up over one front wheel while I scrambled my way up over the other.

The pony, shaggy as a wintering bear, eased himself into a grudging trot, while the boy, bowed over with his cap pulled down over his ears and eyebrows, held the reins slack and fell into a brown study. I studied the harness, a real mystery. It met and clung in all sorts of unexpected places; it parted company in what appeared to be strategic seats of jointure. It was mended sketchily in risky places with bits of hairy rope. Other seemingly unimportant parts were bound together irrevocably with wire. The bridle was too long for the pony's stocky head, so he had shaken the bit out of his mouth at the start, apparently, and went his own way at his own pace.

Our vehicle was an exhausted specimen of something called a spring wagon, who knows why? There were no springs, and the shallow enclosed platform at the back, suitable for carrying various plunder, was worn away until it barely reached midway of the back wheels, one side of it steadily scraping the iron tire. The wheels themselves spun not dully around and around in the way of common wheels, but elliptically, being loosened at the hubs, so that we proceeded with a drunken, hilarious swagger, like the rolling motion of a small boat on a choppy sea.

The soaked brown fields fell away on either side of the lane, all rough with winter-worn stubble ready to sink and become earth again. The scanty leafless woods ran along an edge of the field nearby. There was nothing beautiful in those woods now except the promise of spring, for I detested bleakness, but it gave me pleasure to think that beyond this there might be something else beautiful in its own being, a river shaped and contained by its banks, or a field stripped down to its true meaning, ploughed and ready for the seed. The road turned abruptly and was almost hidden for a moment, and we were going through the woods. Closer sight of the crooked branches assured me that spring was beginning, if sparely, reluctantly: the leaves were budding in tiny cones of watery green besprinkling all the new shoots; a thin sedate rain began again to fall, not so opaque as a fog, but a mist that merely deepened overhead, and lowered, until the clouds became rain in one swathing, delicate grey.

As we emerged from the woods, the boy roused himself and pointed forward, in silence. We were approaching the farm along the skirts of a fine peach orchard, now faintly colored with young bud, but there was nothing to disguise the gaunt and aching ugliness of the farmhouse itself. In this Texas valley, so gently modulated with small crests and shallows, "rolling country" as the farmers say, the house was set on the peak of the barest rise of ground, as if the most infertile spot had been thriftily chosen for building a shelter. It stood there staring and naked, an intruding stranger, strange even beside the barns ranged generously along the back, low-eaved and weathered to the color of stone.

The narrow windows and the steeply sloping roof oppressed me; I wished to turn away and go back. I had come a long way to be so disappointed, I thought, and yet I must go on, for there could be nothing here for me more painful than what I had left. But as we drew near the house, now hardly visible except for the yellow lamplight in the back, perhaps in the kitchen, my feelings changed again toward warmth and tenderness, or perhaps just an apprehension that I could feel so, maybe, again.

The wagon drew up before the porch, and I started climbing down. No sooner had my foot touched ground than an enormous black dog of the detestable German shepherd breed leaped silently at me, and as silently I covered my face with my arms and leaped back. "Kuno, down!" shouted the boy, lunging at him. The front door flew open and a young girl with yellow hair ran down the steps and seized the ugly beast by the scruff. "He does not mean anything." she said seriously in English. "He is only a dog."

Just Louise's darling little puppy Kuno, I thought, a year or so older. Kuno whined, apologized by bowing and scraping one front paw on the ground, and the girl holding his scruff said, shyly and proudly, "I teach him that. He has always such bad manners, but I teach him!"

I had arrived, it seemed, at the moment when the evening chores were about to begin. The entire Müller household streamed out of the door, each man and woman going about the affairs of the moment. The young girl walked with me up the porch and said, "This is my brother Hans," and a young man paused to shake hands and passed by. "This is my brother Fritz," she said, and Fritz took my hand and dropped it as he went. "My sister Annetje," said the young girl, and a quiet young woman with a baby draped loosely like a scarf over her shoulder smiled and held out her hand. Hand after hand went by, their palms variously younger or older, broad or small, male or female, but all thick hard decent peasant hands, warm and strong. And in every face I saw again the pale, tilted eyes, on every head that taffy-colored hair, as though they might all be brothers and sisters, though Annetje's husband and still another daughter's husband had gone by after greeting me. In the wide hall with a door at front and back, full of cloudy light and the smell of soap, the old mother, also on her way out, stopped to offer her hand. She was a tall strong-looking woman wearing a three-cornered black wool shawl on her head, her skirts looped up over a brown flannel petticoat. Not from her did the young ones get those water-clear eyes. Hers were black and shrewd and searching, a band of hair showed black streaked with grey, her seamed dry face was brown as seasoned bark, and she walked in her rubber boots with the stride of a man. She shook my hand briefly and said in German English that I was welcome, smiling and showing her blackened teeth.

"This is my girl Hatsy," she told me, "and she will show you to your room." Hatsy took my hand as if I were a child needing a guide. I followed her up a flight of steps steep as a ladder, and there we were, in Louise's attic room, with the sloping roof. Yes, the shingles were stained all the colors she had said. There were the dime novels heaped in the corner. For once, Louise had got it straight, and it was homely and familiar, as if I had seen it before. "My mother says we could give you a better place on the downstairs," said Hatsy, in her soft blurred English, "but *she* said in her letter you would like it so." I told her indeed I did like it so. She went down the steep stairs then, and her brother came up as if he were climbing a tree, with the trunk on his head and the suitcase in his right hand, and I could not see what kept the trunk from crashing back to the bottom, as he used the left hand to climb with. I wished to offer help but feared to insult him, having noted well the tremendous ease and style with which he had hurled the luggage around before, a strong man doing his turn before a weakling audience. He put his burden down and straightened up, wriggling his shoulders and panting only a little. I thanked him and he pushed his cap back and pulled it forward again, which I took for some sort of polite response, and clattered out hugely. Looking out of my window a few minutes later, I saw him setting off across the fields carrying a lighted lantern and a large steel trap.

I began changing my first letter to Louise. "I'm going to like it here. I don't quite know why, but it's going to be all right. Maybe I can tell you later——"

The sound of the German speech in the household below was part of the pleasantness, for they were not talking to me and did not expect me to answer. All the German I understood then was contained in five small deadly sentimental songs of Heine's, learned by heart; and this was a very different tongue, Low German corrupted by three generations in a foreign country. A dozen miles away, where Texas and Louisiana melted together in a rotting swamp whose sluggish under-tow of decay nourished the roots of pine and cedar, a colony of French emigrants had lived out two hundred years of exile, not wholly incorruptible, but mystically faithful to the marrow of their bones, obstinately speaking their old French by then as strange to the French as it was to the English. I had known many of these families during a certain long summer happily remembered, and here again, listening to another language nobody could understand except those of this small farming community, I knew that I was again in a house of perpetual exile. These were solid, practical, hard-bitten, land-holding German peasants, who struck their mattocks into the earth deep and held fast wherever they were, because to them life and the land were one indivisible thing; but never in any wise did they confuse nationality with habitation.

I liked the thick warm voices, and it was good not to have to understand what they were saying. I loved that silence which means freedom from the constant pressure of other minds and other opinions and other feelings, that freedom to fold up in quiet and go back to my own center, to find out again, for it is always a rediscovery, what kind of creature it is that rules me finally, makes all the decisions no matter who thinks they make them, even I; who little by little takes everything away except the one thing I cannot live without, and who will one day say, "Now I am all you have left—take me." I paused there a good while listening to this muted unknown language which was silence with music in it; I could be moved and touched but not troubled by it, as by the crying of frogs or the wind in the trees.

The catalpa tree at my window would, I noticed, when it came into leaf, shut off my view of the barns and the fields beyond. When in bloom the branches would almost reach through the window. But now they were a thin screen through which the calves, splotchy red and white, moved prettily against the weathered darkness of the sheds. The brown fields would soon be green again; the sheep washed by the rains and become clean grey. All the beauty of the landscape now was in the harmony of the valley rolling fluently away to the wood's edge. It was an inland country, with the forlorn look of all unloved things; winter in this part of the south is a moribund coma, not the northern death sleep with the sure promise of resurrection. But in my south, my loved and never-forgotten country, after her long sickness, with only a slight stirring, an opening of the eyes between one breath and the next, between night and day, the earth revives and bursts into the plenty of spring with fruit and flowers together, spring and summer at once under the hot shimmering blue sky.

The freshening wind promised another light sedate rain

to come at evening. The voices below stairs dispersed, rose
again, separately calling from the yards and barns. The old
woman strode down the path toward the cow sheds, Hatsy
running behind her. The woman wore her wooden yoke,
with the milking pails covered and closed with iron hasps,
slung easily across her shoulders, but her daughter carried
two tin milking pails on her arm. When they pushed back
the bars of cedar which opened onto the fields, the cows
came through lowing and crowding, and the calves scampered each to his own dam with reaching, opened mouths.
Then there was the battle of separating the hungry children
from their mothers when they had taken their scanty share.
The old woman slapped their little haunches with her open
palm, Hatsy dragged at their halters, her feet slipping wide
in the mud, the cows bellowed and brandished their horns,
the calves bawled like rebellious babies. Hatsy's long yellow braids whisked around her shoulders, her laughter was
a shrill streak of gaiety above the angry cow voices and the
raucous shouting of the old woman.

From the kitchen porch below came the sound of splashing water, the creaking of the pump handle, and the stamp-
ing boots of men. I sat in the window watching the darkness come on slowly, while all the lamps were being lighted.
My own small lamp had a handle on the oil bowl, like a
cup's. There was also a lantern with a frosted chimney
hanging by a nail on the wall. A voice called to me from
the foot of my stairs and I looked down into the face of a
dark-skinned, flaxen-haired young woman, far advanced
in pregnancy, and carrying a prosperous year-old boy on
her hip, one arm clutching him to her, the other raised
above her head so that her lantern shone upon their heads.
"The supper is now ready," she said, and waited for me
to come down before turning away.

In the large square room the whole family was gathering
at a long table covered with a red checkered cotton cloth,
with heaped-up platters of steaming food at either end. A
crippled and badly deformed servant girl was setting down

pitchers of milk. Her face was so bowed over it was almost hidden, and her whole body was maimed in some painful, mysterious way, probably congenital, I supposed, though she seemed wiry and tough. Her knotted hands shook continually, her wagging head kept pace with her restless elbows. She ran unsteadily around the table scattering plates, dodging whoever stood in her way; no one moved aside for her, or spoke to her, or even glanced after her when she vanished into the kitchen.

The men then moved forward to their chairs. Father Müller took his patriarch's place at the head of the table, Mother Müller looming behind him like a dark boulder. The younger men ranged themselves about on one side, the married ones with their wives standing back of their chairs to serve them, for three generations in this country had not made them self-conscious or disturbed their ancient customs. The two sons-in-law and three sons rolled down their shirt sleeves before beginning to eat. Their faces were polished with recent scrubbing and their open collars were damp.

Mother Müller pointed to me, then waved her hand at her household, telling off their names rapidly. I was a stranger and a guest, so was seated on the men's side of the table, and Hatsy, whose real name turned out to be Huldah, the maiden of the family, was seated on the children's side of the board, attending to them and keeping them in order. These infants ranged from two years to ten, five in number—not counting the one still straddling his mother's hip behind his father's chair—divided between the two married daughters. The children ravened and gorged and reached their hands into the sugar bowl to sprinkle sugar on everything they ate, solemnly elated over their food and paying no attention to Hatsy who struggled with them only a little less energetically than she did with the calves, and ate almost nothing. She was about seventeen years old, pale-lipped and too thin, and her sleek fine butter-yellow hair, streaked light and dark, real German peasant hair, gave her an air of fragility. But she shared the big-boned structure and the enormous energy and animal force that was like a bodily presence itself in the room; and seeing Father Müller's pale-grey deep-set choleric eyes and high cheekbones, it was easy to trace the family resemblance around the table: it was plain that poor Mother Müller had never had a child of her own—black-eyed, black-haired South Germany people. True, she had borne them, but that was all; they belonged to their father. Even the tawny Gretchen, expecting another baby, obviously the pet of the family, with the sly smiling manner of a spoiled child, who wore the contented air of a lazy, healthy young animal, seeming always about to yawn, had hair like pulled taffy and those slanted clear eyes. She stood now easing the weight of her little boy on her husband's chair back, reaching with her left arm over his shoulder to refill his plate from time to time.

Annetje, the eldest daughter, carried her newly born baby over her shoulder, where he drooled comfortably down her back, while she spooned things from platters and bowls for her husband. Whenever their eyes met, they smiled with a gentle, reserved warmth in their eyes, the smile of long and sure friendship.

Father Müller did not in the least believe in his children's marrying and leaving home. Marry, yes, of course; but must that take a son or daughter from him? He always could provide work and a place in the household for his daughters' husbands, and in time he would do the same for his sons' wives. A new room had lately been built on, to the northeast, Annetje explained to me, leaning above her husband's head and talking across the table, for Hatsy to live in when she should be married. Hatsy turned very beautifully pink and ducked her head almost into her plate, then looked up boldly and said, "Jah, jah, I am marrit now soon!" Everybody laughed except Mother Müller, who said in German that girls at home never knew when they were well off—no, they must go bringing in husbands. This remark did not seem to hurt anybody's feelings, and Gretchen said it was nice that I was going to be here for the wedding. This reminded Annetje of something, and she spoke in English to the table at large, saying that the Lutheran pastor had advised her to attend church oftener and put her young ones in Sunday school, so that God would give her a blessing with her fifth child. I counted around again, and sure enough, with Gretchen's unborn, there were eight children at that table under the age of ten; somebody was going to need a blessing in all that crowd, no doubt. Father Müller delivered a short speech to his daughter in German, then turned to me and said, "What I say iss, it iss all craziness to go to church and pay a preacher goot money to talk his nonsense. Say rather that he pay me to come and lissen, then I vill go!" His eyes glared with sudden fierceness above his square speckled grey and yellow beard that sprouted directly out from the high cheekbones. "He thinks, so, that my time maybe costs nothing? That iss goot! Let him pay me!"

Mother Müller snorted and shuffled her feet. "Ach, you talk, you talk. Now you vill make the pastor goot and mad if he hears. Vot ve do, if he vill not chrissen the babies?"

"You give him goot money, he vill chrissen," shouted Father Müller. "You vait und see!"

"Ah sure, dot iss so," agreed Mother Müller. "Only do not let him hear!"

There was a gust of excited talk in German, with much rapping of knife handles on the table. I gave up trying to understand, but watched their faces. It sounded like a pitched battle, but they were agreeing about something. They were united in their tribal scepticisms, as in everything else. I got a powerful impression that they were all, even the sons-in-law, one human being divided into several separate appearances. The crippled servant girl brought in more food and gathered up plates and went away in her limping run, and she seemed to me the only individual in the house. Even I felt divided into many fragments, having left or lost a part of myself in every place I had travelled, in every life mine had touched, above all, in every death of someone near to me that had carried into the grave some part of my living cells. But the servant, she was whole, and belonged nowhere.

I settled easily enough into the marginal life of the household ways and habits. Day began early at the Müllers', and we ate breakfast by yellow lamplight, with the grey damp winds blowing with spring softness through the open windows. The men swallowed their last cups of steaming coffee standing, with their hats on, and went out to harness the horses to the ploughs at sunrise. Annetje, with her fat baby slung over her shoulder, could sweep a room or make a bed with one hand, all finished before the day was well begun; and she spent the rest of the day outdoors, caring for the chickens and the pigs. Now and then she came in with a shallow boxful of newly hatched chickens, abject dabs of wet fluff, and put them on a table in her bedroom where she might tend them carefully on their first day. Mother Müller strode about hugely, giving orders right and left, while Father Müller, smoothing his whiskers and lighting his pipe, drove away to town with Mother Müller calling out after him final directions and instructions about household needs. He never spoke a word to her and appeared not to be listening, but he always returned in a few hours with every commission and errand performed exactly. After I had made my own bed and set my attic in order, there was nothing at all for me to do, and I walked out of this enthusiastic bustle into the lane, feeling extremely useless. But the repose, the almost mystical inertia of their minds in the midst of this muscular life, communicated itself to me little by little, and I absorbed it gratefully in silence and felt all the hidden knotted painful places in my own mind beginning to loosen. It was easier to breathe, and I might even weep, if I pleased. In a very few days I no longer felt like weeping.

One morning I saw Hatsy spading up the kitchen garden plot, and my offer to help, to spread the seeds and cover them was accepted. We worked at this for several hours each morning, until the warmth of the sun and the stooping posture induced in me a comfortable vertigo. I forgot to count the days, they were one like the other except as the colors of the air changed, deepening and warming to keep step with the advancing season, and the earth grew firmer underfoot with the swelling tangle of crowding roots.

The children, so hungry and noisy at the table, were peaceable little folk who played silent engrossed games in the front yard. They were always kneading mud into loaves and pies and carrying their battered dolls and cotton rag animals through the operations of domestic life. They fed them, put them to bed; they got them up and fed them again, set them to their chores making mud loaves; or they would harness themselves to their carts and gallop away to a great shady chestnut tree on the opposite side of the house. Here the tree became the *Turnverein,* and they themselves were again human beings, solemnly ambling about in a dance and going through the motions of drinking beer. Miraculously changed once more into horses, they harnessed themselves and galloped home. They came at call to be fed and put to sleep with the docility of their own toys or animal playmates. Their mothers handled them with instinctive, constant gentleness; they never seemed to be troubled by them. They were as devoted and caretaking as a cat with her kittens.

Sometimes I took Annetje's next to youngest child, a baby of two years, in her little wagon, and we would go down through the orchard, where the branches were beginning to sprout in cones of watery green, and into the lane for a short distance. I would turn again into a smaller lane, smoother because less travelled, and we would go slowly between the aisle of mulberry trees where the fruit was beginning to hang and curl like green furry worms. The baby would sit in a compact mound of flannel and calico, her pale-blue eyes tilted and shining under her cap, her two lower teeth showing in a rapt smile. Sometimes several of the other children would follow along quietly. When I turned, they all turned without question, and we would proceed back to the house as sedately as we had set out.

The narrow lane, I discovered, led to the river, and it became my favorite walk. Almost every day I went along the edge of the naked wood, passionately occupied with looking for signs of spring. The changes there were so subtle and gradual I found one day that branches of willows and sprays of blackberry vine alike were covered with fine points of green; the color had changed overnight, or so it seemed, and I knew that tomorrow the whole valley and wood and edge of the river would be quick and feathery with golden green blowing in the winds.

And it was so. On that day I did not leave the river until after dark and came home through the marsh with the owls and night jars crying over my head, calling in a strange and broken chorus in the woods until the farthest answering cry was a ghostly echo. When I went through the orchard the trees were all abloom with fireflies. I stopped and looked at it for a long time, then walked slowly, amazed, for I had never seen anything that was more beautiful to me. The trees were freshly budded out with pale bloom, the branches were immobile in the thin darkness, but the flower clusters shivered in a soundless dance of delicately woven light, whirling as airily as leaves in a breeze, as rhythmically as water in a fountain. Every tree was budded out with this living, pulsing fire as fragile and cool as bubbles. When I opened the gate their light shone on my hands like fox fire. When I looked back, the shimmer of golden light was there, it was no dream.

Hatsy was on her knees in the dining room, washing the floor with heavy dark rags. She always did this work at night, so the men with their heavy boots would not be tracking it up again and it would be immaculate in the morning. She turned her young face to me in a stupor of fatigue. "Ottilie! Ottilie!" she called, loudly, and before I could speak, she said, "Ottilie will give you supper. It is waiting, all ready." I tried to tell her that I was not hungry, but she wished to reassure me. "Look, we all must eat. Now or then, it's no trouble." She sat back on her heels, and raising her head, looked over the window sill at the orchard. She smiled and paused for a moment and said happily, "Now it is come spring. Every spring we have that." She bent again over the great pail of water with her mops.

The crippled servant came in, stumbling perilously on the slippery floor, and set a dish before me, lentils with sausage and red chopped cabbage. It was hot and savory and I was truly grateful, for I found I was hungry, after all. I looked at her—so her name was Ottilie?—and said, "Thank you." "She can't talk," said Hatsy, simply stating a fact that need not be emphasized. The blurred, dark face was neither young nor old, but crumpled into criss cross wrinkles, irrelevant either to age or suffering; simply wrinkles, patternless blackened seams as if the perishable flesh had been wrung in a hard cruel fist. Yet in that mutilated face I saw high cheekbones, slanted water-blue eyes, the pupils very large and strained with the anxiety of one peering into a darkness full of danger. She jarred heavily against the table as she turned, her bowed back trembling with the perpetual working of her withered arms, and ran away in aimless, driven haste.

Hatsy sat on her heels again for a moment, tossed her braids back over her shoulder and said, "That is Ottilie. She is not sick now. She is only like that since she was sick when she was a baby. But she can work so well as I can. She cooks. But she cannot talk so you can understand." She went up on her knees, bowed over, and began to scrub again, with new energy. She was really a network of thin taut ligaments and long muscles elastic as woven steel. She would always work too hard, and be tired all her life, and never know that this was anything but perfectly natural;

everybody worked all the time, because there was always more work waiting when they had finished what they were doing then. I ate my supper and took my plate to the kitchen and set it on the table. Ottilie was sitting in a kitchen chair with her feet in the open oven, her arms folded and her head waggling a little. She did not see or hear me.

At home, Hatsy wore an old brown corduroy dress and galoshes without stockings. Her skirts were short enough to show her thin legs, slightly crooked below the knees, as if she had walked too early. "Hatsy, she's a good, quick girl," said Mother Müller, to whom praising anybody or anything did not come easily. On Saturdays, Hatsy took a voluminous bath in a big tub in the closet back of the kitchen, where also were stored the extra chamber pots, slop jars, and water jugs. She then unplaited her yellow hair and bound up the crinkled floss with a wreath of pink cotton rosebuds, put on her pale-blue China silk dress, and went to the *Turnverein* to dance and drink a seidel of dark-brown beer with her suitor, who resembled her brothers enough to be her brother, though I think nobody ever noticed this except myself, and I said nothing because it would have been the remark of a stranger and hopeless outsider. On Sundays, the entire family went to the *Turnverein* after copious washings, getting into starched dresses and shirts, and getting the baskets of food stored in the wagons. The servant, Ottilie, would rush out to see them off, standing with both shaking arms folded over her forehead, shading her troubled eyes to watch them to the turn of the lane. Her muteness seemed nearly absolute; she had no coherent language of signs. Yet three times a day she spread that enormous table with solid food, freshly baked bread, huge platters of vegetables, immoderate roasts of meat, extravagant tarts, strudels, pies—enough for twenty people. If neighbors came in for an afternoon on some holiday, Ottilie would stumble into the big north room, the parlor, with its golden oak melodeon, a harsh-green Brussels carpet, Nottingham lace curtains, crocheted lace antimacassars on the chair backs, to serve them coffee with cream and sugar and thick slices of yellow cake.

Mother Müller sat but seldom in her parlor, and always with an air of formal unease, her knotted big fingers cramped in a cluster. But Father Müller often sat there in the evenings, where no one ventured to follow him unless commanded; he sometimes played chess with his elder son-in-law, who had learned a good while ago that Father Müller was a good player who abhorred an easy victory, and he dared not do less than put up the best fight he was able, but even so, if Father Müller felt himself winning too often, he would roar, "No, you are not trying! You are not doing your best. Now we stop this nonsense!" and his son-in-law would find himself dismissed in temporary disgrace.

Most evenings, however, Father Müller sat by himself and read *Das Kapital*. He would settle deep into the red plush base rocker and spread the volume upon a low table before him. It was an early edition in blotty black German type, stained and ragged in its leather cover, the pages falling apart, a very bible. He knew whole chapters almost by heart, and added nothing to, took nothing from, the canonical, once-delivered text. I cannot say at that time of my life I had never heard of *Das Kapital*, but I had certainly never known anyone who had read it, though if anyone mentioned it, it was always with profound disapproval. It was not a book one had to read in order to reject it. And here was this respectable old farmer who accepted its dogma as a religion—that is to say, its legendary inapplicable precepts were just, right, proper, one must believe in them, of course, but life, everyday living, was another and unrelated thing. Father Müller was the richest man in his community; almost every neighboring farmer rented land from him, and some of them worked it on the share system. He explained this to me one evening after he had given up trying to teach me chess. He was not surprised that I could not learn, at least not in one lesson, and he was not surprised either that I knew nothing about *Das Kapital*. He explained his own arrangements to me thus: "These men, they cannot buy their land. The land must be bought, for Kapital owns it, and Kapital will not give back to the worker the land that is his. Well, somehow, I can always buy land. Why? I do not know. I only know that with my first land here I made good crops to buy more land, and so I rent it cheap, more than anybody else I rent it cheap, I lend money so my neighbors do not fall into the hands of the bank, and so I am not Kapital. Someday these workers, they can buy land from me, for less than they can get it anywhere else. Well, that is what I can do, that is all." He turned over a page, and his angry grey eyes looked out at me under his shaggy brows. "I buy land with my hard work, all my life, and I rent it cheap to my neighbors, and then they say they will not elect my son-in-law, my Annetje's husband, to be sheriff because I am atheist. So then I say, all right, but next year you pay more for your land or more shares for your crops. If I am atheist I will act like one. So, my Annetje's husband is sheriff, that is all."

He had put a stubby forefinger on a line to mark his place, and now he sank himself into his book, and I left quietly without saying good night.

The *Turnverein* was an octagonal pavilion set in a cleared space in a patch of woods belonging to Father Müller. The German colony came here to sit about in the cool shade, while a small brass band played cloppity country dances. The girls danced with energy and direction, their starched petticoats rustling like dry leaves. The boys were more awkward, but willing; they clutched their partners' waists and left crumpled sweaty spots where they clutched. Here Mother Müller took her ease after a hard week. Her gaunt limbs would relax, her knees spread squarely apart, and she would gossip over her beer with the women of her own generation. They would cast an occasional caretaking glance at the children playing nearby, allowing the younger mothers freedom to dance or sit in peace with their own friends.

On the other side of the pavilion, Father Müller would sit with the sober grandfathers, their long curved pipes wagging on their chests as they discussed local politics with profound gravity, their hard peasant fatalism tempered only a little by a shrewd worldly distrust of all officeholders not personally known to them, all political plans except their own immediate ones. When Father Müller talked, they listened respectfully, with faith in him as a strong man, head of his own house and his community. They nodded slowly whenever he took his pipe from his mouth and gestured, holding it by the bowl as if it were a stone he was getting ready to throw. On our way back from the *Turnverein* one evening, Mother Müller said to me, "Well, now, by the grace of Gott it is all settled between Hatsy and her man. It is next Sunday by this time they will be marrit."

All the folk who usually went to the *Turnverein* on Sundays came instead to the Müller house for the wedding. They brought useful presents, mostly bed linen, pillow covers, a white counterpane, with a few ornaments for the bridal chamber—a home-braided round rug in many colors, a brass-bottomed lamp with a round pink chimney decorated with red roses, a stone china washbowl and pitcher also covered with red roses; and the bridegroom's gift to the bride was a necklace, a double string of red coral twigs. Just before the short ceremony began, he slipped the necklace over her head with trembling hands. She smiled up at him shakily and helped him disentangle her short veil from the coral, then they joined hands and turned their faces to the pastor, not letting go until time for the exchange of rings—the widest, thickest, reddest gold bands to be found, no doubt—and at that moment they both stopped smiling and turned a little pale. The groom recovered first, and bent over—he was considerably taller than she—and kissed her on the forehead. His eyes were a deep blue, and his hair not really Müller taffy color, but a light chestnut; a good-looking, gentle-tempered boy, I decided, and he looked at Hatsy as if he liked what he saw. They knelt and clasped hands again for the final prayer, then stood together and exchanged the bridal kiss, a very chaste reserved one, still not on the lips. Then everybody came to shake hands and the men all kissed the bride and the women all kissed the groom. Some of the women whispered in Hatsy's ear, and all burst out laughing except Hatsy, who turned red from her forehead to her throat. She whispered in turn to her husband, who nodded in agreement. She then tried to slip away quietly, but the watchful young girls were after her, and shortly we saw her running through the blossoming orchard, holding up her white ruffled skirts, with all the girls in pursuit, shrieking and calling like excited hunters, for the first to overtake and touch her would be the next bride. They returned, breathless, dragging the lucky one with them, and held her against her ecstatic resistance, while all the young boys kissed her.

The guests stayed on for a huge supper, and Ottilie came in, wearing a fresh blue apron, sweat beaded in the wrinkles of her forehead and around her formless mouth, and passed the food around the table. The men ate first and then Hatsy came in with the women for the first time, still wearing her square little veil of white cotton net bound on her hair with peach blossoms shattered in the bride's race. After supper, one of the girls played waltzes and polkas on the melodeon, and everyone danced. The bridegroom drew gallons of beer from a keg set up in the hall, and at midnight everybody went away, warmly emotional and happy. I went down to the kitchen for a pitcher of hot water. The servant was still setting things to rights, hobbling between table and cupboard. Her face was a brown smudge of anxiety, her eyes were wide and dazed. Her uncertain hands rattled among the pans, but nothing could make her seem real, or in any way connected with the life around her. Yet when I set my pitcher on the stove, she lifted the heavy kettle and poured the scalding water into it without spilling a drop.

The clear honey green of the early morning sky was a mirror of the bright earth. At the edge of the woods there had sprung a reticent blooming of small white and pale-colored flowers. The peach trees were now each a separate nosegay of shell rose and white. I left the house, meaning to take the short path across to the lane of mulberries. The women were deep in the house, the men were away to the fields, the animals were turned into the pastures, and only Ottilie was visible, sitting on the steps of the back porch peeling potatoes. She gazed in my direction with eyes that fell short of me, and seemed to focus on a point midway between us, and gave no sign. Then she dropped her knife and rose, her mouth opened and closed several times, she strained toward me, motioning with her right hand. I went to her, her hands came out and clutched my sleeve, and for a moment I feared to hear her voice. There was no sound from her, but she drew me along after her, full of some mysterious purpose of her own. She opened the door of a dingy bitter-smelling room, windowless, which opened off the kitchen, beside the closet where Hatsy took her baths. A lumpy narrow cot and chest of drawers supporting a blistered looking-glass almost filled the space. Ottilie's lips moved, struggling for speech, as she pulled and tumbled over a heap of rubbish in the top drawer. She took out a photograph and put it in my hands. It was in the old style, faded to a dirty yellow, mounted on cardboard elaborately clipped and gilded at the edges.

I saw a girl child about five years old, a pretty smiling German baby, looking curiously like a slightly elder sister of Annetje's two-year-old, wearing a frilled frock and a prodigious curl of blonde hair, called a roach, on the crown of her head. The strong legs, round as sausages, were encased in long white ribbed stockings, and the square firm feet were laced into old-fashioned soft-soled black boots.

Ottilie peered over the picture, twisted her neck, and looked up into my face. I saw the slanted water-blue eyes and the high cheekbones of the Müllers again, mutilated, almost destroyed, but unmistakable. This child was what she had been, and she was without doubt the elder sister of Annetje and Gretchen and Hatsy; in urgent pantomime she insisted that this was so—she patted the picture and her own face, and strove terribly to speak. She pointed to the name written carefully on the back, Ottilie, and touched her mouth with her bent knuckles. Her head wagged in her perpetual nod; her shaking hand seemed to flap the photograph at me in a roguish humor. The bit of cardboard connected her at once somehow to the world of human beings I knew; for an instant some filament lighter than cobweb spun itself out between that living center in her and in me, a filament from some center that held us all bound to our unescapable common source, so that her life and mine were kin, even a part of each other, and the painfulness and strangeness of her vanished. She knew well that she had been Ottilie, with those steady legs and watching eyes, and she was Ottilie still within herself. For a moment, being alive, she knew she suffered, for she stood and shook with silent crying, smearing away her tears with the open palm of her hand. Even while her cheeks were wet, her face changed. Her eyes cleared and fixed themselves upon that point in space which seemed for her to contain her unaccountable and terrible troubles. She turned her head as if she had heard a voice and disappeared in her staggering run into the kitchen, leaving the drawer open and the photograph face downward on the chest.

At midday meal she came hurrying and splashing coffee on the white floor, restored to her own secret existence of perpetual amazement, and again I had been a stranger to her like all the rest but she was no stranger to me, and could not be again.

The youngest brother came in, holding up an opossum he had caught in his trap. He swung the furry body from side to side, his eyes fairly narrowed with pride as he showed us the mangled creature. "No it is cruel, even for the wild animals," said gentle Annetje to me, "but boys love to kill, they love to hurt things. I am always afraid he will trap poor Kuno." I thought privately that Kuno, a wolfish, ungracious beast, might well prove a match for any trap. Annetje was full of silent, tender solicitudes. The kittens, the puppies, the chicks, the lambs and calves were her special care. She was the only one of the women who caressed the weanling calves when she set the pans of milk before them. Her child seemed as much a part of her as if it were not yet born. Still, she seemed to have forgotten that Ottilie was her sister. So had all the others. I remembered how Hatsy had spoken her name but had not said she was her sister. Their silence about her was, I realized, exactly that—simple forgetfulness. She moved among them as invisible to their imaginations as a ghost. Ottilie their sister was something painful that had happened long ago and now was past and done for; they could not live with that memory or its visible reminder—they forgot her in pure self-defense. But I could not forget her. She drifted into my mind like a bit of weed carried in a current and caught there, floating but fixed, refusing to be carried away. I reasoned it out. The Müllers, what else could they have done with Ottilie? By a physical accident in her childhood she had been stripped of everything but her mere existence. It was not a society or a class that pampered its invalids and the unfit. So long as one lived, one did one's share. This was her place, in this family she had been born and must die; did she suffer? No one asked, no one looked to see. Suffering went with life, suffering and labor. While one lived one worked, that was all, and without complaints, for no one had time to listen, and everybody had his own troubles. So, what else could they have done with Ottilie? As for me, I could do nothing but promise myself that I would forget her, too; and to remember her for the rest of my life.

Sitting at the long table, I would watch Ottilie clattering about in her tormented haste, bringing in that endless food that represented all her life's labors. My mind would follow her into the kitchen where I could see her peering into the great simmering kettles, the crowded oven, her whole body a mere machine of torture. Straight up to the surface of my mind the thought would come urgently, clearly, as if driving time toward the desired event: Let it be now, let it be *now*. Not even tomorrow, no, today. Let her sit down quietly in her rickety chair by the stove and fold those arms, and let us find her there like that, with her head fallen forward on her knees. She will rest then. I would wait, hoping she might not come again, ever again, through the door I gazed at with wincing eyes, as if I might see something unendurable enter through it. Then she would come, and it was only Ottilie, after all, in the bosom of her family, and one of its most useful and competent members; and they with a deep right instinct had learned to live with her disaster on its own terms, and hers; they had accepted and then made use of what was for them only one more painful event in a world full of troubles, many of them much worse than this. So, a step at a time, I followed the Müllers as nearly as I could in their acceptance of Ottilie, and the use they made of her life, for in some way that I could not quite explain to myself, I found great virtue and courage in their steadiness and refusal to feel sorry for anybody, least of all for themselves.

Gretchen bore her child, a son, conveniently between the hours of supper and bedtime, one evening of friendly and domestic-sounding rain. The next day brought neighboring women from miles around, and the child was bandied about among them as if he were a new kind of medicine ball. Sedate and shy at dances, emotional at weddings, they were ribald and jocose at births. Over coffee and beer the talk grew broad, the hearty gutturals were swallowed in the belly of laughter; those honest hard-working wives and mothers saw life for a few hours as a hearty low joke, and it did them good. The baby bawled and suckled like a young calf, and the men of the family came in for a look and added their joyful improprieties.

Cloudy weather drove them home earlier than they had meant to go. The whole sky was lined with smoky black and grey vapor hanging in ragged wisps like soot in a chimney. The edges of the woods turned dull purple as the horizon reddened slowly, then faded, and all across the sky ran a deep shuddering mumble of thunder. All the Müllers hurried about getting into rubber boots and oilcloth overalls, shouting to each other, making their plan of action. The youngest boy came over the ridge of the hill with Kuno helping him to drive the sheep down into the fold. Kuno was barking, the sheep were baaing and bleating, the horses freed from the ploughs were excited; they whinnied and trotted at the lengths of their halters, their ears laid back. The cows were bawling in distress and the calves cried back to them. All the men went out among the animals to round them up and quiet them and get them enclosed safely. Even as Mother Müller, her half-dozen petticoats looped about her thighs and tucked into her hip boots, was striding to join them in the barns, the cloud rack was split end to end by a shattering blow of lightning, and the cloudburst struck the house with the impact of a wave against a ship. The wind broke the window-panes and the floods poured through. The roof beams strained and the walls bent inward, but the house stood to its foundations. The children were huddled into the inner bedroom with Gretchen. "Come and sit on the bed with me now," she told them calmly, "and be still." She sat up with a shawl around her, suckling the baby. Annetje came then and left her baby with Gretchen, too; and standing at the doorsteps with one arm caught over the porch rail, reached down into the furious waters which were rising to the very threshold and dragged in a half-drowned lamb. I followed her. We could not make ourselves heard above the cannonade of thunder, but together we carried the creature into the hall under the stairs, where we rubbed the drowned fleece with rags and pressed his stomach to free him from the water and finally got him sitting up with his feet tucked under him. Annetje was merry with triumph and kept saying in delight, "Alive, alive! look!"

We left him there when we heard the men shouting and beating at the kitchen door and ran to open it for them. They came in, Mother Müller among them, wearing her yoke and milk pails. She stood there with the water pouring from her skirts, the three-cornered piece of black oilcloth on her head dripping, her rubber boots wrinkled down with the weight of her petticoats stuffed into them. She and Father Müller stood near each other, looking like two gnarled lightning-struck old trees, his beard and oilcloth garments streaming, both their faces suddenly dark and old and tired, tired once for all; they would never be rested again in their lives. Father Müller suddenly roared at her, "Go get yourself dry clothes. Do you want to make yourself sick?"

"Ho," she said, taking off her milk yoke and setting the pails on the floor. "Go change yourself. I bring you dry socks." One of the boys told me she had carried a day-old calf on her back up a ladder against the inside wall of the barn and had put it safely in the hayloft behind a barricade of bales. Then she had lined up the cows in the stable, and, sitting on her milking stool in the rising water, she had milked them all. She seemed to think nothing of it.

"Hatsy!" she called, "come help with this milk!" Little pale Hatsy came flying barefoot because she had been called in the midst of taking off her wet shoes, her thick yellow and silver braids thumping on her shoulders as she ran. Her new husband followed her, rather shy of his mother-in-law.

"Let me," he said, wishing to spare his dear bride such heavy work, and started to lift the great pails. "No!" shouted Mother Müller, so the poor young man nearly jumped out of his shirt, "not you. The milk is not business for a man." He fell back and stood there with dark rivulets of mud seeping from his boots, watching Hatsy pour the milk into pans. Mother Müller started to follow her husband to attend him, but said at the door, turning back, "Where is Ottilie?", and no one knew, no one had seen her. "Find her," said Mother Müller, going. "Tell her we want supper now."

Hatsy motioned to her husband, and together they tiptoed to the door of Ottilie's room and opened it silently. The light from the kitchen showed them Ottilie, sitting by herself, folded up on the edge of the bed. Hatsy threw the door wide open for more light and called in a high penetrating voice as if to a deaf person or one at a great distance, "Ottilie! Suppertime. We are hungry!", and the young pair left the kitchen to look under the stairway to see how Annetje's lamb was getting on. Then Annetje, Hatsy, and I got brooms and began sweeping the dirty water and broken glass from the floors of the hall and dining room.

The storm lightened gradually, but the flooding rain continued. At supper there was talk about the loss of animals and their replacement. All the crops must be replanted, the season's labor was for nothing. They were all tired and wet, but they ate heartily and calmly, to strengthen themselves against all the labor of repairing and restoring which must begin early tomorrow morning.

By morning the drumming on the roof had almost ceased; from my window I looked upon a sepia-colored plain of water moving slowly to the valley. The roofs of the barns sagged like the ridge poles of a tent, and a number of drowned animals floated or were caught against the fences. At breakfast Mother Müller sat groaning over her coffee cup. "Ach," she said, "what it is to have such a pain in the head. Here too," she thumped her chest. "All over. Ach, Gott, I'm sick." She got up sighing hoarsely, her cheeks flushed, calling Hatsy and Annetje to help her in the barn.

They all came back very soon, their skirts draggled to the knees, and the two sisters were supporting their mother, who was speechless and could hardly stand. They put her to bed, where she lay without moving, her face scarlet. Everybody was confused, no one knew what to do. They tucked the quilts about her, and she threw them off. They offered her coffee, cold water, beer, but she turned her head. The sons came in and stood beside her, and joined the cry: *"Mutterchen, Mutti, Mutti,* what can we do? Tell us, what you need?" But she could not tell them. It was impossible to ride the twelve miles to town for a doctor; fences and bridges were down, the roads were washed out. The family crowded into the room, unnerved in panic, lost unless the sick woman should come to herself and tell them what to do for her. Father Müller came in and, kneeling beside her, he took hold of her hands and spoke to her most lovingly, and when she did not answer him he broke out crying openly in a loud voice, the great tears rolling, "Ach, Gott, Gott. A hundert tousand tollars in the bank" —he glared around at his family and spoke broken English to them, as if he were a stranger to himself and had forgotten his own language—"and tell me, tell me, what goot does it do?"

This frightened them, and all at once, together, they screamed and called and implored her in a tumult utterly beyond control. The noise of their grief and terror filled the place. In the midst of this, Mother Müller died.

In the midafternoon the rain passed, and the sun was a disc of brass in a cruelly bright sky. The water flowed thickly down to the river, leaving the hill bald and brown, with the fences lying in a flattened tangle, the young peach trees stripped of bloom and sagging at the roots. In the woods had occurred a violent eruption of ripe foliage of a

jungle thickness, glossy and burning, a massing of hot peacock green with cobalt shadows.

The household was in such silence, I had to listen carefully to know that anyone lived there. Everyone, even the
younger children, moved on tiptoe and spoke in whispers.
All afternoon the thud of hammers and the whine of a saw
went on monotonously in the barn loft. At dark, the men
brought in a shiny coffin of new yellow pine with rope
handles and set it in the hall. It lay there on the floor for
an hour or so, where anyone passing had to step over it.
Then Annetje and Hatsy, who had been washing and dressing the body, appeared in the doorway and motioned:
"You may bring it in now."

Mother Müller lay in state in the parlor throughout the
night, in her black silk dress with a scrap of white lace at
the collar and a small lace cap on her hair. Her husband
sat in the plush chair near her, looking at her face, which
was very contemplative, gentle, and remote. He wept at
intervals, silently, wiping his face and head with a big
handkerchief. His daughters brought him coffee from time
to time. He fell asleep there toward morning.

The light burned in the kitchen nearly all night, too, and
the sound of Ottilie's heavy boots thumping about unsteadily was accompanied by the locust whirring of the
coffee mill and the smell of baking bread. Hatsy came to
my room. "There's coffee and cake," she said, "you'd better have some," and turned away crying, crumbling her
slice in her hand. We stood about and ate in silence. Ottilie
brought in a fresh pot of coffee, her eyes bleared and fixed,
her gait as aimless-looking and hurried as ever, and when
she spilled some on her own hand, she did not seem to
feel it.

For a day longer they waited; then the youngest boy
went to fetch the Lutheran pastor, and a few neighbors
came back with them. By noon many more had arrived,
spattered with mud, the horses heaving and sweating. At

every greeting the family gave way and wept afresh, as naturally and openly as children. Their faces were drenched and soft with their tears; there was a comfortable relaxed look in the muscles of their faces. It was good to let go, to have something to weep for that nobody need excuse or explain. Their tears were at once a luxury and a cure of souls. They wept away the hard core of secret trouble that is in the heart of each separate man, secure in a communal grief; in sharing it, they consoled each other. For a while they would visit the grave and remember, and then life would arrange itself again in another order, yet it would be the same. Already the thoughts of the living were turning to tomorrow, when they would be at the work of rebuilding and replanting and repairing—even now, today, they would hurry back from the burial to milk the cows and feed the chickens, and they might weep again and again for several days, until their tears could heal them at last.

On that day I realized, for the first time, not death, but the terror of dying. When they took the coffin out to the little country hearse and I saw that the procession was about to form I went to my room and lay down. Staring at the ceiling, I heard and felt the ominous order and purpose in the movements and sounds below—the creaking harness and hoofbeats and grating wheels, the muted grave voices —and it was as if my blood fainted and receded with fright, while my mind stayed wide awake to receive the awful impress. Yet when I knew they were leaving the yard, the terror began to leave me. As the sounds receded, I lay there not thinking, not feeling, in a mere drowse of relief and weariness.

Through my half-sleep I heard the howling of a dog. It seemed to be a dream, and I was troubled to awaken. I dreamed that Kuno was caught in the trap; then I thought he was really caught, it was no dream and I must wake, because there was no one but me to let him out. I came broad awake, the cry rushed upon me like a wind, and it was not the howl of a dog. I ran downstairs and looked into Gretchen's room. She was curled up around her baby, and they were both asleep. I ran to the kitchen.

Ottilie was sitting in her broken chair with her feet on the edge of the open oven, where the heat had died away. Her hands hung at her sides, the fingers crooked into the palm; her head lay back on her shoulders, and she howled with a great wrench of her body, an upward reach of the neck, without tears. At sight of me she got up and came over to me and laid her head on my breast, and her hands dangled forward a moment. Shuddering, she babbled and howled and waved her arms in a frenzy through the open window over the stripped branches of the orchard toward the lane where the procession had straightened out into formal order. I took hold of her arms where the unnaturally corded muscles clenched and strained under her coarse sleeves; I led her out to the steps and left her sitting there, her head wagging.

In the barnyard there remained only the broken-down spring wagon and the shaggy pony that had brought me to the farm on the first day. The harness was still a mystery, but somehow I managed to join pony, harness, and wagon not too insecurely, or so I could only hope; and I pushed and hauled and tugged at Ottilie and lifted her until she was in the seat and I had the reins in hand. We careened down the road at a grudging trot, the pony jolting like a churn, the wheels spinning elliptically in a truly broad comedy swagger. I watched the jovial antics of those wheels with attention, hoping for the best. We slithered into round pits of green mud, and jogged perilously into culverts where small bridges had been. Once, in what was left of the main road, I stood up to see if I might overtake the funeral train; yes, there it was, going inch-meal up the road over the little hill, a bumbling train of black beetles crawling helter-skelter over clods.

Ottilie, now silent, was doubled upon herself, slipping loosely on the edge of the seat. I caught hold of her stout belt with my free hand, and my fingers slipped between her clothes and bare flesh, ribbed and gaunt and dry against my knuckles. My sense of her realness, her humanity, this shattered being that was a woman, was so shocking to me that a howl as doglike and despairing as her own rose in me unuttered and died again, to be a perpetual ghost. Ottilie slanted her eyes and peered at me, and I gazed back. The knotted wrinkles of her face were grotesquely changed, she gave a choked little whimper, and suddenly she laughed out, a kind of yelp but unmistakably laughter, and clapped her hands for joy, the grinning mouth and suffering eyes turned to the sky. Her head nodded and wagged with the clownish humor of our trundling lurching progress. The feel of the hot sun on her back, the bright air, the jolly senseless staggering of the wheels, the peacock green of the heavens: something of these had reached her. She was happy and gay, and she gurgled and rocked in her seat, leaning upon me and waving loosely around her as if to show me what wonders she saw.

Drawing the pony to a standstill, I studied her face for a while and pondered my ironical mistake. There was nothing I could do for Ottilie, selfishly as I wished to ease my heart of her; she was beyond my reach as well as any other human reach, and yet, had I not come nearer to her than I had to anyone else in my attempt to deny and bridge the distance between us, or rather, her distance from me? Well, we were both equally the fools of life, equally fellow fugitives from death. We had escaped for one day more at least. We would celebrate our good luck, we would have a little stolen holiday, a breath of spring air and freedom on this lovely, festive afternoon.

Ottilie fidgeted, uneasy at our stopping. I flapped the reins, the pony moved on, we turned across the shallow ditch where the small road divided from the main travelled one. I measured the sun westering gently; there would be time enough to drive to the river down the lane of mulberries and to get back to the house before the mourners returned. There would be plenty of time for Ottilie to have a fine supper ready for them. They need not even know she had been gone.

THE RAM IN THE THICKET

by Wright Morris

Wright Morris (1910–   ) is a native of Nebraska, but he has studied at Pomona College and
lived in California for many years. Both areas
have served as background for many of his novels
and short stories. Morris has been a lecturer at
Haveford, Swarthmore, Sarah Lawrence, and
other colleges and is currently teaching at San
Francisco State College. He has been a Guggenheim Fellow three times. He is a prolific writer
whose work has been critically acclaimed for many
years. *Field of Vision* won the National Book
Award in 1956. Among his best-known novels are
Love Among the Cannibals, already an American
classic, and *Cause for Wonder.*

In this dream Mr. Ormsby stood in the yard—at the edge
of the yard where the weeds began—and stared at a figure
that appeared to be on a rise. This figure had the head of a
bird with a crown of bright, exotic plumage—visible, somehow, in spite of the helmet he wore. Wisps of it appeared
at the side, or shot through the top of it like a pillow leaking long sharp spears of yellow straw. Beneath the helmet
was the face of a bird, a long face indescribably solemn,
with eyes so pale they were like openings on the sky. The
figure was clothed in a uniform, a fatigue suit that was dry
at the top but wet and dripping about the waist and knees.
Slung over the left arm, very casually, was a gun. The right

Reprinted by permission of the author.

arm was extended and above it hovered a procession of birds, an endless coming and going of all the birds he had ever seen. The figure did not speak—nor did the pale eyes turn to look at him—although it was for this, this alone, that Mr. Ormsby was there. The only sounds he heard were those his lips made for the birds, a wooing call of irresistible charm. As he stared Mr. Ormsby realized that he was pinned to something, a specimen pinned to a wall that had quietly moved up behind. His hands were fastened over his head and from the weight he felt in his wrists he knew he must be suspended there. He knew he had been brought there to be judged, sentenced, or whatever—and this would happen when the figure looked at him. He waited, but the sky-blue eyes seemed only to focus on the birds, and his lips continued to speak to them wooingly. They came and went, thousands of them, and there were so many, and all so friendly, that Mr. Ormsby, also, extended his hand. He did this although he knew that up to that moment his hands were tied—but strange to relate, in that gesture, he seemed to be free. Without effort he broke the bonds and his hand was free. No birds came—but in his palm he felt the dull drip of the alarm clock and he held it tenderly, like a living thing, until it ran down.

In the morning light the photograph at the foot of his bed was a little startling—for the boy stood alone on a rise, and he held, very casually, a gun. The face beneath the helmet had no features, but Mr. Ormsby would have known it just by the—well, just by the stance. He would have known it just by the way the boy held the gun. He held the gun like some women held their arms when their hands were idle, like parts of their body that for the moment were not much use. Without the gun it was as if some part of the boy had been amputated; the way he stood, even the way he walked was not quite right. But with the gun— what seemed out, fell into place.

He had given the boy a gun because he had never had a gun himself and not because he wanted him to kill anything. The boy didn't want to kill anything either—he couldn't very well with his first gun because of the awful racket the bee-bees made in the barrel. He had given him a thousand-shot gun—but the rattle the bee-bees made in the barrel made it impossible for the boy to get close to anything. And *that* was what had made a hunter out of him. He had to stalk everything in order to get close enough to hit it, and after you stalk it you naturally want to hit something. When he got a gun that would really shoot, and only made a racket after he shot it, it was only natural that he shot it better than anyone else. He said shoot, because the boy never seemed to realize that when he shot and hit something the something was dead. He simply didn't realize this side of things at all. But when he brought a rabbit home and fried it—by himself, for Mother wouldn't let *him* touch it—he never kidded them about the meat they ate themselves. He never really knew whether the boy did that out of kindness for Mother, or simply because he never thought about such things. He never seemed to feel like talking much about anything. He would sit and listen to Mother—he had never once been disrespectful—nor had he ever once heeded anything she said. He would listen, respectfully, and that was all. It was a known fact that Mother knew more about birds and bird migration than anyone in the state of Pennsylvania—except the boy. It was clear to him that the boy knew more, but for years it had been Mother's business and it meant more to her—the business did—than to the boy. But it was only natural that a woman who founded the League for Wild Life Conservation would be upset by a boy who lived with a gun. It was only natural—he was upset himself by the *idea* of it—but the boy and his gun somehow never bothered him. He had never seen a boy and a dog, or a boy and anything any closer —and if the truth were known both the boy's dogs knew it, nearly died of it. Not that he wasn't friendly, or as nice to them as any boy, but they knew they simply didn't rate in a class with his gun. Without that gun the boy himself really looked funny, didn't know how to stand, and nearly fell over if you talked to him. It was only natural that he enlisted, and there was nothing he ever heard that surprised him less than their making a hero out of him. Nothing more natural than that they should name something after him. If the boy had had his choice it would have been a gun rather than a boat, a thousand-shot non-rattle bee-bee gun named Ormsby. But it would kill Mother if she knew —maybe it would kill nearly anybody—what he thought was the most natural thing of all. Let God strike him dead if he had known anything righter, anything more natural, than that the boy should be killed. That was something he could not explain, and would certainly never mention to Mother unless he slipped up some night and talked in his sleep.

He turned slowly on the bed, careful to keep the springs quiet, and as he lowered his feet he scooped his socks from the floor. As a precaution Mother had slept the first few months of their marriage in her corset—as a precaution and as an aid to self-control. In the fall they had ordered twin beds. Carrying his shoes—today, of all days, would be a trial for Mother—he tiptoed to the closet and picked up his shirt and pants. There was simply no reason, as he had explained to her twenty years ago, why she should get up when he could just as well get a bite for himself. He had made that suggestion when the boy was just a baby and she needed her strength. Even as it was she didn't come out of it any too well. The truth was, Mother was so thorough about everything she did that her breakfasts usually took an hour or more. When he did it himself he was out of the kitchen in ten, twelve minutes and without leaving any pile of dishes around. By himself he could quick-rinse them in a little hot water, but with Mother there was the dish pan and all of the suds. Mother had the idea that a meal simply wasn't a meal without setting the table and using half the dishes in the place. It was easier to do it himself, and except for Sunday, when they had brunch, he was out of the house an hour before she got up. He had a bite of lunch at the store and at four o'clock he did the day's shopping since he was right downtown anyway. There was a time he called her up and inquired as to what she thought she wanted, but since he did all the buying he knew that better himself. As secretary for the League of Women Voters she had enough on her mind in times like these without cluttering it up with food. Now that he left the store an hour early he usually got home in the midst of her nap or while she was taking her bath. As he had nothing else to do he prepared the vegetables, and dressed the meat, as Mother had never shown much of a flair for meat. There had been a year—when the boy was small and before he had taken up that gun—when she had made several marvelous lemon meringue pies. But feeling as she did about the gun—and she told them both how she felt about it—she didn't see why she should slave in the kitchen for people like that. She always spoke to them as *they*—or as *you* plural—from the time he had given the boy the gun. Whether this was because they were both men, both culprits, or both something else, they were never entirely separate things again. When she called *they* would both answer, and though the boy had been gone two years he still felt him *there,* right beside him, when Mother said *you.*

For some reason he could not understand—although the rest of the house was as neat as a pin, too neat—the room they *lived* in was always a mess. Mother refused to let the cleaning woman set her foot in it. Whenever she left the house she locked the door. Long, long ago he had said something, and she had said something, and she had said she had wanted one room in the house where she could relax and just let her hair down. That had sounded so wonderfully human, so unusual for Mother, that he had been completely taken with it. As a matter of fact he still didn't know what to say. It was the only room in the house—except for the screened-in porch in the summer

—where he could take off his shoes and open his shirt on his underwear. If the room was *clean,* it would be clean like all of the others, and that would leave him nothing but the basement and the porch. The way the boy took to the out-of-doors—he stopped looking for his cuff links, began to look for pins—was partially because he couldn't find a place in the house to sit down. They had just re-decorated the house—the boy at that time was just a little shaver—and Mother had spread newspapers over every-thing. There hadn't been a chair in the place—except the straight-backed ones at the tables—that hadn't been, that *wasn't* covered with a piece of newspaper. Anyone who had ever scrunched around on a paper knew what that was like. It was at that time that he had got the idea of having his pipe in the basement, reading in the bedroom, and the boy had taken to the out-of-doors. Because he had always wanted a gun himself, and because the boy was alone, with no kids around to play with, he had brought him home that damn gun. A thousand-shot gun by the name of Daisy—funny that he should remember the name —and five thousand bee-bees in a drawstring canvas bag.

That gun had been a mistake—he began to shave him-self in tepid, lukewarm water rather than let it run hot, which would bang the pipes and wake Mother up. That gun had been a mistake—when the telegram came that the boy had been killed Mother hadn't said a word, but she made it clear whose fault it was. There was never any doubt, *any* doubt, as to just whose fault it was.

He stopped thinking while he shaved, attentive to the mole at the edge of his mustache, and leaned to the mirror to avoid dropping suds on the rug. There had been a time when he had wondered about an oriental throw rug in the bathroom, but over twenty years he had become accustomed to it. As a matter of fact he sort of missed it whenever they had guests with children and Mother re-membered to take it up. Without the rug he always felt just a little uneasy, a little naked, in the bathroom, and this made him whistle or turn on the water and let it run. If it hadn't been for that he might not have noticed as soon as he did that Mother did the same thing whenever anybody was in the house. She turned on the water and let it run until she was through with the toilet, then she would flush it before she turned the water off. If you happen to have old-fashioned plumbing, and have lived with a person for twenty years, you can't help noticing little things like that. He had got to be a little like that himself: since the boy had gone he used the one in the basement or waited until he got down to the store. As a matter of fact it was more convenient, didn't wake Mother up, and he could have his pipe while he was sitting there.

With his pants on, but carrying his shirt—for he might get it soiled preparing breakfast—he left the bathroom and tiptoed down the stairs.

Although the boy had gone, was gone, that is, Mother still liked to preserve her slip covers and the kitchen linoleum. It was a good piece, well worth preserving, but unless there were guests in the house he never saw it—he nearly forgot that it was there. The truth was he had to look at it once a week, every time he put down the papers —but right now he couldn't tell you what color that linoleum was! He couldn't do it, and wondering what in the world color it was he bent over and peeked at it—blue. Blue and white, Mother's favorite colors of course.

Suddenly he felt the stirring in his bowels. Usually this occurred while he was rinsing the dishes after his second cup of coffee or after the first long draw on his pipe. He was not supposed to smoke in the morning, but it was more important to be regular that way than irregular with his pipe. Mother had been the first to realize this—not in so many words—but she would rather he did anything than not be able to do *that*.

He measured out a pint and a half of water, put it over a medium fire, and added just a pinch of salt. Then he walked to the top of the basement stairs, turned on the light, and at the bottom turned it off. He dipped his head to pass beneath a sagging line of wash, the sleeves dripping, and with his hands out, for the corner was dark, he entered the cell.

The basement toilet had been put in to accommodate the help, who had to use something, and Mother would not have them on her oriental rug. Until the day he dropped some money out of his pants and had to strike a match to look for it, he had never noticed what kind of a stool it was. Mother had picked it up secondhand—she had never told him where—because she couldn't see buying something new for a place always in the dark. It was very old, with a chain pull, and operated on a principle that invariably produced quite a splash. But in spite of that, he preferred it to the one at the store and very much more than the one upstairs. This was rather hard to explain since the seat was pretty cold in the winter and the water sometimes nearly froze. But it was private like no other room in the house. Considering that the house was as good as empty, that was a strange thing to say, but it was the only way to say how he felt. If he went off for a walk like the boy, Mother would miss him, somebody would see him, and he wouldn't feel right about it anyhow. All he wanted was a dark quiet place and the feeling that for five minutes, just five minutes, nobody would be looking for him. Who would ever believe five minutes like that were so hard to come by? The closest he had ever been to the boy—after he had given him the gun—was the morning he had found him here on the stool. It was then that the boy had said, *et tu, Brutus,* and they had both laughed so hard they had had to hold their sides. The boy had put his head in a basket of wash so Mother wouldn't hear. Like everything the boy said there were two or three ways to take it, and in the dark Mr. Ormsby could not see his face. When he stopped laughing the boy said, *Well Pop, I suppose one flush ought to do,* but Mr. Ormsby had not been able to say anything. To be called Pop made him so weak that he had to sit right down on the stool, just like he was, and support his head in his hands. Just as he had never had a name for the boy, the boy had never had a name for him—none, that is, that Mother would permit him to use. Of all the names Mother couldn't stand, Pop was the worst, and he agreed with her, it was vulgar, common, and used by strangers to intimidate old men. He agreed with her, completely—until he heard the word in the boy's mouth. It was only natural that the boy would use it if he ever had the chance—but he never dreamed that any word, especially *that* word, could mean what it did. It made him weak, he had to sit down and pretend he was going about his business, and what a blessing it was that the place was dark. Nothing more was said, ever, but it remained their most important conversation—so important they were afraid to try and improve on it. Days later he remembered the rest of the boy's sentence, and how shocking it was but without any *sense* of shock. A blow so sharp that he had no sense of pain, only a knowing, as he had under gas, that he had been worked on. For two, maybe three minutes, there in the dark they had been what Mother called them, they were *they*—and they were there in the basement because they were so much alike. When the telegram came, and when he knew what he would find, he had brought it there, had struck a match, and read what it said. The match filled the cell with light and he saw—he couldn't help seeing—piles of tin goods in the space beneath the stairs. Several dozen cans of tuna fish and salmon, and since *he* was the one that had the points, bought the groceries, there was only one place Mother could have got such things. It had been a greater shock than the telegram—that was the honest-to-God's truth and anyone who knew Mother as well as he did would have felt the same. It was unthinkable, but there it was—and there were more on top of the water closet, where he peered while precariously balanced on the stool. Cans of pineapple, crabmeat, and tins of Argentine beef.

He had been stunned, the match had burned down and actually scorched his fingers, and he nearly killed himself when he forgot and stepped off the seat. Only later in the morning—after he had sent the flowers to ease the blow for Mother—did he realize how such a thing *must* have occurred. Mother knew so many influential people, and before the war they gave her so much, that they had very likely given her all of this stuff as well. Rather than turn it down and needlessly alienate people, influential people, Mother had done the next best thing. While the war was on she refused to serve it, or profiteer in any way—and at the same time not alienate people foolishly. It had been an odd thing, certainly, that he should discover all of that by the same match that he read the telegram. Naturally, he never breathed a word of it to Mother, as something like that, even though she was not superstitious, would really upset her. It was one of those things that he and the boy would keep to themselves.

It would be like Mother to think of putting it in here, the very last place that the cleaning woman would look for it. The new cleaning woman would neither go upstairs nor down, and did whatever she did somewhere else. Mr. Ormsby lit a match to see if everything was all right—hastily blew it out when he saw that the can pile had increased. He stood up—then hurried up the stairs without buttoning his pants as he could hear the water boiling. He added half a cup, then measured three heaping tablespoons of coffee into the bottom of the double boiler, buttoned his pants. Looking at his watch he saw that it was seven-thirty-five. As it would be a hard day—sponsoring a boat was a man-size job—he would give Mother another ten minutes or so. He took two bowls from the cupboard, sat them on blue pottery saucers, and with the grapefruit knife in his hand walked to the icebox.

As he put his head in the icebox door—in order to see he had to—Mr. Ormsby stopped breathing and closed his eyes. What had been dying for some time was now dead. He leaned back, inhaled, leaned in again. The floor of the icebox was covered with a fine assortment of jars full of leftovers Mother simply could not throw away. Some of the jars were covered with little oilskin hoods, some with saucers, and some with paper snapped on with a rubber band. It was impossible to tell, from the outside, which one it was. Seating himself on the floor he removed them one at a time, starting at the front and working toward the back. As he had done this many times before, he got well into the problem, near the middle, before troubling to sniff anything. A jar which might have been carrots—it was hard to tell without probing—was now a furry marvel of green mold. It smelled only mildly, however, and Mr. Ormsby remembered that this was penicillin, the life-giver. A spoonful of cabbage—it had been three months since they had had cabbage—had a powerful stench but was still not the one he had in mind. There were two more jars of mold, the one screwed tight he left alone as it had a frosted look and the top of the lid bulged. The culprit, however, was not that at all, but in an open saucer on the next shelf—part of an egg—Mr. Ormsby had beaten the white himself. He placed the saucer on the sink and returned all but two of the jars to the icebox; the cabbage and the explosive looking one. If it smelled he took it out, otherwise Mother had to see for herself as she refused to take *their* word for these things. When he was just a little shaver the boy had walked into the living room full of Mother's guests and showed them something in a jar. Mother had been horrified—but she naturally thought it a frog or something and not a bottle out of her own icebox. When one of the ladies asked the boy where in the world he had found it, he naturally said, *In the icebox.* Mother had never forgiven him. After that she forbade him to look in the box without permission, and the boy had not so much as peeked in it since. He would eat only what he found on the table, or ready to eat in the kitchen—or what he found at the end of those walks he took everywhere.

With the jar of cabbage and furry mold Mr. Ormsby made a trip to the garage, picked up the garden spade, walked around behind. At one time he had emptied the jars and merely buried the contents, but recently, since the war that is, he had buried it all. Part of it was a question of time—he had more work to do at the store—but the bigger part of it was to put an end to the jars. Not that it worked cut that way—all Mother had to do was open a new one—but it gave him a real satisfaction to bury them. Now that the boy and his dogs were gone there was simply no one around the house to eat up all the food Mother saved.

There were worms in the fork of earth he had turned and he stood looking at them—*they* both had loved worms —when he remembered the water boiling on the stove. He dropped everything and ran, ran right into Emil Ludlow, the milkman, before he noticed him. Still on the run he went up the steps and through the screen door into the kitchen—he was clear to the stove before he remembered the door would slam. He started back, but too late, and in the silence that followed the BANG he stood with his eyes tightly closed, his fists clenched. Usually he remained in this condition until a sign from Mother—a thump on the floor or her voice at the top of the stairs. None came, however, only the sound of the milk bottles that Emil Ludlow was leaving on the porch. Mr. Ormsby gave him time to get away, waited until he heard the horse walking, he went out and brought the milk in. At the icebox he remembered the water—why it was he had come running in the first place—and he left the door open and hurried to the stove. It was down to half a cup but not, thank heavens, dry. He added a full pint, then returned and put the milk in the icebox; took out the butter, four eggs, and a Flori-gold grapefruit. Before he cut the grapefruit he looked at his watch and seeing it was ten minutes to eight, an hour before train time, he opened the stairway door.

"Ohhh Mother!" he called, and then he returned to the grapefruit.

Ad astra per aspera, she said, and rose from the bed. In the darkness she felt about for her corset then let herself go completely for the thirty-five seconds it required to get it on. This done, she pulled the cord to the light that hung in the attic, and as it snapped on, in a firm voice she said, *Fiat lux.* Light having been made, Mother opened her eyes.

As the bulb hung in the attic, thirty feet away and out of sight, the closet remained in an afterglow, a twilight zone. It was not light, strictly speaking, but it was all Mother wanted to see. Seated on the attic stairs she trimmed her toenails with a pearl handled knife that Mr. Ormsby had been missing for several years. The blade was not so good any longer and using it too freely had resulted in ingrown nails on both of her big toes. But Mother preferred it to scissors which were proven, along with bathtubs, to be one of the most dangerous things in the home. *Even more than the battlefield, the most dangerous place in the world. Dry feet and hands before turning on lights, dry between toes.*

Without stooping she slipped into her sabots and left the closet, the light burning, and with her eyes dimmed, but not closed, went down the hall. Locking the bathroom door she stepped to the basin and turned on the cold water, then she removed several feet of paper from the toilet paper roll. This took time, as in order to keep the roller from squeaking, it had to be removed from its socket in the wall, then returned. One piece she put in the pocket of her kimono, the other she folded into a wad and used as a blotter to dab up spots on the floor. Turning up the water she sat down on the stool—then she got up to get a pencil and pad from the table near the window. On the first sheet she wrote—

Ars longa, vita brevis
Wildflower club, sun. 4 pm.

She tore this off and filed it, tip showing, right at the front of her corset. On the next page—

ROGER—
Ivory Snow
Sani Flush on thurs.

As she placed this on top of the toilet paper roll she heard him call "First for breakfast." She waited until he closed the stairway door, then she stood up and turned on the shower. As it rained into the tub and splashed behind her in the basin, she lowered the lid, flushed the toilet. Until the water closet had filled, stopped gurgling, she stood at the window watching a squirrel cross the yard from tree to tree. Then she turned the shower off and noisily dragged the shower curtain, on its metal rings, back to the wall. She dampened her shower cap in the basin and hung it on the towel rack to dry, dropping the towel that was there down the laundry chute. This done, she returned to the basin and held her hands under the running water, now cold, until she was awake. With her index finger she massaged her gums—*there is no pyorrhea among the Indians*—and then, with the tips of her fingers, she dampened her eyes.

She drew the blind, and in the half light the room seemed to be full of lukewarm water, greenish in color. With a piece of Kleenex, she dried her eyes, then turned it to gently blow her nose, first the left side, then with a little more blow on the right. There was nothing to speak of, nothing, so she folded the tissue, slipped it into her pocket. Raising the blind, she faced the morning with her eyes softly closed, letting the light come in as prescribed —gradually. Eyes wide, she then stared for a full minute at the yard full of grackles, covered with grackles, before she *discovered* them. Running to the door, her head in the hall, her arm in the bathroom wildly pointing, she tried to whisper, loud-whisper to him, but her voice cracked.

"Roger," she called, a little hoarsely. "The window—run!"

She heard him turn from the stove and skid on the newspapers, bump into the sink, curse, then get up and on again.

"Blackbirds?" he whispered.

"Grackles!" she said, for the thousandth time she said *Grackles*.

"They're pretty!" he said.

"Family—" she said, ignoring him, "family *icteridae* American."

"Well—" he said.

"Roger!" she said, "something's burning."

She heard him leave the window and on his way back to the stove, on the same turn, skid on the papers again. She left him there and went down the hall to the bedroom, closed the door, and passed between the mirrors once more to the closet. From five dresses—*any woman with more than five dresses, at this time, should have the vote taken away from her*—she selected the navy blue sheer with pink lace yoke and kerchief, short bolero. At the back of the closet—but in order to see she had to return to the bathroom, look for the flashlight in the drawer full of rags and old tins of shoe polish—were three shelves, each supporting ten to twelve pairs of shoes, and a large selection of slippers were piled on the floor. On the second shelf were the navy blue pumps—*we all have one weakness, but between men and shoes you can give me shoes*—navy blue pumps with a cuban heel and a small bow. She hung the dress from the neck of the floor lamp, placed the shoes on the bed. From beneath the bed she pulled a hat box—the hat was new. Navy straw with shasta daisies, pink geraniums and a navy blue veil with pink and white fuzzy dots. She held it out where it could be

seen in the mirror, front and side, without seeing herself—
it's not every day that one sponsors a boat. Not every
day, and she turned to the calendar on her night table, a
bird calendar featuring the natural-color male goldfinch
for the month of June. Under the date of June 23rd she
printed the words, *family icteridae—yardful,* and beneath
it—

Met Captain Sudcliffe and gave him U.S.S. *Ormsby*

When he heard Mother's feet on the stairs Mr. Ormsby
cracked her soft boiled eggs and spooned them carefully
into her heated cup. He had spilled his own on the floor
when he had run to look at the black—or whatever color
they were—birds. As they were very, very soft he had
merely wiped them up. As he buttered the toast—the four
burned slices were on the back porch airing—Mother entered the kitchen and said, "Roger—*more* toast?"

"I was watching blackbirds," he said.

"Grack-les," she said, "Any bird is a *black*bird if the
males are largely or entirely black."

Talk about male and female birds really bothered Mr.
Ormsby. Although she was a girl of the old school Mother
never hesitated, *anywhere,* to speak right out about male
and female birds. A cow was a cow, a bull was a bull, but
to Mr. Ormsby a bird was a bird.

"Among the birdfolk," said Mother, "the menfolk, so to
speak, wear the feathers. The female has more serious
work to do."

"How does that fit the blackbirds?" said Mr. Ormsby.

"Every rule," said Mother, "has an exception."

There was no denying the fact that the older Mother
got the more distinguished she appeared. As for himself,
what he saw in the mirror looked very much like the
Roger Ormsby that had married Violet Ames twenty years
ago. As the top of his head got hard the bottom tended
to get a little soft, but otherwise there wasn't much change.

But it was hard to believe that Mother was the pretty little pop-eyed girl—he had thought it was her corset that popped them—whose nipples had been like buttons on her dress. Any other girl would have looked like a you-know—but there wasn't a man in Media county, or anywhere else, who ever mentioned it. A man could think what he would think, but he was the only man who really knew what Mother was like. And how little she was like *that*.

"Three-seven-four east one-one-six," said Mother.

That was the way her mind worked, all over the place in one cup of coffee—birds one moment, Mrs. Dinardo the next.

He got up from the table and went after Mrs. Dinardo's letter—Mother seldom had time to read them unless he read them to her. Returning, he divided the rest of the coffee between them, unequally: three quarters for Mother, a swallow of grounds for himself. He waited a moment, wiping his glasses, while Mother looked through the window at another black bird. "Cowbird," she said, *"Molothrus ater."*

"Dear Mrs. Ormsby," Mr. Ormsby began. Then he stopped to scan the page, as Mrs. Dinardo had a strange style and was not much given to writing letters. "Dear Mrs. Ormsby," he repeated, "I received your letter and I Sure was glad to know that you are both well and I know you often think of me I often think of you too—" He paused to get his breath—Mrs. Dinardo's style was not much for pauses—and to look at Mother. But Mother was still with the cowbird. "Well, Mrs. Ormsby," he continued, "I haven't a thing in a room that I know of the people that will be away from the room will be only a week next month. But come to See me I may have Something if you don't get Something." Mrs. Dinardo, for some reason, always capitalized the letter S which along with everything else didn't make it easier to read. "We are both well and he is Still in the Navy Yard. My I do wish the war was over it is So long. We are So tired of it do come and See us when you give them your boat. Wouldn't a Street be better than a boat? If you are going to name Something why not a Street? Here in my hand is news of a boat Sunk what is wrong with Ormsby on a Street? Well 116 is about the Same we have the river and its nice. If you don't find Something See me I may have something.

> Best love,
> Mrs. Myrtle Dinardo."

It was quite a letter to get from a woman that Mother had known, known Mother, that is, for nearly eighteen years. Brought in to nurse the boy—he could never understand why a woman like Mother, with her figure—but anyhow, Mrs. Dinardo was brought in. Something in her milk, Dr. Paige said, when it was as plain as the nose on your face it was nothing in the milk, but something in the boy. He just refused, plain refused, to nurse with Mother. The way the little rascal would look at her, but not a sound out of him but gurgling when Mrs. Dinardo would scoop him up and go upstairs to their room—the only woman—other woman, that is, that Mother ever let step inside of it. She had answered an ad that Mother had run, on Dr. Paige's suggestion, and they had been like *that* from the first time he saw them.

"I'll telephone," said Mother.

On the slightest provocation Mother would call Mrs. Dinardo by long distance—she had to come down four flights of stairs to answer—and tell her she was going to broadcast over the radio or something. Although Mrs. Dinardo hardly knew one kind of bird from another, Mother sent her printed copies of every single one of her bird-lore lectures. She also sent her hand-pressed flowers from the garden.

"I'll telephone," repeated Mother.

"My own opinion—" began Mr. Ormsby, but stopped when Mother picked up her eggcup, made a pile of her plates, and started toward the sink. "I'll take care of that," he said. "Now you run along and telephone." But Mother walked right by him and took her stand at the sink. With one hand—with the other she held her kimono close about her—she let the water run into the large dish pan. Mr. Ormsby had hoped to avoid this; now he would have to first rinse, then dry, every piece of silver and every dish they had used. As Mother could only use one hand it would be even slower than usual.

"We don't want to miss our local," he said. "You better run along and let me do it."

"Cold water," she said, "for the eggs." He had long ago learned not to argue with Mother about the fine points of washing pots, pans, or dishes with bits of egg. He stood at the sink with the towel while she went about trying to make suds with a piece of stale soap in a little wire cage. As Mother refused to use a fresh piece of soap, nothing remotely like suds ever appeared. For this purpose, he kept a box of Gold Dust Twins concealed beneath the sink, and when Mother turned her back he slipped some in.

"There now," Mother said, and placed the rest of the dishes in the water, rinsed her fingers under the tap, paused to sniff at them.

"My own opinion—" Mr. Ormsby began, but stopped when Mother raised her finger, the index finger with the scar from the wart she once had. They stood quiet, and Mr. Ormsby listened to the water drip in the sink—the night before he had come down in his bare feet to shut it off. All of the taps dripped now and there was just nothing to do about it but put a rag or something beneath it to break the ping.

"Thrush!" said Mother. "Next to the nightingale the most popular of European songbirds."

"Very pretty," he said, although he simply couldn't hear a thing. Mother walked to the window, folding the collar of her kimono over her bosom and drawing the tails into a hammock beneath her behind. Mr. Ormsby modestly turned away. He quick-dipped one hand into the Gold Dust—drawing it out he slipped it into the dish pan and worked up a suds.

As he finished wiping the dishes she came in with a bouquet for Mrs. Dinardo and aranged it, for the moment, in a tall glass.

"According to her letter," Mrs. Ormsby said, "she isn't too sure of having something—"

"Roger!" she said. "You're dripping."

Mr. Ormsby put his hands over the sink and said, "If we're going to be met right at the station I don't see where you're going to see Mrs. Dinardo. You're going to be met at the station and then you're going to sponsor the boat. My own opinion is that after the boat we come on home."

"I know that street of hers," said Mother. "There isn't a wildflower on it!"

On the wall above the icebox was a pad of paper and a blue pencil hanging by a string. As Mother started to write the point broke off, fell behind the icebox.

"Mother," he said, "you ever see my knife?"

"Milkman," said Mother. "If we're staying overnight we won't need milk in the morning."

In jovial tones Mr. Ormsby said, "I'll bet we're right back here before dark." That was all, that was ALL that he said. He had merely meant to call her attention to the fact that Mrs. Dinardo said—all but said—that she didn't have a room for them. But when Mother turned he saw that her mustache was showing, a sure sign that she was mad.

"Well—now," Mother said, and lifting the skirt of her kimono swished around the cabinet and then he heard her on the stairs. From the landing at the top of the stairs she said, "In that case I'm sure there's no need for *my* going. I'm sure the Navy would just as soon have you. After all," she said, "it's *your* name on the boat!"

"Now, Mother," he said, just as she closed the door, *not*

slammed it, just closed it as quiet and nice as you'd please. Although he had been through this a thousand times it seemed he was never ready for it, never knew when it would happen, never felt anything but nearly sick. He went into the front room and sat down on the chair near the piano—then got up to arrange the doily at the back of his head. Ordinarily he could leave the house and after three or four days it would blow over, but in all his life—their life—there had been nothing like this. The Government of the United States—he got up again and called, "OHHhhhh Mother!"

No answer.

He could hear her moving around upstairs, but as she often went back to bed after a spat, just moving around didn't mean much of anything. He came back into the front room and sat down on the milk stool near the fireplace. It was the only seat in the room not protected with newspapers. The only thing the boy ever sat on when he had to sit on something. Somehow, thinking about that made him stand up. He could sit in the lawn swing, in the front yard, if Mother hadn't told everybody in town why it was that he, Roger Ormsby, would have to take the day off—not to sit in the lawn swing, not by a long shot. Everybody knew—Captain Sudcliffe's nice letter had appeared on the first page of the *Graphic,* under a picture of Mother leading a bird-lore hike in the Poconos. This picture bore the title LOCAL WOMAN HEADS DAWN BUSTERS, and marked Mother's appearance on the national bird-lore scene. But it was not one of her best pictures—it dated from way back in the twenties and those hipless dresses and round bucket hats were not Mother's type. Until they saw that picture, and the letter beneath it, some people had forgotten that Virgil was missing, and most of them seemed to think it was a good idea to swap him for a boat. The U.S.S. *Ormsby* was a permanent sort of thing. Although he was born and raised in the town hardly anybody knew very much about Virgil, but they all were pretty familiar with his boat. "How's that boat of yours coming along?" they would say, but in more than twenty years nobody had ever asked him about *his* boy. Whose boy? Well, that was just the point. Everyone agreed Ormsby was a fine name for a boat.

It would be impossible to explain to Mother, maybe to anybody for that matter, what this U.S.S. *Ormsby* business meant to him. "The" boy and "The" *Ormsby*—it was a pretty strange thing that they both had the definite article, and gave him the feeling he was facing a monument.

"Oh Rog-gerrr!" Mother called.

"Coming," he said, and made for the stairs.

From the bedroom Mother said, "However I might feel personally, I do have my *own* name to think of. I am not one of these people who can do as they please—Roger, are you listening?"

"Yes, Mother," he said.

"—with their life."

As he went around the corner he found a note pinned to the door.

> Bathroom window up
> Cellar door down
> Is it blue or brown for Navy?

He stopped on the landing and looked up the stairs.

"Did you say something?" she said.

"No, Mother—" he said, then he added, "It's blue. For the Navy, Mother, it's blue."

AMONG THE DANGS

by George P. Elliott

George P. Elliott (1918–1980). A native of Indiana, Elliott was educated at the University of California, from which he received both his B.A. and his M.A. He was a professor for much of his adult life as well as a prolific writer of stories, poems, essays, and reviews. He was a Guggenheim and a Hudson Review Fellow. He wrote four novels, the last being *Muriel* (1972). The story included here became the title story for one of his short story collections, *Among the Dangs*, published in 1961.

I graduated from Sansom University in 1937 with honors in history, having intended to study law but I had no money and nowhere to get any; by good fortune the anthropology department, which had just been given a grant for research, decided that I could do a job for them. In idle curiosity I had taken a course in anthro, to see what I would have been like had history not catapulted my people a couple of centuries ago up into civilization, but I had not been inclined to enlarge on the sketchy knowledge I got from that course; even yet, when I think about it, I feel like a fraud teaching anthropology. What chiefly recommended me to the department, aside from a friend, was a combination of three attributes: I was a good mimic, a long-distance runner, and black.

Reprinted by permission of Russell & Volkening, Inc. as agents for the author. Copyright © 1958 by George P. Elliott.

The Dangs live in a forested valley in the eastern foot-hills of the Andes. The only white man to report on them (and it was loosely gossiped, the only one to return from them alive), Sir Bewley Morehead in 1910 owed his es-cape to the consternation caused by Halley's Comet. Other-wise, he reported, they would certainly have sacrificed him as they were preparing to do; as it was, they killed the priest who was to have killed him, so he reported, and then burned the temple down. However, Dr. Sorish, our most distinguished Sansom man, in the early Thirties developed an interest in the Dangs which led to my research grant; he had introduced a tribe of Amazonian head-shrinkers to the idea of planting grain instead of just harvesting it, as a result of which they had fattened, taken to drinking brew by the tubful, and elevated Sorish to the rank of new god; the last time he had descended among them—it is Sansom policy to follow through on any primitives we "do"—he had found his worshipers holding a couple of young Dang men captive and preparing for ceremonies which would end only with the processing of their heads; his godhead gave him sufficient power to defer these ceremonies while he made half-a-dozen transcriptions of the men's conversa-tions, and learned their language well enough to arouse the curiosity of his colleagues. The Dangs were handy with blowpipes; no one knew what pleased them; Halley's Comet wasn't due till 1984. But among the recordings Sorish brought back was a legend strangely chanted by one of these young men, whose very head perhaps you can buy today from a natural science company for $150 to $200, and the same youth had given Sorish a sufficient demonstra-tion of the Dang prophetic trance, previously described by Morehead, to whet his appetite.

I was black, true; but, as Sorish pointed out, I looked as though I had been rolled in granite dust and the Dangs as though they had been rolled in brick dust; my hair was short and kinky, theirs long and straight; my lips were thick, theirs thin. It's like dressing a Greek up in reindeer skins, I said, and telling him to go pass himself off as a Lapp in Lapland. Maybe, they countered, but wouldn't he be more likely to get by than a naked Swahili with bones in his nose? I was a long-distance runner, true; but as I pointed out with a good deal of feeling, I didn't know the principles of jungle escape and had no desire to learn them in, as they put it, the field. They would teach me to throw the javelin and wield a machete, they would teach me the elements of judo, and as for poisoned darts and sacrifices they would insure my life—that is, my return within three years—for $5000. I was a good mimic, true; I would be able to reproduce the Dang speech, and especially the trance of the Dang prophets, for the observation of science—"make a genuine contribution to learning." In the Sansom concept, the researcher's experience is an inextricable part of anthropological study, and a good mimic provides the object for others' study as well as for his own. For doing this job I would be given round-trip transportation, an M.S. if I wrote a thesis on the material I gathered, the temporary insurance on my life, and $100 a month for the year I was expected to be gone. After I'd got them to throw in a fellowship of some sort for the following year, I agreed. It would pay for filling the forty cavities in my brothers' and sisters' teeth.

Dr. Sorish and I had to wait at the nearest outstation for a thunderstorm; when it finally blew up, I took off all my clothes, put on a breechcloth and leather apron, put a box of equipment on my head, and trotted after him; his people were holed in from the thunder, and we were in their settlement before they saw us. They were taller than I, they no doubt found my white teeth as disagreeable as I found their stained, filed teeth; but when Sorish spoke to me in English (telling me to pretend indifference to them while they sniffed me over), and in the accents of American acquaintances rather than in the harsh tones of divinity, their eyes filled with awe of me. Their taboo against touching Sorish extended itself to me; when a baby ran up to me and I lifted him up to play with him, his mother crawled to me on her knees beating her head on the ground till I freed him.

The next day was devoted chiefly to selecting the man to fulfill Sorish's formidable command to guide me to the edge of the Dang country. As for running—if those dogs could be got to the next Olympics, Ecuador would take every long-distance medal on the board. I knew I had reached the brow of my valley only because I discovered that my guide, whom I had been lagging behind by forty or fifty feet, at a turn in the path had disappeared into thin brush.

Exhaustion allayed my terror; as I lay in the meager shade recuperating, I remembered to execute the advice I had given myself before coming: to act always as though I were not afraid. What would a brave man do next? Pay no attention to his aching feet, reconnoiter, and cautiously proceed. I climbed a jutting of rock and peered about. It was a wide, scrubby valley; on the banks of the river running down the valley I thought I saw a dozen mounds too regular for stones. I touched the handle of the hunting knife sheathed at my side and trotted down the trackless hill.

The village was deserted, but the huts, though miserable, were clean and in good repair. This meant, according to the movies I had seen, that hostile eyes were watching my every gesture. I had to keep moving in order to avoid trembling. The river was clear and not deep. The unmutilated corpse of a man floated by. I felt like taking the path downstream, but my hypothesized courage drove me up.

In half a mile I came upon a toothless old woman squatting by the track. She did not stop munching when I appeared, nor did she scream, or even stand up. I greeted her in Dang according to the formula I had learned, whereupon she cackled and smiled and nodded as gleefully as though I had just passed a test. She reminded me of my grandmother, rolled in brick dust, minus a corncob pipe between her gums. Presently I heard voices ahead of me. I saw five women carrying branches and walking very slowly. I lurked behind them until they came to a small village, and watched from a bush while they set to work. They stripped the leaves off, carefully did something to them with their fingers, and then dropped them in small-throated pots. Children scrabbled around, and once a couple of them ran up and suckled at one of the women. There remained about an hour till sunset. I prowled, undetected. The women stood, like fashion models, with pelvis abnormally rocked forward; they were wiry, without fat even on their breasts; not even their thighs and hips afforded clean sweeping lines undisturbed by bunched muscles. I saw no men. Before I began to get into a stew about the right tack to take, I stepped into the clearing and uttered their word of salutation. If a strange man should walk in your wife's front door and say, "How do you do," in an accent she did not recognize, simultaneously poking the middle finger at her, her consternation would be something like that of those Dang women; for unthinkingly I had nodded my head when speaking and turned my palm out, as one does in the United States; to them this was a gesture of intimacy, signifying desire. They disappeared into huts, clutching children. I went to the central clearing and sat with my back to a log, knowing they would scrutinize me. I wondered where the men were. I could think of no excuse for having my knife in my hand except to clean my toenails. So astonishing an act was unknown to the Dangs; the women and children gradually approached in silence, watching; I cleaned my fingernails. I said the word for food; no one reacted, but presently a little girl ran up to me holding a fruit in both hands. I took it, snibbed her nose between my fingers, and with a pat on the bottom sent her back to her mother. Upon this there were hostile glances, audible intakes of breath, and a huddling about the baby, who did not understand any more than I did why she was being consoled. While I ate the fruit I determined to leave the next move up to them. I sheathed my knife and squatted on my hunkers, waiting. To disguise my nervousness I fixed my eyes on the ground between my feet, and grasped my ankles from behind in such a way— right ankle with right hand, left with left—as to expose the inner sides of my forearms. Now this was, as I later learned, pretty close to the initial posture taken for the prophetic trance; also I had a blue flower tattooed on my inner right arm and a blue serpent on my left (from the summer I'd gone to sea), the like of which had never been seen in this place. At sundown I heard the men approach; they were anything but stealthy about it; I had the greatest difficulty in suppressing the shivers. In simple fear of showing my fear, I did not look up when the men gathered around; I could understand just enough of what the women were telling the men to realize that they were afraid of me. Even though I was pelted with pebbles and twigs till I was angry, I still did not respond, because I could not think what to do. But then something clammy was plopped onto my back from above and I instantly leaped as high as I could, howling. Their spears were poised before I landed. "Strangers!" I cried, my speech all composed. "Far kinsmen! I come from the mountains!" I had intended to say *from the river lands,* but the excitement tangled my tongue. Their faces remained expressionless, but no spears drove at me, and then, to be doing something, I shoved the guts under the log with my feet.

And saved my life by doing so. That I seemed to have taken, though awkwardly, the prophetic squat; that I bore visible marvels on my arm; that I was fearless and innerly absorbed; that I came from the mountains (their enemies lived toward the river lands); that I wore their apron and spoke their language, albeit poorly; all these disposed them to wonder at this mysterious outlander. Even so, they might very well have captured me, marvelous though I was, possibly useful to them, dangerous to antagonize, had I not been unmaimed, which meant that I was supernaturally guarded. Finally, my scrutinizing the fish guts, daring to smile as I did so, could mean only that I was prophetic; my leap when they had been dropped onto my back was prodigious, "far higher than a man's head," and my howl had been vatic; and my deliberately kicking the guts aside, though an inscrutable act, demonstrated at least that I could touch the entrails of an eel and live.

So I was acceptable to the Dangs. The trouble was, they had no ceremony for naturalizing me. For them, every act had a significance, and here they were faced with a reverse problem, for which nothing had prepared them. They could not possibly just assimilate me without marking the event with an act (that is, a ceremony) signifying my entrance. For them, nothing *just happened*, certainly nothing men did. Meanwhile, I was kept in a sort of quarantine while they deliberated. I did not, to be sure, understand why I was being isolated in a hut by myself, never spoken to except efficiently, watched but not restrained. I swam, slept, scratched, watched, swatted, ate; I was not really alarmed, because they had not restrained me forcibly and they gave me food. I began making friends with some of the small children, especially while swimming, and there were two girls of fifteen or so who found me terribly funny. I wished I had some magic, but I knew only card tricks. The sixth day, swimming, I thought I was being enticed around a point in the river by the two girls, but when I began to chase them they threw good-sized stones at me missing me only because they were such poor shots. A corpse floated by; when they saw it they immediately placed the sole of their right foot on the side of their left knee and stood thus on one leg till the corpse floated out of sight; I followed the girls' example, teetering. I gathered from what they said that some illness was devastating their people; I hoped it was one of the diseases I had been inoculated against. The girls' mothers found them talking with me and cuffed them away. I did not see them for two days, but the night of my eighth day there, the bolder of them hissed me awake at the door of my hut in a way that meant "no danger." I recognized her when she giggled. I was not sure what their customs were in these matters, but while I was deliberating what my course of wisdom should be she crawled into the hut and lay on the mat beside me. She liked me; she was utterly devoid of reticence; I was twenty-one and far from home; even a scabby little knotty-legged fashion model is hard to resist under such circumstances. I learned, before falling asleep, that there was a three-way debate among the men over what to do with me: initiate me according to the prophet-initiation rites, invent a new ceremony, or sacrifice me as propitiation to the disease among them, as was usually done with captives. Each had its advantages and drawbacks; even the news that some of the Dangs wanted to sacrifice me did not excite me as it would have done a week before; now, I half-sympathized with their trouble. I was awakened at dawn by the outraged howl of a man at my door; he was the girl's father; the village men gathered and the girl cowered behind me. They talked for hours outside my hut, men arrived from other villages up and down the valley, and finally they agreed upon a solution to all the problems: they proposed that I should be made one of the tribe by marriage on the same night that I should be initiated into the rites of prophecy.

The new-rite men were satisfied by this arrangement because of the novelty of having a man married and initiated on the same day; but the sacrifice party was visibly unmollified. Noticing this and reflecting that the proposed arrangement would permit me to do all my trance-research under optimum conditions and to accumulate a great deal of sexual data as well, I agreed to it. I would of course only be going through the forms of marriage, not meaning them; as for the girl, I took this vow to myself (meaning without ceremony): "So long as I am a Dang, I shall be formally a correct husband to her." More's a pity.

Fortunately a youth from down the valley already had been chosen as a novice (at least a third of the Dang men enter the novitiate at one time or another, though few make the grade), so that I had not only a companion during the four-month preparation for the vatic rites but also a control upon whom I might check my experience of the stages of the novitiate. My mimetic powers stood me in good stead; I was presumed to have a special prophetic gift and my readiness at assuming the proper stances and properly performing the ritual acts confirmed the Dangs' impressions of my gift; but also, since I was required to proceed no faster than the ritual pace in my learning, I had plenty of leisure in which to observe in the smallest detail what I did and how I, and to some extent my fellow novice, felt. If I had not had this self-observing to relieve the tedium, I think I should have been unable to get through that mindless holding of the same position hour after hour, that mindless repeating of the same act day after day. The Dangs *appear* to be bored much of the time, and my early experience with them was certainly that of ennui, though never again ennui so acute as during this novitiate; yet I doubt that it would be accurate to say they actually are bored, and I am sure that the other novice was not, as a fisherman waiting hours for a strike cannot be said to be bored. The Dangs do not sate themselves on food; the experience which they consider most worth seeking, vision, is one which cannot glut either the prophet or his auditors; they cannot imagine an alternative to living as they live, or, more instantly, to preparing a novice as I was being prepared. The people endure; the prophets, as I have learned, wait for the time to come again, and though they are bitten and stung by ten thousand fears, about this they have no anxiety— the time will surely come again. Boredom implies either satiety, and they were poor and not interested in enriching themselves, or the frustration of impulse, and they were without alternatives and diversions; and that intense boredom which is really a controlled anx-

iety they are protected from by never doubting the worth
of their vision or their power to achieve it.

I was assisted through these difficult months, during
which I was supposed to do nothing but train, by Redadu,
my betrothed. As a novice, I was strictly to abstain from
sexual intercourse; but as betrothed, we were supposed to
make sure before marriage that we satisfied one another,
for adultery by either husband or wife was punishable by
maiming. Naturally, the theologians were much exercised
by this impasse of mine, but while they were arguing,
Redadu and I took the obvious course—we met more or
less surreptitiously. Since my vatic training could not take
place between sunrise and sundown, I assumed that we
could meet in the afternoon when I woke up, but when I
began making plans to this effect, I discovered that she did
not know what I was talking about. It makes as much sense
in Dang to say, "Let's blow poisoned darts at the loss of
the moon," as to say, "Let's make love in broad daylight."
Redadu dissolved in giggles at the absurdity. What to do?
She found us a cave. Everyone must have known what I
was up to, but we were respectable (the Dang term for it
was harsher, *deed-liar*), so we were never disturbed. Redadu's friends would not believe her stories of my luxurious
love ways, especially my biting with lips instead of teeth.
At one time or another she sent four of them to the cave
for me to demonstrate my prowess upon; I was glad that
none of them pleased me as much as she did, for I was beginning to be fond of her. My son has told me that lip-biting
has become, if not a customary, at any rate a possible
caress.

As the night of the double rite approached, a night of
full moon, a new conflict became evident: the marriage
must be consummated exactly at sundown, but the initiation must begin at moonrise, less than two hours later. For
some reason that was not clear to me, preparing for the
initiation would incapacitate me for the consummation. I
refrained from pointing out that it was only technically that

this marriage needed consummating and even from asking why I would not be able to do it. The solution, which displeased everyone, was to defer the rites for three nights, when the moon, though no longer perfectly round, would rise sufficiently late so that I would, by hurrying, be able to perform both of my functions. Redadu's father, who had been of the sacrifice party, waived ahead of time his claim against me: legally he was entitled to annul the marriage if I should leave the marriage hut during the bridal night. And although I in turn could legally annul it if she left the hut, I waived my claim as well so that she might attend my initiation.

The wedding consisted chiefly of our being bound back to back by the elbows and being sung to and danced about all day. At sunset, we were bound face to face by the elbows (most awkward) and sent into our hut. Outside, the two mothers waited—a high prophet's wife took the place of my mother (my Methodist mother!)—until our orgastic cries indicated that the marriage had been consummated, and then came in to sever our bonds and bring us the bridal foods of cold stewed eel and parched seeds. We fed each other bite for bite and gave the scraps to our mothers, who by the formula with which they thanked us pronounced themselves satisfied with us; and then a falsetto voice called to me to hurry to the altar. A man in the mask of a moon slave was standing outside my hut on his left leg with the right foot against his left knee, and he continued to shake his rattle after me so long as I was within earshot of him.

The men were masked. Their voices were all disguised. I wondered whether I was supposed to speak in an altered voice; I knew every stance and gesture I was to make, but nothing of what I was to say; yet surely a prophet must employ words. I had seen some of the masks before—being repaired, being carried from one place to another—but now, faced with them alive in the failing twilight, I was impressed by them in no scientific or aesthetic way: they

terrified and exalted me. I wondered if I would be given a
mask. I began trying to identify such men as I could by their
scars and missing fingers and crooked arms, and noticed
to my distress that they too were all standing one-legged
in my presence. But I had thought that was the stance to
be assumed in the presence of the dead! We were at the
entrance to The Cleft, a dead-end ravine in one of the cliffs
along the valley; my fellow novice and I were each given a
gourdful of some vile-tasting drink and were then taken up
to the end of The Cleft, instructed to assume the first position, and left alone. We squatted as I had been squatting
by the log on my first day, except that my head was cocked
in a certain way and my hands clasped my ankles from the
front. The excitements of the day seemed to have addled
my wits; I could concentrate on nothing, and lost my impulse to observe coolly what was going on; I kept humming *St. James Infirmary* to myself, and though at first I
had been thinking the words, after a while I realized that
I had nothing but the tune left in my head. At moonrise
we were brought another gourd of the liquor to drink, and
were then taken to the mouth of The Cleft again. I did,
easily, whatever I was told. The last thing I remember
seeing before taking the second position was the semicircle
of masked men facing us and chanting, and behind them
the women and children—all standing on the left leg. I lay
on my back with my left ankle on my right and my hands
crossed over my navel, rolled my eyeballs up and held the
lids open without blinking, and breathed in the necessary
rhythm, each breath taking four heartbeats, with an inter-
val of ten heartbeats between each exhalation and the next
inspiration. Then the drug took over. At dawn when a
called command awoke me, I found myself on an islet in the
river dancing with my companion a leaping dance I had not
known or even seen before, and brandishing over my head
a magnificent red and blue, new-made mask of my own.
The shores of the river were lined with the people chanting as we leaped, and all of them were either sitting or else

standing on both feet. If we had been dead the night before, we were alive now. Redadu told me, after I had slept and returned to myself, that my vision was splendid, but of course she was no more permitted to tell me what I had said than I was able to remember it. The Dangs' sense of rhythm is as subtle as their ear for melody is monotonous, and for weeks I kept hearing rhythmic snatches of *St. James Infirmary* scratched on calabash drums and tapped on blocks.

Sorish honored me by rewriting my master's thesis and adding my name as co-author of the resultant essay, which he published in JAFA (*The Journal of American Field Anthropology*): "Techniques of Vatic Hallucinosis Among the Dangs." And the twenty-minute movie I made of a streamlined performance of the rites is still widely used as an audio-visual aid.

By 1939 when I had been cured of the skin disease I had brought back with me and had finished the work for my M.S., I still had no money. I had been working as the assistant curator of the university's Pre-Columbian Museum and had developed a powerful aversion to devoting my life to cataloguing, displaying, restoring, warehousing. But my chances of getting a research job, slight enough with a Ph. D., were nil with only an M.S. The girl I was going with said (I had not told her about Redadu) that if we married she would work as a nurse to support me while I went through law school; I was tempted by the opportunity to fulfill my original ambition, and probably I would have done it had she not pressed too hard; she wanted me to leave anthropology, she wanted me to become a lawyer, she wanted to support me, but what she did not want was to make my intentions, whatever those might be, her own. Therefore, when a new grant gave me the chance to return to the Dangs, I gladly seized it; not only would I be asserting myself against Velma, but also I would be paid for do-ing research for my Ph. D. thesis; besides, I was curious to see the Congo-Maryland-Dang bastard I had left in Reda-du's belly. My assignment was to make a general cultural survey but especially to discover the *content* of the vatic experience—not just the technique, not even the hallucinations and stories, but the qualities of the experience itself. The former would get me a routine degree, but the latter would, if I did it, make me a name and get me a job. After much consultation I decided against taking with me any form of magic, including medicine; the antibiotics had not been invented yet, and even if there had been a simple way to eradicate the fever endemic among the Dangs, my advisers persuaded me that it would be an error to introduce it since the Dangs were barely able to procure food for themselves as it was and since they might worship me for doing it, thereby making it impossible for me to do my research with the proper empathy. I arrived the second time provided only with my knife (which for some reason had not much impressed these stone-agers), some salve to soothe my sores, and the knowledge of how to preserve fish against a lean season, innovation enough but not one likely to divinize me.

I was only slightly worried how I would be received on my return, because of the circumstances under which I had disappeared. I had become a fairly decent hunter—the women gathered grain and fruit—and I had learned to respect the Dangs' tracking abilities enough to have been nervous about getting away safely. While hunting with a companion in the hills south of our valley, I had run into a couple of hunters from an enemy tribe which seldom foraged so far north as this. They probably were as surprised as I and probably would have been glad to leave me unmolested; however, outnumbered and not knowing how many more were with them, I whooped for my companion; one of the hunters in turn, not knowing how many were with me, threw his spear at me. I side-stepped it and reached for my darts and, though I was not very accurate with a blowpipe, I hit him in the thigh: within a minute he was writhing on the ground, for in my haste I had blown a venomous dart at him, and my comrade took his comrade prisoner by surprise. As soon as the man I had hit was dead, I withdrew my dart and cut off his ear for trophy, and we returned with our captive. He told our war chief in sign language that the young man I had killed was the son and heir of their king and that my having mutilated him meant their tribe surely would seek to avenge his death. The next morning a Dang search party was sent out to recover the body so that it might be destroyed and trouble averted, but it had disappeared; war threatened. The day after that I chose to vanish; they would not think of looking for me in the direction of Sorish's tribe, north, but would assume that I had been captured by the southern tribe in retribution for their prince's death. My concern now, two years later, was how to account for not having been maimed or executed; the least I could do was to cut a finger off, but when it came to the point, I could not even bring myself to have a surgeon do it, much less do it myself; I had adequate lies prepared for their other questions, but about this I was a bit nervous. I got there at sundown.

Spying, I did not see Redadu about the village. On the chance, I slipped into our hut when no one was looking; she was there, playing with our child. He was as cute a little preliterate as you ever saw suck a thumb, and it made me chuckle to think he would never be literate either. Redadu's screams when she saw me fetched the women, but when they heard a man's voice they could not intrude. In her joy she lacerated me with her fingernails (the furrows across my shoulder festered for a long time); I could do no less than bite her arm till she bled; the primal scene we treated our son to presumably scarred him for life, though I must say the scars haven't showed up yet. I can't deny I was glad to see her too; for, though I felt for her none of the tender, complex emotions I had been feeling for Velma, emotions which I more or less identified as being love, yet I was so secure with her sexually, I knew so well what to do and what to expect from her in every important matter, that it was an enormous, if cool, comfort to me to be with her. *Comfort* is a dangerous approximation to what I mean; being with her provided, as it were, the condition for doing; in Sansom I did not consider her my wife, and here I did not recognize in myself the American emotions of love or marriage; yet it seemed to me right to be with her; and our son was no bastard. *Cool:* I cannot guarantee that mine was the usual Dang emotion, for it is hard for the cool to gauge the warmth of others; in my reports I have denied any personal experience of love among the Dangs for this reason. When we emerged from the hut, there was amazement and relief among the women; amazement that I had returned and relief that it had not been one of their husbands pleasuring the widow. But the men were more ambiguously pleased to see me: Redadu's scratches were not enough and they doubted my story, that the enemy king had made me his personal slave who must be bodily perfect. They wanted to hear me prophesy.

Redadu told me afterward, hiding her face in my arms for fear of being judged insolent, that I surpassed myself that night, that only the three high prophets had ever been so inspired. And it was true that even the men most hostile to me did not oppose my re-entry into the tribe after they had heard me prophesy: they could have swallowed the story I fed them about my two-year absence only because they believed in me the prophet. Dangs make no separation between fact and fantasy, apparent reality and visionary reality, truth and beauty. I once saw a young would-be prophet shudder away from a stick on the ground, saying it was a snake, and none of the others, except the impressionable, was afraid of the stick; it was said of him that he was a beginner. Another time I saw a prophet scatter the whole congregation, myself included, when he screamed at the sight of a beast which he called a cougar; when sober dawn found the speared creature to be a cur it was said of the prophet that he was strong, and he was honored with

an epithet, Cougar-Dog. My prophesying the first night of
my return must have been of this caliber, though to my dis-
appointment I was given no epithet, not even the nickname
I'd sometimes heard before, Bush-Hair. I knew there was
a third kind of prophesying, the highest, performed only
on the most important occasions in the Cave-Temple where
I had never been. No such occasion had presented itself
during my stay before, and when I asked one of the other
prophets about that ceremony, he put me off with the term
Wind Haired Child of the Sun; from another, I learned
that the name of this sort of prophesying was Stone is Stone.
It would be indiscreet for me to press further; obviously,
I was going to have to stay until I could make sense of
these mysteries.

There was a war party that wanted my support; my
slavery was presumed to have given me knowledge which
would make a raid highly successful; because of this as well
as because I had instigated the conflict by killing the king's
son, I would be made chief of the raiding party. I was uneasy about the fever, which had got rather worse among
them during the previous two years, without risking my
neck against savages who were said always to eat a portion
of their slain enemy's liver raw and whose habitat I knew
nothing of. I persuaded the Dangs, therefore, that they
should not consider attacking before the rains came, because their enemies were now the stronger, having on their
side their protector, the sun. They listened to me, and
waited. Fortunately, it was a long dry season, during which
I had time to find a salt deposit and to teach a few women
the rudiments of drying and salting fish; and during the first
week of the rains, every night there were showers of falling
stars to be seen in the sky; to defend against them absorbed
all energies for weeks, including the warriors'. Even so,
even though I was a prophet, a journeyman prophet as it
were, I was never in on these rites in the Cave-Temple. I
dared not ask many questions. Sir Bewley Morehead had
described a temple, surrounded by seventy-five poles, each

topped by a human head; he could hardly have failed to mention that it was in a cave; yet he made no such mention, and I knew of no temple like the one he had described. At a time of rains and peace in the sky, the war party would importune me. I did not know what to do but wait.

The rains became violent, swamping the villages in the lower valley and destroying a number of huts; yet the rainy season ended abruptly two months before its usual time. Preparations for war had already begun, and day by day as the sun's strength increased and the earth dried, the war party became more impatient; and the preparations in themselves lulled my objections to the raid, even to my leading the raid, and stimulated my desire to make war. But the whole project was canceled a couple of days before we were to attack because of the sudden fever of one of the high prophets; the day after he came down, five others of the tribe fell sick, among them Redadu. There was nothing I could do but sit by her, fanning her and sponging her till she died. Her next older sister took our son to rear. I would allow no one to prepare her body but myself, though her mother was supposed to help; I washed it with the proper infusions of herbs, and at dawn, in the presence of her clan, I laid her body on the river; thank heaven it floated, or I should have had to spend another night preparing it further. I felt like killing someone now; I recklessly called for war now, even though the high prophet had not yet died; I was restrained, not without admiration. I went up into the eastern hills by myself, and returned after a week bearing the hide of a cougar; I had left the head and claws on my trophy, in a way the Dangs had never seen; when I put the skin on in play by daylight and bounded and snarled, only the bravest did not run in terror. They called me Cougar-Man. And Redadu's younger sister came to sleep with me; I did not want her, but she so stubbornly refused to be expelled that I kept her for the night, for the next night, for the next; it was not improper. The high prophet did not die, but lay comatose most of the time. The Dangs have ten master prophets, of whom the specially gifted, whether one or all ten, usually two or three, are high prophets. Fifteen days after Redadu had died, well into the abnormal dry spell, nearly all the large fish seemed to disappear from the river. A sacrifice was necessary. It was only because the old man was so sick that a high prophet was used for this occasion; otherwise a captive or a woman would have served the purpose. A new master prophet must replace him, to keep the complement up to ten. I was chosen.

The exultation I felt when I learned that the master prophets had co-opted me among them was by no means cool and anthropological, for now that I had got what I had come to get, I no longer wanted it for Sansom reasons. *If the conditions of my being elevated,* I said to myself, *are the suffering of the people, Redadu's death, and the sacrifice of an old man, then I must make myself worthy of the great price. Worthy:* a value word, not a scientific one. Of course, my emotions were not the simple pride and fear of a Dang either. I can't say just what sort they were, but I know they were fierce.

At sundown all the Dangs of all the clans were assembled about the entrance to The Cleft. All the prophets, masked, emerged from The Cleft and began the dance in a great wheel. Within this wheel, rotating against it, was the smaller wheel of the nine able-bodied master prophets. At the center, facing the point at which the full moon would rise, I hopped on one leg, then the other. I had been given none of the vatic liquor, that brew which the women, when I had first come among the Dangs, had been preparing in the small-throated pots; and I hoped I should be able to remain conscious throughout the rites. However, at moonrise a moon slave brought me a gourdful to drink without ceasing to dance. I managed to allow a good deal of it to spill unnoticed down with the sweat streaming off me, so that later I was able to remember what had happened, right up to the prophesying itself. The dance continued for at least two more hours; then the drums suddenly stopped and the prophets began to file up The Cleft, me last, dancing after the high prophets. We danced into an opening in the cliff from which a disguising stone had been rolled away; the people were not allowed to follow us. We entered a great cavern illuminated by ten smoking torches. We circled a palisade of stakes; the only sound was the shuffle of our feet and the snorts of our breathing. There were seventy-five stakes, as Morehead had seen, but only on twenty-eight of them were heads impaled, the last few with flesh on them still, not yet skulls cleaned of all but hair. In the center was a huge stone under the middle of which a now dry stream had tunneled a narrow passage; on one side of the stone, above the passage, were two breast-like protuberances, one of which had a recognizable nipple suitably placed. Presently the dancing file reversed so that I was the leader. I had not been taught what to do; I wove the file through the round of stakes, and spiraled inward till we were three deep about The Stone; I straddled the channel, raised my hands till they were touching the breasts and gave a great cry. I was, for reasons I do not understand, shuddering all over; though I was conscious and though I had not been instructed, I was not worried that I might do the wrong thing next; when I touched The Stone, a dread shook me without affecting my exaltation. Two moon slaves seized my arms, took off my mask, and wrapped and bound me, arms at my sides and legs pressed together, in a deer hide, and then laid me on my back in the channel under The Stone with my head only half out, so that I was staring up the sheer side of rock. The dancers continued, though the master prophets had disappeared. My excitement; the new, unused position; being mummied tightly; the weakness of the drug; my will to observe; all kept me conscious for a long time. Gradually, however, my eyes began to roll up into my head, I strained less powerfully against the thongs that bound me, and I felt my breathing approach the vatic rhythm. At this point, I seemed to break out in a new sweat, on my forehead, my throat, in my hair; I could hear a splash; groggily I licked my chin; an odd taste; I wondered if I was bleeding. Of course—it was the blood of the sick old high prophet, who had just been sacrificed on The Stone above me; well, his blood would give me strength; wondering remotely whether his fever could be transmitted by drinking his blood, I entered the trance. At dawn I emerged into consciousness while I was still prophesying; I was on a ledge in the valley above all the people, in my mask again. I listened to myself finish the story I was telling. "He was afraid. A third time a man said to him: 'You are a friend of the most high prophet.' He answered: 'Not me. I do not know that man they are sacrificing.' Then he went into a dark corner; he put his hands over his face all day." When I came to the Resurrection, a sigh blew across the people.

It was the best story they had ever heard. Of course. But I was not really a Christian. For several weeks I fretted over my confusion, this new, unsuspected confusion. I was miserable without Redadu; I let her sister substitute only until I had been elevated, and then I cast her off, promising her however that she and only she might wear an anklet made of my teeth when I should die. Now that I was a master prophet I could not be a warrior; I had had enough hunting, fishing, tedious ceremonies. Hunger from the shortage of fish drove the hunters high into the foothills; there was not enough; they ate my preserved fish, suspiciously, but they ate them. When I left, it was not famine that I was escaping, but my confusion; I was fleeing to the classrooms and the cool museums where I should be neither a leftover Christian nor a mimic of a Dang.

My academic peace lasted for just two years, during which time I wrote five articles on my researches, publishing them this time under my name only, did some of the work for my doctorate, and married Velma. Then came World War II, in which my right hand was severed above the wrist; I was provided with an artificial hand and given enough money so that I could afford to finish my degree in style. We had two daughters and I was given a job at Sansom. There was no longer a question of my returning to the Dangs. I would become a settled anthropologist; teach, and quarrel with my colleagues in the learned journals. But by the time the Korean War came along and robbed us of a lot of students, my situation at the university had changed considerably. Few of my theoretical and disputatious articles were printed in the journals, and I hated writing them; I was not given tenure and there were some hints to the effect that I was considered a one-shot man, a flash-in-the-pan; Velma nagged for more money and higher rank. My only recourse was further research, and when I thought of starting all over again with some other tribe—in Northern Australia, along the Zambesi, on an African Island—my heart sank. The gossip was not far from the mark—I was not one hundred per cent the scientist and never would be. I had just enough reputation and influential recommendations to be awarded a Guggenheim Fellowship; supplemented by a travel grant from the university, this made it possible for me to leave my family comfortably provided for and to return to the Dangs.

A former student now in Standard Oil in Venezuela arranged to have me parachuted among them from an S.O. plane; there was the real danger that they would kill me before they recognized me, but if I arrived in a less spectacular fashion I was pretty sure they would sacrifice me for their safety's sake. This time, being middle-aged, I left my hunting knife and brought instead at my belt a pouch filled with penicillin and salves. I had a hard time identifying the valley from the air; it took me so long that it was sunset before I jumped; I knew how the Dangs were enraged by airplanes, especially by the winking lights of night fliers, and I knew they would come for

me if they saw me billowing down. Fortunately, I landed
in the river, for, though I was nearly drowned before I
disentangled my parachute harness, I was also out of
range of the blowpipes. I finally identified myself to the
warriors brandishing their spears along the shore; they
had not quite dared to swim out after so prodigious a
being; even after they knew who I said I was and allowed
me to swim to shore, they saw me less as myself than as
a supernatural being. I was recognized by newcomers
who had not seen me so closely swinging from the parachute (the cloud); on the spot my epithet became, as it
remained, Sky-Cougar. Even so, no one dared touch me
till the high prophet—there was only one now—had
arrived and talked with me; my artificial hand seemed to
him an extension of the snake tattooed onto my skin; he
would not touch it; I suddenly struck him with it and
pinched his arm. "Pinchers," I said, using the word for a
crayfish claw; and he laughed. He said there was no way
of telling whether I was what I seemed to be until he had
heard me prophesy; if I prophesied as I had done before
I had disappeared, I must be what I seemed to be; meanwhile, for the three weeks till full moon, I was to be kept
in the hut for captives.

At first I was furious at being imprisoned, and when
mothers brought their children from miles about to peek
through the stakes at the man with the snake-hand, I
snarled or sulked like a caged wolf. But I became conscious that a youth, squatting in a quiet place, had been
watching me for hours, and demanded of him who he
was. He said, "I am your son," but he did not treat me
as his father. To be sure, he could not have remembered
what I looked like; my very identity was doubted; even
if I were myself, I was legendary, a stranger who had
become a Dang and had been held by an enemy as captive slave for two years and had then become a master
prophet with the most wonderful vision anyone knew.
Yet he came to me every day and answered all the ques-

tions I put to him. It was, I believe, my artificial hand
that finally kept him aloof from me; no amount of ac-
quaintance could accustom him to that. By the end of the
first week it was clear to me that if I wanted to survive—
not to be accepted as I once had been, just to survive
—I would have to prophesy the Passion again. And how
could I determine what I would say when under the
vatic drug? I imagined a dozen schemes for substituting
colored water for the drug, but I would need an accom-
plice for that and I knew that not even my own son
would serve me in so forbidden an act.

I called for the high prophet. I announced to him in
tones all the more arrogant because of my trepidations
that I would prophesy without the vatic liquor. His response to my announcement astonished me: he fell upon
his knees, bowed his head, and rubbed dust into his hair.
He was the most powerful man among the Dangs, except
in time of war when the war chief took over, and furthermore he was an old man of personal dignity; yet here he
was abasing himself before me and, worse, rubbing dust
in his hair as was proper in the presence of the very sick
to help them in their dying. He told me why: prophesying
successfully from a voluntary trance was the test which I
must pass to become a high prophet; normally a master
prophet was forced to this, for the penalty for failing it
was death. I dismissed him with a wave of my claw.

I had five days to wait until full moon. The thought of
the risk I was running was more than I could handle
consciously; to avoid the jitters, I performed over and
over all the techniques of preparing for the trance, though
I carefully avoided entering it. I was not sure I was able
to enter it alone, but whether I could or not I knew I
wanted to conserve my forces for the great test. At first
during those five days I would remind myself once in a
while of my scientific purpose in going into the trance
consciously; at other times I would assure myself that it
was for the good of the Dangs I was doing it, since it was

not wise or safe for them to have only one high prophet.
Both of these reasons were true enough, but not very
important. As scientist, I should tell them some new myth,
say the story of Abraham and Isaac or of Oedipus, so
that I could compare its effect on them with that of the
Passion; as master prophet, I should ennoble my people
if I could. However, thinking these matters over as I held
my vatic squat hour after hour, visited and poked at by
prying eyes, I could find no myth to satisfy me: either,
as in the case of Abraham, it involved a concept of God
which the Dangs could not reach, or else, as with Oedipus,
it necessitated more drastic changes than I trusted myself
to keep straight while prophesying—that Oedipus should
mutilate himself was unthinkable to the Dangs and that
the gods should be represented as able to forgive him for
it was impious. Furthermore, I did not think, basically,
that any story I could tell them would in fact ennoble
them. I was out to save my own skin.

The story of Christ I knew by heart; it had worked for
me once, perhaps more than once; it would work again.
I rehearsed it over and over, from the Immaculate Conception to the Ascension. But such was the force of that
story on me that by the fifth day my cynicism had disappeared along with my scientism, and I believed, not
that the myth itself was true, but that relating it to my
people was the best thing it was possible for me to do for
them. I remember telling myself that this story would help
raise them toward monotheism, a necessary stage in the
evolution toward freedom. I felt a certain satisfaction in
the thought that some of the skulls on the stakes in the
Cave-Temple were very likely those of missionaries who
had failed to convert these heathen.

At sundown of the fifth day, I was taken by moon
slaves to a cave near The Cleft, where I was left in peace.
I fell into a troubled sleep, from which I awoke in a sweat:
"Where am I? What am I about to do?" It seemed to
me dreadfully wrong that I should be telling these, my

people, a myth in whose power, but not in whose truth, I believed. Why should I want to free them from superstition up into monotheism and thence up into my total freedom, when I myself was half-returning, voluntarily, down the layers again? The energy for these sweating questions came, no doubt, from my anxiety about how I was going to perform that night, but I did not recognize this fact at the time. Then, I thought it was my conscience speaking, and that I had no right to open to the Dangs a freedom I myself was rejecting. It was too late to alter my course; honesty required me, and I resolved courageously, not to prophesy at all.

When I was fetched out, the people were already in assembly at The Cleft and the wheel of master prophets was revolving against the greater wheel of dancers. I was given my cougar skin. Hung from a stake, in the center where I was to hop, was a huge, terrific mask I had never seen before. As the moon rose, her slaves hung this mask on me; the thong cut into the back of my neck cruelly, and at the bottom the mask came to a point that pressed my belly; it was so wide my arms could only move laterally. It had no eyeholes; I broke into a sweat wondering how I should be able to follow the prophets into the Cave-Temple. It turned out to be no problem: the two moon slaves, one on each side, guided me by prodding spears in my ribs. Once in the cave, they guided me to the back side of The Stone and drove me to climb it, my feet groping for steps I could not see; once, when I lost my balance, the spears' pressure kept me from falling backward. By the time I reached the top of The Stone, I was bleeding and dizzy. With one arm I kept the mask from gouging my belly while with the other I helped my aching neck support the mask. I did not know what to do next. Tears of pain and anger poured from my eyes. I began hopping. I should have been moving my arms in counterpoint to the rhythm of my hop, but I could not bear the thought of letting the mask cut into me more. I kept hopping in the same place, for fear of falling off; I had not been noticing the sounds of the other prophets, but suddenly I became conscious that they were making no sounds whatever. In my alarm at this I lurched to the side, and cut my foot on a sharp break in the rock. Pain converted my panic to rage.

I lifted the mask and held it flat above my head. I threw my head back and howled as I had never howled in my life, through a constricted, gradually opening throat, until at the end I was roaring; when I gasped in my breath, I made a barking noise. I leaped and leaped, relieved of pain, confident. I punched my knee desecratingly through the brittle hide of the mask, and threw it behind me off The Stone. I tore off my cougar skin and, holding it with my claw by the tip of its tail, I whirled it around my head. The prophets, massed below me, fell onto their knees. I felt their fear. Howling, I soared the skin out over them; one of those on whom it landed screamed hideously. A commotion started; I could not see very well what was happening. I barked and they turned toward me again. I leaped three times and then, howling, jumped wide-armed off The Stone. The twelve-foot drop hurt severely my already cut foot. I rolled exhausted into the channel in the cave floor.

Moon slaves with trembling hands mummied me in the deerskin and shoved me under The Stone with only my head sticking out. They brought two spears with darts tied to the points; rolling my head to watch them do this, I saw that the prophets were kneeling over and rubbing dirt into their hair; then the slaves laid the spears alongside the base of The Stone with the poisoned pricks pointed at my temples; exactly how close they were I could not be sure, but close enough so that I dared not move my head. In all my preparations I had, as I had been trained to do, rocked and wove at least my head; now, rigidity, live rigidity. A movement would scratch me and a scratch would kill me.

I pressed my hook into my thigh, curled my toes, and pressed my tongue against my teeth till my throat ached. I did not dare relieve myself even with a howl, for I might toss my head fatally. I strained against my thongs to the verge of apoplexy. For a while, I was unable to see, for sheer rage. Fatigue collapsed me. Yet I dared not relax my vigilance over my movements. My consciousness sealed me off. Those stone protuberances up between which I had to stare in the flickering light were merely chance processes on a boulder, similes to breasts. The one thing I might not become unconscious of was the pair of darts waiting for me to err. For a long time I thought of piercing my head against them, for relief, for spite. Hours passed. I was carefully watched.

I do not know what wild scheme I had had in mind when I had earlier resolved not to prophesy, what confrontation or escape; it had had the pure magnificence of a fantasy-resolution. But the reality, which I had not seriously tried to evade, was that I must prophesy or die. I kept lapsing from English into a delirium of Dang. By the greatest effort of will, I looked about me rationally: I wondered whether the return of Halley's Comet, at which time all the stakes should be mounted by skulls, would make the Dangs destroy the Cave-Temple and erect a new one; I observed the straight, indented seam of sandstone running slantwise up the boulder over me and wondered how many eons this rotting piece of granite had been tumbled about by water; I reflected that I was unworthy both as a Christian and as a Dang to prophesy the life of Jesus, but I convinced myself that I was a trivial matter since to the Christians it was the telling more than the teller that counted and to the Dangs this myth would serve as a civilizing force they needed. Surely, I thought, my hypocrisy could be forgiven me, especially since I resolved to punish myself for it by leaving the Dangs forever as soon as I could. Having reached this rational solution, I smiled and gestured to the high prophet with my eyes;

he did not move a muscle. When I realized that nothing to do with hypocrisy would unbind me, desperation swarmed in my guts and mounted toward my brain; with this question it took me over: *How can I make myself believe it is true?* I needed to catch hold of myself again. I dug my hook so hard into my leg—it was the only action I was able to take—that I gasped with pain; the pain I wanted. I did not speculate on the consequences of gouging my leg, tearing a furrow in my thigh muscle, hurting by the same act the stump of my arm to which the hook was attached; just as I knew that the prophets, the torches, the poisoned darts were there in the cave, so also I knew that far far back in my mind I had good enough reasons to be hurting myself, reasons which I could find out if I wanted to, but which it was not worth my trouble to discover; I even allowed the knowledge that I myself was causing the pain to drift back in my mind. The pain itself, only the pain, became my consciousness, purging all else. Then, as the pain subsided, leaving me free and equipoised, awareness of the stone arched over me flooded my mind. Because it had been invested by the people with a great mystery, it was an incarnation; the power of their faith made it the moon, who was female; at the same time it was only a boulder. I understood Stone is Stone, and that understanding became my consciousness.

My muscles ceased straining against the bonds, nor did they slump; they ceased aching, they were at ease, they were ready. I said nothing, I did not change the upward direction of my glance, I did not smile; yet at this moment the high prophet removed the spears and had the moon slaves unbind me. I did not feel stiff nor did my wounds bother me, and when I put on my cougar skin and leaped, pulled the head over my face and roared, all the prophets fell onto their faces before me. I began chanting and I knew I was doing it all the better for knowing what I was about; I led them back out to the waiting people, and until dawn I chanted the story of the birth, prophesying, betrayal, sacrifice, and victory of the most high prophet. I am a good mimic, I was thoroughly trained, the story is the best; what I gave them was, for them, as good as a vision. I did not know the difference myself.

But the next evening I knew the difference. While I performed my ablutions and the routine ceremonies to the full moon, I thought with increasing horror of my state of mind during my conscious trance. What my state of mind actually had been I cannot with confidence now represent, for what I know of it is colored by my reaction against it the next day. I had remained conscious, in that I could recall what happened; yet that observer and commentator in myself, of whose existence I had scarcely been aware, but whom I had always taken for my consciousness, had vanished; I no longer had been thinking, but had lost control so that my consciousness had become what I was doing; and, almost worse, when I had been telling the story of Christ, I had done it not because I had wanted to or believed in it, but because, in some obscure sense, I had had to. Thinking about it afterward, I did not understand or want to understand what I was drifting toward, but I knew it was something that I feared. And I got out of there as soon as I was physically able.

For here in Sansom, what I have learned has provided me with material for an honorable contribution to knowledge, has given me a tenure to a professorship, thereby pleasing my wife; whereas if I had stayed there among the Dangs much longer I would have reverted until I had become one of them, might not have minded when the time came to die under the sacrificial knife, would have taken in all ways the risk of prophecy, as my Dang son intends to do, until I had lost myself utterly.

THE GONZAGA MANUSCRIPTS

by Saul Bellow

Saul Bellow (1915–   ) was born in Quebec,
the son of Russian-Jewish parents who emigrated
to Canada. His family moved to Chicago when he
was still a child, and he still considers that his
home. Bellow graduated from Northwestern University with honors in anthropology and sociology
but decided on a literary rather than an academic
career. *The Adventures of Augie March* won the
National Book Award for 1953, and among his
subsequent novels, *Henderson the Rain King*,
Herzog, and *Humboldt's Gift* have raised him to
the front rank of American novelists. In 1976 he
won both the Pulitzer Prize and the Nobel Prize.

Buttoned to the throat in a long, soft overcoat, dark
green, Clarence Feiler got off the Hendaye Express in the
Madrid station. It was late afternoon and it was raining,
and the station with its throng and its dim orange lights
seemed sunken under darkness and noise. The gaunt
horselike Spanish locomotives screamed off their steam
and the hurrying passengers struggled in the narrow gates.
Porters and touts approached Clarence, obviously a foreigner by his small blond beard, blue eyes, almost brim-
less hat, long coat and crepe-soled shoes. But he carried

From *Seize the Day* by Saul Bellow. Copyright 1954 by Saul Bellow.
Reprinted by permission of The Viking Press, Inc.

his own bag and had no need of them. This was not his first visit to Madrid. An old limousine took him to the Pension La Granja, where he had a room reserved. This limousine probably had run on the boulevards of Madrid before Clarence was born but it was mechanically still beautiful. In the spacious darkness of the back seat the windows were like the glass of an old cabinet, and he listened happily to the voice of the wonderful old motor. Where could you get another ride like this, on such an evening, through such a place? Clarence loved Spanish cities, even the poorest and barrenest, and the capitals stirred his heart as no other places did. He had first come as an undergraduate, a mere kid, studying Spanish literature at the University of Minnesota; and then he had come again and seen the ruins of the Civil War. This time he came not as a tourist but on a quest. He had heard from a Spanish Republican refugee in California, where he now lived, that there were more than a hundred poems by Manuel Gonzaga somewhere in Madrid. Not a single Spanish publishing house could print them because they were so critical of the Army and the state. It was hard to believe that poems by one of the greatest of modern Spanish geniuses could be suppressed, but the refugee gave Clarence reliable proof that it was so. He showed him letters to one of Gonzaga's nephews from a man named Gúzman del Nido, Gonzaga's friend and literary executor, with whom he had served in North Africa, admitting that he had once had the poems but had given them up to a certain Countess del Camino since most of them were love poems addressed to her. The countess had died during the war, her home had been looted, and he didn't know what had become of the poems.

"Perhaps he doesn't care, either," said the refugee. "He's one of these people who think everything has come to an end anyway, and they might as well live comfortably. Gúzman del Nido lives very comfortably. He's rich. He is a member of the Cortes."

"Money doesn't have to do that to you," said Clarence, who had a little money himself. He was not exactly a rich man, but he didn't have to work for a living. "He must have a bad character not to care about his friend's work. And such work! You know, I was just killing time in graduate school till I came across Gonzaga. The year I spent doing my thesis on *Los Huesos Secos* was the first good year I had had since I was a boy. There hasn't been anything like it since. I'm not much on modern poetry in English. Some of it is very fine, of course, but it doesn't express much wish to live. To live as a creature, that is. As if it were not good enough. But the first time I opened Gonzaga I read:

> *These few bits of calcium my teeth are,*
> *And these few ohms my brain is,*
> *May make you think I am nothing but puny.*
> *Let me tell you, sir,*
> *I am like any creature—*
> *A creature.*

I felt right away and in spite of this ironical turn that I was in touch with a poet who could show me how to go on, and what attitude to take toward life. The great, passionate poems carried me away, like 'The Poem of Night,' which I still know by heart from beginning to end and which often seems like the only thing I really have got—" Clarence was sometimes given to exaggerating. "Or take the poem called 'Confession,' the one that goes:

> *I used to welcome all*
> *And now I fear all.*
> *If it rained it was comforting*
> *And if it shone, comforting,*
> *But now my very weight is dreadful . . .*

When I read that, Gonzaga made me understand how we lose everything by trying to become everything. This was the most valuable lesson of my life, I think. Gosh! There should be someone trying to find those posthumous poems. They ought not to be given up. They must be marvelous."

He felt, suddenly, as if he had been thrown into a race, terribly excited, full of effort, feverish—and profoundly grateful. For Clarence had not found his occupation and had nothing to do. He did not think it right to marry until he had found something and could offer a wife leadership. His beard was grown not to hide weaknesses but as a project, to give his life shape. He was becoming an eccentric; it was all he could do with his good impulses. As yet he did not realize that these impulses were religious. He was too timid to say he believed in God, and he couldn't think that it would matter to anyone what he believed. Since he was weak, it would be said, he must have some such belief. However, he was really enthusiastic about Gonzaga, and to recover this inspired Spaniard's poems was something that mattered. And "Does it really matter?" was always the test question. It filled Clarence with secret pleasure to know that he was not indifferent, at bottom pretending. It *did* matter, and what mattered might save him. He was in Madrid not to perform an act of cultural piety but to do a decent and necessary thing, namely, bring the testimony of a great man before the world. Which certainly could use it.

As soon as he arrived at the Pension La Granja and the lamps were lit in his room, a comfortable large room with balconies facing the trees of the Retiro, Madrid's biggest park, Clarence called for the porter and sent off two letters. One was addressed to Gúzman del Nido, Gonzaga's comrade-in-arms of the Moroccan War and literary executor, and the other to a Miss Faith Ungar on García de Paredes Street. This Miss Ungar was an art student, or rather student of art history; her fiancé was an airplane pilot who brought in cheaper pesetas from Tangiers. Clarence disliked black-marketing, but the legal rate of exchange was ridiculous; he was prepared to pay a lot of money for those manuscripts and at eighteen to one he might spend a small fortune.

His landlady came to welcome him to the pension—a pale, big woman with a sort of turban of hair wound spirally to a point. She came also to collect his passport and other travel papers for police inspection and to give him a briefing on her guests. A retired general was the oldest. She had also some people from British Shell and the widow of a Minister and six members of a Brazilian trade delegation, so the dining room was full. "And are you a tourist?" she said, glancing at the *triptico,* the elaborate police document all travelers have to carry in Spain.

"In a way," said Clarence, guardedly. He didn't like to be thought of as a tourist, and yet secrecy was necessary. Gonzaga's poems, though unpublished, would probably come under the head of national treasures.

"Oh have you come to study something?"

"Yes, that's it."

"There's a great deal here to interest people from a country as new as yours."

"There certainly is," he said, his rosy beard-lengthened face turned to her, seeming perfectly sincere. The color of his mouth was especially vivid in the lamplight. It was not yet full evening and the rain was stopping. Beyond the trees of the Retiro the sky was making itself clear of clouds, and a last yellow daylight pierced the water-gray. Trolley sparks scratched green within the locust trees.

A bell rang, an old handbell, announcing dinner. A maid passed, ringing it proudly, her shoulders thrown back.

The guests were eating soup in the dining room, an interior room, not very airy, with dark red, cloth-covered walls. The Brazilians were having a lively conversation. The old general, feeble-headed, eyes nearly extinct, was bothering the soup with his spoon but not eating. Doña

Elvia seated Clarence with a hefty British lady; he knew he must expect to have trouble with her. She was in a bad way. Her face was heavily made up; she thought she was a person of charm, and she did have a certain charm, but her eyes were burning. Tresses of dark-reddish hair fought strongly for position on her head.

"If you came here with the intention of having fun, you won't have it in Madrid. I've been here twenty years and never had any," she said. "By now I'm so tired out I don't even look for any. I don't read any books, I don't go to the cinema, and I can just barely stand to read *Coyote* and look at the funnies. I can't understand why so many Americans want to come here. They're all over the place. One of your bishops was arrested at Santander for bathing without the top of his costume."

"Really?"

"They're very strict in Spain about dress. I suppose if they had known he was a bishop they would have let him alone. However, in the water . . ."

"It's strange," said Clarence. "Well, anyway, he's not one of *my* bishops. I have no bishops."

"You do have Congressmen, though. Two of those had their pants stolen while taking a nap on the Barcelona Express. The thieves reached into the compartment from the roof. It happened in broad daylight. They carried about two thousand dollars each. Don't they have pocket-books? Why do they carry so much money in their pockets?"

Clarence frowned. "Yes, I read about that," he said. "I can't tell you why they carry so much money in their trouser pockets. Maybe that's the custom down South. It's none of my business, though."

"I'm afraid I'm annoying you," she said. She was not afraid at all; a bold look of enjoyment had entered her eyes. She was trying to bait him. Why? he wondered; he found no ready answer.

"You're not annoying me."

"If I am," she said, "it's not absolutely my fault. You know Stendhal once wrote there was a secret principle of unhappiness in the English."

"Is that so?" he said. He looked at her with deep interest. What a busted-up face; full of unhappy vigor and directionless intelligence. Yes, she was astonishing. He felt sorry for her and yet lucky to have met her, in spite of everything.

"He may have been right. You see, I used to read widely once. I was a cultivated person. But the reason for it was sex, and that went."

"Oh, come, I wouldn't say—"

"I shouldn't be talking like this. It's partly the weather. It's been raining so hard. It isn't supposed to rain like this in the summer. I've never seen so much damned rain. You people may be to blame for that."

"*Who* people? Which people?"

"It could be because of the atom bomb," she said. "The weather has never been normal since the atom thing started. Nobody can tell what this radioactive stuff is doing. Perhaps it's the beginning of the end."

"You make me feel very strange," said Clarence. "But why are the American bombs the dangerous ones? There are others."

"Because one always reads of the Americans exploding them. They do it under water. Holes are torn in the ocean bottom. The cold water rushes in and cools the core of the earth. Then the surface shrinks. No one can tell what will happen. It's affected the weather already."

Clarence's color grew very high and he looked dazed. He paid no attention to his broiled meat and french-fried potatoes. "I don't keep up much with science," he said. "I remember I did read somewhere that industry gives off six billion tons of carbon dioxide every year and so the earth is growing warmer because the carbon dioxide in the air is opaque to heat radiation. All that means that the glaciers won't be coming back."

"Yes, but what about Carbon Fourteen? You Americans are filling the air with Carbon Fourteen, which is very dangerous."

"I don't know about it. I am not all Americans. You are not all the English. You didn't lick the Armada, I didn't open the West. You are not Winston Churchill, I am not the Pentagon."

"I believe you are some sort of fanatic," she announced.

"And I believe you're a nasty old bag!" he said, enraged. He left the table and went to his room.

Half an hour later she knocked at his door. "I'm terribly sorry," she said. "I suppose I did go too far. But it's all right, we're friends now, aren't we? It does you so much good to be angry. It really is good." She did, now, look very friendly and happy.

"It's all right. I'm sorry too," he said.

After all, how would feuding with this Englishwoman help him with his quest? And then there were wrong ways and right ways of going about it. Gonzaga's poems should be recovered in the spirit of Gonzaga himself. Otherwise, what was the use?

Considering it all next morning, he saw that this Miss Walsh, the Englishwoman, had done him a service by baiting him. Unwittingly, she offered a test of his motive. He could not come to Spain and act badly, blindly. So he was deepened in his thought and in his purpose, and felt an increased debt to Gonzaga and to those poems.

He was in a hurry next morning to get to a bookstore and see what Gonzaga items there were in print. Impatiently he turned himself out of the comfortable bed, pulled on his underpants, dealt nervously with his cuff-buttons, washed at his little sink with the glass shelves and pointed faucets, and combed his hair and whiskers with his palms. Odors of soil and flowers came from the Retiro across the freshly watered street. The morning was clear, still and blue. He took one bite of the brick bits of toast the maid brought, sipped from the immense cup of bitter café-au-lait, and then rushed out to find a bookstore.

At Bucholz's he found only a single volume he had not seen before, a collection of letters from Gonzaga to his father. The frontispiece showed Gonzaga in his lieutenant's uniform—a small man, by Clarence's standard—sitting up straight at the keyboard of an old-fashioned piano, his large eyes opened directly into the camera. Underneath he had noted, "Whenever I am lucky enough to come upon a piano in one of these Moroccan towns, I can, after playing for ten or fifteen minutes, discover how I really feel. Otherwise I am ignorant." Clarence's face colored with satisfaction as he stooped and looked. What a man this Gonzaga was—what a personality! On the very first page was an early version of a poem he had always admired, the one that began:

> Let me hear a sound
> Truly not my own;
> The voice of another,
> Truly other. . . .

The book engrossed him entirely until eleven o'clock. With a sort of hungry emotion, he sat at a café table and read it from cover to cover. It was beautiful. He thanked God for sending him the Republican refugee who had given him the idea of coming to Spain.

Reluctantly he left the café and took a cab to García de Paredes Street, where Miss Ungar lived. He hated to do it, but he needed the pesetas, and it was unavoidable.

Again he was lucky. She was not at all the kind of person you would have expected a black-marketing art student to be; she was young and unusually attractive with a long, intelligent white face. Her hair was drawn tightly back over her elongated head and tied off in an arched, sparkling tail. Her eyes were extremely clear. Clarence was greatly taken with her. Even the fact that her teeth, because of the contrast with her very fair skin, were not too bright, impressed him. It proved to him that she was genuine. On a ribbon round her neck she wore a large silver medal.

"Is that a religious thing you're wearing?"

"No. Do you want to look at it?" She bent forward so that it swung free. He picked up the warm piece of silver and read: *Helena Waite Award for Historical Studies*.

"You won it?"

"Yes."

"Then why are you in this kind of business?"

"And what did you come here for?" she said.

"I need pesetas."

"And we need dollars. My fiancé and I want to buy a house."

"I see."

"Besides, it's a way of meeting a lot of people. You'd be surprised how few interesting people an American woman in Madrid can meet. I can't spend all my time in the Prado or at the Library. The embassy people are about as interesting as a plate of cold cuts. My fiancé only gets here twice a month. Are you on a holiday?"

"Sort of."

She didn't believe him. She knew he had come with a definite purpose. He could not say why, but this pleased him.

"How do you like the Granja?"

"It's all right. An Englishwoman there lammed into me last night, first about the atom bomb and then saying that I must be a fanatic. She thought I was peculiar."

"Everybody has to make it as he can," she said.

"That's exactly the way I feel about it."

He had thought that the kind of woman who became engaged to an airline pilot might look down on him. She didn't, not in the least. Soon he was wondering how that sort of man could interest her.

"If you have no other plans, why don't you come to lunch with me," he said "and save me from that Miss Walsh?"

They went out to eat. Though the day had grown hot, she stopped in the courtyard to put on a pair of net gloves; women without gloves were considered common in Madrid. For his part Clarence thought the momentary grasp of her fingers as she worked them into the gloves was wonderful; what a lot of life she had! Her white face gave off a pleasant heat. As they walked, she told him she couldn't give him many pesetas just yet; she'd pay whatever rate was quoted in the *Tribune* on the day the money arrived. That day, Clarence reflected, would also be the day on which her pilot arrived; he had no business to be disturbed by that, and yet it did disturb him.

Near the Naval Ministry they were stopped by a procession. Priests with banners led it, and after them came a statue of the Virgin carried by four men. A group of barefooted widows followed in their mourning with black mantillas. Old women passed, carrying tapers. Most of these appeared to be old maids, and the flames made a clear additional light near each face. A band played Beethoven's Funeral March. Above the walls of the ministry trees shot their leaves; there was the same odor of flowers and soil that Clarence had smelled that morning, of graves, of summer pines. Across the square, on the car tracks, a welding arc hummed and scalded. The dazzling mouths of the horns were carried past and the fire in the daylight moved away, but it was the bare white feet of the widows, treading on the dusty asphalt paving that Clarence watched, and when they were gone he said to Miss Ungar, "Wasn't that splendid? I'm glad I'm here."

His brows had risen; his face was so lively that Miss Ungar laughed and said, "You take it big. I like the way you take it. You ought to be sure to visit Toledo. Have you ever been there?"

"No."

"I go often. I'm doing a study. Come with me next time I go. I can show you lots of things there."

"There's nothing I'd like better. When do you go next?"

"Tomorrow."

He was disappointed. "Oh, I'm sorry, I can't make it tomorrow," he said. "I arrived yesterday and I'm going to be very busy for a while. Just give me a rain-check, will you? I'll hold you to this. But there is something special I came to do—you guessed it, I suppose—and I can't take the time to go anywhere now. I'm all keyed up."

"Is this mission of yours a secret?"

"In a way. There's an illegal side to it, probably. But I don't think you'd tell on me, and I'm so full of it I'm willing to talk. Have you ever heard of a poet named Gonzaga?"

"Gonzaga? I must have. But I don't think I ever read his poems."

"You should read them. He was very great, one of the most original of modern Spanish poets, and in the class of Juan Ramón Jiménez, Lorca, and Machado. I studied him at school and he means a lot to me. To understand what he did, you have to think first of modern literature as a sort of grand council considering what mankind should do next, how they should fill their mortal time, what they should feel, what they should see, where they should get their courage, how they should love, how they should be pure or great, and all the rest. This advice of literature has never done much good. But you see God doesn't rule over men as he used to, and for a long time people haven't been able to feel that life was firmly attached at both ends so that they could stand confidently in the middle and trust the place where they were. That kind of faith is missing, and for many years poets have tried to supply a substitute. Like 'the unacknowledged legislators' or 'the best is yet to be,' or Walt Whitman saying that whoever touched him could be sure he was touching a man. Some have stood up for beauty, and some have stood up for perfect proportion, and the very best have soon gotten tired of art for its own sake. Some took it as their duty to behave like brave performers who try to hold down panic during a theater fire. Very great ones have quit, like Tolstoi, who became a reformer, or like Rimbaud, who went to Abyssinia, and at the end of his life was begging of a priest, '*Montrez-moi. Montrez . . .* Show me something.' Frightening, the lives some of these geniuses led. Maybe they assumed too much responsibility. They knew that if by their poems and novels *they* were fixing values, there must be something wrong with the values. One man can't furnish them. Oh, he may try, if his inspiration is for values, but not if his inspiration is for words. If you throw the full responsibility for meaning and for the establishing of good and evil on poets, they are doomed to go down. However, the poets reflected what was happening to everyone. There are people who feel that they are responsible for *everything*. Gonzaga is free from this, and that's why I love him. Here. See what he says in some of these letters. I found this marvelous collection this morning."

His long hands shaking, he pressed flat the little book on the table of the restaurant. Miss Ungar's quiet face expressed more than intellectual interest. "Listen. He writes to his father: 'Many feel they must say it all, whereas all has been said, unsaid, resaid so many times that we are bound to feel futile unless we understand that we are merely adding our voices. Adding them when moved by the spirit. Then and then only.' Or this: 'A poem may outlive its subject—say, my poem about the girl who sang songs on the train—but the poet has no right to expect this. The poem has no greater privilege than the girl.' You see what kind of man he was?"

"Impressive—really!" she said. "I see that."

"I've come to Spain to find some of his unpublished poems. I have some money, and I've never really been able to find the thing that I wanted to do. I'm not original myself, except in some minor way. Anyhow, that's why

I'm here. Lots of people call themselves leaders, healers, priests, and spokesmen for God, prophets or witnesses, but Gonzaga was a human being who spoke only as a human being; there was nothing spurious about him. He tried never to misrepresent; he wanted to see. To move you he didn't have to do anything, he merely had to be. We've made the most natural things the hardest of all. Unfortunately for us all, he was killed while still young. But he left some poems to a certain Countess del Camino, and I'm here to locate them."

"It's a grand thing. I wish you luck. I hope people will help you."

"Why shouldn't they?"

"I don't know, but don't you expect to run into trouble?"

"Do you think I ought to expect to?"

"If you want my honest opinion, yes."

"I may get the poems—why, just like that," he said. "You never can tell."

"Started, by God!" he said when he received an answer from Gúzman del Nido. The member of the Cortes invited him to dinner. All that day he was in a state, and the weather was peculiarly thick, first glaring sunshine, then explosive rains. "See what I told you," said Miss Walsh. But when Clarence went out late in the afternoon, the sky was clear and pale again and the Palm Sunday leaves braided in the ironwork of balconies were withering in the sunlight. He walked to the Puerta del Sol with its crowd of pleasure-seekers, beggars, curb-haunters, wealthy women, soldiers, cops, lottery-ticket and fountain-pen peddlers, and priests, humble door-openers, chair-menders and musicians. At seven-thirty he boarded a streetcar, following directions; it seemed to take him to every other point of the city first. Finally, with the wisp of trolley paper still in his hand, he got off and mounted a bare stony alley at the top of which was the del Nido villa. Suddenly there was another cloudburst—*una tormenta* was what the

Madrileños called it. No doorway offered cover and he was drenched. At the gate he had to wait a long while for the porter to answer his ring, perhaps five minutes in the hard rain. This would probably give comfort to the Englishwoman with her atomic theories. His nervous long eyes seemed to catch some of the slaty blue of the pouring rain-cloud; his blond beard darkened, and he pulled in his shoulders. The tall gate opened. The porter held out an umbrella in his brown fist. Clarence walked past him to the door of the house. The rain stopped when he was halfway up the path.

So he was at a disadvantage when Gúzman del Nido came forward to meet him. He walked clumsily in his sodden wool suit. It had a shameful smell, like a wet dog.

"How do you do, Señor Feiler. What a shame about the rain. It has ruined your suit but it gives your face a fine color."

They shook hands, and it came over Clarence with a thrill as he looked at the high-bridged nose and dark, fine-textured skin of del Nido that he was in touch with Gonzaga himself—this round-shouldered man in his linen suit, bowing his sloping head, smiling with sharp teeth, with his hairless hand and big-boned wrist and his awkward fanny, he had been Gonzaga's friend and belonged within the legend. Clarence at once sensed that he would make him look foolish if he could, through the irony of his very complete manners. He also realized that del Nido was the sort of person who cut everyone down to size, Gonzaga included; precisely the sort of man to whom Gonzaga had written: *"Go away! You have no holy ones."*

"The letter I sent you—" Clarence managed to begin. They were hurrying toward the dining room; other guests were waiting.

"We can discuss it later."

"I understand you gave certain poems to the Countess del Camino," he said.

But del Nido was speaking with another guest. The candles were lit and the company sat down.

Clarence had no appetite.

He was sitting between an Italian Monsignore and an Egyptian lady who had lived in New York and spoke a very slangy English. There was a German gentleman, too, who headed some insurance company; he sat between Señora del Nido and her daughter. From his end of the table, del Nido with his narrow sleek head and his forward-curved teeth shining with valuable crowns, dominated the conversation. About his eyes the skin was twisted in curious laugh-wrinkles. Impressed, appalled, too, Clarence asked himself again and again how Gonzaga could have trusted such a person. A maker of witticisms, as Pascal had said, a bad character. When these words of Pascal came into his head, Clarence turned to the Monsignore as a man to whom this might make sense. But the Monsignore was interested mostly in stamp-collecting. Clarence was not, so the Monsignore had nothing further to say to him. He was a gloomy, fleshy man whose hair grew strongly and low over the single deep wrinkle of his forehead.

Gúzman del Nido kept on talking. He talked about modern painting, about mystery stories, about old Russia, about the movies, about Nietzsche. Dreamy-looking, the daughter seemed not to listen; his wife expanded some of his remarks. The daughter stared with close-set eyes into the candle flames. The Egyptian lady was amused by the strong smell of Clarence's rain-shrinking clothes. She made a remark about wet wool. He was grateful for the absence of electric lights.

"An American was arrested in Córdoba," said Gúzman del Nido. "He stole the hat of a *Guardia Civil* for a souvenir."

"Isn't that unusual!"

"He'll find the jail smaller than the jails at home. I

hope you won't mind if I tell a story about Americans and the size of things in Spain."

"Why should I mind?" said Clarence.

"Splendid. Well, there was an American whose Spanish host could not impress him. Everything was larger in America. The skyscrapers were bigger than the palaces. The cars were bigger. The cats were bigger. At last his host placed a lobster between his sheets and when the horrified American saw it his host said, 'This is one of our bedbugs. I don't think you can beat that.'"

For some reason this fetched Clarence more than it did the others. He uttered a bark of laughter that made the candlelights bend and flutter.

"Perhaps you'll tell us an American story," said del Nido.

Clarence thought. "Well, here's one," he said. "Two dogs meet in the street. Old friends. One says, 'Hello.' The other answers, 'Cock-a-doodle-do!' 'What does that mean? What's this cock-a-doodle-do stuff?' 'Oh,' says he, 'I've been studying foreign languages.'"

Dead silence. No one laughed. The Egyptian lady said, "I'm afraid you laid an egg." Clarence was angry.

"Is this story told in English or in American?" del Nido asked.

That started a discussion. Was American really a sort of English? Was it a language? No one seemed sure, and Clarence at last said, "I don't know whether or not it is a language, but there is *something* spoken. I've seen people cry in it and so forth, just as elsewhere."

"We deserved that," said del Nido. "It's true, we're not fair to Americans. In reality the only true Europeans left are Americans."

"How so?"

"The Europeans themselves do not have the peace of mind to appreciate what's best. Life is too hard for us, society too unstable."

Clarence realized that he was being shafted; del Nido was satirizing his guest; he undoubtedly meant that Clarence could not comprehend Gonzaga's poems. An ugly hatred for del Nido grew and knotted in his breast. He wanted to hit him, to strangle him, to trample him, to pick him up and hurl him at the wall. Luckily del Nido was called to the phone, and Clarence stared out his rage at the empty place, the napkin, the silver, the crest of the chair. Only Señorita del Nido seemed aware that he was offended.

Once more Clarence told himself that there was a wrong way to go about obtaining the poems, a way contrary to their spirit. That did much to calm him. He managed to get down a few spoonfuls of ice cream and mastered himself.

"Why are you so interested in Gonzaga?" said del Nido to him later in the garden, under the date palms with their remote leaves.

"I studied Spanish literature in college and became a Gonzagian."

"Wasn't that rather strange, though? You must forgive me, but I see my poor old friend Gonzaga, who was Spanish of the Spanish, in that terrible uniform we used to wear, and our hands and faces bruised and baked and chapped by the desert sun, and I ask myself why he should have had an effect . . ."

"I don't know why. I'd like to understand it myself; but the fact that he did is what you start with."

"I have made an interesting observation about poets and their lives. Some are better in real life than in their work. You read bitter poems and then you find the poet is personally very happy and good-tempered. Some are worse in their personality than you would guess from their work. They are luckier, in a way, because they have a chance to correct their faults and improve themselves. Best of all are the ones who are exactly the same inside and out, in the spoken word and the written. To be what you seem to be is the objective of true culture.. Gonzaga was of the second type."

"Was he?" It occurred to Clarence that del Nido was trying to make himself more interesting to him than Gonzaga could be, to push Gonzaga out.

"I think I can tell you one reason why Gonzaga appeals to me," said Clarence. "He got away from solving *his* own problem. I often feel this way about it: a poem is great because it is absolutely necessary. Before it came silence. After it comes more silence. It begins when it must and ends when it must, and therefore it's not personal. It's 'the sound truly not my own.'" Now he was proving to del Nido that he *could* comprehend; at the same time he knew that he was throwing away his effort. Gúzman del Nido was fundamentally indifferent. Indifferent, indifferent, indifferent! He fundamentally did not care. What can you do with people who don't fundamentally care! "But you know why I came to you. I want to know what became of Gonzaga's last poems. What were they like?"

"They were superb love poems. But I don't know where they are now. They were dedicated to the Countess del Camino and I was supposed to hand them on to her. Which I did."

"There aren't any copies?" said Clarence, trembling as del Nido spoke of the poems.

"No. They were for the countess."

"Of course. But they were also for everyone else."

"There's plenty of poetry already, for everyone. Homer, Dante, Calderón, Shakespeare. Have you noticed how much difference it makes?"

"It should make a difference. Besides, Calderón wasn't your friend. But Gonzaga was. Where's the countess now? The poor woman is dead, isn't she? And what happened to those poems? Where do you think the poems can be?"

"I don't know. She had a secretary named Polvo, a fine old man. A few years ago he died, too. The old man's

nephews live in Alcalá de Henares. Where Cervantes was
born, you know. They're in the civil service, and they're
very decent people, I hear."

"You never even asked them what happened to your
friend's poems?" cried Clarence, astonished. "Didn't you
want to find them?"

"I thought eventually I'd try to trace them. I'm sure the
countess would have taken good care of her poems."

This was where the discussion stopped, and Clarence was
just as glad that it couldn't continue; he sensed that Gúzman del Nido would have liked to give him the dirt on Gonzaga—revelations involving women, drunkenness and dope-
taking, bribery, gonorrhea, or even murder. Gonzaga had
escaped into the army; that was notorious. But Clarence
didn't want to hear del Nido's reminiscences.

It's natural to suppose, because a man is great, that the
people around him must have known how to respond to
greatness, but when those people turn out to be no better
than Gúzman del Nido you wonder what response greatness
really needs.

This was what Clarence was saying to Miss Ungar several days later.

"He's glad he doesn't have the poems," said Miss Ungar.
"If he had them he'd feel obligated to do something about
them, and he's afraid of that because of his official position."

"That's right. Exactly," said Clarence. "But he did me
one favor anyway. He put me on to the countess's secretary's nephews. I've written to them and they've invited me
to Alcalá de Henares. They didn't mention the poems but
maybe they were just being discreet. I'd better start being
more discreet myself. There's something unpleasant going
on, lately."

"What is it?"

"I think the police have an eye on me."

"Oh, come!"

"I do. I'm serious. My room was searched yesterday. I

know it was. My landlady didn't answer one way or another when I asked her. She didn't even bother."

"It's too peculiar for anything," Miss Ungar said, laughing in amazement. "But why should they search? What for?"

"I suppose I just inspire suspicion. And then I made a mistake with my landlady the day after my visit to del Nido. She's a very patriotic character. She has a retired general in the pension, too. Well, she was talking to me the other morning and among other things she told me how healthy she was, strong as a rock—*una roca*—a sort of Gibraltar. And like a dumbbell I said, without even thinking, '*Gibraltar Español!*' That was an awful boner."

"Why?"

"During the war, you see, when the British were taking such a pounding there was a great agitation for the return of Gibraltar to Spain. The slogan was *Gibraltar Español!* Of course they don't like to be reminded that they were dying for the British to get it good and hot from Germany. Well, she probably thinks I'm a political secret somebody. And she was just plain offended."

"But what difference does it really make, as long as you don't do anything illegal?"

"When you're watched closely you're bound sooner or later to do *something*," he said.

He went out to Alcalá on a Sunday afternoon and met the two nephews of Don Francisco Polvo and their wives and daughters.

They proved to be a family of laughers. They laughed when they spoke and when you answered. You saw nothing in the town but sleepy walls, and parched trees and stones. The brothers were squat, sandy-haired, broad-bellied men.

"We're having tea in the garden," said Don Luis Polvo. He was called "the Englishman" by the others because he had lived in London for several months twenty years ago; they addressed him as "My Lord," and he obliged them by acting like an *Inglés*. He even owned a scotch terrier named *Duglas*. The family cried to him, "Now's your chance to speak English, Luis. Speak to him!"

"Jolly country, eh?" Luis said. That was about all he could manage.

"Very."

"More, more!"

"Charing Cross."

"Go on, Luis, say more."

"Piccadilly. And that's all I can remember."

The tea was served. Clarence drank and sweltered. Lizards raced in the knotty grapevines and by the well. . . . The wives were embroidering. The laughing daughters were conversing in French, obviously about Clarence. Nobody appeared to believe what he said. Lanky and pained he sat in what looked to be a suit made of burlap, with his tea. Instead of a saucer, he felt as though he were holding on to the rim of Saturn.

After tea they showed him through the house. It was huge, old, bare, thick-walled and chill, and it was filled with the portraits and the clothing of ancestors—weapons, breastplates, helmets, daggers, guns. In one room where the picture of a general in the Napoleonic Wars was hung, a fun-making mood seized the brothers. They tried on plumed hats, then sabers, and finally full uniforms. Wearing spurs, medals, musty gloves, they went running back to the terrace where the women sat. Don Luis dragged a sword, his seat hung down and the cocked hat sagged broken, opening in the middle of his sandy baldness. With a Napoleonic musket, full of self-mockery, he performed the manual-at-arms to uproarious laughter. Clarence laughed, too, his cheeks creased; he couldn't explain however why his heart was growing heavier by the minute.

Don Luis aimed the musket and shouted, *"La bomba atómica! Poum!"*

The hit he scored with this was enormous. The women shrieked, swiveling their fans, and his brother fell on his behind in the sanded path, weeping with laughter. The terrier *Duglas* leaped into Don Luis's face, fiercely excited.

Don Luis threw a stick and cried, "Fetch, fetch, *Duglas! La bomba atómica! La bomba atómica!*"

The blood stormed Clarence's head so furiously he heard the strange noise of it. This was another assault on him. Oh! he thought frantically, the things he had to bear! The punishment he had to take trying to salvage those poems!

As if in the distance, the voice of Don Luis cried, "Hiroshima! Nagasaki! Bikini! Good show!" He flung the stick and the dog bounded on taut legs, little *Duglas,* from the diminished figure of his master and back—the tiny white and brown animal, while laughter incessantly pierced the dry air of the garden.

It was not a decent joke, even though Don Luis in that split hat and the withered coat was mocking the dead military grandeur of his own country. That didn't even the score. The hideous stun of the bomb and its unbearable, death-brilliant mushroom cloud filled Clarence's brain. This was not right.

He managed to stop Don Luis. He approached him, laid a hand on the musket, and asked to speak with him privately. It made the others laugh. The ladies started to murmur about him. An older woman said, *"Es gracioso"*; the girls seemed to disagree. He heard one of them answer, *"Non, il n'est pas gentil."* Proudly polite, Clarence faced it out. "Damn their damn tea!" he said to himself. His shirt was sticking to his back.

"We did not inherit my uncle's papers," said Don Luis. "Enough, *Duglas!*" He threw the stick down the well. "My brother and I inherited this old house and other land but if there were papers they probably went to my cousin Pedro Alvarez-Polvo who lives in Segovia. He's a very interesting fellow. He works for the *Banco Español* but is a cultivated person. The countess had no family. She was fond of my uncle. My uncle was extremely fond of Alvarez-Polvo. They shared the same interests."

"Did your uncle ever speak of Gonzaga?"

"I don't recall. The countess had a large number of artistic admirers. This Gonzaga interests you very much, doesn't he?"

"Yes. Why shouldn't I be interested in him? You may some day be interested in an American poet."

"*I*? No!" Don Luis laughed, but he was startled.

What people! Damn these dirty laughers! Clarence waited until Don Luis's shocked and latterly somewhat guilty laughter ended, and his broad yap, with spacious teeth, closed—his lips shook with resistance to closing, and finally remained closed.

"Do you think your cousin Alvarez-Polvo would know . . ."

"He would know a lot," said Don Luis, composed. "My uncle confided in him. *He* can tell you something definite, you can count on him. I'll give you a letter of introduction to him."

"If it's not too much trouble."

"No, no, the pleasure is mine." Don Luis was all courtesy.

After returning to Madrid on the bus through the baking plain of Castile, Clarence phoned Miss Ungar. He wanted her sympathy and comfort. But she didn't invite him to come over. She said, "I can give you the pesetas tomorrow." That was her tactful way of informing him that the pilot had landed, and he thought she sounded regretful. Perhaps she was not really in love with her fiancé. Clarence now had the impression that the black-marketing was not her idea but the pilot's. It embarrassed her, but she was too loyal to admit it to him.

"I'll come by later in the week. There's no hurry," he said. "I'm busy anyway."

It would hurt him to do it, but he'd cash a check at the American Express tomorrow at the preposterous legal rate of exchange.

Disappointed, Clarence hung up. *He* should have a woman like that. It passed dimly over his mind that a live woman would make a better quest than a dead poet. But the poet was already *there;* the woman not. He sent a letter to Alvarez-Polvo, washed all over, and lay reading Gonzaga by a buzzing light under the canopy of his bed.

He arrived in Segovia early one Sunday morning. It was filled with sunlight, the clouds were silk-white in the mountain air. Their shadows wandered over the slopes of the bare sierra like creatures that crept and warmed themselves on the soil and rock. All over the old valley were convents, hermitages, churches, towers, the graves of San Juan and other mystical saints. At the highest point of Segovia was the Alcázar of Isabella the Catholic. And passing over the town with its many knobby granite curves that divided the sky was the aqueduct, this noble Roman remnant, as bushy as old men's ears. Clarence stood at the window of his hotel and looked at this conjured rise of stones that bridged the streets. It got him, all of it—the ancient mountain slopes worn as if by the struggles of Jacob with the angel, the spires, the dry glistening of the atmosphere, the hermit places in green hideaways, the sheep bells' clunk, the cistern water dropping, while beams came as straight as harp-wires from the sun. All of this, like a mild weight, seemed to press on him; it opened him up. He felt his breath creep within him like a tiny pet animal.

He went down through the courtyard. There the cistern of fat stone held green water, full of bottom-radiations from the golden brass of the faucets. Framed above it in an archway were ladies' hair styles of twenty years ago—a brilliantine advertisement. Ten or so beautiful señoritas with bangs, shingles, and windswept bobs smiled like various priestesses of love. Therefore Clarence had the idea that this cistern was the Fountain of Youth. And also that it was something Arcadian. He said, " 'Ye glorious nymphs!' " and burst out laughing. He felt happy—magnificent! The sun poured over his head and embraced his back hotly.

Smiling, he rambled up and down the streets. He went to the Alcázar. Soldiers in German helmets were on guard. He went to the cathedral. It was ancient but the stones looked brand-new. After lunch he sat at the café in front of the aqueduct waiting for Alvarez-Polvo. On the wide sloping sidewalk there were hundreds of folding chairs, empty, the paint blazed off them and the wood emerging as gray as silverfish. The long low windows were open, so that inside and outside mingled their air, the yellow and the sombre, the bar brown and the sky clear blue. A gypsy woman came out and gave Clarence the eye. She was an entertainer, but whether a real gypsy or not was conjectural. In the phrase he had heard, some of these girls were *Gitanas de miedo,* or strictly from hunger. But he sat and studied the aqueduct, trying to imagine what sort of machinery they could have used to raise the stones.

A black hearse with mourners who trod after it slowly, and with all the plumes, and carvings of angels and death-grimacers, went through the main arch to the cemetery. After ten minutes it came galloping back with furious lashing of the horses, the silk-hatted coachman standing, yacking at them. Only a little later the same hearse returned with another procession of mourners who supported one another, weeping aloud, grief pushing on their backs. Through the arch again. And once more the hearse came flying back. With a sudden tightness of the guts Clarence thought, Why all these burials at once? Was this a plague? He looked at the frothy edge of his glass with horror.

But Alvarez-Polvo set his mind at rest. He said, "The hearse was broken all week. It has just been repaired."

He was a strange-looking man. His face seemed to have been worked by three or four diseases and then abandoned. His nose swelled out and shrunk his eyes. He had a huge mouth, like his cousin Don Luis. He wore a beret, and a yellow silk sash was wound around his belly. Clarence often had noticed that short men with big bellies sometimes held their arms ready for defense as they walked, but at heart expected defeat. Alvarez-Polvo, too, had that posture. However, his brown, mottled, creased, sunlit face with kinky gray hair escaping from the beret seemed to declare that he had a soul like a drum. If you struck, you wouldn't injure him. You'd hear a sound.

"You know what I've come for?" said Clarence.

"Yes, I do know. But let's not start talking business right away. You've never been in Segovia before, I assume, and you must let me be hospitable. I'm a proud Segoviano —proud of this ancient, beautiful city, and it would give me pleasure to show you the principal places."

At the words "talking business" Clarence's heart rose a notch. Was it only a matter of settling the price? Then he had the poems! Something in Clarence flapped with eager joy, like a flag in the wind.

"By all means. For a while. It is beautiful. Never in my life have I seen anything so gorgeous as Segovia."

Alvarez-Polvo took his arm.

"With me you will not only see, you will also understand. I have made a study of it. I'm a lover of such things. I seldom have an opportunity to express it. Wherever I take my wife, she is interested only in *novelas morbosas*. At Versailles she sat and read Ellery Queen. In Paris, the same. In Rome, the same. If she lives to the end of time, she will never run out of *novelas morbosas*."

From this remark, without notice, he took a deep plunge into the subject of women, and he carried Clarence with him. Women, women, women! All types of Spanish beauty. The Granadinas, the Malagueñas, the Castellanas, the Cataluñas. And then the Germans, the Greeks, the French, the Swedes! He tightened his hold on Clarence and pulled him close as he boasted and complained and catalogued and confessed. He was ruined! They had taken his money, his health, his time, his years, his life, women had—innocent, mindless, beautiful, ravaging, insidious, malevolent, chestnut, blond, red, black. . . . Clarence felt hemmed in by women's faces, and by women's bodies.

"I suppose you'd call this a Romanesque church, wouldn't you?" Clarence said, stopping.

"Of course it is," said Alvarez-Polvo. "Just notice how the Renaissance building next to it was designed to harmonize with it."

Clarence was looking at the pillars and their blunted faces of humorous, devil-beast humanities, the stone birds, demon lollers, apostles. Two men carried by a spring and mattress in a pushcart. They looked like the kings of Shinar and Elam defeated by Abraham.

"Come, have a glass of wine," said Alvarez-Polvo. "I'm not allowed to drink since my operation, but you must have something."

When could they begin to talk about the poems? Clarence was impatient. Gonzaga's poems would mean little if anything to a man like this, but in spite of his endless gallant bunk and his swagger and his complaints about having broken his springs in the service of love and beauty, he was probably a very cunning old fuff. He wanted to stall Clarence and find out what the poems were worth to him. And so Clarence gazed, or blinked, straight ahead, and kept a tight grip on his feelings.

In the *bodega* were huge barrels, copper fittings, innumerable bottles duplicated in the purple mirror, platters of *mariscos,* crawfish bugging their eyes on stalks, their feelers cooked into various last shapes. From the middle of the floor rose a narrow spiral staircase. It mounted—who-knew-where? Clarence tried to see but couldn't. A little torn-frocked beggar child came selling lottery tickets. The old chaser petted her; she wheedled; she took his small hand and laid her cheek to it. Still talking, he felt her hair. He stroked his fill and sent her away with a coin.

Clarence drank down the sweet, yellow Malaga.

"Now," said Alvarez-Polvo, "I will show you a church few visitors ever see."

They descended to the lower part of town, down littered stairways of stone, by cavelike homes and a lot where runty boys were passing a football with their heads, and dribbling and hooking it with their boots.

"Here," Alvarez-Polvo said. "This wall is of the tenth century and this one of the seventeenth."

The air inside the church was dark, cool, thick as ointment. Hollows of dark red and dark blue and heavy yellow slowly took shape, and Clarence began to see the altar, the columns.

Alvarez-Polvo was silent. The two men were standing before a harshly crowned Christ. The figure was gored deeply in the side, rust-blooded. The head-cover of thorns was too wide and heavy to be borne. As he confronted it, Clarence felt that it threatened to scratch the life out of him, to scratch him to the heart.

"The matter that interests us both . . ." Alvarez-Polvo then said.

"Yes, yes, let's go somewhere and have a talk about it. You got the poems among your uncle's papers. Do you have them here in Segovia?"

"Poems?" said Alvarez-Polvo, turning the dark and ruined face from the aisle. "That's a strange word to use for them."

"Do you mean they're not in that form? What are they, then? What are they written in?"

"Why, the usual legal language. According to law."

"I don't understand."

"Neither do I. But I can show you what I'm talking about. Here. I have one with me. I brought it along." He drew a document from his pocket.

Clarence held it, trembling. It was heavy, glossy and heavy. He felt an embossed surface. Yes, there was a seal on it. What had the countess done with the poems? This paper was emblazoned with a gilt star. He sought light and read, within an elaborate border of wavy green, *Compañia de Minas, S.A.*

"Is this— It can't be. You've given me the wrong thing." His heart was racing. "Look in your pocket again."

"The wrong thing?"

"It looks like shares of stock."

"Then it isn't the wrong thing. It's what it's supposed to be, mining stock. Isn't that what you're interested in?"

"Of course not! Certainly not! What kind of mine?"

"It's a pitchblende mine in Morocco, that's what it is."

"What in the name of anything do I want with pitch-blende!" Clarence shouted.

"What any sensible man would want. To sell it. Pitch-blende has uranium in it. Uranium is used in atom bombs."

Oh, dear God!

"Claro. Para la bomba atómica."

"What have I to do with atom bombs? What do I care about atom bombs! To hell with atom bombs!" Clarence cried out, furious.

"I understood you were a financier."

"Me? Do I look like one?"

"Yes, of course you do. More English than American, I thought. But a financier. Aren't you?"

"I am not. I came about the poems of Gonzaga, the poems owned by the Countess del Camino. Love poems dedicated to her by the poet Manuel Gonzaga."

"Manuel? The soldier? The little fellow? The one that was her lover in nineteen-twenty-eight? He was killed in Morocco."

"Yes, yes! What did your uncle do with the poems?"

"Oh, that's what you were talking about. Why, my uncle did nothing with them. The countess did, herself. She had them buried with her. She took them to the grave."

"Buried! With her, you say! And no copies?"

"I doubt it. My uncle had instructions from her, and he was very loyal. He lived by loyalty. My uncle—"

"Oh, damn! Oh, damn it! And didn't he leave you any-thing in that collection of papers that has to do with Gonzaga? No journals, no letters that mention Gonzaga? Nothing?"

"He left me these shares in the mine. They're valuable. Not yet, but they will be if I can get capital. But you can't raise money in Spain. Spanish capital is cowardly, ignorant of science. It is still in the Counter-Reformation. Let me show you the location of this mine." He opened a map and began to explain the geography of the Atlas Mountains.

Clarence walked out on him—ran, rather than walked. He had to get out of Segovia. Quickly. Panting, enraged, choking, he clambered from the lower town.

As soon as he entered his room at the hotel he knew that his valise had been searched. Storming, he slammed it shut and dragged it down the stairs, past the cistern, and into the lobby.

He called in a shout to the manager, "Why must the police come and turn my things upside down?"

White-faced and stern, the manager said, "You must be mistaken, señor."

"I am not mistaken. Why must the police bother foreign visitors?"

A man rose angrily from a chair in the lobby. He wore an old suit with a mourning band on the arm.

"These Englishmen!" he said with fury. "They don't know what hospitality is. They come here and enjoy them-selves, and criticize our country, and complain about po-lice. What hypocrisy! There are more police in England. The whole world knows you have a huge jail in Liverpool, filled with Masons. Five thousand Masons are *encarcelados* in Liverpool alone."

Clarence couldn't reply. He stared. The he paid his bill and left. All the way to Madrid he sat numb and motion-less in his second-class seat.

As the train left the mountains, the heavens seemed to

split; a rain began to fall, heavy and sudden, boiling on the wide plain.

He knew what to expect from that redheaded Miss Walsh at dinner.

PRINCE OF DARKNESS

by J. F. Powers

James Farl Powers (1917–   ) is a Roman
Catholic with, as the story below indicates, a sharp
and perceptive eye for the real life within that
church and the often strained relations between
the clerical and the secular life. Born in Illinois,
Powers attended Northwestern but did not finish
his degree. He is married and the father of five
children.

It was not until 1943 that his literary excellence
was recognized with the publication of "Lions,
Harts, Leaping Does" in *Accent*. The story was
chosen for the 1944 O'Henry collection. Powers
was a Guggenheim Fellow in 1948, and his novel
Morte d'Urban won the National Book Award for
1963. His short story collection, *Look How the
Fish Live,* appeared in 1975.

1. MORNING

"I should've known you'd be eating breakfast, Father. But
I was at your Mass and I said to myself that must be
Father Burner. Then I stayed a few minutes after Mass to
make my thanksgiving."

"Fine," Father Burner said. "Breakfast?"

"Had it, Father, thanking you all the same. It's the regret
of my life that I can't be a daily communicant. Doctor forbids it. 'Fast every day and see how long you last,' he tells
me. But I do make it to Mass."

"Fine. You say you live in Father Desmond's parish?"

"Yes, Father. And sometimes I think Father Desmond does too much. All the societies to look after. Plus the Scouts and the Legion. Of course Father Kells being so elderly and all . . ."

"We're all busy these days."

"It's the poor parish priest's day that's never done, I always say, Father, not meaning to slight the ladies, God love 'em."

Father Burner's sausage fingers, spelling his impatience over and over, worked up sweat in the folds of the napkin which he kept in view to provoke an early departure. "About this matter you say Father Desmond thought I might be interested in—"

"The Plan, Father." Mr. Tracy lifted his seersucker trousers by the creases, crossed his shining two-tone shoes and rolled warmly forward. "Father . . ."

Father Burner met his look briefly. He was wary of the fatherers. A backslider he could handle, it was the old story, but a red hot believer, especially a talkative one, could be a devilish nuisance. This kind might be driven away only by prayer and fasting, and he was not adept at either.

"I guess security's one thing we're all after."

Father Burner grunted. Mr. Tracy was too familiar to suit him. He liked his parishioners to be retiring, dumb or frightened. There were too many references made to the priest's hard lot. Not so many poor souls as all that passed away in the wee hours, nor was there so much bad weather to brave. Mr. Tracy's heart bled for priests. That in itself was a suspicious thing in a layman. It all led up to the Plan.

"Here's the Plan, Father . . ." Father Burner watched his eye peel down to naked intimacy. Then, half listening, he gazed about the room. He hated it too. A fabulous brown rummage of encyclopedias, world globes, maps, photographs, holy pictures, mirrors, crucifixes, tropical fish and too much furniture. The room reproduced the world in exact scale, all wonders and horrors seemingly, less land than water. From the faded precipices of the walls photographs viewed each other for the most part genially across time. Three popes, successively thinner, raised hands to bless their departed painters. The world globes simpered in the shadows, heavy-headed idiot boys, listening. A bird in a blacked-out cage scratched among its offal. An anomalous buddha peeked beyond his dusty umbilicus at the trampled figures in the rug. The fish swam on, the mirrors and encyclopedias turned in upon themselves, the earless boys heard everything and understood nothing. Father Burner put his big black shoe on a moth and sent dust flecks crowding up a shaft of sunlight to the distant ceiling.

"Say you pay in $22.50 every month, can be paid semi-annually or as you please, policy matures in twenty years and pays you $35.67 a month for twenty years or as long as you live. That's the deal for you, Father. It beats the deal Father Desmond's got, although he's got a darned good one, and I hope he keeps it up. But we've gone ahead in the last few years, Father. Utilities are sounder, bonds are more secure and this new legislation protects you one hundred per cent."

"You say Ed—Father Desmond—has the Plan?"

"Oh, indeed, Father." Mr. Tracy had to laugh. "I hope you don't think I'm trying to high-pressure you, Father. It's not just a piece of business with me, the Plan."

"No?"

"No. You see, it's more or less a pet project of mine. Hardly make a cent on it. Looking out after the fathers, you might say, so they'll maybe look out after me—spiritually. I call it heavenly life insurance."

Slightly repelled, Father Burner nodded.

"Not a few priests that I've sold the Plan to remember me at the altar daily. I guess prayer's one thing we can all use. Anyway it's why I take a hand in putting boys through seminary."

With that Mr. Tracy shed his shabby anonymity and

drew executive markings for Father Burner. He became the one and only Thomas Nash Tracy—T. N. T. It was impossible to read the papers and not know a few things about T. N. T. He was in small loans and insurance. His company's advertising smothered the town and country; everybody knew the slogan T. N. T. spells Security. He figured in any financial drive undertaken by the diocese, was caught by photographers in orphanages and sat at the heavy end of the table at communion breakfasts. Hundreds of nuns, thanks to his thoughtfulness, ate capon on Christmas Day and a few priests of the right sort received baskets of scotch. He was a B. C. L., a Big Catholic Layman, and now Father Burner could see why. Father Burner's countenance softened at this intelligence and T. N. T. proceeded with more assurance.

"And don't call it charity, Father. Insurance, as I said, is a better name for it. I have a little money, Father, which makes it possible." He turned his voice down to a whisper. "You might say I'm moderately wealthy." He looked sharply at Father Burner, not sure of his man. "But I'm told there isn't any crime in that."

"I believe you need not fear for your soul on that account."

"Glad to hear it from you, a priest, Father. Oft times it's thrown up to me." He came to terms with reality, smiling. "I wasn't always so well off myself, so I can understand the temptation to knock the other fellow."

"Fine."

"But that's still not to say that water's not wet or that names don't hurt sometimes, whatever the bard said to the contrary."

"What bard?"

" 'Sticks and stones—' "

"Oh."

"If this were a matter of Faith and Morals, Father, I'd be the one to sit back and let you do the talking. But it's a case of common sense, Father, and I think I can safely say if you listen to me you'll not lose by it in the long run."

"It could be."

"May I ask you a personal question, Father?"

Father Burner searched T. N. T.'s face. "Go ahead, Mr. Tracy."

"Do you bank, Father?"

"*Bank?* Oh, bank—no. Why?"

"Let's admit it, Father," T. N. T. coaxed, frankly amused. "Priests as a class are an improvident lot—our records show it—and you're no exception. But that, I think, explains the glory of the Church down through the ages."

"The Church is divine," Father Burner corrected. "And the concept of poverty isn't exactly foreign to Christianity or even to the priesthood."

"Exactly," T. N. T. agreed, pinked. "But think of the future, Father."

Nowadays when Father Burner thought of the future it required a firm act of imagination. As a seminarian twenty years ago, it had all been plain: ordination, roughly ten years as a curate somewhere (he was not the kind to be sent to Rome for further study), a church of his own to follow, the fruitful years, then retirement, pastor emeritus, with assistants doing the spade work, leaving the fine touches to him, still a hearty old man very much alive. It was not an uncommon hope and in fact all around him it had materialized for his friends. But for him it was only a bad memory growing worse. He was the desperate assistant now, the angry functionary aging in the outer office. One day he would wake up and find himself old, as the morning finds itself covered with snow. The future had assumed the forgotten character of a dream, so that he could not be sure that he had ever truly had one.

T. N. T. talked on and Father Burner felt a mist generating on his forehead. He tore his damp hands apart and put the napkin aside. Yes, yes, it was true a priest received miserably little, but then that was the whole idea. He did not comment, dreading T. N. T.'s foaming compassion, to be spat upon with charity. Yes, as a matter of fact, it would be easier to face old age with something more to draw upon than what the ecclesiastical authorities deemed sufficient and would provide. Also, as T. N. T. pointed out, one never knew when he might come down with an expensive illness. T. N. T., despite himself, had something . . . The Plan, in itself, was not bad. He must not reject the olive branch because it came by buzzard. But still Father Burner was a little bothered by the idea of a priest feathering his nest. Why? In other problems he was never the one to take the ascetic interpretation.

"You must be between thirty-five and forty, Father."

"I'll never see forty again."

"I'd never believe it from anyone else. You sure don't look it, Father."

"Maybe not. But I feel it."

"Worries, Father. And one big one is the future, Father. You'll get to be fifty, sixty, seventy—and what have you got?—not a penny saved. You look around and say to yourself—where did it go?"

T. N. T. had the trained voice of the good and faithful servant, supple from many such dealings. And still from time to time a faint draught of contempt seemed to pass through it which had something to do with his eyes. Here, Father Burner thought, was the latest thing in simony, unnecessary, inspired from without, participated in spiritlessly by the priest who must yet suffer the brunt of the blame and ultimately do the penance. Father Burner felt mysteriously purchasable. He was involved in an exchange of confidences which impoverished him mortally. In T. N. T. he sensed free will in its senility or the infinite capacity for equating evil with good—or with nothing, the same thing, only easier. Here was one more word in the history of the worm's progress, another wave on the dry flood that kept rising, the constant aggrandizement of decay. In the end it must touch the world and everything at the heart. Father Burner felt weak from a nameless loss.

"I think I can do us both a service, Father."

"I don't say you can't." Father Burner rose quickly. "I'll have to think about it, Mr. Tracy."

"To be sure, Father." He produced a glossy circular. "Just let me leave this literature with you."

Father Burner, leading him to the door, prevented further talk by reading the circular. It was printed in a churchy type, all purple and gold, a dummy leaf from a medieval hymnal, and entitled, "A Silver Lining in the Sky." It was evidently meant for clergymen only, though not necessarily priests, as Father Burner could instantly see from its general tone.

"Very interesting," he said.

"My business phone is right on the back, Father. But if you'd rather call me at my home some night—"

"No thanks, Mr. Tracy."

"Allow me to repeat, Father, this isn't just business with me."

"I understand." He opened the door too soon for T. N. T. "Glad to have met you."

"Glad to have met you, Father."

Father Burner went back to the table. The coffee needed warming up and the butter had vanished into the toast. "Mary," he called. Then he heard them come gabbing into the rectory, Quinlan and his friend Keefe, also newly ordained.

They were hardly inside the dining room before he was explaining how he came to be eating breakfast so late— so late, see?—not *still*.

"You protest too much, Father," Quinlan said. "The Angelic Doctor himself weighed three hundred pounds and I'll wager he didn't get it all from prayer and fasting."

"A pituitary condition," Keefe interjected, faltering. "Don't you think?"

"Yah, yah, Father, you'll wager"—Father Burner, eyes malignant, leaned on his knife, the blade bowing out bright and buttery beneath his fist—"and I'll wager you'll be the first saint to reach heaven with a flannel mouth!" Rising from the table, he shook Keefe's hand, which was damp from his pocket, and experienced a surge of strength, the fat man's contempt and envy for the thin man. He thought he might break Keefe's hand off at the wrist without drawing a drop of blood.

Quinlan stood aside, six inches or more below them, gazing up, as at two impossibly heroic figures in a hotel mural. Reading the caption under them, he mused, "Father Burner meets Father Keefe."

"I've heard about you, Father," Keefe said, plying him with a warmth beyond his means.

"Bound to be the case in a diocese as overstocked with magpies as this one." Father Burner threw a fresh napkin at a plate. "But be seated, Father Keefe." Keefe, yes, he had seen him before, a nobody in a crowd, some affair . . . the K. C. barbecue, the Youth Center? No, probably not, not Keefe, who was obviously not the type, too crabbed and introversive for Catholic Action. "I suppose," he said, "you've heard the latest definition of Catholic Action— the interference of the laity with the inactivity of the hierarchy."

"Very good," Keefe said uneasily.

Quinlan yanked off his collar and churned his neck up and down to get circulation. "Dean in the house? No? Good." He pitched the collar at one of the candles on the buffet for a ringer. "That turkey we met coming out the front door—think I've seen his face somewhere."

"Thomas Nash Tracy," Keefe said. "I thought you knew."

"The prominent lay priest and usurer?"

Keefe coughed. "They say he's done a lot of good."

Quinlan spoke to Father Burner: "Did you take out a policy, Father?"

"One of the sixth-graders threw a rock through his windshield," Father Burner said. "He was very nice about it."

"Muldoon or Ciesniewski?"

"A new kid. Public school transfer." Father Burner patted the napkin to his chin. "Not that I see anything wrong with insurance."

Quinlan laughed. "Let Walter tell you what happened to him a few days ago. Go ahead, Walter," he said to Keefe.

"Oh, that." Keefe fidgeted and seemingly against his better judgment began. "I had a little accident—was it Wednesday it rained so? I had the misfortune to skid into a fellow parked on Fairmount. Dented his fender." Keefe stopped and then, as though impelled by the memory of it, went on. "The fellow came raging out of his car at me. I thought there'd be serious trouble. Then he must have seen I was a priest, the way he calmed down, I mean. I had a funny feeling it wasn't because he was a Catholic or anything like that. As a matter of fact he wore a Masonic button." Keefe sighed. "I guess he saw I was a priest and . . . ergo knew I'd have insurance."

"Take nothing for your journey, neither staff, nor scrip," Quinlan said, "words taken from today's gospel."

Father Burner spoke in a level tone: "Not that I *still* see anything wrong with insurance. It's awfully easy," he continued, hating himself for talking such drivel, "to make too much of little things." With Quinlan around he played the conservative; among the real righthanders he was the enfant terrible. He operated on the principle of discord at any cost. He did not know why. It was a habit. Perhaps it had something to do with being overweight.

Arranging the Dean's chair, which had arms, for himself, Quinlan sank into it, giving Keefe the Irish whisper. "Grace, Father."

Keefe addressed the usual words to God concerning the gifts they were about to receive. During the prayer Father Burner stopped chewing and did not reach for anything. He noted once more that Quinlan crossed himself sloppily enough to be a bishop.

Keefe nervously cleared the entire length of his throat.

"It's a beautiful church you have here at Saint Patrick's, Father." A lukewarm light appeared in his eyes, flickered, sputtered out, leaving them blank and blue. His endless fingers felt for his receding chin in the onslaught of silence.

"*I* have?" Father Burner turned his spoon abasingly to his bosom, "*Me?*" He jabbed at the grapefruit before him, his second, demolishing its perfect rose window. "I don't know why it is the Irish without exception are always laying personal claim to church property. The Dean is forever saying *my* church, *my* school, *my* furnace . . ."

"I'm sorry, Father," Keefe said, flushing. "And I'll confess I did think he virtually built Saint Patrick's."

"Out of the slime of the earth, I know. A common error." With sudden, unabated displeasure Father Burner recalled how the Dean, one of the last of the old brick and mortar pastors, had built the church, school, sisters' house and rectory, and had named the whole thing through the lavish pretense of a popular contest. Opposed bitterly by Polish, German and Italian minorities, he had effected a compromise between their bad taste (Saint Stanislaus, Saint Boniface, Saint Anthony) and his own better judgment in the choice of Saint Patrick's.

Quinlan, snorting, blurted: "Well, he did build it, didn't he?"

Father Burner smiled at them from the other world. "Only, if you please, in a manner of speaking."

"True," Keefe murmured humbly.

"Nuts," Quinlan said. "It's hard for me to see God in a few buildings paid for by the funds of the faithful and put up by a mick contractor. A burning bush, yes."

Father Burner, lips parched to speak an unsummonable cruelty, settled for a smouldering aside to the kitchen. "Mary, more eggs here."

A stuffed moose of a warm woman with a tabbycat face charged in on swollen feet. She stood wavering in shoes sliced fiercely for corns. With the back of her hand she wiped some cream from the fuzz ringing her baby-pink mouth. Her hair poked through a broken net like stunted antlers. Father Burner pointed to the empty platter.

"Eggs," he said.

"Eggs!" she cried, tumbling her eyes like great blue dice among them. She seized up the platter and carried it whirling with grease into the kitchen.

Father Burner put aside the grapefruit. He smiled and spoke calmly. "I'll have to let the Dean know, Father, how much you like *his* plant."

"Do, Father. A beautiful church . . . 'a poem in stone'—was it Ruskin?"

"Ruskin? *Stones of Venice,*" Father Burner grumbled. "*Sesame and Lilies,* I know . . . but I never cared for his *style.*" He passed the knife lovingly over the pancakes on his plate and watched the butter bubble at the pores. "So much sweetness, so much light, I'm afraid, made Jack a dull boy."

Quinlan slapped all his pockets. "Pencil and paper, quick!"

"And yet . . ." Keefe cocked his long head, brow fretted, and complained to his upturned hands. "Don't understand how he stayed outside the Church." He glanced up hopefully. "I wonder if Chesterton gives us a clue."

Father Burner, deaf to such precious speculation, said: "In the 19th century Francis Thompson was the only limey worth his salt. It's true." He quartered the pancakes. "Of course, Newman."

"Hopkins has some good things."

"Good—yes, if you like jabberwocky and jebbies! I don't care for either." He dispatched a look of indictment at Quinlan.

"What a pity," Quinlan murmured, "Oliver Wendell couldn't be at table this morning."

"No, Father, you can have your Hopkins, you and Father Quinlan here. Include me out, as Sam Goldwyn says. Poetry, I'll take my poetry the way I take my liquor, neat."

Mary brought in the platter oozing with bacon and eggs.

"Good for you, Mary," Quinlan said. "I'll pray for you."

"Thank you, Father," Mary said.

Quinlan dipped the platter with a trace of obeisance to Father Burner.

"No thanks."

Quinlan scooped up the coffeepot in a fearsome rush and held it high at Father Burner, his arm so atremble the lid rattled dangerously. "Sure and will you be about having a sup of coffee now, Father?"

"Not now. And do you mind not playing the wild Irish wit so early in the day, Father?"

"That I don't. *But a relentless fate pursuing good Father Quinlan, he was thrown in among hardened clerics where but for the grace of God that saintly priest, so little understood, so much maligned . . .*" Quinlan poured two cups and passed one to Keefe. "For yourself, Father."

Father Burner nudged the toast to Keefe. "Father Quinlan, that saintly priest, models his life after the Rover Boys, particularly Sam, the fun-loving one."

Quinlan dealt himself a mighty mea culpa.

Father Burner grimaced, the flesh rising in sweet concentric tiers around his mouth, and said in a tone entrusting and ennobling Keefe with his confidence: "The syrup, if you please, Father." Keefe passed the silver pitcher which was running at the mouth. Father Burner reimmersed the doughy remains on his plate until the butter began to float around the edges as in a moat. He felt them both watching the butter. Regretting that he had not foreseen this attraction, he cast about in his mind for something to divert them and found the morning sun coming in too strongly. He got up and pulled down the shade. He returned to his place and settled himself in such a way that a new chapter was indicated. "Don't believe I know where you're located, Father."

"Saint Jerome's," Keefe said. "Monsignor Fiedler's."

"One of those P. N. places, eh? Is the Boss sorry he ever started it? I know some of them are."

Keefe's lips popped apart. "I don't quite understand."

Quinlan prompted: "P. N.—Perpetual Novena."

"Oh, I never heard him say."

"You wouldn't, of course. But I know a lot of them that are." Father Burner stuck a morsel on his fork and swirled it against the tide of syrup. "It's a real problem all right. I was all out for a P. N. here during the depression. Thought it might help. The Dean was against it."

"I can tell you this," Keefe said. "Attendance was down from what it used to be until the casualties began to come in. Now it's going up."

"I was just going to say the war ought to take the place of the depression." Father Burner fell silent. "Terrible thing, war. Hard to know what to do about it. I tried to sell the Dean the idea of a victory altar. You've seen them. Vigil lights—"

"At a dollar a throw," Quinlan said.

"Vigil lights in the form of a V, names of the men in the service and all that. But even that, I guess—Well, like I said, I tried . . ."

"Yes, it is hard," Keefe said.

"God, the Home and the Flag," Quinlan said. "The poets don't make the wars."

Father Burner ignored that. "Lately, though, I can't say how I feel about P. N.'s. Admit I'm not so strong for them as I was once. Ought to be some way of terminating them, you know, but then they wouldn't be perpetual, would they?"

"No, they wouldn't," Keefe said.

"Of course the term itself, perpetual novena, is preposterous, a solecism. Possibly dispensation lies in that direction. I'm not theologian enough to say. Fortunately it's not a problem we have to decide." He laid his knife and fork across the plate. "Many are the consolations of the lowly curate. No decisions, no money worries."

"We still have to count the sugar," Quinlan said. "And put up the card tables."

"Reminds me," Father Burner said earnestly. "Father Desmond at Assumption was telling me they've got a new machine does all that."

"Puts up card tables?" Quinlan inquired.

"Counts the collection, wraps the silver," Father Burner explained, "so it's all ready for the bank. Mean to mention it to the Dean, if I can catch him right."

"I'm afraid, Father, he knows about it already."

Father Burner regarded Quinlan sceptically. "Does? I suppose he's against it."

"I heard him tell the salesman that's what he had his assistants for."

"Assistant, Father, not assistants. You count the collection, not me. I was only thinking of you."

"I was only quoting him, Father. *Sic.* Sorry."

"Not at all. I haven't forgotten the days I had to do it. It's a job has to be done and nothing to be ashamed of. Wouldn't you say, Father Keefe?"

"I daresay that's true."

Quinlan, with Father Burner still molesting him with his eyes, poured out a glass of water and drank it all. "I still think we could do with a lot less calculating. I notice the only time we get rid of the parish paper is when the new lists are published—the official standings. Of course it's a lousy sheet anyway."

Father Burner, as editor of the paper, replied: "Yes, yes, Father. We all know how easy it is to be wrathful or fastidious about these things—or whatever the hell it is you are. And we all know there *are* abuses. But contributing to the support of the Church is still one of her commandments."

"Peace, Pere," Quinlan said.

"Figures don't lie."

"Somebody was telling me just last night that figures do lie. He looked a lot like you."

Father Burner found his cigarettes and shuffled a couple half out of the pack. He eyed Quinlan and the cigarettes as though it were as simple to discipline the one as to smoke the others. "For some reason, Father, you're damned fond of those particular figures."

Keefe stirred. "Which particular figures, Father?"

"It's the figures put out by the Cardinal of Toledo on how many made their Easter duty last year." Father Burner offered Keefe a cigarette. "I discussed the whole thing with Father Quinlan last night. It's his latest thesis. Have a cigarette?"

"No, thanks," Keefe said.

"So you don't smoke?" Father Burner looked from Keefe to Quinlan, blacklisting them together. He held the cigarette hesitantly at his lips. "It's all right, isn't it?" He laughed and touched off the match with his thumbnail.

"His Eminence," Quinlan said, "reports only fifteen per cent of the women and five per cent of the men made their Easter duty last year."

"So that's only three times as many women as men," Father Burner said with buried gaiety. "Certainly to be expected in any Latin country."

"But fifteen per cent, Father! And five per cent! Just think of it!" Keefe glanced up at the ceiling and at the souvenir plates on the moulding, as though to see inscribed along with scenes from the Columbian Exposition the day and hour the end of the world would begin. He finally stared deep into the goldfish tank in the window.

Father Burner ploughed up the silence, talking with a mouthful of smoke. "All right, all right, I'll say what I said in the first place. There's something wrong with the figures. A country as overwhelmingly Catholic as Spain!" He sniffed, pursed his lips, and said: "Pooh!"

"Yes," Keefe said, still balking. "But it *is* disturbing, Father Burner."

"Sure it's disturbing, Father Keefe. *Lots* of things *are.*"

A big faded goldfish paused to stare through the glass at them and then with a single lob of its tail slipped into a dark green corner.

Quinlan said, "Father Burner belongs to the school that's always seeing a great renascence of faith in the offing. The hour before dawn and all that. Tell it to Rotary on Tuesday, Father."

Father Burner countered with a frosty pink smile. "What would I ever do without you, Father? If you're trying to say I'm a dreadful optimist, you're right and I don't mind at all. I am—and proud of it!"

Ascending to his feet, he went to the right side of the buffet, took down the card index to parishioners and returned with it to his place. He pushed his dishes aside and began to sort out the deadheads to be called on personally by him or Quinlan. The Dean, like all pastors, he reflected, left the dirty work to the assistants. "Why doesn't he pull them," he snapped, tearing up a card, "when they kick off! Can't very well forward them to the next world. Say, how many Gradys live at 909 South Vine? Here's Anna, Catherine, Clement, Gerald, Harvey, James A., James F.—which James is the one they call 'Bum'?"

"James F.," Quinlan said. "Can't you tell from the take? The other James works."

"John, Margaret, Matthew—that's ten, no eleven. Here's Dennis out of place. Patrick, Rita and William—fourteen of them, no birth control there, and they all give. Except Bum. Nice account otherwise. Can't we find Bum a job? What's it with him, drink?"

Now he came to Maple Street. These cards were the remains of little Father Vicci's work among the magdalens. Ann Mason, Estelle Rogers, May Miller, Billie Starr. The names had the generic ring. Great givers when they gave —Christmas, $25.00; Easter, $20.00; Propagation of the Faith, $10.00; Catholic University, $10.00—but not much since Father Vicci was exiled to the sticks. He put Maple Street aside for a thorough sifting.

The doorbell rang. Father Burner leaned around in his chair. "Mary." The doorbell rang again. Father Burner bellowed. "Mary!"

Quinlan pushed his chair away from the table. "I'll get it."

Father Burner blocked him. "Oh, I'll get it! Hell of a bell! Why does he have a bell like that!" Father Burner opened the door to a middle-aged woman whose name he had forgotten or never known. "Good morning," he said. "Will you step in?"

She stayed where she was and said, "Father, it's about the servicemen's flag in church. My son Stanley—you know him—"

Father Burner, who did not know him, half nodded. "Yes, how is Stanley?" He gazed over her shoulder at the lawn, at the dandelions turning into poppies before his eyes.

"You know he was drafted last October, Father, and I been watching that flag you got in church ever since and it's still the same, five hundred thirty-six stars. I thought you said you put a star up for all them that's gone in the service, Father."

Now the poppies were dandelions again. He could afford to be firm with her. "We can't spend all our time putting up stars. Sometimes we fall behind. Besides, a lot of the boys are being discharged."

"You mean there's just as many going in as coming out, so you don't have to change the flag?"

"Something like that."

"I see." He was sorry for her. They had run out of stars. He had tried to get the Dean to order some more, had even offered . . . and the Dean had said they could use up the gold ones first. When Father Burner had objected, telling him what it would mean, he had suggested that Father Burner apply for the curatorship of the armory.

"The Pastor will be glad to explain how it works the next time you see him."

"Well, Father, if that's the way it is . . ." She was fading down the steps. "I just thought I'd ask."

"That's right. There's no harm in asking. How's Stanley?"

"Fine, and thank you, Father, for your trouble."

"No trouble."

When he came back to the table they were talking about the junior clergymen's examinations which they would take for the first time next week. Father Burner interrupted: "The Dean conducts the history end of it, you know."

"I say!" Keefe said. "Any idea what we can expect?"

"You have nothing to fear. Nothing."

"Really?"

"Really. Last year, I remember, there were five questions and the last four depended on the first. So it was really only one question—if you knew it. I imagine you would've." He paused, making Keefe ask for it.

"Perhaps you can recall the question, Father?"

"Perfectly, Father. 'What event in the American history of the Church took place in 1541?' " Father Burner, slumping in his chair, smirked at Keefe pondering for likely martyrs and church legislation. He imagined him skipping among the tomes and statuary of his mind, winnowing dates and little known facts like mad, only at last to emerge dusty and downcast. Father Burner sat up with a jerk and assaulted the table with the flat of his hand. "Time's up. Answer: 'De Soto sailed up the Mississippi.' "

Quinlan snorted, Keefe sat very ill, incredulous, silent, utterly unable to digest the answer, finally croaking, "How odd." Father Burner saw in him the boy whose marks in school had always been a consolation to his parents.

"So you don't have to worry, Father. No sense in preparing for it. Take in a couple of movies instead. And cheer up! The Dean's been examining the junior clergy for twenty-five years and nobody ever passed history yet. You wouldn't want to be the first one."

Father Burner said grace and made the sign of the cross with slow distinction. "And, Father," he said, standing, extending his hand to Keefe, who also rose, "I'm glad to have met you." He withdrew his hand before Keefe was through with it and stood against the table knocking toast crumbs onto his plate. "Ever play any golf? No? Well, come and see us for conversation then. You don't have anything against talking, do you?"

"Well, of course, Father, I . . ."

Father Burner gave Keefe's arm a rousing clutch. "Do that!"

"I will, Father. It's been a pleasure."

"Speaking of pleasure," Father Burner said, tossing Quinlan a stack of cards, "I've picked out a few lost sheep for you to see on Maple Street, Father."

2. NOON

He hung his best black trousers on a hanger in the closet and took down another pair, also black. He tossed them out behind him and they fell patched at the cuffs and baggy across his unmade bed. His old suede jacket, following, slid dumpily to the floor. He stood gaping in his clerical vest and undershorts, knees knocking and pimply, thinking . . . what else? His aviator's helmet. He felt all the hooks blindly in the darkness. It was not there. "Oh, hell!" he groaned, sinking to his knees. He pawed among the old shoes and boxes and wrapping paper and string that he was always going to need. Under his golf bag he found it. So Mary had cleaned yesterday.

There was also a golf ball unknown to him, a Royal Bomber, with one small hickey in it. Father Desmond, he remembered, had received a box of Royal Bombers from a thoughtful parishioner. He stuck the helmet on his balding head to get it out of the way and took the putter from the bag. He dropped the ball at the door of the closet. Taking his own eccentric stance—a perversion of what the pro recommended and a dozen books on the subject— he putted the ball across the room at a dirty collar lying against the bookcase. A thready place in the carpet caused the ball to jump the collar and to loose a pamphlet from the top of the bookcase. He restored the pamphlet—Pius XI on "Atheistic Communism"—and poked the ball back to the door of the closet. Then, allowing for the carpet, he drove the ball straight, *click,* through the collar, *clop.* Still had his old putting eye. And his irons had always been steady if not exactly crashing. It was his woods, the tee shots, that ruined his game. He'd give a lot to be able to hit his woods properly, not to dub his drives, if only on the first tee—where there was always a crowd (mixed).

At one time or another he had played every hole at the country club in par or less. Put all those pars and birdies together, adding in the only two eagles he'd ever had, and you had the winning round in the state open, write-ups and action shots in the papers—photo shows Rev. Ernest "Boomer" Burner, par-shattering padre, blasting out of a trap. He needed only practice perhaps and at his earliest opportunity he would entice some of the eighth-grade boys over into the park to shag balls. He sank one more for good measure, winning a buck from Ed Desmond who would have bet against it, and put the club away.

Crossing the room for his trousers he noticed himself in the mirror with the helmet on and got a mild surprise. He scratched a little hair down from underneath the helmet to offset the egg effect. He searched his eyes in the mirror for a sign of ill health. He walked away from the mirror, as though done with it, only to wheel sharply so as to see himself as others saw him, front and profile, not wanting to catch his eyes, just to see himself . . .

Out of the top drawer of the dresser he drew a clean white silk handkerchief and wiped the shine from his nose. He chased his eyes over into the corner of the mirror and saw nothing. Then, succumbing to his original intention, he knotted the handkerchief at the crown of the helmet and completed the transformation of time and place and person by humming, vibrato. "Jeannine, I dream of lilac time," remembering the old movie. He saw himself over his shoulder in the mirror, a sad war ace. It reminded him that his name was not Burner, but Boerner, an impediment removed at the outset of the first world war by his father. In a way he resented the old man for it. They had laughed at the seminary; the war, except as theory, hardly entered there. In perverse homage to the old Boerner, to which he now affixed a proud "von," he dropped the fair-minded American look he had and faced the mirror sneering, scar-cheeked and black of heart, the flying Junker who might have been. "Himmelkreuzdonnerwetter! When you hear the word 'culture,'" he snarled, hearing it in German, "reach for your revolver."

Reluctantly he pulled on his black trousers, falling across the bed to do so, as though felled, legs heaving up like howitzers.

He lay still for a moment, panting, and then let the innerspring mattress bounce him to his feet, a fighter coming off the ropes. He stood looking out the window, buckling his belt, and then down at the buckle, chins kneading softly with the effort, and was pleased to see that he was holding his own on the belt, still a good half inch away from last winter's high water mark.

At the sound of high heels approaching on the front walk below, he turned firmly away from the window and considered for the first time since he posted it on the wall the prayer for priests sent him by a candle concern. "Remember, O most compassionate God, that they are but weak and frail human beings. Stir up in them the grace of their vocation which is in them by the imposition of the Bishop's hands. Keep them close to Thee, lest the enemy prevail against them, so that they may never do anything in the slightest degree unworthy of their sublime . . ." His eyes raced through the prayer and out the window . . .

He was suddenly inspired to write another letter to the Archbishop. He sat down at his desk, slipped a piece of paper into his portable, dated it with the saint's day it was, and wrote, "Your Excellency: Thinking my letter of some months ago may have gone amiss, or perhaps due to the press of business—" He ripped the paper from the portable and typed the same thing on a fresh sheet until he came to "business," using instead "affairs of the Church." He went on to signify—it was considered all right to "signify," but to resignify?—that he was still of the humble opinion that he needed a change of location and had decided, since he believed himself ready for a parish of his own, a rural one might be best, all things considered (by which he meant easier to get). He, unlike some priests of urban upbringing and experience, would have no objection to the country. He begged to be graced with an early reply. That line, for all its seeming docility, was full of dynamite and ought to break the episcopal silence into which the first letter had dissolved. This was a much stronger job. He thought it better for two reasons: the Archbishop was supposed to like outspoken people, or, that being only more propaganda talked up by the syncophants, then it ought to bring a reply which would reveal once and for all his prospects. Long overdue for the routine promotion, he had a just cause. He addressed the letter and placed it in his coat. He went to the bathroom. When he came back he put on the coat, picked up the suede jacket and helmet, looked around for something he might have forgot, a book of chances, a box of Sunday envelopes to be delivered, some copy for the printer, but there was nothing. He lit a cigarette at the door and not caring to throw the match on the floor or look for the ashtray, which was out of sight again, he dropped it in the empty holy water font.

Downstairs he paused at the telephone in the hall, scribbled "Airport" on the message pad, thought of crossing it out or tearing off the page, but since it was dated he let it stand and added "Visiting the sick," signing his initials, *E. B.*

He went through the wicker basket for mail. A card from the Book-of-the-Month Club. So it was going to be another war book selection this month. Well, they knew what they could do with it. He wished the Club would wake up and select some dandies, as they had in the past. He thought of *Studs Lonigan*—there was a book, the best thing since the Bible.

An oblique curve in the road: perfect, wheels parallel with the center line. So many drivers took a curve like that way over on the other fellow's side. Father Burner touched the lighter on the dashboard to his cigarette and plunged his hams deeper into the cushions. A cloud of smoke whirled about the little Saint Christopher garroted from the ceiling. Father Burner tugged viciously at both knees, loosening the binding black cloth, easing the seat. Now that he was in open country he wanted to enjoy the scenery—God's majesty. How about a sermon that would liken the things in the landscape to the people in a church? All different, all the same handiwork of God. Moral: it is right and meet for rocks to be rocks, trees to be trees, pigs to be pigs, but—and here the small gesture that says so much—what did that mean that men, created in the image and likeness of God, should be? And what—He thrust the sermon out of mind, tired of it. He relaxed, as before an open fireplace, the weight of dogma off his shoulders. Then he grabbed at his knees again, cursing. Did the tailor skimp on the cloth because of the ecclesiastical discount?

A billboard inquired—"Pimples?" Yes, he had a few, but he blamed them on the climate, the humidity. Awfully hard for a priest to transfer out of a diocese. He remembered the plan he had never gone through with. Would it work after all? Would another doctor recommend a change? Why? He would only want to know why, like the last bastard. Just a slight case of obesity, Reverend. Knew he was a non-Catholic when he said Reverend. Couldn't trust a Catholic one. Some of them were thicker than thieves with the clergy. Wouldn't want to be known as a malingerer, along with everything else.

Another billboard—"Need Cash? See T. N. T."

Rain. He knew it. No flying for him today. One more day between him and a pilot's license. Thirteen hours yet and it might have been twelve. Raining so, and with no flying, the world seemed to him . . . a valley of tears. He would drive on past the airport for a hamburger. If he had known, he would have brought along one of the eighth-grade boys. They were always bragging among themselves about how many he had bought them, keeping score. One of them, the Cannon kid, had got too serious from the hamburgers. When he said he was "contemplating the priesthood" Father Burner, wanting to spare him the terrible thing a false vocation could be, had told him to take up aviation instead. He could not forget the boy's reply: *But couldn't I be a priest like you, Father?*

On the other hand, he was glad to be out driving alone. Never had got the bang out of playing with the kids a priest in this country was supposed to. The failure of the Tom Playfair tradition. He hated most sports, Ed Desmond was a sight at a ball game. Running up and down base lines, giving the umpires hell, busting all the buttons off his cassock. Assumption rectory smelled like a locker room from all the equipment. Poor Ed.

The rain drummed on the engine hood. The windshield wiper sliced back and forth, reminding him a little of a guillotine. Yes, if he had to, he would die for the Faith.

From here to the hamburger place it was asphalt and slicker than concrete. Careful. Slick. Asphalt. Remembered . . . Quinlan coming into his room one afternoon last winter when it was snowing, the idiot, prating:

Here were decent godless people:
Their only monument the asphalt road
And a thousand lost golf balls . . .

That was Quinlan for you; always spouting against the
status quo without having anything better to offer. Told
him that. Told him golfers, funny as it might seem to
some people, have souls and who's to save them? John
Bosco worked wonders in taverns, which was not to say
Father Burner thought he was a saint, but rather only that
he was not too proud to meet souls half-way wherever it
might be, in the confessional or on the fairways. Saint
Ernest Burner, Help of Golfers, Pray for Us! (Quinlan's
come back.) Quinlan gave him a pain. Keefe, now that he
knew what he was like, ditto. Non-smokers. Jansenists.
First fervor is false fervor. They would cool. He would
not judge them, however.

He slowed down and executed a sweeping turn into the
parking lot reserved for patrons of the hamburger. He
honked his horn his way, three shorts and a long—victory.
She would see his car or know his honk and bring out
two hamburgers, medium well, onions, pickle, relish, tomato, catsup, his way.

She came out now, carrying an umbrella, holding it os-
tensibly more over the hamburgers than herself. He took
the tray from her. She waited dumbly, her eyes at a level
with his collar.

"What's to drink?"

"We got pop, milk, coffee . . ." Here she faltered, as
he knew she would, washing her hands of what recurrent
revelation, rather than experience, told her was to follow.

"A nice cold bottle of beer." Delivered of the fatal
words, Father Burner bit into the smoking hamburger.
The woman turned sorrowfully away. He put her down
again for native Protestant stock.

When she returned, sheltering the bottle under the umbrella, Father Burner had to smile at her not letting pious

scruples interfere with business, another fruit of the so-called Reformation. Watch that smile, he warned himself, or she'll take it for carnal. He received the bottle from her hands. For all his familiarity with the type, he was uneasy. Her lowered eyes informed him of his guilt.

Was he immoderate? Who on earth could say? *In dubiis libertas,* not? He recalled his first church supper at Saint Patrick's, a mother bringing her child to the Dean's table. She's going to be confirmed next month, Monsignor. Indeed? Then tell me, young lady, what are the seven capital sins? Pride, Covetousness . . . Lust, Anger. Uh. The child's mother, one of those Irish females built like a robin, worried to death, lips silently forming the other sins for her daughter. Go ahead, dear. Envy. Proceed child. Yes, Monsignor. Uh . . . Sloth. To be sure. That's six. One more. And . . . uh. Fear of the Lord, perhaps? Meekness? Hey, Monsignor, ain't them the Divine Counsels! The Dean, smiling, looking at Father Burner's plate, covered with chicken bones, at his stomach, fighting his vest, and for a second into the child's eyes, slipping her the seventh sin. *Gluttony,* Monsignor! The Dean gave her a coin for her trouble. She stood awkwardly in front of Father Burner, lingering, twisting her gaze from his plate to his stomach, to his eyes, finally quacking, Oh Fawther!

Now he began to brood upon his failure as a priest. There was no sense in applying the consolations of an anchorite to himself. He wanted to know one thing: when would he get a pastorate? When would he make the great metamorphosis from assistant to pastor, from mouse to rat, as the saying went? He was forty-three, four times transferred, seventeen years an ordained priest, a curate yet and only. He was the only one of his class still without a parish. The only one . . . and in his pocket, three days unopened, was another letter from his mother, kept waiting all these years, who was to have been his housekeeper. He could not bear to warm up her expectations again.

Be a chaplain? That would take him away from it all and there was the possibility of meeting a remote and glorious death carrying the Holy Eucharist to a dying soldier. It would take something like that to make him come out even, but then that too, he knew in a corner of his heart, would be only exterior justification for him, a last bid for public approbation, a short cut to nothing. And the chaplain's job, it was whispered, could be an ordeal both ignominious and tragic. It would be just his luck to draw an assignment in a rehabilitation center, racking pool balls and repairing ping pong bats for the boys—the apostolic game-room attendant and toastmaster. Sure, Sarge, I'll lay you even money the Sox make it three straight in Philly and spot you a run a game to boot. You win, I lose a carton of Chesters—I win, you go to Mass every day for a week! Hard-headed holiness . . .

There was the painful matter of the appointment to Saint Patrick's. The Dean, an irremovable pastor, and the Archbishop had argued over funds and the cemetery association. And the Archbishop, losing though he won, took his revenge, it was rumored, by appointing Father Burner as the Dean's assistant. It was their second encounter. In the first days of his succession, the Archbishop heard that the Dean always said a green Mass on Saint Patrick's Day, thus setting the rubrics at nought. Furious, he summoned the Dean into his presence, but stymied by the total strangeness of him and his great age, he had talked of something else. The Dean took a different view of his narrow escape, which is what the chancery office gossips called it, and now every year, on repeating the error, he would say to the uneasy nuns, "Sure and nobody ever crashed the gates of hell for the wearing of the green." (Otherwise it was not often he did something to delight the hearts of the professional Irish.)

In the Dean's presence Father Burner often had the sensation of confusion, a feeling that someone besides them stood listening in the room. To free himself he would say things he neither meant nor believed. The Dean would take the other side and then . . . there they were again. The Dean's position in these bouts was roughly that of the old saints famous for their faculty of smelling sins and Father Burner played the role of the one smelled. It was no contest. If the Archbishop could find no words for the Dean there was nothing he might do. He might continue to peck away at a few stray foibles behind the Dean's back. He might point out how familiar the Dean was with the Protestant clergy about town. He did. It suited his occasional orthodoxy (reserved mostly to confound his critics and others much worse, like Quinlan, whom he suspected of having him under observation for humorous purposes) to disapprove of all such questionable ties, as though the Dean were entertaining heresy or at least felt kindly toward this new "interfaith" nonsense so dear to the reformed Jews and freshwater sects. It was very small game, however. And the merest brush with the Dean might bring any one of a hundred embarrassing occasions back to life, and it was easy for him to burn all over again.

When he got his dark room rigged up in the rectory the Dean had come snooping around and inquired without staying for an answer if the making of tin-types demanded that a man shun the light to the extent Father Burner appeared to. Now and again, hearkening back to this episode, the Dean referred to him as the Prince of Darkness. It did not end there. The title caught on all over the diocese. It was not the only one he had.

In reviewing a new historical work for a national Catholic magazine, he had attempted to get back at two Jesuits he knew in town, calling attention to certain tendencies —he meant nothing so gross as "order pride"—which, if not necessarily characteristic of any religious congregation within the Church, were still too often to be seen in any long view of history (which the book at hand did not pretend to take), and whereas the secular clergy, *per se,* had much to answer for, was it not true, though certainly not through any superior virtue, nor even as a consequence of their secularity—indeed he would be a fool to dream that such orders as those founded, for instance, by Saint Benedict, Saint Francis and Saint Dominic (Saint Ignatius was not instanced) were without their places in the heart of the Church, even today, when perhaps . . .

Anyway "secular" turned up once as "circular" in the review. The local Jesuits, writing in to the magazine as a group of innocent bystanders, made many subtle plays upon the unfortunate "circular" and its possible application to the person of the reviewer (their absolute unfamiliarity with the reviewer, they explained, enabled them to indulge in such conceivably dangerous whimsy). But the direction of his utterances, they thought, seemed clear, and they regretted more than they could say that the editors of an otherwise distinguished journal had found space for them, especially in wartime, or perhaps they did not rightly comprehend the course—was it something new?—set upon by the editors and if so . . .

So Father Burner was also known as "the circular priest" and he had not reviewed anything since for that magazine.

The mark of the true priest was heavy on the Dean. The mark was on Quinlan, it was on Keefe. It was on every priest he could think of, including a few on the bum and his good friend and bad companion Father Desmond. But it was not on him, not properly. They, the others, were stained with it beyond all disguise or disfigurement—indelibly, as indeed Holy Orders by its sacramental nature must stain, for keeps in this world and the one to come. "Thou art a priest forever." With him, however, it was something else and less, a mask or badge which he could and did remove at will, a temporal part to be played, almost only a doctor's or lawyer's. They, the others, would be lost in any persecution. The mark would doom them. But he, if that *dies irae* ever came—and it was every plump seminarian's apple-cheeked dream—could pass as the most harmless and useful of humans, a mailman, a bus rider, a husband. But would he? No. They would see. I, he would say, appearing unsought before the judging rabble, am a priest, of the order of Melchisedech. Take me. I am ready *Deo gratias*.

Father Burner got out the money to pay and honked his horn. The woman, coming for the bottle and tray, took his money without acknowledging the tip. She stood aside, the bottle held gingerly between offended fingers, final illustration of her lambishness, and watched him drive away. Father Burner, applying a cloven foot to the pedal, gave it the gas. He sensed the woman hoping in her simple heart to see him wreck the car and meet instant death in an unpostponed act of God.

Under the steadying influence of his stomach thrust against the wheel, the car proceeded while he searched himself for a cigarette. He passed a hitch-hiker, saw him fade out of view in the mirror overhead, gesticulate wetly in the distance. Was the son of a gun thumbing his nose? Anti-clericalism. But pray that your flight be not in the winter . . . No, wrong text: he would not run away.

The road skirted a tourist village. He wondered who stayed in those places and seemed to remember a story in one of the religion scandal sheets . . . ILLICIT LOVE in steaming red type.

A billboard cried out, "Get in the scrap and—get in the scrap!" Some of this advertising, he thought, was pretty slick. Put out probably by big New York and Chicago agencies with crack men on their staffs, fellows who had studied at *Time*. How would it be to write advertising? He knew a few things about lay-out and type faces from editing the parish paper. He had read somewhere about the best men of our time being in advertising, the air corps of business. There was room for better taste in the Catholic magazines, for someone with a name in the secular field to step in and drive out the moneychangers with their trusses, corn cures, non-tangle rosary beads and crosses that glow in the dark. It was a thought.

Coming into the city limits, he glanced at his watch, but neglected to notice the time. The new gold strap got his eye. The watch itself, a priceless pyx, held the hour (time is money) sacred, like a host. He had chosen it for an ordination gift rather than the usual chalice. It took the kind of courage he had to go against the grain there.

"I'm a dirty stinker!" Father Desmond flung his arms out hard against the mattress. His fists opened on the sheet, hungry for the spikes, meek and ready. "I'm a dirty stinker, Ernest!"

Father Burner, seated deep in a red leather chair at the sick man's bedside, crossed his legs forcefully. "Now don't take on so, Father."

"Don't call me 'Father'!" Father Desmond's eyes fluttered open momentarily, but closed again on the reality of it all. "I don't deserve it. I'm a disgrace to the priesthood! I am not worthy! Lord, I am not worthy!"

A nurse entered and stuck a thermometer in Father Desmond's mouth.

Father Burner smiled at the nurse. He lit a cigarette and wondered if she understood. The chart probably bore the diagnosis "pneumonia," but if she had been a nurse very long she would know all about that. She released Father Desmond's wrist and recorded his pulse on her pad. She took the thermometer and left the room.

Father Desmond surged up in bed and flopped, turning with a wrench of the covers, on his stomach. He lay gasping like a fish out of water. Father Burner could smell it on his breath yet.

"Do you want to go to confession?"

"No! I'm not ready for it. I want to remember this time!"

"Oh, all right." It was funny, if a little tiresome, the way the Irish could exaggerate a situation. They all had access to the same two or three emotions. They all played the same battered barrel organ handed down through generations. Dying, fighting, talking, drinking, praying . . . wakes, wars, politics, pubs, church. The fates were decimated and hamstrung among them. They loved monotony.

Father Desmond, doing the poor soul uttering his last words in italics, said: "We make too good a thing out of confession, Ernest! Ever think of that, Ernest!" He wagged a nicotined finger. Some of his self-contempt seemed to overshoot its mark and include Father Burner.

Father Burner honked his lips—plutt! "Hire a hall, Ed." Father Desmond clawed a rosary out from under his pillow.

Father Burner left.

He put the car in the garage. On the way to his room he passed voices in the Dean's office.

"Father Burner!" the Dean called through the door.

Father Burner stayed in the hallway, only peeping in, indicating numerous commitments elsewhere. Quinlan and Keefe were with the Dean.

"Apparently, Father, you failed to kill yourself." Then, for Keefe, the Dean said: "Father Burner fulfils the dream of the American hierarchy and the principle of historical localization. He's been up in his flying machine all morning."

"I didn't go up." Sullenness came and went in his voice. "It rained." He shuffled one foot, about to leave, when the Dean's left eyebrow wriggled up, warning, holding him.

"I don't believe you've had the pleasure." The Dean gave Keefe to Father Burner. "Father Keefe, sir, went through school with Father Quinlan—from the grades through the priesthood." The Dean described an arc with his breviary, dripping with ribbons, to show the passing years. Father Burner nodded.

"Well?" The Dean frowned at Father Burner. "Has the

cat got your tongue, sir? Why don't you be about greeting Father O'Keefe—or Keefe is it?"

"Keefe," Keefe said.

Father Burner, caught in the old amber of his inadequacy, stepped over and shook Keefe's hand once.

Quinlan stood by and let the drama play itself out.

Keefe, smiling a curious mixture more anxiety than amusement, said: "It's a pleasure, Father."

"Same here," Father Burner said.

"Well, good day, sirs!" The Dean cracked open his breviary and began to read, lips twitching.

Father Burner waited for them in the hall. Before he could explain that he thought too much of the Dean not to humor him and that besides the old fool was out of his head, the Dean proclaimed after them: "The Chancery phoned, Father Burner. You will hear confessions there tonight. I suppose one of those Cathedral jokers lost his faculties."

Yes, Father Burner knew, it was common procedure all right for the Archbishop to confer promotions by private interview, but every time a priest got called to the Cathedral it did not mean simply that. Many received sermons and it was most likely now someone was needed to hear confessions. And still Father Burner, feeling his pocket, was glad he had not remembered to mail the letter. He would not bother to speak to Quinlan and Keefe now.

3. NIGHT

"And for your penance say five Our Fathers and five Hail Mary's and pray for my intention. And now make a good act of contrition. *Misereatur tui omnipatens Deus dimissis peccatis tuis . . .*" Father Burner swept out into the current of the prayer, stroking strongly in Latin, while the penitent, a miserable boy coming into puberty, paddled as fast as he could along the shore in English.

Finishing first, Father Burner waited for the boy to conclude. When, breathless, he did, Father Burner anointed the air and shot a whisper, "God bless you," kicking the window shut with the heel of his hand, ejecting the boy, an ear of corn husked clean, into the world again. There was nobody on the other side of the confessional, so Father Burner turned on the signal light. A spider drowsy in his web, drugged with heat and sins, he sat waiting for the next one to be hurled into his presence by guilt ruddy ripe, as with the boy, or, as with the old ladies who come early and try to stay late, by the spiritual famine of their lives or simply the desire to tell secrets in the dark.

He held his wrist in such a way as to see the sweat gleaming in the hairs. He looked at his watch. He had been at it since seven and now it was after nine. If there were no more kneeling in his section of the Cathedral at 9:30 he could close up and have a cigarette. He was too weary to read his Office, though he had the Little Hours, Vespers and Compline still to go. It was the last minutes in the confessional that got him—the insensible end of the excursion that begins with so many sinewy sensations and good intentions to look sharp at the landscape. In the last minutes how many priests, would-be surgeons of the soul, ended as blacksmiths, hammering out absolution anyway?

A few of the Cathedral familiars still drifted around the floor. They were day and night in the shadows praying. Meeting one of them, Father Burner always wanted to get away. They were collectors of priests' blessings in a day when most priests felt ashamed to raise their hands to God outside the ceremonies. Their respect for a priest was fanatic, that of the unworldly, the martyrs, for an emissary of heaven. They were so desperately disposed to death that the manner of dying was their greatest concern. But Father Burner had an idea there were more dull pretenders than saints among them. They inspired no unearthly feelings in him, as true sanctity was supposed to, and he felt it was all right not to like them. They spoke of God, the

Blessed Virgin, of miracles, cures and visitations, as of people and items in the news, which was annoying. The Cathedral because of its location, described by brokers as exclusive, was not so much frequented by these wretches as it would have been if more convenient to the slums. But nevertheless a few came there, like the diarrhetic pigeons, also a scandal to the neighborhood, and would not go away. Father Burner, from his glancing contact with them, had concluded that body odor is the real odor of sanctity.

Through the grating now Father Burner saw the young Vicar General stop a little distance up the aisle and speak to a couple of people who were possible prospects for Father Burner. "Anyone desiring to go to confession should do so at once. In a few minutes the priests will be gone from the confessionals." He crossed to the other side of the Cathedral.

Father Burner did not like to compare his career with the Vicar General's. The Archbishop had taken the Vicar General, a younger man than Father Burner by at least fifteen years, direct from the seminary. After a period of trial as Chancellor, he was raised to his present eminence —for reasons much pondered by the clergy and more difficult to discern than those obviously accounted for by intelligence, appearance and, post facto, the loyalty consequent upon his selection over many older and possibly abler men. It was a medieval act of preference, a slap in the face to the monsignori, a rebuke to the principle of advancement by years applied elsewhere. The Vicar General had the quality of inscrutability in an ideal measure. He did not seem at all given to gossip or conspiracy or even to that owlish secrecy peculiar to secretaries and so exasperating to others. He had possibly no enemies and certainly no intimates. In time he would be a bishop unless, as was breathed wherever the Cloth gathered over food and drink, he really was "troubled with sanctity," which might lead to anything else, the cloister or insanity.

The Vicar General appeared at the door of Father Burner's compartment. "The Archbishop will see you, Father, before you leave tonight." He went up the aisle, genuflected before the main altar, opened as a gate one of the host of brass angels surrounding the sanctuary, and entered the sacristies.

Before he would let hope have its way with him, Father Burner sought to recast the expression on the Vicar General's face. He could recall nothing significant. Very probably there had been nothing to see. Then, with a rush, he permitted himself to think this was his lucky day. Already he was formulating the way he would let the news out, providing he decided not to keep it a secret for a time. He might do that. It would be delicious to go about his business until the very last minute, to savour the old aggravations and feel none of the sting, to receive the old quips and smiles with good grace and know them to be toothless. The news, once out, would fly through the diocese. Hear about Burner at Saint Pat's, Tom? Finally landed himself a parish. Yeah, I just had it from Mc-Kenna. So I guess the A. B. wasn't so sore at the Round One after all. Well, he's just ornery enough to make a go of it.

Father Burner, earlier in the evening, had smoked a cigarette with one of the younger priests attached to the Cathedral (a classmate of Quinlan's but not half the prig), stalling, hoping someone would come and say the Archbishop wanted to see him. When nothing happened except the usual small talk and introduction to a couple of missionaries stopping over, he had given up hope easily. He had seen the basis for his expectations as folly once more. It did not bother him after the fact was certain. He was amenable to any kind of finality. He had a light heart for a . . . an American of German descent. And his hopes rose higher each time and with less cause. He was a ball that bounced up only. He had kept faith. And now—his just reward.

A little surprised he had not thought of her first, he admitted his mother into the new order of things. He wanted to open the letter from her, still in his coat, and late as it was send her a wire, which would do her more good than a night's sleep. He thought of himself back in her kitchen, home from the sem for the holidays, a bruiser in a tight black suit, his feet heavy on the oven door. She was fussing at the stove and he was promising her a porcelain one as big as a house after he got his parish. But he let her know, kidding on the square, that he would be running things at the rectory. It would not be the old story of the priest taking orders from his housekeeper, even if she was his mother (seminarians, from winter evenings of shooting the bull, knew only too well the pitfalls of parish life), or as with Ed Desmond, a few years ago when his father was still living with him, the old man losing his marbles one by one, butting in when people came for advice and instruction, finally coming to believe he was the one to say Mass in his son's absence, no need to get a strange priest in, and sneaking into the box to hear confessions the day before they took him away.

He would be gentle with his mother, however, even if she talked too much, as he recalled she did the last time he saw her. She was well-preserved and strong for her age and ought to be able to keep the house up. Once involved in the social life of the parish she could be a valuable agent in coping with any lay opposition, which was too often the case when a new priest took over.

He resolved to show no nervousness before the Archbishop. A trifle surprised, yes—the Archbishop must have his due—but not overly affected by good fortune. If questioned, he would display a lot of easy confidence not unaccompanied by a touch of humility, a phrase or two like "God willing," or "with the help of Almighty God and your prayers, Your Excellency." He would also not forget to look the part, reliable, casual, cool, an iceberg, only the tip of his true worth showing.

At precisely 9:30 Father Burner picked up his breviary
and backed out of the stall. But then there was the scuff of
a foot and the tap of one of the confessional doors closing
and then, to tell him the last penitent was a woman, the
scent of apple blossoms. He turned off the light, saying
"Damn!" to himself, and sat down again inside. He threw
back the partition and led off, "Yes?" He placed his hand
alongside his head and listened, looking down into the
deeper darkness of his cassock sleeve.

"I . . ."

"Yes?" At the heart of the apple blossoms another scent
bloomed: gin and vermouth.

"Bless me, Father, I . . . have sinned."

Father Burner knew this kind. They would always wait
until the last moment. How they managed to get themselves
into church at all, and then into the confessional, was a
mystery. Sometimes liquor thawed them out. This one was
evidently young, nubile. He had a feeling it was going to
be adultery. He guessed it was—and up to him to get her
underway.

"How long since your last confession?"

"I don't know . . ."

"Have you been away from the Church?"

"Yes."

"Are you married?"

"Yes."

"To a Catholic?"

"No."

"Protestant?"

"No."

"Jew?"

"No."

"Atheist?"

"No—nothing."

"Were you married by a priest?"

"Yes."

"How long ago was that?"

"Four years."

"Any children?"

"No."

"Practice birth control?"

"Yes, sometimes."

"Don't you know it's a crime against nature and the Church forbids it?"

"Yes."

"Don't you know that France fell because of birth control?"

"No."

"Well, it did. Was it your husband's fault?"

"You mean—the birth control?"

"Yes."

"Not wholly."

"And you've been away from the Church ever since your marriage?"

"Yes."

"Now you see why the Church is against mixed marriages. All right, go on. What else?"

"I don't know . . ."

"Is that what you came to confess?"

"No. Yes. I'm sorry, I'm afraid that's all."

"Do you have a problem?"

"I think that's all, Father."

"Remember, it is your obligation, and not mine, to examine your conscience. The task of instructing persons with regard to these delicate matters—I refer to the connubial relationship—is not an easy one. Nevertheless, since there is a grave obligation imposed by God, it cannot be shirked. If you have a problem—"

"I don't have a *problem*."

"Remember, God never commands what is impossible and so if you make use of the sacraments regularly you have every reason to be confident that you will be able to overcome this evil successfully, with His help. I hope this is all clear to you."

"All clear."

"Then if you are heartily sorry for your sins for your penance say the rosary daily for one week and remember it is the law of the Church that you attend Mass on Sundays and holy days and receive the sacraments at least once a year. It's better to receive them often. Ask your pastor about birth control if it's still not clear to you. Or read a Catholic book on the subject. And now make a good act of contrition . . ."

Father Burner climbed the three flights of narrow stairs. He waited a moment in silence, catching his breath. He knocked on the door and was suddenly afraid its density prevented him from being heard and that he might be found standing there, like a fool or a spy. But to knock again, if heard the first time, would seem importunate.

"Come in, Father."

At the other end of the long study the Archbishop sat behind an ebony desk. Father Burner waited before him as though expecting not to be asked to sit down. The only light in the room, a lamp on the desk, was so set that it kept the Archbishop's face in the dark, fell with a gentle sparkle upon his pectoral cross and was absorbed all around by the fabric of the piped cloth he wore. Father Burner's eyes came to rest upon the Archbishop's freckled hand, ringed, square and healthy.

"Be seated, Father."

"Thank you, Your Excellency."

"Oh, sit in this chair, Father." There were two chairs. Father Burner changed to the soft one. He had a suspicion that in choosing the other side he had fallen into a silly trap, that it was a game the Archbishop played with his visitors: the innocent ones, seeing no issue, would take the soft chair, because handier; the guilty would go a step out of their way to take the hard one. "I called Saint Patrick's this morning, Father, but you were . . . out."

"I was visiting Father Desmond, Your Excellency."

"Father Desmond . . ."

"He's in the hospital."

"I know. Friend of his, are you, Father?"

"No, Your Excellency. Well"—Father Burner waited for the cock to crow the third time—"yes, I *know* the man." At once he regretted the scriptural complexion of the words and wondered if it were possible for the Archbishop not to be thinking of the earlier betrayal.

"It was good of you to visit Father Desmond, especially since you are not close to him. I hope he is better, Father."

"He is, Your Excellency."

The Archbishop got up and went across the room to a cabinet. "Will you have a little glass of wine, Father?"

"No. No, thanks, Your Excellency." Immediately he realized it could be another trap and, if so, he was caught again.

"Then I'll have a drop . . . *solus.*" The Archbishop poured a glass and brought it back to the desk. "A little wine for the stomach's sake, Father."

Father Burner, not sure what he was expected to say to that, nodded gravely and said, "Yes, Your Excellency." He had seen that the Archbishop wore carpet slippers and that they had holes in both toes.

"But perhaps you've read Saint Bernard, Father, and recall where he says we priests remember well enough the apostolic counsel to use wine, but overlook the adjective 'little.' "

"I must confess I haven't read Saint Bernard lately, Your Excellency." Father Burner believed this was somehow in his favor. "Since seminary, in fact."

"Not all priests, Father, have need of him. A hard saint . . . for hardened sinners. What is your estimate of Saint Paul?"

Father Burner felt familiar ground under his feet at last. There were the Pauline and Petrine factions—a futile business, he thought—but he knew where the Archbishop stood and exclaimed: "One of the greatest—"

"Really! So many young men today consider him . . .

a bore. It's always the deep-breathing ones, I notice. They say he cuts it too fine."

"I've never thought so, Your Excellency."

"Indeed? Well, it's a question I like to ask my priests. Perhaps you knew that."

"No, I didn't, Your Excellency."

"So much the better then . . . but I see you appraising the melodeon, Father. Are you musical?"

"Not at all, Your Excellency. Violin lessons as a child." Father Burner laughed quickly, as though it were nothing.

"But you didn't go on with them?"

"No, Your Excellency." He did not mean it to sound as sad as it came out.

"What a pity."

"No great loss, Your Excellency."

"You are too . . . modest, Father. But perhaps the violin was not your instrument."

"I guess it wasn't, Your Excellency." Father Burner laughed out too loud.

"And you have the choir at Saint Patrick's, Father?"

"Not this year, Your Excellency. Father Quinlan has it."

"Now I recall . . ."

"Yes." So far as he was concerned, and there were plenty of others who thought so too, Quinlan had played hell with the choir, canning all the women, some of them members for fifteen and twenty years, a couple even longer and practically living for it, and none of them as bad as Quinlan said. The liturgical stuff that Quinlan tried to pull off was all right in monasteries, where they had the time to train for it, but in a parish it sounded stodgy to ears used to the radio and split up the activity along sexual lines, which was really old hat in the modern world. The Dean liked it though. He called it "honest" and eulogized the men from the pulpit—not a sign that he heard how they brayed and whinnied and just gave out or failed to start—and each time it happened ladies in the congregation were sick and upset for days afterward, for he inevitably ended up by attacking women, pants, cocktails, communism, cigarettes and running around half naked. The women looked at the men in the choir, all pretty in surplices, and said to themselves they knew plenty about some of them and what they had done to some women.

"He's tried a little Gregorian, hasn't he—Father Quinlan?"

"Yes, Your Excellency," Father Burner said. "He has."

"Would you say it's been a success—or perhaps I should ask you first if you care for Gregorian, Father."

"Oh, yes, Your Excellency. Very much."

"Many, I know, don't . . . I've been told our chant sounds like a wild bull in a red barn of consumptives coughing into a bottle, but I will have it in the Cathedral, Father. Other places, I am aware, have done well with . . . light opera."

Father Burner frowned.

"We are told the people prefer and understand it. But at the risk of seeming reactionary, a fate my office prevents me from escaping in any event, I say we spend more time listening to the voice of the people than is good for either it or us. We have been too generous with our ears, Father. We have handed over our tongues also. When they are restored to us I wonder if we shall not find our ears more itching than before and our tongues more tied than ever."

Father Burner nodded in the affirmative.

"We are now entering the whale's tail, Father. We must go back the way we came in." The Archbishop lifted the lid of the humidor on the desk. "Will you smoke, Father?"

"No, thanks, Your Excellency."

The Archbishop let the lid drop. "Today there are few saints, fewer sinners and everybody is already saved. We are all heroes in search of an underdog. As for villains, the classic kind with no illusions about themselves, they are . . . extinct. The very devil, for instance, where the devil is the devil today, Father?"

Father Burner, as the Archbishop continued to look at

him, bit his lips for the answer, secretly injured that he should be expected to know, bewildered even as the children he toyed with in catechism.

The Archbishop smiled, but Father Burner was not sure at what, whether at him or what had been said. "Did you see, Father, where our brother Bishop Buckles said Hitler remains the one power on earth against the Church?"

Yes, Father Burner remembered seeing it in the paper; it was the sort of thing that kept Quinlan talking for days. "I did, Your Excellency."

"Alas, poor Buckles! He's a better croquet player than that." The Archbishop's hands unclasped suddenly and fell upon his memo pad. He tore off about a week and seemed to feel better for it. His hands, with no hint of violence about them now, came together again. "We look hard to the right and left, Father. It is rather to the center, I think, we should look, to ourselves, the devil in us."

Father Burner knew the cue for humility when he heard it. "Yes, Your Excellency."

With his chubby fingers the Archbishop made a steeple that was more like a dome. His eyes were reading the memo. "For instance, Father, I sometimes appear at banquets— when they can't line up a good foreign correspondent— banquets at which the poor are never present and at which I am unfailingly confronted by someone exceedingly well off who is moved to inform me that 'religion' is a great consolation to him. Opium, rather, I always think, perhaps wrongfully and borrowing a word from one of our late competitors, which is most imprudent of me, a bishop."

The Archbishop opened a drawer and drew out a sheet of paper and an envelope. "Yes, the rich have souls," he said softly, answering an imaginary objection which happened to be Father Burner's. "But if they had Christ they would not be themselves, that is to say, rich."

"Very true, Your Excellency," Father Burner said.

The Archbishop faced sideways to use an old typewriter. "And likewise, lest we forget, we would not be ourselves,

that is to say—what? For we square the circle beautifully
in almost every country on earth. We bring neither peace
nor a sword. The rich give us money. We give them consolation and make of the eye of the needle a gate. Together
we try to reduce the Church, the Bride of Christ, to a
streetwalker." The Archbishop rattled the paper, Father
Burner's future, into place and rolled it crookedly into the
typewriter. "Unfortunately for us, it doesn't end there. The
penance will not be shared so equitably. Your Christian
name, Father, is—?"

"Ernest, Your Excellency."

The Archbishop typed several words and stopped, looking over at Father Burner. "I can't call to mind a single
Saint Ernest, Father. Can you help me?"

"There were two, I believe, Your Excellency, but Butler
leaves them out of his *Lives.*"

"They would be German saints, Father?"

"Yes, Your Excellency. There was one an abbot and the
other an archbishop."

"If Butler had been Irish, as the name has come to indicate, I'd say that's an Irishman for you, Father. He does
not forget to include a power of Irish saints." The Archbishop was Irish himself. Father Burner begged to differ
with him, believing here was a wrong deliberately set up
for him to right. "I am not Irish myself, Your Excellency,
but some of my best friends are."

"Tut, tut, Father. Such tolerance will be the death of
you." The Archbishop, typing a few words, removed the
paper, signed it and placed it in the envelope. He got up
and took down a book from the shelves. He flipped it open,
glanced through several pages and returned it to its place.
"No Ernests in Baring-Gould either. Well, Father, it looks
as if you have a clear field."

The Archbishop came from behind the desk and Father
Burner, knowing the interview was over, rose. The Archbishop handed him the envelope. Father Burner stuffed it
hastily in his pocket and knelt, the really important thing,

to kiss the Archbishop's ring and receive his blessing. They walked together toward the door.

"Do you care for pictures, Father?"

"Oh, yes, Your Excellency."

The Archbishop, touching him lightly on the arm, stopped before a reproduction of Raphael's Sistine Madonna. "There is a good peasant woman, Father, and a nice fat baby." Father Burner nodded his appreciation. "She could be Our Blessed Mother, Father, though I doubt it. There is no question about the baby. He is not Christ." The Archbishop moved to another picture. "Rembrandt had the right idea, Father. See the gentleman pushing Christ up on the cross? That is Rembrandt, a self portrait." Father Burner thought of some of the stories about the Archbishop, that he slept on a cot, stood in line with people sometimes to go to confession, that he fasted on alternate days the year round. Father Burner was thankful for such men as the Archbishop. "But here is Christ, Father." This time it was a glassy-eyed Christ whose head lay against the rough wood of the cross he was carrying. "That is Christ, Father. The Greek painted Our Saviour."

The Archbishop opened the door for Father Burner, saying, "And, Father, you will please not open the envelope until after your Mass tomorrow."

Father Burner went swiftly down the stairs. Before he got into his car he looked up at the Cathedral. He could scarcely see the cross glowing on the dome. It seemed as far away as the stars. The cross needed a brighter light or the dome ought to be painted gold and lit up like the state capital, so people would see it. He drove a couple of blocks down the street, pulled up to the curb, opened the envelope, which had not been sealed, and read: "You will report on August 8 to the Reverend Michael Furlong, to begin your duties on that day as his assistant. I trust that in your new appointment you will find not peace but a sword."

ENCORE

by James Purdy

James Purdy (1923–   ). A Midwesterner from Ohio, Purdy holds an M.A. from the University of Chicago and has studied at the University of Madrid. In 1957 his collection of short stories, *Color of Darkness*, was published. His first novel, *Malcolm*, won much critical esteem as a satire on the spiritual sterility of modern urban America, a subject which bulks large in his writing. Mr. Purdy has since published several novels and volumes of short stories of great power and poignance.

"He's in that Greek restaurant every night. I thought you knew that," Merta told her brother.

"What does he do in it?" Spence said, wearily attentive.

"I don't go to Greek restaurants and I don't spy on him," she said.

"Then how do you know so certainly he is there every night?"

"How do you know anything? He's not popular at the college. He says he likes to talk to Spyro, the restaurant owner's son, about painting. I don't know what they do!"

"Well, don't tell me if you don't know," her brother said. He got up and took his hat to go.

"Of course," she continued, anxiously stepping in front of him to detain his going, "it isn't so much that Spyro is all at fault, you know. There are things wrong with Gibbs, too. As I said, he's not popular at the college. He wasn't asked to join a fraternity, you know. And the restaurant has made up for that, I suppose. It's always open for him day or night."

"Maybe you should make your own home more of a place he could bring his friends to," Spence said, a kind of cold expressionless tone in his voice.

"You would say that," she repeated almost without emotion. "I don't suppose you ever half considered what it is, I mean this home. It's not a home. It's a flat, and I'm a woman without a husband."

"I know, I know, Merta. You've done it all alone. Nobody's lifted a finger but you." His weariness itself seemed to collapse when he said this, and he looked at her with genuine feeling.

"I'm not trying to get your pity. I wanted to tell somebody what was going on at Spyro's is all. I needed to talk to somebody."

"I think Spyro's is the best place he could go," Spence said.

"And Spyro's awful father and grandfather!" she cried as though seeing something from far back of dread and ugliness.

"The Matsoukases?" Spence was surprised at her vehemence.

"Yes, the Matsoukases! With their immense eyes and black beards. Old Mr. Matsoukas, the grandfather, came here one evening, and tried to get fresh with me."

"I can hardly believe it," Spence said.

"You mean I am making it up," she accused him.

"No, no, I just can't visualize it."

"And now," she returned to the only subject which interested her, "Gibbs is there all the time as though it was his home."

"Do you talk to him about it, Merta?"

"I can't. I can't tell him and nag him about not going to the Greek restaurant at night. It's glamor and life to him, I suppose, and I suppose it *is* different. A different sort of place. The old man hasn't allowed them to put in juke boxes or television or anything, and you know Gibbs likes anything funny or different, and there isn't anything funny or different but maybe Spyro's. None of the college crowd goes there, and Gibbs feels he's safe there from their criticism and can drink his coffee in peace."

"Well it sounds so dull, drinking coffee in a seedy Greek restaurant, I don't see why a mother should worry about her son going there. And call me out of bed to talk about it!"

"Oh Spence," she said urgently again, "he shouldn't go there. Don't you see? He shouldn't be there."

"I don't see that at all," Spence said. "And, Merta, I wish you would quit calling me up at this hour of the night to talk about your son, who is nearly a grown man by now. After all I have my profession to worry about too. . . ."

She stared at him.

"I had to talk with somebody about Spyro," she said.

"Oh, it's Spyro then you wanted to talk about," Spence said, the irritation growing in his manner.

"Spyro," she said vaguely, as though it were Spence who himself had mentioned him and thus brought him to mind. "I never cared much for that young man."

"Why not?" Spence was swift to hold her to anything vague and indirect because he felt that vagueness and indirectness was her method.

"Well, Spyro does all those paintings and drawings that are so bizarre."

"Bizarre," he paused on the word. "They're nearly *good,* if you ask me."

"I don't like Spyro," she said.

"Why don't you invite him here, if your son likes him?" he put the whole matter in her hands.

"When I work in a factory all day long, Spence. . . ."

"You don't feel like doing anything but working in a factory," he said irritably.

"I thought my own brother would be a little more understanding," she said coldly angry.

"I wish you would be of Gibbs," he told her.

"Oh Spence, please, please."

"Please, nothing. You always have a problem, but the problem is you, Merta. You're old and tired and complaining, and because you can't put your finger on what's wrong you've decided that there's something wrong with your son because he goes, of all places, to a Greek restaurant and talks to Spyro who draws rather well and who is now making a portrait of your son."

"Spence! Don't tell me that!"

"You dear old fool, Merta," he said and he put on his hat now, which she looked at, he thought, rather critically and also with a certain envy.

"That's a nice hat," she forced herself to say at last.

"Well a doctor can't look like a nobody," he said, and then winced at his own words.

"What you should do, Merta," he hurried on with another speech, "is get some sort of hobby, become a lady bowler, get on the old women's curling team, or meet up with some gent your own age. And let your son go his own way."

"You are comforting," Merta said, pretending to find humor in his words.

"Was that Spence leaving just now?" Gibbs said, putting down some books.

Merta held her face up to be kissed by him, which he did in a manner resembling someone surreptitiously spitting out a seed.

"And how was Spyro tonight?" she said in a booming encouraging voice whose suddenness and loudness perhaps surprised even her.

He looked at her much as he had when as a small boy she had suddenly burst into the front room and asked him what he was being so very still for.

"Spyro is doing a portrait of me," he told her.

"A portrait," Merta said, trying hard to keep the disapproval out of her voice.

"That's what it is," Gibbs said, sitting down at the far end of the room and taking out his harmonica.

She closed her eyes in displeasure, but said nothing as he played "How High the Moon." He always played, it seemed, when she wanted to talk to him.

"Would you like Spyro to come to visit us some day?" she said.

"Visit us?"

"Pay a call," she smiled, closing her eyes.

"What would he pay us a call for?" he wondered. Seeing her pained hurt look, he expanded: "I mean what would he get to see here."

"Oh me," she replied laughing. "I'm so beautiful."

"Spyro thinks you don't like him," Gibbs said, and while she was saying *Tommyrot!* Gibbs went on: "In fact, he thinks everybody in this town dislikes him."

"They *are* the only Greeks, it's true," Merta said.

"And we're such a front family in town, of course!" he said with sudden fire.

"Well, your Uncle Spence is somebody," she began, white, and her mouth gaping a little, but Gibbs started to play on the harmonica again, cutting her off.

She tried to control her feelings tonight, partly because she had such a splitting headache.

"Would you like a dish of strawberry jello?" Merta said above the sound of the harmonica playing.

"What?" he cried.

"Some strawberry jello," she repeated, a little embarrassment now in her voice.

"What would I want that for?" he asked, putting down the harmonica with impatience.

"I suddenly got hungry for some, and went out there and made it. It's set by now and ready to eat."

There was such a look of total defeat on her old gray face that Gibbs said he would have some.

"I've some fresh coffee too," she said, a touch of sophistication in her voice, as if coffee here were unusual and exotic also.

"I've had my coffee," he said. "Just the jello, thank you."

"Does Spyro always serve you coffee?" she said, her bitterness returning now against her will as they stood in the kitchen.

"I don't know," he said belligerently.

"But I thought you saw him every evening," she feigned sweet casualness.

"I never notice what he serves," Spence said loudly and indifferently.

"Would you like a large dish or a small dish of jello?" she said heavily.

"Small, for Christ's sake," he told her.

"Gibbs!" she cried. Then, catching herself, she said, "Small it will be, dear."

"What have you got to say that you can't bring it out!" he suddenly turned on her, and taking the dish of jello from her hand he put it down with a bang on the oilcloth covering of the tiny kitchen table.

"Gibbs, let's not have any trouble. Mother has a terrible headache tonight."

"Well, why don't you go to bed then," he said in his stentorian voice.

"Perhaps I will," she said weakly. She sat down and began eating right out of the jello bowl. She ate nearly all the rubbery stiff red imitation strawberry jello and drank in hurried gulps the coffee loaded with condensed milk.

"Spence gave me hell all evening," she said eating. "He thinks I would be happier if I found a fellow!"

She laughed but her laughter brought no response from Gibbs.

"I know I have nothing to offer anybody. Let's face it."

"Why do you have to say *let's face it!*" Gibbs snapped at her.

"Is there something wrong grammatically with it?" she wondered taking her spoon out of her mouth.

"Every dumb son of a bitch in the world is always saying *let's face it.*"

"And your own language is quite refined," she countered.

"Yes, let's face it, it is," he said, a bit weakly, and he took out the harmonica from his pocket, looked at it, and put it down noiselessly on the oilcloth.

"I've always wanted to do right by you, Gibbs. Since you was a little boy, I have tried. But no father around, and all. . . ."

"Mom, we've been over this ten thousand times. Can't we just forget I didn't have an old man, and you worked like a team of dogs to make up for everything."

"Yes, let's do. Let's forget it all. For heaven's sake, I'm eating all this jello," she said gaily.

"Yes, I noticed," he said.

"But I want to do for you," she told him suddenly again with passion, forgetting everything but her one feeling now, and she put out her hand to him. "You're all I have, Gibbs."

He stared at her. She was weeping.

"I've never been able to do anything for you," she said. "I know I'm not someone you want to bring your friends home to see."

"Mom, for Christ's sake," he said.

"Don't swear," she said. "I may not know grammar or English, but I'm not profane and I never taught you to be. So there," she said, and she brought out her handkerchief and wiped her eyes, making them, he saw, even older and more worn with the rubbing.

"Mom," he said, picking up the harmonica again, "I don't *have* any friends."

"No?" she said laughing a little. Then understanding his remark more clearly as her weeping calmed itself, she said, commanding again, "What do you mean now by that?"

"Just what I said, Mom. I don't have any friends. Except maybe Spyro."

"Oh that Greek boy. We would come back to him."

"How could I have friends, do you think. After all. . . ."

"Don't you go to college like everybody else," she said hurriedly. "Aren't we making the attempt, Gibbs?"

"Don't get so excited. I don't care because I don't have any friends. I wasn't accusing you of anything."

"You go to college and you ought to have friends," she said. "Isn't that right?"

"Look, for Christ's sake, just going to college doesn't bring you friends. Especially a guy like me with. . . ."

"What's wrong with you," she said. "You're handsome. You're a beautiful boy."

"Mom, Je-sus."

"No wonder that Greek is painting you. You're a fine-looking boy."

"Oh it isn't that way at all," he said, bored. "Spyro has to paint somebody."

"I don't know why you don't have friends," she said. "You have everything. Good looks, intelligence, and you can speak and act refined when you want to. . . ."

"You have to be rich at that college. And your parents have to be. . . ."

"Is that *all* then?" she said, suddenly very white and facing him.

"Mom, I didn't mean anything about you. I didn't say any of this to make you feel. . . ."

"Be quiet," she said. "Don't talk."

"Maybe we *should* talk about it, Mom."

"I can't help what happened. What was *was,* the past is the past. Whatever wrong I may have done, the circumstances of your birth, Gibbs. . . ."

"Mom, please, this isn't about you at all."

"I've stood by you, Gibbs," she hurried on as if testifying before a deaf judge. "You can never deny that." She stared at him as though she had lost her reason.

"I'd like to have seen those rich women with their fat manicured husbands do what I've done," she said now as though powerless to stop, words coming out of her mouth that she usually kept and nursed for her long nights of sleeplessness and hate.

She stood up quickly as if to leave the room.

"With no husband or father to boot in this house! I'd like to see *them* do what I did. God damn them," she said.

Gibbs waited there, pale now as she was, and somehow much smaller before her wrath.

"God damn everybody!" she cried. "God damn everybody."

She sat down and began weeping furiously.

"I can't help it if you don't have friends," she told him, quieting herself with a last supreme effort. "I can't help it at all."

"Mom," he said. He wanted to weep too, but there was something too rocklike, too bitter and immovable inside him to let tears come loose. Often at night as he lay in his bed knowing that Merta was lying in the next room sleepless, he had wanted to get up and go to her and let them both weep together, but he could not.

"Is there anything I could do to change things here at home for you?" she said suddenly wiping away the tears, and tensing her breast to keep more of the torrent from gathering inside herself. "Anything at all I can do, I will," she said.

"Mom," he said, and he got up and as he did so the harmonica fell to the linoleum floor.

"You dropped your little . . . toy," she said tightening her mouth.

"It's not a toy," he began. "This is," he began again. "You see, this is the kind the professionals play on the stage . . . and everywhere."

"I see," she said, struggling to keep the storm within her quiet, the storm that now if it broke might sweep everything within her away, might rage and rage until only dying itself could stop it.

"Play something on it, Gibbs darling," she said.

He wanted to ask her if she was all right.

"Play, play," she said desperately.

"What do you want me to play, Mom?" he said, deathly pale.

"Just play any number you like," she suggested.

He began then to play "How High the Moon" but his lips trembled too much.

"Keep playing," she said beating her hands with the heavy veins and the fingers without rings or embellishment.

He looked at her hands as his lips struggled to keep themselves on the tiny worn openings of the harmonica which he had described as the instrument of the professionals.

"What a funny tune," she said. "I never listened to it right before. What did you say they called it?"

"Mom," he said. "Please!"

He stretched out his hand.

"Don't now, don't," she commanded. "Just play. Keep playing."

TELL ME A RIDDLE

by Tillie Olsen

Tillie Olsen (1913–   ), like Wright Morris, was born in Nebraska and now lives in San Francisco. She is married and the mother of four children. At various times in her career she has been secretary and transcriber in industry, Resident Scholar at Radcliffe Institute for Independent Studies, and Creative Writing Fellow at Stanford University. She received a Ford grant in 1959, and the story included here, "Tell Me a Riddle," was chosen best story of the year for the *O'Henry Prize Stories* of 1961. She is the author of several volumes of non-fiction, as well as the novel *Yonnondio: From the Thirties* (1974), a powerful evocation of an impoverished world.

1.

For forty-seven years they had been married. How deep back the stubborn, gnarled roots of the quarrel reached, no one could say—but only now, when tending to the needs of others no longer shackled them together, the roots swelled up visible, split the earth between them, and the tearing shook even to the children, long since grown.

Why now, why now? wailed Hannah.

As if when we grew up weren't enough, said Paul.

Poor Ma. Poor Dad. It hurts so for both of them, said Vivi. They never had very much; at least in old age they should be happy.

Knock their heads together, insisted Sammy; tell 'em: you're too old for this kind of thing; no reason not to get along now.

Lennie wrote to Clara: They've lived over so much together; what could possibly tear them apart?

Something tangible enough.

Arthritic hands, and such work as he got, occasional. Poverty all his life, and there was little breath left for the running. He could not, could not turn away from this desire: to have the troubling of responsibility, the fretting with money, over and done with; to be free, to be *care*free where success was not measured by accumulation, and there was use for the vitality still in him.

There was a way. They could sell the house, and with the money join his lodge's Haven, cooperative for the aged. Happy communal life, and was he not already an official; had he not helped organize it, raise funds, served as a trustee?

But she—would not consider it.

"What do we need all this for?" he would ask loudly, for her hearing aid was turned down and the vacuum was shrilling. "Five rooms" (pushing the sofa so she could get into the corner) "furniture" (smoothing down the rug) "floors and surfaces to make work. Tell me, why do we need it?" And he was glad he could ask in a scream.

"Because I'm use't."

"Because you're use't. This is a reason, Mrs. Word Miser? Used to can get unused!"

"Enough unused I have to get used to already . . . Not enough words?" turning off the vacuum a moment to hear herself answer. "Because soon enough we'll need only a little closet, no windows, no furniture, nothing to make work but for worms. Because now I want room . . . Screech and blow like you're doing, you'll need that closet even sooner . . . Ha, again!" for the vacuum bag wailed, puffed half up, hung stubbornly limp. "This time fix it so it stays; quick before the phone rings and you get too important-busy."

But while he struggled with the motor, it seethed in him. Why fix it? Why have to bother? And if it can't be fixed, have to wring the mind with how to pay the repair? At the Haven they come in with their own machines to clean your room or your cottage; you fish, or play cards, or make jokes in the sun, not with knotty fingers fight to mend vacuums.

Over the dishes, coaxingly: "For once in your life, to be free, to have everything done for you, like a queen."

"I never liked queens."

"No dishes, no garbage, no towel to sop, no worry what to buy, what to eat."

"And what else would I do with my empty hands? Better to eat at my own table when I want, and to cook and eat how I want."

"In the cottages they buy what you ask, and cook it how you like. *You* are the one who always used to say: better mankind born without mouths and stomachs than always to worry for money to buy, to shop, to fix, to cook, to wash, to clean."

"How cleverly you hid that you heard. I said it then because eighteen hours a day I ran. And you never scraped a carrot or knew a dish towel sops. Now—for you and me —who cares? A herring out of a jar is enough. But when *I* want, and nobody to bother." And she turned off her ear button, so she would not have to hear.

But as *he* had no peace, juggling and rejuggling the money to figure: how will I pay for this now?: prying out the storm windows (there they take care of this); jolting in the streetcar on errands (there I would not have to ride to take care of this or that); fending the patronizing of relatives just back from Florida (there it matters what one is, not what one can afford), he gave *her* no peace.

"Look! in their bulletin. A reading circle. Twice a week it meets."

"Haumm," her answer of not listening.

"A reading circle. Chekhov they read that you like, and Peretz. Cultured people at the Haven that you would enjoy."

"Enjoy!" She tasted the word. "Now, when it pleases you, you find a reading circle for me. And forty years ago when the children were morsels and there was a Circle, did you stay home with them once so I could go? Even once? You trained me well. I do not need others to enjoy. Others!" Her voice trembled. "Because *you* want to be there with others. Already it makes me sick to think of you always around others. Clown, grimacer, floormat, yesman, entertainer, whatever they want of you."

And now it was he who turned on the television loud so he need not hear.

Old scar tissue ruptured and the wounds festered anew. Chekhov indeed. She thought without softness of that young wife, who in the deep night hours while she nursed the current baby, and perhaps held another in her lap, would try to stay awake for the only time there was to read. She would feel again the weather of the outside on his cheek when, coming late from a meeting, he would find her so, and stimulated and ardent, sniffing her skin, coax: "I'll put the baby to bed, and you—put the book away, don't read, don't read."

That had been the most beguiling of all the "don't read, put your book away" her life had been. Chekhov indeed!

"Money?" She shrugged him off. "Could we get poorer than once we were? And in America, who starves?"

But as still he pressed:

"Let me alone about money. Was there ever enough? Seven little ones—for every penny I had to ask—and sometimes, remember, there was nothing. But always *I* had to manage. Now *you* manage. Rub your nose in it good."

But from those years she had had to manage, old humiliations and terrors rose up, lived again, and forced her to relive them. The children's needings; that grocer's face or this merchant's wife she had had to beg credit from when credit was a disgrace, the scenery of the long blocks walked around when she could not pay; school coming, and the desperate going over the old to see what could yet be remade; the soups of meat bones begged "for-the-dog" one winter . . .

Enough. Now they had no children. Let *him* wrack his head for how they would live. She would not exchange her solitude for anything. *Never again to be forced to move to the rhythms of others.*

For in this solitude she had won to a reconciled peace.

Tranquillity from having the empty house no longer an enemy, for it stayed clean—not as in the days when (by the perverse logic of exhausted housewifery) it was her family, the life in it, that had seemed the enemy: tracking, smudging, littering, dirtying, engaging her in endless defeating battle—and on whom her endless defeat had been spewed.

The few old books, memorized from rereading; the pictures to ponder (the magnifying glass superimposed on her heavy eyeglasses). Or if she wishes, when he is gone, the phonograph, that if she turns up very loud and strains, she can hear: the ordered sounds, and the struggling.

Out in the garden, growing things to nurture. Birds to be kept out of the pear tree, and when the pears are heavy and ripe, the old fury of work, for all must be canned, nothing wasted.

And her one social duty (for she will not go to luncheons or meetings) the boxes of old clothes left with her, as with a life-practiced eye for finding what is still wearable within the worn (again the magnifying glass superimposed on the heavy glasses) she scans and sorts—this for rag or rummage, that for mending and cleaning, and this for sending abroad.

Being able at last to live within, and not move to the rhythms of others, as life had helped her to: denying; removing; isolating; taking the children one by one; then deafening, half-blinding—and at last, presenting her solitude.

And in it she had won to a reconciled peace.

Now he was violating it with his constant campaigning: *Sell the house and move to the Haven.* (You sit, you sit—there too you could sit like a stone.) He was making of her a battleground where old grievances tore. (Turn on your ear button—I am talking.) And stubbornly she resisted—so that from wheedling, reasoning, manipulation, it was bitterness he now started with.

And it came to where every happening lashed up a quarrel.

"I will sell the house anyway," he flung at her one night. "I am putting it up for sale. There will be a way to make you sign."

The television blared, as always it did on the evenings he stayed home, and as always it reached her only as noise. She did not know if the tumult was in her or outside. Snap! she turned the sound off. "Shadows," she whispered to him, pointing to the screen, "look, it is only shadows." And in a scream: "Did you say that you will sell the house? Look at me, not at that. I am no shadow. You cannot sell without me."

"Leave on the television. I am watching."

"Like Paulie, like Jenny, a four-year-old. Staring at shadows. *You cannot sell the house.*"

"I will. We are going to the Haven. There you would not have the television when you do not want it. I could sit in the social room and watch. You could lock yourself up to smell your unpleasantness in a room by yourself—for who would want to come near you?"

"No, no selling." A whisper now.

"The television is shadows. Mrs. Enlightened! Mrs. Cultured! A world comes into your house—and it is shadows. People you would never meet in a thousand lifetimes. Wonders. When you were four years old, yes, like Paulie, like Jenny, did you know of Indian dances, alligators, how they use bamboo in Malaya? No, you scratched in your dirt with the chickens and thought Olshana was the world. Yes, Mrs. Unpleasant, I will sell the house, for there better can we be rid of each other than here."

She did not know if the tumult was outside, or in her. Always a ravening inside, a pull to the bed, to lie down, to succumb.

"Have you thought maybe Ma should let a doctor have a look at her?" asked their son Paul after Sunday dinner, regarding his mother crumpled on the couch, instead of, as was her custom, busying herself in Nancy's kitchen.

"Why not the President too?"

"Seriously, Dad. This is the third Sunday she's lain down like that after dinner. Is she that way at home?"

"A regular love affair with the bed. Every time I start to talk to her."

Good protective reaction, observed Nancy to herself. The workings of hos-til-ity.

"Nancy could take her. I just don't like how she looks. Let's have Nancy arrange an appointment."

"You think she'll go?" regarding his wife gloomily. "All right, we have to have doctor bills, we have to have doctor bills." Loudly: "Something hurts you?"

She startled, looked to his lips. He repeated: "Mrs. Take It Easy, something hurts?"

"Nothing . . . Only you."

"A woman of honey. That's why you're lying down?"

"Soon I'll get up to do the dishes, Nancy."

"Leave them, Mother, I like it better this way."

"Mrs. Take It Easy, Paul says you should start ballet. You should go see a doctor and ask: how soon can you start ballet?"

"A doctor?" she begged. "Ballet?"

"We were talking, Ma," explained Paul, "you don't seem any too well. It would be a good idea for you to see a doctor for a checkup."

"I get up now to do the kitchen. Doctors are bills and foolishness, my son. I need no doctors."

"At the Haven," he could not resist pointing out, "a doctor is *not* bills. He lives beside you. You start to sneeze, he is there before you open up a Kleenex. You can be sick there for free, all you want."

"Diarrhea of the mouth, is there a doctor to make you dumb?"

"Ma. Promise me you'll go. Nancy will arrange it."

"It's all of a piece when you think of it," said Nancy, "the way she attacks my kitchen, scrubbing under every cup hook, doing the inside of the oven so I can't enjoy Sunday dinner, knowing that half-blind or not, she's going to find every speck of dirt . . ."

"Don't, Nancy, I've told you—it's the only way she knows to be useful. What did the *doctor* say?"

"A real fatherly lecture. Sixty-nine is young these days. Go out, enjoy life, find interests. Get a new hearing aid, this one is antiquated. Old age is sickness only if one makes it so. Geriatrics, Inc."

"So there was nothing physical."

"Of course there was. How can you live to yourself like she does without there being? Evidence of a kidney disorder, and her blood count is low. He gave her a diet, and she's to come back for follow-up and lab work . . . But he was clear enough: Number One prescription—start living like a human being. When I think of your dad, who could really play the invalid with that arthritis of his, as active as a teenager, and twice as much fun . . ."

"You didn't tell me the doctor says your sickness is in you, how you live." He pushed his advantage. "Life and enjoyments you need better than medicine. And this diet, how can you keep it? To weigh each morsel and scrape away the bits of fat to make this soup, that pudding. There, at the Haven, they have a dietician, they would do it for you."

She is silent.

"You would feel better there, I know it," he says gently. "There there is life and enjoyments all around."

"What is the matter, Mr. Importantbusy, you have no card game or meeting you can go to?"—turning her face to the pillow.

For a while he cut his meetings and going out, fussed over her diet, tried to wheedle her into leaving the house, brought in visitors:

"I should come to a fashion tea. I should sit and look at pretty babies in clothes I cannot buy. This is pleasure?"

"Always you are better than everyone else. The doctor said you should go out. Mrs. Brem comes to you with goodness and you turn her away."

"Because *you* asked her to, she asked me."

"They won't come back. People you need, the doctor said. Your own cousins I asked; they were willing to come and make peace as if nothing had happened . . ."

"No more crushers of people, pushers, hypocrites, around me. No more in *my* house. You go to them if you like."

"Kind he is to visit. And you, like ice."

"A babbler. All my life around babblers. Enough!"

"She's even worse, Dad? Then let her stew a while," advised Nancy. "You can't let it destroy you; it's a psychological thing, maybe too far gone for any of us to help."

So he let her stew. More and more she lay silent in bed, and sometimes did not even get up to make the meals. No longer was the tongue-lashing inevitable if he left the coffee cup where it did not belong, or forgot to take out the garbage or mislaid the broom. The birds grew bold that summer and for once pocked the pears, undisturbed.

A bellyful of bitterness, and every day the same quarrel in a new way and a different old grievance the quarrel forced her to enter and relive. And the new torment: I am not really sick, the doctor said it, then why do I feel so sick?

One night she asked him: "You have a meeting tonight? Do not go. Stay . . . with me."

He had planned to watch "This Is Your Life" anyway, but half sick himself from the heavy heat, and sickening therefore the more after the brooks and woods of the Haven, with satisfaction he grated:

"Hah, Mrs. Live Alone And Like It wants company all of a sudden. It doesn't seem so good the time of solitary when she was a girl exile in Siberia. 'Do not go. Stay with me.' A new song for Mrs. Free As A Bird. Yes, I am going out, and while I am gone chew this aloneness good, and think how you keep us both from where if you want people you do not need to be alone."

"Go, go. All your life you have gone without me."

After him she sobbed curses he had not heard in years, old-country curses from their childhood: Grow, oh shall you grow like an onion, with your head in the ground. Like the hide of a drum shall you be, beaten in life, beaten in death. Oh shall you be like a chandelier, to hang and to burn . . .

She was not in their bed when he came back. She lay on the cot on the sun porch. All week she did not speak or come near him; nor did he try to make peace or care for her.

He slept badly, so used to her next to him. After all the years, old harmonies and dependencies deep in their bodies; she curled to him, or he coiled to her, each warmed, warming, turning as the other turned, the nights a long embrace.

It was not the empty bed or the storm that woke him, but a faint singing. *She* was singing. Shaking off the drops of rain, the lightning riving her lifted face, he saw her so; the cot covers on the floor.

"This is a private concert?" he asked. "Come in, you are wet."

"I can breathe now," she answered; "my lungs are rich." Though indeed the sound was hardly a breath.

"Come in, come in." Loosing the bamboo shades. "Look how wet you are." Half helping, half carrying her, still faint-breathing her song.

A Russian love song of fifty years ago.

He had found a buyer, but before he told her, he called together those children who were close enough to come. Paul, of course, Sammy from New Jersey, Hannah from Connecticut, Vivi from Ohio.

With a kindling of energy for her beloved visitors, she arrayed the house, cooked and baked. She was not prepared for the solemn after-dinner conclave, they too probing in and tearing. Her frightened eyes watched from mouth to mouth as each spoke.

His stories were eloquent and funny of her refusal to go back to the doctor; of the scorned invitations; of her stubborn silences or the bile "like a Niagara"; of her contrariness: "If I clean it's no good how I cleaned; if I don't clean, I'm still a master who thinks he has a slave."

("Vinegar he poured on me all his life; I am well marinated; how can I be honey now?")

Deftly he marched in the rightness for moving to the Haven; their money from social security free for visiting the children, not sucked into daily needs and into the house; the activities in the Haven for him; but mostly the Haven for *her:* her health, her need of care, distraction, amusement, friends who shared her interests.

"This does offer an outlet for Dad," said Paul; "he's

always been an active person. And economic peace of
mind isn't to be sneezed at, either. I could use a little of
that myself."

But when they asked: "And you, Ma, how do you feel
about it?" she could only whisper:

"For him it is good. It is not for me. I can no longer
live between people."

"You lived all your life *for* people," Vivi cried.

"Not with." Suffering doubly for the unhappiness on her
children's faces.

"You have to find some compromise," Sammy insisted.
"Maybe sell the house and buy a trailer. After forty-seven
years there's surely some way you can find to live in
peace."

"There is no help, my children. Different things we
need."

"Then live alone!" He could control himself no longer.
"I have a buyer for the house. Half the money for you,
half for me. Either alone or with me to the Haven. You
think I can live any longer as we are doing now?"

"Ma doesn't have to make a decision this minute, however you feel, Dad," Paul said quickly, "and you wouldn't
want her to. Let's let it lay a few months, and then talk
some more.

"I think I can work it out to take Mother home with
me for a while," Hannah said. "You both look terrible,
but especially you, Mother. I'm going to ask Phil to have
a look at you."

"Sure," cracked Sammy. "What's the use of a doctor
husband if you can't get free service out of him once in a
while for the family? And absence might make the heart
. . . you know."

"There was something after all," Paul told Nancy in a
colorless voice. "That was Hannah's Phil calling. Her gall
bladder . . . Surgery."

"Her *gall* bladder. If that isn't classic. 'Bitter as gall'—talk of psychosom—"

He stepped closer, put his hand over her mouth and said in the same colorless, plodding voice, "We have to get Dad. They operated at once. The cancer was everywhere, surrounding the liver, everywhere. They did what they could . . . at best she has a year. Dad . . . we have to tell him."

2.

Honest in his weakness when they told him, and that she was not to know. "I'm not an actor. She'll know right away by how I am. O that poor woman. I am old too, it will break me into pieces. O that poor woman. She will spit on me: 'So my sickness was how I live.' O Paulie, how she will be, that poor woman. Only she should not suffer . . . I can't stand sickness, Paulie, I can't go with you."

But went. And play-acted.

"A grand opening and you did not even wait for me . . . A good thing Hannah took you with her."

"Fashion teas I needed. They cut out what tore in me; just in my throat something hurts yet . . . Look! so many flowers, like a funeral. Vivi called, did Hannah tell you? And Lennie from San Francisco, and Clara; and Sammy is coming." Her gnome's face pressed happily into the flowers.

It is impossible to predict in these cases, but once over the immediate effects of the operation, she should have several months of comparative well-being.
The money, where will come the money?
Travel with her, Dad. Don't take her home to the old associations. The other children will want to see her.
The money, where will I wring the money?

Whatever happens, she is not to know. No, you can't ask her to sign papers to sell the house; nothing to upset her. Borrow instead, then after . . . *I had wanted to leave you each a few dollars to make life easier, as other fathers do. There will be nothing left now. (Failure! you and your "business is exploitation." Why didn't you make it when it could be made?—Is that what you're thinking Sammy?)* Sure she's unreasonable, Dad —but you have to stay with her; if there's to be any happiness in what's left of her life, it depends on you. *Prop me up children, think of me, too. Shuffled, chained with her, bitter woman. No Haven, and the little money going . . . How happy she looks, poor creature.*

The look of excitement. The straining to hear everything (the new hearing aid turned full). Why are you so happy, dying woman?

How the petals are, fold on fold, and the gladioli color. The autumn air.

Stranger grandsons, tall above the little gnome grandmother, the little spry grandfather. Paul in a frenzy of picture-taking before going.

She, wandering the great house. Feeling the books; laughing at the maple shoemaker's bench of a hundred years ago used as a table. The ear turned to music.

"Let us go home. See how good I walk now." "One step from the hospital," he answers, "and she wants to fly. Wait till Doctor Phil says."

"Look—the birds too are flying home. Very good Phil is and will not show it, but he is sick of sickness by the time he comes home."

"Mrs. Telepathy, to read minds," he answers; "read mine what it says: when the trunks of medicines become a suitcase, then we will go."

The grandboys, they do not know what to say to us . . . Hannah, she runs around here, there, when is there time for herself?

Let us go home. Let us go home.

Musing; gentleness—*but for the incidents of the rabbi
in the hospital, and of the candles of benediction.
Of the rabbi in the hospital:*

Now tell me what happened, Mother.

From the sleep I awoke, Hannah's Phil, and he stands
there like a devil in a dream and calls me by name. I
cannot hear. I think he prays. Go away please, I tell him,
I am not a believer. Still he stands, while my heart
knocks with fright.

You scared *him,* Mother. He thought you were delirious.

Who sent him? Why did he come to me?

It is a custom. The men of God come to visit those of
their religion they might help. Jew, Protestant, Catholic,
the hospital makes up the list for them, and you are
on the Jewish list.

Not for rabbis. At once go and make them change. Tell
them to write: Born, human; Religion, none.

And of the candles of benediction:

Look how you have upset yourself, Mrs. Excited Over
Nothing. Pleasant memories you should leave.

Go in, go back to Hannah and the lights. Two weeks I
saw the candles and said nothing. But she asked me.

So what was so terrible? She forgets you never did, she
asks you to light the Friday candles and say the benediction like Phil's mother when she visits. If the candles
give her pleasure, why shouldn't she have the pleasure?

Not for pleasure she does it. For emptiness. Because his
family does. Because all around her do.

That is not a good reason too? But you did not hear her.
For heritage, she told you. For the boys, from the past
they should have tradition.

Superstition! From the savages, afraid of the dark, of themselves: mumbo words and magic lights to scare away ghosts.

She told you: how it started does not take away the goodness. For centuries, peace in the house it means.

Swindler! does she look back on the dark centuries? Candles bought instead of bread and stuck into a potato for a candlestick? Religion that stifled and said: in Paradise, woman, you will be the footstool of your husband, and in life—poor chosen Jew—ground under, despised, trembling in cellars. And cremated. And cremated.

This is religion's fault? You think you are still an orator of the 1905 revolution? Where are the pills for quieting? Which are they?

Heritage. How have we come from savages, how no longer to be savages—this to teach. To look back and learn what ennobles man—this to teach. To smash all ghettos that divide man—not to go back, not to go back —this to teach. Learned books in the home, will man live or die, and she gives to her boys—superstition.

Hannah that is so good to you. Take your pill, Mrs. Excited For Nothing, swallow.

Heritage! But when did I have time to teach? Of Hannah I asked only hands to help.

Swallow.

Otherwise—musing; gentleness.

Not to travel. To go home.

The children want to see you. We have to show them you are as thorny a flower as ever.

Not to travel.

Vivi wants you should see her new baby. She sent the tickets—airplane tickets—a Mrs. Roosevelt she wants to make of you. To Vivi's we have to go.

A new baby. How many warm, seductive babies. She holds him stiffly, *away* from her, so that he wails. And a long shudder begins, and the sweat beads on her forehead.

"Hush, shush," croons the grandfather, lifting him back. "You should forgive your grandmamma, little prince, she has never held a baby before, only seen them in glass cases. Hush, shush."

"You're tired, Ma," says Vivi. "The travel and the noisy dinner. I'll take you to lie down."

(A long travel from, to, what the feel of a baby evokes.)

In the airplane, cunningly designed to encase from motion (no wind, no feel of flight), she had sat severely and still, her face turned to the sky through which they cleaved and left no scar.

So this was how it looked, the determining, the crucial sky, and this was how man moved through it, remote above the dwindled earth, the concealed human life. Vulnerable life, that could scar.

There was a steerage ship of memory that shook across a great, circular sea: clustered, ill human beings; and through the thick-stained air, tiny fretting waters in a window round like the airplane's—sun round, moon round. (The round thatched hut roofs of Olshana.) Eye round—like the smaller window that framed distance the solitary year of exile when only her eyes could travel, and no voice spoke. And the polar winds hurled themselves across snow trackless and endless and white—like the clouds which had closed together below and hidden the earth.

Now they put a baby in her lap. Do not ask me, she would have liked to beg. Enough the worn face of Vivi, the remembered grandchildren. I cannot, cannot . . .

Cannot what? Unnatural grandmother, not able to make herself embrace a baby.

She lay there in the bed of the two little girls, her new

hearing aid turned full, listening to the sound of the children going to sleep, the baby's fretful crying and hushing, the clatter of dishes being washed and put away. They thought she slept. Still she rode on.

It was not that she had not loved her babies, her children. The love—the passion of tending—had risen with the need like a torrent; and like a torrent drowned and immolated all else. But when the need was done—o the power that was lost in the painful damming back and drying up of what still surged, but had nowhere to go. Only the thin pulsing left that could not quiet, suffering over lives one felt, but could no longer hold nor help.

On that torrent she had borne them to their own lives, and the riverbed was desert long years now. Not there would she dwell, a memoried wraith. Surely that was not all, surely there was more. Still the springs, the springs were in her seeking. Somewhere an older power that beat for life. Somewhere coherence, transport, meaning. If they would but leave her in the air now stilled of clamor, in the reconciled solitude, to journey to her self.

And they put a baby in her lap. Immediately to embrace, and the breath of *that* past: warm flesh like this that had claims and nuzzled away all else and with lovely mouths devoured; hot-living like an animal—intensely and now; the turning maze; the long drunkenness; the drowning into needing and being needed. Severely she looked back—and the shudder seized her again, and the sweat. Not that way. Not there, not now could she, not yet . . .

And all that visit, she could not touch the baby.

"Daddy, is it the . . . sickness she's like that?" asked Vivi. "I was so glad to be having the baby—for her. I told Tim, it'll give her more happiness than anything, being around a baby again. And she hasn't played with him once."

He was not listening, "Aahh little seed of life, little charmer," he crooned, "Hollywood should see you. A heart

of ice you would melt. Kick, kick. The future you'll have
for a ball. In 2050 still kick. Kick for your granddaddy
then."

Attentive with the older children; sat through their per-
formances (command performance; we command you to
be the audience); helped Ann sort autumn leaves to find
the best for a school program; listened gravely to Richard
tell about his rock collection, while her lips mutely formed
the words to remember: *igneous, sedimentary, metamor-
phic;* looked for missing socks, books and bus tickets;
watched the children whoop after their grandfather who
knew how to tickle, chuck, lift, toss, do tricks, tell secrets,
make jokes, match riddle for riddle. (Tell me a riddle,
Granny. I know no riddles, child.) Scrubbed sills and
woodwork and furniture in every room; folded the laundry;
straightened drawers; emptied the heaped baskets waiting
for ironing (while he or Vivi or Tim nagged: You're supposed to rest here, you've been sick) but to none tended
or gave food—and could not touch the baby.

After a week she said: "Let us go home. Today call
about the tickets."

"You have important business, Mrs. Inahurry? The
President waits to consult with you?" He shouted, for the
fear of the future raced in him. "The clothes are still warm
from the suitcase, your children cannot show enough how
glad they are to see you, and you want home. There is
plenty of time for home. We cannot be with the children
at home."

"Blind to around you as always: the little ones sleep
four in a room because we take their bed. We are two more
people in a house with a new baby, and no help."

"Vivi is happy so. The children should have their grandparents a while, she told to me. I should have my mommy
and daddy . . ."

"Babbler and blind. Do you look at her so tired? How

she starts to talk and she cries? I am not strong enough yet
to help. Let us go home."

(To reconciled solitude.)

*For it seemed to her the crowded noisy house was
listening to her, listening for her. She could feel it like a
great ear pressed under her heart. And everything knocked:
quick constant raps: let me in, let me in.*

*How was it that soft reaching tendrils also became
blows that knocked?*

C'mon Grandma, I want to show you . . .

Tell me a riddle, Grandma. (*I know no riddles*)

Look Grammy, he's so dumb he can't even find his
hands. (Dody and the baby on a blanket over the fer-
menting autumn mound)

I made it—for you (Flat paper dolls and aprons that
lifted on scalloped skirts that lifted on flowered pants;
hair of yarn and great ringed questioning eyes) (Ann)

Watch me, Grandma. (Richard snaking up the tree,
hanging exultant, free, and with one hand at the top.
Below Dody hunching over in pretend-cooking.)
(Climb too, Dody, climb and look)

Be my nap bed, Granny. (The "No!" too late.) Morty's
abandoned heaviness, while his fingers ladder up and
down her hearing-aid cord to his drowsy chant:
eentsiebeentsiespider. (*Children trust*)

It's to start off your own rock collection, Grandma.
That's a trilobite fossil, 200 million years old (millions
of years on a boy's mouth) and that one's obsidian,
black glass.

Knocked and knocked.

Mother, I *told* you the teacher said we had to bring it
back all filled out this morning. Didn't you even ask
Daddy? Then tell *me* which plan and I'll check it: evacu-

ate or stay in the city or wait for you to come and take me away. (Seeing the look of straining to hear) It's for Disaster, Grandma. *(Children trust)*

Vivi in the maze of the long, the lovely drunkenness. The old old noises: baby sounds; screaming of a mother flayed to exasperation; children quarreling; children playing; singing; laughter.

And Vivi's tears and memories, spilling so fast, half the words not understood.

She had started remembering out loud deliberately, so her mother would know the past was cherished, still lived in her.

Nursing the baby: My friends marvel, and I tell them, oh it's easy to be such a cow. I remember how beautiful my mother seemed nursing my brother, and the milk just flows . . . Was that Davy? It must have been Davy . . .

Lowering a hem: How did you ever . . . when I think how you made everything we wore . . . Tim, just think, seven kids and Mommy sewed everything . . . do I remember you sang while you sewed? That white dress with the red apples on the skirt you fixed over for me, was it Hannah's or Clara's before it was mine?

Washing sweaters: Ma, I'll never forget, one of those days so nice you washed clothes outside; one of the first spring days it must have been. The bubbles just danced up and down while you scrubbed, and we chased after, and you stopped to show us how to blow our own bubbles with green onion stalks . . . you always . . .

"Strong onion, to still make you cry after so many years," her father said, to turn the tears into laughter.

While Richard bent over his homework: Where is it now, do we still have it, the Book of the Martyrs? It always seemed so, well—exalted, when you'd put it on the round table and we'd all look at it together; there was even a halo from the lamp. The lamp with the beaded fringe you could move up and down; they're in style again, pulley lamps like that, but without the fringe. You know the book I'm talking about, Daddy, the Book of the Martyrs, the first picture was a bust of Socrates? I wish there was something like that for the children, Mommy, to give them what you . . . (And the tears splashed again)

(What I intended and did not? Stop it, daughter, stop it, leave that time. And he, the hypocrite, sitting there with tears in his eyes too—it was nothing to you then, nothing.)

. . . The time you came to school and I almost died of shame because of your accent and because I knew you knew I was ashamed; how could I? . . . Sammy's harmonica and you danced to it once, yes you did, you and Davy squealing in your arms . . . That time you bundled us up and walked us down to the railroad station to stay the night 'cause it was heated and we didn't have any coal, that winter of the strike, you didn't think I remembered that, did you, Mommy? . . . How you'd call us out to see the sunsets . . .

Day after day, the spilling memories. Worse now, questions, too. Even the grandchildren: Grandma, in the olden days, when you were little . . .

It was the afternoons that saved.

While they thought she napped, she would leave the mosaic on the wall (of children's drawings, maps, calendars, pictures, Ann's cardboard dolls with their great ringed questioning eyes) and hunch in the girls' closet, on the low shelf where the shoes stood, and the girls' dresses covered.

For that while she would painfully sheathe against the listening house, the tendrils and noises that knocked, and Vivi's spilling memories. Sometimes it helped to braid and unbraid the sashes that dangled, or to trace the pattern on the hoop slips.

Today she had jacks and children under jet trails to

forget. Last night, Ann and Dody silhouetted in the window against a sunset of flaming man-made clouds of jet trail, their jacks ball accenting the peaceful noise of dinner being made. Had she told them, yes she had told them of how they played jacks in her village though there was no ball, no jacks. Six stones, round and flat, toss them out, the seventh on the back of the hand, toss, catch and swoop up as many as possible, toss again . . .

Of stones (repeating Richard) there are three kinds: earth's fire jetting; rock of layered centuries; crucibled new out of the old. But there was that other—frozen to black glass, never to transform or hold the fossil memory . . . (let not my seed fall on stone). There was an ancient man who fought to heights a great rock that crashed back down eternally—eternal labor, freedom, labor . . . (stone will perish, but the word remain). And you, David, who with a stone slew, screaming: Lord, take my heart of stone and give me flesh.

Who was screaming? Why was she back in the common room of the prison, the sun motes dancing in the shafts of light, and the informer being brought in, a prisoner now, like themselves. And Lisa leaping, yes, Lisa, the gentle and tender, biting at the betrayer's jugular. Screaming and screaming.

No, it is the children screaming. Another of Paul and Sammy's terrible fights?

In Vivi's house. Severely: you are in Vivi's house.

Blows, scream, a call: "Grandma!" For her? O please not for her. Hide, hunch behind the dresses deeper. But a trembling little body hurls itself beside her—surprised, smothered laughter, arms surround her neck, tears rub dry on her cheek, and words too soft to understand whisper into her ear (Is this where you hide too, Grammy? It's my secret place, we have a secret now.)

And the sweat beads, and the long shudder seizes.

It seemed the great ear pressed inside now, and the

knocking. "We have to go home," she told him, "I grow ill here."

"It is your own fault, Mrs. Bodybusy, you do not rest, you do too much." He raged, but the fear was in his eyes. "It was a serious operation, they told you to take care . . . All right, we will go to where you can rest."

But where? Not home to death, not yet. He had thought to Lennie's, to Clara's; beautiful visits with each of the children. She would have to rest first, be stronger. If they could but go to Florida—it glittered before him, the never-realized promise of Florida. California: of course. (The money, the money dwindling!) Los Angeles first for sun and rest, then to Lennie's in San Francisco.

He told her the next day. "You saw what Nancy wrote: snow and wind back home, a terrible winter. And look at you—all bones and a swollen belly. I called Phil: he said: 'A prescription, Los Angeles sun and rest.'"

She watched the words on his lips. "You have sold the house," she cried, "that is why we do not go home. That is why you talk no more of the Haven. Why there is money for travel. After the children you will drag me to the Haven."

"The Haven! Who thinks of the Haven any more? Tell her, Vivi, tell Mrs. Suspicious: a prescription, sun and rest, to make you healthy . . . And how could I sell the house without *you*?"

At the place of farewells and greetings, of winds of coming and winds of going, they say their good-bys.

They look back at her with the eyes of others before them: Richard with her own blue blaze; Ann with the Nordic eyes of Tim; Morty's dreaming brown of a great-grandmother he will never know; Dody with the laughing eyes of him who had been her springtime love (who stands beside her now); Vivi's all tears.

The baby's eyes are closed in sleep.

Good-by, my children.

3.

It is to the back of the great city he brought her, to the dwelling places of the cast-off old. Bounded by two lines of amusement piers to the north and to the south, and between a long straight paving rimmed wtih black benches facing the sand—sands so wide the ocean is only a far fluting.

In the brief vacation season, some of the boarded stores fronting the sands open, and families, young people and children, may be seen. A little tasseled tram shuttles between the piers, and the lights of roller coasters prink and tweak over those who come to have sensation made in them.

The rest of the year it is abandoned to the old, all else boarded up and still; seemingly empty, except the occasional days and hours when the sun, like a tide, sucks them out of the low rooming houses, casts them onto the benches and sandy rim of the walk—and sweeps them into decaying enclosures back again.

A few newer apartments glint among the low bleached squares. It is in one of these Lennie's Jeannie has arranged their rooms. "Only a few miles north and south people pay hundreds of dollars a month for just this gorgeous air, Granddaddy, just this ocean closeness."

She had been ill on the plane, lay ill for days in the unfamiliar room. Several times the doctor came by—left medicine she would not take. Several times Jeannie drove in the twenty miles from work, still in her Visiting Nurse uniform, the lightness and brightness of her like a healing.

"Who can believe it is winter?" he said one morning. "Beautiful it is outside like an ad. Come, Mrs. Invalid, come to taste it. You are well enough to sit in here, you are well enough to sit outside. The doctor said it too."

But the benches were encrusted with people, and the sands at the sidewalk's edge. Besides, she had seen the far

ruffle of the sea: "there take me," and though she leaned
against him it was she who led.

Plodding and plodding, sitting often to rest, he grumbling. Patting the sand so warm. Once she scooped up a
handful, cradling it close to her better eye; peered, and
flung it back. And as they came almost to the brink and
she could see the glistening wet, she sat down, pulled off
her shoes and stockings, left him and began to run. "You'll
catch cold," he screamed, but the sand in his shoes weighed
him down—he who had always been the agile one—and
already the white spray creamed her feet.

He pulled her back, took a handkerchief to wipe off the
wet and the sand. "O no," she said, "the sun will dry,"
seized the square and smoothed it flat, dropped on it a
mound of sand, knotted the kerchief corners and tied it
into a bag—"to look at with the strong glass" (for the
first time in years explaining an action of hers)—and lay
down with the little bag against her cheek, looking toward
the shore that nurtured life as it first crawled toward
consciousness the millions of years ago.

He took her one Sunday in the evil-smelling bus, past
flat miles of blister houses, to the home of relatives. O
what is this? she cried as the light began to smoke and
the houses to dim and recede. Smog, he said, everyone
knows but you . . . Outside he kept his arms about her,
but she walked with hands pushing the heavy air as if to
open it, whispered: who has done this? sat down suddenly
to vomit at the curb and for a long while refused to rise.

*One's age as seen on the altered face of those known in
youth.* Is this they he has come to visit? This Max and
Rose, smooth and pleasant, introducing them to polite
children, disinterested grandchildren, "the whole family,
once a month on Sundays. And why not? We have the
room, the help, the food."

Talk of cars, of houses, of success: this son that, that
daughter this. And *your* children? Hastily skimped over,

the intermarriages, the obscure work—"my doctor son-in-law, Phil"—all he has to offer. She silent in a corner. (Car-sick like a baby, he explains.) Years since he has taken her to visit anyone but the children, and old apprehensions prickle: "no incidents," he silently begs, "no incidents." He itched to tell them. "A very sick woman," significantly, indicating her with his eyes, "a very sick woman." Their restricted faces did not react. "Have you thought maybe she'd do better at Palm Springs?" Rose asked. "Or at least a nicer section of the beach, nicer people, a pool." Not to have to say "money" he said instead: "would she have sand to look at through a magnifying glass?" and went on, detail after detail, the old habit betraying of parading queerness of her for laughter.

After dinner—the others into the living room in men- or women-clusters, or into the den to watch TV—the four of them alone. She sat close to him, and did not speak. Jokes, stories, people they had known, beginning of reminiscence, Russia fifty-sixty years ago. Strange words across the Duncan Phyfe table: *hunger; secret meetings; human rights; spies; betrayals; prison; escape*—interrupted by one of the grandchildren: "Commercial's on; any Coke left? Gee, you're missing a real hair-raiser." And then a granddaughter (Max proudly: "look at her, an American queen") drove them home on her way back to U.C.L.A. No incident—except that there had been no incidents.

The first few mornings she had taken with her the magnifying glass, but he would sit only on the benches, so she rested at the foot, where slatted bench shadows fell, and unless she turned her hearing aid down, other voices invaded.

Now on the days when the sun shone and she felt well enough, he took her on the tram to where the benches ranged in oblongs, some with tables for checkers or cards. Again the blanket on the sand in the striped shadows, but she no longer brought the magnifying glass. He played

cards, and she lay in the sun and looked toward the waters;
or they walked—two blocks down to the scaling hotel, two
blocks back—past chili-hamburger stands, open-doored
bars, Next to New and Perpetual Rummage Sale stores.

Once, out of the aimless walkers, slow and shuffling like
themselves, someone ran unevenly toward them, embraced,
kissed, wept: "dear friends, old friends." A friend of *hers,*
not his: Mrs. Mays who had lived next door to them in
Denver when the children were small.

Thirty years are compressed into a dozen sentences; and
the present, not even in three. All is told: the children
scattered; the husband dead; she lives in a room two
blocks up from the sing hall—and points to the domed
auditorium jutting before the pier. The leg? phlebitis; the
heavy breathing? that, one does not ask. She too comes
to the benches each nice day to sit. And tomorrow, tomorrow, are they going to the community sing? Of course he
would have heard of it, everybody goes—the big doings
they wait for all week. They have never been? She will
come to them for dinner tomorrow and they will all go
together.

*So it is that she sits in the wind of the singing, among
the thousand various faces of age.*

*She had turned off her hearing aid at once they came
into the auditorium—as she would have wished to turn
off sight.*

*One by one they streamed by and imprinted on her—
and though the savage zest of their singing came voice-
lessly soft and distant, the faces still roared—the faces
densened the air—chorded*

> children-chants, mother-croons, singing of the
>   chained;
> love serenades, Beethoven storms, mad Lucia's
>   scream;

drunken joy-songs, keens for the dead, work-
    singing

*while from floor to balcony to dome a bare-footed
sore-covered little girl threaded the sound-thronged
tumult, danced her ecstasy of grimace to flutes that
scratched at a crossroads village wedding*

*Yes, faces became sound, and the sound became faces;
and faces and sound became weight—pushed, pressed*

"Air"—her hand claws his.

"Whenever I enjoy myself . . ." Then he saw the gray
sweat on her face. "Here. Up. Help me, Mrs. Mays," and
they support her out to where she can gulp the air in sob
after sob.

"A doctor, we should get for her a doctor."

"Tch, it's nothing," says Ellen Mays, "I get it all the
time . . . You've missed the tram; come to my place . . .
close . . . tea. My view. See, she *wants* to come. Steady
now, that's how." Adding mysteriously: "Remember your
advice, easy to keep your head above water, empty things
float. Float."

The singing a fading march for them, tall woman with a
swollen leg, weaving little man, and the swollen thinness
they help between.

The stench in the hall: mildew? decay? "We sit and
rest then climb. My gorgeous view. We help each other
and here we are."

The stench along into the slab of room. A washstand
for a sink, a box with oilcloth tacked around for a cupboard, a three-burner gas plate. Artificial flowers, colorless
with dust. Everywhere pictures foaming: wedding, baby,
party, vacation, graduation, family pictures. From the narrow couch under a slit of window, sure enough the view:
lurching rooftops and a scallop of ocean heaving, preen-
ing, twitching under the moon.

"While the water heats. Excuse me . . . down the hall."
Ellen Mays has gone.

"You'll live?" he asks mechanically, sat down to feel
his fright; tried to pull her alongside.

She pushed him away. "For air," she said; stood clinging to the dresser. Then, in a terrible voice:

After a lifetime of room. Of many rooms.

Shhh.

You remember how she lived. Eight children. And now
one room like a coffin. Shrinking the life of her into one
room

She pays rent!

Like a coffin. Rooms and rooms like this. I lie on the
quilt and hear them talk Once you went for coffee I
walked I saw A Balzac a Chekhov to write it Rum-
rage Alone On scraps

Shhh, Mrs. Orator Without Breath. Better here old than
in the old country.

And they sang like . . . like . . . Wondrous. *Man, one
has to believe.* So strong. For what? To rot not grow?

Your poor lungs beg you: *Please.* They sob between
each word.

Singing. Unused the life in them. She in this poor
room with her pictures. Max You The children. Everywhere. And who has meaning? Century after century
still all in man not to grow?

Coffins, rummage, plants: sick woman. O lay down. We
will get for you the doctor.

"And when will it end. O, *the end.*" *That* nightmare
thought, and this time she writhed, crumpled beside him,
seized his hand (for a moment again the weight, the soft
distant roaring of humanity) and on the strangled-for
breath, begged: "Man . . . will destroy ourselves?"

And looking for answer—in the helpless pity and fear
for her (for *her*) that distorted his face—she understood
the last months, and knew that she was dying.

4.

"Let us go home," she said after several days.

"You are in training for a cross-country trip? That is why you do not even walk across the room? Here, like a prescription Phil said, till you are stronger from the operation. You want to break doctor's orders?"

She saw the fiction was necessary to him, was silent; then: "At home I will get better. If the doctor here says?"

"And winter? And the visits to Lennie and to Clara? All right," for he saw the tears in her eyes, "I will write Phil, and talk to the doctor."

Days passed. He reported nothing. Jeannie came and took her out for air, past the boarded concessions, the hooded and tented amusement rides, to the end of the pier. They watched the spent waves feeding the new, the gulls in the clouded sky even up where they sat, the windblown sand stung.

She did not ask to go down the crooked steps to the sea.

Back in her bed, while he was gone to the store, she said: "Jeannie, this doctor, he is not one I can ask questions. Ask him for me, can I go home?"

Jeannie looked at her, said quickly: "Of course, poor Granny, you want your own things around you, don't you? I'll call him tonight . . . Look, I've something to show you," and from her purse unwrapped a large cookie, intricately shaped like a little girl. "Look at the curls—can you hear me well, Granny?—and the darling eyelashes. I just came from a house where they were baking them."

"The dimples," she marveled, "there in the knees," holding it to the better light, turning, studying, "like art. Each singly they cut, or a mold?"

"Singly," said Jeannie, "and if it is a child only the mother can make them. O Granny, it's the likeness of a real little girl who died yesterday—Rosita. She was three years old, *Pan del Muerto,* the Bread of the Dead. It was the custom in the part of Mexico they came from."

Still she turned and inspected. "Look, the hollow in the throat, the little cross necklace . . . I think for the mother it is a good thing to be busy with such bread. You know the family?"

Jeannie nodded. "On my rounds. I nursed . . . O Granny, it is like a party; they play songs she liked to dance to. The coffin is lined with pink velvet and she wears a white dress. There are candles . . ."

"In the house?" Surprised, "They keep her in the house?"

"Yes," said Jeannie, "and it is against the health law. I think she is . . . prepared there. The father said it will be sad to bury her in this country; in Mazatlán they have a feast night with candles each year; everyone picnics on the graves of those they loved until dawn."

"Yes Jeannie, the living must comfort themselves." And closed her eyes.

"You want to sleep, Granny?"

"Yes, tired from the pleasure of you. I may keep the Rosita? There stand it, on the dresser, where I can see; something of my own around me."

In the kitchenette, helping her grandfather unpack the groceries, Jeannie said in her light voice:

"I'm resigning my job, Granddaddy."

"Ah, the lucky young man. Which one is he?"

"Too late. You're spoken for." She made a pyramid of cans, unstacked, and built again.

"Something is wrong with the job?"

"With me. I can't be"—she searched for the word—"professional enough. I let myself feel things. And tomorrow I have to report a family . . ." The cans clicked again. "It's not that, either. I just don't know what I want to do, maybe go back to school, maybe go to art school. I thought if you went to San Francisco I'd come along and talk it over with Mommy and Daddy. But I don't see how you can go. She wants to go home. She asked me to ask the doctor."

The doctor told her himself. "Next week you may travel, when you are a little stronger." But next week there was the fever of an infection, and by the time that was over, she could not leave the bed—a rented hospital bed that stood beside the double bed he slept in alone now.

Outwardly the days repeated themselves. Every other afternoon and evening he went out to his new-found cronies, to talk and play cards. Twice a week, Mrs. Mays came. And the rest of the time, Jeannie was there.

By the sickbed stood Jeannie's FM radio. Often into the room the shapes of music came. She would lie curled on her side, her knees drawn up, intense in listening (Jeannie sketched her so, coiled, convoluted like an ear), then thresh her hand out and abruptly snap the radio mute— still to lie in her attitude of listening, concealing tears.

Once Jeannie brought in a young Marine to visit, a friend from high-school days she had found wandering near the empty pier. Because Jeannie asked him to, gravely, without self-consciousness, he sat himself cross-legged on the floor and performed for them a dance of his native Samoa.

Long after they left, a tiny thrumming sound could be heard where, in her bed, she strove to repeat the beckon, flight, surrender of his hands, the fluttering footbeats, and his low plaintive calls.

Hannah and Phil sent flowers. To deepen her pleasure, he placed one in her hair. "Like a girl," he said, and brought the hand mirror so she could see. She looked at the pulsing red flower, the yellow skull face; a desolate, excited laugh shuddered from her, and she pushed the mirror away—but let the flower burn.

The week Lennie and Helen came, the fever returned. With it the excited laugh, and incessant words. She, who in

her life had spoken but seldom and then only when necessary (never having learned the easy, social uses of words),
now in dying, spoke incessantly.

In a half-whisper: "Like Lisa, she is, your Jeannie.
Have I told you of Lisa, she who taught me to read? Of the
high-born she was, but noble in herself. I was sixteen;
they beat me; my father beat me so I would not go to
her. It was forbidden, she was a Tolstoyan. At night, past
dogs that howled, terrible dogs, my son, in the snows of
winter to the road, I to ride in her carriage like a lady, to
books. To her, life was holy, knowledge was holy, and she
taught me to read. They hung her. Everything that happens one must try to understand why. She killed one who
betrayed many. Because of betrayal, betrayed all she lived
and believed. In one minute she killed, before my eyes
(there is so much blood in a human being, my son), in
prison with me. All that happens, one must try to understand.

"The name?" Her lips would work."The name that was
their pole star; the doors of the death houses fixed to open
on it; I read of it my year of penal servitude. Thuban!"
very excited, "Thuban, in ancient Egypt the pole star. Can
you see, look out to see it, Jeannie, if it swings around
our pole star that seems to *us* not to move.

"Yes, Jeannie, at your age my mother and grandmother
had already buried children . . . yes, Jeannie, it is more
than oceans between Olshana and you . . . yes, Jeannie,
they danced, and for all the bodies they had they might
as well be chickens, and indeed, they scratched and flapped
their arms and hopped.

"And Andrei Yefimitch, who for twenty years had never
known of it and never wanted to know, said as if he
wanted to cry: but why my dear friend this malicious
laughter?" Telling to herself half-memorized phrases from
her few books. "Pain I answer with tears and cries, base-
ness with indignation, meanness with repulsion . . . for
life may be hated or wearied of, but never despised."

Delirious: "Tell me, my neighbor, Mrs. Mays, the pictures never lived, but what of the flowers? Tell them who ask: no rabbis, no ministers, no priests, no speeches, no ceremonies: ah, false—let the living please themselves. Tell Sammy's boy, he who flies, tell him to go to Stuttgart and see where Davy has no grave. And what?" A conspirator's laugh. "And what? where million's have no graves."

In delirium or not, wanting the radio on; not seeming to listen, the words still jetting, wanting the music on. Once, silencing it abruptly as of old, she began to cry, unconcealed tears this time. "You have pain, Granny?" Jeannie asked.

"The music," she said, "still it is there and we do not hear; knocks, and our poor human ears too weak. What else, what else we do not hear?"

Once she knocked his hand aside as he gave her a pill, swept the bottles from her bedside table: "no pills, let me feel what I feel," and laughed as on his hands and knees he groped to pick them up.

Nighttimes her hand reached across the bed to hold his.

A constant retching began. Her breath was too faint for sustained speech now, but still the lips moved:

When no longer necessary to injure others
Pick   pick pick   Blind chicken
As a human being   responsibility for

"David!" imperious, "Basin!" and she would vomit, rinse her mouth, the wasted throat working to swallow, and begin the chant again.

She will be better off in the hospital now, the doctor said.
He sent the telegrams to the children, was packing her suitcase, when her hoarse voice startled. She had roused, was pulling herself to sitting.

"Where now?" she asked. "Where now do you drag me?"

"You do not even have to have a baby to go this time,"

he soothed, looking for the brush to pack. "Remember, after Davy you told me—worthy to have a baby for the pleasure of the hospital?"

"Where now? Not home yet?" Her voice mourned. "Where *is* my home?"

He rose to ease her back. "The doctor, the hospital," he started to explain, but deftly, like a snake, she had slithered out of bed and stood swaying, propped behind the night table.

"Coward," she hissed, "runner."

"You stand," he said senselessly.

"To take me there and run. Afraid of a little vomit."

He reached her as she fell. She struggled against him, half slipped from his arms, pulled herself up again.

"Weakling," she taunted, "to leave me there and run. Betrayer. All your life you have run."

He sobbed, telling Jeannie. "A Marilyn Monroe to run for her virtue. Fifty-nine pounds she weighs, the doctor said, and she beats at me like a Dempsey. Betrayer, she cries, and I running like a dog when she calls; day and night, running to her, her vomit, the bedpan . . ."

"She wants you, Granddaddy," said Jeannie. "Isn't that what they call love? I'll see if she sleeps, and if she does, poor worn-out darling, we'll have a party, you and I; I brought us rum babas."

They did not move her. By her bed now stood the tall hooked pillar that held the solutions—blood and dextrose —to feed her veins. Jeannie moved down the hall to take over the sickroom, her face so radiant, her grandfather asked her once: "you are in love?" (Shameful the joy, the pure overwhelming joy from being with her grandmother; the peace, the serenity that breathed.) "My darling escape," she answered incoherently, "my darling Granny"— as if that explained.

Now one by one the children came, those that were able.

Hannah, Paul, Sammy. Too late to ask: and what did you learn with your living, Mother, and what do we need to know?

Clara, the eldest, clenched:

> *Pay me back, Mother, pay me back for all you took from me. Those others you crowded into your heart. The hands I needed to be for you, the heaviness, the responsibility.*
>
> *Is this she? Noises the dying make, the crablike hands crawling over the covers. The ethereal singing.*
>
> *She hears that music, that singing from childhood; forgotten sound—not heard since, since . . . And the hardness breaks like a cry: Where did we lose each other, first mother, singing mother?*
>
> *Annulled: the quarrels, the gibing, the harshness between; the fall into silence and the withdrawal.*
>
> *I do not know you, Mother. Mother, I never knew you.*

Lennie, suffering not alone for her who was dying, but for that in her which never lived (for that which in him might never live). From him too, unspoken words: *goodby mother who taught me to mother myself.*

Not Vivi, who must stay with her children; not Davy, but he is already here, having to die again with *her* this time, for the living take their dead with them when they die.

Light she grew, like a bird, and, like a bird, sound bubbled in her throat while the body fluttered in agony. Night and day, asleep or awake (though indeed there was no difference now) the songs and the phrases leaping.

And he, who had once dreaded a long dying (from fear of himself, from horror of the dwindling money) now desired her quick death profoundly, for *her* sake. He no longer went out, except when Jeannie forced him; no longer laughed, except when, in the bright kitchenette, Jeannie coaxed his laughter (and she, who seemed to hear nothing else, would laugh too, conspiratorial wisps of laughter).

Light, like a bird, the fluttering body, the little claw hands, the beaked shadow on her face; and the throat, bubbling, straining:

He tried not to listen, as he tried not to look on the face in which only the forehead remained familiar, but trapped with her the long nights in that little room, the sounds worked themselves into his consciousness, with their punctuation of death swallows, whimpers, gurglings.

Even in reality (swallow) *life's lack of it*
The bell   Summon   what ennobles
78,000 in one minute (whisper of a scream) *78,000 human beings   destroy ourselves?*

"Aah, Mrs. Miserable," he said, as if she could hear, "all your life working, and now in bed you lie, servants to tend, you do not even need to call to be tended, and still you work. Such hard work it is to die? Such hard work?"

The body threshed, her hand clung in his. A melody, ghost-thin, hovered on her lips, and like a guilty ghost, the vision of her bent in listening to it, silencing the record instantly he was near. Now, heedless of his presence, she floated the melody on and on.

"Hid it from me," he complained, "how many times you listened to remember it so?" And tried to think when she had first played it, or first begun to silence her few records when he came near—but could reconstruct nothing. There was only this room with its tall hooked pillar and its swarm of sounds.

An unexamined life   not worth
Strong   with the not yet   in the now
Dogma dead   war dead   one country

"It helps, Mrs. Philosopher, words from books? It helps?" And it seemed to him that for seventy years she had hidden a tape recorder, infinitely microscopic, within her, that it had coiled infinite mile on mile, trapping every song, every melody, every word read, heard and spoken—and that maliciously she was playing back only what said nothing of him, of the children, of their intimate life together.

"Left us indeed, Mrs. Babbler," he reproached, "you who called others babbler and cunningly saved your words. A lifetime you tended and loved, and now not a word of us, for us. Left us indeed? Left me."

And he took out his solitaire deck, shuffled the cards loudly, slapped them down.

Lift high   banner of reason (tatter of an orator's voice) *justice   freedom and light*

Mankind   life worthy   heroic capacities

Seeks (blur of shudder) *belong   human being*

"Words, words," he accused, "and what human beings did *you* seek around you, Mrs. Live Alone, and what mankind think worthy?"

Though even as he spoke, he remembered she had not always been isolated, had not always wanted to be alone (as he knew there had been a voice before this gossamer one; before the hoarse voice that broke from silence to lash, make incidents, shame him—a girl's voice of eloquence that spoke their holiest dreams). But again he could reconstruct, image, nothing of what had been before, or when, or how, it had changed.

Ace, queen, jack. The pillar shadow fell, so, in two tracks; in the mirror depths glistened a moon-like blob, the empty solution bottle. And it worked in him: *of reason and justice and freedom. Dogma dead:* he remembered the quotation, laughed bitterly. "Hah, good you do not know what you say; good Victor Hugo died and did not see it, his twentieth century."

Deuce, ten, five. Dauntlessly she began a song of their youth of belief:

> *These things shall be, a loftier race*
> *than e'er the world hath known shall rise*
> *with flame of freedom in their souls*
> *and light of knowledge in their eyes*

King, four, jack. "In the twentieth century, hah!"

> *They shall be gentle, brave and strong*
> *to spill no drop of blood, but dare*
> *all that may plant man's lordship firm*
> *on earth and fire and sea and air*

"To spill no drop of blood, hah! So, cadaver, and you too, cadaver Hugo, 'in the twentieth century ignorance will be dead, dogma will be dead, war will be dead, and for all mankind one country—of fulfillment.' Hah!"

> *And every life* (long strangling cough) *shall*
> *be a song*

The cards fell from his fingers. Without warning, the bereavement and betrayal he had sheltered—compounded through the years—hidden even from himself—revealed itself,
>   uncoiled,
>   released,
>   *sprung*

and with it the monstrous shapes of what had actually happened in the century.

A ravening hunger or thirst seized him. He groped into the kitchenette, switched on all three lights, piled a tray— "you have finished your night snack Mrs. Cadaver, now I will have mine." And he was shocked at the tears that splashed on the tray.

"Salt tears. For free. I forgot to shake on salt?"

Whispered: "Lost, how much I lost."

Escaped to the grandchildren whose childhoods were childish, who had never hungered, who lived unravaged by disease in warm houses of many rooms, had all the school for which they cared, could walk on any street, stood a head taller than their grandparents, towered above—beautiful skins, straight backs, clear straightforward eyes. "Yes, you in Olshana," he said to the town of sixty years ago, "they would be nobility to you."

And was this not the dream then, come true in ways undreamed? he asked.

And are there no other children in the world? he answered, as if in her harsh voice.

And the flame of freedom, the light of knowledge?
And the drop, the drop of blood?

And he thought that at six Jeannie would get up and it would be his turn to go to her room and sleep, and he could press the buzzer and she would come now; that in the afternoon Ellen Mays was coming, and this time they would play cards and he could marvel at how rouge can stand half an inch on the cheek; that in the evening the doctor would come, and he could beg him to be merciful, to stop the feeding solutions, to let her die.

To let her die, and with her their youth of belief out of which her bright, betrayed words foamed; stained words, that on her working lips came stainless.

Hours yet before Jeannie's turn. He could press the buzzer and wake her to come now; he could take a pill, and with it sleep; he could pour more brandy into his milk glass, though what he had poured was not yet touched.

Instead he went back, checked her pulse, gently tended with his knotty fingers as Jeannie had taught.

She was whimpering; her hand crawled across the covers for his. Compassionately he enfolded it, and with his free hand gathered up the cards again. Still was there thirst or hunger ravening in him.

That world of their youth—dark, ignorant, terrible with hate and disease—how was it that living in it, in the midst of corruption, filth, treachery, degradation, they had not mistrusted man nor themselves; had believed so beautifully, so . . . falsely?

"Aaah, children," he said out loud, "how we believed, how we belonged." And he yearned to package for each of the children, the grandchildren, for everyone, *that joyous certainty, that sense of mattering, of moving and being moved, of being one and indivisible with the great of the past, with all that freed, ennobled man*. Package it, stand on corners, in front of stadiums and on crowded beaches, knock on doors, give it as a fabled gift.

"And why not in cereal boxes, in soap packages?" he mocked himself. "Aah. You have taken my senses, cadaver."

Words foamed, died unsounded. Her body writhed; she made kissing motions with her mouth. (Her lips moving as she read, poring over the Book of the Martyrs, the magnifying glass superimposed over the heavy eyeglasses.) *Still she had believed?* "Eva!" he whispered. "Still you believed? You lived by it? These Things Shall Be?"

"One pound soup meat," she answered distinctly, "one soup bone."

"My ears heard you. Ellen Mays was witness: 'Man . . . one has to believe.'" Imploringly: "Eva!"

"Bread, day-old." She was mumbling. "Please, in a wooden box . . . for kindling. The thread, hah, the thread breaks. Cheap thread"—and a gurgling, enormously loud, began in her throat.

"I ask for stone; she gives me bread—day-old." He pulled his hand away, shouted: "Who wanted questions? Everything you have to wake?" Then dully, "Ah, let me help you turn, poor creature."

Words jumbled, cleared. In a voice of crowded terror:

"Paul, Sammy, don't fight.

"Hannah, have I ten hands?

"How can I give it, Clara, how can I give it if I don't have?"

"You lie," he said sturdily, "there was joy too." Bitterly: "Ah how cheap you speak of us at the last."

As if to rebuke him, as if her voice had no relationship with her flailing body, she sang clearly, beautifully, a school

song the children had taught her when they were little;
begged:

"Not look   my hair   where they cut . . ."

(The crown of braids shorn.) And instantly he left the
mute old woman poring over the Book of the Martyrs; went
past the mother treadling at the sewing machine, singing
with the children; past the girl in her wrinkled prison dress,
hiding her hair with scarred hands, lifting to him her awkward, shamed, imploring eyes of love; and took her in his
arms, dear, personal, fleshed, in all the heavy passion he
had loved to rouse from her.

"Eva!"

Her little claw hand beat the covers. How much, how
much can a man stand? He took up the cards, put them
down, circled the beds, walked to the dresser, opened, shut
drawers, brushed his hair, moved his hand bit by bit over
the mirror to see what of the reflection he could blot out
with each move, and felt that at any moment he would
die of what was unendurable. Went to press the buzzer to
wake Jeannie, looked down, saw on Jeannie's sketch pad
the hospital bed, with *her;* the double bed alongside, with
him; the tall pillar feeding into her veins, and their hands,
his and hers, clasped, feeding each other. And as if he had
been instructed he went to his bed, lay down, holding the
sketch as if it could shield against the monstrous shapes of
loss, of betrayal, of death—and with his free hand took hers
back into his.

So Jeannie found them in the morning.

That last day the agony was perpetual. Time after time
it lifted her almost off the bed, so they had to fight to hold
her down. He could not endure and left the room; wept as if
there never would be tears enough.

Jeannie came to comfort him. In her light voice she said:
Granddaddy, Granddaddy don't cry. She is not there, she
promised me. On the last day, she said she would go back
to when she first heard music, a little girl on the road of the

village where she was born. She promised me. It is a wedding and they dance, while the flutes so joyous and vibrant tremble in the air. Leave her there, Granddaddy, it is all right. She promised me. Come back, come back and help her poor body to die.

For two of that generation
Seevya and Genya
Infinite, dauntless, incorruptible.

Death deepens the wonder

I LOOK OUT FOR ED WOLFE

by Stanley Elkin

Stanley Elkin (1930–   ), a native of New York
City, received a Ph.D. from the University of Illinois. Since 1960 he has been an assistant professor
at Washington University in Missouri. *The Paris
Review* gave Elkin its humor prize for 1964. He
was also granted the Longfellow Foundation
Award for 1961. Elkin's published works include
novels and stories, often hilarious and surreal
images of modern life.

He was an orphan, and, to himself, he seemed like one,
looked like one. His orphan's features were as true of himself as are their pale, pinched faces to the blind. At twenty-
seven he was a neat, thin young man in white shirts and
light suits with lintless pockets. Something about him suggested the ruthless isolation, the hard self-sufficiency of the
orphaned, the peculiar dignity of men seen eating alone in
restaurants on national holidays. Yet it was this perhaps
which shamed him chiefly, for there was a suggestion, too,
that his impregnability was a myth, a smell not of the furnished room which he did not inhabit, but of the three-room
apartment on a good street which he did. The very excel-

lence of his taste, conditioned by need and lack, lent to him the odd, maidenly primness of the lonely.

He saved the photographs of strangers and imprisoned them behind clear plastic windows in his wallet. In the sound of his own voice he detected the accent of the night school and the correspondence course, and nothing of the fat, sunny ring of the world's casually afternooned. He strove against himself, a supererogatory enemy, and sought by a kind of helpless abrasion, as one rubs wood, the gleaming self beneath. An orphan's thinness, he thought, was no accident.

Returning from lunch he entered the office building where he worked. It was an old building, squat and gargoyled, brightly patched where sandblasters had once worked and then quit before they had finished. He entered the lobby, which smelled always of disinfectant, and walked past the wide, dirty glass of the cigarette and candy counter to the single elevator, as thickly barred as a cell.

The building was an outlaw. Low rents and a downtown address and the landlord's indifference had brought together from the peripheries of business and professionalism a strange band of entrepreneurs and visionaries, men desperately but imaginatively failing: an eye doctor who corrected vision by massage; a radio evangelist; a black-belt judo champion; a self-help organization for crippled veterans; dealers in pornographic books, in paper flowers, in fireworks, in plastic jewelry, in the artificial, in the artfully made, in the imitated, in the copied, in the stolen, the unreal, the perversion, the plastic, the *schlack*.

On the sixth floor the elevator opened and the young man, Ed Wolfe, stepped out.

He passed the Association for the Indians, passed Plasti-Pens, passed *Coffin & Tombstone*, passed Soldier Toys, passed Prayer-a-Day. He walked by the opened door of C. Morris Brut, Chiropractor, and saw him, alone, standing at a mad attention, framed in the arching golden nimbus of his inverted name on the window, squeezing handballs.

He looked quickly away but Dr. Brut saw him and came toward him, putting the handballs in his shirt pocket where they bulged awkwardly. He held him by the elbow. Ed Wolfe looked at the yellowing tile beneath his feet, infinitely diamonded, chipped, the floor of a public toilet, and saw Dr. Brut's dusty shoes. He stared sadly at the jagged, broken glass of the mail chute.

"Ed Wolfe, take care of yourself," Dr. Brut said.

"Right."

"Regard your posture in life. A tall man like yourself looks terrible when he slumps. Don't be a *schlump*. It's no good for the organs."

"I'll watch it."

"When the organs get out of line the man begins to die."

"I know."

"You say so. How many guys make promises. Brains in the brain-pan. Balls in the strap. The bastards downtown." He meant doctors in hospitals, in clinics, on boards, non-orphans with M.D. degrees and special license plates and respectable patients who had Blue Cross, charts, died in clean hospital rooms. They were the bastards downtown, his personal New Deal, his neighborhood Wall Street banker. A disease cartel. "They won't tell you. The white bread kills you. The cigarettes. The whiskey. The sneakers. The high heels. They won't tell you. Me, *I'll* tell you."

"I appreciate it."

"Wise guy. Punk. I'm a friend. I give a father's advice."

"I'm an orphan."

"I'll adopt you."

"I'm late to work."

"We'll open a clinic. 'C. Morris Brut and Adopted Son.' "

"It's something to think about."

"Poetry," Dr. Brut said and walked back to his office, his posture stiff, awkward, a man in a million who knew how to hold himself.

Ed Wolfe went on to his own office. He walked in. The sad-faced telephone girl was saying, "Cornucopia Finance

Corporation." She pulled the wire out of the board and slipped her headset around her neck where it hung like a delicate horse collar. "Mr. La Meck wants to see you. But don't go in yet. He's talking to somebody."

He went toward his desk at one end of the big main office. Standing, fists on the desk, he turned to the girl. "What happened to my call cards?"

"Mr. La Meck took them," the girl said.

"Give me the carbons," Ed Wolfe said. "I've got to make some calls."

She looked embarrassed. The face went through a weird change, the sadness taking on an impossible burden of shame so that she seemed massively tragic, like a hit-and-run driver. "I'll get them," she said, moving out of the chair heavily. Ed Wolfe thought of Dr. Brut.

He took the carbons and fanned them out on the desk. He picked one in an intense, random gesture like someone drawing a number on a public stage. He dialed rapidly.

As the phone buzzed brokenly in his ear he felt the old excitement. Someone at the other end greeted him sleepily.

"Mr. Flay? This is Ed Wolfe at Cornucopia Finance." (Can you cope, can you cope? he hummed to himself.)

"Who?"

"Ed Wolfe. I've got an unpleasant duty," he began pleasantly. "You've skipped two payments."

"I didn't skip nothing. I called the girl. She said it was okay."

"That was three months ago. She meant it was all right to miss a few days. Listen, Mr. Flay, we've got that call recorded, too. Nothing gets by."

"I'm a little short."

"Grow."

"I couldn't help it," the man said. Ed Wolfe didn't like the cringing tone. Petulance and anger he could meet with his own petulance, his own anger. But guilt would have to be met with his own guilt and that, here, was irrelevant.

"Don't con me, Flay. You're a trouble-maker. What are

you, Flay, a Polish person? Flay isn't a Polish name, but your address . . ."

"What's that?"

"What are you? Are you Polish?"

"What's that to you? What difference does it make?" That was more like it, Ed Wolfe thought warmly.

"That's what you are, Flay. You're a Pole. It's guys like you who give your race a bad name. Half our bugouts are Polish persons."

"Listen. You can't . . ."

He began to shout. "*You* listen. You wanted the car. The refrigerator. The chintzy furniture. The sectional you saw in the funny papers. And we paid for it, right?"

"Listen. The money I owe is one thing, the way . . ."

"We paid for it, right?"

"That doesn't . . ."

"Right? Right?"

"Yes, you . . ."

"Okay. You're in trouble, Warsaw. You're in trouble trouble. It means a lien. A judgment. We've got lawyers. You've got nothing. We'll pull the furniture the hell out of there. The car. Everything."

"Wait," he said. "Listen, my brother-in-law . . ."

Ed Wolfe broke in sharply. "He's got some money?"

"I don't know. A little. I don't know."

"Get it. If you're short, grow. This is America."

"I don't know if he'll let me have it."

"Steal it. This is America. Goodbye."

"Wait a minute. Please."

"That's it. There are other Polish persons on my list. This time it was just a friendly warning. Cornucopia wants its money. Cornucopia. Can you cope? Can you cope? Just a friendly warning, Polish-American. Next time we come with the lawyers and the machine guns. Am I making myself clear?"

"I'll try to get it to you."

Ed Wolfe hung up. He pulled a handkerchief from his

drawer and wiped his face. His chest was heaving. He took another call card. The girl came by and stood beside his desk. "Mr. La Meck can see you now," she mourned.

"Later. I'm calling." The number was already ringing.

"Please, Mr. Wolfe."

"Later, I said. In a minute." The girl went away. "Hello. Let me speak with your husband, madam. I am Ed Wolfe of Cornucopia Finance. He can't cope. Your husband can't cope."

The woman said something, made an excuse. "Put him on, goddamn it. We know he's out of work. Nothing gets by. Nothing." There was a hand on the receiver beside his own, the wide male fingers pink and vaguely perfumed, the nails manicured. For a moment he struggled with it fitfully, as though the hand itself were all he had to contend with. He recognized La Meck and let go. La Meck pulled the phone quickly toward his mouth and spoke softly into it, words of apology, some ingenious excuse Ed Wolfe couldn't hear. He put the receiver down beside the phone itself and Ed Wolfe picked it up and returned it to its cradle.

"Ed," La Meck said, "come into the office with me."

Ed Wolfe followed La Meck, his eyes on La Meck's behind.

La Meck stopped at his office door. Looking around he shook his head sadly and Ed Wolfe nodded in agreement. La Meck let Ed Wolfe pass in first. While La Meck stood, Ed Wolfe could discern a kind of sadness in his slouch, but once La Meck was seated behind his desk he seemed restored, once again certain of the world's soundness. "All right," La Meck began, "I won't lie to you."

Lie to me. Lie to me, Ed Wolfe prayed silently.

"You're in here for me to fire you. You're not being laid off. I'm not going to tell you that I think you'd be happier someplace else, that the collection business isn't your game, that profits don't justify our keeping you around. Profits are terrific, and if collection isn't your game it's because you haven't got a game. As far as your being happier someplace else, that's bullshit. You're not supposed to be happy. It isn't in the cards for you. You're a fall-guy type, God bless you, and though I like you personally I've got no use for you in my office."

I'd like to get you on the other end of a telephone some day, Ed Wolfe thought miserably.

"Don't ask me for a reference," La Meck said. "I couldn't give you one."

"No, no," Ed Wolfe said. "I wouldn't ask you for a reference." A helpless civility was all he was capable of. If you're going to suffer, *suffer,* he told himself.

"Look," La Meck said, his tone changing, shifting from brutality to compassion as though there were no difference between the two, "you've got a kind of quality, a real feeling for collection. I'm frank to tell you, when you first came to work for us I figured you wouldn't last. I put you on the phones because I wanted you to see the toughest part first. A lot of people can't do it. You take a guy who's down and bury him deeper. It's heart-wringing work. But you, you were amazing. An artist. You had a real thing for the dead-beat soul, I thought. But we started to get complaints, and I had to warn you. Didn't I warn you? I should have suspected something when the delinquent accounts started to turn over again. It was like rancid butter turning sweet. So I don't say this to knock your technique. Your technique's terrific. With you around we could have laid off the lawyers. But Ed, you're a gangster. A gangster."

That's it, Ed Wolfe thought. I'm a gangster. Babyface Wolfe at nobody's door.

"Well," La Meck said, "I guess we owe you some money."

"Two weeks' pay," Ed Wolfe said.

"And two weeks in lieu of notice," La Meck said grandly.

"And a week's pay for my vacation."

"You haven't been here a year," La Meck said.

"It would have been a year in another month. I've earned the vacation."

"What the hell," La Meck said. "A week's pay for vacation."

La Meck figured on a pad and tearing off a sheet handed it to Ed Wolfe. "Does that check with your figures?" he asked.

Ed Wolfe, who had no figures, was amazed to see that his check was so large. Leaving off the deductions he made $92.73 a week. Five $92.73's was evidently $463.65. It was a lot of money. "That seems to be right," he told La Meck.

La Meck gave him a check and Ed Wolfe got up. Already it was as though he had never worked there. When La Meck handed him the check he almost couldn't think what it was for. It was as if there should have been a photographer there to record the ceremony. ORPHAN AWARDED CHECK BY BUSINESSMAN.

"Goodbye, Mr. La Meck," he said. "It has been an interesting association," he added foolishly.

"Goodbye, Ed," La Meck answered, putting his arm around Ed Wolfe's shoulders and leading him to the door. "I'm sorry it had to end this way." He shook Ed Wolfe's hand seriously and looked into his eyes. He had a hard grip.

Quantity and quality, Ed Wolfe thought.

"One thing, Ed. Watch yourself. Your mistake here was that you took the job too seriously. You hated the chiselers."

No, no, I loved them, he thought.

"You've got to watch it. Don't love. Don't hate. That's the secret. Detachment and caution. Look out for Ed Wolfe."

"I'll watch out for him," he said giddily and in a moment he was out of La Meck's office, and the main office, and the elevator, and the building itself, loose in the world, as cautious and as detached as La Meck could want him.

He took the car from the parking lot, handing the attendant the two dollars. The man gave him fifty cents back. "That's right," Ed Wolfe said, "it's only two o'clock." He put the half dollar in his pocket, and, on an impulse, took out his wallet. He had twelve dollars. He counted his change. Eighty-two cents. With his fingers, on the dusty dashboard, he added $12.82 to $463.65. He had $476.47. Does that check with your figures? he asked himself and drove into the crowded traffic.

Proceeding slowly, past his old building, past garages, past bar and grills, past second-rate hotels, he followed the traffic further downtown. He drove into the deepest part of the city, down and downtown to the bottom, the foundation, the city's navel. He watched the shoppers and tourists and messengers and men with appointments. He was tranquil, serene. It was something he would be content to do forever. He could use his check to buy gas, to take his meals at drive-in restaurants, to pay tolls. It would be a pleasant life, a great life, and he contemplated it thoughtfully. To drive at fifteen or twenty miles an hour through eternity, stopping at stoplights and signs, pulling over to the curb at the sound of sirens and the sight of funerals, obeying all traffic laws, making obedience to them his very code. Ed Wolfe, the Flying Dutchman, the Wandering Jew, the Off and Running Orphan, "Look Out for Ed Wolfe," a ghostly wailing down the city's corridors. What would be bad? he thought.

In the morning, out of habit, he dressed himself in a white shirt and light suit. Before he went downstairs he saw that his check and his twelve dollars were still in his wallet. Carefully he counted the eighty-two cents that he had placed on the dresser the night before, put the coins in his pocket, and went downstairs to his car.

Something green had been shoved under the wiper blade on the driver's side.

YOUR CAR WILL NEVER BE WORTH MORE THAN IT IS WORTH RIGHT NOW! WHY WAIT FOR DEPRECIATION TO MAKE YOU AUTOMOTIVELY BANKRUPT? I WILL BUY THIS CAR AND PAY YOU CASH! I WILL NOT CHEAT YOU!

Ed Wolfe considered his car thoughtfully a moment and got in. He drove that day through the city playing the car radio softly. He heard the news each hour and each half hour. He listened to Arthur Godfrey far away and in another world. He heard Bing Crosby's ancient voice, and thought sadly, Depreciation. When his tank was almost empty he thought wearily of having to have it filled and could see himself, bored and discontented behind the bug-stained glass, forced into a patience he did not feel, having to decide whether to take the Green Stamps the attendant tried to extend. Put money in your purse, Ed Wolfe, he thought. Cash! he thought with passion.

He went to the address on the circular.

He drove up onto the gravel lot but remained in his car. In a moment a man came out of a small wooden shack and walked toward Ed Wolfe's car. If he was appraising it he gave no sign. He stood at the side of the automobile and waited while Ed Wolfe got out.

"Look around," the man said. "No pennants, no strings of electric lights." He saw the advertisement in Ed Wolfe's hand. "I ran the ad off on my brother-in-law's mimeograph. My kid stole the paper from his school."

Ed Wolfe looked at him.

"The place looks like a goddamn parking lot. When the snow starts falling I get rid of the cars and move the Christmas trees right onto it. No overhead. That's the beauty of a volume business."

Ed Wolfe looked pointedly at the nearly empty lot.

"That's right," the man said. "It's slow. I'm giving the policy one more chance. Then I cheat the public just like everybody else. You're just in time. Come on, I'll show you a beautiful car."

"I want to sell my car," Ed Wolfe said.

"Sure, sure," the man said. "You want to trade with me. I give top allowances, I play fair."

"I want you to buy my car."

The man looked at him closely. "What do you want? You

want me to go into the office and put on the ten-gallon hat? It's my only overhead so I guess you're entitled to see it. You're paying for it. I put on this big frigging hat, see, and I become Texas Willie Waxelman, the Mad Cowboy. If that's what you want, I can get it in a minute."

It was incredible, Ed Wolfe thought. There were bastards everywhere who hated other bastards downtown everywhere. "I don't want to trade my car in," Ed Wolfe said, "I want to sell it. I, too, want to reduce my inventory."

The man smiled sadly. "You want me to buy *your* car. You run in and put on the hat. I'm an automobile *salesman,* kid."

"No, you're not," Ed Wolfe said. "I was with Cornucopia Finance. We handled your paper. You're an automobile buyer. Your business is in buying up four- and five-year-old cars like mine from people who need dough fast and then auctioning them off to the trade."

The man turned away and Ed Wolfe followed him. Inside the shack the man said, "I'll give you two hundred."

"I need six hundred," Ed Wolfe said.

"I'll lend you the hat. Hold up a goddamn stagecoach."

"Give me five."

"I'll give you two fifty and we'll part friends."

"Four hundred and fifty."

"Three hundred. Here," the man said, reaching his hand into an opened safe and taking out three sheaves of thick, banded bills. He held the money out to Ed Wolfe. "Go ahead, count it."

Absently Ed Wolfe took the money. The bills were stiff, like money in a teller's drawer, their value as decorous and untapped as a sheet of postage stamps. He held the money, pleased by its weight. "Tens and fives," he said, grinning.

"You bet," the man said, taking the money back. "You want to sell your car?"

"Yes," Ed Wolfe said. "Give me the money," he said hoarsely.

He had been to the bank, had stood in the patient, slow, money-conscious line, had presented his formidable check to the impassive teller, hoping the four hundred and sixty-three dollars and sixty-five cents she counted out would seem his week's salary to the man who waited behind him. Fool, he thought, it will seem two weeks' pay and two weeks in lieu of notice and a week for vacation for the hell of it, the three-week margin of an orphan.

"Thank you," the teller said, already looking beyond Ed Wolfe to the man behind him.

"Wait," Ed Wolfe said. "Here." He handed her a white withdrawal slip.

She took it impatiently and walked to a file. "You're closing your savings account?" she asked loudly.

"Yes," Ed Wolfe answered, embarrassed.

"I'll have a cashier's check made out for this."

"No, no," Ed Wolfe said desperately. "Give me cash."

"Sir, we make out a cashier's check and cash it for you," the teller explained.

"Oh," Ed Wolfe said. "I see."

When the teller had given him the two hundred fourteen dollars and twenty-three cents, he went to the next window where he made out a check for $38.91. It was what he had in his checking account.

On Ed Wolfe's kitchen table was a thousand dollars. That day he had spent a dollar and ninety cents. He had twenty-seven dollars and seventy-one cents in his pocket. For expenses. "For attrition," he said aloud. "The cost of living. For streetcars and newspapers and half gallons of milk and loaves of white bread. For the movies. For a cup of coffee." He went to his pantry. He counted the cans and packages, the boxes and bottles. "The three weeks again," he said. "The orphan's nutritional margin." He looked in his icebox. In the freezer he poked around among white packages of frozen meat. He looked brightly into the vegetable tray. A whole lettuce. Five tomatoes. Several slices of cucumber. Browning celery. On another shelf four bananas. Three and a half apples. A cut pineapple. Some grapes, loose and collapsing darkly in a white bowl. A quarter pound of butter. A few eggs. Another egg, broken last week, congealing in a blue dish. Things in plastic bowls, in jars, forgotten, faintly mysterious left-overs, faintly rotten, vaguely futured, equivocal garbage. He closed the door, feeling a draft. "Really," he said, "it's quite cozy." He looked at the thousand dollars on the kitchen table. "It's not enough," he said. "It's not enough," he shouted. "It's not enough to be cautious on. La Meck, you bastard, detachment comes higher, what do you think? You think it's cheap?" He raged against himself. It was the way he used to speak to people on the telephone. "Wake up. Orphan! Jerk! Wake up. It costs to be detached."

He moved solidly through the small apartment and lay down on his bed with his shoes still on, putting his hands behind his head luxuriously. It's marvelous, he thought. Tomorrow I'll buy a trench coat. I'll take my meals in piano bars. He lighted a cigarette. "I'll never smile again," he sang, smiling. "All right, Eddie, play it again," he said. "Mistuh Wuf, you don' wan' ta heah dat ol' song no maw. You know whut it do to you. She ain' wuth it, Mistuh Wuf." He nodded. "Again, Eddie." Eddie played his black ass off. "The way I see it, Eddie," he said, taking a long, sad drink of warm Scotch, "there are orphans and there are orphans." The overhead fan chuffed slowly, stirring the potted palmetto leaves.

He sat up in the bed, grinding his heels across the sheets. "There are orphans and there are orphans," he said. "I'll move. I'll liquidate. I'll sell out."

He went to the phone and called his landlady and made an appointment to see her.

It was a time of ruthless parting from his things, but there was no bitterness in it. He was a born salesman, he told himself. A disposer, a natural dumper. He administered severance. As detached as a funeral director, what he had learned was to say goodbye. It was a talent of a sort. And he had never felt quite so interested. He supposed he was doing what he had been meant for, what, perhaps, everyone was meant for. He sold and he sold, each day spinning off, reeling off little pieces of himself, like controlled explosions of the sun. Now his life was a series of speeches, of nearly earnest pitches. What he remembered of the day was what he had said. What others said to him, or even whether they spoke at all, he was unsure of.

Tuesday he told his landlady, "Buy my furniture. It's new. It's good stuff. It's expensive. You can forget about that. Put it out of your mind. I want to sell it. I'll show you bills for over seven hundred dollars. Forget the bills. Consider my character. Consider the man. Only the man. That's how to get your bargains. Examine, Examine. I could tell you about inner springs; I could talk to you of leather. But I won't. I don't. I smoke, but I'm careful. I can show you the ashtrays. You won't find cigarette holes in *my* tables. Examine. I drink. I'm a drinker. I drink. But I hold it. You won't find alcohol stains. May I be frank? I make love. Again, I could show you the bills. But I'm cautious. My sheets are virginal, white.

"Two hundred fifty dollars, landlady. Sit on that sofa. That chair. Buy my furniture. Rent the apartment furnished. Deduct what you pay from your taxes. Collect additional rents. Realize enormous profits. Wallow in gravy. Get it, landlady? Get it? Just two hundred fifty dollars. Don't disclose the figure or my name. I want to remain anonymous."

He took her into his bedroom. "The piece of resistance, landlady. What you're really buying is the bedroom stuff. I'm selling you your own bare floor. What charm. Charm? Elegance. Elegance! I throw in the living-room rug. That I throw in. You have to take that or it's no deal. Give me cash and I move tomorrow."

Wednesday he said, "I heard you buy books. That must be interesting. And sad. It must be very sad. A man who loves books doesn't like to sell them. It would be the last thing. Excuse me. I've got no right to talk to you this way. You buy books and I've got books to sell. There. It's business now. As it should be. My library—" He smiled helplessly. "Excuse me. Such a grand name. Library." He began again slowly. "My books, my books are in there. Look them over. I'm afraid my taste has been rather eclectic. You see, my education has not been formal. There are over eleven hundred. Of course many are paperbacks. Well, you can see that. I feel as if I'm selling my mind."

The book buyer gave Ed Wolfe one hundred twenty dollars for his mind.

On Thursday he wrote a letter:

American Annuity & Life Insurance Company,
Suite 410,
Lipton-Hill Building,
2007 Bevero Street, S.W.,
Boston 19, Massachusetts

Dear Sirs,

I am writing in regard to Policy Number 593-000-34-78, a $5,000, twenty-year annuity held by Edward Wolfe of the address below.

Although only four payments having been made, sixteen years remain before the policy matures, I find I must make application for the immediate return of my payments and cancel the policy.

I have read the "In event of cancellation" clause in my policy, and realize that I am entitled to only a flat three percent interest on the "total paid-in amount of the partial amortizement." Your records will show that I have made four payments of $198.45 each. If your figures check with mine this would come to $793.80. Adding three percent interest to the amount ($23.81), your company owes me $817.61.

Your prompt attention to my request would be gratefully

appreciated, although I feel, frankly, as though I were selling my future.

On Monday someone came to buy his record collection. "What do you want to hear? I'll put something comfortable on while we talk. What do you like? Here, try this. Go ahead, put it on the machine. By the edges, man. By the edges! I feel as if I'm selling my throat. Never mind about that. Dig the sounds. Orphans up from Orleans singing the news of chain gangs to café society. You can smell the freight trains, man. Recorded during actual performance. You can hear the ice cubes clinkin' in the glasses, the waiters picking up their tips. I have jazz. Folk. Classical. Broadway. Spoken Word. Spoken Word, man! I feel as though I'm selling my ears. The stuff lives in my heart or I wouldn't sell. I have a one-price throat, one-price ears. Sixty dollars for the noise the world makes, man. But remember. I'll be watching. By the edges. Only by the edges!"

On Friday he went to a pawnshop in a Checker Cab.

"You? You buy gold? You buy clothes? You buy Hawaiian guitars? You buy pistols for resale to suicides? I wouldn't have recognized you. Where's the skullcap, the garters around the sleeves? The cigar I wouldn't ask you about. You look like anybody. You look like everybody. I don't know what to say. I'm stuck. I don't know how to deal with you. I was going to tell you something sordid, you know? You know what I mean? Okay, I'll give you facts.

"The fact is, I'm the average man. That's what the fact is. Eleven shirts, 15 neck, 34 sleeve. Six slacks, 32 waist. Five suits at 38 long. Shoes 10-C. A 7½ hat. You know something? Those marginal restaurants where you can never remember whether they'll let you in without a jacket? Well the jackets they lend you in those places always fit me. That's the kind of guy you're dealing with. You can have confidence. Look at the clothes. Feel the material. And there's one thing about me. I'm fastidious. Fastidious. Immaculate.

You think I'd be clumsy. A fall guy falls down, right? There's not a mark on the clothes. Inside? Inside it's another story. I don't speak of inside. Inside it's all Band-Aids, plaster, iodine, sticky stuff for burns. But outside—fastidiousness, immaculation, reality! My clothes will fly off your racks. I promise. I feel as if I'm selling my skin. Does that check with your figures?

"So now you know. It's me, Ed Wolfe. Ed Wolfe, the orphan? I lived in the orphanage for sixteen years. They gave me a name. It was a Jewish orphanage so they gave me a Jewish name. Almost. That is they couldn't know for sure themselves so they kept it deliberately vague. I'm a foundling. A lostling. Who needs it? right? Who the hell needs it? I'm at loose ends, pawnbroker. I'm at loose ends out of looser beginnings. I need the money to stay alive. All you can give me.

"Here's a good watch. Here's a bad one. For good times and bad. That's life, right? You can sell them as a package deal. Here are radios. I'll miss the radios. A phonograph. Automatic. Three speeds. Two speakers. The politic bastard shuts itself off. And a pressure cooker. It's valueless to me, frankly. No pressure. I can live only on cold meals. Spartan. Spartan.

"I feel as if I'm selling—this is the last of it, I have no more things—I feel as if I'm selling my things."

On Saturday he called the phone company: "Operator? Let me speak to your supervisor, please.

"Supervisor? Supervisor, I am Ed Wolfe, your subscriber at TErrace 7-3572. There is nothing wrong with the service. The service has been excellent. No one calls, but you can have nothing to do with that. However, I must cancel. I find that I no longer have any need of a telephone. Please connect me with the business office.

"Business office? Business office, this is Ed Wolfe. My telephone number is TErrace 7-3572. I am closing my account with you. When the service was first installed I had to surrender a twenty-five dollars' deposit to your company.

It was understood that the deposit was to be refunded when
our connection with each other had been terminated. Dis-
connect me. Deduct what I owe on my current account from
my deposit and refund the rest immediately. Business office,
I feel as if I'm selling my mouth."

When he had nothing left to sell, when that was finally
that, he stayed until he had finished all the food and then
moved from his old apartment into a small, thinly furnished
room. He took with him a single carton of clothing—the
suit, the few shirts, the socks, the pajamas, the underwear
and overcoat he did not sell. It was in preparing this carton
that he discovered the hangers. There were hundreds of
them. His own. Previous tenants'. Hundreds. In each closet
on rods, in dark, dark corners was this anonymous residue
of all their lives. He unpacked his carton and put the hangers
inside. They made a weight. He took them to the pawnshop
and demanded a dollar for them. They were worth, he
argued, more. In an A&P he got another carton free and
went back to repack his clothes.

At the new place the landlord gave him his key.

"You got anything else?" the landlord asked. "I could
give you a hand."

"No," he said. "Nothing."

Following the landlord up the deep stairs he was conscious of the $2,479.03 he had packed into the pockets of
the suit and shirts and pajamas and overcoat inside the carton. It was like carrying a community of economically viable
dolls.

When the landlord left him he opened the carton and
gathered all his money together. In fading light he reviewed
the figures he had entered in the pages of an old spiral
notebook:

Pay $463.65
Cash 12.82
Car 300.00

Savings	$214.23
Checking	38.91
Furniture (& bedding)	250.00
Books	120.00
Insurance	817.61
Records	60.00
Pawned:	
Clothes	$110.00
2 watches	18.00
2 radios	12.00
Phonograph	35.00
Pressure Cooker	6.00
Phone deposit (less bill)	19.81
Hangers	1.00
Total	$2,479.03

So, he thought, that was what he was worth. That was the going rate for orphans in a wicked world. Something under $2,500. He took his pencil and lined through all the nouns on his list. He tore the list carefully from top to bottom and crumpled the half which inventoried his ex-possessions. Then he crumpled the other half.

He went to the window and pushed the loose, broken shade. He opened the window and set both lists on the ledge. He made a ring of his forefinger and thumb and flicked the paper balls into the street. "Look out for Ed Wolfe," he said softly.

In six weeks the season changed. The afternoons failed. The steam failed. He was as unafraid of the dark as he had been of the sunlight. He longed for a special grief, to be touched by anguish or terror, but when he saw the others in the street, in the cafeteria, in the theatre, in the hallway, on the stairs, at the newsstand, in the basement rushing their fouled linen from basket to machine, he stood, as indifferent to their errand, their appetite, their joy, their greeting, their effort, their curiosity, their grime, as he was to his own. No envy wrenched him, no despair unhoped him, but, gradually, he became restless.

He began to spend, not recklessly so much as indifferently. At first he was able to recall for weeks what he spent on a given day. It was his way of telling time. Now he had difficulty remembering and could tell how much his life was costing only by subtracting what he had left from his original two thousand four hundred seventy-nine dollars and three cents. In eleven weeks he had spent six hundred seventy-seven dollars and thirty-four cents. It was almost three times more than he had planned. He became panicky. He had come to think of his money as his life. Spending it was the abrasion again, the old habit of self-buffing to come to the thing beneath. He could not draw indefinitely on his credit. It was limited. Limited. He checked his figures. He had eighteen hundred and one dollars, sixty-nine cents. He warned himself, "Rothschild, child. Rockefeller, feller. Look out, Ed Wolfe. Look out."

He argued with his landlord, won a five-dollar reduction in his rent. He was constantly hungry, wore clothes stingily, realized an odd reassurance in his thin pain, his vague fetidness. He surrendered his dimes, his quarters, his half-dollars in a kind of sober anger. In seven weeks he spent only one hundred thirty dollars, fifty-one cents. He checked his figures. He had sixteen hundred seventy-one dollars, eighteen cents. He had spent almost twice what he had anticipated. "It's all right," he said. "I've reversed the trend. I can catch up." He held the money in his hand. He could smell his soiled underwear. "Nah, nah," he said. "It's not enough."

It was not enough, it was not enough, it was not enough. He had painted himself into a corner. Death by *cul-de-sac*. He had nothing left to sell, the born salesman. The born champion, long-distance, Ed Wolfe of a salesman, and he lay in his room winded, wounded, wondering where his next pitch was coming from, at one with the ages.

He put on his suit, took his sixteen hundred seventy-one dollars and eighteen cents and went down into the street. It was a warm night. He would walk downtown. The ice which just days before had covered the sidewalk was dissolved to slush. In darkness he walked through a thawing, melting world. There was, on the edge of the air, something, the warm, moist odor of the change of the season. He was, despite himself, touched. "I'll take a bus," he threatened. "I'll take a bus and close the windows and ride over the wheel."

He had dinner and some drinks in a hotel. When he finished he was feeling pretty good. He didn't want to go back. He looked at the bills thick in his wallet and went over to the desk clerk. "Where's the action?" he whispered. The clerk looked at him, startled. He went over to the bell captain. "Where's the action?" he asked and gave the man a dollar. He winked. The man stared at him helplessly.

"Sir?" the bell captain said, looking at the dollar.

Ed Wolfe nudged him in his gold buttons. He winked again. "Nice town you got here," he said expansively. "I'm a salesman, you understand, and this is new territory for me. Now if I were in Beantown or Philly or L. A. or Vegas or Big D or Frisco or Cincy, why I'd know what was what. I'd be okay, you know what I mean?" He winked once more. "Keep the buck, kid," he said. "Keep it, keep it," he said, walking off.

In the lobby a man sat in a deep chair, *The Wall Street Journal* opened widely across his face. "Where's the action?" Ed Wolfe said, peering over the top of the paper into the crown of the man's hat.

"What's that?" the man asked.

Ed Wolfe, surprised, saw that the man was a Negro.

"What's that?" the man repeated, vaguely nervous. Embarrassed, Ed Wolfe watched him guiltily, as though he had been caught in an act of bigotry.

"I thought you were someone else," he said lamely. The man smiled and lifted the paper to his face. Ed Wolfe stood before the man's opened paper, conscious of mildly teetering. He felt lousy, awkward, complicatedly irritated and

ashamed, the mere act of hurting someone's feelings suddenly the most that could be held against him. It came to
him how completely he had failed to make himself felt.
"Look out for Ed Wolfe, indeed," he said aloud. The man
lowered his paper. "Some of my best friends are Coman-
ches," Ed Wolfe said. "Can I buy you a drink?"

"No," the man said.

"Resistance, eh?" Ed Wolfe said. "That's good. Resistance is good. A deal closed without resistance is no deal.
Let me introduce myself. I'm Ed Wolfe. What's your
name?"

"Please, I'm not bothering anybody. Leave me alone."

"Why?" Ed Wolfe asked.

The man stared at him and Ed Wolfe sat suddenly down
beside him. "I won't press it," he said generously. "Where's
the action? Where *is* it? Fold the paper, man. You're playing somebody else's gig." He leaned across the space between them and took the man by the arm. He pulled at
him gently, awed by his own boldness. It was the first time
since he had shaken hands with La Meck that he had
touched anyone physically. What he was risking surprised
and puzzled him. In all those months to have touched only
two people, to have touched even two people! To feel their
life, even, as now, through the unyielding wool of clothing,
was disturbing. He was unused to it, frightened and oddly
moved. The man, bewildered, looked at Ed Wolfe timidly
and allowed himself to be taken toward the cocktail lounge.

They took a table near the bar. There, in an alcoholic
dark, within earshot of the easy banter of the regulars, Ed
Wolfe seated the Negro and then himself. He looked around
the room and listened for a moment. He turned back to
the Negro. Smoothly boozy, he pledged the man's health
when the girl brought their drinks. He drank stolidly,
abstractedly. Coming to life briefly, he indicated the men
and women around them, their sun-tans apparent even in the
dark. "Pilots," he said. "All of them. Airline pilots. The girls
are all stewardesses and the pilots lay them." He ordered

more drinks. He did not like liquor and liberally poured ginger ale into his bourbon. He ordered more drinks and forgot the ginger ale. *"Goyim,"* he said. "White *goyim.* American *goyim.*" He stared at the Negro. "These are the people, man. The mothered and fathered people." He leaned across the table. "Little Orphan Annie, what the hell kind of an orphan is that with all her millions and her white American *goyim* friends to bail her out?"

He watched them narrowly, drunkenly. He had seen them before—in good motels, in airports, in bars—and he wondered about them, seeing them, he supposed, as Negroes or children of the poor must have seen him when he had had his car and driven sometimes through slums. They were removed, aloof—he meant it—a different breed. He turned and saw the Negro and could not think for a moment what the man could have been doing there. The Negro slouched in his chair, his great white eyes hooded. "You want to hang around here?" Ed Wolfe asked him.

"It's your party," the man said.

"Then let's go someplace else," Ed Wolfe said. "I get nervous here."

"I know a place," the Negro said.

"You know a place. You're a stranger here."

"No, man," the Negro said. "This is my hometown. I come down here sometimes just to sit in the lobby and read the newspapers. It looks good, you know what I mean? It looks good for the race."

"The *Wall Street Journal?* You're kidding Ed Wolfe. Watch that."

"No," the Negro said. "Honest."

"I'll be damned," Ed Wolfe said. "I come for the same reasons."

"Yeah," the Negro said. "No shit."

"Sure, the same reasons." He laughed. "Let's get out of here." He tried to stand, but fell back again in his chair. "Hey, help me up," he said loudly. The Negro got up and came around to Ed Wolfe's side of the table. Leaning over, he raised him to his feet. Some of the others in the room looked at them curiously. "It's all right," Ed Wolfe said. "He's my man. I take him with me everywhere. It looks good for the race." With their arms around each other's shoulders they stumbled out of the room and through the lobby.

In the street Ed Wolfe leaned against the building and the Negro hailed a cab, the dark left hand shooting up boldly, the long black body stretching forward, raised on tip-toes, the head turned sharply along the left shoulder. Ed Wolfe knew he had never done it before. The Negro came up beside Ed Wolfe and guided him toward the curb. Holding the door open he shoved him into the cab with his left hand. Ed Wolfe lurched against the cushioned seat awkwardly. The Negro gave the driver an address and the cab moved off. Ed Wolfe reached for the window handle and rolled it down rapidly. He shoved his head out the window of the taxi and smiled and waved at the people along the curb.

"Hey, man. Close the window," the Negro said after a moment. "Close the window. The cops, the cops."

Ed Wolfe lay his head along the edge of the taxi window and looked up at the Negro who was leaning over him and smiling and seemed trying to tell him something.

"Where we going, man?" he asked.

"We're there," the Negro said, sliding along the seat toward the door.

"One ninety-five," the driver said.

"It's your party," Ed Wolfe told the Negro, waving away responsibility.

The Negro looked disappointed, but reached into his pocket to pull out his wallet.

Did he see what I had on me? Ed Wolfe wondered anxiously. Jerk, drunk, you'll be rolled. They'll cut your throat and then they'll leave your skin in an alley. Be careful.

"Come on, Ed," the Negro said. He took him by the arm and got him out of the taxi.

Fake. Fake, Ed Wolfe thought. Murderer. Nigger. Razor man.

The Negro pulled Ed Wolfe toward a doorway. "You'll meet my friends," he said.

"Yeah, yeah," Ed Wolfe said. "I've heard so much about them."

"Hold it a second," the Negro said. He went up to the window and pressed his ear against the opaque glass.

Ed Wolfe watched him without making a move.

"Here's the place," the Negro said proudly.

"Sure," Ed Wolfe said. "Sure it is."

"Come on, man," the Negro urged him.

"I'm coming, I'm coming," Ed Wolfe mumbled, "but my head is bending low."

The Negro took out a ring of keys, selected one, and put it in the door. Ed Wolfe followed him through.

"Hey, Oliver," somebody called. "Hey, baby, it's Oliver. Oliver looks good. He looks *good.*"

"Hello, Mopiani," the Negro said to a short black man.

"How is stuff, Oliver?" Mopiani said to him.

"How's the market?" a man next to Mopiani asked with a laugh.

"Ain't no mahket, baby, it's a *sto'*," somebody else said.

A woman stopped, looked at Ed Wolfe for a moment, and asked: "Who's the ofay, Oliver?"

"That's Oliver's broker, baby."

"Oliver's broker looks good," Mopiani said. "He looks *good.*"

"This is my friend, Mr. Ed Wolfe," Oliver told them.

"Hey, there," Mopiani said.

"Charmed," Ed Wolfe said.

"How's it going, man," a Negro said indifferently.

"Delighted," Ed Wolfe said.

He let Oliver lead him to a table.

"I'll get the drinks, Ed," Oliver said, leaving him.

Ed Wolfe looked at the room glumly. People were drinking steadily, gaily. They kept their bottles under their chairs in paper bags. Ed Wolfe watched a man take a bag from beneath his chair, raise it, and twist the open end of the bag carefully around the neck of the bottle so that it resembled a bottle of champagne swaddled in its toweling. The man poured into his glass grandly. At the dark far end of the room some musicians were playing and three or four couples danced dreamily in front of them. He watched the musicians closely and was vaguely reminded of the airline pilots.

In a few minutes Oliver returned with a paper bag and some glasses. A girl was with him. "Mary Roberta, Ed Wolfe," he said, very pleased. Ed Wolfe stood up clumsily and the girl nodded.

"No more ice," Oliver explained.

"What the hell," Ed Wolfe said.

Mary Roberta sat down and Oliver pushed her chair up to the table. She sat with her hands in her lap and Oliver pushed her as though she were a cripple.

"Real nice little place here, Ollie," Ed Wolfe said.

"Oh, it's just the club," Oliver said.

"Real nice," Ed Wolfe said.

Oliver opened the bottle and poured liquor in their glasses and put the paper bag under his chair. Oliver raised his glass. Ed Wolfe touched it lamely with his own and leaned back, drinking. When he put it down empty, Oliver filled it again from the paper bag. He drank sluggishly, like one falling asleep, and listened, numbed, to Oliver and the girl. His glass never seemed to be empty anymore. He drank steadily but the liquor seemed to remain at the same level in the glass. He was conscious that someone else had joined them at the table. "Oliver's broker looks good," he heard somebody say. Mopiani. Warm and drowsy and gently detached, he listened, feeling as he had in barbershops, having his hair cut, conscious of the barber, unseen behind him. touching his hair and scalp with his warm fingers. "You see Bert? He looks good," Mopiani was saying.

With great effort Ed Wolfe shifted in his chair, turning to the girl.

"Thought you were giving out on us, Ed," Oliver said. "That's it. That's it."

The girl sat with her hands folded in her lap.

"Mary Roberta," Ed Wolfe said.

"Uh huh," the girl said.

"Mary Roberta."

"Yes," the girl said. "That's right."

"You want to dance?" Ed Wolfe asked.

"All right," she said. "I guess so."

"That's it, that's it," Oliver said. "Stir yourself."

He got up clumsily, cautioned, like one standing in a stalled Ferris wheel, and went around behind her chair, pulling it far back from the table with the girl in it. He took her warm, bare arm and moved toward the dancers. Mopiani passed them with a bottle. "Looks good, looks good," Mopiani said approvingly. He pulled her against him to let Mopiani pass, tightening the grip of his pale hand on her brown arm. A muscle leaped beneath the girl's smooth skin, filling his palm. At the edge of the dance floor Ed Wolfe leaned forward into the girl's arms and they moved slowly, thickly across the floor. He held the girl close, conscious of her weight, the life beneath her body, just under her skin. Sick, he remembered a jumping bean he had held once in his palm, awed and frightened by the invisible life, jerking and hysterical, inside the stony shell. The girl moved with him in the music, Ed Wolfe astonished by the burden of her life. He stumbled away from her deliberately. Grinning, he moved ungently back against her. "Look out for Ed Wolfe," he crooned.

The girl stiffened and held him away from her, dancing self-consciously. Ed Wolfe, brooding, tried to concentrate on the lost rhythm. They danced in silence for a while.

"What do you do?" she asked him finally.

"I'm a salesman," he told her gloomily.

"Door to door?"

"Floor to ceiling. Wall to wall."

"Too much," she said.

"I'm a pusher," he said, suddenly angry. She looked frightened. "But I'm not hooked myself. It's a weakness in my character. I can't get hooked. Ach, what would you *goyim* know about it?"

"Take it easy," she said. "What's the matter with you? Do you want to sit down?"

"I can't push sitting down," he said.

"Hey," she said, "don't talk so loud."

"Boy," he said, "you black Protestants. What's that song you people sing?"

"Come on," she said.

"Sometimes I feel like a motherless child," he sang roughly. The other dancers watched him nervously. "That's our national anthem, man," he said to a couple that had stopped dancing to look at him. "That's our song, sweethearts," he said, looking around him. "All right, mine then. I'm an orphan."

"Oh, come on," the girl said, exasperated, "an orphan. A grown man."

He pulled away from her. The band stopped playing. "Hell," he said loudly, "from the beginning. Orphan. Bachelor. Widower. Only child. All my names scorn me. I'm a survivor. I'm a goddamned survivor, that's what." The other couples crowded around him now. People got up from their tables. He could see them, on tiptoes, stretching their necks over the heads of the dancers. *No,* he thought. No, no. Detachment and caution. The La Meck Plan. They'll kill you. They'll kill you and kill you. He edged away from them, moving carefully backward against the bandstand. People pushed forward onto the dance floor to watch him. He could hear their questions, could see heads darting from behind backs and suddenly appearing over shoulders as they strained to get a look at him.

He grabbed Mary Roberta's hand, pulling her to him fiercely. He pulled and pushed her up onto the bandstand

and then climbed up beside her. The trumpet player, bewildered, made room for them. "Tell you what I'm going to do," he shouted over their heads. "Tell you what I'm going to do."

Everyone was listening to him now.

"Tell you what I'm going to do," he began again.

Quietly they waited for him to go on.

"I don't *know* what I'm going to do," he shouted. "I don't *know* what I'm going to do. Isn't that a hell of a note?

"Isn't it?" he demanded.

"Brothers and sisters," he shouted, "and as an only child bachelor orphan I used the term playfully you understand. Brothers and sisters, I tell you what I'm *not* going to do. I'm no consumer. Nobody's death can make me that. I won't consume. I mean it's a question of identity, right? Closer, come up closer, buddies. You don't want to miss any of this."

"Oliver's broker looks good up there. Mary Roberta looks good. She looks good," Mopiani said below him.

"Right, Mopiani. She looks good, she looks *good*," Ed Wolfe called loudly. "So I tell you what I'm going to do. What am I bid? What am I bid for this fine strong wench? Daughter of a chief, masters. Dear dark daughter of a dead dinge chief. Look at those arms. Those arms, those arms. What am I bid?"

They looked at him, astonished.

"What am I bid?" he demanded. "Reluctant, masters? Reluctant masters, masters? Say, what's the matter with you darkies? Come on, what am I bid?" He turned to the girl. "No one wants you, honey," he said. "Folks, folks, I'd buy her myself, but I've already told you. I'm not a consumer. Please forgive me, miss."

He heard them shifting uncomfortably.

"Look," he said patiently, "the management has asked me to remind you that this is a living human being. This is the real thing, the genuine article, the goods. Oh, I told them I wasn't the right man for this job. As an orphan I have no conviction about the product. Now you should have seen me in my old job. I could be rough. Rough. I hurt people. Can you imagine? I actually caused them pain. I mean, what the hell, I was an orphan. I *could* hurt people. An orphan doesn't have to bother with love. An orphan's like a nigger in that respect. Emancipated. But you people are another problem entirely. That's why I came here tonight. There are parents among you. I can feel it. There's even a sense of parents behind those parents. My God, don't any of you folks ever die? So what's holding us up? We're not making any money. Come on, what am I bid?"

"Shut up, mister." The voice was raised hollowly someplace in the back of the crowd.

Ed Wolfe could not see the owner of the voice.

"He's not in," Ed Wolfe said.

"Shut up. What right you got to come down here and speak to us like that?"

"He's not in, I tell you. I'm his brother."

"You're a guest. A guest got no call to talk like that."

"He's out. I'm his father. He didn't tell me and I don't know when he'll be back."

"You can't make fun of us," the voice said.

"He isn't here. I'm his son."

"Bring that girl down off that stage!"

"Speaking," Ed Wolfe said.

"Let go of that girl!" someone called angrily.

The girl moved closer to him.

"She's mine," Ed Wolfe said. "I danced with her."

"Get her down from there!"

"Okay," he said giddily. "Okay. All right." He let go of the girl's hand and pulled out his wallet. The girl did not move. He took out the bills and dropped the wallet to the floor.

"Damned drunk!" someone shouted.

"That white man's crazy," somone else said.

"Here," Ed Wolfe said. "There's over sixteen hundred dollars here," he yelled, waving the money. It was, for him, like holding so much paper. "I'll start the bidding. I hear over sixteen hundred dollars once. I hear over sixteen hundred dollars twice. I hear it three times. Sold! A deal's a deal," he cried, flinging the money high over their heads. He saw them reach helplessly, noiselessly toward the bills, heard distinctly the sound of paper tearing.

He faced the girl. "Goodbye," he said.

She reached forward, taking his hand.

"Goodbye," he said again, "I'm leaving."

She held his, squeezing it. He looked down at the luxuriant brown hand, seeing beneath it the fine articulation of bones, the rich sudden rush of muscle. Inside her own he saw, indifferently, his own pale hand, lifeless and serene, still and infinitely free.

A SHOWER OF GOLD

by Donald Barthelme

Donald Barthelme (1933–   ) has had a varied
career as newspaper reporter, magazine editor, and
museum director and has served in the army in
Korea and Japan. Born in Texas, Mr. Barthelme
now lives in New York City. His avant-garde fiction has appeared in many magazines, most regularly in *The New Yorker*. His stories have been
collected in several volumes. They are often wildly humorous, but full of thoughtful and even
tragic suggestiveness.

Because he needed the money Peterson answered an ad that
said *"We'll pay you* to be on TV if your opinions are strong
enough or your personal experiences have a flavor of the
unusual." He called the number and was told to come to
Room 1551 in the Graybar Building on Lexington. This he
did and after spending twenty minutes with a Miss Arbor
who asked him if he had ever been in analysis was okayed
for a program called *Who Am I?* "What do you have strong
opinions about?" Miss Arbor asked. "Art," Peterson said,
"life, money." "For instance?" "I believe," Peterson said,
"that the learning ability of mice can be lowered or increased by regulating the amount of serotonin in the brain.
I believe that schizophrenics have a high incidence of unusual fingerprints, including lines that make almost complete circles. I believe that the dreamer watches his dream

in sleep, by moving his eyes." *"That's very interesting!"* Miss Arbor cried. "It's all in the *World Almanac,"* Peterson replied.

"I see you're a sculptor," Miss Arbor said, "that's wonderful." "What is the nature of the program?" Peterson asked. "I've never seen it. Let me answer your question with another question," Miss Arbor said. "Mr. Peterson, are you absurd?" Her enormous lips were smeared with a glowing white cream. "I beg your pardon?" "I mean," Miss Arbor said earnestly, "do you encounter your own existence as gratuitous? Do you feel *de trop?* Is there nausea?" "I have an enlarged liver," Peterson offered. "That's *excellent!"* Miss Arbor exclaimed. "That's a *very* good beginning! *Who Am I?* tries, Mr. Peterson, to discover what people *really are.* People today, we feel, are hidden away inside themselves, alienated, desperate, living in anguish, despair and bad faith. Why have we been thrown here, and abandoned? That's the question we try to answer, Mr. Peterson. Man stands alone in a featureless, anonymous landscape, in fear and trembling and sickness unto death. God is dead. Nothingness everywhere. Dread. Estrangement. Finitude. *Who Am I?* approaches these problems in a root radical way." "On television?" "We're interested in basics, Mr. Peterson. We don't play around." "I see," Peterson said, wondering about the amount of the fee. "What I want to know now, Mr. Peterson, is this: are you *interested* in absurdity?" "Miss Arbor," he said, "to tell you the truth, I don't know. I'm not sure I believe in it." "Oh, Mr. Peterson!" Miss Arbor said, shocked. "Don't *say* that! You'll be . . ." "Punished?" Peterson suggested. *"You* may not be interested in absurdity," she said firmly, "but absurdity is interested in *you."* "I have a lot of problems, if that helps," Peterson said. "Existence is problematic for you," Miss Arbor said, relieved. "The fee is two hundred dollars."

"I'm going to be on television," Peterson said to his dealer. "A terrible shame," Jean-Claude responded. "Is it unavoidable?". "It's unavoidable," Peterson said, "if I want to eat." "How much?" Jean-Claude asked and Peterson said: "Two hundred." He looked around the gallery to see if any of his works were on display. "A ridiculous compensation considering the infamy. Are you using your own name?" "You haven't by any chance . . ." "No one is buying," Jean-Claude said. "Undoubtedly it is the weather. People are thinking in terms of—what do you call those things?—Chris-Crafts. To boat with. You would not consider again what I spoke to you about before?" "No," Peterson said, "I wouldn't consider it." "Two little ones would move much, much faster than a single huge big one," Jean-Claude said, looking away. "To saw it across the middle would be a very simple matter." "It's supposed to be a work of art," Peterson said, as calmly as possible. "You don't go around sawing works of art across the middle, remember?" "That place where it saws," Jean-Claude said, "is not very difficult. I can put my two hands around it." He made a circle with his two hands to demonstrate. "Invariably when I look at that piece I see two pieces. Are you absolutely sure you didn't conceive it wrongly in the first instance?" "Absolutely," Peterson said. Not a single piece of his was on view, and his liver expanded in rage and hatred. "You have a very romantic impulse," Jean-Claude said. "I admire, dimly, the posture. You read too much in the history of art. It estranges you from those possibilities for authentic selfhood that inhere in the present century." "I know," Peterson said, "could you let me have twenty until the first?"

Peterson sat in his loft on lower Broadway drinking Rheingold and thinking about the President. He had always felt close to the President but felt now that he had, in agreeing to appear on the television program, done something slightly disgraceful, of which the President would not approve. But I needed the money, he told himself, the telephone is turned off and the kitten is crying for milk. And

I'm running out of beer. The President feels that the arts should be encouraged, Peterson reflected, surely he doesn't want me to go without beer? He wondered if what he was feeling was simple guilt at having sold himself to television or something more elegant: nausea? His liver groaned within him and he considered a situation in which his new relationship with the President was announced. He was working in the loft. The piece in hand was to be called *Season's Greetings* and combined three auto radiators, one from a Chevrolet Tudor, one from a Ford pickup, one from a 1932 Essex, with part of a former telephone switchboard and other items. The arrangement seemed right and he began welding. After a time the mass was freestanding. A couple of hours had passed. He put down the torch, lifted off the mask. He walked over to the refrigerator and found a sandwich left by a friendly junk dealer. It was a sandwich made hastily and without inspiration: a thin slice of ham between two pieces of bread. He ate it gratefully nevertheless. He stood looking at the work, moving from time to time so as to view it from a new angle. Then the door to the loft burst open and the President ran in, trailing a sixteen-pound sledge. His first blow cracked the principal weld in *Season's Greetings,* the two halves parting like lovers, clinging for a moment and then rushing off in opposite directions. Twelve Secret Service men held Peterson in a paralyzing combination of secret grips. He's looking good, Peterson thought, very good, healthy, mature, fit, trustworthy. I like his suit. The President's second and third blows smashed the Essex radiator and the Chevrolet radiator. Then he attacked the welding torch, the plaster sketches on the workbench, the Rodin cast and the Giacometti stickman Peterson had bought in Paris. *"But Mr. President!"* Peterson shouted. *"I thought we were friends!"* A Secret Service man bit him in the back of the neck. Then the President lifted the sledge high in the air, turned toward Peterson, and said: "Your liver is diseased? That's a good sign. You're making progress. You're thinking."

"I happen to think that guy in the White House is doing a pretty darn good job." Peterson's barber, a man named Kitchen who was also a lay analyst and the author of four books titled *The Decision To Be,* was the only person in the world to whom he had confided his former sense of community with the President. "As far as his relationship with you personally goes," the barber continued, "it's essentially a kind of I-Thou relationship, if you know what I mean. You got to handle it with full awareness of the implications. In the end one experiences only oneself, Nietzsche said. When you're angry with the President, what you experience is self-as-angry-with-the-President. When things are okay between you and him, what you experience is self-as-swinging-with-the-President. Well and good. *But,*" Kitchen said, lathering up, "you want the relationship to be such that what you experience is the-President-as-swinging-with-you. You want *his* reality, get it? So that you can break out of the hell of solipsism. How about a little more off the sides?" "Everybody knows the language but me," Peterson said irritably. "Look," Kitchen said, "when you talk about me to somebody else, you say 'my barber,' don't you? Sure you do. In the same way, I look at you as being 'my customer,' get it? But you don't regard yourself as being 'my' customer and I don't regard myself as 'your' barber. Oh, it's hell all right." The razor moved like a switchblade across the back of Peterson's neck. "Like Pascal said: 'The natural misfortune of our mortal and feeble condition is so wretched that when we consider it closely, nothing can console us.' " The razor rocketed around an ear. "Listen," Peterson said, "what do you think of this television program called *Who Am I?* Ever seen it?" "Frankly," the barber said, "it smells of the library. But they do a job on those people, I'll tell you that." "What do you mean?" Peterson said excitedly. "What kind of a job?" The cloth was whisked away and shaken with a sharp popping sound. "It's too horrible even to talk about," Kitchen said. "But it's what they deserve, those crumbs." "Which crumbs?" Peterson asked.

That night a tall foreign-looking man with a switchblade big as a butcherknife open in his hand walked into the loft without knocking and said "Good evening, Mr. Peterson, I am the cat-piano player, is there anything you'd particularly like to hear?" "Cat-piano?" Peterson said, gasping, shrinking from the knife. "What are you talking about? What do you want?" A biography of Nolde slid from his lap to the floor. "The cat-piano," said the visitor, "is an instrument of the devil, a diabolical instrument. You needn't sweat quite so much," he added, sounding aggrieved. Peterson tried to be brave. "I don't understand," he said. "Let me explain," the tall foreign-looking man said graciously. "The keyboard consists of eight cats—the octave—encased in the body of the instrument in such a way that only their heads and forepaws protrude. The player presses upon the appropriate paws, and the appropriate cats respond—with a kind of shriek. There is also provision made for pulling their tails. A tail-puller, or perhaps I should say tail *player*" (he smiled a disingenuous smile) "is stationed at the rear of the instrument, where the tails are. At the correct moment the tail-puller pulls the correct tail. The tail-note is of course quite different from the paw-note and produces sounds in the upper registers. Have you ever seen such an instrument, Mr. Peterson?" "No, and I don't believe it exists," Peterson said heroically. "There is an excellent early seventeenth-century engraving by Franz van der Wyngaert, Mr. Peterson, in which a cat-piano appears. Played, as it happens, by a man with a wooden leg. You will observe my own leg." The cat-piano player hoisted his trousers and a leg-like contraption of wood, metal and plastic appeared. "And now, would you like to make a request? 'The Martyrdom of St. Sebastian'? The 'Romeo and Juliet' overture? 'Holiday for Strings?' " "But why—" Peterson began.

"The kitten is crying for milk, Mr. Peterson. And whenever a kitten cries, the cat-piano plays." "But it's not my kitten," Peterson said reasonably. "It's just a kitten that wished itself on me. I've been trying to give it away. I'm not sure it's still around. I haven't seen it since the day before yesterday." The kitten appeared, looked at Peterson reproachfully, and then rubbed itself against the cat-piano player's mechanical leg. "Wait a minute!" Peterson exclaimed. "This thing is rigged! That cat hasn't been here in two days. What do you want from me? What am I supposed to do?" "Choices, Mr. Peterson, choices. You *chose* that kitten as a way of encountering that which you are not, that is to say, kitten. An effort on the part of the *pour-soi* to—" "But it chose me!" Peterson cried, "the door was open and the first thing I knew it was lying in my bed, under the Army blanket. I didn't have anything to do with it!" The cat-piano player repeated his disingenuous smile. "Yes, Mr. Peterson, I know, I know. Things are done to you, it is all a gigantic conspiracy. I've heard the story a hundred times. But the kitten is here, is it not? The kitten is weeping, is it not?" Peterson looked at the kitten, which was crying huge tigerish tears into its empty dish. *"Listen* Mr. Peterson," the cat-piano player said, *"listen!"* The blade of his immense knife jumped back into the handle with a thwack! and the hideous music began.

The day after the hideous music began the three girls from California arrived. Peterson opened his door, hesitantly, in response to an insistent ringing, and found himself being stared at by three girls in blue jeans and heavy sweaters, carrying suitcases. "I'm Sherry," the first girl said, "and this is Ann and this is Louise. We're from California and we need a place to stay." They were homely and extremely purposeful. "I'm sorry," Peterson said, "I can't—" "We sleep anywhere," Sherry said, looking past him into the vastness of his loft, "on the floor if we have to. We've done it before." Ann and Louise stood on their toes to get a good look. "What's that funny music?" Sherry asked, "it sounds pretty far-out. We really won't be any trouble at all and it'll just be a little while until we make a connection." "Yes," Peterson said, "but why me?" "You're an artist," Sherry said sternly, "we saw the A.I.R. sign downstairs." Peterson cursed the fire laws which made posting of the signs obligatory. "Listen," he said, "I can't even feed the cat. I can't even keep myself in beer. This is not the place. You won't be happy here. My work isn't authentic. I'm a minor artist." "The natural misfortune of our mortal and feeble condition is so wretched that when we consider it closely, nothing can console us," Sherry said. "That's Pascal." "I know," Peterson said, weakly. "Where is the john?" Louise asked. Ann marched into the kitchen and began to prepare, from supplies removed from her rucksack, something called *veal engagé*. "Kiss me," Sherry said, "I need love." Peterson flew to his friendly neighborhood bar, ordered a double brandy, and wedged himself into a telephone booth. "Miss Arbor? This is Hank Peterson. Listen, Miss Arbor, I can't do it. No, I mean really. I'm being punished horribly for even thinking about it. No, I mean it. You can't imagine what's going on around here. Please, get somebody else? I'd regard it as a great personal favor. Miss Arbor? Please?"

The other contestants were a young man in white pajamas named Arthur Pick, a karate expert, and an airline pilot in full uniform, Wallace E. Rice. "Just be natural," Miss Arbor said, "and of course be frank. We score on the basis of the validity of your answers, and of course that's measured by the polygraph." "What's this about a polygraph?" the airline pilot said. "The polygraph measures the validity of your answers," Miss Arbor said, her lips glowing whitely. "How else are we going to know if you're . . ." "Lying?" Wallace E. Rice supplied. The contestants were connected to the machine and the machine to a large illuminated tote board hanging over their heads. The master of ceremonies, Peterson noted without pleas-

ure, resembled the President and did not look at all
friendly.

The program began with Arthur Pick. Arthur Pick got
up in his white pajamas and gave a karate demonstration
in which he broke three half-inch pine boards with a single
kick of his naked left foot. Then he told how he had dis-
armed a bandit, late at night at the A&P where he was an
assistant manager, with a maneuver called a "rip-choong"
which he demonstrated on the announcer. "How about
that?" the announcer caroled. "Isn't that something? Audience?" The audience responded enthusiastically and
Arthur Pick stood modestly with his hands behind his
back. "Now," the announcer said, "let's play *Who Am I?*
And here's your host, *Bill Lemmon!*" No, he doesn't look
like the President, Peterson decided. "Arthur," Bill Lemmon said, "for twenty dollars—do you love your mother?"
"Yes," Arthur Pick said. "Yes, of course." A bell rang,
the tote board flashed, and the audience screamed. "He's
lying!" the announcer shouted, "lying! lying! lying!"
"Arthur," Bill Lemmon said, looking at his index cards,
"the polygraph shows that the validity of your answer is
. . . questionable. Would you like to try it again? Take
another crack at it?" "You're crazy," Arthur Pick said.
"Of course I love my mother." He was fishing around inside his pajamas for a handkerchief. "Is your mother
watching the show tonight, Arthur?" "Yes, Bill, she is."
"How long have you been studying karate?" "Two years,
Bill." "And who paid for the lessons?" Arthur Pick hesitated. Then he said: "My mother, Bill." "They were pretty
expensive, weren't they, Arthur?" "Yes, Bill, they were."
"How expensive?" "Five dollars an hour." "Your mother
doesn't make very much money, does she, Arthur?" "No,
Bill, she doesn't." "Arthur, what does your mother do for
a living?" "She's a garment worker, Bill. In the garment
district." "And how long has she worked down there?"
"All her life, I guess. Since my old man died." "And she
doesn't make very much money, you said." "No. But she

wanted to pay for the lessons. She *insisted* on it." Bill Lemmon said: "She wanted a son who could break boards with his feet?" Peterson's liver leaped and the tote board spelled out, in huge, glowing white letters, the words BAD FAITH. The airline pilot, Wallace E. Rice, was led to reveal that he had been caught, on a flight from Omaha to Miami, with a stewardess sitting on his lap and wearing his captain's cap, that the flight engineer had taken a Polaroid picture, and that he had been given involuntary retirement after nineteen years of faithful service. "It was perfectly safe," Wallace E. Rice said, "you don't understand, the automatic pilot can fly that plane better than I can." He further confessed to a lifelong and intolerable itch after stewardesses which had much to do, he said, with the way their jackets fell just on top of their hips, and his own jacket with the three gold stripes on the sleeve darkened with sweat until it was black.

I was wrong, Peterson thought, the world is absurd. The absurdity is punishing me for not believing in it. I affirm the absurdity. On the other hand, absurdity is itself absurd. Before the emcee could ask the first question, Peterson began to talk. "Yesterday," Peterson said to the television audience, "in the typewriter in front of the Olivetti showroom on Fifth Avenue, I found a recipe for Ten Ingredient Soup that included a stone from a toad's head. And while I stood there marveling a nice old lady pasted on the elbow of my best Haspel suit a little blue sticker reading THIS INDIVIDUAL IS A PART OF THE COMMUNIST CONSPIRACY FOR GLOBAL DOMINATION OF THE ENTIRE GLOBE. Coming home I passed a sign that said in ten-foot letters COWARD SHOES and heard a man singing "Golden Earrings" in a horrible voice, and last night I dreamed there was a shoot-out at our house on Meat Street and my mother shoved me in a closet to get me out of the line of fire." The emcee waved at the floor manager to turn Peterson off, but Peterson kept talking. "In this kind of a world," Peterson said, "absurd if you will, possibilities nevertheless proliferate and escalate all around us and there are opportunities for beginning again. I am a minor artist and my dealer won't even display my work if he can help it but minor is as minor does and lightning may strike even yet. Don't be reconciled. Turn off your television sets," Peterson said, "cash in your life insurance, indulge in a mindless optimism. Visit girls at dusk. Play the guitar. How can you be alienated without first having been connected? Think back and remember how it was." A man on the floor in front of Peterson was waving a piece of cardboard on which something threatening was written but Peterson ignored him and concentrated on the camera with the little red light. The little red light jumped from camera to camera in an attempt to throw him off balance but Peterson was too smart for it and followed wherever it went. "My mother was a royal virgin," Peterson said, "and my father a shower of gold. My childhood was pastoral and energetic and rich in experiences which developed my character. As a young man I was noble in reason, infinite in faculty, in form express and admirable, and in apprehension . . ." Peterson went on and on and although he was, in a sense, lying, in a sense he was not.